BLUE BEECH SERIES

JUST NEIGHBORS - JUST ROOMMATES - JUST FRIENDS

BOOKS 4 - 6

USA TODAY BESTSELLING AUTHOR
CHARITY FERRELL

JUST NEIGHBORS

CHAPTER ONE

CHLOE

Every day, without fail, my hot neighbor tells me good morning. And, every morning, I tell him to fuck off.

Today will be no different.

"Good morning, Chloe!"

The abrupt sound of his voice cuts through the morning air and slices away my good mood. His deep voice brims with authority and masculinity, and I clench my jaw in irritation. His voice and I share a love-hate relationship. It makes my panties wet, but I wish it belonged to someone who wasn't an asshole.

I rush down the stairs, my coffee mug clutched in my hand, and speed-walk toward my car. I pause on my way for what I give in to every morning, and my pride flips me off the second I cast a glance in his direction.

I can't restrain myself. His voice demands attention, as if he were a king, and shamelessly, I need to worship the view of him. He's standing in his daily spot on his porch—shirtless, no doubt another device to make me miserable. It's fall, and the weather is peaking in the low sixties. No sane person hangs out on display this time of year. I'm curious if he'll carry on his half-naked greeting when winter hits.

Fingers crossed his balls freeze off, and he learns his lesson.

Gray sweatpants hang low on his waist, the drawstring loosely tied, putting his six-pack on display. My pride then rolls in its grave when my thighs clench together under my pencil skirt as my gaze falls to the deep V disappearing beneath the waistband. His chestnut-colored hair is a tousled mess, as if someone were pulling it all night—which wouldn't be a shocker to the world. There's been a regular cycle of women coming and going from his home.

He's Blue Beech's favorite bachelor. It's unfortunate the people who worship him don't know what a terrible person he is. This crazy-attractive man has done nothing but ruin my life and reputation.

My cheeks blush when he confirms he caught me checking him out with a mischievous smile.

"Fuck off!" I yell when I pass him.

He ignores my response and whistles loudly as if I'd catcalled him back. "Looking professional today, babe. I prefer today's skirt to yesterday's. It's tighter. Shorter. Sexier."

Arrogant prick.

I grip the door handle and stop before getting in. It's a dangerous game to play with him, but I can't stop myself. "I don't care what you prefer, jerk. I don't dress to please you."

Mental note: buy fifty of the skirts worn yesterday and burn this one.

I slide into my car while ignoring his laughter, slam the door shut, and situate my bag and coffee. I hold my hand up and flip the bird when I cruise past him. He only laughs.

Kyle Lane, the man I've despised since sophomore year of high school, moved into the house next door three months, six days, and twenty hours ago. The jerk wore out his welcome within five seconds.

Correction: he was never welcome in my neighborhood.

If I had known the world's biggest jackass was shacking up next door, I'd have burned it to the ground. Being around him is the equivalent of menstrual cramps.

His irritating morning game began our first day as neighbors. He scared the shit out of me the first few times, and I made a fool of myself—tripping, spilling my coffee on my white blouse, spraining my ankle once.

Initially, I ignored him, assuming it'd last a few days, but here we are—three months into me possibly being on my way to prison for neighbor homicide.

Kyle does it for his sick entertainment.

The man gets off on making me miserable.

I brake at a Stop sign and scrub my hands over my face while taking a deep breath. If there's any day I don't want to deal with his bullshit, it's today. I've been dreading this day, stabbed it on my desk calendar with a red pen as if it'd declared when I'd die.

But there's no avoiding it.

———

My office is on the second floor of the building.

I pass crowds of people and separate offices on my way there. To dodge the curious stares often filled with pity, I take the stairs in favor of the elevator. Cardio isn't my favorite morning routine, so my ass had better thank me for it later.

"Nuh-uh, nope. You turn around before I drag you outside and shove you in the trunk of my car, and we take a paid vacation until tomorrow," Melanie, my assistant, declares when I shuffle into the office, resembling a frazzled mess.

I drop my keys in my bag. "I'm not running from my problems."

"Maybe you should. Running from your problems is better than committing murder."

I groan. "Oh my God, I'm not running away or killing anyone today."

She raises a brow. "Though, tomorrow, it's a possibility?"

I signal to her computer with my coffee while passing her desk on the way to my office. "Work on a new résumé. I'm firing you."

She flips her shiny blonde hair over her shoulder. "Don't dial my number when the new one is lame and won't help you bury a body." A smile dances on her lips when I glance at her.

"I appreciate your loyalty, Melanie. You've earned yourself another week of employment."

"And I appreciate yours for not firing me after the six hundredth threat." She swivels her chair and looks at me. "Are you taking calls today?"

I shrug—an attempt to fake indifference. "Yes. I doubt anyone will call."

"More reason for us to haul ass out of here."

I sigh. "I'll be in my office if you need me."

But please don't.

I have a bag of mini Snickers, plenty of coffee, and a flask if worse comes to worst to survive this day.

She salutes me. "Sounds good, boss. I'll be on Pornhub, so please don't need me."

I can't stop myself from cracking a smile while shaking my head. "One of these days, I'm going to fire you."

"And that will be the worst day of your life."

"Yeah, yeah, yeah," I mutter before disappearing into the solitude of my office.

I shut the door, collapse in the uncomfortable chair behind my desk, and vacantly stare at the stack of papers in need of editing. This office is what I've wanted for years, what I've worked my ass off for. I'm the editor in chief of *The Blue Beech Register*. The number of scandalous stories in our small town is that of *Sesame Street*, but it's given me a job, experience on my résumé, and the opportunity to move up in the field.

———

"What the fuck, Chloe?"

I hear the very familiar and very pissed off voice in the reception area outside my office, and my back stiffens in my chair. His tone is the opposite of what it was this morning when he was hanging out, half-naked, on his porch.

I toss the pen in my hand on my desk, preparing myself for the incoming shitshow when my office door flies open.

I need that flask, stat.

I straighten myself, squaring up my shoulders, and scowl at the man taking residence in the doorway. "Excuse you. Who do you think you are, barging into my office?"

Melanie is definitely getting fired.

The next task on my to-do list is hiring a secretary who hates my neighbor and won't mind taking a criminal charge for kicking him in the nuts.

The walls vibrate when Kyle slams the door shut as if he owned the place, and he stalks the few steps until he's directly in front of my desk. He spreads his feet and crosses his arms across his broad chest. "Your neighbor. Your proclaimed enemy. The man whose dick you've wanted to ride since sophomore year."

Oh, this motherfucker.

"True. True." I sneer at him in repulsion. "And *you wish.*"

He stares me down, and his tone turns serious-slash-pissed again. "Word is, you're poking around about Lauren Barnes's assault, so you can publish about it in your pitiful paper. What the fuck?"

I've been dreading this conversation. I knew he'd come roaring in here, prepared for war, and he wouldn't understand my reasoning for writing the details of what happened to his best friend's fiancée.

"It's a story worth reading," I reluctantly answer.

Kyle's hands move from his chest to his pockets, and he shuts up long enough for me to appreciate the sight of him in his police uniform. I'm positive they're tailored to fit every inch of his tall, muscular stature. His hair is now brushed, and a light scruff scattered along his cheeks complements his stupidly handsome face. A small cleft rests in the center of his chin, and he has cheekbones any Real Housewife would beg their plastic surgeon for. The early morning, shirtless view of Kyle is nice, but, *damn,* so is this. I hate my attraction to him.

My eye-fucking assault breaks when he starts bitching again.

"It's a desperate attempt to publish something *scandalous.*" He says the last word dramatically. "It's bullshit. Stick to your boring stories about food drives and petty crimes and keep your mouth shut about anyone close to me."

I wince at his insult but compose myself. "It's not a *desperate* attempt. The man was running drugs in this town, harassing women, and assaulted your best friend's fiancée and his father. They're giving him a slap on the wrist because his family is loaded, and that's bullshit. I'm a journalist, Kyle. Reporting these stories is my job."

"Find another story." His strong jaw clenches. "You publish it, and I swear to God, I will ruin your life in every way possible."

"Are you threatening me?" I swallow hard.

He leans forward and plants his hands on my desk, the smell of teakwood and citrus taking over my space. "Consider it more than a threat. What happened between us in the past will seem like a fairy tale compared to what I'll do. I will arrest every person you love. Every day, your mother and sister will get a visit from an officer. Do not fuck with me on this."

I straighten my palms and flatten my hands on my desk, mirroring his stance. "Acting like a dick isn't helping your case in getting what you want."

He scoffs and shifts closer. His cool, minty breath brushes the side of my face. "I'm not one to beg, but I am one to make a point. Don't act like you don't know that I can destroy a person in one night, *Fieldgain*."

I flinch. It's known I despise my last name. I've never liked it because of the people I share it with, but my hatred for it increased after it was turned into a taunt—thanks to him.

Our lips are inches apart with neither of us dropping eye contact. This will result in one of three ways: one of us killing the other, us fucking each other, or me kicking him out of my office before either of the first two happens.

I pull away with the hope he'll do the same and sit back in my chair. "Leave my office, or I'll write a story about you."

He remains in his stance and releases a hard laugh. "Oh, sweet Chloe, you're smart enough to know you can't touch me. Don't act clueless to that fact and make sure you remember it. I will always have more power than you do in this town. Period."

That's not a lie.

But I hate him for pointing it out.

Kyle is Blue Beech's golden boy and man-slut, and he's basically royalty here.

He pulls away from my desk and takes a step back with tightness in his eyes. He knows this story will kill Lauren and Gage. "Don't fucking run it, Chloe. Unless you want hell to pay."

"The story goes out in two days," I argue. "I need a front-page story."

"Print one about fucking puppies for all I care." He turns to leave but halts to throw me a cold smile. "And have a *good day.* It's a special one, isn't it?" He snaps his fingers and points one at me. "Shouldn't you be in a wedding dress?" He snaps again and places his fist to his lips, letting out an amused laugh. "Oh shit, wrong girl."

"Fuck you," I bite out while gripping the arms of my chair.

"Word is, we've already done that." He winks.

Oh, this motherfucker.

"I hate you!" I pick up the first thing I can—a stapler—and fling it his way.

Okay, not at him.

I can't exactly assault a police officer.

It hits the wall, leaving a mark, and falls to the floor.

"Whoa, I should arrest you." He grabs the handcuffs from his belt and holds them in the air. "You ever worn a pair of these?"

I flip him off.

"Is that an offer?" He swings the cuffs back and forth like a pendulum. "We can put these to enjoyable use."

I point to the door. "Get out."

"By the way, work on your aim." He smiles, taps my door with his knuckles, and leaves the room without shutting the door.

I take a few minutes to make sure he's gone before jumping up from my seat and charging into the reception area. "You're fired, Melanie. Quit watching porn and watch who comes into my office instead."

Melanie peeks up from her desk, faking innocence. "I wasn't watching porn. I was waiting to hear a live show while you two screwed in there. Figured it'd be much more entertaining."

I shoot her an annoyed glare. "Shut it."

"The sexual tension bled through these walls and practically gave me an orgasm."

"You can't have *sexual tension* with a man you hate."

"That's where you're wrong, boss lady. Hate sex is the best sex."

I retreat to my office and grab the flask.

Screw it.

———

I'm Chloe Fieldgain, and I am a walking, talking cliché.

I caught my boyfriend cheating—and I stupidly forgave him.

He proposed—and I stupidly said yes.

I caught him cheating again—and I stopped being an idiot and dumped his ass.

And what do I earn for my train wreck of a five-year relationship? Hearing the gag-worthy story of him proposing in Town Square to the woman he cheated with, and the second embarrassment of knowing that they're tying the knot today—four months after we broke off our engagement.

Today is the wedding, and no amount of alcohol will help me forget.

That doesn't stop me from trying, and where better than in a public place? That's why I'm stupidly getting my drink on at the Down Home Pub—the only bar in Blue Beech.

I took a sip from my flask after Kyle's departure earlier today and then put it back in case anything work-related dropped onto my desk. When five o'clock hit, I headed straight to the pub, and I'm now sitting at the bar in the corner where the brokenhearted linger.

A slight buzz is hitting me as I trace the names scratched into the wood of the bar with my finger. All day, I've forced myself to remember the worst of Kent—the cheating, him being not so great in bed, and his shitty sense of humor. My intoxicated mind needs to be reminded that dropping him was the best thing to happen to me.

Who wants to live the rest of their life with shitty sex and a cheating bastard of a boyfriend?

Not this girl.

"Well, well, well, if it's not-my-favorite reporter. You here, stalking around, waiting for someone to create a scene, so you can write an article about it tomorrow?"

That motherfucking voice.

I knock back the rest of my drink, needing the liquid courage, and tilt my gaze forward to find Kyle sitting a few stools down from mine. Unlike me, he's changed out of his work clothes and into something more comfortable. A red buffalo plaid flannel covers his shoulders, and a backward ball cap hides his hair.

"If it's not-my-favorite asshole," I reply before swirling my tongue in my mouth to capture any lingering excess alcohol. To deal with him, I need to be as drunk as possible.

"Oh, *favorite*? I like that." He winks, stands up, and comes my way even though I'm not sending an *I want company* vibe. "Maybe I'll work my way up to your favorite fuck."

I roll my eyes. "I take it back. Just asshole, delete the prefix."

His scent and proximity drag me into a high stronger than anything behind the bar will.

"What do you want, Kyle?"

He smirks—a sign he came over to fuck with me. "Didn't expect you to show your face in public tonight."

"Fuck off."

"You're plastered," he states.

I shoot him a glare. "And you're an asshole. A smart one, with your very intelligent revelation, but still a definite asshole."

He rests his elbow on the bar and leans into it while facing me. "Are *asshole* and *fuck* your favorite words in the dictionary?"

"Only when it comes to you."

He places his palm over his chest. "Aw, I'm flattered I have a special place in your brain."

"Fuck off."

"And there you go, thinking about me again."

"What do you want?" I repeat. "You want to rub my shitty life in my face?" I pause. "Wait, why are you here? Isn't everyone and their damn dressed-up dog attending the stupid wedding of the cheaters?"

His eyes meet mine with humor. "Shouldn't you be there, objecting?"

"I hate you," I grumble.

"Good." He sets his beer down and situates himself into the seat next to mine as if my insult were an invite.

"*Now*, what are you doing?" *Why am I constantly asking him this?*

"I'm giving you the pleasure of my company to help clear your head," he says as if it were as obvious as my Social Security number.

I hold my empty glass up. "I've already found the solution. Go annoy another poor soul." I'm not surprised when he makes himself comfortable.

"You know what would do an *even better* job?" he asks.

I hold my cup up. "Shattering this glass and then slicing your genitals off with a broken piece?"

"Damn, you're brutal." His attention swings from me to the bartender, Maliki. He yells out an order of fries and water.

Maliki nods in response and then calls out the order to the kitchen. Maliki owns the Down Home Pub and insisted all drinks were on him tonight when I plopped down earlier.

Kyle stays quiet while sipping his beer, and I play with my glass, uncertain if I should order another vodka I can barely stomach.

What's his play here?

He doesn't speak again until Maliki slides the fries and water down the bar, and they land in front of me. I glance over at Kyle in question, and he snags a fry before holding one out to me.

"Eat up, drunkie," he demands. "And drink the water if you don't want a hangover tomorrow and risk oversleeping. It'd be an unpleasant start to my day if I couldn't annoy your ass while enjoying my coffee."

I narrow my eyes at him but bite off the end of a fry. He's right, but I won't admit that to him. When I finish the fry, he pours ketchup on the side of the basket and slides it closer to me. My stomach growls. I had no appetite earlier and worked through lunch and dinner.

He snags a few fries, and we eat in silence until his arrogant voice breaks through.

"Aw, we're sharing a meal, Fieldgain," he teases. "Consider this our first date. Do I get laid?"

I wince at his comment. It sickens me more than the alcohol and breakup heartbreak combined. He had to bring up our history, knowing today is already hell for me.

I throw down the fry in my hand, sick and tired of his games. "Did you forget that happened years ago?"

The playfulness on his face falls into regret. "Chloe."

I brush my hands together, removing the salt on my fingertips, and push the basket of fries toward him. "Save it. I don't want to think about it tonight. I have enough disturbing memories to drink away. I don't need another on my list."

He leans back and snags another fry. "Fine by me. I'd prefer not to talk about it either unless you give me the chance to explain myself."

"Hard pass."

He grabs the water and hands it to me. "How about we make a toast?"

I take it from him with a frown. At least he's changing the subject. "No."

He grabs my wrist, pulls my hand up, and clinks my water against his beer. "What if we toast to douchebags?"

"To you then."

He shrugs. "I was thinking more of your ex, but I'll take your verbal abuse because I'm a nice guy." He sets his glass down to settle his elbow on the bar again and puts his attention on me. "Why are you upset though? Word is, you cheated on Kent before he fucked around with Lacy."

"Cheated?" I scoff. I'm tired of Kent using it as an excuse for his unfaithfulness. "I hardly believe it's cheating when it's with yourself."

His head cocks to the side as he blinks in confusion. "I'm sorry, what?"

I want to stop talking, but the alcohol forces me to defend myself. "I *cheated* on Kent with myself."

His lips curve into a wicked smile. "Explain, please."

Oh shit, Chloe. Abort confession. A-fucking-bort confession.

The confession pouring from my mouth seconds later informs me that I'm no longer sober enough to make responsible decisions. "He caught me, uh … pleasuring myself … you know … doing his job." The words come out in slow stutters.

His mouth drops open at the same time he knocks over his drink with his elbow. I've never seen him so flustered before. I smile, knowing I caught him off guard.

He stares at me with interest. "Are you telling me, he got pissed at you for playing with your pussy?" He grins. "Damn, I thought I was possessive."

"Don't say it like that," I grumble, wishing I could cut and run from this conversation. Unfortunately, I'm certain I can't even get off my stool without falling on my face.

He grabs a napkin and cleans up his mess. "So, he's labeling you a cheater for getting yourself off?"

I avert eye contact. "Yes."

Half his body slides off his seat when he moves in closer. "Can you please provide details of what happened, so I can determine if he's correct?"

I press him into his own space. "I gave you the details."

"You didn't give me shit for details. Was it with your hand? A sex toy?" He tilts his head back and groans. "Fuck, this makes my night."

I hold my hand up as a flush of embarrassment hits my cheeks. "Oh my God, I'm not doing this with you."

He runs his tongue over his lips. "Come on," he begs. "Give my imagination something pleasurable to think about when I'm home with my hand around my dick."

Oh my God.

I shut my eyes and pull at the collar of my top, suddenly burning up.

Is he saying he'll jack off to whatever I confess?

"I'm not giving you any *details*. I don't want to conduct a casual conversation with you, let alone one about my sex life." I shove his shoulder. "And don't talk about having your hand on your dick around me."

He eyeballs the bar. "Why? It's not out of the ordinary to play with your pussy. Ask anyone in here."

"Quit calling it playing with my pussy!" I hiss. "And I'd rather not poll that right now … or ever."

He chuckles. "You masturbate. Good for you. I do it on the regular *right next door*. I've made it clear how much I love those skirts of yours."

I'll smack myself for this tomorrow. "We were, uh … you know …"

Thankfully, he catches my drift in seconds. "Fucking?"

"Yes, *fucking*. It was in the morning, before work. He got off. I didn't. When he left, I grabbed the vibrator he knew nothing about from my bedside drawer."

He grins, eating this up. "Wait, so this happened frequently?" He appears baffled, disgusted, and entertained, all at the same time.

"Quit interrupting, or I'll stop," I warn.

He holds his hands up. "My bad, my bad. Do continue the Chloe Masturbation Saga."

"So, I started to, uh … take matters into my own hands."

"You played with your pussy," he corrects.

I push him again and shyly glance away. "Yes. I didn't hear the front door open. I was almost there, and next thing I knew, he came barging into the bedroom. He'd forgotten his wallet."

"And, also, to give you an orgasm."

"He got pissed, accused me of emasculating him, and called it cheating, arguing he should be the one giving me orgasms. He'd already been sleeping with Lacy, but he uses that as an excuse to make me the bad guy. Kent knows I won't defend myself and tell people he caught me masturbating, not cheating."

I cover my mouth with my hand and want to curl away in embarrassment when I realize what I confessed and *who* I confessed it to. Kyle is the last person I should've told. I wait for the snide comments from him, but they never come.

He licks his lips and stares at me in fascination. "If you were mine, I would've sat down and enjoyed the show. That's *after* I had given you the best orgasm of your life. Then, you'd go to work, missing my cock and rubbing your thighs together, anticipating me doing it again. During your lunch break, I'd visit you in your office, spread you out on top of your desk, and eat your pussy. Later, when we were in bed, I'd fuck you all over again."

Jesus. This man and his words.

Those words in that voice.

Heat shoots up my spine while I fumble for a response. My heart races as I imagine him doing all those things.

Maybe a one-night stand will help rid me of my thoughts of Kent the Cheater.

No. Nope.

This is Kyle Lane.

I clear my throat when our eyes meet, hoping it will kill my dirty imagination. "So ..." I stutter out. "That's how I cheated."

"It's not cheating, but at least it helped you dodge a bullet with that one. Dude is an asshole. He was the backup to the backup quarterback in high school. The fuck were you thinking, being with him?"

I narrow my eyes at him. "He was the only guy who'd talk to me, thanks to you."

Guilt creeps up his face again. "Returning to the subject at hand ... *your hand* on ... or in your pussy."

I cover my entire face with my hands this time.

He removes them one by one.

"Can we not talk about this ... or act like we never *did* talk about it?"

"There is no chance in hell I'll forget this conversation." He winks. "I'm starting to like you more, dear neighbor."

———

I'm drunk off my ass with the man I hate sitting at my side.

Last time we hung out, it crushed me.

Kyle chuckles, drags my drink away from me, and sets it out of my reach. "Cut-off time for Chloe."

I scowl at him and gesture to the bar. "Look at that, ladies and gents. The life of the party has graduated to the party pooper. Is the music too loud for you? Should I ask Maliki to turn it down a notch, so you can get your full eight hours of sleep?"

"I love wasted, smart-ass Chloe." He smirks.

I'm clueless as to how long we've been sitting here with each other. Kyle's company has outshone every thought of Kent. Being around him is entertaining and much better than drinking myself into a stupor alone. I'm an emotional drunk. The first time I got wasted, I blubbered about losing a pet goldfish before puking and passing out.

Hanging out with Kyle—if that's what you can call it—has been interesting. We argued when I attempted to order a drink stronger than the vodka in front of me. Five minutes later, I realized I had no choice. When I yelled my order to Maliki, Kyle shook his head, and Maliki turned around like a traitorous little shit.

Somehow, Kyle volunteered for Chloe babysitting duty—not surprising. He's always enjoyed being in charge and bossing people around. Sober me does not like him being in charge and bossy. But drunk me—good ole stupid, drunk me—loves his authority.

Somehow, the liquor numbs my hate for him. His attractiveness is the culprit of my sliding closer to him as the night grows later. My attention closes in on his hair as I think of how amazing it'd be to mess it up, run my hands through it, while he touched me in places he shouldn't. The flannel hugging his muscular arms looked hot when he sat down, but my mouth watered when he unbuttoned it later and revealed a black V-neck tee. He hung the flannel on the back of his stool and stretched his arms out on the bar.

I knew vodka went straight to the head, but I didn't know it messed with your head like this.

Maybe I should drink away those thoughts.
Excellent idea.
I need to up my alcohol intake.

I reach for the half-full glass of vodka soda he confiscated, but he grabs my hand. His finger massages the space between my thumb and finger before sliding the drink farther away from me.

"Nice try," he says.

"But it's half-full!" I argue as if he took my favorite toy. "Isn't that a drinking foul?"

"True, but you're *way* over being tipsy." His response drips with authority, and I shiver.

"*Duh*. It was my game plan tonight."

He cocks his head toward the door. "Come on, my drunk Nancy Drew. I'll drive you home."

I cross my arms. "No."

"Yes."

"I can find my way home."

He snorts. "It's not like it's out of my way or anything."

"I'm not getting in the car with my archnemesis."

"Archnemesis?" he scoffs. "What are we, a fucking high school drama?"

"Piss off."

"Come on, I'm a nice guy. I ordered you fries. Mean people don't order other people fries. They keep them to themselves." He elbows me. "So, admit it. I'm a nice fucking dude."

I reach for my water, which he allows, and play with the straw, staring at it instead of him. "Maybe now … but not then."

His eyes narrow my way. "I was a stupid teenager, Chloe. Get over it."

"*Get over it?* You don't understand the consequences I had to deal with because of your *stupid teenager* actions."

He throws cash onto the bar and rises from his stool. "Stand up before I call your ex-fiancé and ask if he'll ditch his wedding to pick you and your vibrator-loving pussy up." He pauses and grabs his flannel, throwing it on over his tee. Then, he leans in. "On second thought, I won't even need to call him. The groom's party walked in. Now, you can either leave with me and not face your ex and his new wife or you can keep your ass in this corner and watch their happiness. It's up to you."

I glance up to see Kent's best man walking to the bar with a brides-maid at his side.

This is where they chose to reception it up?

I grab my purse. "Fine, but how am I getting my car in the morning?"

"I rode with my sister. She helps Maliki close sometimes. I'll drive your car." He holds out his hand. "Keys, neighbor dearest."

I roll my eyes but grab them from my bag and shove them in his hand. "Can we go out another way, so they don't see me?"

He nods toward the back exit and grabs my water. "Sure can."

I allow him to take my hand, and he guides me down a dimly lit hallway. My head spins, and I use the wall and him to level myself. The chilly night hits me when we make it outside, and my car headlights blink when he hits the unlock button on my key.

Opening the passenger door, he assists me into the seat and then moves to the driver's side.

He hands me the water and helps me with my seat belt. "Drink this," he orders.

I gulp it down, realizing how thirsty I am.

He rests his hand on the top of my seat while reversing out of the parking spot. "See, I'm a nice guy, babe."

"Fries and rides don't make everything better," I mutter. "They don't erase my hate for you, so, no, you're still not a nice guy."

"I'll prove it to you then."

I narrow my eyes at him. "What does that mean?"

"You shall see, dear neighbor."

CHAPTER TWO

KYLE

Five days out of the week, my mornings consist of showering, pouring myself a cup of coffee, and then walking outside to fuck with Chloe before she leaves for work.

I consider it our cute little routine.

She most likely thinks of it as a prologue to the day she murders my ass.

I tap my fingers against the steering wheel of Chloe's Honda and peek over at her slouched in the passenger seat. She's desperate if she's publicly drinking and allowing me to drive her home.

I ditched the guys as soon as I caught sight of her sitting in the back of the bar, resembling an old heartbreak country song. Gage gave me a glare and then a sly smirk when I instructed him to bury my body next to my grandmother's in case she killed me, and my sister sent me five smile emojis after I sent her a text saying I didn't need a ride home. They've been up my ass about getting a girlfriend, like it will establish world peace.

"Quit staring at me like that," she snarls.

"Like what?" I ask.

"Like you pity me."

"I don't pity you." I stop to correct myself. "Scratch that. I do pity you."

"Someone grew up and put their honest undies on."

I soften my tone and explain myself. "I don't pity you for the reason you think. I pity you for having a boyfriend who failed to get you off."

My response is met with silence.

"Was it every time?"

Groaning, she shifts her neck from side to side as if it's sore. "I'm not discussing this with you. I should've never told you in the first place."

"Jesus, Chloe, I won't tell anyone you own a vibrator. It's not uncommon, but if you're ashamed of your sexuality—"

"I'm not ashamed of my sexuality," she snaps with a sneer.

"Appears that way to me. You pleasure yourself. Who the fuck cares? I'm more concerned that you consider it weird that you masturbate but not weird that your boyfriend didn't give two shits if you were satisfied."

"Contrary to your belief, not every relationship is about sex."

"True, but Kent not giving a shit about satisfying you wasn't a healthy relationship. It was a selfish one."

"I don't like being around you," she huffs out.

"Tough shit. We're neighbors. Get used to it."

She shifts in her seat to face me. "Speaking of that, why would you buy the house next door? What's your play here?"

"Don't flatter yourself by thinking I'm secretly in love with you," I say with a laugh. "It's a nice home in a decent neighborhood with great landscaping."

Lies. The landscaping sucks ass.

"Oh, look, we're here," I say while pulling into her driveway. "No more time for your paranoia of me moving in to ruin your life."

"Until you tell me why, it's what I'm assuming."

I park the car. "Keep assuming wrong then."

She starts to talk, no doubt to continue this ridiculous argument, but her hand closes over her mouth. "Oh shit," she groans.

Fuck!

Those are never good words to hear from a drunk person with, most likely, a low alcohol tolerance.

I turn off the car. "Oh shit, what?"

The door flies open, and her head disappears from my view.

Motherfucker.

She's a damn puker.

I unbuckle my seat belt and walk to her side. Sure enough, there's vomit. It's not just outside but also on the side of her mouth and on her top.

I drag my flannel off, step to the side of the puke, and wipe her mouth with it. "Swear to God, you'd better not fucking flip me off tomorrow morning."

After I'm finished using my favorite shirt as a puke rag, I assist her out of the car. She doesn't argue, doesn't fight me, but I can see the humiliation on her face. I'm the last person she wants help from. My arm is on her shoulder, the other at the dip of her back, and her side is resting against mine. She points to the door key on the ring, and I unlock the door before walking in. A lamp in the room's corner provides light for me to walk through without running into furniture.

"I'm usually not up for drunk babysitting," I say when she points toward what I'm guessing is her bedroom. "Not even for my little sister, who can hold her liquor better than you. Jesus, you damn lightweight."

She argues with a groan and a tip of her middle finger, and I can't stop myself from laughing.

This is my first time stepping into her house. It's nice—plenty of feminine shit everywhere. We pass a child's room, and she points to an open doorway. I flip on the light and take in her bedroom. It's not what I expected from her—not uptight. It's bright purple with gold accents scattered throughout.

"Come on, let's get you in bed," I say, jerking my head toward it.

My statement is more of a guess.

Does she want to go to bed?

Shower?

Sleep by the toilet?

I take the bed as her decision when she allows me to lead her there and grab her waist to steady her. The way I deposit her on the bed is far from graceful, and I hear a thud when her head hits the headboard.

Whoops.

I'm not trying to be Mr. Romantic over here anyway.

She rubs her head while chewing on her lower lip. "I'm going to bed alone."

I hold my hands up and grimace. "The frilly-ass bed is all yours. Taking advantage of puking, drunk chicks isn't a hobby of mine. I wouldn't kiss you right now if you begged me. French-fry vomit is not a turn-on."

She makes herself comfortable, still wearing her clothes and shoes, and I wonder if it's how she'll sleep. I'd offer her help, but I'm not risking her losing her shit on me. She stretches out on the bed and pulls the blanket until it smacks her chin. Her blonde hair is half-smashed against the headboard and half-down in tangles, and she stares at me with mascara smudged around her baby-blue eyes.

Even when she's a drunken mess, there's no mistake that Chloe is fucking gorgeous in every sense with her light skin, freckles scattered along her nose and cheeks, and plump lips that tasted like candy the first and only time we kissed. I wonder if they still taste the same.

"I thought any woman willing to sleep with you was a turn-on," she replies, proud of her comeback.

"As usual, your thoughts are inaccurate, Nancy Drew." I do a sweeping gesture to the hallway. "By the way, are you hiding children in here?"

She could be dating someone with kids. But he'd have to be against staying over or going out in public with her because I've never seen anyone.

She shakes her head and then hiccups. "I help my sister with my niece and nephew."

I draw in a breath. "Ah, I've seen her drop them off a few times."

"You need to quit stalking me."

"You need to quit thinking I find you important enough to stalk."

That shuts her up real quick.

I walk backward while staring at her. "Anything else you need?"

"Nope. I'm good."

"You sure? Water? Advil? Your vibrator?"

She grabs a pillow and hurls it at me. "Get out!"

I turn around but glance over my shoulder at her before taking off. My voice softens. "And, Chloe, thank you for not running the story."

I asked a woman who works at the printing company, and she confirmed Lauren's name was nowhere in the paper.

Her eyes narrow in my path. "You're not welcome. I'm risking a potential promotion—all because you threatened to blackmail me."

She's right.

It didn't feel good, threatening her, but I protect the people I care about.

I turn on my heel, her keys still in my hand, and leave the room. I lock her front door behind me, the key ring swinging around my finger on my short walk home.

I started my day telling Chloe good morning.

I'm ending my day telling her good night.

Tomorrow, she'll tell me to fuck off.

It's the circle of us—enemies since my balls dropped.

———

My phone vibrates with a text as soon as I stroll through my front door.

Gage: You home?

I drop both our keys into my designated key bowl before replying.

Me: Just walked in. What's up?

Gage: You home alone?

Me: Why? Does Lauren want to come over and give me company?

My phone vibrates in my hand seconds later, and I answer it after two rings.

"Say something like that again, and I'll come over and beat your ass," Gage warns as soon as I pick up.

I chuckle. "You're not doing a satisfactory job as a fiancé if you're calling me this late and not snuggled up with her … or whatever you lame, monogamous people do these days."

"I don't share my bedroom talk."

Gage is my best friend, but Lauren is a delicate subject for him. He loves her more than anyone—has since we were kids.

I fake offense. "Not even your best friend?"

"Especially not with my best friend, who referred to her as Satan for years."

"Some would find the name flattering. Now, to what do I owe the pleasure of a call so urgent that it couldn't wait until tomorrow?"

Gage is my partner, and I'll see him bright and early in the morning, so we rarely do nightcap conversations.

"Call me curious, but I was wondering if you were sleeping over at your neighbor's."

I stroll into the kitchen, snag a bottle of water, and head to my bedroom. "Mrs. Kettle? We went to school with her son. Gross, man."

He laughs. "Hey, maybe it's time for you to change your type. Nothing else has worked out for you."

I'm not looking for anything serious and unsure if I'll ever be. "I'm not at Chloe's. Drunk chicks who can hardly walk don't make my dick hard."

He releases a long breath before responding. "Jesus, Kyle. I wasn't referring to you fucking her. I want to know where her head is regarding publishing the story."

I toss my puke-decorated flannel into the hamper and undress. "You're asking if I questioned her while she vomited?"

"No. I'm asking if you questioned her when you visited her office *or* when you spent your night canoodling with her in the pub's corner. Please make sure the story isn't run."

"I know for sure she's not running it in this week's paper. How did you know I was in her office today?"

"Her assistant, Melanie."

"Is Lauren aware you're chatting it up with Chloe's assistant, Melanie?"

"I'm not *chatting it up* with anyone. Melanie is fooling around with Joey and told him. Joey relayed the message to me."

Damn Joey.

No more women advice from me for him.

"So, you used Joey's big mouth to your advantage?" I ask.

"Obviously." He sighs. "Give me the fucking details on what's running through her head."

"I was hoping for a bedtime story first."

"Once upon a time, a dude needed to give his friend details. He didn't. Got his fucking head ripped off. The end."

"I love a happy ever after." I grab a towel and turn on the shower. "I think I made myself clear, but I'll talk to her again, okay?"

"Thank you." He sighs again. "Tell her she owes you a favor for your drunk babysitting."

I grin. "Don't worry; I intend on letting her know."

CHAPTER THREE

CHLOE

Yesterday morning, I thought my ex tying the knot would be the lowest thing to happen to me. I was so wrong. Somehow, my mission to escape thoughts of Kent derailed me straight into the company of a man I'd been avoiding for years.

I drank with him, allowed him to drive me home, and gave him the keys to my house to escort me inside.

He was in my bedroom, for Christ's sake.

I'm appalled at myself for admitting how I received most of my orgasms in my last relationship.

Today's to-do list: research realtors and vacate my ass out of here ASAP.

While I shower, my head pounds with a reminder of every sip I took last night, praying Kyle doesn't deliver his morning greeting. Maybe he'll see me as a weird, self-pleasuring freak he no longer wants to live next to.

Maybe he'll move.

Fingers crossed.

Doubt it.

He pressed me for every detail about the morning Kent had walked in on me. I don't know if it was the drinks I'd consumed or Kyle seeming sincere for once in his life that drove me to spill the embarrassing story.

I get dressed and opt for flats rather than heels. It's easier to run in them. Operation Avoid Kyle is now in full force, and my first mission is to sprint to my car as soon as I open my door. I find my bag on the couch and shuffle through it in search of my keys.

Nothing.

Maybe he left them in my car.

I suck in a calming breath and open my front door.

"Good morning!" His voice is louder than usual, closer than usual, more annoying than usual.

I shriek, my coffee falling from my hand and splattering onto my porch, and my heart stops in my chest.

Kyle is standing on *my* front porch, smiling in front of me.

My mouth drops open. "You've got to be kidding me," I mutter under my breath. I guess I didn't scare him away last night. "This is getting out of hand," I add when he bends down to pick up my coffee mug. "And stalker-like."

He sets the cup and lid on the porch railing, and there's mischief in his smile.

Oh shit.

"What? You spilling your coffee? It is clumsy, you know."

"No. You showing up at my door."

"I was in your bedroom last night."

"That doesn't sound less stalker-like."

His smile turns playful. "Shut it, Fieldgain. I didn't come over to admit I peeped through your windows and sniffed your panties. I came for reimbursement."

I blink. "I'm sorry, reimbursement?"

He nods. "Yes. It's time to pay your debt."

"Excuse me? I don't owe you shit unless it's a swift kick in the nuts for being on my property, *uninvited.*"

He appears entertained while leaning back on his heels. "I was invited last night. The invite is valid for a full twenty-four hours."

I roll my eyes. "Seriously?"

"Yes. You told me to stop by whenever I wanted, remember?"

I park my hands on my hips. "Those words left my mouth alongside the vomit?"

"You. Owe. Me. Now, I have a few options on payment."

I scoff, "I owe you for being a decent human being?"

He points to me and snaps his fingers. "Correct."

I clench my teeth and tap my foot. "I can't believe I'm entertaining this, but what are my *options*?"

He holds a finger up. "One: we have morning sex."

I snort. "Not happening."

He holds up a second finger. "Two: we have sex after work this evening."

"Next."

He adds another finger to the mix. "Three: you take me to breakfast." When I don't answer, he gestures to my empty cup. "Unless you plan on slurping it from the ground, you need a fresh cup."

While taking my sweet time to determine my next move with him, I get chills when I realize he's not bare-chested today.

What a shame.

Instead, he's giving me the gorgeous view of him in his blue uniform again—another one fitting him perfectly.

Definitely not a shame.

Whichever sight he delivers never fails to turn me on. My nipples tighten, and I wonder what it'd be like to strip his uniform off and for him to use his handcuffs on me.

I nearly fall over in embarrassment, and my eyes meet his at the sound of him clearing his throat.

A cocky smirk plays at his lips. "Chloe, while I appreciate you checking me out, unless you plan on doing something about it, let's not make my dick hard, okay?"

It takes me a moment to pull myself together, and I gesture to the door. "If breakfast is what you want, come on in. There are Cheerios and Pop-Tarts in my pantry. Have at it."

Here I go again, being stupid.

Who invites their enemy into their home *again*?

People in horror movies who wind up murdered—that's who.

"As much as I'd love to come in and have you serve me breakfast —" he begins.

"Serve?" I interrupt with a snort. "I'd throw it to you and walk out the door."

My answer further amuses him. "Shirley's Diner. I can drive us, or you can meet me there in five."

I feign annoyance.

He grins.

"Fine," I deadpan. "Thirty minutes. One pancake."

"Forty minutes. *Two* pancakes."

"Jesus. Just fucking follow me." I yell his name to stop him, and he turns to leave.

"Decide on a better offer, one involving us in your bed?" he asks with a raised brow.

"You wish. Where are my keys?"

"I might know the answer to your question."

"Are you kidding me?" I screech. "You jacked my keys?"

"Technically, you gave them to me, but I kept them to lock your door on my way out. You should thank me for eliminating the risk of you being executed in your sleep."

I push my open palm his way. "Hand them over."

He pats the pocket by his groin, and I notice the outline of keys underneath the fabric. "I'd prefer if you grabbed them. The pockets are tiny, so smaller hands would do better to rescue them."

I take a deep breath. "The longer you play your games, the shorter time we spend at breakfast. Choose your battles, Lane."

My mouth waters at the idea of going forward and startling him by grabbing my keys. I'd love to watch his reaction if I did reach in, graze his cock, and then pull them out slowly and torturously.

I don't though because not only am I a chickenshit, but he also drags them out and dumps them in my hand seconds later.

"I hope you bring your appetite." He shifts around and strides to his new Jeep.

I further check him out and shrug with no shame before walking to my car.

Shirley's Diner is packed with people stuffing their stomachs with every breakfast food imaginable. The diner has been a staple here for longer than I've been alive. Blue Beech, Iowa, is a small town where everybody knows everybody. Most residents reside in town, in comfortable neighborhoods void of dilapidated homes, or are lucky to own acres of land.

Me? I was raised on the outskirts, given the name West Side Trash decades ago. There's no cute '50s-themed diner within walking distance of the west side. It's at least a mile walk anywhere—the school, Town Square, any stores.

I pledged I'd move from the west side trailer park I had grown up in when I made enough money. I did. Unfortunately, my sister and mother refuse to do the same. They both live in the same run-down double-wide with my niece and nephew. Don't get me wrong. I don't judge people from there, but it's where most of the crime takes place.

Shirley gives Kyle a grin when we walk in and seats us, muttering something about giving us his favorite booth.

Of course he has a favorite.

Unlike other patrons who aren't the biggest fans of my family, she greets me with a friendly smile while we sit down, and she takes our orders.

No matter what other people think about my family, Shirley has never let outside influence change her opinion of me. In high school, I'd come to the diner to do homework, and Shirley always brought me free milkshakes.

I order a coffee, scrambled eggs, and toast. If I'm stuck with him, I might as well eat.

"What's your favorite breakfast food?" Kyle asks from across the booth when our food is dropped off.

"I don't have one," I answer with honesty.

He dramatically gasps at my answer. "What? Who doesn't have a favorite breakfast food? Pancakes or waffles with delicious maple syrup." He tips his head back and groans. "Mmm … chicken and waffles."

Goose bumps run up my arms. His food-loving groan turns me on.

I am ridiculous.

When he glimpses at me, I shrug, acting like I wasn't imagining him making the same groan while inside me. "I grew up on generic cereal and toast, so I wouldn't consider any of those as my favorite."

Even now that I can afford decent breakfast foods, it's never been my thing—most likely because of skipping meals in college in favor of studying.

His eyebrows scrunch together. "I'm sorry, but what does that have to do with not having a favorite breakfast food?"

I straighten my napkin in my lap. "I'm not a breakfast person. Sue me."

He points his fork in my direction, syrup dripping from the ends. "One day, I'll make you breakfast in bed. You'll eat my pancakes while naked and love every bite. Watch and see."

I snort. "You've lost your mind."

This conversation needs to take a different turn, pronto. It's making me imagine things I shouldn't. Eating his pancakes while naked *does* sound like a fun time.

He drops his fork and focuses all his attention on me. "All right then. Chloe Fieldgain is not a breakfast person; got it. Let's move on to the next question. What is your favorite food then?"

I chew on my lower lip. "I don't have a favorite food."

I'm not a foodie. I live on a diet of salads and quick meals. It's not entertaining, cooking for one.

He gapes at me. "Everyone has a favorite food, Chloe. If you picked one thing to eat for the rest of your life, what would it be?"

I hate the question. It's a typical first-date question that no one has ever asked me.

Shit.

This is most definitely not a date.

I drum my fingers against the table while thinking. "Uh … grilled chicken, I guess."

"Grilled chicken?" he slowly repeats in a disapproving tone, making me feel judged. "Grilled chicken is the one thing you'd pick to eat for the rest of your life?"

I shrug. "Why not? It's healthy and easy to make."

I had my fair share of cooking for four when I was younger. It's a chore now.

He gives me a confident smile. "Jesus, as your neighbor, I'm officially taking it upon myself to change your favorite meal into something less boring."

I glare at him in reluctance. "All right then, favorite meal judge, what's yours?"

It doesn't take him but a second to answer. "Pussy." The word falls from his lips with pride and no shame, as if he'd said it was chocolate cake.

The one word causes me to spit out my coffee.

He smirks at my reaction. "It's organic."

I cover my face with my napkin and shake my head before cleaning up the mess. "There are so many things disturbing about your answer … about your *favorite food*."

"*Disturbing?*" He raises his brow as a teasing smile plays over his lips. Yes, the man loves fucking with me. "What is so *disturbing* about it?"

I start to answer, but he cuts me off and continues talking. "I'm not surprised that someone whose boyfriend never sufficiently ate her pussy would find my answer disturbing. I'm sorry your orgasm-abandoned personality finds it disturbing, but a quick tip for when you find another boyfriend: you'd better pray it's his favorite meal." He grabs his coffee and leans back in the booth. "I'd suggest making it a first-date question."

I can't stop from smiling even though he just talked shit about me and insulted my personality. *Orgasm-abandoned? Who says that? Hell, what does it even mean?*

"You're seriously depraved." I grab my coffee and rest my elbows on the table as the cup dangles from my fingers. I take a slow drink and continue. "Maybe it's why I've hated you all these years."

He sets his mug down and leans across the table, lowering his voice so that only I hear. "You didn't hate me that night."

I push against his forehead with my palm, and he relaxes in the booth, not one bit alarmed I forehead-slapped him.

"You need to quit with that bullshit before I throw my coffee in your face."

He drapes his arm along the booth. "In high school ... I did a shitty thing."

"No shit, Sherlock."

As painfully as I want to deny it, regret is on his face.

"I've felt like a douchebag since then."

"You should."

My gaze lowers to my eggs before reaching Kyle's eyes again. We're inches apart, and it takes us seconds for our gazes to connect. I can't resist pouring all my emotions out, needing him to witness the hurt he caused me, and we create the connection I wanted with him so many years ago.

"You could've fixed it, you know," I say, soft-spoken.

He doesn't look away. "It wasn't that simple."

"It was that simple."

He gulps, his Adam's apple bobbing. "I'm sorry."

A child screaming in the background breaks our connection, and I shut my eyes, shake my head, and withdraw, my back against the booth again.

"Whatever," I finally mutter, opening my eyes. "It doesn't matter anymore."

"Obviously, it does since you bring it up every time we talk." His face remains serious, and he pinches the bridge of his nose. "I'm fucking sorry, Chloe. I don't know how many more times you want me to say it. Tell me what I need to do to make it up to you. Go ahead. As long as it's not cutting off my balls or some shit, I'm willing."

There's nothing he can do to change it now. The damage is done.

Although this is the first time he's offered to make up for what he did instead of giving me a simple apology.

"I don't like this Kyle," I grumble. I need the smart-ass Kyle who's easier to hate to return—not the guy who takes care of me when I'm drunk and then insists on having breakfast together.

He raises a brow while studying me. "What Kyle?"

"The nice, no-ulterior-motive Kyle."

He takes a bite of his neglected breakfast and swallows it down. "How do you know I don't have an ulterior motive?"

"Do you?"

He shrugs. "Possibly."

I glare at him. "Of course you do. You want to make sure I don't run the story about Lauren." I shake my head and roll my eyes. *Go figure.* "We've been neighbors for months, and you've never invited me to breakfast. Will you threaten and harass me about her story until the day I die?"

"Technically, you telling me to fuck off daily never gave me the notion you'd enjoy a meal with me, but last night confirmed you don't hate me as much as you lead on." He smirks. "And we both know you're smart enough not to run the story since I made myself clear on the repercussions."

I narrow my eyes his way. "What makes you so sure I won't?"

He shrugs and settles back so casually that you'd think we were discussing the weather. "You're smart. Always have been."

"Except when I hang out with you."

"No, that's smart. Who doesn't want to hang out with me? You seemed to enjoy it last night. I'm cool as shit."

"Negative. Men who are *cool as shit* don't do what you did, and they most definitely don't threaten women not to publish stories in what you so kindly referred to as a *pitiful* newspaper. So, what gives?"

"I was a fucking kid, Chloe, for the millionth goddamn time. Kids do stupid shit."

"You're right. Kids toilet-paper houses or sneak out. They don't cross lines like you did."

He pushes his plate forward and stares at me with intent and annoyance. "My only *ulterior motive* is convincing you to get to know me and realize I'm not the villain you paint me out to be. I want us to share some meals and *maybe* share some orgasms. You know, I've wanted to finish what we started in high school."

I pour more sugar into my coffee even though it's unnecessary. His words piss me off. "Your behavior didn't show that."

"True, but I'll make it up to you. Don't waste orgasms by giving them to a vibrator."

I take a drink and cringe at the sweetness. "How do you know I don't have a boyfriend?"

"I was the one who took you home and tucked you in last night, and you're having breakfast with me. If you do, he's another shit boyfriend you should dump."

"And what?" I raise a brow. "Sleep with you?"

"If it's what you need, I don't mind taking on the job." He holds his hand up but drops it as soon as his phone buzzes with a text. "It's Gage. He'll be here in five to pick me up."

"In the squad car?" I question.

He nods.

"Does he always drive?"

I've seen them come and go, and Kyle always seems to be riding passenger. I'm not sure why I've paid attention. It could be because Kyle enjoys being in charge, which means, being in the driver's seat, so it makes me wonder why he doesn't ever drive.

He nods again.

"Do you feel emasculated?" *Ugh, I sound like Kent. Ew.*

"For not driving? Fuck no. Gage has gone through some rough shit. If driving helps him, he can have the keys anytime he wants."

"Things like what?" I've heard the rumors but never known what was true and what wasn't. I considered writing a piece on it but decided against it after no one would say a word to me.

"I would never put my best friend's business out there. Loyalty is a big deal to me."

"But you had no problem putting my business out there," I fire back. "You had no problem with people talking about *me*."

"You weren't and aren't my best friend." He says it matter-of-factly, no bullshit, like his loyalty only falls on those he deems worthy.

"Glad to know. I'll be sure to never tell you my personal business."

He cocks his head to the side and smirks. "Earn my loyalty, and you can."

I ignore his comment and take another drink of the Candy Land–tasting coffee. Our teenage waitress, who should probably be on her way to high school, hands him the bill without even glancing at me.

He pulls it away when I go to grab it.

"I've got this," I say in a demanding tone. I try to snatch it from his hand but with no success. "You said *I* owed you breakfast."

"Did I?" He fakes confusion and scratches his head. "I thought I said I'd take you to breakfast."

I push my hand out further. "Give me the damn bill."

"How about … no?" He pulls out his wallet and drags out a fifty without bothering to glance at the bill. "Keep the change," he says, handing it to the waitress.

She gives him a girlie smile I would've given every Backstreet Boy in my day. "Thank you so much, Kyle."

He smiles in return—not in a disturbing, *I like to creep on younger girls* way, but more of a genuine one. "You're welcome."

What gives?

Why would he tip a pre-algebra student so much money?

The waitress skips away in excitement, and I scoff.

He flinches. "What?"

"Look at you, Mr. Dreamy Eyes Keep the Change."

"Mad I'm not making dreamy eyes at you?" He inches forward. "I'm not hitting on her. Her father walked out on the family a few weeks ago. Her mother works here as well, and they're barely making ends meet. If an extra tip helps them out, then I'll give her an extra tip."

I hate that this turns me on. "That's, uh … very nice of you."

"Again, I've tried to tell you that I'm a nice guy. Let me know when you're done lying to yourself."

I roll my eyes. "Okay, okay, you're *such a nice guy*, Kyle. There's no other man nicer than you. When people tell tales about this century, you'll be the man they call the *nicest*. You will be put in history books as Mr. Nice Guy."

He grins. "Quit giving me the sarcastic attitude, Chloe. It makes me want you more."

My stomach flutters, and my gaze on him softens.

God, why do I have to hate this man?

Why can't he stay Voldemort evil?

I push my coffee up the table and set my napkin next to it. "I need to get to work. We've shared a meal. Now, we're even."

He shakes his head and clicks his tongue against the roof of his mouth. "Wrong. We're nowhere near even."

"The hell?" I do a sweeping gesture of me in the booth. "This was my payback."

"No. Breakfast was for me driving you home. You still owe me for dealing with your puking ass. Three shared meals in return for my kindness."

"Are you kidding me?" I yelp. "You never mentioned there were numerous debts owed."

He bites into his lower lip in humor. "I must've forgotten that part."

I throw my arms up and then drop them to my sides. "I don't have time to play games with you. I have a job to get to."

"Second order of business: as previously discussed, no digging up information on people I care about. Promise me."

So, this is why I'm getting nice Kyle.

Duh. He's not doing this for no reason.

"You know damn well I can't promise that."

"Actually, it's quite simple for you."

"*Fine*, I won't publish any stories."

He nods, accepting my answer as if he were my authority. "Third order of business: have dinner with me tonight."

"Not happening."

He crosses his arms behind his neck. "I'll visit you at work for lunch then. We'll enjoy a romantic picnic in your office. I'll find a basket and a red tablecloth to set the mood."

My gaze darts around the diner. Briefly, I forgot we weren't alone. "Fine, dinner at *your* house."

"Cool. See you at six."

"Whatever. I have work to do."

He tilts his head toward the window when Gage pulls up. "Me, too. See you tonight." He winks. "Wear one of those cute skirts I like."

"Wear that muzzle I like."

He grins. "I love when you get kinky on me."

CHAPTER FOUR

CHLOE

AGE THIRTEEN

Dear Diary,
  I hate my bedroom.
My friend Holly's is prettier.
It's pink, and she has a real bed, not a mattress on the floor like mine.
She lives in the same trailer court. Her parents are poor, too, but at least they give her something pretty.

Meanwhile, my bedroom walls are a dingy yellow from cigarette smoke.

I throw my diary down and lower my head, glaring at the worn, stained comforter.

Ugh. Just writing about it makes me hate my life more.

I pick up the book next to me and open it.

Time to take myself to a happier place where I have a father, a mother who doesn't suck, and an older sister who isn't mean fifty times a day for no reason.

"Hey, Chloe. What are you reading there?"

I peek up from my book to find my sister's boyfriend, Sam, standing in the cramped doorway. I smile before holding up the book, so he can read the cover.

"*The Lion, The Witch, and The Wardrobe*, huh?" he asks. "Your sister said you enjoyed reading."

"I love to read." I wait for him to make fun of me like Claudia, my sister, does.

She's been dating Sam for a few months now. I only saw him a few times before, but lately, he's been coming around more. My mother hated him at first, calling him filthy names and then sinking so low as to demand he pay her to see my sister. She needed the money to buy drugs and alcohol.

He pays her now—most likely because my sister is younger, and I'd guess he's around my mother's age. Now, she doesn't mind as much.

Neither do I.

Sam is handsome. He reminds me of a character from some of the romance novels I shouldn't check out of the library. He's tall with dark hair and broad shoulders and maturer than my sister. It's not unusual for her to date older men, but she's never brought someone home like Sam. He doesn't lick his lips or ogle me, making me uncomfortable because my mom won't buy me a training bra, and my nipples poke through my shirts.

He leans against the doorframe. "Girls who like to read are those with a bright future ahead of them. Their imaginations can take them anywhere."

I crawl to the edge of the mattress and settle myself Indian-style. "My sister doesn't like to read."

He chuckles. "Yes, I am well aware."

"Why do you like her then?"

Claudia is gorgeous, and even at eighteen, she could pass for someone old enough to get into bars. Mama lets her go with her sometimes, too. Claudia is also mean and selfish, and she isn't the big sister girls dream of.

"Your sister excels in other areas," he replies.

"Like sex?"

My response surprises him.

He raises a brow and points to my book. "Keep reading. Excel at that."

He walks away before I can reply.

The next day, he returns with a box of books—brand-new books!

"These are for you," he says. "Keep reading, Chloe."

"Thank you!" I squeal, hastily searching through the box. I grab a copy of a Sarah Dessen book and hug it to my chest. "Thank you so much!" The book hits the floor with a thud when I jump up to give him a hug.

When he leaves, I grab my diary and write about how nice Sam is.

CHAPTER FIVE
CHLOE

My stomach fills with dread when I see the name flashing across my phone screen. My finger wavers over the Ignore button for a few seconds but eventually moves to answer it.

I clench the phone in my hand. "Hello?"

"What is wrong with you?" Claudia shrieks on the other line. "Marsha said she saw you having breakfast with Kyle Lane this morning."

My sister is best known for her overdramatic behavior.

Scratch that.

She's best known as being a scam artist.

An alcoholic.

An opportunist.

Overdramatic runs in fourth.

"Good morning to you, too," I grumble, rubbing my forehead.

I can't share pancakes with someone without it being talked about.

Good thing I run the headlines in this town.

"Did you fall and smack your head? I know you're still mourning the loss of your snooze-fest relationship with Kent, but Kyle Lane is bad news."

"Noted."

She's irritated, but her not continuing her rant confirms this isn't a courtesy call. She wants something from me.

"Go ahead and say it," I finally mutter.

"I need you to watch the kids tonight."

"I can't. I have plans."

I'm not a fan of helping and enabling her, but normally, I have no problem with babysitting my niece and nephew, Gloria and Trey. I wish she'd act like a mom and take responsibility for them instead of putting it all on me.

"With who?" she snaps, the attitude resurfacing. "*Kyle?*"

Even though she can't see me, I tip my chin up. "My plans are none of your business."

We've never had a relationship where we share beauty secrets or boy advice. We only share conversations when it concerns the kids or she needs money.

"Do those *plans* involve Kyle?"

I release a long sigh. "It's a work thing, not that it's any of your concern. I'm available after seven."

"Cool. I'll drop them off then."

The line goes dead.

Claudia is as grateful to me for watching her kids as those obnoxious twits on *My Super Sweet 16* for their extravagant birthday parties.

Helping her is expected of me—has been for years. Like my mother, whose demise will be her strict diet of vodka and endless opiates, she's entitled. If someone has something of value, she demands a slice. Free rides are hitting the jackpot, and Claudia views me as her money train to support her partying.

I drop my phone in my bag before getting out of my car and heading to my office. My head throbs with every step I take up the stairs. It's not even lunchtime, and I've already dealt with Kyle and Claudia.

"Homegirl, you are in *trouble*," Melanie sings as soon as I walk in, her feet kicked up on the desk.

Her loud voice makes my head hurt, but it's nothing compared to the shrill of Claudia's.

I shrug off my jacket and settle it on my arm. "I can be late for once."

She snorts and drops her feet, smoothing out her skirt. "I don't give two shits about your punctuality. What I'm referring to is, you looking like you were up all night, drinking or sexing it up—or possibly both."

"You have no idea," I grumble while heading toward my office.

"The rumors are true then?"

I stop mid-step. "What rumors?"

She sits on the edge of her chair in excitement. "Word is, you left Down Home with Kyle last night and then had breakfast with him this morning."

Seriously?

Joke's on me. The woman who writes other people's stories is now the face of the town gossip.

"Word is, people need to mind their damn business," I grumble.

This is not what my hangover needs at the moment.

"He took me home and left last night. This morning, I spilled my coffee when he came over to give me my keys, and he offered to buy me another. Just two neighbors sharing a meal. No biggie."

She glowers, confirming I'm full of bullshit, before her face turns somewhat serious. "You know I'm all for you getting laid, but make him a booty call only. That's it. You get an orgasm and get the hell out of there, girlfriend. His family is no joke about protecting their image and not letting outsiders in."

She's right. Like Kyle, his family is royalty here. His dad is the mayor, his grandfather a judge, and his mother the biggest philanthropist in the town. Blue Beech isn't full of people with money, except the Lane family. They've owned this town for decades.

"Trust me," I say. "There's nothing going on between us."

———

I don't wear one of those skirts he likes.

I wear yoga pants and an old tee.

"I'm actually doing this," I say to myself while pulling my hair into a sloppy ponytail.

Sure, I've shared drinks and meals with Kyle, but dinner at his home is intimate. There will be no crowd around and no puking involved. Kyle obviously wants to have sex, and I'd be a liar if I said I didn't want the same.

Last time we had dinner, it ruined me. No one was supposed to find out, but they did.

When they did, Kyle came out unscathed.

Everyone loved him, his family, and their wealth.

Guys wanted to be his best friend. Girls wanted to be his girlfriend or current screw. Even I was guilty of the last two, which was what pulled me into the mess of him. He was nice when no one else even glimpsed in my direction.

Turned out, he wasn't the nice guy he'd played off to be, and I'm scared he's playing the same deprived game.

I walk through Kyle's front door without bothering to knock. He doesn't respect my privacy. Therefore, he doesn't deserve his. I check out the living room after the door shuts behind me. I expected the interior of Kyle's home to scream bachelor pad with neon signs and poker tables, but it's nowhere close. While there is a flat screen TV set up on the wall and a saddle-brown leather sofa, it's clean with dark pillows and a bookcase filled with books and pictures of him and his family.

I follow the noise of dishes clinking and the scent of food into the kitchen to find Kyle standing at the island with a beer in his fist and dishes set out in front of him. I figured we'd have pizza or takeout, but it smells of comfort food—similar to how Kent's mother's would when she spent all day in the kitchen.

What the ...

Surely, he didn't cook for us.

"We need to make this quick," I say.

He grins as if my outburst wasn't rude. "Mmm ... I'm not normally into quick the first time, but I'll make an exception for you."

"Hilarious," I deadpan. "I'm babysitting in an hour."

"Not cool. You agreed to dinner." He's scolding me as if I were a child, like he's the one who has to babysit *me*.

I throw my hands up. "I'm here, aren't I?"

He sets his beer down and walks around the island, resting against the counter and pushing his hands into his pockets. He's in jeans, a tee fitting the vast expanse of his chest, and barefoot. "And? Our dinner will take longer than an hour."

I blow out a frustrated breath. "Wrong. Whatever you're cooking will take me ten minutes to eat." I smile. "I'm a fast eater."

He tsks under his breath. "You're lucky your escape plan is kid-sitting. Otherwise, I'd make you cancel."

Make me?

He's given himself the control tonight, and apparently, my spine has flattened because the urge to take that control back is nonexistent.

"How sweet of you," I mutter.

He shoves off the counter, takes the few steps separating us, and captures my chin in his hand.

I draw in a breath and surprisingly don't jerk away.

He uses one finger to tilt my chin up before cupping it, his finger sweeping along my skin, and his emerald-green eyes scream determination while he appraises me as if I were an expensive item he was debating on purchasing. "I'm sweet when necessary, dear neighbor, and as you're well aware, not sweet when necessary."

Is he flirting with me or threatening me?

I don't catch my breath until he drops my chin and turns away. I glance around the kitchen, debating on if I should leave.

"We should get started. You're not bailing before dessert," he says. He snatches his beer again and points at me with it. "What's your drink of choice?"

"Water, please."

Alcohol combined with Kyle is a bad idea unless my plan is to drop my panties or throw up on him—or possibly both.

"Water it is." He opens the fridge and draws out a bottle of water *and* a wine cooler before holding the cooler up. "In case you do want a drink, I snagged a few of these. When my sister was a teenager, she'd sneak and drink them. There's hardly any alcohol in them. Serving you anything stronger might result in you painting my walls with the wonderful dinner I've prepared for us."

His joke eases me, and I smile. "With the hangover I'm suffering from, I don't even want to think about consuming alcohol."

He settles the drinks down in front of me, and a pleasant smell covers the room when he opens the oven, drags out a pan, and places it on the island. I push forward on my toes to get a better view.

My attention flies to him. "You cooked this?" *There's no way.*

Chicken coated with spices, vegetables, and potatoes are in the pan. My stomach growls at the sight. I haven't had a home-cooked meal like this since last Christmas with Kent's parents.

"Negative," he answers. "My mother did. I'm heating it up. It has to count for something, right?"

I can't help but smirk. "Aw, how cute. His mommy made dinner for his forced non-date."

He drops the oven gloves on the counter and smiles at me. "Shove it, Fieldgain. My mother's cooking is the fucking best and is better than anything I can pull together. I prefer to impress you, not give you food poisoning."

I tilt my head his way. "Appreciate that."

I drag out a breath, watching Kyle move around the room to gather up everything. It's hot. He's not the chef tonight, but he's no stranger to the kitchen.

He prepares our plates, grabs the silverware, and directs me to the four-person table across the room.

He takes the chair next to me when everything is situated. "How was your day, honey?" His fingers circle around the neck of his beer, and he takes a drink while waiting for me to answer.

I narrow my eyes his way. "Don't make this all domestic."

He's not thrown off his game at my response. "All right then, how the fuck was your day, you goddamn pain in the ass?"

I shrug. "Now, that brings me back to my dinners as a child." At least, when my mother wasn't too drunk to sit with us.

"Same."

I raise a brow at the same time I snort. "Yeah, right. The Lanes are the picture-perfect family." I cough. "I mean, it's what everyone says. I wouldn't know."

He sets down his beer and leans back in the chair. "Looking in from the outside? Sure. Inside? No. My mother and father despise each other. They're experts at hiding it in public."

His parents not having a healthy relationship isn't surprising. His father is an asshole. Most people in this town, friend or foe, wouldn't dare mutter a bad word about the mayor. The people on the lower end of the totem pole, we speak about him. It might be in hushed whispers, but it's known that his father isn't a stand-up gentleman.

"Dig in," he says, breaking me away from my thoughts. "We only have an hour."

I take the first bite and moan.

It's delicious.

I'd so hire Kyle's mom as my chef if I ever won the lottery.

"This is amazing," I comment before taking another bite.

He sticks his chest out in mock over-the-top pride. "Ding! One point for Kyle."

"One point for Kyle's mom," I correct.

"Give a man credit now. You said your favorite meal was grilled chicken. I made sure that's what you got." He shrugs and moves in closer until our elbows are touching. His eyes meet mine. "Maybe I'll get my favorite meal tonight, too."

I nearly choke on my bite and use my water to help me swallow it down while he laughs in the background. "You enjoy catching me off guard, don't you?"

"I enjoy it more than you think. Hearing you tell me to fuck off is music to my ears."

I take another drink of my water. "Subject change, please." I glance at my watch. "You're running low on time, Officer Lane."

"Okay, Miss Fast Eater, let's see the proof."

I take a huge bite, and he laughs.

He's hardly touched his food. All he's doing is giving me the same deep stare he gave me earlier when I first walked in. His gaze is intense, but his words are playful. "Any hot plans this weekend? Going out, searching for a new boyfriend?"

I swallow down my bite. "Hey now, someone who's single can't talk shit about a fellow single person. At least I've been in a long-term relationship."

"How do you know I haven't had or am not in one now?"

That shuts my ass up for a moment.

He laughs. "Wow, I've never heard you go so quiet before. I'm patiently waiting for your smart-ass response." He takes a drink. "And for your information, I have had a serious relationship. Becky Binds, to be exact," he says proudly. "You going to run a story about that? I can give you plenty of details if need be."

I snort. "That does *not* qualify as a long-term relationship."

"Why, Ms. Relationship Expert 101?"

"It wasn't real. It was superficial and lasted, like, three months." I slam my mouth shut. *Oh shit.* Now, I seem like a total stalker. It's embarrassing, but I paid attention to Kyle and his relationships after our fallout happened.

"Is there a statute of limitations for relationships?" he asks.

I'm relieved at his lack of teasing about my knowledge of his bull-shit relationship statuses in high school. I hated Becky's guts. They dated after our incident, and she made it her mission to make my life a living hell, even spreading rumors about me and creating the not-so-original, taunting chant that followed me down the high school hallways.

"High school relationships don't count," I state. "Are you currently the boyfriend of a poor girl who needs to find better taste?"

"*Poor girl?* Interesting, coming from a woman having dinner with me at my house, and even more interesting since said chick had drinks with me last night."

"The woman who was *forced* to come to dinner and can leave at any time," I correct with a cold glare.

"No one forced you to walk your sexy ass over here. You could've easily stood me up."

I hate that he's right. "*Fine*, I was hungry. Now, any crazy girlfriends I should worry about that will make it their mission to ruin my life if they find out I'm having dinner here?"

He lets out a breath. "Not dating anyone, so I'm all yours, babe."

I ignore the *all yours* comment. "I was right then."

"Not entirely. I recently ended a relationship."

I perk up in my seat. "Why?"

He shrugs. "It wasn't there."

"Do I know her?"

"No. Lauren set me up with a nurse from the hospital. It was fun for a while, but our schedules were chaotic and made it difficult to see each other. She wasn't next door and available whenever I needed her."

"I'm not sleeping with you, so if that's your game plan here, you're wasting your time. I'm sure it won't be hard for you to find another Becky Binds."

He strokes his chin and laughs. "My sweet Chloe, were you jealous of Becky Binds for having me?"

I fake a grimace. "Negative. How could I be jealous of someone who possibly had chlamydia and was a terrible person in high school? Again, I'm not sleeping with you." My repetition is to also convince myself.

"We don't have to sleep together. We can do other things and then go sleep in our own beds."

I suck in a breath. The thought of not sleeping but sleeping together turns me on more than it should. "You'd better quit before I leave."

He holds his hands up. "Okay, okay. Let's eat."

Our conversation takes a turn, and I'm surprised by how comfortable we are with each other. He tells me about the police station drama, and I complain about my office being a snooze-fest. As our plates clear, we take things to a more personal level, and I tell him about Gloria and Trey and how they're the reason I'm still in Blue Beech. I don't trust Claudia to care for them. Kyle has still made his fair share of smart-ass comments, but nothing to make me want to kick him in the balls for.

My phone beeps in my bag. There hasn't been one boring minute with us, so there was no need to check it.

"Check it," Kyle says, referring to it.

I grab it to find a text.

Claudia: Be there in 20.

"Your sister?" he asks.

I slip my phone into my bag. "Yep."

He wipes his mouth with a napkin. "How much time do we have?"

"Twenty minutes." I stop and hold up a finger. "Fifteen. She can't see me leaving your house."

"That pipes up a man's ego."

"She'll give me shit. She hates you."

He scrunches his face up. "She has no reason to hate me."

"She hates you by proxy. I hate you, so she hates you."

I set my phone down without bothering to text her back and grab my plate to clean up.

Kyle rises from his chair. "Don't worry about it."

I shake my head. "Nope. You cooked—*heated up*." I laugh. "It's only fair I clean."

I move faster than him, but he catches up seconds later and grabs the plate from my hand at the same time I'm about to set it on the counter.

He whips me around to face him and stands inches from me. "I'll let you clean next time."

"Whoa," I say, forcing myself to make my response sound like a joke, but inside, my heart is racing. "What makes you so sure there will be a next time?"

His hands go to each side of me, his palms resting on the surface of the counter, and his arms block me from moving around him. I inhale his masculine scent before peeking up at him in time to catch the way his eyes skim up and down my body.

"You promised me three dates, sweet Chloe," he whispers, tipping his head down and burying his face in the curve of my neck.

Goose bumps travel down my spine, and my traitorous body aches for him to touch me, to kiss me, to do all the things he's made comments about doing.

I gulp, fighting to stand my ground. "Three meals," I correct.

He groans into my neck before dropping kisses along my sensitive skin. "Fine, three *meals*, but you're bailing early on this one. So, you owe me another half." He sucks on my skin next, as if he wants to mark me.

I release a heavy breath and throw my head back, stupidly giving him better access.

Jesus, why am I allowing myself to get caught up in him like this? Why am I so weak?

I clear my throat. "Why are you so adamant on hanging out with me, Kyle?"

"Why are you so adamant on not being around me, Chloe?" he whispers into my ear before nibbling my earlobe.

"You know why," I hiss, balancing myself against the counter. My knees are weak, and if I fall, it'll put me in line with Kyle's waist—with his crotch.

"Why?" he asks. "Is it because you hate me *or* because you can't control yourself when I'm around?" He skims his hands up my sides, causing me to let out a light whimper. "You're so used to being in control—in charge of your emotions, your life, every single thing. You've never handed control over to anyone else, have you?"

Desire rushes through me, and I blow out a nervous breath when he withdraws to lock eyes with me.

"Yes," I stutter out. "Once. I gave it to you."

He flinches but recovers. His fingers curl around my waist, and I gasp when his erection presses hard against my core.

"Do you remember how good it felt, losing control?" he asks.

I inspect the floor, but he grabs my chin again, forcing me to meet his eyes—the same as earlier.

"Be honest. I won't judge you. I'll never judge you."

His deep-set eyes impale mine. This is too personal, and I've never been this charged up before, not even with Kent—the man I planned to marry.

I finally gain the courage to say, "I'm not going there."

Before I can say or do anything, his lips capture mine.

And, just like that, I'm gone for him.

I exhale a sharp breath, and he wastes no time before sliding his tongue into my mouth. He tastes of beer and is skilled as we make out against the counter, his excitement rubbing against mine ever so slightly. I drop my head back when his lips return to my neck, sucking and licking.

"I wish I could take my time in pleasuring you," he whispers into my ear. "Unfortunately, we don't have that. You're about to receive the fastest orgasm you've ever had."

I open my mouth to object but moan instead. I could use an orgasm right now. It's been a while since I've had one not given via the vibrator Kent resented. There's no objecting to Kyle having his way with me, so I allow him to take control.

Seconds later, his fingers dip underneath the hem of my yoga pants, and he stretches them out far enough to dive straight into my panties.

"So wet for someone you hate," he says, running a finger through my drenched slit. "You might think you hate me, sweet Chloe, but your pussy seems to like me. Maybe next time, I'll bring my dick out to play."

I open my mouth to question the *next time* comment but whimper when he tugs my pants down.

"Spread your legs wider and let me get one leg out," he demands.

I do as I was told. Denying him isn't an option, but I'll regret this in the morning.

"How much easier would this have been if you'd worn the skirt like I said?"

"Quit bitching," I mutter. "We're running out of time."

And I desperately need an orgasm right now.

"Oh, how the tables have turned, my dear neighbor." He plunges a finger inside me before adding another seconds later, sliding them in and out of me. His fingers are thick and skilled, hitting me in all the right places.

I should unbuckle his pants and return the favor, but I'm too caught up in the moment. I rest my hands on his shoulders as he finger-fucks me hard.

"Does that feel good?" he whispers against my lips as he uses his thumb to circle my clit.

I nod.

"Wait until you find out how good my cock feels."

I stop myself from telling him it won't be happening, but hell, at the rate we're going, his cock will probably end up in every hole of my body.

"I need to taste you. *Fuck*."

I moan.

"Fuck it."

My breathing hitches at the loss of his fingers, and he drops to his knees. He braces one hand against my thigh, and I shiver when he plants a kiss at my opening. There isn't a long wait until his tongue dips in and out of me, and I throw my head back. It's fast. We're both sweating, and I grip the edge of the counter when his fingers work me again. His tongue moves from my slit to my clit, from my clit to my slit, repeating the teasing action.

It doesn't take long to set me off, and I'm shaking with an orgasm. He grips the outside of my thighs and holds me up.

"Holy shit," I say, catching my breath.

I glance down to find him staring at me with a wide grin and a face filled with need. He kisses both of my thighs before standing up, his hands moving to my waist.

"Holy shit," I repeat. "I cannot believe we did that."

He kisses my forehead and I'm thankful when he pulls my pants up because, right now, my body is useless.

"It's hard not to believe it when your body is trembling, and if I wasn't holding you up, you'd most likely fall to the floor."

"God, I hate you," I say with a shudder.

"I'll take that as a compliment since you just had an orgasm as a result of my tongue-fucking you." He nuzzles his head in my neck while I pull myself together. "Thank you for letting me play with your pussy tonight and for bringing dessert." He kisses my cheek. "Time for you to babysit."

I turn away in embarrassment when he draws back. "Thanks for, uh … dinner." I clear my throat. "I guess I'll see you tomorrow morning."

"See you then."

He doesn't kiss me again or make another move while I straighten myself out, grab my bag, and head to the door with so many thoughts spiraling through me.

"Oh, wait," he finally says as I'm about to walk out.

I turn around, and he hands me a plate full of brownies.

"Dessert. The kids will enjoy these."

My phone beeps.

Claudia: About to pull up.

Fuck!

"They will. Thank you." I rush out of the house and make it to my porch at the same time she arrives.

What in the flying fuck happened?

———

Claudia is two hours late to pick up the kids.

No surprise there.

She dropped them off without dinner in their bellies, so I took them to the diner. When we returned to my house, they devoured a brownie each, and then I went into full parent mode. With Gloria being four, she needs more attention than Trey. I gave her a bath and then read her a story before she crashed out in the bedroom. Trey has graduated to the guest room with a bigger bed and a smart TV.

"Is your homework finished?" I ask when I walk into the living room.

A glass of milk is in his hand, and a brownie sits on the table next to him.

He groans. "Yes, boss woman. I'm not dumb enough to bail on homework with you. Mom, yes. You, nope."

"Smart boy." I sit down on the couch across from him and cross my legs, a mug of tea in my hand.

Trey is fourteen and at the age where he'll pick up on the environment he's living in. He'll do one of two things—want a better life for himself or fall into the black hole. My sister had him young, so he grew up faster than most kids. Him being born also made me grow up faster. I fled that life as soon as I could, and I want him to be able to do the same.

"How's everything going at home?" I ask.

"Mom has a new boyfriend," he states with a straight face.

"I'm sure he's a real winner," I mutter before I can stop myself. Even though it's difficult, I try not to talk shit about Claudia in front of him.

He snorts. "Oh, yes, like all her others." He frowns. "Are you sure there's nothing you can do for us to live here?"

As much as Claudia loves to pawn her children off on me, she refuses to grant me custody. She uses them as a power trip and exploits my love and concern for them to her advantage. If it wasn't for the children, I'd have nothing to do with her.

"Trust me, buddy, I've tried," I answer with disappointment. It hurts my heart as much as it hurts theirs.

"I know," he says with a hint of a frown.

He picks a channel, a show of viral videos of people's failed stunts, and I grab my laptop to get some work done.

An hour later, Claudia pulls up. I make sure she's not high or drunk before letting the kids know she's here.

"You're late," I say when I step outside.

She brushes away her bleach-blonde hair from her face and takes another puff of her cigarette. "Shit happens, Chloe. Damn. This is your niece and nephew. Don't you love spending time with them?"

I fan the air in front of me to get rid of her cigarette smoke and draw back. "Don't patronize me. I spend more time with them than you do. Tonight, Gloria asked me why you never want to be around her like other mommies and their kids at her school. Get your shit together."

"Or what? You'll ask for custody like always?"

"I don't understand why you won't." I lower my voice. "You obviously have no interest in being a mother."

She sneers. "You're jealous." She tosses her cigarette on the ground and stomps on it with her heel. "You're childless, and your fiancé left you for another woman. Maybe you need to pay attention to your pathetic life before insulting mine."

"Fuck you, Claudia," is all I say before turning around.

I don't want my niece and nephew for my lack of children. I want to protect them from the life she's giving them.

I've adapted to her and my mother's insults, and mostly, I have become immune to them, but there are still times—*times like this*—that remind me of my misfortunes. She uses it to trigger me even though I've done nothing but help her.

People can be assholes. People can throw your misfortune in your face, even when it's unnecessary, even when you've done nothing to them. Some people aren't nice, and if there's anything I've learned from my chaotic childhood, it's that hurt people hurt other people. Misery loves company, and my family is always ready to hurl insults.

"I'm sorry. That was harsh," she calls out.

"It's nothing worse than what you've said before," I mutter while shaking my head.

I grab Gloria when she and Trey step outside and help her into her carseat while Claudia lights another cigarette and stands to the side. When she's finished, I stand on my porch and wave good-bye as they pull away. I take a deep breath and am about to go in when I hear it.

"Good night, Chloe!"

The words shoot through the night from Kyle's front porch. I glance over to find him standing beneath his bright porch light, shirtless, with a bottle of water in his hand. I shake my head, fight my smile, and flip him off before walking into my house.

At least he made me smile after the Claudia Horror Show.

CHAPTER SIX

KYLE

I'm waiting for Chloe as soon as she steps out onto her porch. From now on, I will deliver my good mornings face-to-face.

"Good morning, my dearest neighbor," I greet, not startling her this time. "I enjoyed our dinner. Next time, maybe you can bring your vibrator as the guest of honor."

I can't stop thinking about last night.

Like yesterday, I'm dressed in my uniform. I promised Gage I'd come in early and help with extra paperwork, but I didn't want to miss seeing her.

"Fuck off," she replies, fighting a smile.

Another one of those black skirts I love hugs her hourglass curves and stops at her knees, and though it's not revealing, it's sexy. Her white button-down blouse is thin, and evidence of her hard nipples shows through.

"I was down for it last night and will be later this evening. Care to make a date for it?"

She hands me her coffee tumbler and tugs her jacket over her shoulders. "Last night was a mistake, and I'd appreciate us acting like it never happened."

"A mistake I'd love to make again." I inch closer. "I'll relive it repeatedly. My brain will never forget the sound and sight of you coming for me.”

Flustered, she snatches her coffee back. “I’m being serious.”

“Let me remind you that, every time I’ve touched you, you’ve enjoyed it. Keep attempting to persuade yourself otherwise, but we both know you love my hands on you.”

She blushes. “You’re right. I enjoy you touching me. The problem is, I’ve never enjoyed the consequences.”

We’re side by side as we step off her porch and walk to her car.

“I see you still hate me for that.”

“I will always hate you for that.”

“Hate is an expensive grievance to carry in life. It shortens your life span, triggers depression, interrupts sleep—”

“I’ve hated you for years, so what harm is a little more?” she interrupts.

“Do you know what *does* lengthen your life span? Orgasms—”

She interrupts me again. “This is the part of the morning where I instruct you to fuck off.”

“You already said it.”

“Then, *fuck off* again.”

“Wow, Chloe, way to make a man feel used,” I say when we reach her car.

Instead of getting in, she rests against it, grips her coffee, and stares at me, not interested in ending our conversation.

“I seriously hate you more than the Grinch hates Christmas.”

“You need to work on your insult game. That was the worst I’ve ever heard.” I smile. “All joking aside, have dinner with me again tonight.”

She smiles back, surprising me. “*Fine*, I’ll do dinner with you tonight at *my* house, but keep your hands to yourself. Got it? This is because I don’t make deals with people and not keep them.”

I hold my hands up. “These bad boys will stay to themselves— unless you beg me for them. Deal?”

“Yeah,” she draws out, “not happening.”

I open the car door for her and help her in like the upstanding gentleman I most certainly am not, and she slides in.

I wiggle my fingers. "We'll see. Next time, you might ask for another body part of mine."

She swats at my hand holding the car door open. "You're seriously a child."

"You know that's not true." I wink and turn around at the sound of Gage pulling into my driveway. "I need to get to work now and make the world a better place. You can reward me for it later."

Fucking with Chloe Fieldgain is fun.

I wonder what fucking her will be like.

———

Gage exchanges a glance with me when I'm inside the car. "I see your neighbor has yet to murder you. First, you're having breakfast with her, and now, you're walking her to her car in the morning. What's up with that?"

"Good morning to you, too," I answer, grabbing the coffee he brought for me from the cupholder. "Jealous I didn't have breakfast with you or walk you to your car?"

"Hardly. I'll let you keep those favors for girls you tormented in high school."

"I didn't torment her. We had a rivalry."

He snorts. "Some rivalry. You wanted to bang her. She wanted to kill you."

I shrug. "Something along those lines, yes."

"She forgive you?"

"I'm working on it."

"You're wasting your time. She's despised you for over a decade. *A fucking decade.*"

"How do you know she still hates me? Until recently, you were MIA from this place for years."

He grabs his coffee and takes a drink. "Hmm … I didn't notice, dipshit."

"Don't take it as an insult. I'm damn happy you're back. Focus on our current conversation."

"I was updated on all Blue Beech–related drama," he grumbles, not impressed.

Like me, Gage couldn't give two shits about gossip.

"The big-mouthed future baby mama? I told you she was trouble."

"Shut up before I throw you out of this car."

"Yeah, yeah, yeah, so you tell me daily," I joke. "Chloe has no reason to hate me now. We're mature adults."

He gawks at me. "Holy shit, you're banging her, aren't you?"

"If only," I mutter.

He narrows his eyes and studies me. "Correction: you haven't screwed her, *but* something happened between you two, considering she didn't have a gun to your balls seconds ago." He lowers his voice. "I hate to bring this up, but do you think … *dating* her will cause tension with your father?"

"I don't give a fuck what he thinks."

The mood turns somber. "You and your dad still not speaking?"

"When necessary … for my mom." Not that I have an issue with that. The less I talk to my dad, the better my day goes.

"Maybe your relationship will get better over time—you know, like your and Chloe's."

"My relationship with him gets worse with time, and unlike Chloe, I don't want to be around him."

"I understand, man. So, you're into her, huh? I knew you crushed on her in high school, even after she told you to get fucked, but I thought you had grown out of it. You're like a kid on the playground again. How many valentines are you putting in her basket this year?"

"Piss off."

"My best friend is infatuated with a chick who hates him."

———

I smile before answering the phone. "Hello, world's best mother."

"Hi, honey," she says on the other line. "Can you pick up a few things for me at the store before coming over tonight?"

I stop walking on my journey to my desk at the station. "Tonight?"

"Yes, for your sister's birthday dinner."

I frown and pull my phone away to check my Calendar app. "Her birthday isn't for another three days."

"She has plans with Devin, so we're doing it tonight."

Devin the Douchebag.

My younger sister lives for dating the wrong dudes. They're not even the bad boys, more along the lines of fuck boys who wear sweaters with cardigans over their shoulders—which is surprising. She's the wild child out of the bunch.

"I'll be there. Send me a list of what you want me to pick up. Seven?"

"Yes, seven. I'll see you then."

I need to tell Chloe about our change of plans. I open the database and find her phone number—perk of being in law enforcement.

If texting doesn't work, I can persuade her better in person; I wouldn't mind stopping by her office for a quick visit.

CHAPTER SEVEN

CHLOE

I grab my phone from my desk when it beeps with a text.

Unknown: Hey, gorgeous.

I hit reply.

Me: Who is this?

I'm certain I know the answer to my question.

Unknown: Your favorite neighbor.

Me: Mrs. Davis?

Unknown: Let me elaborate. The neighbor who made you come last night.

Me: Mr. Davis?

The Davises are my eighty-year-old neighbors.

Unknown: Hmm … seems you need to be reminded of who your orgasms belong to. A do-over is in the works.

I sigh. I'd love for a *do-over*, but I'm not sure if sleeping with him would get in the way of my job. Not to mention, what it would do to my heart. I vowed to never let Kyle in my heart, and here I am, practically handing it over to him on a platter, ready for him to shatter it.

Me: What do you want, Kyle?

Kyle: This is a reminder of our dinner plans tonight.

Me: I don't need a reminder. I've been dreading it since this morning.

Kyle: Aw. I'm looking forward to it, too. I'll pick you up at 6:30.

Whoa. Whoa. Whoa.

Me: Pick me up? You're coming to my house, remember?

Kyle: Change of plans, sweetheart.

Me: I'm not going to your house or anywhere in public with you.

Kyle: What about my parents'?

Me: HELL TO THE NO!

I wait for his response but nothing.

Melanie groaning drags my attention from the phone to her as she staggers into my office with her hands filled with file folders.

"Hey, here are the documents you asked for," she says.

I stand to gather some from her hands and settle them down on my desk while she does the same with hers. "Thank you."

Her green eyes study me in interest. "Damn, you look hot this morning. You're sporting a special *glow*. Did you finally bang Kyle?" She winks and places one hand in a circular motion before putting her finger through it.

I came in early, so she lost her chance to interrogate me this morning.

"God, why do I like *and* employ you?"

"Because I'm awesome … and my stalking skills are legit."

She leaves when my phone rings, and I pick it up, expecting it to be Kyle, but it's someone I'd rather not talk to more than him. I roll my eyes before accepting the call.

"Hey, I need you to babysit," Claudia says as soon as I answer. "I'll drop the kids off at five."

"I have plans."

"Seriously? I need you, Chloe. I need to work to make money to take care of my family like you've lectured me about."

I scoff. "Quit lying. Your boss sent me your schedule."

"That motherfucker," she hisses. "*Fine,* I have a date."

"So do I," I lie. I have to *hang out* with Kyle.

"With who?"

My tone turns sharp. "None of your business. Maybe you should spend time with your kids for a change."

"Oh, here she goes again, Ms. I'm Better Than You."

"Never said that."

"Fuck you! I won't ask for your help again."

The line goes dead.

Doubt it will happen.

———

"Hello, dearest neighbor."

My heart races, and I jump up from my chair. I was so preoccupied with my work that I didn't hear my office door open.

"Melanie! You're fired!" I yell when I recover.

"Melanie is going out for lunch and has seen nothing," she yells from the reception area. "You kids have fun! I'll be back in *one hour*, so make it quick."

I cross my arms and settle down in my chair. "What are you doing here? We've been seeing each other more than necessary, and I'm not a fan."

Kyle smirks, shuts the door, and stands at the head of my desk. Earlier, his demeanor was carefree. Now, he looks determined with his eyes on me.

"You're not a fan of having lunch with someone?" he asks.

I gulp but hold myself together. Why does him looming over me like this make me nervous? "I prefer to eat solo, like I did throughout high school."

He shrugs off my response. "Good thing we're not in high school anymore."

"I'm not hungry for your food or your games, Kyle. I have work to do."

"So selfish," he says, casually strolling around my desk. "What if *I'm* hungry?"

I tense up but keep my voice level. "Go feed yourself then. I'm not your mom who will bake chicken whenever you ask. Go find yourself a nice Martha Stewart to hang out with because it will not be me."

"Now, why would I want a woman who cooks when I can have that smart-ass mouth of yours? Keep throwing the attitude at me. It makes me want you more."

I gulp. "The feeling is not mutual."

I hold in a gasp when he grabs the chair and turns me to face him.

"What time do you want me to pick you up? Dinner is at seven, but we can spend time together beforehand if you'd like. Maybe a quickie in my backseat?"

"Never o'clock."

"Come on, Chloe. You *loved* my mother's food along with some other perks I won't specify in your workplace. Don't you want more of that?"

What's disturbing is, I *do* want more, and him standing in front of me with his crotch practically in my face isn't helping the matter.

"What is wrong with you?" I ask, irritated. "You want me to go to the house of the man who proposed moving city lines, so the neighborhood I grew up in wouldn't be in it? He called us scums of the sewer."

"My father won't be there. He doesn't show up to family functions."

"Still not happening."

Heat spreads through my chest when he drops to his knees and glances up at me with a grin. My skin flushes when he grabs the hem of my skirt, and a chill hits me when he yanks it up. He's keeping a slight distance between us—most likely in case I kick him in the face.

"What do you think you're doing?" I hiss. My stomach tightens, and instead of kicking him in the face, I want it between my legs.

I'm frozen in place when his hands splay across my bare thighs, leading my breathing to rise while I await his next move.

"I told you, I'm hungry," he mutters. He shoves my skirt until it's scrunched around my waist, and he settles himself closer. His mouth is so close to my core that I feel his breath against it. He groans. "And no panties. I love it when you leave my snack unwrapped."

I hold in a breath when he tilts his head forward to flick his tongue up my slit.

"Oh my God," I moan.

"Spread them wider," he demands before sucking on my clit.

He grips my waist to lift me enough to adjust my skirt, settling it underneath my ass and against my back, until I'm exposed for him.

"Good girl," he praises.

His attention sets on my core before he buries his face there. I throw my head back when he dips his tongue inside me.

"How do you like me tasting your pussy?"

I answer by rocking my hips forward to meet his tongue and can tell he approves of my response when he slides a finger inside me, causing me to lose a breath.

He caresses me a few times with that single finger before dragging it out and glancing up at me. "Tell me, sweet Chloe, if I reward you with my mouth, will you come with me tonight?"

"Reward me?" I raise a brow. "You came into my office. It seems like I'm doing *you* a favor, Officer."

He chuckles, his finger running along the seam of my opening but not pushing inside, teasing me. "Oh, trust me; you're definitely doing me a favor by letting me lick this pussy. *But* I'm not asking for anything sexual in return. Like last night, I'll deal with my blue balls. All I'm asking for is your company tonight."

"My company, so you won't end up with blue balls again?"

"Blue balls and I will become great friends the more I hang out with you." His head lowers again to suck on my slit while his finger continues to torture me. "Say you'll come with me tonight, Chloe." His mouth moves to my thigh, raining it with light kisses while refusing me what I want.

"It's not a good idea," I stutter. I reach down and wrap my fingers around his neck, sinking my fingernails into his skin, attempting to push his face closer.

Instead of giving in, he retreats more.

Well, that sure backfired on me.

"But you think me giving you an orgasm is a good idea?"

"Obviously." I snort. "Why else would I allow your face in my lap?"

"Then, say you'll come with me, and I'll give you an orgasm."

I dig my nails harder into his skin. "Not fair. You can't extort me to go to dinner with you by orgasm."

"I can convince you to do anything I want with my fingers." He pushes his finger inside me again. "With my tongue." He licks the inside of my thigh. "And with my cock when the time comes. I can do whatever I want, Chloe. It's the first thing you need to accept in our relationship."

"We don't have a relationship." *I cannot believe we're having this conversation with his head between my legs. What is really going on?*

"I'm about to eat your pussy. Do you not have a relationship with other people who stick their tongue in your pussy?"

"Please," I whisper. *No! What am I doing? I do not beg Kyle for anything.*

"You want me to finish what I started? Then, say you'll come to dinner at my parents' tonight."

"Fine."

I grip his neck, and this time, he allows me to pull him in closer.

I might hate the man, but I love his mouth between my legs. His mouth goes straight to my opening, his tongue diving in and out, before he slips two fingers … then three into me. He rotates them to the side when he knows I'm about to come. The pad of his thumb goes straight to my clit, massaging it. He's everywhere, touching me in all the right places. Seconds later, I cover my mouth when I come apart.

He waits until I stop shaking before placing a single kiss to my clit while I collapse in my chair. He stands, and I fight to control my breathing. He wipes his mouth with the back of his hand. When my arms are no longer shaking, I hastily pull down my skirt in embarrassment, like he didn't just have his face buried between my thighs.

He watches me pull myself together as if I were his favorite show. I catch my breath as he licks his lips.

"Thank you for lunch. I enjoyed it."

My gaze drops down his body, and I notice the bulge between his legs. This time, I lick my lips as my mouth salivates for him.

He drops a kiss onto my forehead, his crotch nearly shoved in my face. "See you tonight." The erection in my view leaves when he turns away.

I grab his hand to stop him. "Wait."

He stares at me with interest.

"Don't you want me to …" I nod to his waist.

"Return the favor?" he clarifies.

"Yeah … I mean, I know you said blue balls and you would become friends, but …" I lower my gaze while the words stutter from my lips, as if I were twelve and had never seen a cock before.

He shrugs casually, as if he were asked the question daily. "I won't stop you, but it's not why I came. I had a craving for your pussy. If you have a craving for some dick-sucking, mine is all yours."

My gaze slightly moves up, and I bite into the edge of my lip when I notice his handcuffs. If we ever have sex, I want us to use them. I shut my eyes and imagine the things he'd do with me.

I rest my eyes on Kyle's lap as if it were *my* favorite meal.

I stand up, surprised I can support my weight after the mind-blowing orgasm he gave me, and his eyes widen in interest as I take the small step to him. They turn hungry when I sink down to my knees, and they harden while he watches me unbuckle his duty belt.

His hand folds over mine, stopping me, and I peek up at him as he drags the belt off—along with his gun—and carefully sets it on the corner of my desk. This gives me better access to unzip his pants, and I easily tug them down along with his briefs until they hit his knees. My mouth falls open when his cock comes level with my face.

The asshole has a perfect cock, too.

Go figure.

He's huge and engorged, the tip of it red and glistening with pre-cum.

I settle my knees on his boots to give me better height and wrap my fingers around his dick. It jerks under my palm. When I glance up, his wild eyes meet mine.

"This never happened. Do you hear me?"

His cock twitches.

He holds his hands up. "Chloe never had her hand wrapped around my cock; got it. Can we also act like your lips around my cock didn't happen either?"

Instead of answering him, I take him fully in my mouth, causing him to gasp. I nearly choke when the tip of him hits the back of my throat. I try to stop myself from gagging, and before it happens, his cock slowly moves out until the tip is at my lips.

"Shit, Chloe," Kyle croaks out. "You don't have to swallow my cock. Make yourself comfortable. Relax your jaw. Do it the way you want to."

It's like he read my mind. I shut my eyes and do as he said, slowly sliding my mouth up and down his length. With every stroke, I grow more comfortable. His hand dives into my hair, but he lets me keep my pace. I pray to God Melanie or anyone else doesn't walk in. The door is closed, but not everyone is polite enough to knock.

I know he's close by his breathing and the shaking of his legs.

"Fuck, Chloe," he hisses. "Let me fuck you. *Please*, let me fuck you." His pleading turns me on more.

I shake my head, and his cock slips from my lips. "No." I return to the task at hand.

I *want* to have sex with him. But I can't.

"Your mouth is amazing." He winces when I take him deeper. "We've already crossed a line. What's one more?" He groans. "We can say it never happened."

That awful idea turns into a good one at the sound of his moaning.

I keep sucking him without answering and smile in satisfaction when he releases in my mouth.

I'm forming a relationship with Kyle, but it's only sexual.

We have a relationship based on oral sex.

We're oral sex buddies.

And I intend to keep it that way.

What harm can a few shared orgasms do?

———

"Are you sure me coming is a good idea?" I ask from the passenger seat of Kyle's truck. "Your father despises me."

He glances over at me and raises a brow. "My father doesn't know you. How could he hate you?"

I run my hand up and down the seat belt. "Correction: he hates everyone *like me*."

"No, he doesn't."

"He refers to us as scum of the city. Dirtbags. Cockroaches. Along with some other choice words."

He winces at his father's comments. "He won't be there. My mom said he's attending a work event."

I deviate the conversation to one I've been wondering about after hearing the gossip around town. "Was he mad when you didn't go into the line of work he wanted you to?"

Everyone knows Kyle had been groomed to go into law and politics like his father. He went as far as attending law school before dropping out his first year.

"How did you go from future attorney to a police officer?"

"Because it's what I wanted to do, and I won't allow anyone else to declare my future. Was he happy about it? No. But I am, and that's all that matters."

"Your father seems like an asshole who always gets his way."

He chuckles. "You must know my father."

Everyone has their opinion of Michael Lane. Some glowing. Some distasteful.

In my opinion, Michael Lane is trash.

But most of Blue Beech practically worships their beloved mayor.

"I've heard rumors. How mad was he when you dropped out of law school?"

"We barely speak," he answers, rubbing the back of his neck.

My face falls. "I'm sorry."

He's not upset—annoyed if anything. "Don't be. Hearing less of my dad's voice is a goddamn blessing."

I chuckle to lighten the mood. "I take it, you aren't a daddy's boy?"

"Never have been. Never will be."

I can't stop the grin playing at my lips. "So, you're a mama's boy?"

His voice turns humorless, surprising me. "I love my mother more than anything. If it classifies me as a *mama's boy*, so be it. She doesn't pay my bills, but I will damn sure always protect her."

All right then.

Let's add protective and sweet to Kyle's Pros.

We pull into the nicest neighborhood in Blue Beech, and he rounds a corner before parking in a circular drive of the largest home on the block.

"This is it."

I eyeball my surroundings before glimpsing his way. "Why don't you live in this neighborhood?"

He raises a brow in confusion.

"You can obviously afford to live in a nicer neighborhood than mine."

"You do realize I'm a police officer, right? We're not raking in the money."

"Yes," I draw out. "But your family is loaded."

"Doesn't mean I am, nor do I want their money."

I snap my mouth shut and unbuckle my seat belt, feeling awkward over my question. Of course Kyle, as a grown man, doesn't allow his family to support him.

"And to feed your curiosity, I moved there because it was the house my grandmother grew up in. She talked about it all the time and how she missed living in a simple neighborhood. Someone bought it and renovated it. I put in an offer when it went back on the market. Trust me; it wasn't because you lived next door even though it is a plus." He winks before opening his door and getting out.

Circling around the truck, he opens my door next before offering his hand.

"Are you doing this to make sure I don't get out and make a run for it?" I ask.

He chuckles. "No. I'm doing it because I'm romantic as fuck."

I grab his hand with reluctance.

"I promise it won't be dreadful. I enjoy your company, and deny it all you want, but you also enjoy mine. We'll eat dinner, sing 'Happy Birthday' to my sister, and then bail. If you're uncomfortable, we'll leave."

I release an overly exaggerated breath and hop out of the truck.

———

Kyle's introduces me to his family. His mother, Nancy. His younger brother, Rex. The birthday girl and younger sister, Sierra. And the youngest girl, Cassidy. Sierra's boyfriend is here, appearing nothing like I'd imagine her with by looking at her. Sierra is sporting a black leather jacket and bright red lips, and she's wearing heels. Her boyfriend is in a sweater and a pair of Sperry slip-ons.

Sometimes, opposites do attract.

No Michael Lane in sight. Good. My appetite won't be ruined.

We're seated at the table, about to dig in, when the front door slams.

Uh-oh. Front doors slamming are never a good sign.

The room goes silent.

No one takes a bite or drink.

"Sorry I'm late."

I stiffen at the sound of his voice.

Shit.

I hold my breath, awaiting his entrance. He stands in the entry, arms broad with an expensive suit and a face full of smugness. For a small-town mayor, he thinks he's hotter shit than he is. He hardly has any pull, but word is, he's trying to move up the totem pole and make it to Governor of Iowa. Then, Senate. Then, however higher he can manipulate his way up.

He walks around the table, giving his wife a kiss on the cheek before doing the same to Sierra and Cassidy. He gives Sierra's boyfriend a head nod but pays no attention to Rex or Kyle before taking the empty chair at the head of the table.

"I thought you couldn't make it?" Kyle asks with a slight hiss in his tone.

Michael gives a crooked politician's smile. "Didn't think I could, but there was a break in my schedule, so I figured, *Why not?*"

I'm not sure if he's noticed my presence.

Rex snorts. "Yeah, why not show up to your daughter's birthday dinner?"

"Rex," Michael warns.

I like Rex and his little smart mouth.

"Don't get mad at me for stating the obvious," Rex argues.

"Some of us work for a living to provide for a son who wants to take a year to defer from college to jerk around," Michael bites out with a glare toward Rex.

"Or maybe your son decided he won't be a puppet and follow in his father's footsteps. I'm not attending the college or majoring in what you want. Just like Kyle, I don't want to be Michael Lane's protégé. You've shown me firsthand your *business*, and politics are something I never want to be a part of."

This sure is fun.

Very entertaining.

I'm at the best dinner show, and I didn't pay for a ticket.

"Everyone, shut up," Kyle finally snaps. "This is Sierra's birthday dinner, not a pissing match. If we want to do that shit, we'll do it later. So, eat your fucking dinner and shut your fucking mouths unless it's to wish her a happy birthday."

Well, damn.

"Thank you," Sierra says.

Kyle glances over at Nancy. "Sorry, Mom."

I don't pay attention to Nancy. My eyes stay on Michael. I watch the way his upper lip snarls at Kyle. He clearly likes to be the one in charge. He's about to most likely lay into him until his eyes flicker my way. I receive a dirtier look than anyone at this table so far.

"I see we have company," Michael says, jerking his chin toward me.

"Yes, sorry for the lack of introduction while you came in, talking shit," Kyle says.

I've never seen him like this—so condescending and defiant. It's a major turn-on, given he's being a total dick to an asshole I don't like.

Kyle tips his head my way. "Chloe, Mayor Lane." Then, he tips his head toward his father. "Mayor Lane, Chloe."

Michael rubs his chin. "Welcome to my home." He says it with such distaste that more than one person at the table flinches.

"Dad," Kyle warns, "you're not even supposed to be here. If you plan to insult people, leave."

His glare confirms I'm not welcome here.

———

"How long have you been dating my brother?" Sierra asks when I walk out of the bathroom and into the hallway.

I don't see Kyle anywhere in sight.

Dinner was awkward, to say the least. Nancy forced conversation, asking what everyone had been up to. Sierra recently graduated from college. So did her boyfriend. Cassidy's college choice was met with approval from Michael. Rex got skipped, considering he'd already told Michael to get fucked. The same with Kyle. When Nancy came to me, Michael interrupted the conversation and began discussing a charity function.

I nearly fall on my face at her question. "Negative thirty minutes."

She blinks. "Huh?"

"We're not dating."

"So ... just friends?" she asks.

I shrug. "Just neighbors."

She leans against the wall, and I don't know if she was passing by when I walked out of the bathroom or if she was waiting for me.

"I think you two would make a cute couple."

I shake my head. "No. It's a bad idea."

"Hmm ... doesn't seem that way, but if you saying that makes you feel better …" she says before smoothing a hand down her blonde hair. "Thanks for coming to my birthday dinner."

With that, her boyfriend appears, and she leaves with him.

I walk down the hall and out the front door, in need of fresh air. I inhale deep breaths while standing on the front porch.

"How dare you step foot into my home," Michael says, coming to my side.

He was waiting for the perfect time to pounce.

"I'm unsure of why you're so angry about it," I reply, trying to keep my voice as firm as I can. *You don't scare me.*

He rests his elbows on the railing next to me. From the outside, we resemble two friends sharing a friendly conversation, and I hate how close he is.

"You don't belong here. My son hanging out with you will tarnish my family's image."

"Your son is a big boy who can make his own decisions. Maybe you should look in the mirror and realize what a deceptive liar you are."

He lets out an arrogant laugh. "That's where you're wrong, Chloe. I'm not a deceptive man. I'm a man who wants the best for the town he's in charge of, and if I have to get rid of the people who pollute it, it's what I'll do."

"I wouldn't brag about that."

"Oh, really?"

I stare straight ahead. "You're a *fighter* who will do anything to get what he wants even if it means stepping on the less fortunate. As our mayor, maybe you should fight for them instead."

"Life isn't fair. Accept it. It's a lesson you should've learned early, but I'm sure your single, drug-addicted mother didn't instill it." He cracks a smile.

I push off the railing. "Don't talk about my mother. Don't talk about my family. Matter of fact, don't come near me again."

"Chloe. No one cares about your dysfunctional family. You're the one who stepped into my home, unwelcome. I'm well aware that you see my son as an opportunity. I guess the apple doesn't fall far from the tree, seeing as you're trying to fuck your way into getting my son's money."

"You don't know what you're talking about."

"You of all people should know how powerful I am. Remember Sam?"

I wince at the name. "Go fuck yourself, Mayor Lane."

He laughs while I walk away.

CHAPTER EIGHT

KYLE

There's a knock on my office door.

My father walks in.

Great. He's most likely not here to ask for my Christmas wish list.

"What's up?" This conversation needs to be as short as possible.

He shuts the door behind him and takes a seat. "I don't think it's a good idea for you to be hanging out with Chloe Fieldgain."

Ah, there it is. This isn't a social hello, unsurprisingly. I expected a call, but it seems he felt the need to show his face instead.

The tension between my dad and Chloe was strong, and I can't blame her. Even with my mom's discouragement, he judges those less fortunate in our town.

Last night, I could tell we were both exhausted, so I didn't ask Chloe to hang out, and we went into our own homes.

"Who I hang out with is none of your business," I reply.

He laughs. "Tell me it's only sex and you're using condoms."

"It's not only sex, and we're not using condoms. I'm hoping to give you fifteen grandchildren with her." *Take that, asshole.*

"Son, if you're having an issue getting women to sleep with you, I can find someone to help get your rocks off."

I hold my hand up and cringe. *Fucking gross.* "Calm down. I'm not sleeping with Chloe."

"Good. You might be smarter than I thought."

I scoff. "Smart because I'm not sleeping with someone?"

"Smart, like your father, who knows where he sticks his dick is important."

"That's where you're wrong. I never want to be a man like you."

"A man like me?" he asks, insulted.

"Yes. A shitty husband. A shitty dad. A man so hungry for power that he can't realize his plate is already full."

He pulls at the collar of his suit. "I'm beginning to think my daughters carry more balls than my sons. Rex wants to be … fuck, I don't know what, and you want to screw a woman who grew up in the trailer park."

"*Again,* I'm not fucking Chloe. We're friends and neighbors."

He smiles. "Be safe with her. The last thing you need is a baby with the woman. Fuck her all you want, but be careful."

"Leave her alone," I instruct. "Don't you dare give her the same warning, or there will be problems."

He huffs. "Since when do you think you have authority over me?"

"Since I decided I'm not afraid of you and not a puppet under your bullshit. I thought I'd already proved that to you. It's been fun." I tip my head toward the door. "You know the way out."

"Selfish bastard."

"I wish I were a bastard."

―――――

"And there's our favorite third wheel," Lauren sings.

"Piss off," I grumble when I slide into the backseat of Gage's truck. "If you two weren't forcing me to come, I wouldn't be a third wheel. My mom, who is the queen of throwing parties, never had a gender reveal party. Next, you two will be drinking hipster beer and eating avocado toast."

"Avocado toast is amazing, for your information," Lauren replies with a laugh. "Stop being a hater."

I run my hands through my hair. "Can't you post the baby's sex on Facebook like normal people do? Why are you throwing a big party?"

I'm curious as to whether I'm having a godson or goddaughter, but they want to find out the sex with balloons filled with confetti. Chloe wouldn't be into this shit. I pause.

Why am I thinking about her and what she'd do if she were pregnant?

"Lauren wanted a party. We're having a party, so shut your mouth, or you won't be the godfather," Gage replies.

Lauren glances at me from the passenger seat and scrunches her face up. "You wouldn't be a third wheel if you found a girlfriend."

"I told you to find me a girlfriend. Not my problem you failed."

"Been there. Done that. Had to listen to too many women cry over the phone about you breaking their hearts. My job as your matchmaker is over. I'd love to say it's been fun, but I'd be lying." She studies me for a few moments. "Do you not want a relationship? Does commitment scare you?"

"It's not at the top of my priority list," I answer with no shame.

Commitment scares the shit out of me. I've never witnessed it first-hand. My mother turns a blind eye to my father's affairs. Every Lane man has been an adulterer. The only man I'm close with who I've seen is capable of staying faithful is Gage.

I'm not against commitment. I'm afraid I'll fail at it.

A hint of disappointment crosses her face before she sets her attention on Gage. "I told you he'd die old and alone." She squeals. "I cannot wait to decorate my beachside villa in ten years." She winks at me before whipping back around in her seat.

"What does my love life and a beachside villa have to do with shit?" I question with confusion.

Gage chuckles. "My girl over here made me bet that you wouldn't have a serious relationship in the next ten years. If you don't, I somehow owe her a beachside villa. Whatever the hell it is, it sounds expensive as fuck."

"You two bet on my love life?" I ask before rubbing my chin. "Better yet, why are you creeps *talking* about my love life? Has your bedroom talk become that boring?"

"Far from it," Gage answers. "Trust me; I couldn't give two shits about who you're banging or marrying, but she wouldn't shut up about it. It's easier to agree, so it's what I did. If you ever do settle down, you'll understand."

Lauren pats his shoulder. "Good man." Her attention bounces to me. "So, keep being a heartbreaking whore."

"Oh, babe, say good-bye to your beachside shit. Kyle will be tied down before then," Gage tells her.

"And how are you so certain?" she asks with a raised brow.

"He's trying to get into his neighbor's panties."

"Neighbor?" Lauren asks. "I need a name."

"Chloe Fieldgain," Gage answers before I get the chance to tell him to keep out of my love life.

"Uh … doesn't she hate your guts?" Lauren questions.

Lauren is unaware that Chloe was writing a story about her being assaulted by her old landlord. So far, with her family's influence and our jobs, we've kept the details to a minimum. People know something happened, but unless Lauren opens up, they'll never know everything.

I grin. "You hated me once, and here we are, headed to a whatever-you-called-it party."

She narrows her eyes. "A *gender reveal* party." She perks up in her seat. "Now, didn't you and Chloe have a thing in high school that went south? Yes! I love me a good second-chance romance." She kisses Gage's shoulder. "Don't I, babe?"

Gage brakes at a Stop sign and stares at her with affection. "I wouldn't call it a thing."

"Fuck off," I hiss.

"People call her the ice queen," Lauren comments. "Like, all she does is hide behind her books and the newspaper she works for."

"I'm trying to break through the frost," I explain.

"You should invite her on a double date."

"He should the fuck not," Gage says. "I'd rather buy you a beach-side villa than be involved in Kyle's girl drama like we're teenagers."

That's Gage. He'll tell me when I'm being an idiot, but he isn't one for heart-to-hearts unless it's with Lauren.

"Invite her on a double date," Lauren demands.

Gage smiles over at his fiancée. "The queen has spoken."

———

The party is being held on Lauren's family's property. There's an endless amount of food, and I watch my best friend and his fiancée pop the balloon.

Does Chloe want kids? My guess is yes since it seems like she frequently helps with her sister's kids.

The confetti is pink. The cake is pink.

I'm having a goddaughter.

By the end of the car ride home, I've decided I'm going to ask Chloe on a double date.

CHAPTER NINE
CHLOE

*K*yle Calling.

The Ignore button is hit.

I need space to get my head straight before we talk. We haven't done much of that since dinner at his parents'. He still tells me good morning, but it's brief before he leaves for work. His truck was in the drive, but no lights were on in his house when I got home yesterday.

Hours later, Gage's truck pulled up, and Kyle stepped out. When he was unlocking his front door, Lauren yelled his name, ran up the porch steps, and handed him a pink balloon.

He grabbed it, laughed, and hugged her.

My phone rings again.

Kyle Calling.

I hit Ignore.

It rings once more.

Kyle again.

"Jesus, what?" I answer.

"You need to get to Garfield's Grocery," he says in a serious tone.

"Why? I'm working."

"Trey was busted for shoplifting."

"Shit! Give me ten."

"Park in the rear lot, so no one sees you, and I'll let you in."

———

Kyle is waiting for me when I pull into the parking lot. I speed-walk his way, and he moves to the side, letting me in without speaking. I curse with every step as I walk down a hallway lined with loaves of bread and pastries.

Damn it, Trey.

Why did he shoplift?

Why didn't he come to me if he needed money?

Kyle leads me into a dimly lit office reeking of mothballs. Trey is sitting in a chair, and surprisingly, he's not wearing handcuffs. Mr. Garfield, the store's owner, is at his side, worry lining his wrinkled face. His wife is sitting in a chair behind an old desk, looking like she's ready to rip Trey's head off.

I cast them a glance of apology, but only Mr. Garfield will make eye contact. Today isn't the first time someone from my family has shoplifted from here. My mom and sister were regular thieves. Mr. Garfield let it slide for a while but eventually started calling the cops. They ended up banned from the store after the tenth occurrence. I haven't been banned yet, but Mrs. Garfield keeps a watchful eye on me. Every visit, I slip extra cash in the tip jars at the registers to make up for my family's theft. Mr. Garfield's soul is kinder than his wife's.

"Seriously, Trey?" I snap with a stressed sigh as soon as the door slams shut behind me.

Regret is clear on his face. Trey isn't a troublemaker, but he's a survivor.

"Your family is filth," Mrs. Garfield hisses. "Thinking they can take whatever they want." Her glare cuts to Kyle. "I don't know why this young man is helping you and that *thief*."

My apologetic face turns cold, and my nails bite into my palms as I clench my fists. *Don't say anything.*

If I lose my cool, she'll take it out on Trey.

"Enough, Mary," Mr. Garfield warns his wife.

Kyle steps to my side and looks in her direction. "Mrs. Garfield, don't act like you've never needed a handout in your life."

I cringe at the word *handout.*

My blood pressure rises. We don't need *handouts.*

"I think they've had enough *handouts,*" Mary answers with a sneer.

"And I think you need to grow a heart," Kyle says.

Mary strokes her throat and grimaces. "No offense, Officer, but you're not the one losing money."

Tears prick at my eyes, but none of them will see them fall.

"Money or not," Kyle says, "he's a kid."

I open my mouth, wanting to say something, but I'm not sure how I can justify Trey's actions. They're inexcusable.

"Kid or not, he's not innocent," she continues. "Her family teaches their kids to become criminals at a young age."

Kyle looks at Trey. "Come on, let's get out of here, so we don't waste any more of their time."

Trey nervously stands up. He looks down in shame when our eyes meet, and my heart hurts for him. That was me so many years ago—surviving by any means necessary. The difference is, I had no one to go to for help. He has me.

"What are you going to do with him?" I ask Kyle, finally gaining the ability to speak before opening my purse. "I'll pay for whatever he took and extra for the inconvenience."

Kyle waves away my offer. "Don't worry about it. I'm not arresting him." He tilts his head toward Trey. "Stay out of trouble, or next time, I won't be as nice."

"What?" I blurt out.

"Officer Lane paid for what your nephew stole and extra for our troubles," Mr. Garfield explains with a nervous smile. "We won't be pressing charges against Trey."

I let out a huge breath. "Thank you so much. I'm so sorry, and it won't happen again."

"I understand struggle, dear," Mr. Garfield says. "Don't let my wife get you down. She's having a rough day. We both know you're a good girl."

I look at Mary and lock eyes with her, hoping she'll see my gratitude. "Thank you again."

She looks away as if the sight of me disgusts her and snarls at Trey. My anger heightens. I hate being looked at as if I'm beneath someone, but it *really* pisses me off when that disdain is directed at someone I care about.

The three of us rush down the hall, and I don't speak again until we've made it outside.

"What the hell were you thinking?" I yell at Trey as we head to my car. "You could've been arrested!"

Trey looks at me, his eyes flickering with regret and humiliation. "Gloria needed supplies for daycare and food. Mom wouldn't give me the money, so I had to get them another way."

I swallow hard. "Why didn't you come to me?"

"I can't always come to you. You bought us new clothes *and* paid for my football equipment. It's not fair to always ask you for money." His attention goes to the ground, and he kicks at pebbles with his shoe. "It's pathetic enough that Mom always begs you for it and then spends it on booze."

"I would much rather give you the money than her, Trey. I give her money to help you and Gloria. Don't ever feel ashamed about asking me for help. Do you hear me? If you or Gloria need something, you come to *me*. You don't shoplift!"

Kyle clears his throat, and we both look at him. I forgot he was here.

He tips his head toward the corner of the parking lot and focuses on me. "Can I talk to you for a sec?"

"Of course." I grab my keys from my purse and hand them to Trey. "I'll meet you in the car in a minute."

Trey grabs them and walks away. I scrub at my eyes before dragging my hands over my face and meet Kyle. We're facing each other, and his hands settle on my shoulders before he takes a step back, as if he's inspecting me.

"You okay?" he asks.

I nod. "Yes, just a little pissed off. I can't believe Trey would shoplift. I've told him a million times, if he needs something, call me. Instead, he steals, proving to everyone that we're all the same."

He lowers his hands to run them over my arms. "Don't you dare listen to that old bat, you hear me? Block out every fucking word she said to you."

"What she said wasn't a lie," I mutter.

"The fuck it is. The mistakes and wrongdoings of your family don't define you. Who they are is not *you*. What I see when I look at you is a strong woman, a woman who fights for what she wants and takes on responsibilities that aren't hers to make children's lives better."

I don't want his words to make me feel better, but they do.

He's giving me all the feels.

How is this asshole I thought I hated giving me all these good feels?

I inhale a deep breath, and when I move to open my purse, his hands drop, breaking our connection.

"How much do I owe you?"

He shakes his head. "Don't worry about it."

"I can pay for my family's shit, Kyle."

His eyes soften. "I never said you couldn't. It's already taken care of." He whistles and tilts his head toward my car. "Get Trey out of here before Mrs. Garfield comes out with her shotgun."

I frown and hitch my bag up my shoulder. "Fine, but we're talking about this later."

He smiles. "You're always welcome in my home."

CHAPTER TEN

CHLOE

AGE FOURTEEN

My sister is having a baby.

A baby boy, to be exact.

She won't tell me who the father is, but I've heard her scream at him and demand money over the phone.

Since Claudia doesn't know anything about babies, I checked out books from the library for her, receiving quite the curious look from the assistant librarian. Claudia threw them across the room and said she'd know how to take care of her baby when he got here. So, I took them to my room and read them myself.

Someone in this house needs to be educated on what to do with a newborn.

Sam's visits are limited now. All they do is argue when he comes over. Him not coming around makes me sad. He is nice to me and helps me with my homework. He cares about my interests and never tells me my dreams are stupid. Sam is who I want my father to be.

A month later, Sam stops coming over permanently.

———

AGE FIFTEEN

"Hey there, stranger."

My head flies up at the sound of the voice I've missed.

Sam stands in my doorway, looking clean-cut in a suit and with a ball cap over his head. It's rare seeing him without a hat on.

"Hi," I answer in surprise, unable to hide my excitement. "Long time no see."

He has been nonexistent in our lives for nearly a year. I thought he was gone for good, so the sight of him brings nothing but joy to my face. He's never met Trey, who came into the world three months ago. He did send a care package with no return address. A note was attached, saying he wanted Trey to have the baby essentials.

"Sorry about that," he answers. "Life gets in the way sometimes."

I nod, though I don't understand. Something I've come to learn is, if someone wants time with someone, they make it, no matter what. That means Sam didn't want to spend time with anyone in our home —including me.

Having men come and go isn't out of the ordinary. I've never met my father. My knowledge of him is through old photographs and the few choice words my mother shouts when I ask about him.

Sam steps farther into my room. "Your sister said you're very helpful with Trey."

The baby books I read have been put to good use since I'm Trey's main caretaker. Not his mother. I get up with him at night and change all his diapers, and since she refuses to breastfeed, in fear it will mess up her "good tits," I feed him his formula.

I shrug and hold back the urge to tell Sam that. I want him to be proud of me, but Claudia will kill me. "I try."

He smiles. "You're such a good girl, Chloe. I'm sure she appreciates your help greatly."

I snort. "Claudia doesn't appreciate anything."

"That's the understatement of the year."

I tuck my legs underneath my butt. "So then, why do you like her? Why don't you find a nicer girlfriend?"

It's been a while since I've asked him, but I don't understand how a decent man like him can like her. There must be something wrong with him. Broken people seek out other broken people. I see it every day of my life and wonder how I'm ever going to find someone nice to take on the job of being with someone as broken as I am.

He shrugs. "People like people for different reasons."

"You like her because she's pretty … and she has sex with you."

He chuckles and slides his hands into his pants pockets.

"You two seem so different," I go on.

"Opposites attract sometimes," he argues.

"Duh," I say with a roll of my eyes. "Opposites have sex with each other, but—"

He cuts me off. "You seem to know an awful lot about sex for someone your age."

I point out my bedroom door. "Uh … have you seen the people I live with?"

He walks into my room and sits down on the edge of the bed, concern now etched on his face. "None of their boyfriends have ever … they've never touched you or talked to you inappropriately, have they?"

"No," I rush out.

They've looked but never touched.

"You'll tell me if they do, right?"

"Yes."

"You promise?"

"I promise," I say softly.

He gives me a gentle smile. "You know, you're going to make something of yourself when you get older. I'm certain of it."

His words come out with pride.

They fill me with pride.

"Thank you," I whisper. "I want to be a writer when I grow up."

This spikes his interest. I love when he seems interested in me.

"Yeah? What type of writer?"

"I don't know. I like reading the newspapers."

He chuckles. "Whoa. The pay for the amount of work is chump change."

I frown. "Not everything is always about money."

He rubs his hand over his clean-shaven cheek. "If there's anything you learn from me, Chloe, it's that life is always about money."

CHAPTER ELEVEN

KYLE

A towel is wrapped around my waist after the post-gym shower, and I walk through the living room at the sound of the doorbell. The realization that I'm about to answer my door half-naked doesn't hit me until I'm standing in front of it. I look out the peephole and smile at the sight of Chloe standing at my door, glancing around in annoyance.

As soon as I swing the door open, I lean against the doorframe, leveling my arm above me while a grin plays at my lips. "Hello, my favorite neighbor. Care to borrow some sugar?"

Unfortunately for me, the expression on Chloe's face isn't screaming that she's down for having a good time. Her chin is jutted into the air, and her pretty little lips are pinched together.

A wad of cash is shoved into my chest. "This is for whatever Trey took," she says. "Let me know if it's not enough."

Whoa. Whoa. Whoa.

I shake my head while ignoring the cash. "I'm not taking your money."

"Why?" she snaps.

"I don't need to give you a reason."

"Bullshit!" She inches the cash further. "Now, tell me how much, Kyle."

I wave for her to come in, and surprisingly, she does. She crosses her arms as soon as the door shuts.

"Why'd you do it? Why are you being so nice to me, inviting me to your fucking family dinner, and helping my family?"

"I told you, I'm a nice person."

She snorts. "People don't do things to be *nice*. There's always an underlying reason."

I throw my hands up. "Do I need a reason to be nice to someone? I'm fucking attracted to you, Chloe! I wish I could take what happened between us back every single day. When I see you in the morning, I wonder where we'd be if I hadn't been such a dumb shit then."

This isn't how everything was supposed to go down.

I take a step forward, grab the back of her head, and pull her to me. "Maybe it's time I find out."

CHAPTER TWELVE
CHLOE

I can't digest Kyle's words before his lips crash into mine, and I'm pushed against the door. The money slips from my fingers, and I draw in a gasp when his excitement rubs against my thigh over my pants.

I could've thrown the cash at him and walked away. It'd have been the smart response. I might be book smart, but I'm sure as hell not emotionally smart. My emotions have no sense of rationality around him.

So, instead of being smart and fleeing the scene, I walked in, asking for trouble. Our kiss confirms everything I've feared. This is what I want. *He's* what I want, and I'm not strong enough to continue pushing him away.

Sleeping with Kyle doesn't mean we need to have a relationship—or hell, even like each other. The only way sex can happen with us is if it's no-strings attached and with no expectations. With every kiss and touch, I'm allowing him in deeper, knowing I'll be left with emptiness when everything crashes between us.

The gasp escapes me when his tongue dips between the seam of my lips, and his fingers plunge into the base of my ponytail, roughly raking through the strands and then tugging at the ends. This man has fingered me and gone down on me, but those times were always about my orgasm, about him proving he could get me off.

This is different. Our kiss is laced with desperation and urgency, and with tentative fingers, I stroke him over the towel.

He moans into my mouth when I gain the courage to tug on the towel until it falls at our feet.

"Tell me this is happening," he says. "Let me have all of you."

I run my tongue over his bottom lip and wrap my fingers around his bare, swollen length, sliding them along the tip, spreading his pre-cum. "Does this answer your question?"

His chest moves against mine when he chuckles. "So far, it's looking pretty damn promising."

"Very promising," I whisper with a smile.

"There's one problem."

"What's that?"

He knots my ponytail around his fist, forcing my head back, and kisses up my throat. "I'm the only one naked." He licks the curve of my neck before releasing me, and I lose my hold on him when he withdraws a step. "Strip for me."

I steady myself against the door at his command, my breathing ragged, and I take in his naked body in all its glory. The finely sculpted muscles of his chest and arms are no stranger to me, and even though I've given him a blow job, there wasn't much time to take in his swollen, thick cock before.

When my eyes meet his again, I find him intensely watching me, almost daring me to disobey him.

"Strip, Chloe," he demands again. "Get naked. I won't ask you again."

I hold in a breath before grabbing the hem of my shirt and hurriedly ripping it over my head. My heart rapidly pounds against my chest, and it takes only seconds for me to step out of my yoga pants. My attention closes in on him, waiting for approval, but he gives nothing.

I haven't given him all of me yet.

I lock eyes with him, and his gaze turns wicked when I unhook my bra, my breasts spilling forward. Still, not a single word from him. Neither do I get one after dragging my panties down my weak legs and kicking them away from my feet.

This is the first time Kyle has seen me fully naked. My heart is beating wildly, like I was working out for hours, and I've never felt so exposed.

"Take your hair down."

I do as I was told.

He inches closer while drinking me in, his eyes roaming up and down my body. He runs his hand over his face, stopping at his chin, and bites into his thumb.

And, finally—*fucking finally*—he's directly in front of me. "You're beautiful. Absolutely stunning, Chloe." His compliment sparks through me stronger than anything I've felt with another man.

His hand then moves to my chin, and he strokes it. "Can I ask you a question?"

"Uh … yes?"

"Do you want me to fuck you, or do you want to fuck me?"

Holy motherfucking hell.

I gulp, suddenly feeling out of breath. "I want to fuck you."

He smiles in satisfaction before capturing my hand, jerking me into the living room, and then collapses on the sofa. He gestures to his cock and spreads his legs. "Fuck me then."

I eye the cleft in his chin and take a deep breath. *This will change everything.*

It's one thing, giving in to my desire when he's the initiator, but another to climb onto his lap and ride him. To fuck him. He's forcing me to make every decision on whether we cross this line.

Deep breaths expel from his lips while he awaits my next move, and the shock on his face when I fall to my knees at his feet satisfies me.

"*Fuck*," he hisses with a clenched jaw.

It's time for me not to play fair. I waste no time in tightening my fingers around his cock again, and it twitches in my hand. I slowly stroke him, and with deep pleasure, I watch the torture on his face—torture of not being in control.

He hisses through his teeth when I bend forward to rub his cock against my nipple back and forth before releasing it as my mouth waters. I lick up his cock before sucking on the base at the bottom, and then I slide my tongue up, licking and sucking on his tip.

He bites into his lower lip and sucks in a breath. He tilts his hips up, asking for more.

I'm aching for him to be inside me but also throbbing to taste him again. I swallow before taking him fully in my mouth, sliding my tongue along the length, and then I bob my head up and down. My hands rest on his strong thighs for me to get the right angle to suck him perfectly. When I glimpse up at him, I see Kyle with his hands laced behind his neck as he stares at me with desperation.

I feel like I'm on a caffeine buzz, and I'm soaked between my legs.

"Yes, just like that, baby," he groans. "Don't stop. *Fuck*. Don't stop."

I pause. "What if I want to stop to ride your cock?"

His hand drops to massage my cheek, and his face turns soft. "Chloe, anytime you want to ride my cock, I give you permission to always stop what you're doing."

The compassionate look on his face mixed with his dirty words captivates me, and I take a deep breath before standing tall while his cock stands before me.

This is it.

No going back.

I can no longer say I resisted the temptation of Kyle Lane.

I'm throwing down the white flag with no apologies.

I can't help but grin at his surprise when I crawl up his lap, grab him by the base, and slowly lower myself down on him, my thighs hitting his with a smack. He fills me up perfectly, like he's always belonged there, already hitting my spots before I've even moved. I use his shoulders for support to lift myself up and then fall down. One of his hands spans over my hip while the other cups my chin, pulling me in for a kiss.

"Fuck me like you said you would," he demands, pulling away before pushing me back against his mouth.

Our kiss is deep, and the hand resting on my chin lowers to my breast, cupping it. He slowly strokes my nipple with his thumb before pinching it. As I set my pace, Kyle uses his hands as a weapon, moving them everywhere—from my hips to my breasts and then to my back.

"You feel so good," he says into my mouth, meeting my thrusts as I ride him. "Better than I imagined."

I circle my hips, alternating between bouncing up and down and then grinding hard, making it my mission to fuck him better than any other woman has.

"Fuck, shit, Chloe," he bites out. "I'm going to come." His finger goes to my clit, and he's rough as he works it.

I crush my mouth to his, his words setting a fire inside me. "Then, come."

My heart slams against my chest as I pull away and wait for it. I want to see. I *need* to witness the evidence of me riding Kyle into an orgasm. For reasons unknown, a surge of pride rolls through me.

I'm good enough to make him lose control like this. I'm strong enough to make him feel this way.

But it doesn't happen. As I wait for it, an arm spans around my waist, and he clutches my hips, halting me from making another move.

What the …

"I'm bare," he says in a thick voice. "We forgot a condom, so hop off me before I fill you with my cum."

"No, it's fine," I reply in a comforting tone.

The mood is lifting, cooling down, and I'm afraid it'll burn out.

"I'm on the pill," I whisper with reassurance. "It's fine. I promise." I peel his arm off me and grind on him.

He raises a brow. "You sure you're okay with this?"

"I'm positive."

Is he sure about this?

I'm answered when his hips surge up, his cock hitting me in all the right places.

"I can't believe I'm going to fill you up. *Fuuuccck.* You have no idea how long I've wanted this."

And, as cliché as it sounds, we get off at the same time. He explodes inside me as I arch my back and call out his name. I suddenly feel light-headed before shaking against Kyle as he goes slack. I can feel his heart beating just as wildly. My hands cling to his shoulders as if I can't hold myself up.

"Now, it's my turn to fuck you." He grabs my waist, hauls me over his shoulder, and rushes down the hallway before depositing me on what I assume is his bed.

I watch him from the foot of the bed and rub my legs together. "Let's see if you're as good as you've led on to be."

He's already proven it in his kitchen … in my office … on his couch.

"Don't worry, Chloe. I'm about to prove myself to you in every way possible, so you'll never doubt me again."

It terrifies me.

He crawls up my body, and I gasp when his tongue slides up my stomach and to my neck, slowly reaching my mouth.

"I'm going to fuck you how I've imagined every day since I saw you walk out of your house, wearing one of those skirts I love so much."

"Show me then."

————

I collapse on my back while working to catch my breath. "Holy shit," I say between pants. "Holy motherfucking shit." I cast a glance to Kyle next to me to find him doing the same.

I just had the best sex of my life. Kyle bringing me to his bed and having his way with me was even better than me riding him. Screw Kent and his half-assed screws. I'll be sending his new wife a thank-you card for their affair. Maybe even a gift card, so she can invest in a good vibrator as a complimentary, shitty sex-stealer gift.

Kyle blows out a strong breath and then chuckles. "That's exactly what a man likes to hear after giving a woman a dozen of orgasms."

I turn my head and glare over at him. "It wasn't a *dozen.*"

Sweat drips from his forehead, and red scratches are visible on his shoulders. He doesn't even seem fazed by my marking him. "Somewhere along those lines, babe."

I lean up on my elbow to look at him, briefly forgetting I'm naked and putting myself on display. I've suddenly become comfortable with him. "Don't flatter yourself."

"I thought you knew me well enough to know that I *always* flatter myself." He stands up, his cock semi-hard with the cum-filled condom attached, and goes to the bathroom to dispose of it.

Even though I'd told him I was on the pill in the living room, he snagged a condom from the nightstand drawer during round two.

He falls down next to me with a wicked grin on his face. "Flattery is the best compliment. If you agree to a dozen, next time, I'll shoot for *two dozen.* It ends in your favor."

"I don't know if we should let this happen again. Don't you think it will make things more complicated for us?"

I'm afraid he'll hurt me, afraid I'll fall for him and get hurt again. If he learns my secret, he'll walk away with my heart and hate me.

He pulls himself out of bed, moves around the room, and snags an abandoned shirt off the floor. "Fine, if it's what you want. I'll get dressed. You get dressed. I'll see you tomorrow morning."

My mouth falls open. "What? Are you kicking me out of your bed?"

He tosses the shirt on the floor while shaking his head, a smile twitching at his lips—his swollen lips a result of me biting into them every time he hit the right spot. "What? You keep talking like us having sex was a mistake. What do you think a man wants to do with that ego booster? Leave me be with my hurt feelings."

I grab a pillow and throw it at him. "I hate you."

"Your moans prove otherwise." He jerks his thumb toward the door. "Now, do you want me to go on an exploration for your panties or stay in here where you will not need them?"

I stare at him in response.

"Answer me. Would you rather me find your panties or your G-spot again?" He points to his watch-less wrist. "Time is ticking, babe."

I shoot him an annoyed look. "Seriously, you're giving me a time limit on my choice to receive an orgasm or not?"

"I am."

I tap the bed. "Hang out here for a sec. You probably need to rest and not search your house at the moment."

"Perfect. Chloe code for fucking her again." He returns to bed.

I hold myself up with my elbow and stare at him. "You don't find this weird?"

He mirrors my stance and gives me his full attention, his eyes staring at mine and not roaming over my naked body. "No. We're two people sexually attracted to each other. Two people who get along and vibe. Why is that weird?"

I signal between the two of us. "You're *you*, and I'm *me*."

He clicks his tongue against the roof of his mouth. "Good observation."

I push his shoulder. "I never thought …" I stop to shake my head and don't finish my sentence.

"You never thought you'd give in to the sexual chemistry between us, begging to be discovered since high school?"

I shrug. "Something like that."

He snags my waist and pulls me into him. "I'm still sensing some of that chemistry. Shall we try another go? See if we can fuck it out?"

That's what we do.

Kyle has been inside me five times.

Five times.

The stamina on this man is unbelievable.

Hell, the stamina in myself is surprising.

We've slept together, shared meals, watched TV, and carried on conversations I never thought we would.

Kyle takes a drink of his water and looks away from his sandwich to me. We're at the kitchen table, devouring the grilled cheeses he made for us.

I shyly look away when I realize he's practically studying me. "What?" I mutter, feeling too on display.

"I like seeing you in my house, in my kitchen, in *my bed*." He shrugs. "I like seeing you here in general. I love you opening up to me and allowing me to see the real Chloe. I like *you*, Chloe. And, even if we weren't sleeping together, if we were sitting in my living room, watching paint dry, I'd still want you to be here."

His words send chills down my body, and goose bumps form on my bare legs. I'm wearing a pair of panties and his tee.

"I don't understand." I shut my eyes, and the next words come out in stutters. "Why? Why me?"

His face scrunches in confusion. "Why *not* you? Why would you ever question why anyone would want to hang out with you? The better question is, why are *you* hanging out with me? Don't sell yourself short on how fucking amazing you are."

I blush while processing his words.

A playful grin is on his face.

"What? Why are you looking at me like that?"

"Watching you blush is sexy."

I cover my face. "Or so embarrassing."

He plucks my hands from my face one by one and caresses my jaw. It seems to be his thing. "Nope. Sexy. I love it. Your pale cheeks turn this rosy color. Your eyes widen. Your lips pucker up. It's why I do everything in my power to make you do it."

I groan. "Stop being sweet. This Kyle is too much for me."

He chuckles. "Never."

I take a bite of my sandwich to hide my smile. "You were born to drive me crazy, weren't you?"

"No, I was born to be a police officer, *but* being able to hang out with you and drive you crazy is a plus. What a perfect life I have." He slides his plate up the table. "Now, what do I need to do for you to take my next question seriously?"

"Not ask it."

He laughs. "Seriously. Don't immediately answer. I know your lips are set to an automatic *no* whenever I ask you to do something."

"Incoming question is now scaring the shit out of me."

He inhales a deep breath. "Want to go on a double date with Gage and Lauren?"

Wow, I was expecting something along the lines of trying anal.

Not that.

Shoot, maybe I'd rather him ask me about anal.

"Uh …" I draw out. "We're not dating, let alone *double* dating."

"What makes you think we aren't dating? Is neighbor-fucking a regular thing for you?"

"Possibly."

His questions are throwing me off my game.

"Bullshit."

I give him a forced glare. "Excuse me, how do you know what I do with my personal life?"

"I know you."

I snort. "You know nothing about me, Kyle Lane."

His voice softens. "Then, tell me more about you."

"Hard pass."

He laughs. "Looks like we need to work our way up to having a serious a conversation. We've had sex, but God forbid, we get into a too-personal conversation."

"Sounds like a good plan to me."

He groans. "You confuse me."

"Then, let me spell it out for you. This is sex. No dating. You should know this. I've seen the women coming and going from here. You do casual sex. If you want to keep doing *this*"—I gesture between the two of us—"casual is what we have to be. We're casually hanging out, which means no double dating."

"Fine, then have a *casual* hang-out with Lauren and Gage."

I frown. "They hate me." *That should save me from his little group date … hang-out.*

"They don't."

My frown stays intact. "They should, considering I was going to publish a story about her."

"Lauren doesn't hate anyone, except for any girl who touches Gage and his ex-wife. And you're neither one of those. We never told her about the story. Only Gage knows, and eventually, he'll warm up to you."

"Warm up to me? That's convincing."

"Trust me; he's grateful you didn't publish the story." He tickles my side, causing me to laugh. "So, what do you say, Fieldgain? You. Me. Casually hanging out with friends."

"I'll think about it."

He grins.

"Hey now, that's not me agreeing to it."

He grins wider. "We shall see, dear neighbor."

CHAPTER THIRTEEN

AGE FIFTEEN

I toss my backpack on my bed and do a happy dance.

I got asked to the homecoming dance.

Me!

The poor girl with the junkie mother, the absent father, and sister knocked up with an illegitimate son was asked to the homecoming dance.

Holy yay!

This weekend, I'm forgetting about my crappy life. This weekend, I won't be the girl living in filth—well, what filth I can't clean. This weekend, I won't be the outsider who yearns to fit in but is unable to afford every puzzle piece.

I wasn't just asked. I was asked by Kyle Lane. The hottest and coolest guy wants to go out with the class loner. I was shocked when he asked. We'd only spoken a few times, and those were to compare test scores.

This is going to be the best day of my life.

———

All my homecoming excitement ends when I tell my mother.

"Why would a boy invite you to the dance?" she snarls, as if it were the most disturbing idea in the world. "He must want to get in your panties."

"Or he might like me," I snap.

She snorts and takes another drink of vodka.

I hate my mother and don't care if I'm judged for it. You don't have to like someone because you're related.

An hour later, my mom passes out in her bedroom, and I play with Trey on the floor.

"I'm sorry about Mom," Claudia says, surprising me. "It's no fun when she treats you like a whore. She's done it to me all my life, too."

I rise up onto my knees. "Did you ever go to a high school dance?"

"A few times, yes."

A twinge of jealousy hits me, and I bite into my bottom lip. "How did you afford the dresses?"

"I stole them."

I briefly consider this.

"You can't pull off shoplifting, Chloe. You're too obvious."

"Maybe I'll find some fabric and make my own."

She reclines in her chair and crosses her arms. "I'll try to pull something together for you, okay?"

I nod, knowing I shouldn't agree to my sister stealing something for me, but this might be the biggest night of my life.

———

I'm searching the couch cushions for spare change to purchase fabric from the store. Our neighbor said I could borrow her sewing machine. I taught myself to use it a few years ago to fix the holes in my clothes, and eventually, I even made a baby blanket for Trey.

"Hey there, Chloe."

His voice surprises me. I drop the cushion to find Sam with a shopping bag in his hand.

"Hi," I say.

Normally, I'm excited to see him, but he hasn't been around lately, *and* there's not even one penny in the couch. There's no way I'll find enough money for fabric.

"Your sister said you got asked to the dance this weekend."

I brightly smile until I remember my lack of funds. "I did, but I'm not going."

"Why? Isn't every teenage girl's dream to go to homecoming?"

I bite into my lip as tears swell in my eyes. "I don't …" I lower my gaze in embarrassment. "I can't afford a dress."

He holds up the bag. "Lucky for you, I'm here to solve that problem."

"Really?" A few tears fall down my cheek, and I blink them away, making certain this is real.

No one has ever done anything this kind for me.

He hands me the bag. "Go try it on to make sure it fits. Your sister wasn't sure about your size."

I grab the bag, race to my bedroom, and drag the dress from the bag. I run my hands over it and admire the sparkly pink fabric. It feels and looks expensive. I inspect the tag. *Holy wow.* It is expensive. I hold it against my chest and squeal in excitement. Also in the bag is a pair of silver flats decorated with pink stars and a heart necklace.

This will be the best night ever.

I put my dress on, tying it around my neck, and hurry into the living room. Claudia and Sam are waiting for me. She's on the couch, and he's standing in the corner, his hands in his black dress slacks. He never sits down, like he thinks we're contaminated and he'll catch something.

"I love it!" I say, rushing over to him.

He seems surprised when I wrap my arms around him but loosens up and hugs me back, patting my shoulder. "You're welcome."

"Cute. Not my style but whatever," Claudia comments when I pull away.

"Shut the hell up, Claudia," he snaps, taking me aback, and he straightens out his shirt.

Claudia slams her mouth shut and rolls her eyes.

"Thank you so much," I tell him.

"You're welcome." He shoots Claudia a dirty look. "You look very pretty." He points at me. "Remember, boys are bad."

"I'm fifteen," I answer. "I don't need to worry about boys."

Claudia glowers at Sam. "High school boys are never who you need to worry about."

Sam ignores her comment, shoots me a smile, and then leaves.

I jump up and down and smile at Claudia. "Thank you *so, so, so* much for asking him to buy me a dress."

She smiles back. "It's no problem. Don't tell Mom, okay?"

"I won't! Gosh, I wish I had a boyfriend like Sam. He's so cool and nice."

She frowns. "You need to be careful around him, Chloe."

"What do you mean?"

"Sam isn't as perfect as he leads on, okay? We only know him in this trailer. Otherwise, he doesn't exist to us."

I don't ask her what she means. I don't want the moment to be ruined.

———

Tonight has been nothing short of a fairy tale. I've pinched myself to confirm it's not a dream.

I didn't want Kyle to see where I lived, so I had him meet me at the school instead of picking me up. We went to dinner and then rode back to school in a limo—a freaking *white limousine!* I felt like a movie star.

Kyle introduced me to his friends. I've received a few dirty looks from cheerleaders, but it won't kill my high of tonight. He asked *me* to the dance, not them.

Kyle holds his hand out. "Take a walk with me."

I nod and try to mask the excitement barreling through me.

Looking so handsome in his suit, he can ask me anything right now, and I'll say yes.

Can I have a kidney?

Yes!

Will you sell me your soul?

Duh!

I wipe my sweaty hands down my dress before taking his, and he leads us off our gym's makeshift dance floor. The room is filled with pink streamers, and the DJ has played "Cha Cha Slide" three times too many. Wandering eyes follow our every step as we make our way outside, and I'm surprised when he walks us to the football field.

We don't stop until we're in the center of the field, and he stares at me under the bright stadium lights before taking my other hand, too. "Can I kiss you, Chloe?"

"Yes," I answer with no delay. I lick my lips.

We're going to kiss!

Best. Freaking. Night. Ever!

He releases my hands and steps closer, so close that our lips are already nearly touching.

"Is this your first kiss?"

I swallow. "No."

I don't ask him the same. The stories of his player ways roam through the hallways more than students running late to class, and I've spotted him sucking face with his fair share of cheerleaders. He's experienced. There's no question about it—as experienced as a high school guy can be. I won't put my money on him being Claudia-level experienced.

I play off more confidence than I have. Our kiss will be my second. My first was with Marvin, the boy down the road. His tongue was sloppy, and his breath smelled like Cheetos—not a good time. I should've known a kiss with a boy named after a Martian would be nothing to party about.

Kissing Kyle will be different, not sloppy or gross. The girls I've seen him with always seem to be enjoying themselves and look far from grossed out.

Kyle stares down at me with a genuine smile, and all the anxiousness inside me melts away.

"You're adorable when you're nervous."

"It's *so* not adorable," I mutter. *More like pathetic. Who's afraid of a kiss?*

Goose bumps prick my skin when he cups my chin in his hand and drags my face up until we're making strong eye contact. He grins before tilting his head down, and then he softly presses his lips against mine.

It's perfect.

His lips are like super-soft pillows.

He slightly pulls away to eye me, awaiting my reaction, and when I stare at him, practically panting, he leans in for another kiss. He slides his tongue inside my mouth this time, and I gasp before doing the same.

No Cheetos breath on this guy.

He tastes like peppermint and spiked fruit punch.

I lose track of how long we make out before he stops to sit on the grass and pulls me down with him. My dress hikes up, and I know it's getting dirty. Briefly, I wonder how hard it will be to clean off grass stains because I am *so* keeping this dress for the rest of my life.

He gives me one last kiss before lowering me onto my back. He moves on top of me, holding himself up with his arm. "Is this okay?"

"Yes," I say in surprise.

I spread my legs for him to adjust himself between them, and my heart races when he lightly brushes strands of my hair off my shoulder. He plants kisses along my neck before dropping his mouth down to my cleavage.

"Your skin is so soft," he mutters, sucking the exposed skin between my breasts before cupping one in his hand.

My dress lifts more, and when I move to situate it, his pants-covered erection slides against my core.

Holy crap.

I've never experienced anything like this, never felt this tingling between my legs. I tilt my hips up to meet his, wanting more.

Okay, maybe he's more experienced than I thought.

He lets out a low moan before pressing against me, and his lips meet mine again.

His hands anchor around my hips. I thrust upward while he rocks against me over and over again as we make out on the field. I slightly pull away when his metal belt buckle hits my core.

"Do you want to stop?" he asks, pulling away and catching his breath.

I shake my head, and with unsteady hands, I unbuckle his belt. I settle myself on my back against the grass when I'm finished and smile. "Much better."

He grins, and our next kiss is rougher. His movements are more hurried as he pushes my dress up to my waist and exposes me, my red panties on display for him. After I fail to lower his pants with my feet, he pushes them down his thighs. We're so close that his breaths are hitting mine. My breathing is ragged when his erection under his boxers slides against my panties. My heart is racing like I ran a mile in gym class.

His fingers hook around the side of my panties, but he suddenly stops. "Have you done this before?" He peeks down at me with bright green eyes.

Am I that obvious?

"Does it matter?" I whisper.

He flinches and rests his hands on my thighs. "I'm not taking your virginity on a football field, Chloe."

I was so worked up that I forgot we were in public. Not just in public, but at our freaking *school.* Who dry-humps someone at school?

"It's … it's okay," I assure, struggling to keep my voice strong. *What are you thinking? Your sister was a pregnant teen!* "You have a condom, right?"

He keeps staring, contemplating his next move, and I rock against him to convince him to pop my cherry.

"Are you sure about this?"

I nod. "As long as you have protection."

"I do."

I miss his touch when he pulls away to grab his wallet, and the sound of him opening the condom cuts through our heavy breathing.

Then, that sound is overtaken by shrills of laughter.

"Holy fucking shit, ladies and gentlemen! Get a load of this! Lane is about to fuck Little Miss Trailer Trash!"

Kyle jerks my dress down and stands to pull his pants up before holding his hand out to me. I glare at him before moving my attention to the crowd around me. My chest tightens with embarrassment. My fellow classmates, clad in their formal attire, are pointing and laughing at me. They're holding their cell phones in my direction, no doubt recording my humiliation. The flashes of cameras nearly blind me.

I'm collapsed in the middle of the football field in a wrinkled, dirty dress, and the condom Kyle planned to wear while taking my virginity is lying beside me. There will be photographic evidence of this forever.

Tears prick at my eyes while the insults continue.

"I can't believe you'd touch her!" a girl yells. "Haven't you seen her sister? She has, like, ninety STDs. You can get them from sharing a toilet, you know."

"Now, I know why he asked her to the dance!" another shouts.

"We knew you could do it, man! See, there's no stick up her ass, only your cock!" adds another.

More laughter erupts.

I cover my face in embarrassment, forcing myself to breathe, and tears stream down my cheeks. I kick off my flats, jump up, and sprint away from them with Kyle on my trail, screaming my name. When we're out of earshot from the mocking crowd, I whip around and face him.

"Chloe," he says, taking a hesitant step forward.

I bend down at the waist and catch my breath while holding my hand out to stop him. "You stay away from me."

"Let me explain."

"No. You're like the rest of them."

I push him, and while he catches his step, I take off running in the opposite direction. I go this way to school every day, so I can walk it with my eyes closed. When I hear his steps and voice still calling my name, I duck behind a bush. I wait until I only hear the leaves rustling with the wind before standing up and starting the walk home.

I sniffle and wipe my eyes with every step.

I'm naive and stupid.

The loser never gets the fairy tale.

She gets the nightmare.

———

I'm ten minutes away from home when a car pulls up behind me.

My back goes straight while I contemplate whether to take off running or turn around.

This is it.

Straight out of a horror movie, this will be the night of my death. I say a silent prayer when I hear a door slam. Even if I wanted to make a run for it, my feet don't want to move.

"Chloe!"

I whip around and zero in on the man headed in my direction. My heart pounds, but as he moves closer, I grow more comfortable.

"What are you doing out here?" he yells when he's steps away. "You're going to get yourself run over!"

I wipe away my never-ending tears, and my body trembles when I blow out a shaky breath. "I … I don't want to talk about it."

Sam stops and stares down at me. "What were you thinking?" He takes me in. He shoots a glance toward his car running, and then his attention moves back to me. "Come on. I'll take you home, but you can't say a fucking word. Do you hear me?" His face is laced with concern, but his voice is harsh.

I look past him toward the car, and my eyes widen. "I don't need a ride."

A head pokes out of the window. "Who is she?" he yells.

I squint, taking in the people in the vehicle before dragging my eyes to Sam. I'm just as confused as the voice asking who I am. "Who are those people?"

"It doesn't matter," he barks. "Now, do you want a ride or not?"

My lower lip trembles, and I want to wrap my arms around him. I want to tell him how terrible my night has been because Sam is my only friend. But I don't. I don't because, right now, this isn't the Sam I know, and I'm not getting into a car with those people.

"No, I'm okay."

"Chloe," he warns.

"I'm fine," I snap.

He stands tall. "This is the last offer I'm giving you."

"I appreciate the offer, Sam, but I'm okay."

He leans down to whisper in my ear, "Don't say a word about this. You never saw this. You never saw me *or them*. Do you understand me?"

I nod, and the tears continue to fall.

I don't start walking again until he pulls away.

When I get home, I throw the dress in the trash.

———

When I return to school, I'm no longer the class loner no one pays attention to.

I'm the joke. They laugh and point at me. I'm called the same names my sister is called. A photo of yours truly is plastered against my locker. The pain hits me as I take in the picture of me on the football field, and I cringe at the horror on my face in the photo.

"Chloe Fieldgain gave pussy on the football field," is chanted down the hallway.

I slam my locker shut and flee to the restroom, locking myself in a stall as I cry *again*.

I've lived up to my family name because of him.

After the bell rings, I wipe my eyes and leave the restroom, unsure of what my next move will be.

Do I leave or cut class?

I round the corner to find Kyle waiting for me.

He's in his football jersey, his hair is messy, and his green eyes are wide. He halts, glancing to each side of the hallway, and then moves closer.

"Chloe," he draws out.

"You stay away from me," I warn.

He takes another step until he's standing in front of me. "Let me explain …"

The few people lingering in the hall gasp when I smack him across the face. "Go to hell, Kyle."

I whip around and start walking away.

"Dude, she smoked you!" I hear a guy say to him in the background.

"She came to me, begging for a second round, and was pissed I told her to kick rocks," Kyle says. "They always come back, wanting more."

I freeze in my step, and my heart nearly explodes out of my chest. *Is he kidding me?*

"Dude, you'd better go get checked after that one."

I hear someone smack him on the back.

"I always wrap it up," he replies.

I cringe and ball my knuckles into fists while I talk myself out of turning around and punching him in the face this time.

I go home and vow to hate Kyle for the rest of my life.

As time passes, I learn to ignore the names, the rude gestures, and the condoms stuck to my locker.

I'm now known as the girl who gave it up to Kyle Lane on the football field.

CHAPTER FOURTEEN

KYLE

I admire Chloe in my bed like a stalker from a Lifetime movie. The sheet is pushed up her chest as she faces me, sleeping. I'm pushing a strong eight on the creep scale. I don't stare at women like this.

She's beautiful—drop-dead fucking gorgeous.

The first time I saw her was in elementary school. She was front and center of the classroom, sitting there before anyone else arrived, with her attention on the book sitting on her desk. She was a stranger. I'd never seen her at any birthday parties or playdates. I was nervous when I took the seat next to her, but she never once glimpsed in my direction.

Her social isolation continued into middle school. Anytime I attempted to strike up a conversation, I was given short responses, and then she would go back into her shell of solitude.

Then, high school hit, and she talked to me. It wasn't the conversation I had been hoping for. It was about grades. We held the top GPAs in our class, and grades were something she took seriously. She studied her ass off. Her attention was always focused on school, and everyone knew her end game was to be valedictorian. She wanted it enough to step out of her comfort zone and ask me to compare test grades.

She needed to become valedictorian more than me. You didn't need to know her backstory to know she wasn't as fortunate as I was.

She walked to school, her off-brand sneakers were always in poor condition, and she never attended a field trip. She needed the scholarships more than me. I was headed to college whether or not I had them, so at times, I'd answer questions wrong to lower my test scores.

I liked her. I wanted to know more about her. She was naturally beautiful, both inside and out, and intelligent. She was kind to everyone, not just to those she deemed worthy, like most kids in my circle.

I finally gained the courage to ask her to the dance after Gage told me to stop pussyfooting around. He knew I crushed on her, and like me, he didn't give a shit about outside influence. When she said yes, I was ecstatic. Sure, a few assholes made snide comments, but I didn't care. I wanted to know more about Chloe Fieldgain, about the girl who seemed to be a shining star among others who dimmed with nothing.

Then, everything fell apart. I hate myself for how it went down.

After the dance, I had no way to contact her. She had no phone or email, and all anyone knew was that she lived in a trailer court on the west side.

It got worse when she came back to school and gave me the smack I deserved. I was pissed, my friends were making fun of me, and I was a stupid-ass teenager, so I lied. I joked at her expense because of my embarrassment that she wanted nothing to do with me.

Over time, we became rivals. I led her to believe I was vying for valedictorian while still throwing tests. On the day of graduation, when she shyly gave a short speech, I grinned.

Chloe isn't just an attractive woman. I liked her before I knew about sex or relationships or status. I wanted her to be my girlfriend then. Now, I want to make her more. After having all of her, there's no way I'm letting her go this time.

I've never touched skin as soft as hers or experienced a connection so strong with someone—both inside and outside of the bedroom. I've never had sex without a condom or wanted to keep a woman in my bed, like I do her.

Fuck me. My feelings for her are stronger than I thought.

She stirs when I press my lips against her cheek.

"Good morning," I whisper.

Her eyes don't open, but she releases a sleepy laugh. "Fuck off."

"As much as I love our porch routine, I love this one *so much* better. Say fuck in this bed as often as you like."

Her eyes stay closed, and she grins.

"Call into work today," I say when her eyes flutter open. Correction: I fucking plead.

She yawns and keeps her head rested on the pillow. "As much as I'd love to, I can't. Neither can you. You need to stop the criminals."

We're facing each other, our eyes locked and cheeks against pillows.

"I work second shift," I say, stretching forward to brush back a strand of her hair. "Did you decide about *hanging out* with Gage and Lauren? They're going to the city for a night and invited us."

"Are you sure they didn't invite *you*, and you're asking me to tag along?"

"Babe, I doubt they'd invite me out on the town as a third wheel. They want you to come."

She pulls in a breath, and I take in the beauty of her blonde hair against the pillowcase and the light freckles sprinkled across her nose. "I don't know."

"Give me your reasons for not wanting to go," I challenge.

"People are already gossiping about us hanging out. Imagine what they'll say when we *double date* with your best friend."

I want to say, *Let them talk*, but don't. She's Chloe, and Chloe overthinks.

"It's out of town. No one will know us. Trust me."

She bites into her plump bottom lip.

"Come on," I tease. "It'll be fun."

She throws her head back. "All right, you've talked me into it."

My eyes widen. "You do know all right means yes?"

She laughs. "Yes, I'm well aware of what all right means. Why are you so shocked?"

"You said yes to double-dating with me."

She points her finger my way. "No, I agreed to double *hanging out* with you."

"It's a date. Admit it."

She holds in a smile while shaking her head.

I slide out of bed. "I'm going to shower. Care to join?"

She turns on her back and stretches. "A hot shower sounds amazing right now."

I walk around the bed to her side and hold out my hand. "I'll be nice and share my shower with you on one condition."

She rises up. "What's that?"

"Admit we're going on a date. I'll share my shower, wash your hair, and then, if you're good, give you an idea of what to look forward to on our double date."

She sits on the edge of the bed and stares up at me. "Maybe I'll shower when you're done."

"I'll be sure to run *all* the hot water out. If you like taking cold showers, it'll be all yours, babe."

She stares at me with reluctance.

"Say it," I tease. "You know you want to."

"Fine. I'll go on a *double date* with you."

I grab her around the waist and throw her over my shoulder. "All right, since you insist, I'll go on a double date with you!"

———

"I told you I'd make you breakfast in bed one day," I say, shooting a glance over at Chloe. "I have a future breakfast lover in my bed."

Plates with pancakes and eggs are balanced on our sheet-covered legs, and our backs are resting against the headboard.

"Maybe I don't want to be a breakfast person," she comments, turning to grab her cup of coffee from the nightstand and taking a drink.

"What's your beef with breakfast, huh?" I ask. I cut into my pancake, smother it in syrup, and take a bite.

She sets her cup down and shrugs. "It's not my thing. Sometimes, I'll grab something while on the go, but it's not a meal I've ever looked forward to. My mom didn't bother with feeding us well-balanced meals, and we were stuck with what the food pantry handed out. Most of the time, it was plain, generic cereal that I grew tired of."

If there wasn't a plate of food on her lap, I'd drag her to my side and collect her in my arms. I wish I could've helped her when we were younger, given her someone to ask for help when she needed a cheeseburger or a friend. I should've never taken the broken girl to the football field and shattered her more. I never planned for us to hook up, and contrary to what Chloe believes, I never meant for anyone to follow us. All I wanted was to kiss her, but one thing led to another, and the horny teenager in me was game for whatever she'd allow.

"I will make you breakfast every morning in exchange for you not telling me to fuck off." I playfully elbow her. "Deal?"

She glances at me sideways and points to me with her fork. "I'll get back to you on that, Officer." She takes a giant bite and nods while chewing it up. "And, since you're always asking me for favors, I have one to ask of you."

"Lay it on me. Getting a yes from me will be more effortless than getting one from you."

She nervously looks away.

"Spit it out. You asking for my firstborn?"

I've come to realize Chloe never asks anyone for anything. This must be important to her.

She takes in a quick breath. "Trey has a football game tomorrow. He asked me to invite you."

That's it? She's nervous about a football game? The fuck?

"I'll be there."

She squints at me. "What? That was too easy."

"Did you want it to be complicated? He has a football game. I don't have plans. Why would I say no?"

She shrugs. "Kent never wanted anything to do with Trey or Gloria." She frowns. "Sometimes, he acted like they were more of an inconvenience."

I like kids and consider myself a good big brother. Trey seems like he can use a good big brother influence.

"You *still* haven't realized that Kent is an asshole? Him bailing on

Trey's games isn't a surprise," I say. "I don't blame him for bailing. He didn't like being reminded of how he couldn't catch a football to save his life."

"Oh my God, you're terrible!"

A piece of pancake falls from her mouth when she snorts, and I laugh as she stares at me in horror. I shrug it off, not wanting her to feel uncomfortable about it, and she grabs her napkin to clean up her mess.

"In the beginning, it was a healthy relationship. He was a good boyfriend," she says. "He wasn't a cheater or so self-centered. Maybe it was a game to him. Men seem to enjoy games." She throws me a dirty look.

"A boyfriend who can't give you an orgasm isn't a good boyfriend," I counter.

"It wasn't like that *every time*, only a few. Women don't *always* get off, Kyle. Google it if you doubt me."

I grab her empty plate, set it on top of mine, and place them on the nightstand. I don't regularly leave dirty dishes in my bedroom, but I'll take care of them as soon as we're done with this stupid conversation about her lame-ass ex.

"A few times he didn't give you an orgasm or a few times he did?"

She scowls and folds her arms across my tee she's wearing. "I'm not talking about my old sex partner with my new sex partner."

I hold my hand up. "Please do not refer to me as your new sex partner again."

"Then, what would you like me to refer to you as? My booty call? My neighbor dick?"

I start counting out the names on my fingers. "The guy who gives you the best orgasms. Your favorite dick. The guy you are *kind of* dating but don't want to admit it. Refer to Kent as your sex partner all you want—your inadequate sex partner—but not me."

She rolls her eyes. "Don't be so mean."

"Don't defend a chump, and I won't be."

"He was the only guy who'd speak to me after what you did, you know."

I gape at her. "Wow. Did you know he never once stood up for you in the locker room? In fact, not to hurt your feelings, but he cracked plenty of jokes at your expense. Plenty."

She waves off my information. "He was a stupid high school boy. We didn't start dating until after college."

"He gets to be a *stupid high school boy*, but I'm fucking Satan?"

"The rumors started because of you." She fixes her stare on me but isn't as pissed as she normally is when we talk about this. Hurt is clear on her face, but now, there's a thin layer of understanding. She's lowering her walls, trusting me, and finally giving me a chance to explain myself. "You could've changed everything and stopped your friends and *girlfriend* from making my life miserable."

I suck my cheeks in. "You wouldn't speak to me!"

"Why would I?" she snaps. "You set me up!"

I repeatedly shake my head. "I never set you up. That's bullshit."

She snorts. "Oh, come on. We're hooking up, and then, *boom*, your asshole posse of friends shows up to take humiliating pictures of me. I used to think you were this amazing guy. I can't even explain how excited I was when you invited me to the dance. It was my first dance and turned out to be utter hell—because of you, Kyle. I was stupid enough to believe you liked me."

Whoa. What?

I glance at her and refuse to continue our conversation until her eyes meet mine. Hers are sad. Understandably, this conversation hurts her, but I'm glad we're finally talking this out. There's a thickness in my throat when I respond. Even though I couldn't stop them from finding us, she's right that I could've attempted to stop their teasing. Chloe hurt me, and I let my stupid male ego stand in the way of realizing I could've stood up for her.

"Chloe," I gently say, "I would've never asked you to the dance if I didn't like you."

She scoffs as an attempt to hide the hurt. "You invited me as a joke, as a prank."

I wince. *She thinks it was a prank?*

"Chloe, I swear to you, me inviting you to the dance was not a prank. Should I have taken you to the field? No. I wanted to kiss you, and it sounded better, maybe even romantic in my teenage eyes, than in some supply closet or a bedroom at an after-party where my friends were taking their dates. I never brought you there to put on a show for the school. They also took pictures of me with my pants down."

"Which made the girls want you more," she cuts in.

Shame fills me. It's true.

"Why would I take you as a prank? I could've had anyone go with me."

She throws her hands up. "Oh, wow, everyone. Let's welcome Kyle's ego to the conversation."

"I didn't say it to brag but to make a point. I sincerely liked you. You intrigued me. You were smart and fucking gorgeous, and your personality was genuine. You never said a distasteful word about anyone, and you worked hard for everything you had." I blow out a stressed breath. "Did it piss me off when you wouldn't even let me explain myself? Yes. Did it piss me off when you slapped me in front of my friends? Yes. So, I decided, *Fuck it. If she wants nothing to do with me, then it is what it is.*"

"You let them make my life a living hell," she grinds out.

I situate myself, so I'm sitting in front of her when I notice tears slipping down her cheeks. *Shit.* I don't want to make her cry, especially in my bed.

She attempts to look away and hide her swollen face and tears, but I don't allow it. Her eyes dart toward the bathroom door and then the hallway, searching for an escape plan so that I don't see her without her armor on.

"Fuck," I hiss, cupping her face with my hands. "Please don't cry. I'm sorry. Tell me what I can do to make it better. You want me to put an ad out in the paper? Wear a tee with an apology letter on it?"

She sniffles but is no longer trying to pull away. I still haven't earned eye contact yet though.

"It doesn't matter. It's over with."

I grimace and soften my tone. "If it still hurts you, then it matters.

I'm sorry, Chloe. I was a stupid little prick who didn't think about where my actions would lead. I'm sorry."

She inhales a few calming breaths before releasing a nervous laugh. "Thank you. Even though we can't go back in time, I'm glad we talked about it. It was long overdue, and I should've come to you about it. You also should've grown some balls and made an announcement or even put out a stupid ad, you prick."

"If it counts for anything, I broke up with Becky Binds after she wrote *slut* on your locker. Oh, and I punched Daniel Moore for asking me if I'd put in a good word with you for him to get into your panties."

"Wow, that makes sense now. While I appreciate the attempt and your intentions might have been pure, you breaking up with her made her hate me more."

"Shit, that sure backfired on me, didn't it?"

She nods.

"I can still put out an ad now, you know?" I stretch forward and grab my phone from the nightstand. "Let me call Melanie and see who's in charge of advertising in *The Blue Beech Register*. I'll ask them to draft up something." I hold my phone up. "Do you think we can have it in this week's paper?"

She snatches my phone from me. "Oh God, no! I was kidding!" She points it at me. "Swear to God, if there's *anything* with my name in the paper tomorrow, I'm killing you. I can see Melanie being sneaky and allowing you to do it."

"So, you're done hating me now?" I attempt the best look of innocence I can manage.

"No matter how I feel toward you now, I will always hate you for it." A smile plays at her lips, and she pinches two fingers together while shutting one eye. "A little less now."

I grip her waist and draw her toward me. "Let me fuck all that hate out of you, and you can work on loving me."

We both flinch at my words.

Oh fuck.

That was the worst thing to say.

I have feelings for her but can't love her.

We hardly know each other.

I've never been in love with a chick.

In high school, I thought I was in love a few times, but again, I was a dumb fucking teenager.

I act like the words never came out of my mouth and kiss her, hoping my dick will help her forget them.

CHAPTER FIFTEEN

KYLE

"What are you doing here?"

I turn around to find a woman I vaguely recognize. I know her from somewhere but can't pinpoint exactly where. Her blonde hair is teased, her top is low-cut enough to show me her push-up bra, and hints of red lipstick decorate her front teeth.

"And you are?" I question.

"I'm Claudia, Chloe's sister," she answers with a snarl.

Ah, yes.

I've arrested her a few times. She's called me every name in the book and then some I've never heard before. Chick might be a junkie, but she's creative as fuck with her insults.

"You need to leave," she demands with a hostility I don't understand.

Chloe said her sister hated my guts, but damn, this is overboard.

We're in a crowd of people, and my hands are full with concession stand snacks. This isn't the best place to hold this conversation.

"I'm here for the same reason you are," I answer. "To watch the football game."

Her shoulders slightly relax, but her tone is still louder than necessary. "Trey said you got him off the hook for stealing from that Garfield bitch."

People stop at her words, and they glance at us with curiosity, some even with disgust.

I lower my voice, hoping she'll do the same. "I helped him out, yes."

"Why?"

"I like to help people."

She takes a step toward me. "Is that what you're doing? Helping my sister like you're goddamn Superman? Do not use my children as a pawn to fuck her." She shakes her head. "I know your type. Your stuck-up wife who can't suck dick properly bores you in the bedroom, so you come to us *trash* to entertain you instead. When you're finished getting your rocks off, we get thrown away."

Fuck, the shit Chloe has to put up with from this woman.

No wonder she's always stressed the fuck out. This chick has raised my blood pressure after a five-minute conversation. I can't imagine what it's like to live around her. I need to help Chloe remove some of her sister's weight off her shoulders, maybe help out with the kids.

"Sorry to burst your bubble, Claudia, but there's no boring housewife sitting at home, so I don't understand what you're talking about," I reply with a smile. "And I doubt I'll ever grow bored with her."

She winces and takes a moment to come up with a response. She didn't expect my answer. "You'll have one eventually and then throw my sister away. I'm here to stop that."

"It won't happen, so do yourself a favor and stop worrying about Chloe. Pass your worries onto your children. Now, let's go enjoy your son's game."

I walk away before she can respond and head toward the bleachers where Gloria and Chloe are waiting. I hand them their goods and take a seat next to Chloe. Minutes later, Claudia and a man sit down in the row behind us.

"Kyle," Chloe says, gesturing to them, "this is my sister and her friend—"

"My *boyfriend*, Roger," Claudia corrects.

"Right, Roger," Chloe replies.

I give them a nod. "It's nice to meet you."

Claudia gives me a cold glare. "Really, asshole? You going to act like we didn't share words back there?"

Chloe earmuffs Gloria with her hands.

"No, I wasn't going to mention you going nuts on me, but fine." I move my gaze from her to Chloe. "Your sister is convinced I have an imaginary wife and need to stay away from you."

Chloe's face shades in embarrassment. I didn't need to say her sister's words for her to understand.

"Claudia," she warns, "this is not the place for one of your scenes."

Too late for that.

"I don't want him or his stuck-up family around my children," she snarls.

"Relax. He wants to help Trey stay out of trouble. Trey didn't get a shoplifting charge because of Kyle. You should be thanking him instead of giving him a rough time."

"Roger can help Trey stay out of trouble."

I can't stop myself from laughing, and I hold my hand over my mouth to hide it. I don't do it well though. I can tell Chloe is biting her tongue from doing the same. Roger is the last person I'd want as a role model for my son. I've picked him up for petty crimes. Dude also has sticky fingers.

Claudia leans forward and sticks her head between Chloe and me. "He thinks he's better than us."

"No, *he* doesn't," I correct.

"He doesn't. Kyle is trying to help," Chloe says. "Like I said, this isn't the place."

"It's never the place to state my opinion with you. No one is allowed to embarrass precious Chloe and her perfect reputation." She lets out a sarcastic laugh and fixes her attention on me. "Oh, wait, some asshole already tarnished your reputation. Now, you're fucking him and making a fool of yourself. Don't come running to me when you find out he's using you for pussy."

She sure puts a somber mood on shit.

Claudia was kind enough to raise her voice louder than the announcer, so all eyes are now on us. Chloe is pulling her jacket tighter around her body, and her eyes won't meet mine—no doubt, out of embarrassment.

I stand. "I'll go."

Chloe brings her hand up to stop me. "No." She glances over at Claudia. "Trey wanted Kyle to come. Let's not disappoint him more than we already have, okay?"

"Wanted him to come?" Claudia says, appalled. "Okay, whatever." Her glare turns to me. "Stay away from my children. This will be the last time my son will want to hang out with you after I tell him what you did to his aunt." Her glare goes back to Chloe. "Here I am, trying to show up and be a good mom, and you do this."

I ignore Claudia and focus on Chloe, forcing a smile before leaning in so that only she can hear me. "I'll stay, but I'm going to watch from somewhere else."

"Thank you," she whispers.

I ignore Claudia's shit-talking as I walk away. As I'm looking for a new seat, I spot Gage and Lauren in the stands. They exchange a confused glance when I sit down. I failed to tell them I was coming.

"I see you party animals are enjoying your Friday night," I say. "What are you guys doing here?"

"Dude, what better way is there to spend a Friday night than watching high school kids kick ass in football?" Gage replies with a grin.

"The better question is, what are you doing here?" Lauren says. "Normally, you spend your Fridays at Down Home with the guys."

I nod toward the field. "Chloe said Trey asked for me to come."

"Trey as in Chloe's nephew?" Gage questions, the words slowly leaving his mouth.

"Yes."

"You're so damn screwed," he mutters.

"She agreed to a double date," I inform them. "So, please act normal for once."

Lauren fakes offense. "What? I'm always normal."

Gage snorts while I chuckle.

She rolls her eyes and slaps Gage on his shoulder, resulting in a laugh and kiss from him.

I sit back and watch the game.

Trey is the JV quarterback and has talent. I watch him play while also keeping my eye on Chloe. She's trying but not doing a great job of hiding how miserable she is with her sister and Roger.

———

"Pizza! I love pizza!" Gloria sings while skipping into the pizza shop with Chloe at her side.

Trey's team won. After the game ended, Chloe texted, saying Gloria was hungry and cranky, so they were leaving, and she thanked me for coming. As soon as I saw them get up, I jumped up from my seat and followed her down the bleachers.

Not in a stalker way, I swear it.

I stayed to the side while Chloe and Claudia talked near the entrance, but Claudia's loud mouth made it possible for me—along with everyone around—to hear her every word. From what it sounded like, she was skipping out on Trey's celebratory pizza dinner in exchange for having a drink with good ole Roger. I'm a drinker. I don't care who else drinks, but don't ditch your kid who played his ass off for a few beers.

Because crazy Claudia bailed, I had the opportunity to invite myself.

So, here we are.

Pizza-ing it up.

Gloria and Trey squeeze into one side of the booth while Chloe and I do the same across from them. I rub my hands together after ordering drinks and study the menu even though I've eaten here hundreds of times. It's the only pizza joint in town.

"So," I say, setting the menu to the side, "your aunt Chloe said we're getting extra anchovies on our pizza."

I'm good with kids. We hold events and fundraisers at the station all the time, and when my siblings and I were growing up, my mom insisted we do our fair share of charity, most of them involving children from bad upbringings.

"Heck no!" Trey exclaims, shaking his head. "I'm not eating that nasty crap."

Gloria peers up at me, her blonde hair back in French braids and finished off with red bows. "What are anchovies?"

"Dead Nemos," Trey replies.

"Trey!" Chloe warns. "Not funny."

"What?" Trey questions. "I'd prefer not to enjoy Nemo with my extra cheese."

Gloria appears close to tears.

Shit. Maybe I'm not good with kids anymore.

She's thinking we're devouring cartoon characters tonight. "But … but I love Nemo."

Chloe shoots Trey a stern look. "Your brother is kidding, honey." She slides crayons to her. "Now, show me how well you color."

Chloe's attention moves to entertaining her niece and taking her mind away from eating striped fish.

"You played a good game tonight," I tell Trey.

He grins and perks up in his seat. "Thanks, dude. I'm hoping they move me up to varsity. It'd be awesome!"

"Kyle played varsity," Chloe says, bumping my shoulder.

Whoa. Is this about to finish with a compliment or a smart-ass comment about jocks?

"Cool!" Trey says with wide eyes. "What position did you play?"

I scratch my neck. "Quarterback."

"I bet you got laid all the time," Trey comments.

"Seriously, Trey," Chloe says, gesturing to Gloria.

He shrugs. "It's the truth. Dudes on varsity get so many chicks, and considering there's not much else going for me, I need all the help I can get."

Chloe flinches next to me at the same time I frown.

"What does that mean?" she snaps.

Uh-oh.

Trey plays with the straw in his drink and looks down in shame when answering, "Come on, you know our family and where we live. Girls don't want to date guys who come from the trailer park or ones with no money. So, if I make it to varsity, they'll like me more."

I open my mouth to assure him it's not true, but a response coming from me isn't appropriate. I hate he's going through it, but I've never experienced that struggle. The best person to tell him not to look at himself that way and ensure it gets better is the woman sitting next to me—a woman who was raised in it, struggled with it, and then rose from it. Chloe is living evidence you can't control the cards you're dealt, but you can control how you play them.

Hurt and resentment are clear on her face, but her voice is soft when she speaks, "That's not true."

I wait for her to say more, but there's nothing. Maybe it's a sensitive subject for her. Shit, *maybe* is an understatement. I've talked to children who live there, and their lives aren't pretty.

I point to Trey and decide to brighten the somber mood the best I can. "I'd suggest not pursuing a girl who dates you because you either made it to varsity or have money. She's not the type who will end up being a good girlfriend."

"Plus," Chloe adds before Trey can reply, "I thought you were dating a girl from the neighborhood?"

He shrugs. "I was."

"And?" she questions.

"She's not ..." He pauses to shake his head, as if he's debating whether to continue. "People make fun of her. People make fun of *me* for hanging out with her."

I look over at Chloe in fear for myself. Her attitude is sexy but can also be scary as hell. Her eyes are closed, and a mixture of pain and fury flashes across her face. Trey's attention goes to his drink. He's taking loud sips, realizing it's better to keep his mouth shut sometimes.

"Let me guess," Chloe finally snaps, and she peeks over at Gloria before continuing her ass-chewing. "Earmuffs, sweetie."

Gloria drops her crayons and places her hands over her ears.

Chloe clears her throat, lubricating her impending lecture. "Let me guess; she's called trailer trash for where she lives—side note, which is also where *you* live—and for her parents being poor. She doesn't own brand-name shoes or have the extra funds to go on class trips, so they sneer at her in disgust, as if she were scum beneath their shoes." She focuses on him in disappointment. "Don't you dare judge or hurtfully treat a girl—better yet, *anyone* for that. Do you hear me?" She rests her elbows on the table, leans in, and lowers her voice. "Let me tell you something. I was that girl they're teasing. Do it again, and I will ground you for so long; you'll be eighty before you see a varsity jersey."

Da-yum.

Chloe came in with the kill shot.

Trey struggles for a response. "I … I didn't mean it like that."

"Yes, you did," she says within seconds.

He looks at us, embarrassed. "It's hard here." He shakes his head. "Forget it. Remind me not to talk about my girl problems with you."

"You can bring up your girl problems with me anytime," Chloe says. "I'd prefer it, so you don't make decisions like that again."

"Or ask me," I add. "I happen to be very educated on the ladies."

Chloe elbows me. "He is not very educated on the ladies, hence why he's still single." Her eyes focus on Trey. "Don't be an asshole to her, you hear me? I will make it my mission to check up with her regularly to make sure you're not."

"I understand," Trey says. "I know it's wrong. I'll talk to her tomorrow and apologize."

Chloe leans forward to remove Gloria's earmuffs.

Dinner has taken a sad turn. I frown. Chloe's reaction hit a chord. A thickness forms in my throat for not treating her better or for not sticking up for her, so she wouldn't feel like *that girl.*

"Now that that's over, let's change the subject to rainbows and butterflies, okay?" Chloe says, her mood turning the opposite in seconds. She grins at Gloria and starts coloring with her again.

We order our food. I talk football with Trey while Chloe and Gloria color until our pizza comes. Pepperoni, no anchovies.

The mood lightens as we eat. Gloria talks about how much she loves her preschool teacher and how her class loved the pink boots

Chloe had gotten her. Trey talks about his grades and how he aced his last few tests.

They're good kids.

Good kids limited on opportunity because of their background.

And that fucking sucks.

Being a police officer has matured me and opened my eyes to how others aren't born into privileged lives like I was. I see these kids who go without. If it looks like they need food, I'll buy them something at the diner, or I'll slip them some candy. But I've never heard their stories like this.

This dinner has enlightened me.

———

Trey slams my Jeep door shut at the same time I get out, and we walk over to Chloe's house from my drive. He asked to ride with me after pizza. It's unfortunate the people in this town label kids like him as delinquents without knowing their stories. Trey isn't trouble. He's a kid who needs direction and a good role model, and I'm up for helping anyone I can.

"Dude," he says next to me. He's a teenager and already nearly six feet tall. "You'd better be coming over and hanging out with us tonight."

We walk up the porch steps where Chloe is jamming her key into the front door lock while Gloria stands next to her, holding a doll sporting ratty hair.

"I'm not sure about that, buddy," I answer. I have no problem with coming over uninvited when it's just Chloe home but not when the kids are over.

"Come on," Trey argues with a face full of determination. "I have the best Netflix watch list. Plus, it's not like you old folks have anything better to do on a Friday night. You're going to go home, get rid of the corns on your feet, and then clean your dentures."

Trey is a little smart-ass.

He reminds me of myself at his age.

Chloe helps Gloria inside the house and starts flipping on lights when we walk in. "Hey now," she calls out to Trey, "we are not that old."

"You two are freaking ancient," Trey continues before glancing at me. "There's no way you're going to bed this early."

I peer over at Chloe and wait for her permission. Yes, fucking wait for her permission like I'm the same age as Trey.

"Yes, Kyle, you don't want them to think we're *too old*," she replies in a playful tone. "Let's show these youngins that we can totally hang."

"Never say *totally hang* again," I say, winking. "You're already making us look old."

Trey slaps me on the back. "I'll be on popcorn duty. Kyle, make yourself comfortable!"

Gloria plops down on the couch and situates her baby next to her. "*The Grinch*!" she squeals. "I want to watch *The Grinch*!"

I sit down in an abandoned chair across from her. "*The Grinch*?" I question. "It's October."

"Gloria requests to watch it every day of the year," Chloe says around a sigh. "Netflix won't take it down." She sits down and starts carefully unbraiding Gloria's hair. "It's your bedtime, honey. How about we put your pajamas on, and I'll read *The Grinch* to you before bed?"

"Okay!" Gloria says with excitement. "Can I wear my princess pajamas?"

"Of course." Chloe peeks over at me. "Let me get her situated for bed. I'll be back."

I nod. "Take your time."

I've never seen this side of Chloe. I've seen the competitive, pissed off side of her. All she cared about was her grades in high school, so they called her the ice queen. She went to one school dance—the one with me. She didn't attend field trips, parties, games—anything. From the looks of it, she had no social life. Also, from the looks of it now, she still doesn't.

Trey returns with drinks and a large bowl of popcorn. "Here, dude." He tosses me a can of Coke. "This cool?"

I pop open the tab. "Sure is."

He takes Gloria's abandoned seat. "Aunt Chloe's ex was a Coke drinker, too, which I liked."

I raise a brow. *Not sure why the kid is bringing up Kent the Buzzkill.*

"Dude, you're way cooler than him," he quickly adds, as if reading my annoyance. "What I meant was, I like hanging out with someone who can have a good time without drinking beer and getting wasted—like all my mom's boyfriends do. I've drunk beer a few times. It tastes like cow piss." He peers at the hallway, making sure Chloe isn't within earshot. "Now, vodka, on the other hand …"

Shit. How do I tell this kid not to drink vodka when I was chugging the shit in high school? Fuck, I am not ready to be a dad yet. But, as a cop, I've given the same speech numerous times. Bonging a few beers didn't affect me when I was younger, but I can't say the same for others.

"This is much more satisfying than alcohol, I promise. Not to mention, safer."

He chuckles, shaking his head. "You have to say that as a grown-up and cop."

I lean back in my chair. "I'm not trying to be a dick, but look at your mother's boyfriends. Are they who you want to be like?"

He points his Coke to me and grins. "Good point."

I hold up my can in a cheers gesture.

He props his feet up onto the coffee table. "Thanks for coming to my game tonight."

"No problem. I had fun. Thanks for inviting me and letting me crash your pizza party."

"Crash our parties anytime, dude."

He pulls his phone from his pocket when it rings. "Shit," he whispers under his breath when he glances at the screen.

"What?" *I mean, watch your mouth.*

All playfulness is gone. "It's my mom."

He hits the Ignore button and shoves it back into his pocket. Can't say I blame the guy.

What seems like a minute later, Chloe returns to the living room with a ringing phone in her hand.

"Let me guess," Trey huffs out. "It's her."

Chloe's smile is gone. "I'm sorry, buddy," she replies with a strained voice.

"Ignore it, like I did," he replies.

Her face falls. "We both know what happens when I do that." She repeatedly shakes her head while moving out of the room and heading back down the hallway.

"What happens?" I ask Trey when she's gone.

He scrubs his hand over his chin, debating on whether to tell me. "Mom shows up here with her boyfriend of the week, and it ends up turning into some big drama-fest."

"Ah. No one likes drama-fests."

He uneasily glances around. "I hate her."

I wince. *Damn.* "Now, that's harsh."

He shrugs. "Maybe it is, but I do."

"I understand, but parents make mistakes, and eventually, maybe she'll learn from them."

"No, she won't." His voice is tense.

The little guy hates his mother. Even though my relationship with my father is strained, I love my parents. I have a good fucking mother who'd do anything for her children, whose world is wrapped around her children. It saddens me that he doesn't.

"Sorry, guys, but your mom wants you to come home," Chloe says, coming back into the room.

"Seriously?" Trey groans. "We just got here, and it's not a school night."

"I tried explaining, but she said she had plans for you in the morning," Chloe answers.

Trey rolls his eyes. "Yeah, right. Plans for us to make her and her boyfriend breakfast." His breathing shakes. "No. She chose not to go to dinner. Tell her we're staying here tonight."

Chloe looks at him in devastation. "I'm sorry, buddy. I tried. Now, grab your bag. Maybe I can pick you up tomorrow and we can do something, okay?"

She turns around, walks down the hall, and returns with Gloria in her arms.

"I'll drive you," I say, jumping up from the couch.

She shakes her head. "You don't need to do that."

I start following them outside. "I want to."

She sighs. "It will be a pain in the butt to move the car seat."

"Then, we'll take your car." I wink. "It won't be the first time I've driven it."

She shuts her eyes and sighs, as if she's lost all energy to carry on our conversation. "*Fine,* but I'll drive since I know where it is. You can ride passenger."

Her giving in so easily surprises me. "Works for me."

The four of us load into the car, and everyone is quiet as she makes her way out of town. I've answered police calls in this neighborhood plenty of times. Sadly, it's where most of our crime comes from—the outskirts of Blue Beech.

Chloe parks in front of a run-down brown trailer, unbuckles her seat belt, and then glances at me. "I need to go in and make sure everything is okay."

"What do you mean, make sure everything is okay?" I ask before she gets out.

"She needs to go in and make sure Mom isn't drunk, or it's an unsafe situation for us to be in," Trey answers for her.

She looks back and gives him a look, saying he shouldn't have said that.

I clutch my door handle. "Let me come with you."

She grabs my shoulder to stop me. "Definitely not a good idea. It'd make things worse. Stay here. I'll be back."

I don't settle in my seat. "The fact that the three of you could possibly walk into an *unsafe* situation makes me uncomfortable, and there's no way I can sit here. I'll stand on the porch, out of the way. No one will even know I'm there."

She opens her mouth to argue, but her phone starts ringing. I see Claudia's name on the screen.

"Fine," she says with a groan.

She helps Gloria out of her car seat while I grab her bag, and we walk up the creaky porch steps. I hand Trey Gloria's bag, and a whiff of cigarette smoke and mold hits me when they open the door. I stand out of view and watch through the torn blinds. Claudia is sitting on the couch with a cigarette in her hand, talking to Chloe about needing money for food. Roger is spread out next to her with a beer in one hand and a slice of pizza in the other. Claudia must be too dumb to realize that asking for food money when there's an open pizza box in front of him isn't helping her case.

"You've tapped me out this month," Chloe says with a stressed breath.

"Don't act like you've forgotten who took care of you when Mom didn't," Claudia snaps.

"I took care of myself, but thank you for the reminder," Chloe replies.

Claudia puts out her cigarette while Trey helps Gloria out of her coat. "When will you have it then?"

"I will go buy you groceries in the morning," Chloe says.

"I like doing it myself. You buy too much healthy stuff for our liking."

"I'll drop off groceries tomorrow, Claudia. I'm not arguing with you tonight." Chloe kisses Gloria and then Trey on their heads. "Good night, guys. Call if you need anything."

"They won't need anything, *Chloe*! I'm their mother. If they do, they can ask me," Claudia shouts to her back.

Chloe nods and walks out the door.

I rest my hand on her back as we walk down the steps to the car. I get into the driver's side while she takes passenger. She doesn't fight it. I see the defeat in her eyes.

I blow out a breath as I pull out of the neighborhood. "Chloe, I don't know how you do it."

She peeks over at me. "Do what?"

"Deal with her."

"I do it for the kids. Not her."

"I'm surprised she didn't let them stay. She seemed like she didn't want to spend another minute with them at the game."

"Trust me; it wasn't her wanting to spend time with them."

"What do you mean?"

"When she called, she asked me to borrow a few hundred dollars. I told her I didn't have it. She demanded I bring the children home, or she was calling the cops."

Wow. The nerve of her sister. "Babe, in case you haven't realized it, I am the cops. Did you tell her there was already one there?"

She gives me a look. "I don't want to drag you or any other law enforcement into my family's drama. Not to mention, people talk. She already causes enough problems for me, just being her. There doesn't need to be record of endless police visits to my house."

"Maybe you should take her to court and fight for custody."

"I've tried, but there's nothing I can do. She's passing drug tests. I have no power, and if I take it too far, the kids might end up in foster care before the process of adoption goes through. *If* I'm even able to adopt them. It's complicated. The system wants to keep children with their parents. Claudia uses it to her advantage with me."

"You ever walked into something you'd refer to as an unsafe situation with Claudia before?"

"A few times, yes."

"And?"

She fiddles with a ring on her finger. "I threatened to call the cops if she didn't let me leave with the kids. Claudia is not a fan of the police," she says, glancing over at me.

I grip the steering wheel. "Shocker."

"Big time."

"I need you to make me a promise." It's dark in the car, so I can't see the expression on her face.

"What's that?"

"Anytime you go over there, to make sure the kids or you aren't walking into a dangerous setting, you call me to come with you."

"I'm a big girl, Kyle," she replies with a thick voice.

"I'm well aware that you're strong as fuck, Chloe, but you're not invincible. Neither are those children."

"Okay."

I briefly scope her out. "Okay, what?"

"I'll call you before visiting any seedy trailers."

Her giving in without another argument surprises me.

When we get back to her house, I follow her into the kitchen where she grabs us a few waters from the fridge and then leads me back into the living room. I sit down next to her on the couch, and she tucks her feet underneath her ass, slightly facing me.

"If you also don't mind me asking, where's their father?" I ask, grabbing some popcorn from the bowl Trey brought out earlier.

Chloe shrugs. "They have different ones, and to be honest, I don't know."

"You don't know who they are or where they are?"

"Last I heard, Gloria's was in prison, and Trey's was a deadbeat asshole who chose not to be in his life." She rolls her eyes. "Exactly my sister's type."

"Has it always been this way? Her running to you every time she needs something? Being neglectful and expecting you to fix the problem?"

"For as long as I can remember."

I rest my arm on the back of the couch and study her. "If you ever need help with them, let me know."

She gives me a small smile. "They'd probably enjoy it, to be honest." She takes a long drink of water and rubs at her bottom lip. "Trey likes you, and I think you'd be a good influence on him."

I smirk arrogantly. "What's there not to like, babe?"

She shoves my chest.

"Maybe I'll ask him to put a good word in for me with his aunt."

"Hmm … you might already be putting in a good word for yourself," she whispers.

Surprising me again, she straddles my lap and circles her arms around my neck. I shut my eyes as she slightly grinds against me, her core rubbing against my now-growing cock.

I smile and run my fingers over the slit between her lips. "You know, I've realized something."

"What's that, *Officer?*"

I massage her breasts over her top, moving in a circular motion. "You haven't introduced me to your bed." I drag my fingers through her soft hair. "It seems unfair since you've become so familiar with mine."

My cock throbs when she slides off my lap and holds out her hand.

"Let me introduce you to it then."

My attention stays plastered to her ass, and I'm surprised I don't run into a wall as she leads me to her bedroom. The room brightens with the switch of the light, and she wastes no time before undressing. Chloe needs this tonight—needs to forget, to let loose, to be free of her problems.

What better way to make her feel good than with my fingers, my tongue, my cock?

I open my mouth to disclose all the dirty things I'll be doing to her body tonight when a thought pops into my head. *Yes.* Instead of my original plan of throwing her on the bed and devouring her pussy, I head to her nightstand while she stands, watching me.

She stops mid-unsnap of her bra. "What are you doing?"

"Oh, nothing. Proceed as you were," I answer with a grin, my attention staying on the drawer. I push away panties and bras until I find what I'm looking for. Her face reddens when I turn around and hold up her vibrator. "I want you to show me how you use this, Chloe."

She stands frozen, catching her breath, as the blush on her face grows redder. "What?" The word stutters from her plump lips.

I hold out the vibrator to her. "Show me what you like."

Her mouth falls open, and she rakes a hand through her hair. As she moves, her bra falls to the floor, and I lick my lips at the sight of her perfect breasts. I want to suck on them, suck on her, *fuck her*, but the urge to watch her play with herself overrides all those cravings—for the time being.

I inch forward, and she shivers when I run my hand over her hip.

"Chloe, I never want you to feel uncomfortable with me. I'll never judge you for what you like and don't like in the bedroom." I turn the vibrator on, rub it up her stomach, and then lower it to her core, running it over her panties. "If you want to show me, I'd love it. If not, we can do anything else you want."

I use my free hand to cup her breast, sliding my tongue against her perky nipple before wrapping my lips around it while continuing to stroke her with the vibrator. I lose my hold when she rips it from my hand and steps back. She's hesitant as she climbs up her bed, but as she watches me stare at her with desire, her confidence builds.

Fucking yes.

"Shit, Chloe," I say. "You are so fucking sexy, baby."

My words give her more courage, and she slips her panties down her legs, kicking them off her feet. I grab the ottoman sitting in the corner of the room and slide it in front of the bed, taking a seat and preparing for the most spectacular show I'll ever see.

"I've been dreaming of this."

It takes me seconds to unbuckle my pants, and my hand is wrapped around my cock before they even fall to the floor. She opens her legs and puts herself on full display for me—*for motherfucking me.* I'm close to exploding before giving myself the first stroke. How I got lucky enough for a sight and experience like this is beyond me. She caresses her clit with the vibrator first, then her slit, and then slowly plants it inside herself. I throw my shirt off and keep my eyes glued on her.

"Yes, God, that's so fucking hot," I pant.

I'm hypnotized, watching her pleasure herself. I keep the same pace, jerking myself off. It's torture to stop myself from coming. She rocks her hips up, her back arching, and I know she's close.

My voice falters when I tell her to stop.

I have to do it with her.

I want to do it with her.

On her.

A wild grin is on her face when she crawls to the end of the bed. She arches a finger, gesturing for me to come forward, and my cock twitches. I lick my lips, and my cock aches when I stop stroking it. She situates herself on her knees when I reach her and wait for her next move. Her gaze locks on mine when she rubs the vibrator along my lips.

"I've never done anything like this before," she whispers before handing me the vibrator and spreading her legs.

I caress her clit with it and then slide it inside her. Her hands grip my shoulders as I fuck her with it.

Her nails dig into my skin. "Have you … ever watched another woman do this?"

I drag away the vibrator, rest my palm on her stomach, and push her back before meeting her on the bed, my body over hers. "Nope, and don't care to. Only you." I groan when I push my cock inside her. "Only you, Chloe."

She whimpers as I stay in place, not moving, and I stare down at her. We make the strongest eye contact I've ever experienced.

Tonight was a big step for Chloe. She's never opened herself up like that to anyone else, not even to men she's opened her heart to.

I shiver when she runs her hands up and down my arms. "And trust me; you will be the only man who's ever watched me."

"Thank fuck."

Her confirmation sets me on fire. I grab her thighs, situate them on my shoulders, pull out, and thrust back into her. We find our release, and I fall down next to her.

I roll off and catch my breath as she rests her head on my chest.

"Thank you for everything tonight. For going to Trey's game, for the pizza party, and for giving me an orgasm." She snuggles tightly into my side. "And for tagging along to Claudia's. I feel safe with you."

I squeeze her tight. "And thank you for tonight—for letting me crash your party and be there for you, for fucking yourself in front of me and then letting me fuck you." I sigh. "And, even if you hadn't agreed, I would've followed you to Claudia's."

She holds herself up to look at me in question. "Why didn't I know you were this sweet?"

"You were too busy telling me to fuck off to give me the chance to show you the real me."

She laughs. "Oh, yeah, right."

Her lips meet mine through a smile.

CHAPTER SIXTEEN

CHLOE

Kyle walks into my living room and frowns while eyeing me. "I have to say, I'm a little disappointed."

"What? Why?" I question.

I peek down at myself. I appear the same as I did when I left his house this morning for work. Sleepovers at his place are now an everyday occurrence, and instead of saying good morning from his porch, he says it from next to me in bed.

"I was hoping you were dressed up."

I throw him an annoyed expression. "And what are you? Where's your *sexy* cop costume?"

"At my house. I'm saving it for later." He winks. "When I handcuff you to my bed."

I can't hold back my grin.

"Yes, handcuffing you to my bed is definitely tonight's plan."

Gloria stomping into the kitchen ends our flirt-fest. "Look at me, Aunt Chloe!" she squeals. She gives Kyle a lopsided smile when she spots him. "Can you guess what I am?"

He settles his finger on his chin. "Hmm … are you … the Tin Man?"

Gloria laughs and shakes her head. "No, silly!"

Kyle squints at her. "Are you the Cowardly Lion?"

Her smile widens. "No!"

"Then, you must be Dorothy!"

She hops up and down. "Yes." She holds her basket up and snatches the stuffed dog inside. "And this is Toto."

Kyle kneels, so he's eye-level with her. "Hello, Dorothy and Toto. It's nice to meet you." He shakes her hand before petting Toto on the head. "I'll give you extra candy when you stop by my house later."

"Yay!" She claps her hands. "I can't wait for all my candy."

"All right, Dorothy," I say, resting my palm on her back. "Let's do your pigtails."

We gather in the living room, and I sit down on the couch while Gloria plops onto the floor in front of me.

"What made you be Dorothy?" Kyle asks Gloria, resting in a chair. "Is that your favorite movie?"

Gloria nods. "My favorite in the entire world!" She kicks her feet back and forth, showing off her sparkly red shoes. "Do you like my shoes?"

"Very much," Kyle answers before lifting his leg. "Much cooler than these Nikes I'm sporting."

Gloria squeals. "What's your favorite movie?"

He glances around the room. "Promise not to tell anyone?"

Gloria holds her pinkie out. "I pinkie promise to infinity."

He leans in as if telling her a secret and then loops their fingers together. "It's *The Wizard of Oz*."

She claps her hands again. "Yay!"

I finish her pigtails at the same time Trey walks in, wearing his football gear.

Gloria frowns at the sight of him. "Where's your costume? You're supposed to be the Scarecrow!"

Trey's shoulders slump. "I told you, I'm not trick-or-treating this year."

Gloria crosses her arms and sulks. "And I said you have to."

"Sorry, but I'm too old for trick-or-treating," Trey answers.

She hops up and looks close to tears when she stomps her foot. "That's not fair!"

I stand and drape my arm around her. "Let's have a girls' Halloween night."

She sniffles and scowls at Trey, shooting him a stare that'd force me to cave in seconds. "You always come with me!"

He offers her an apologetic smile. "Sorry, Glor-Bear. Aunt Chloe said she'd take you though."

"Fine, I don't want you to come anymore," she declares, hiding her face in my waist.

"What about this?" Kyle comments. "I'm handing out candy at my house." He signals between Gloria and Chloe. "You two trick-or-treat it up." He winks at Gloria. "Save me the Reese's Cups, and Trey can hang out at my house. I made tacos, so come over when you're finished."

Trey gives Kyle a glance. "You made tacos?"

"Sure did."

"His mother made tacos," I correct with a smile.

"Your mom still cooks for you, bro?" Trey asks. "That's lame."

"For your information, *I* made the tacos tonight. My mom only makes my date-night meals," Kyle argues.

"That's even lamer," Trey comments. "You're supposed to impress chicks."

Trey goes to Kyle's, and Gloria and I go trick-or-treating for a good hour before we go to Kyle's for tacos. Trey might be too old for trick-or-treating, but he has no problem with raiding Gloria's candy bag.

Claudia picks the kids up late, and then I let Kyle use his hand-cuffs on me.

"I love this place," Lauren sings out, skipping into the restaurant. "Oh, the memories here will last a lifetime."

A prominent magazine I'd kill to write for has chosen Clayton's as one of the finest restaurants in Iowa for the past four years. I came here with Kent for all of our celebration dinners—our birthdays, anniversaries, and promotions. The restaurant is an hour out of Blue Beech, and we're staying in a hotel in the city for the night. It's nice, not worrying about nosy people gawking at you.

"Yes, such romantic memories." Gage chuckles before kissing Lauren.

Lauren glances at me while we make our way to the hostess stand. "When Gage came home, he followed me here. He also brought a date in a desperate attempt to make me jealous."

Gage ruffles his hand through Lauren's hair, resulting in a glare from her. "Why don't you elaborate on the story, babe? Tell her how you deceived me into thinking you were having an affair with a married man. Come to find out, you were here, celebrating your friend's birthday with his husband."

"Wow," I say while laughing.

I envy Lauren and Gage's relationship. They were high school sweethearts, and even though they broke up and he moved away, they reconciled. Now, she's pregnant, and they're engaged.

Lauren is wearing a red dress, her baby bump on display, and her black heels don't bring her close to Gage's stature. Her dark hair is down in curls, and Gage's is messy as he protectively settles his strong arm around her.

I'm dressed in a simple black dress with black heels. My blonde hair is straightened, and the only makeup I'm wearing is a bright red lip. Kyle is sporting a white button-down shirt with a hint of color on the collar and cuffs and dark jeans. Like his uniforms, the shirt perfectly fits him and showcases his broad shoulders and muscles.

In high school, I had no friends. All my dinner companions tonight were in the cool crowd. I never spoke to Gage. He spent most of his time with Kyle, and anyone who hung out with Kyle was an enemy. Lauren was always nice to me and once even picked me as her Chemistry partner when she realized I was always picked last.

Kyle wraps his arm around my shoulders. "Come on, let's grab a drink from the bar."

I stop him and nudge my head toward Lauren.

She waves away my concern. "Don't worry about me. I take notes of all the delicious-looking martinis and will come back when there isn't a little one in my stomach. I'm totally cool with you guys drinking without me."

Kyle takes my hand and leads me to a small open section at the bar.

"The bartender is not even paying attention to us," Lauren whines.

"You're pregnant and at the bar," Gage says.

Lauren glares and then kisses him. "Go get the bartender's attention, Kyle."

"Be right back," Kyle tells us, giving my side a squeeze. "He's giving the other side all his attention."

I lean forward and rest my elbows on the bar while observing him move around the bar. I bite into my lip when I catch women staring at him as if they want him as their dessert. There's a bridal party assembled around the bar, attempting to capture his attention, but he ignores them. I beam with pride. He's overlooking them because of me. He wants me.

"Wow, you're here with *him*?"

I tense and immediately know who said that.

"With fucking Kyle Lane?" Kent snarls.

I turn to scowl at him and notice his wedding ring. There's no bitterness. Kent stands in front of me, and I feel nothing toward him, not hurt or regret.

He sets his drink on the bar and nudges closer by bumping the person next to me. "I need not go into details about why being around him is a vile fucking idea."

"And you cheating on me with another chick was a vile fucking idea, but you did. Now, you're *married* to the woman you swore you weren't touching while I'm sharing a meal with the man you warned me away from. Oh, how the motherfucking world turns," I snap with no hesitation.

He snatches his drink up and chugs it before slamming it down. "Don't come running to me when he screws you over."

My eyes narrow his way as we form strong eye contact. "Trust me; don't concern yourself with that. Go back to your wife. Maybe you can be a not-so-shitty partner to her."

I tense up when I see Kyle approach us. He doesn't look threatened my Kent's presence. Kyle slaps Kent on the back, bumps his shoulder when stepping around him, and places our drinks on the bar before dragging me into his side.

A hard expression spreads across Kent's face.

"Good to see you, man," Kyle addresses him. "I hope you're doing well. Thank you for cheating on Chloe to give me the opportunity to make her happy—*very* happy."

"Fuck you," Kent scowls.

Kyle laughs coldly. "Nah, I'd rather have fun with Chloe. Appreciate the offer though."

"Why do you even care who I'm here with?" I ask Kent.

"I still care about you! I don't want to see you get used by this"—he tosses his hands out to signal Kyle—"asshole who has already hurt you once. Don't trust him. You think he'll ever want to be with you? Look, he took you out of Blue Beech for your date, so no one would see you together."

Kyle's fingers curl around my waist. "Fuck you. Don't assume shit you know nothing about."

Gage steps between them. "Enough. Both of you, walk away, and we'll all enjoy a nice dinner."

Kent furiously shakes his head. "Go ahead, Chloe. Let him treat you like the whore he always made you out to be. I guess your little nickname suited you." His nostrils flare.

My cheeks redden in embarrassment.

Kyle settles me behind him, blocking me from Kent. I attempt to go around him to give Kent a good ass-kicking, but it's too late. One second, my ex's mouth is talking shit about me, and the next, Kyle's fist is hitting it, preventing him from talking more shit about me.

People step out of the way when Kent cries out and holds his nose.

"That's assault!" he screams. "You assaulted me!"

"It was a love tap, Kent," Kyle replies with annoyance, as if he were scolding a child. "No damage was done."

With that, Kyle grips my hand and leads me toward the exit. As we pass the restrooms, I bump into Kent's wife, and she blinks a few times, as if she were imagining me. When she realizes I'm real and I'm unable to move, her attention then swings to Kyle, and I grin.

I pat her shoulder. "Thank you so much for stealing Kent away from me, Lacy."

"Screw you, Chloe." An evil smirk stretches across her lips. "Maybe I'll be able to give him babies, you barren bitch."

Oh, this bitch.

Hell no.

Sadness and rage consume me at her words. At this moment, two things can happen: I could burst into tears or punch Lacy. I raise my hand, ready for a catfight, but Kyle grabs it and leads me out of the restaurant while I attempt to jerk away.

"Hey," I yell, swatting at him when we make it outside to the valet. "Why are you allowed to hit someone, but I'm not?"

He whips around to look at me, his face filled with irritation. "That can get you into tough shit."

I tap my heel against the ground. "Uh, in case you forgot, you're a *police officer.* That can get you into some tough shit."

His hand leaves mine when he holds up a finger. "First, if it does, it does." Another finger goes up. "Second, I made sure not to do any damage."

"Damn it, Kyle, you couldn't wait to punch him until *after* we ate?" Lauren yells, stomping her feet and shaking her head until they make it to us.

Kyle rubs the back of his neck and throws Lauren an apologetic look. "My apologies. Go yell at Kent for not waiting to talk shit until *after* we ate."

I wipe away the tears over Lacy's words, and my mouth goes dry as I stare at Lauren. "I'm sorry."

Lauren glances at me. "No, don't you apologize." She points to Kyle with her chin. "Now, you need to be sorry, stupid. You're a cop. You can get in serious trouble for that."

"I'm sorry," Kyle states. "You two go eat. We'll figure something out."

"Nah," Gage cuts in, looking indifferent. "It's too busy in there anyway. Where's our next choice of food?"

"I have an idea," Kyle says, chewing on his lip. "How about we hit that arcade in the mall?"

"What are we, twelve?" Lauren asks.

"No, smart-ass," Kyle replies. "At night, it turns into adults only. They serve food and alcohol. It's a good time."

"I'm game," Gage responds with a shrug. "It'd be nice to do something different and low-key."

"We need to stop by the hotel, so we can change then," Lauren says. "These heels are killing my feet. I live in scrubs, so I need jeans ASAP."

"Totally agree," I say.

Lauren gives me a bright grin.

———

When we walk into the hotel's lobby, Kyle heads to the counter for our room keys.

"I know the night is still young and all," Lauren says around a groan when she stops next to me while Gage joins Kyle. "But can it be young for only you and Kyle? I'm a prude who wants to order room service and go to bed."

I frown. "I'm sorry about dinner."

She waves away my apology. "Girl, don't worry about that. I feel terrible, so you did us a favor."

The guys come back with key cards and grab our luggage.

"Change of plans," Lauren tells Kyle. "Gage and I are going to our room, calling room service, and passing out."

Gage strokes her back and seems fine with not going out.

Kyle offers a warm smile. "Tell them to charge it to my room."

Lauren starts to object, but Gage smacks Kyle on the back.

"How kind of you to offer. I'll be sure to inform them." He glances at Lauren. "My girl is eating for two, so I apologize in advance for the bill. You two have a nice night and don't get in too much trouble."

We crowd into the elevator, and our rooms are next to each other. After Kyle unlocks our door, I toss my bag on the bed, collapse on it, and unstrap my heels.

"My feet are killing me." I drop them to the floor when I'm finished. I open my suitcase and select a pair of flats. "So, we're going to an arcade?"

Kyle nods.

"One where you play Skee-Ball, win tickets, and select cheap prizes?"

Kyle sets his bag down and grins. "It'll be fun. I promise."

"Is it weird that a woman pushing thirty is excited to go to an arcade?"

"As weird as it is that a guy pushing thirty is excited to go to an arcade." He snags a shirt and flashes me a look. "Excited to go because of who his company will be."

I change my clothes in excitement.

I throw my arms up and jump up and down. "Winner, winner, chicken dinner!"

We came, ate arcade food, drank, and now, we're playing games.

There's been a gleam in Kyle's eyes all night. We've had a blast, and I'm thankful we came. I would've never gone if he hadn't recommended it.

"I'm officially wiped out." I yawn as my buzz flutters through my belly.

"Let's cash in our tickets." He snags my hand in his. "My guess is, you won enough for a new car."

Kyle let me win all the games. I had no idea what I was doing while he explained them. We leave the mall where the arcade is, and the chill of the night smacks into us. The mall is down the street from our hotel, so we walked.

I hook my arm through Kyle's and skip forward as if I were Gloria's age. "Thank you, thank you. I had so much fun!" I scrunch my nose up. "The arcade part, not the Kent part."

He chuckles while dragging me closer, and I inhale the masculine scent of him.

God, I love his smell.

"You having fun was my goal for tonight, so that makes me happy."

I peek up at him. "You know, I've never acted like a kid before. It was freeing, not worrying about everything and having fun. I don't remember the last time I did that."

He tightens his hold, and we stroll past a couple making out. "We can go back whenever you want. Next time, we can bring the kids. They'd have a blast."

My heart flutters, and we don't lose contact.

"Why are you so good to me and my family?"

"Family means everything. My brother, my sisters, my mom—they mean the world to me. I like you. That means, I like your family." He clicks his tongue. "With the exception of your sister—no offense."

I laugh. "We can't love them all."

I love that he thinks about that stuff, that he thinks about Trey and Gloria being like me—children never given the chance to do anything like go to an arcade. Sure, I give them more than I had while growing up. We've seen movies and gone to fairs, and I've taken them shopping but never anything like the arcade.

This, I would've remembered as a kid.

This, I'll remember as a grown-up.

I realize three things as I walk down the street with him.

1. I never want Kyle to leave.

2. I'm falling for him.

3. I'm terrified of losing him when he learns my secret.

———

I kick off my shoes when we make it back into the hotel room and collapse on the bed. "Kyle Lane, you let me drink too much tonight," I sing—no, slur. "I will be placing all blame on you for tomorrow's hangover grumpiness."

He chuckles and heads over to our luggage. "Hey, you're the one who insisted on three margaritas while we played Whac-A-Mole. That's all on you, babe."

I glare at him with just one eye. "Don't blame a girl for having a good time."

He grabs our bags and sets them on the luggage rack. "Trust me; I love watching you enjoy yourself. Now, what do you want to sleep in tonight?" He unzips my bag and shuffles through it. "Did you pack pajamas?"

I drag myself up to look at him. "Huh?"

He continues searching through my bag until he pulls out a pair of pajamas. "You sleep nude when we're together, but what about when you're traveling … not naked?"

I jerk my head toward the pajamas in his hand. "Those."

He tosses them to me.

"You're okay with me sleeping in these?"

He stops going through his bag to look at me. "I'm sorry, am I okay with what?"

"With me not sleeping nude," I clarify.

He blinks. "I'm still not following, babe."

"We're usually naked when we're in bed together."

He inhales a deep breath when he understands what I'm saying, and he tosses the shirt in his hand back into his bag. "Chloe, what the fuck? I'm not hanging out with you for sex. If I only wanted quick pussy, I could get it anywhere, at any time."

"Full of yourself much?" I mutter.

He stares at me with frustration and hurt. "Not saying it to pipe my ego. I'm saying it to prove my point to you." He signals to the pajamas at my side. "Sleep in those. Sleep in my sweatpants. Sleep in a fucking Halloween costume. Either way, it won't change my mind about being next to you."

His response shocks me. At first, I played it off as a joke, but deep down, it's been bothering me, not knowing if that's all he wants. From the beginning, we've made it clear this is sex and then we go our separate ways. And I said the same. I was adamant on no double dating or getting too close.

The truth keeps hitting me tonight. I was afraid of expressing myself and wanting more in fear of Kyle hurting me again. I didn't want him in case he didn't want me.

But it seems like … he does.

My life gets more complicated.

"Now …" he says, breaking me out of my thoughts. He's holding up a pair of his sweats when I look over at him. "Are these okay for me to sleep in?"

I flip him the bird. "Funny."

I grab my pajamas, and he comes over to play assistant while I struggle to get undressed.

So, it is about sex, I wonder when he drops to his knees and drags my pants off. I'm thinking the same when he helps me with my shirt and bra, my boobs bouncing free.

So, maybe it isn't about sex, I wonder when he grabs my pajamas and dresses me.

He returns to our bags to grab our toothbrushes from *his* bag. My drunken lips curl into a smile. He texted me, asking what my favorite color was after my first weekend at his house. The next day, there sat a new toothbrush of the same color on his bedroom vanity. Neither one of us mentioned it, but he smiles and winks every time I pick it up.

"You need me to brush yours?" he asks, handing mine over.

I laugh and lead us to the bathroom. "Hopefully, I can manage this one by myself."

"Tell me if you change your mind. I've never brushed anyone else's teeth, but I don't mind getting that personal with you."

We share the sink and brush our teeth in silence. Next, we floss. He leaves when I ask him for my makeup wipes. He drops them off and then goes back into the bedroom. When I walk out, he's already changed into sweatpants with no shirt on and in bed, his back against the headboard.

Sharing a bed with him and not for sexual reasons makes my

stomach flip-flop. Sure, we sleep in the same one during sleepovers, but that's after sex. This is different. This is comfortable. This feels like we're in a relationship.

I shake my head. *Quit questioning this. He'll probably jump on you as soon as you get in.*

I wouldn't object to it.

He taps the spot next to him. "Come here."

When I crawl in, he pulls the sheet to our waists, snatches my hips, and drags me to his side. I rest my head on his shoulder.

A pained breath leaves him. "I want to tell you something."

I perk up in his arms. "What's up?"

His voice turns gentle. "Kent's words … they keep creeping up on me."

"Kyle, he was mad and talking shit."

"He said I'd treat you like a whore." He leans us forward, so he can settle his arm behind me, and then he runs his fingers through my hair, untangling the mess. "I never want you to feel like that, Chloe. I've never and I will never think of you that way."

"Kyle," I cut in.

"No, let me finish."

I shut my mouth.

"If you ever, for even one second, feel like that, you tell me … and slap me in the face. I'm not only here for sex. You're not my whore. I'm a fan of dirty talk, yes, but us having sex isn't what this is all about."

My heart races at his confession, and I struggle for words while staring at him. "So, this isn't just casual sex between two neighbors?"

His lips tilt into a smile.

I give him a cheesy smile in return.

"Absolutely fucking not. Again, I can find sex anywhere." He squeezes me.

If I could see my heart, it'd be glowing.

I make myself comfortable, and he rests his hand on my waist. The warmth of his skin relaxes me.

The room turns quiet, the TV he turned on the only noise, and he scratches his jaw before speaking. "Can I ask you a question?"

"Depends on what it is," I mutter.

His hand moves and begins stroking my shoulder. "Hey, don't blame a man for being curious about the woman in his bed."

"I'm close to drunk, so ask away."

"What made you decide to be a writer?"

I gulp. I hate being asked that question, and I normally lie. I don't to him. "Because of Trey's dad."

He tenses. "The deadbeat asshole?"

I nod. "He was the only guy of my sister's who was nice to me." I hold a finger up. "Correction: he was nice *then*."

He tightens his hold, expecting a bad story.

"He helped me with my homework and talked to me about my goals. I only got books from him or the library, so when I was running low, I read the newspaper. It was a national paper, and I loved reading the articles. He told me writers got paid pennies and to choose a better career path. I won't lie and say I didn't change my mind, but then he broke my heart. I went to my journal and wrote about him, wishing I could publish it so that everyone else would know, too. I signed up for the newspaper to spite him, not caring if I'd make money, and I fell in love with it."

"What did he do to hurt you?"

I rub my forehead, and the memories of fear and hurt play through my mind. "He was the same as all her other boyfriends. He was better at putting up a front. He hurt me, he hurt Trey, and I'll never forgive him for that."

He grits his teeth. "What do you mean, he hurt you?"

"No, no, nothing like that. More like hurt my feelings."

He presses his lips to my cheek, then my nose, and then pulls back with a gentle smile. "I'm sorry that happened."

I duck my head down. I hate talking about Sam. "Why were you so hell-bent on not going into law and politics?"

"I was expected to grow up in my father's shadow. Instead, I decided I wanted to be a police officer. It pissed him off, but I didn't care."

"I like that you followed your heart."

"I'm glad you followed yours. Fuck Trey's dad." His chest moves when he chuckles. "When you became editor of the school paper, Ms. Sanders allowed me to read your unapproved articles."

Embarrassment and shock trickle up my spine. "What?"

There's playfulness in his tone. "I was her TA, and she talked about how you wanted to create controversy with your articles. You never cared about speaking the truth, no matter how many toes you stepped on."

"Nope. The truth will set you free."

"If I recall, you wrote an interesting article about me."

My face reddens. *Shit. Shit. Shit.* "No, she didn't."

"She did."

"Isn't that against code of conduct?"

"Like it mattered. She let me do whatever I wanted."

"Oh my God, did you sleep with our teacher?"

"Why would you think that?"

"She was young and hot, and why else wouldn't she have approved my articles about you?" I elbow him. "That's against the law, you know. My next article will be about Ms. Sanders, the woman married to the principal, who was biased against my articles because you were banging her."

He holds his hand up. "Whoa, hold on, killer. She wasn't breaking laws and banging me."

I snort.

"We slept together once *after* I graduated and was eighteen. She wasn't married then."

"Eh, whatever. I'll be digging up dirt on her. I can't believe you didn't kill me for writing up the article."

"Sweet Chloe, who would want to be upset someone wrote an article about them being a bully?"

"I never said your name."

"The description fit me to a tee. A *young athlete* with a father *in power* receives favor from the principal and teachers and drinks underage at parties."

"Why didn't you say anything?"

"It didn't get published, did it?"

"It could've."

He shrugs. "I like that you thought about me enough to write an article." He kisses the top of my head. "You're a skilled writer. I read everything you wrote. Don't think I'm a stalker."

"Really?"

He nods. "Everything that did and didn't get published."

"Why? Some of them were boring as shit."

"I won't deny that." Quick breaths leave him. "You've always intrigued and interested me, Chloe. You wrote from the heart, whether people liked it or not. Gage gave me so much shit for reading them. You hated me, but those articles allowed me to learn more about you."

I see the sincerity and honesty in his eyes.

He's not lying.

He blows out a breath. "We've been drinking, so I'll do a drunk confession, and if you don't like it, maybe you'll forget about it in the morning."

"How about we make this a night of drunk confessions?" I stupidly reply.

His next words leave his mouth seconds later, as if he was waiting to release them. "I don't think I like you anymore. It's more than that now. Stronger than that. I'm fucking falling for you faster and harder than I have with anyone." He grabs my face, rubbing small circles with his finger on the top of my cheek. "Please tell me if you feel it, too."

My heart hammers against my chest, and fear sets in. "I do … I feel the same way."

He grins but still looks concerned. "You can ruin me. Please don't."

It's weird, seeing Kyle like this, so open, vulnerable, and not the strong, joking guy he always is. His feelings for me scare him.

"I won't."

And, just like that, I lied straight to his face.

CHAPTER SEVENTEEN

The morning sun beams through the curtains. We're at the hotel, and I don't want to leave this room, where we poured more secrets in one night than our entire relationship.

Relationship.

Is that what we are?

In a relationship?

The idea of us being more than casual fuck buddies is exciting, but what happens when we return to the reality of Blue Beech?

What happens when what I'm hiding comes to light?

My back is against Kyle's chest. We stayed in this position all night, and today feels different from any other morning we've woken up side by side.

His fingers lace around my stomach, and the sound of him yawning hits my ear. I somehow manage to twist in his arms through the tight confinement he has me in until I'm facing him, chest-to-chest, our mouths inches apart.

I love the view of his handsome face in the morning. His hair is unruly. Day-old scruff sits on his cheeks of perfection. He's so carefree in the morning. Hell, he's so carefree in life. That balance is nice because I am so the opposite. Kyle puts me at ease when the rest of the world tears me down. The corners of his eyes crinkle when he notices me studying him.

"Good morning," I whisper.

"Good morning, gorgeous girl," he answers with a smile. "As much as I love saying those words to you, it's nice to hear them first. How did you sleep?"

I respond with an easy smile. "Perfect."

He rubs his hand over his scruff before leaning in to kiss me. "Any hangover signs yet?"

"So far, so good."

Except for my word vomit last night.

He chuckles. "Your chest of secrets feel lighter this morning?"

Yes. No. Maybe.

"For the most part, yes."

He snorts. "Only you would say *for the most part.*"

"What do you mean?"

"You're a glass ball of mysteries and secrets, but soon, you'll let me crack each one open. You'll see."

"Pretty sure of yourself, aren't you?"

"How many things did I say would happen between us while you stayed adamant they wouldn't? All of them. Us in bed together—*check.* Serving you breakfast in bed—*check.* You opening up to me"—he playfully squeezes me—"in more ways than one—*check.*"

I slap his arm. "Eventually, you'll need to buy my place in order to house your entire ego."

I shiver at his hand sliding up and down my arm.

"Fine by me. How about you stay at my house and my ego takes residence at yours?"

"Are you still nervous to have sex?" I ask teasingly.

"I'm not *nervous* to have sex with you. What's worrying me is what your dumbass ex said."

"You don't make me feel like a whore, I promise." With that, I grab his cock over his sweats. "In fact, maybe you should worry about me treating you like *my* whore."

We drag our pants down at the same time. His nails bite into my waist when he thrusts inside me.

"I see no problem with that."

I moan at his first thrust. We're close—*so close*—and I've never had sex like this before. He cups my ass to yank me deeper into everything that is him before dragging his hand to my breast, cupping it.

Then, he stops me. "Can I ask you another question?"

Jesus. This man and his goddamn questions.

I attempt to move, but he doesn't allow it. "Let's save the question for when your cock isn't inside me." It's never fair on my end.

"Why? I'm much more persuasive when my cock is inside you."

I'm well aware.

"That's where you're wrong," I lie.

"That's untrue. My cock was inside you when I asked if you wanted me to fuck you harder. You said yes. My cock was inside your mouth when I asked you if you wanted me to fuck your face harder. You said yes. My cock was inside you—"

I dramatically tilt my head back. "All right, all right, I get your point. Spit it out."

His hand rides up to my back as he lightly caresses it. "Dallas Barnes, Lauren's brother, is tying the knot next weekend. Want to be my wedding date?"

I've heard about the wedding. It's had bigger buzz than my ex's. Dallas and Willow's story is more beautiful than my ex's. No affairs present in their situation. Dallas lost his wife to cancer. It was tragic. I went to the funeral, and he was devastated. Willow saved him and his daughter from a lonely life.

I shove my face into his neck. "I don't think that's such a good idea."

He pulls out of me, and I fall to my back as he hovers above me, making strong eye contact. "*Au contraire*, I think it's a great one."

I bite into my lower lip. "People will talk."

"Hopefully. I doubt anyone will be up for a mute wedding, but I'll put in a request if it'll make you more comfortable. Do you know sign language?"

I smack his shoulder. "You know what I mean."

"No, I don't."

"You're you … and I'm me," I stutter out.

"Yes … I didn't know you weren't aware of that."

"You're a Lane. I'm a Fieldgain. We don't go together."

He slides back inside me and raises his hips, resulting in a gasp from me. "Wrong. We sure seem to go together pretty damn well right now."

"To the outside world, we don't go together." *And to me.*

His hand reaches up to cup my breast, lightly squeezing it, and then his lips head to my ear. "Why do you care so much about what the outside world thinks?"

I caress his chest. "Says the guy who the entire town loves."

"Says the girl this guy is falling for."

My heart flutters, and my breathing is heavy as I smash my mouth to his.

All wedding talk disappears as he takes me away into another world, both physically and emotionally.

———

I'm exhausted.

We're back at my house.

We ate breakfast with Gage and Lauren before leaving the hotel early this morning. It's nice having a social life. Before Kent, it was nonexistent and went back to that after our breakup.

Kyle grabs my foot in his lap and massages it. "This weekend was fun. Thank you again." He smiles. "Let's figure out a weekend we can take the kids."

I love that he thinks of things like that.

That's when it hits me.

Kyle is great with kids. I saw it with Trey and Gloria. He'll be a great father to lucky kids someday.

"Do you want kids?" I rush out before I lose the guts to ask.

His hand on my foot stops, and he uses the free one to scratch the back of his neck. "Maybe. Possibly. If it happens, it happens. Maybe adoption is a good idea for me."

His answer seems rehearsed, as if he conjured up the right words for when I asked him. Sure, he most likely does get asked if he wants to be a father, *but* what guy says he wants kids but is considering taking the adoption route? A guy who's had to think about it.

Anxiety twists in my gut. "Don't bullshit me."

He winces at my response and peers over at me in confusion. "What?"

"You heard Kent's bitch wife call me barren."

He nods. "I did, but it's not my place to bring it up. It's a personal issue for you, and when you're ready to trust me with it, you'll come to me." He squeezes my foot. "I don't mind waiting for you to reveal all parts of yourself to me. Do it piece by piece; that's cool with me."

"I can't have children," I whisper. I told him I was on birth control the first time we had sex because I was afraid of telling him this.

People aren't sure how to respond when they hear a woman say infertility. Hell, before, *I* wouldn't have known how to respond with that statement.

He nods again, processing what I said without showing an ounce of emotion. Lowering his voice, he says, "You love children."

"I do," I answer with a choked-up voice, and my anxiety rushes harder as the tears start.

"I'm sorry, Chloe." He grabs my arm and pulls me onto his lap.

I stare down and gulp. "That's why you said you were up for adopting, isn't it?"

He delves his hand through my hair before lowering it and using the tip of his finger to drag my chin up. "Hey, you don't know that. Maybe I've always wanted to adopt."

"Always as in the last twelve hours after you heard what Lacy said?"

I sniffle, and my breakdown is coming. My hurt normally comes when I'm alone, and no one's here to judge me. They can't see my pain —not my doctor, not my mother or sister, not Kent.

It's thrown in my face—by my mother, by my sister when I ask her for the children, by Kent when we broke up. Pissed off people never fail to throw other's misfortune in their faces.

He wipes away my tears. "That doesn't matter."

I keep my gaze on him. "So, you did say it because you knew there was a possibility of that. You said it, so you wouldn't hurt my feelings."

"True, but I also said it because I *mean* it. I see a future with you. Shit, I want a future with you." He places a hand over his heart and gives me a smile. "If adopting a child is how we have children, then I'm down."

I wind my arms around his neck. "I guess I'll have you."

He gives me a gentle smile, grabs my hand, and kisses it. "Do you want to tell me why you can't?"

"I have endometriosis," I tell him. "It's a health condition that can cause infertility in women and issues that can result in having their uterus removed. I was one of those women."

He rubs my back as compassion crosses his features. "I'm so sorry."

I'm not sure what starts it, maybe because I'm *finally* opening up to someone, but all my emotions, all my thoughts, suddenly spill out—in front of a man I'm finding myself trusting more than anyone. "It kills me," I say around a groan and a sob. "I see so many women, my sister being one, who don't deserve—" I pause to correct myself. "That's mean of me to say. I see these women who don't *want* to be mothers or take care of their children, and it kills me to see them take it for granted." Sadness overcomes me. "God, what I'd kill for that."

"Babe," he says, continuing to rub my back.

I wipe away the tears while Kyle stares at me, giving me his undivided attention with a concerned face. Shame corrodes my insides. "It's what a woman was created to do, right? Our bodies are made to bear babies. As little girls, it's what we look into our future for, hoping for. I remember when I took care of Trey when I was fifteen. Sometimes, I'd act like he was *my* baby. I couldn't wait to be a mother someday." Pain grips my chest as my throat thickens with sobs. "All that was taken from me by a simple diagnosis. Sometimes, I don't even feel like a woman. Sometimes, I hate my body for being this way, for doing this to me."

Kent's mother helped me post-surgery. She was kind but couldn't hide the sadness in her eyes that I wouldn't be giving her a grandbaby. Coming to terms with my infertility is hard enough, but seeing the disappointment and judgment on others makes it so much worse.

Kyle is quiet. He never cuts me off, never tries to justify what I'm feeling. He listens and takes my pain in. "Don't you dare base your worth off your ability to have children. You're still a woman—a strong, compassionate, sexy woman who gives out unconditional love for so many people. Why aren't you giving that same love to yourself?" He strokes my face, collecting all my tears with his fingers. "You, along with other women, weren't put here for that. Period. You're over here, helping Trey and Gloria and taking a job that pays half of what it should. Anyone who makes you believe any different shouldn't be in your life."

I gulp, unable to produce any words. I'm not withdrawn from him like when I told Kent.

"There are alternatives," he goes on. "Adoption. Surrogate. Don't let your diagnosis stop you from being a mother if it's what you want."

I nod. Adoption crossed my mind, but worry set in that it'd be selfish for me to bring a child into a single-parent home. I grew up without a father, and it hurt. I want to give a child that perfect life— mother, father, stability, white picket fence, all that. Right now, I can't.

Kyle isn't finished speaking. My honesty with my confession opened up the emotional floodgates. He doesn't blink as we make steady eye contact, and my body feels weak as he looks at me with … I'm not even sure *what* it is.

His voice is rich with emotion when he finally talks. "Chloe, last night, we wanted alcohol in our systems to speak our sober thoughts, but speaking honestly, no bullshit, I'm falling in love with you. I'll say it drunk, sober, today, tomorrow, and every day for the rest of my life. I want to make this official. I'm done pretending like we're just casual sex friends. I want you to be mine, and in the future, if we make it there, we can adopt all the babies in the world."

Kent never talked about it with me; he'd shut down when it was brought up. He was pissed about his life plan changing drastically. It scared me to hear another person call me a failure, so those wounds always stayed with me.

Kyle wanted this conversation with me.

Kyle will never put me down for flaws I can't control.

He'll stay by my side, exploring every alternative.

Kyle will stand by my side always … until he learns my lie.

CHAPTER EIGHTEEN

KYLE

I've been on shift for three hours. So far, we've settled a domestic dispute with exes fighting over custody of their golden retriever and handled another where a woman slapped a man for rear-ending her car.

I'm thankful the crime rate in Blue Beech barely exists, and because of that, there's a great deal of downtime during our shifts. Gage is definitely grateful for it. He worked for Chicago PD before returning to Blue Beech and had no downtime on the job. I've considered moving out of Blue Beech and taking a job where I can save more lives and make a bigger difference, but I could never leave my family.

Gage thrums his fingers against the table and smirks my way. We're at the diner, having dinner. We're regulars here when our shift is slow, and we need a bite to eat. If we receive a call, Shirley will sometimes keep our food and heat it up when we come back.

"Why are you looking at me like that?" I question before taking the last bite of my cheeseburger.

He tilts his head to the side, as if he's studying me. "Lauren ordered me to inspect you."

The fuck?

I raise a brow. "Inspect me?"

"Yes. She's curious if you're looking or behaving differently."

I scratch my head. "Why is your girlfriend worried about me looking or behaving differently?"

"She enjoyed our little double date and believes you and Chloe will make a good couple."

I snort loudly. "You two bailed before the night started."

After the Kent drama, the four of us went to breakfast the next day. I'd woken up with a sense of relief that morning. My talk with Chloe had answered questions I'd wondered about since our night at the bar.

I joke about sex and our relationship, but deep down, I want more. My feelings for her build the more she lets me in and opens herself up to me.

We shared more in one night at the hotel than we had in weeks. I had been outraged when Kent accused me of using Chloe as my whore. Sure, in the beginning, we'd shared orgasms more than feelings, but sex isn't all we're about; it wasn't ever what I wanted us to be all about.

"We were doing you a favor," Gage says.

"Or you two are lame," I counter.

"Yes, my *pregnant* fiancée was tired, but she wanted to give you two alone time since you hadn't been out much. When you'd suggested the arcade, she'd found the perfect opportunity for you to have fun without worrying about the curious eyes of Blue Beech residents. If we had been there, it would've interfered."

I grab my napkin and wipe my mouth. "I wasn't aware they taught relationship expertise in nursing school."

I appear uninterested but have always appreciated Lauren's advice about women. She's played a role in successful relationships in our town.

"She has statistics to back up her claims. Dallas and Willow had town gossip issues. She was an out-of-towner, pregnant with Blue Beech's attractive widower. It helped their relationship when they got out of town." He shrugs. "Plus, Lauren offered room service, crime TV, and sex. I was down for whatever she suggested."

"You're always down for whatever she suggests."

"Welcome to being in love, man. Get ready for it."

I snort.

"I almost shot Lauren's landlord in the head after he hurt her. You punched Kent after he insulted Chloe. A man only interested in sex doesn't fight over a chick he's not falling for. You like your neighbor, and for Lord knows what reason, she likes you. Happiness and possibly *falling in love* looks good on you, man."

I grab my water and suck the rest of it down. There's no disputing his claims. Even though Chloe and I haven't labeled our relationship, every token of us having one is there. We spend all our free time together, have expressed our feelings toward the other, and aren't interested in dating anyone else.

There's no denying it now.

Chloe Fieldgain is no doubt my motherfucking girlfriend.

I can't help but smile.

Now, I need to convince her to let her guard down and realize it, too.

Gage yawns and goes for his coffee, but the static of our portable radio stops him. The dispatcher reports a public disturbance call. Gage flashes me a concerned look, and my stomach knots when she states the address.

He tells her we're on it, and I throw down cash to cover our bill before we jump into the car. Gage flips on the sirens and races toward my neighborhood while I fish my phone from my pocket and dial Chloe's number.

No answer.

Dial it again.

No answer.

"Any idea?" Gage asks, his eyes not leaving the road.

"Her sister gives her trouble sometimes," I answer.

"Domestic problems—my favorite," Gage grumbles.

A beat-up truck is in Chloe's driveway, and Claudia and Roger are standing in her yard. Chloe is on the front porch, her arms folded in disdain. All attention deviates to us, and I'm positive this calm scene isn't what it was five minutes ago.

"The sister, I take it?" Gage asks.

My eyes harden, and I nod.

"I've picked up the guy a few times."

"It's her boyfriend."

I draw in a steady breath and step out of the car. My anger heightens the closer we get. Roger is pacing in front of the house. Claudia flicks her cigarette onto the ground and lights another.

"What's the problem here?" Gage asks.

Roger laughs coldly with bloodshot eyes when he sees me. "You've got to be shitting me! The boyfriend has arrived to play hero. What a fucking joke."

"Not here to play hero." I glower. "Only here to do my job."

If I wasn't in my uniform and on the clock, my answer would be different. We're steps away, but Roger reeks of alcohol as if it's a second skin. A public intoxication arrest might be in the works. Roger and Claudia not fleeing is odd. Most arrestee regulars avoid contact with us at all costs.

I'm grinding my teeth when I dart up Chloe's porch stairs to be with her. "What is going on?"

She shakes her head in agitation. "This is so damn embarrassing," she rasps out. "You, my neighbors—everyone in this godforsaken neighborhood is being treated to a front-row seat to my family drama."

I nod in understanding but have to do my job at the same time. "Give me the details, so I can get this figured out for you."

Claudia has the right to take her kids, and there isn't a damn thing Chloe can do. In fact, I'd have to break her heart and let her take them from Chloe's home.

"I want my goddamn children!" Claudia shouts before Chloe can answer me, and she signals to Chloe with a snarl. "That's illegal, you know." Her attention turns to me. "I'd like to report her for kidnapping."

Jesus Christ.

Exactly what I was afraid of.

When I said I wanted less downtime, I wasn't referring to dealing with Claudia's crazy-ass antics.

Chloe tenses, and I can't stop myself from stepping closer to her, my hips meeting hers.

I tip my head down to whisper in her ear, "She's right."

Chloe blows out a series of short breaths before shouting to Claudia, "You've been drinking. Our deal from day one has been I keep them when you've been drinking. I don't trust you to make responsible decisions!"

"I had two beers!" Claudia screams. As much as I want to dispute it, she's not displaying any signs of being overly-intoxicated. "I'm not drunk!"

"I'll be right back," Gage cuts in.

He knows the easiest solution to our problem. Everyone is quiet while he walks to the car and then comes back with a Breathalyzer test in his hand.

"Let's make this easy, so we can all be on our way. If you're under the legal limit, you're good to go." His gaze cuts to Chloe, and he delivers the news with apology. "And I'm sorry, but unless there's a court order, she can take the children with her."

Chloe clenches her fists when Gage tests Claudia first. We are silent as she blows into the tube and wait for her results.

Gage inspects the numbers. "She's good," he calls out.

Chloe curses under her breath. She's so pissed. I wouldn't be shocked if she marched down the stairs and fought Claudia.

"Told you I'm not drunk!" Claudia yells to her.

I drape my arm around Chloe's waist in case she makes an attempt to charge Claudia.

"Not drunk doesn't mean you haven't been drinking *or* that the kids won't be around your hotheaded boyfriend who tends to get angry after drinking too much," Chloe screams back, all worries about neighbors listening be damned.

Roger steps forward while Gage prepares the test for him. "Fuck you, you dumb bitch!"

Gage reaches out, his arm hitting Roger's chest, to stop him from advancing our way. Roger retreats from Gage and sends us a poisonous glare, mainly focused on Chloe.

He then angles his eyes toward me. "Dude," he spits out, "do you know how stupid you look, protecting her?" He's now screaming at the top of his lungs. "She is *using* you! Has she told you her little family secret?" His glare moves back to Chloe. "Of course not. Otherwise, he wouldn't be at your side, you dumb bitch!"

"Kyle," Gage draws out in warning, reading my mind to stop me from impulsively punching Roger in the face harder than I did Kent.

"Shut your goddamn mouth, Roger," Claudia warns, rushing to his side in alarm. She throws down her new cigarette and attempts to pull him away.

Roger doesn't allow it. "Why? The bitch has done nothing to help you."

Gage says my name again as I loom closer to Roger. I'm gulping down my anger, but it's growing more difficult.

Curiosity creeps through me when I peek at Chloe. Her hands are cupped around her mouth, and her face is paler than usual.

Roger uses the back of his arm to wipe his nose before pointing at me. "You sure you don't want to walk in the house, so you can take care of your little brother?" He lets out a sinister laugh. "*Or* maybe it's time your father steps up and supports his bastard son better! Maybe you can be the one deciding who Trey goes home with, considering you're just as much family as Chloe is!"

What the fuck?

My eyes return to Chloe in question. "What is he talking about?"

She's staring at me, shocked and speechless.

"He's drunk," Claudia says, attempting to shoo Roger back to the truck. "Don't listen to a word he says."

"Listen to every word I say, man," Roger replies. "I'm the only person you'll get the truth from, not these two! They've been blackmailing your father for years, ever since Trey was a baby, and accepting checks from him in exchange for their silence!"

I'm not dumb. It's clear what Roger is insinuating. I wouldn't believe a word falling out of his mouth if Chloe didn't look like she was close to passing out and if Claudia didn't appear close to a panic attack.

"Come on, Roger," I say with annoyance. "Stop hinting around the bullshit. Are you saying that Trey is my father's son? That he's my brother?"

They all appear shocked that I was so up-front in questioning his allegations.

"I, uh …" Roger stutters out, suddenly realizing the consequences of his fuckup.

Gage's jaw is dropped open, and he's repeatedly looking from me to Chloe to Roger.

"You need to leave," Chloe croaks out loud enough for everyone to hear. "The kids are sleeping. You've done enough damage for one night. Call me tomorrow to pick up the children."

Claudia and Roger turn around to leave, and Claudia slaps Roger in the back of his head. "You stupid idiot! If I'm cut off, you'd better get a job to make up for the money he gives me!" She hits his back next. "Congratulations! Your big mouth fucked up our lives!"

Gage waits until they leave, Claudia in the driver's seat, and eyes Chloe with a scowl. "I'll be in the car," he informs me without granting Chloe another look.

I wait until he's in the car before turning to start my cycle of questions. "I take it what Roger claims is true? My father is Trey's dad?"

She scrubs her hands over her eyes. "Kyle, it's complicated."

"No, it's really not," I fire back in seconds. "It's a quick yes or no answer."

She nods slowly. "Yes."

I stare at her in disbelief. So much damage to our relationship has happened in ten minutes.

How did I miss this? How didn't I know?

"And why did you keep it from me?"

She's silent as she racks her mind for the best answer, her face unreadable. Chloe is an expert at hiding every emotion flowing through her.

My police radio beeps with a call.

I hold my hand up to stop her. "I need to go. It seems like you need time to come up with your answer. Don't worry about it. I don't fucking care."

With that, I turn around and walk away.

———

Gage's face is contorted in what almost looks like disgust when I slip back into the car. "Wow," he draws out, as if, like Chloe, he's at a loss for words. "I'm not sure what to say to you right now, except for I'm fucking sorry and I'm here for you, man."

I only nod.

The rest of our shift passes in a blur.

No one gets arrested.

Gage doesn't bring the conversation back up until he pulls into my driveway when our shift ends.

"What are you going to do?" he asks, shifting into park.

My mind races with the endless questions I have for people—Chloe, my dad, my mom, Trey.

"I have no fucking idea," I mutter.

He rubs the back of his neck and moves it from side to side. "Maybe there is a reason she kept it from you."

I scratch my cheek and give him a silent look.

"You know why Lauren kept her secret from me."

"That's different, man. She lied to protect someone you love."

"Chloe lying saved your mom from heartbreak and humiliation," he adds. "There had to be a reason for it."

I scoff. "That'll change tonight. Roger might as well have shouted it from a microphone. People will know, and if Chloe had been up-front with me, we could've talked about it. Roger wouldn't have seen the confusion on my face, and the chances of him running his mouth would've been lower." I shake my head. "I can't be with a liar. I've given her nothing but honesty since we've been together and received nothing but lies and walls up from her. And, not to mention, her taking money from my father in exchange for her silence." I shudder.

He nods. "I understand. Let me know if you need anything, okay? And keep me updated."

"I will."

I open the door and step out, and a heavy feeling knots in my stomach when I glance at Chloe's house. The living room light is the only one on. I contemplate whether to talk to her, but my phone rings, breaking my thoughts, and I tug it out of my pocket.

"Good job with selecting your girlfriend," Sierra yells on the other line when I answer. "Word has already spread about Dad's love child. Cassidy said Mom's crying in her bedroom."

Shit.

My anger flares, and I scowl at Chloe's before walking into my home. "Call Dad and yell at him."

My father cheating on my mom with Claudia—how the fuck that happened is another story in itself—isn't Chloe's fault; I'm well aware of that. Him impregnating Claudia isn't Chloe's fault. I can't be pissed at her for any of those things, but I can be pissed for lying, and I can be pissed that her actions caused my mother pain.

If I hadn't been there, Roger would've never said it. If I hadn't forced myself into her life, this wouldn't be happening. If she had told me, I could've figured out a better way to relay the information to my mother.

But no.

Now, we're in a shitshow.

Roger was told but not me.

How the fuck was he trusted over me?

"Trust me," Sierra says, interrupting my thoughts. "I've called him fifteen times. He's not answering. My issue isn't with Chloe particularly. It's the fact that she came to our house and looked our mother in the eyes without caring about her hoe sister being a homewrecker."

I toss my keys in the bowl and go straight to the fridge for a beer but stop myself. Tonight calls for something stronger. I snag a bottle of Jack, grab a Coke, and make myself a nice, strong drink. "I know. I know. Any advice?"

She blows out a frustrated breath. "It depends on how much you like her. Me? I don't know if I could forgive a guy whose cracked-out sister's boyfriend did what he did. Not to mention, the cracked-out sister's boyfriend said that they'd been blackmailing Dad for money. That's not cool. I need answers. Get answers from her, Kyle."

I grit my teeth and grip my drink as I go to my bedroom to change out of my uniform. "I'm carrying too much anger to ask for answers from her or him at the moment."

She releases a stressed breath. She's as protective of our family as I am. "Understandable. I will blow his phone up all night and am prepared to sit in his office if need be."

I put her on speakerphone to remove my gun from the holster. I slip it in the nightstand drawer and throw on a tee and sweatpants. "Doubt he'll come home tonight."

"He has to eventually."

I down my drink. "Maybe I should join you."

"Not happening. We can't add the mayor's son giving him an ass-kicking on top of the mayor having a love child all in one night."

I make another drink when we end the call.

My next incoming call is from my mom.

I chug my whiskey and pour another when she asks me to stay on the phone with her as she cries and rants about how much she hates my father. I stop myself from throwing the glass across the room.

CHAPTER NINETEEN
CHLOE

AGE FIFTEEN

I didn't go to school today.

I *never* miss school if I can help it.

Today, I couldn't help it.

Couldn't *mentally* survive another day of the taunting.

I made it through yesterday, tears blinding my eyes as I walked home, and cursed Kyle Lane with every step I took. I ate lunch in the restroom and sped to my classes before anyone could see me in the hall. I haven't seen Kyle once after I slapped him.

A few days off from school will prepare me for becoming the target of my bullying classmates.

Kyle has made everyone believe we had sex and that I wanted a *round two*. Heck, I'm glad we never made it to *round one*. Giving him my virginity would've been a giant mistake on top of going to the dance with him.

No more dances or school functions for me.

I slapped him and he deserved it. He had taken me to the dance as a prank straight out of a '90s chick flick—ask the geek to the dance as a joke and then publicly humiliate her.

I'm in my bedroom, reading to Trey, when I hear the front door slam shut. Fear spirals through me. My mother is at her boyfriend's for the week, and it's too early for Claudia to be out of bed. I drop my book at the sound of roaring footsteps and scurry to the corner of my room where a baseball bat is hidden. I settle Trey into the closet behind my clothes and tell him to shush. My sister hangs out with sketchy people, and I've prepared myself in case she pushes one to flip their lid and hurt us.

My door flies open, and Sam stands in my doorway.

"Chloe!" he shouts. "What were you fucking thinking?"

His face is red, fury in his eyes, and a vein in his neck is twitching underneath the skin.

This isn't the Sam I know.

No.

This crazy, irate man isn't him.

"What … what are you talking about?" I stutter.

"Going to the dance with my son!"

Whoa. What?

"Wait … Kyle is your son?"

He winces. "How could you not know that?"

I shrug. "I've never seen you two together."

"His mother was in the car with me," he grinds out.

I met Kyle's mom when we went to his house to take pictures before the dance. I didn't notice she was the woman in the passenger seat of Sam's car, but I knew there was one *and* children in the back-seat. None of them were Kyle, so I had no idea they were his siblings. I'm not dumb. As soon as I saw them in the car, I knew Sam's secret. He has a family. I said nothing to Claudia, in fear of her flipping out on me or anyone else.

Sam is the least of my worries at the moment.

Well, he was … *until* now.

I gulp. "I didn't know he was your son."

Sam shakes his head and continues to talk, frustration lining his features. "You know now, and I know why he's been depressed, wallowing around the house with a broken heart. I'm sure it's over you and the fact that I saw you walking home in the middle of the night for who the fuck knows what reason." He snarls. "Looks like the apple doesn't fall far from the tree with us interested in trailer trash."

I flinch at his words.

Sam has never made me feel ashamed of where I live. That's something I always admired about him.

The tears falling down my face seem to shake off some of his temper.

He bends down in front of me on one knee. "Chloe, I don't want to be mean, but keep your mouth shut about me and your sister. It could end harmful to you."

I silently stare at him.

"You've never seen me here. Got it?"

"I'm sorry …" Tears fall faster with each word. "I didn't know!"

"What the fuck is going on?" Claudia yells, stomping into my room. She stops with her arms crossed. Her eyes turn cold and suspicious when she notices Sam next to me. "What the fuck are you doing in my sister's room?"

Sam stands and wipes his hands down his pants. He points to the closet and keeps his attention on me, ignoring Claudia. "Trey, the whimpering baby you're trying to hide in the closet, *I'm* his father." His finger swings around to the corner of the room where I keep all Trey's essentials. "You see those diapers? *I* pay for them." He gestures to my bedroom. "You like your home?"

Not particularly.

"I'm the one who helps pay the bills here," he says louder before pointing to my sister. "I'm the one who takes care of her *and* puts food in this house."

"You son of a bitch," Claudia yells.

Sam leans back down to meet my eyes. His tone is softer, but his eyes are full of warning. "Chloe, if you say one word about me ever stepping foot inside here, you'll regret it. You and your entire white-trash family will regret living in this town. Same goes for Trey. If you want him to be safe and well taken care of, you'll keep to yourself. The only times you'll go to school is to learn, and then you'll come back home. Stay away, or you'll be put away."

My heart slams against my chest. *What is going on?*

"I thought you were a good person."

"Here's a quick life lesson for you, Chloe: quit thinking people are good. All you're going to get is let down."

He steps away, bumping into my sister while walking out of my bedroom, and I jump at the sound of the door slamming. I run out into the living room to make sure he's gone.

"Good job, you dumb bitch!" Claudia screams behind me. "Whatever it is he's pissed about, you keep your goddamn mouth shut about it, okay? Sam is someone you don't want to cross. He'll ruin our lives and take Trey from us. Do you want that to happen?"

I shake my head, blinded by tears. "No … no, of course not."

"Then, what you saw, you take to the grave. Understood?"

"But … but—"

"There are no *buts*. Now, go to your room and read or whatever the fuck you do." She pauses. "Hold that thought. Watch Trey for a while. I need to blow off some steam after the problems you caused today."

CHAPTER TWENTY

Anxiousness crawls through me when I lock my front door and take small steps over to Kyle's.

It's four in the morning, and I can't sleep. All I can think about is where his head is, though I'm not sure I'll be able to sleep even when I find out.

I want to kick Claudia's ass for telling Roger about Michael being Trey's father. Roger's outburst cost everyone so much. When Michael finds out people know about his secret child, he'll cut Claudia off. She no longer holds any leverage over him. No longer will the *I'll call your wife and expose you* threats work. Michael has supported Trey since his birth, supported our family, and all that will be gone.

Eventually, I came to learn that Sam wasn't Sam's real name. It was Michael. *Mayor Michael Lane,* to be exact. I was shocked at first, but it taught me a valuable lesson—not to trust anyone.

Michael's attorney signed and sent out all payments, so there'd be no trace of Michael being involved. His money put food on the table, gave Trey what he needed, and paid our bills. He promised this in exchange for our silence. When I turned sixteen, those checks were no longer made out to Claudia. My name was on them, and I cashed them with guilt.

After I graduated from college and started making decent money, I stopped accepting his money. Claudia's threats never stopped, so the checks went back to her.

I can grasp Kyle's anger. I was searching for the right time to tell him. With every call, hang-out, and touch, the desire to unmask the truth was like a knife to my throat. It wasn't my life I would be hurting if I opened my mouth, so it was too risky. Kyle would've confronted his father.

He sees me as a liar and someone who blackmailed his father for financial gain.

"I know it's late, but we need to talk," I say as soon as he answers the door.

I smell the liquor on his breath when he steps to the side to allow me entrance. His glossy eyes confirm that not only can't he sleep, too, but he's also wasted—something I've never seen from him.

There's a glass in his hand, and he takes a drink before replying. "There's nothing to say, Chloe."

I stop, knowing I need to be careful with my words. "If you'll let me explain …" I should've thought this through before coming over.

"Let you explain?" he shouts, his voice cold and callous. "Let you explain how I spent an hour on the phone with my heartbroken mother, how she's embarrassed the entire town knows, how you chose to keep it from me, *or* how you've been blackmailing my father for *fourteen fucking years?*" He scoffs. "Unless it's to explain any of that, I don't want to hear shit from you." He downs his drink and sets it down. "Were you ever going to tell me?"

I bite into the edge of my lip. "I … I think so."

"You think so?" he repeats slowly. "When? A year? Two? Never?"

Tears glisten in my eyes. "I can't answer that because I don't know."

"You've been lying this entire time."

I shake my head. "When you asked who Trey and Gloria's father was, I never said I didn't know. I never lied."

His upper lip curls. "Wow, really? I didn't find it necessary to specify *my father*, but I did ask who his dad was."

He did, and I was careful with my wording for this reason.

"I told you he was a deadbeat asshole. That's the truth in my opinion—no offense."

My answer isn't met with approval.

"You also said you didn't know where he was."

Again, I was careful with my words.

"At the time, I didn't know where he was." I press my lips together.

My response only pisses him off further. "Bullshit, Chloe!"

"I never lied to you." I fight to keep my voice strong.

"You selectively left out details."

"I still didn't lie."

He glares. "You've had years to tell me."

Anger surfaces, and I push through the incoming tears. "There was never a reason to tell you! I hated you!"

He lifts his chin. "So, when you were in my bed, you hated me. While I was going to *my brother's* football games, you hated me. When you told me you had feelings for me, it was all a lie, and you hated me?"

I press my finger into my chest. "You came to me, Kyle! I didn't come knocking on your door, asking you to hang out." I swallow hard, and tears are streaming down my face. "I did hate you. I never pursued you in the beginning."

"And perusing you was a big fucking mistake!"

I jump when he throws his glass across the room, and it hits a picture of his family, shattering it.

"One big fucking mistake!" He points to the door. "Leave, Chloe. I don't want you here, and I don't trust you."

I wipe away tears, forcing myself to not give up yet, to not give up on us. "Can you please hear me out?"

"Like you heard me out years ago?" He deepens his tone. "Please, Chloe, it took you years to finally *hear me out*. You had all this time to say something, anything, and you said nothing." A cold laugh rumbles from his throat. "And here I thought, I was falling in love with you." He holds up a finger. "I thought *we* were falling for each other. I'll never trust you again. Mark my fucking words. My father confessed everything to my mother. You and your sister blackmailed him for years, accepting over a hundred thousand dollars, and it didn't stop when we began dating. That's where you crossed the goddamn line. Now, get the fuck out of my house."

"*Please*," I beg. Salty tears hit my lips, and my chin quivers. I've never been so terrified of losing someone in my life. I inhale a pained breath. "I'm sorry, I really am, but I was protecting my family."

"And that's what I'm doing." He glares at me. "My guilt for what happened in high school is gone. Looks like you got your revenge. Con-fucking-gratulations. Now, you can fuck off."

CHAPTER TWENTY-ONE

CHLOE

I never thought I'd miss Kyle telling me good morning.

It's been two days since we talked. After our four a.m. conversation, I left with tears in my eyes. He was drunk, and there was nothing else I could say to change his mind. I stayed positive, hoping he'd calm down and we'd talk the next day, but nothing.

Claudia is furious, and I'm sure Roger got an ass-kicking when they got back to the trailer. You don't mess with Claudia's money. She told me she'd been blowing up Michael's phone but hadn't heard back from him. I'm surprised he hasn't paid her a visit about her boyfriend spilling the beans. Michael made it clear from day one that, if a word was muttered, his checkbook was closed.

His silence means the Bank of Michael is out of business.

I ignore the looks and whispers when I walk into my office building, but there's no ignoring Melanie. As soon as she sees me, she demands I tell her everything. I do. At least someone will hear me out.

I answer the phone when I see Trey's name flashing across the screen.

"Hey, buddy!"

"I hate you!" he screams on the other end.

"Whoa," I say. "What is going on?"

"How could you know and not tell me?" Hurt is clear in his voice.

If I could see his face right now, I'd be in tears.

"How could you not tell me who my father is … that Kyle is my big brother? How could you?"

I open my mouth to speak, but he cuts me off. "I had to find out at school where everyone is calling my mom a homewrecker. I didn't believe it until Cassidy came barreling down the hall in tears, calling Mom the same thing." His voice breaks. "You listened to me ask about my father for years when I was younger, and you told me he was gone. He was in the same town. I could've known him all along."

"I'm sorry," I choke out.

"Did Kyle know?"

"No. He's just as mad."

"Tell him I never want to see him again. He and his family are terrible. And, right now, so are you."

The line goes dead.

———

The sound of my phone ringing drags me away from the article I'm writing. I stretch across the table to grab it.

Kyle Calling.

Maybe he is drunk and wants to remind me of how much he hates me.

Or maybe he's ready to hear me out.

I take a deep breath of courage before answering, "Hello?"

"We have a situation."

A crappy situation from the tone of his voice.

"Jesus, did Trey get busted shoplifting again?"

"It's your sister."

My blood runs cold anytime those words are spoken. "What?"

He groans, and I can imagine him running his hand along his forehead like he does when he's stressed.

"She got picked up for possession. With her record, she's most likely not going home tonight." He pauses as faint yelling comes from the other side of the phone. "She wants to talk to you."

Of course the screaming maniac is her.

Her inebriated voice suddenly slurring on the other line stops me from telling him I have nothing to say to her.

"Chloe! Tell your boyfriend to get me out of this hellhole!"

Oh, now, she wants me to date Kyle.

"He's not my boyfriend," I answer flatly. *Unfortunately.*

"Your fuck buddy. Whatever," she counters with urgency.

I frown. She's saying this in front of people in the station.

Perfect.

"Where are the kids?" is all I answer.

"The kids? You're worried about them when I'm about to go to *jail!* What kind of sister are you?"

Jesus. This chick. How are we related?

"Yes, I'm worried about your children. I need to pick them up, considering you won't be able to," I reply, not bothering to answer about helping her out. Let her sit there all night or longer for all I care. She's not my main concern.

"They're at school," she finally answers.

"It's too late for them to be at school."

"Then, I'm not quite sure where they are at the moment. You know their schedule better than I do."

"Jesus. I need to go. Hand the phone back to Kyle."

"No! Not until you fix this for me!"

I hang up.

A few minutes later, my phone rings again.

"This'd better be Kyle, or I'm disconnecting the call again."

"It's me," he answers. "Never thought I'd hear you say that on the other line."

"Me either," I mutter. "So?"

"She won't see a judge until tomorrow, concerning her bail ... if she'll even receive one. The guys who arrested her said she asked her boyfriend to look after the kids."

"So, she knows where the kids are. She just wouldn't tell me."

"Or she doesn't remember. She's drugged out of her mind. I'm surprised she knew who *you* were. Roger somehow wasn't carrying anything. My guess is, he gave it to Claudia, so we couldn't book him, too. You and I both know that dude isn't someone I'd trust with my children. Call Trey and pick them up. Gage can go with you if you're concerned about your safety. I'll have someone keep you updated about Claudia."

"Don't worry about sending Gage. I'll be fine and figure everything out."

"Good luck, Chloe." His tone isn't one filled with intimacy. He's concerned but still cold. He's doing his job, treating me as he would anyone else in this situation, but it's not the man who told me he was falling in love with me. He's no longer the man I was falling in love with.

"And, Kyle?" I say, hoping to catch him before he hangs up.

"Yes?"

"Thank you."

"I'm not doing this for you. I'm doing it for the kids, and it's my job."

I grab my purse and keep my phone to my ear while walking to my car. "Right ... I guess." I stop to find the right words. "Do you ... do you think you can stop by and talk tonight or tomorrow?"

"There's nothing to talk about."

And it's his turn to end the call.

———

I call Trey as soon as I get in my car, and he answers with the first ring.

"Where are you?" I ask.

"Mom's," he mutters.

"Who's there with you?"

"No one. We got back from the Y a few hours ago."

Claudia and I set up a schedule where we take turns picking them up from school or the after-school program.

I start the car and reverse out of my driveway. "How did you get home?"

"We walked."

I'm going to kick Claudia's ass. She could've at least asked me to pick them up.

"Why didn't you ask me for a ride?"

"I don't want to call you all the time, and I'm mad at you at the moment."

"I'm coming to get you. Your mom has to go out of town for a few days, so you get to stay with me."

He sighs and lowers his voice. "I already know she was arrested." His voice is filled with disappointment, and I have a feeling it's more for me lying to him *again* than Claudia's arrest.

"Yes, she was arrested. How did you find out?"

"It was here in the trailer park."

"You were home?"

"No, but everyone told me when we got home. Roger said we're supposed to stay with him and not to call you. He left for a beer run about ten minutes ago."

"I'm on my way. Get yourself and Gloria ready."

When I pull up, they're waiting for me outside with bags in their hands. I wish I could say this was the first time we'd done this, but it isn't. Call it a routine for us Fieldgains.

"Mommy's boyfriend told us not to leave!" Gloria says when I get out of my car.

"Yeah, well, Mommy's boyfriend can get over it," I tell her, scooping her up in my arms.

I turn around and notice the squad car pull up across the street. I see Gage on the driver's side.

I strap Gloria into her car seat while Trey gets in.

"Give me a sec," I tell them before heading over to the squad car.

Gage rolls down his window. "He's not here, if that's what you're wondering."

I shake my head and lie. "I wanted to say thank you."

His face turns neutral, but his words are harsh. "You should've told him, you know."

I sigh. "It's complicated."

He nods. "I understand complicated. I've told him to talk to you, but he's stubborn. Don't give up though."

"Aunt Chloe!" Trey yells.

I turn around to look at him.

"We'd better get going before Roger gets back!"

I nod and then glance back at Gage. "Thank you—again."

———

Trey is sitting in my living room, throwing a football in the air and catching it, when I walk in after putting Gloria to bed.

He sets the ball aside. "So, uh … the mayor is my dad?"

I tighten my sweater around my chest and slump down on the couch.

I called Trey after he hung up earlier. He's young and confused. He didn't answer my call, but he did text, saying he was okay but needed time to clear his head and had a test to study for. I told him okay, but I'm still not prepared to have this conversation.

"Yes," I reply.

He slowly shakes his head in disbelief. "How? I don't understand. He's … *him* … and Mom is *Mom*."

"Trust me; you're not the only one confused."

When I was sixteen, Claudia got drunk and opened up about her relationship with Michael. They'd met at a job fair. Claudia's probation officer had forced her to go look for a job. Instead, she sat in the back parking lot and smoked. That was where she met Michael, who was sneaking out to do the same. They'd talked, hit it off, and exchanged numbers.

He hesitates before asking his next question. "Is it true you made him pay you money not to tell anyone?"

I grimace. "I don't think this is an appropriate conversation for a teenager."

He appears annoyed at my response. "I already know you did."

"It sounds worse than what it was. We didn't hold a gun to his head. He'd offered. He wanted to make sure you were taken care of."

That's the truth. Michael paid Claudia from the beginning, but she took it upon herself to demand more with the threats. With how much money he's given her, I'm surprised he hasn't gone bankrupt.

His face scrunches up. "Is Kyle mad that I'm his brother?"

"Of course not," I assure with a soothing voice. "Everyone was just taken by surprise."

"Did you break up because of it?"

I suck in my cheeks and tilt my head toward his book bag on the floor. "You need to do your homework, and we'll talk about this another time. It's been a long night."

"Kyle was a good dude. Too bad he couldn't be my big brother when I was growing up."

I clutch my sweater around myself tighter, nearly ripping it. "I'm sorry for keeping it from you."

He only nods, grabs his book bag, and pulls out a notebook. "What happens next ... with the whole Mom situation?"

Ease pumps through me for him not asking more Michael-related questions.

"You'll stay here until we figure something out," I state.

His face brightens and then falls. "Roger said Mom told him we could only stay with you if you paid her bail and got Kyle to drop the charges on her."

"I can't convince anyone to drop drug-possession charges."

A flicker of a smile passes over his lips, but he attempts to hide it. "Maybe, we can stay with you now."

CHAPTER TWENTY-TWO

KYLE

So much has happened in the past few days.

The town is torn on their thoughts about my father. His scandal is nothing out of the ordinary with politics, so him having an affair and illegitimate son won't affect him professionally, but those secrets will alter his public image—our family's public image.

My father left town *for a conference* and won't be back for a few days. He hasn't answered my calls but did take Sierra's. She was a daddy's girl growing up, and I think his affair has hurt her more than the rest of us children. He apologized profusely.

When I visited my mom, she was in the kitchen, and stacks of papers sat in front of her—legal documents, receipts of money transactions, and papers covered with texts. She demanded the documents or threatened a divorce. My father surprisingly had his attorney drop off everything. When I asked if she was leaving him, she only shook her head and grabbed another piece of damning evidence against Chloe.

I sat down and skimmed through them with her, grimacing with every check made out to Chloe for thousands and thousands of dollars. My mom hasn't commented on my involvement with her, but I won't be inviting her to dinner in my mother's home again. *Shit.* Inviting her to dinner, *period.*

When I went back to work, all eyes were on me. People had questions but were too timid to ask them. Then, Claudia was brought in, making everything worse. She talked shit to me the entire time the arresting officers booked her. She announced I was having sex with her sister and threatened to release more family secrets if I didn't get her out of trouble.

I didn't.

Her threats only sped up her booking process.

———

"Give them to me, you stupid cunt!"

The loud voice wakes me. I throw some clothes on, grab my gun, badge, and phone, and rush outside to find Roger standing in front of Chloe's house, throwing rocks at it.

Not again.

I look away from him to see Chloe standing on the porch in her robe, begging him to leave.

I walk closer, and it's no surprise Roger is wasted off his ass. He drops the rocks in his hand when he notices me approaching.

"What's going on here?" I ask.

"He's trying to make me give him the kids," Chloe shouts, worry clear in her voice.

Roger takes a step forward, causing me to do the same and block him from getting closer to Chloe.

"I told the little shitheads not to leave," Roger slurs. "Claudia said they couldn't stay unless she bailed her out. She didn't, so I'm here to collect the brats."

"They're not going anywhere with you," Chloe answers, her hands going to her hips. "Keep throwing rocks at my house all you want. I'll call the cops."

"Why *haven't* you called the cops?" I ask her.

She shrugs. "I didn't know what was going on at first. I came out here, saw him, and figured asking him to leave would be easier than involving the police and having every town bigmouth talking about it tomorrow."

"Roger, you need to call someone to pick you up," I demand. I want him gone, but he's too drunk to drive anywhere.

"Fuck you, dude," he spits. "Go back home. You have nothing to do with this. Don't you hate her now?"

"I'll call one of my friends and ask them to pick you up then." I grab my phone. "You can keep your girlfriend company."

He lets out a cruel laugh. "At least my girlfriend doesn't keep secrets from me."

I freeze up at his words.

I can't help but laugh at myself for my stupidity.

I pull out my phone and call the station while making my way up to Chloe's porch. Douchebag can't say or do anything. Dude is dumb but not dumb enough to fuck with a police officer.

The police cruiser pulls up five minutes later, and they arrest him for public intoxication and disturbing the peace. Chances are, he'll be out tomorrow if he makes bail.

———

"Thank you," Chloe says when Cliff and Pete leave, Roger in the back of their cop car.

Standing on her porch, I nod in response. I should walk away and go back to my house, but for unexplained reasons, I can't. The need to make sure she's okay, not shaken up, is there … and so is the need to be near her.

I'm so fucking conflicted, and I'd be lying to myself if I said I didn't miss her.

Fuck, do I miss her.

I miss our mornings, both before and after we started a relationship, our arguing, our sex, the conversations that somehow convinced her to open up to me.

I miss Chloe Fieldgain, but I fucking hate her at the same time.

The porch light shines over us as she leans back against the front door, and I take in the fluffy pink slippers on her feet.

"Are you ready to let me explain myself?" she asks, letting out a breath. "I gave you that chance."

I slip her a glare. "You did, after a goddamn decade, so I'll call you when that time comes."

She grimaces. "Grow up, Kyle, and let's act like adults about this, okay? We've both made mistakes."

"What's there to explain?" I snap back. "It's clear as motherfucking day. I pissed you off in high school, so you got your revenge by blackmailing my family."

She advances a step from the door into my space. "You think that's why I cashed the checks *he offered* us? Over teenage heartbreak?"

A chill hits my core. "I want you to be honest with me."

"Always," she says with no hesitation.

Liar.

I decide against calling her out for it. "Were you ever going to tell me?"

"I don't know. The more I trusted you, I think, yes, I would've eventually." She peeks up at me with a sad face. "Thank you for controlling Roger."

"I did it for the kids," I halfway lie.

"I'm sorry for all this, you know. I never wanted to hurt you or your family. That was never my intention. My feelings for you have been pure from the very beginning. It's going to kill me to watch you walk away from me."

She stands up on her tiptoes and presses her face into my neck. I can't stop myself from cupping her ass and shifting her close. Her teeth tug at my earlobe, and I don't hesitate to follow her when she leads me into the house to her bedroom.

CHAPTER TWENTY-THREE
CHLOE

I have no idea what I'm doing.

I don't seduce men.

I mean, I didn't until now.

A lamp shines in the corner of the room next to my bed, giving me a good view of him. I place my hand over Kyle's mouth as soon as he shuts the door behind us and push him against it. I'll prove to him in every way possible that our feelings are real and not to walk away.

He removes my hand. "You're the screamer, babe. I'll be the one forcing you to be quiet."

Facts.

I smile in return. He doesn't do the same. The stare on his face is packed with pain and desire. He wants me but doesn't. He believes me but doesn't. He wants to work this out but doesn't.

Everything I'm reading on Kyle is confliction.

Let me prove it to you.

I sink to my knees, hastily undo his pants, and lick the length of his cock the moment it springs free. A deep groan leaves his mouth before he catches himself and bites into his lower lip, masking the sounds of his pleasure. It's a shame. I want to hear every word and moan leaving him, but the kids can't hear us. I capture him in my mouth, sucking hard, and hope to erase the hate he has for me. He's smooth as I attempt to use his dick to deep-throat my way back into his heart, as pathetic as it sounds. He won my forgiveness by orgasm; maybe I can do the same with him.

He grows harder with every stroke from my mouth. I get lost in the act and don't tear myself away until he speaks. "Stop, Chloe. This isn't going to finish with my cock in your mouth."

When I stare up at him, he's taking me in with cold eyes and a guarded look. That's when I realize he hasn't touched me. His hands aren't in my hair. This is the first time he's never touched me. Instead, he's made this impersonal, as if I were a random chick he was about to fuck in the restroom of a bar.

I need to give him more.

I rise up on my knees, gripping his thighs, and kiss up his chest— over his tee, his neck, his jaw, moving my way toward his lips. He subtly turns his face away from me.

"Kiss me, Kyle," I embarrassingly plead. "Touch me." *Forgive me.* "Fuck me."

My last two words do the trick. He grips my waist and kisses my hair before crashing his lips to mine. He breaks away to remove his shirt and then palms my breast over my robe.

"Is this what you want?" he whispers into my mouth.

"More than anything," I reply.

He wastes no time before pushing me back toward my bed. My shoulders tighten as he takes me in, and I lose a breath when he harshly tugs the ties of my robe, releasing it, and then tosses it across the room. My panties are torn and flung in the opposite direction.

He twists me around, my back facing him, his broad chest pushing up against me. My knees hit the bed, and I shiver when he reaches out and tucks my hair behind my shoulder.

"You always seem to get what you want, don't you, Chloe?" he hisses in my ear before running his tongue along the lobe.

I gasp when he grips my waist and rubs his hard cock against my ass. I press against him at the same time he guides us up my bed. He lifts himself on all fours while I stay on my stomach, and he lightly feathers a finger down my spine.

"Chloe, how you've ruined me," he says, his finger still skimming my skin.

My hips are raised, and with no warning, he slams inside me before lowering me so that I'm flat on my stomach again. Our legs tangle together, and I'm already close to getting off as he balances himself over me. Our bodies rub against each other's with every stroke, and I don't have the power to move. He carries our weight as he slams into me.

I shove my face into my pillow to mask my moans. I've never had sex like this before. It's angry. It's raw. It's rough. This is a pure hate fuck.

I move my head to the side and bite into his arm as I grow closer, and his hands grab mine, squeezing them as he nears his release.

"Yes, fucking mark me," he grinds out.

He grips harder, and I bite deeper with every push and pull from him.

My pussy constricts against his cock as waves of pleasure hit me, and then I shudder out my orgasm while his hips continue to slam into me until it's his turn to come. When it's time, he pulls out and releases on my back, like I'm some random whore he only wants to come all over.

He falls to the side of me as we fight to catch our breaths, and I already miss the heat and sweat of his body when he rolls off the bed. I start to turn around to see him but jump when he slaps my ass.

"Thanks for the fuck, neighbor," he comments. "I've needed some release."

I jump up to my knees. "Excuse me?"

He grabs his shirt from the floor and then his pants.

"You're not spending the night?"

He throws his shirt over his head without glancing in my direction. "I'll pass. Like I said, I appreciate the fuck. This was fun. Next time you want a quick, meaningless fuck, you know where to find me."

"You're an asshole," I hiss.

"You thought I was an asshole then? Just wait." He leans onto my bed with his palms on each side of me. "You know what's funny? You're exactly like him. A manipulative liar."

With that, he turns around and leaves.

———

I stomp into my office with fury in my eyes. Fury in my *sleepy* eyes. I was up all night, pissed about Kyle.

"Whoa, killer. Who's on the murder list today?" Melanie asks.

"Kyle motherfucking Lane," I grit out. "I hate him!"

She holds her hand up to stop me and narrows her eyes at me in confusion. "Hold up. Last time we talked, you said you wanted him, and he hated you. Now, you hate him, too? What happened?" She leans back in her chair. "This is getting *very* interesting."

"He came over last night, and we had sex," I confess.

She tilts her head to the side. "Isn't that what you wanted?" She stops to study me for a moment, as if she's missing something. "Was it bad sex or something? Did he leave before getting you off? Start some kinky shit you weren't okay with?"

"No! It was amazing sex!"

"Good boy," she comments with a pleased smile. "So, what's the problem then?"

"The *problem* is, after we finished, he slapped my ass, said thank you, and then left!" I throw my hands up in the air and throw my bag onto the floor. "Who the fuck does that?"

"I told you, hate sex is the best sex," she replies. "Nothing beats pent-up frustration like rough sex that ends with someone telling the other to fuck off." She chews on the pen in her hand as if this isn't a big deal.

I grab my bag from the floor while still looking at her. "Remind me why I talk to you about my problems. Hate sex might be *the best sex*, but the after-party of hate sex fucking sucks."

She shrugs. "Look on the bright side; you guys are making progress in the shitshow that is Kyle and Chloe's relationship. Yesterday morning, he wanted nothing to do with you. Now, he's jamming his cock into your vagina. Things are looking up, my friend."

"No. Things are looking more along the lines of homicide. Be prepared to finally get a new job because I'll be in prison."

She laughs before her face turns soft. "Give him time, Chloe. Was it a dick move? Absolutely. The man is pissed, and his ego is bruised."

"I'm not giving him shit, except sliced tires, so do you have any better advice?"

"At the moment, no, but let me drink some coffee, answer some emails, and take a two-hour lunch break, and then I'll get back to you."

"I'm screwed," I mutter before walking into my office.

CHAPTER TWENTY-FOUR
CHLOE

Claudia Calling.

I hit Ignore.

It's her fifth call in a row.

I don't have time for her bullshit games today.

My phone beeps with a text.

Claudia: Quit ignoring my calls!

They released her from jail days ago. Surprisingly, the judge had granted her bail. Also surprisingly, Roger had paid it. She hasn't seen the kids or picked them up from my house, but the weekend is over. Claudia always waits until the weekend ends to threaten me with seeing them if I don't give her money.

An hour later, Claudia comes storming into my office with Melanie on her trail.

"I tried to stop her," Melanie says, shooting Claudia a scowl before looking at me. "But I figured you'd frown upon me tackling your sister to the ground."

A smile twitches at my lips. *Right now, probably not.*

"I appreciate that."

Melanie isn't a Claudia fan, and this isn't the first time my sister has barged into my office, barking out demands.

Melanie throws Claudia another dirty look before leaving and makes sure to shut the door behind her. Claudia tends to get loud during her visits.

Claudia plops down on the chair in front of my desk. She's sporting the hungover look, complete with dark circles under her blue eyes and last night's makeup smudged across her face.

"Your secretary is a bitch," she snarls.

I fold my hands together, set them on my desk, and lean forward. "No, she isn't. Now, what's so important that you felt the need to visit me at my work, which I've asked you numerous times not to? This is a public office, not a place for me to handle my family issues."

Claudia has never taken my job seriously. Oftentimes, it seems like she *wants* me to lose it.

She rolls her eyes. "I need money."

I cut her off before she can elaborate. "No."

She winces. "But—"

I interrupt her again. "I said, no."

"You're a goddamn bitch," she seethes. "I hate you."

The feeling is mutual.

I shrug. "If that's how you feel, then that's how you feel."

She bows her head. "I'm in trouble, and Michael still isn't answering my calls."

"That's nothing new, Claudia. You're always in trouble, and your reasoning for needing money is never-ending, dramatic, Shakespearian bullshit. If Michael isn't giving you money, go back to the job you quit."

She lifts her chin and glares at me while I'm fighting with myself not to cave in. I'm a habitual pushover when it comes to Claudia. Eventually, I grow tired of her pleading and give in. That's not happening today.

She lowers her voice. "Roger and I owe some men money." She continues before I get the chance to confirm she won't receive a cent from me. "Roger borrowed additional money on top of our debt to pay my bail!"

"How precious of him," I mutter. "He lives in your home, rent-free. He should help you."

"They're dangerous, Chloe. They can hurt me!"

"You are adults and capable of paying your own debts. I'm done bailing you out of your messes. Last time, when I said it was the last time, I wasn't lying." I push my hands forward before doing a scraping them clean motion. "No more."

"What about the kids then, huh? Are you not concerned with their safety?"

"They are safe at my house."

"*Please*, Chloe." She's close to tears, and I'm close to caving. It happens every single time. She knows what works on me. "*Please.*"

Don't do it. Don't do it.

"I've given you thousands of dollars to help you, and you've done nothing but blow it on booze and taking care of your deadbeat boyfriends. No more. Nothing."

"My kids need to eat," she grits out before pushing her fingers through her greasy hair.

"Then, I will buy them food."

"They need heat and electricity."

"I have both at my house. They can stay with me."

"What about me, huh? Do you not care if I'm cold and hungry?"

"If you need to sleep in my spare bedroom, you can, but you'll be pulling your shit together. No drugs. No Roger. There will be rules." I shut my eyes in dread. Babysitting Claudia is harder than babysitting both Trey and Gloria.

"I don't want to live with you," she snaps.

I fix my stare on her. "That wasn't a friendly invite. It was a desperate offer."

She jumps up from the chair and wags her finger in my direction. "Fuck you, Chloe! Fuck you! Expect not to see the kids this week *or ever!*"

My blood pressure rises with every second we're speaking. "Don't make the children suffer out of spite and deprive them of a life we wanted when we were children."

Her hand splays across her chest. "Are you saying you'd be a better mother for them?"

I rub my forehead. "I'm not trying to be their mother. I'm trying to give them a better life—whether it's as their aunt or even their friend. They are my number one priority, and they will always be my number one priority. *Period.*"

Her lipstick-messy lip curls up as she releases a hard laugh. "God, you're so desperate for children that you'd even take someone else's."

I slam my hand down on my desk and stand. "Now, it's my turn to say fuck you." I jerk my finger toward the door. "Leave my office."

She scrambles back, and regret flashes across her face. It takes her a few moments to plaster on a fake smile. "Sorry, that was wrong of me to say."

I shake my head and keep my finger pointed. "Save your apology. You meant it. You've meant it every time you've said it. Shove that apology up your ass."

She uses both hands to flip me off, dropping one momentarily to open the door, and then puts them back in the position as she walks backward out of my office, and from the sound of Melanie's laughter, I'm assuming she's doing the same to her.

I'm still standing when Melanie wanders into my office minutes later.

"You should've let me tackle her, babe," she says before circling around the desk to droop her arm over my shoulders. "You are one strong-as-hell woman, and I'm so fucking proud of you for not letting her walk all over you." She squeezes my shoulder before stepping back. "If you need help with the kids, I'm here." Her head tilts to the side. "None of them are in diapers, right?"

"One hundred percent potty-trained."

"Perfect. If you need help with the kids, you let me know."

I smile. "Your bad humor is always what I need on stressful days."

"I'm here all day, folks." She stops to correct herself. "Or at least until five."

She scurries away at the sound of the front desk phone ringing, and I snatch up my phone to text Trey. It's his lunch hour, so hopefully, he has his phone.

Me: I'll pick you up after school today.

My phone beeps with a response seconds later.

Trey: Mom said to go with Roger.

Me: I'll deal with your mom and Roger.

They're always tardy, picking them up from school. If Claudia wants the kids, she'll come to my house. Today isn't the first time Claudia has said her life is in danger. Normally, when she says that, I grab my wallet. Even though I don't one hundred percent believe her, doubt is still in the back of my mind, and I worry about the kids' safety. Hell, I'm *always* concerned with their safety.

Let them come to my house.

I'll be ready for that fight.

———

I'm not surprised when Roger and Claudia show up at my doorstep hours after school let out. Their breath reeks of alcohol, and the dilated pupils and scabs on Roger's face confirm my suspicions that he's using more than alcohol for getting high.

"I want my goddamn children," Claudia screeches as soon as they come in.

I cross my arms. "Tough shit."

I gulp and stand straight even though my heart is pounding when Roger lunges my way. Him coming closer results in Trey stepping to my side. Claudia scoffs, and a cynical laugh leaves Roger at Trey's protective gesture.

This isn't going to end well.

"Look at this badass," Roger barks out, signaling to a fuming Trey.

Trey's jaw is clenched, and his hands are knotted into fists. There's a *finally fed up* expression on his face. Roger pressing him will make things worse between everyone.

"Fuck you," Trey bites out. "We don't want to leave with you." His attention swings to Claudia. "I refuse to stay with you and your"—he tips his head toward Roger—"piece-of-shit boyfriend. You'll have to drag me out."

"That can be arranged, you little asshole," Roger grits out before lunging toward Trey.

I kick my foot out, tripping Roger, and the floor vibrates when his body hits it. I use Trey's shirt to pull him to the other side of the room while Roger gets up, and I rush to my purse.

"Stop!" I yell. "I'll give you the fucking money. Hold on!"

The angry look on Roger's face is why I'm giving in. I'm not risking the kids' or my safety.

"Twenty-two hundred dollars," Claudia demands, kissing Roger's cheek in celebration of their win. "We'd prefer cash, but a check will do if you don't have that much on you."

"I'm not giving you twenty-two hundred dollars," I say, shuffling through my bag until I find my wallet.

"If you want to keep them, that's how much I want," Claudia replies. "Take it or leave it."

Trey takes a step forward and scowls at his mother in repulsion. "Whoa, whoa. Are you *selling* us for twenty-two hundred dollars?" He peers over at me with disbelief. "Is that what you're giving her the money for? So we can stay here?"

Instead of answering him, I collect all the bills from my wallet, step forward, and shove it into Claudia's chest. "There's three hundred dollars. That's all I have and all you're getting. If you take it, you'll leave and let the children stay here. You will not come tomorrow, begging for more money. This is your one chance. Take it or leave it."

Roger snatches the money from her hand, counts it, and motions to the door.

"Fine," Claudia draws out. "But I want them for the holidays."

I nod. "I'll let them spend a few hours with you."

"I'm not spending a minute with her!" Trey screams.

"I don't want to spend the holiday with your selfish ass," Claudia spits out. "I only want to see your sister."

"I want to see Mommy!"

Our attention goes to the hallway where Gloria is standing.

Perfect.

Hopefully, she didn't witness too much of what just happened.

"Of course, honey," Claudia says, leaning down and gesturing for Gloria to come over. "I'll be here to pick you up."

Gloria barrels down the hallway, right into her arms, giving her a hug. Claudia wraps her arms around her and squeezes her tight. It's moments like this: where Claudia attempts to be a decent and loving parent that I somewhat feel bad for her, but then I remember how she operates. She'll promise Gloria everything under the sun and then disappoint her. Then, I'll be the one to pick up the pieces.

Gloria is the only person who says good-bye when they leave.

CHAPTER TWENTY-FIVE

KYLE

TWO WEEKS LATER

Unless fireworks are involved, holiday shifts are uneventful.

So far, this Thanksgiving, there hasn't even been a failed deep-fried turkey attempt, so for the past two hours, Gage and I have been sitting idle in the car, talking shit to each other.

"Go talk to Chloe," Gage says, repeating the same thing he's said daily. "You look like hell."

I take a swig of my coffee and settle it in the holder before answering him. "I look like hell because I had to survive a family dinner where the table conversation involved my ex-girlfriend's family blackmailing my father out of thousands of dollars."

He nods in understanding, but his words are the opposite of that. "A—quit being so dramatic. I know it fucking hurts to be lied to, but it happened. B—listen to her side of the story. You've only heard your father's, who's a man you can't stand, by the way." He sighs. "Do you remember what happened when Lauren hid secrets from me and wouldn't explain herself?"

"Yes, you skipped town for years." I grab my coffee and bump his shoulder with the side of the cup. "Is that what I'm supposed to do?"

"No, that's what I don't want to happen. Skip that part. From experience, I can tell you, it's miserable. Talk to her. Maybe you can work shit out."

"Even if we do work shit out, what am I supposed to tell my family? They hate her."

"Your family is understanding and forgiving."

"And you're usually not, so what gives? Why are you all of a sudden Team Chloe?"

"Let me make this clear; I'm always Team Motherfucking Kyle. *Always*. As for that, I see this is tearing you apart. You liked her, or still like her, but won't listen to her side of the story. No matter what, you owe her that." He inhales a deep breath. "When everything came to the surface with why Lauren did what she did, a heavy weight was lifted off our shoulders. It was the push we needed to move on and be happy. Be grateful Chloe isn't making you wait years." He blows out a breath. "I'm not telling you to get back with her. All I'm saying is, clear the air. You're pissed, I get it, but all of this is because of your father."

"I hate when you're right," I grumble. "Maybe—" I'm interrupted by the dispatcher's voice on the police radio, informing us of a car accident report.

"On it," Gage replies to her. "We're only minutes away from the scene. Call the medics just in case."

He flips the lights, and the car sirens blare through the dark streets and pouring rain. It becomes difficult to see once we hit the unlit back road.

"There," I say, pointing to the view of bright headlights.

He swerves over to the side of the road, and we both jump out as soon as the car is in park. An old sedan is crashed into a tree, the lights shining bright, and smoke is coming from the hood. We sprint through the field to the car, hostile rain showering down on us.

I'm there first, and I shine my flashlight into the driver's side to find a woman. She's motionless, her forehead resting on the steering wheel. A bottle of opened vodka and drug paraphernalia is in the passenger seat. I hold the light while Gage manages to open the door.

He rushes to take her pulse. "Still alive."

A rush of relief hits me. "Thank God." I move my attention to the backseat. "There's a passenger."

I'm soaked, blinking away the drops hitting me, and the door creaks when I open it. I flash my light on the backseat, and fear twists through my stomach. A chill colder than the icy rain pelting my face runs through my veins. My heart sinks into my stomach while an intense pain hits me.

"No!" I scream with a shaky voice while crawling to the body slumped against the backseat. She's half off the seat, and her cheek is resting against the floor. "No!"

"Motherfucker!" Gage yells behind me, and I hold a breath before checking her pulse. "Kyle, talk to me!"

I cradle the body in my arms, my chin trembling, and I look back to see EMTs running our way with a gurney.

"Here!" I scream at the top of my lungs. "Here now! Help me!"

I crawl out and carefully help them pull the limp body from the car.

The EMT looks at me with dread and confirms what I already know. "DOA."

I step in front of them, and my breathing is ragged as I attempt to do CPR.

Gage comes to my side, grabs my elbow, and stops me. "Brother, don't."

"No!" I yell, my hands going back to her chest. "Let me try! I can fix this!"

"I'm sorry," the EMT says. "Even with CPR, which will do more damage to her body, there's nothing we can do to save her. There's severe blunt force trauma to the head, and she's lost too much blood."

She looks at me with wide eyes filled with sadness. "Trust me, if there was anything I could do, I'd be fighting for it right now."

I scrub my hand over my face and scream before looking at the EMTs helping the driver onto another gurney.

"You stupid bitch!" I yell, advancing toward her.

All my morals dissipate in this moment, and it's scary to say there's no doubt in my mind that I could walk away from this scene without giving the driver a second look.

Gage throws his arm out to stop me while the EMTs look at me as if I've lost my mind. "Kyle, calm down!" He tilts his head toward the EMTs moving the passenger up the hill. "Help them get her into the ambulance!"

I nod, turn around, and run up the hill. Even though putting her in the ambulance won't stop the outcome of tonight, she deserves to be out of the rain, deserves a lot more than this. I don't slide into the warmth of the car after I help them. They shut the door in my face, the sirens wailing through the unlit road.

Gage helps the medics with the driver when the second ambulance leaves shortly after the first. We silently stand there, soaked, staring at the scene, wishing we could've changed it, that we could've driven faster, run faster, saved her.

"You need to go, Kyle," Gage finally says. "The investigators are on their way to the hospital, and I'll meet them there to tell them everything. If they need any additional information, they'll call you."

"No," I grit out. "I want to be there."

"You're too pissed to go there, and the investigators will immediately make you go home out of conflict of interest. Monroe is on his way here, and we're driving to the hospital. You have somewhere else to be."

I get into the car, drive home, and sprint to a porch that isn't mine.

The door swings open.

"Kyle?"

CHAPTER TWENTY-SIX
CHLOE

I blink a few times as if I'm imagining Kyle standing in front of me. Water drips from every inch of him, and my stomach knots at the sight of his trembling hands. Anguish covers his face like a blanket while he stares at me with fear-stricken eyes.

What the …

This is unexpected.

"Chloe. Can I come in?"

His question snaps me to my senses. "Of course," I answer, moving aside to allow him room to step into the entryway. "You must be freezing." I shut the door behind us. "Let me grab you a towel." I'm stopped when he reaches out and closes his cold hand around mine.

"I don't need a towel." He squeezes my hand, and water falls along my bare toes when I look into his damp-lashed eyes. "We need to talk."

This isn't a courtesy visit.

"What's going on, Kyle?" I question.

Do I want to know?

Instead of answering me, he lightly touches my shoulder with his free hand and brushes away a strand of loose hair fallen from my pony-tail. "Let's sit down."

Dread falls upon me as he leads me to the couch, and I sit on the edge of the cushion. "Please tell me what's going on," I stammer out. "You're scaring me."

He retreats a step and casts me a terrified glance. "There was an accident."

The tone of his voice heightens my panic. This *accident* will affect me. I don't speak. I wait for him to continue. I wait for him to break me down more than what I already am.

He drops to his knees only inches away and clears his throat. He blinks away tears before using his arm to wipe them away again.

He stares up at me with a pale face, and his voice cracks as he prepares to deliver bad news. "Your sister ..." He pauses, as if searching for the right words. "She hit a tree while driving."

I jerk my head back. "What? Is she going to be okay?"

His jaw clenches. "She's on her way to the hospital right now."

A burst of relief hits me. "Thank God." That relief suddenly filters into dread. "Gloria ... Gloria is with her tonight. Is she at the hospital with her? Is everything all right?" I pull away from him and jump up in search of my purse. "I need to go get her."

Kyle stands. "Chloe ..." He says my name in caution, as if I were about to walk off a cliff.

My heart caves into my chest as dread sets in. "I have to go to the hospital. I need to get Gloria."

"Chloe ..." His voice deepens as he erases the gap between us.

I push his chest and hold my finger up in front of him. "Don't." I walk away from him, and my voice trembles. "Don't you dare fucking say it!"

He grabs my shoulders, turns me around, and drags me into his chest. "Gloria was in the car with her."

"Don't you say it," I whisper, stifling a scream. "Don't you dare fucking say it!"

His hold on me tightens, and his lips brush against my hair. "I'm so sorry, Chloe."

"No! No!" I yell, flares of anger shooting through me as he grasps me. I struggle to break free. "Let me leave, Kyle!" My arms fly in every direction, and I'm certain they've made contact with him a few times, but he doesn't flinch, just keeps a secure hold on me.

"You're not driving in this condition," he says.

My body shakes. "I need to go to her!"

He pulls in a thick breath. "There's nowhere to go for her."

Kyle doesn't have to tell me. I already know.

"Whoa, whoa," Trey interrupts while stepping into the room, yawning. "What's going on in here?" He shoots Kyle a hard glare before puffing out his chest.

Kyle loosens his hold on me and makes sure I'm not a runner before releasing me completely. "Hey, buddy. Why don't you go to your room for a minute?" he tells Trey.

I rub my face, my eyes, my arms. My hands need to be busy or else I'll throw something across the room.

"I'm not going anywhere," Trey replies with a clenched jaw when he notices the condition I'm in. "Why are you here?"

I gulp and press my hand into Kyle's stomach, stopping him from telling Trey. I need to do it. I have to do it. Kyle only nods, and I make my way to Trey.

"There was an accident with your mom and Gloria," I whisper. "A car accident."

Trey tenses but stays quiet.

"Gloria ..."

Concern flickers across his face. He helped raise Gloria and was more of a father to her than her own. He was the one who made sure she went to school, had every meal, and did her homework.

"What happened to her?" Trey grits out with knotted fists.

"I'm sorry, honey, but Gloria ..." I glance over at Kyle for confirmation, just in case I'm wrong, and he gives me a solemn nod. I shake my head before giving him a look of desperation. I need him to say it, to make the final call, because those words can't leave my mouth. I'm too weak.

Kyle gives me another nod and steps to my side. "Gloria passed away tonight, Trey." His tone isn't one of a policeman breaking the news to an unsuspecting family. He's heartbroken. He feels for Trey. For *us. For Gloria.*

Trey's face twists in pain as he registers Kyle's statement, and his hands start shaking. "What? How? No, this can't be true. I saw her earlier today. She was fine. We went on a walk, and she told me about the new book she checked out from the library! She was fine!" His eyes change from a hardened state to a fearful one. "You're wrong, man. You're wrong!" Trey says with tears streaming down his face.

I rush forward to hug him. He shrugs away and pulls his phone from his pocket but is unable to hold it with his shaking hands. It falls to the floor, the thud ringing out through the grave silence, and he reaches down and picks it up in haste.

"I'm calling Mom," he explains, punching his fingers against the screen. "She'll tell you everything is okay. They're probably eating ice cream while Gloria talks about her dolls."

"Trey," Kyle says softly.

"No!" he screams. "I'm calling her! You've made a mistake!"

He holds the phone to his ear as tears slide down his face. "Pick up, Mom. Please. Just pick up the phone." His shouts grow louder. "Pick up!"

I know it goes to voice mail when he blurts out, "Goddamn it."

He starts to dial again, but Kyle takes the phone from him.

Surprisingly, Trey doesn't fight him for it back. Instead, he sinks down on the couch, his face stricken with tears. I rush over, wrapping my arms around him, capturing his loud sobs in my shoulder.

"I'm so sorry," I say over and over again while brushing my hand over his hair. "I'm so sorry, Trey."

His face is red when he pulls away. "Mom?"

"She's in the hospital right now. I'm not sure what's going on, but she's alive," I answer.

"I want to kill her," Trey blurts out. "I don't care what anyone says! She deserves to die for taking my sister away from me!" It's sad that Trey knows his mother well enough to know she played a part in Gloria's death—a destructive part.

I stroke Trey's back while he attempts to contain his hurt. When he starts to calm down, I inhale a deep breath and look at Kyle. I forgot he was there while I consoled Trey.

I calm my voice, and it turns flat. "I need you to drive me to the hospital, please. I need someone to scream at, and that somebody is Claudia."

Tears threaten his eyes as he stares at me. "I can't do that, Chloe. Even if I could, you wouldn't be able to see her since it's an ongoing investigation," he says, his voice almost cracking mid-sentence.

I ask, "When did it happen?" at the same time Trey asks, "How?"

He comes closer. "We're not entirely sure yet. Claudia was driving. Gloria was in the backseat, unbuckled, and there was no car seat either. The details are limited, and normally, we aren't supposed to notify anyone until all the details are confirmed, but I couldn't do that to you."

I nod—a silent thank-you. He nods back—a silent you're welcome.

"This is all my fault," Trey mutters. "It's all my fault for refusing to go with Mom tonight for her visitation. If I had been there, I could've stopped it from happening. I could've protected my baby sister."

I wrap my arm around Trey's shoulder and drag him into me again. "Trey, listen to me. This is in no way your fault."

It's my fault.

I allowed her to go with Claudia against my better judgment. Claudia was doing better after I gave her the cash. She dumped Roger. She threw no tantrums, no asking for money and no threatening to take the kids. She was sober and excited to spend time with Gloria when I dropped her off at the trailer. She never mentioned them leaving.

Kyle kneels down in front of Trey. He's fighting back his own pain. He didn't know Gloria for long, but the expression on his face shows he cared for her.

"We don't know if it's anyone's fault yet," he replies in a soothing voice. "It could've been weather or vehicle-related."

It was Claudia.

It's always fucking Claudia.

Even if the accident wasn't her fault, losing Gloria was. Claudia didn't have her in a car seat. She didn't protect her.

"Was she drunk? High?" I question.

"We won't know anything until the toxicology reports come back," Kyle answers.

"Don't bullshit me," I snap.

He sighs, terrified to tell me. "There was an opened alcohol bottle and drug paraphernalia in the vehicle." His voice softens. "I know there's nothing I can say or do for you"—his attention moves to Trey —"but I'm here. If you need *anything,* I'm right here."

No. He's not hitting me with this nightmare and then ending the conversation like this. I will not be given the *I'm sorry for your loss; I'm here* bullshit. I want my goddamn niece back in her goddamn bed with her goddamn dolls. I want goddamn answers.

I jump up from my seat. "Watch Trey." I sprint across the room and snag my keys. "I'm going to the hospital."

I make it outside, nearly to my car, when Kyle stops me. I fight him again, soaking wet this time, as he drags me back inside, slides my keys into his pocket, and locks the door.

"Chloe, you can't do that right now. As soon as the doctors give us the go-ahead, we can question her. Until then, it's better for us to sit here and wait."

"Sit here and wait?" I scream. "Claudia is not getting out of this, Kyle. She does not get to heal or rest. She doesn't even deserve another ounce of breath for what she did! You know who deserves that?" I seethe. "*The little girl she neglected!* That *I* neglected. That's who deserves it. Not you." I push him back again. "Not me." My finger shoves into my chest. "She was only four fucking years old!"

Kyle lets me take my anger out on him and waits until I'm finished before speaking. "As soon as I can, I'll take you to her. I swear it. I'll let you say whatever you need to without anyone stopping you, okay?"

"Where do we go from here?" I whisper.

"You grieve and let me handle the rest." He tilts his head toward Trey. "You two take care of each other."

He moves from me to Trey and pulls him into a hug. "I'll be home all night. Come over. Call. Anything you need, I'm here."

"Will you … will you hang out here longer?" Trey asks, peering up at him.

"Of course," Kyle answers. He says it with no question, no hesitation, no asking for permission.

The rest of the night, I'm numb. Angry. Like I'm not even present or alive. I walk through my house, emotionless, consoling Trey. I take phone calls, give police information, and answer as many questions as I can, but mentally, I'm checked out, not with it. I feel nothing, and along with feeling nothing, I can't process my loss.

I go to bed with tears in my eyes.

When Kyle comes into my bedroom later, I don't stop him.

When he holds me as I fight myself to sleep, I don't stop him.

When I do fall asleep and wake up in the middle of the night, jerking from a nightmare, and he tightens his hold on me, I don't stop him.

He does it again and again.

His arms never leave my body. His voice in my ear is soothing.

And that confirms more than I already know.

This man I love has a heart of gold and deserves someone less messed up, less deceitful than me.

CHAPTER TWENTY-SEVEN
CHLOE

The warmth of Kyle's chest brushes against my back when I wake up, and his arm is draped along my waist—a security blanket. My heart sinks, the tears simmering, when my memory is refreshed from last night's nightmare. It wasn't a nightmare. It was my reality.

I wince and inhale a sharp breath, feeling too numb to move.

Grief. Hurt. Regret.

They sucker-punch me. It seems surreal, and I'm nearly tempted to roll out of bed, pad down the hallway, and go to her room in hopes that I'll find her sleeping. But it'd break me more. She's gone. I failed her.

His arm tightens around me when he realizes I'm awake.

"Hi," he simply says in a subdued voice.

I swallow. Even though his nearness provides comfort, it won't erase what he said and did the last time he was here. That's not important to bring up right now though. I'm too exhausted to fight, to nearly speak.

The sheets fall down my body, and his arms leave me when I sit up. My head spins, and seconds later, I'm close to falling back down. His arm curls around my stomach just in time, and a glass of water is offered my way.

"Here, drink this," he whispers as I turn to face him.

"Thank you." I gulp it down, realizing how dry my mouth was.

"What do you need me to do for you?" he asks, his tone gentle and kind, as if he's prepared to pull the weight of my pain off me.

"I need to see Claudia," is all I answer.

She got last night—more time than she deserved—and there's no way I can make it through the day without confronting her.

He nods. "Do you want me to stay with Trey?"

"Please."

"Of course. Anything you need, I'm here, Chloe."

"Thank you."

"Always."

———

I wait for Trey to wake up before leaving for the hospital. He walks into the kitchen with droopy shoulders, red eyes, and a puffy face, wearing the same clothes from last night. Even now, he looks to be on the verge of tears.

An hour after Kyle arrived and told us about the accident, Trey left for his bedroom with a bowed spine, and this is the first time I've seen him since.

I checked on him before going to bed, asking if he was all right through his closed door, and received a simple, "I'm fine."

He opens the fridge, snags a bottle of water, and leans back against the door after shutting it. "Are you going to see her today?"

I nod while sitting at the kitchen table. "I am."

I eventually pulled myself together, showered while having practice conversations in my head of what I wanted to say when confronting Claudia, and then dressed before walking into the kitchen. Kyle was waiting with a coffee cup in his hand, and worry lined his features.

"Tell her I hate her fucking guts," Trey says in a flat, monotone voice, not seeming apologetic or concerned for his language.

I don't scold him because I don't blame him. Those words have been on the tip of my tongue since last night.

"I want you to say it," he goes on. "Word for word. Tell her I'm no longer her son and to forget about me." Tears lace his eyes again. "Tell her I'll never forgive her for taking my baby sister away from me. If there's anything you can do for me right now, Aunt Chloe, it's to relay that message to her. If you don't, I'll call an Uber and do it myself."

I gulp and stumble for the right words before speaking. "Do you want to go to the hospital with me?" *Say no.*

Even though I don't want him to, he deserves the choice. It's his mother. It was his sister she killed. He deserves it just as much as I do.

He shakes his head while tightly gripping the water bottle in his hand. "I never want to see her again. She should've died instead of Gloria. She's the one who deserved it."

Kyle finally steps into the conversation, clearly uncomfortable with Trey's choice of words. "I know you're angry."

Trey interrupts him. "No, dude, don't even. There's no talking me down from my hate toward her. I've thought about it all night. I couldn't sleep because all I could think about was, it's her fault I'll never see my sister again. She's not my mother. She's nothing to me." His sadness turns into anger. "I need to shower."

I stand up when Trey starts to leave the kitchen. "Trey."

He holds his palm out. "Just leave me alone for a while, okay?"

Kyle pulls out the chair next to mine when Trey leaves. "Are you sure you're ready to do this?"

"I was ready for it last night." I tilt my chin up to stare at him. "You need to swear to me, she won't get off the hook for this."

He takes my hand in his. "I promise I'll do everything I can for her to get what she deserves."

———

I'm filled with fury when I slam the door shut behind me, and I don't care who can hear when I scream my words out, "I fucking hate you!"

Claudia is in front of me, relaxing in a hospital bed, with IVs in her arm. One of her hands is cuffed to the bed rail. I don't know her condition or diagnosis, and I don't know if she'll even tell me. Right now, I don't even care.

A large bandage is stretched along her forehead, a dark bruise is around her eye, and there are scratches and cuts along her neck. Her blonde hair is matted along her hairline, and her eyes are slanted. I hate that she's here, hate that she was saved and given treatment even though she killed Gloria.

She looks down, playing with her hands, and shrugs. "What's new, Chloe?" The regret is clear on her face. She knows what she did, the part she played in Gloria's death. "You think I don't feel bad?" she yells. "You think I don't have to live with this guilt every day?"

I swallow. "Good. I hope it haunts you until you take your last breath." I step closer to her bed, and she tenses up. "Not only were you driving under the influence, but you were also too lazy and stupid to put her in a car seat. What were you thinking? I told you I'd pick her up after you were finished visiting!" I curl my hands into fists and stop myself from punching her in the face, my anger getting the best of me.

She rubs her head. "I wanted to take her out for a drive. I wanted to be a normal mom for once and drive my daughter around."

"Stop with the fucking lies! They found your phone. You were meeting a drug dealer." I grip my hands around the bed rails and tilt my head forward until I'm in her face, not even bothered that she might be the one to punch me. "She's gone because you needed to get high."

"Fuck you!" Spit flies out with her words. "She was my child!"

I draw back, and my lips curl. "A child you never bothered to take care of. A child you failed."

"I want you to leave."

"I don't care what you want. You're going to lie there and listen to every single word I say because this will be the last visit I'll ever give you. If they give you a trial, which I'll fight for, I'll be there, but this will be our last conversation. Do you hear me?" I point my finger at her. "So, sit back, shut up, and listen to me tell you how much I fucking hate you. Listen to me tell you I will fight until the death of me to make sure you get in trouble for this."

She scratches her head. "Say whatever you want, Chloe. Make me feel like a piece of shit, like you've done since you were a kid."

I pace in front of her bed, holding my tongue the best that I can.

"I want to see Trey," she says, her voice scratchy. "I want to tell him I'm sorry and see him one more time."

That catches my attention, and I shift to face her. "Tough shit. He doesn't want to see you."

"Don't lie to me," she bites out.

"If he decides he wants to see you at any time, I'll give him that." I pause while briefly debating on whether to relay the message he gave me. "He said he hates your guts and you're dead to him." I'll give that to Trey. Right or wrong, he deserves to have his voice.

Her face and tone turn spiteful. "He might hate me, but as a minor, he has no say in what happens in his life. He can't stop me from demanding he live with his father instead of you."

I stumble back a step, her words catching me off guard. I pull in a sharp breath and straighten my back, appearing to brush off the threat lined between her words. "Not only is there no physical proof that Michael is Trey's father, I doubt he'll step up. Nice try though."

She shakes her head. "That's where you're wrong. Michael's name is on the birth certificate."

I gulp. "You're lying."

The corners of her mouth tilt up in a cold smirk. "He made me take a DNA test to prove Trey was his before supporting us. They already paid me a visit. They want to take him now that I'll be in jail."

"Bullshit. Michael never wanted Trey."

"True, but Michael is eating crow to regain his wife's trust, *and* how bad will it look if he turns his back on his son? They'll give him a stable home environment."

My snorting interrupts her. *Stable my ass.*

"I'll do everything in my power to make that happen."

"Don't. You know I've been there for Trey since day one."

"And, now, it's time for someone better to do it."

My heart races as fear sets in. "Fuck you, Claudia."

I charge out of the hospital with tears in my eyes.

More tears fall, and I scream to the emptiness of my car when I catch sight of a couple I recognize walking into the hospital.

CHAPTER TWENTY-EIGHT

KYLE

I grab my phone from the coffee table when it buzzes with a text.

Gage: We're en route to Chloe's with food.

He called earlier to check on me, asked about Chloe, and said him and Lauren would be over with enough baked goods to last a month—all prepared by Lauren's mother. I asked them to make a pit stop at the diner and pick up a takeout order for Trey and me.

I haven't heard from Chloe since she left for the hospital. She needs time and space to process everything.

Eventually, Trey wandered into the living room with a blank stare on his face. I handed him the remote when he sat down on the other end of the couch. He chose the movie, and we sat in silence while watching it. Just like with Chloe, I'm giving him time.

We haven't discussed us being brothers, but I'll approach the conversation when the time is right. The day after losing his sister isn't. I've been a good brother to my siblings, and I don't mind being the same for Trey.

My fallout with Chloe won't stop me from comforting her while she endures her loss. Have I forgotten about the chaos her family has caused mine? No. Right now, that issue isn't at the top of my priority list.

I didn't know Gloria long, but I cared for her. This morning, when

Chloe asked me to shut Gloria's bedroom door, tears threatened my eyes when I noticed the sparkly red shoes in the corner and the stuffed Toto on the bed. My throat choked up as I took in the dolls, the coloring books, all the memories and toys of a sweet girl taken away too early.

Fuck. I want to kill Claudia myself.

Lauren wraps me in a hug as soon as I answer the door. She was on shift when Claudia was brought into the ER and assigned her nurse until she was transferred to another floor. Lauren said her tongue hurt from biting it all night while caring for her.

Claudia's toxicology report came back, confirming alcohol and heroin flowed through her bloodstream at the time of the accident. She'd fallen asleep at the wheel and suffered minor injuries—a concussion and internal bleeding. She'll be taken straight to the county jail upon her release.

Lauren and Gage don't stay long, and Trey devours his cheeseburger before moving on to the cupcakes. An hour later, he's asleep on the couch, and it's time for me to leave for work. Both my lieutenant and Gage offered to give me the evening off, but I declined. No one could cover my shift, and I wasn't going to leave Gage to work alone.

I text Chloe before leaving, telling her, if she needs anything, don't hesitate to call, but receive nothing back.

It's the same when my shift ends at midnight.

———

Chloe's car is in the driveway when Gage drops me off, and I dig out the house key she gave me earlier today after asking if I'd come over later. I was reluctant to come so late since she still hadn't returned my text, but my house key is here, so I have no choice.

The house is quiet when I walk in, and a light shines from the kitchen. I tiptoe down the hall to find Chloe sitting at the table, staring blankly at the papers and documents scattered along it. It appears to be work files, paperwork she was given last night regarding Claudia, Gloria, the accident, and bills. I stop mid-step when I notice what's in her hand—a packet regarding funeral arrangements.

She chokes out a cry, unaware I'm here, and slams her hand over her mouth, as if it were a crime for her to break down. I hesitate before moving closer, and she takes in my presence in discomfort.

"Chloe, talk to me," I beg.

She stiffens in her chair and avoids eye contact. "You don't have to be here." The words leave her mouth calmly but chillingly.

Where is this coming from?

Before she left for the hospital, she thanked me for being there for her and Trey. All of a sudden, in a ten-hour span, everything has changed.

Something happened.

I draw in closer and stop in front of the table. "I know, but I want to be here."

She stands, almost robotically. She grabs a bottle of water from the refrigerator and rests with her back against the cabinet. "Don't feel sorry for me. I don't need you to feel sorry for me."

"Feel sorry for you?" I throw back. "I'm hurting that you're hurting. Your heart is broken, and all I want to do is help! To make you feel better!"

She throws the bottle across the room before thrusting her finger in my direction. "Fuck you! You wanted nothing to do with me before Gloria's death. You came into my bedroom, fucked me, and then told me to *get fucked!* Don't think you can step in here and act like you're some hero. I can do it on my own! I can save myself. Now, I'm kindly asking you to leave."

It takes me what feels like a minute to speak. "Chloe."

She vacantly stares at me. "Leave."

My eyes lock with hers. "I'm sorry." Regret lodges in my throat. "I'm sorry," I repeat, not moving any closer to her. "I'm fucking sorry for not allowing you to explain yourself. It was my mistake, and I'm willing to listen when you're ready, but right now, right fucking now, that's the last of my concern. Does that mean I'll forget what went down? No, but you need a friend, and I'm here."

That vacant stare turns into one of defeat. "No, Kyle, I don't want to be *your friend.* I don't want anything to do with you or your family!"

I throw my arms up in the air. "Here we fucking go again with your fucking obsession with my family! The truth is out! It's over now!"

She lets out a cold laugh. "No, it's not over! You want to know why?" She advances my way. "Because, now that your father's secret is out, your parents want custody of Trey. They can provide a *better environment* for him."

Whoa. What?

"Who told you this?"

"Claudia."

I scowl. "You're believing *her* out of all people?" I rub at my brow. "Chloe, if my mother even *considered* taking custody of Trey, she would've told me. Claudia said that to hurt you."

"Really?" She raises her voice. "Did she tell you she visited Claudia in the hospital?"

I slam my mouth shut. "No."

"I saw them, Kyle! Your mom and dad were there!"

"Maybe for another reason. There's more than one patient in that hospital," I stupidly reply. "My mom does charity work there."

Annoyance floods her face.

I scrub my hands over my face. "Chloe … we … this." I'm at a loss for words. "Let me talk to my mother." I can't deny it because it sounds like my mother—always wanting to fix the problem and create a better life for someone. She sees Trey as a charity case.

She gestures between us. "This has to be done. Too much terrible shit has happened for us to ever have a healthy relationship. From what happened in high school to the secret about your father and now this. Too much damage has been done. We need to stop kidding ourselves that we'd ever work out."

My heart rages in my chest. *Is she fucking kidding me?* "Or maybe it's time to stop kidding ourselves and realize this can work between us. How about that, huh?"

She frantically shakes her head. "No. It'll never work. I'm asking you to leave."

"Chloe," I beg, another attempt for her to understand what she's doing.

"Leave!" she screams.

Anger crushes through me like a bullet. "Fine, keep pushing people away. Don't be upset when you're alone and nursing a broken heart for the rest of your life because you're so goddamn stubborn."

My words seem to add more power to her anger. "No, I'm being smart to stop my heartache. It's time I stop letting people in. All I get is pain and hurt."

"What have I done to hurt you? *What the flying fuck have I done?* I did something shitty in high school that I *thought* we'd moved on from. I said some stupid shit to you. Now, let's take a step back and talk about what you've done to hurt me. You've done nothing but lie to me—about my father, about me having a brother I never knew about, about my father fucking your sister behind my mother's back! I'm the one taking the risk with you, not the other way around."

"And I didn't know your mother would take custody of Trey!"

"Whoa, whoa. Who's taking custody of me?"

I whip around and spot Trey standing feet away from me with a dumbfounded look on his face.

He whips his arm out to me. "Your mom is trying to take me away from Aunt Chloe?"

I hold my palm out and shake my head. "It's a big misunderstanding."

"It's not," Chloe counters. "I called the social worker. They've talked to her, and with your parents' influence, cheating scandal or not, they have more power."

Horror flashes through Trey's eyes. "I'll never live with anyone else. Fuck that."

"Trey, watch your mouth," Chloe warns.

He shrugs. "Ground me. Do whatever. I've already lost enough anyway."

Chloe looks at me. "Kyle, please leave. It's over. We're over. Thank you for all you've done, but please, go home."

"Chloe." I draw out her name while fighting for the right words.

"Please," she begs.

It's too late. Even if I find the words, it's done.

I nod. "Thank you for clarifying all I needed to know. I'm glad this meant nothing to you."

With that, I grab my shit and leave.

CHAPTER TWENTY-NINE

S *miles.*

Funerals are full of them.

An entire range of smiles is what I've received today.

I never want to smile and thank someone for coming again.

The church is filled with people smiling while paying their respects. It should make me feel good for the support, but instead, it angers me. Most of these people didn't care about her kind until tragedy hit. Parents are here, who denied their children playdates with her because of where she came from. Even Mrs. Garfield shoots me an apologetic smile, a hint of shame in her eyes, when it's her turn to give her condolences.

Gloria's casket is small, and the bright pink flowers Trey picked out lie atop it. She's wearing her Dorothy costume, and her stuffed Toto is nestled at her side. I came early before the showing, sat in front of her casket, and apologized. I should've never trusted Claudia with her. *Never.* That's on me. Our little Dorothy will be buried today because of my stupid judgment.

When I look at her, it's a deeper cut into my heart, but I won't quit torturing myself. Every heart-shattering glance is worth it because, after today, I'll never be able to do it again. All I'll have is photos.

Adjusting to life without Gloria is a mixture of emotions—denial, disbelief, anger, regret, and sadness. As she was the youngest, Trey and I made Gloria the priority of our lives, and now, she's gone even though all the evidence of the space she filled in our hearts is everywhere.

Claudia put in a request to attend the funeral, but it was denied. Denied by *Mayor Lane.* She's facing a long list of charges for Gloria's death, including vehicular manslaughter. I haven't visited her again and don't plan to. Trey's attitude hasn't changed in the matter either.

I take a seat in the front row and look over to the corner where Kyle has stood since he came in. He's kept his distance, but even that is comforting. I never doubted he'd show.

I catch a glimpse of his family a few rows back—including his father. Sierra reached out to Trey a few days ago, inviting him over to her house for dinner. I'm not dumb. They want to warm themselves up to him. He declined, but he was nice about it. It's his sister, and he's having trouble coming to terms with that. He lost a sister, and now, a new one is coming around.

I've felt guilt over my wanting custody of him. He'll have more money, growing up as a Lane, but I can't lose him. I've already lost Gloria, and I won't survive another loss. I'm also not too selfish; if the time comes and Trey does want to live with them, I'd let him go.

I'd let him go because, unlike everyone else, it's his happiness that matters to me.

I look over when Kyle sits down next to me. There's been an empty chair there since I sat down. It's almost as if no one dared to take it.

"Hi," he says.

Him being at my side eases me.

"Hi," I reply.

When the service starts and the tears hit, he grabs my hand. I squeeze it tight. Trey gives the eulogy, keeping his sobs together to say his words. I'm mentally and physically depleted when it ends.

"Thank you for coming," I whisper as people clear out of the church.

"Always," he says.

The three of us stand, and Kyle looks from me to Trey. "I'm right next door and not going anywhere. If you need anything—sugar, a friend, a hug—you guys come knocking, okay?"

Trey and I nod.

His offer makes me smile for a brief moment—something I haven't done in what seems like weeks.

———

The loss of Gloria hits Trey the hardest when we arrive home.

He plucks a picture of her from the fridge, sets it down on the table next to the pizza we picked up, and stares at it, tears resurfacing. "I wouldn't even dress up as a stupid scarecrow for her!" he says through sobs. "That's all she wanted—for her big brother to go trick-or-treating with her—and I let her down because I was being a stupid hard-ass." He ducks his head down in humiliation … anger … sadness. "God, what I'd do to have her back. I'd dress up as a scarecrow every day of my life. I'd do anything—*anything*—for her to be next to me right now."

I get up from my chair, stand behind him, and wrap my arms around his shoulders.

I don't know how long we cry and stare at her.

When Trey goes to bed, the pizza untouched, I tread into my bedroom.

Reality sinks through, drowning me like an anchor, and I don't know if I'll ever be able to reach the surface again. I slide down the wall, raise my knees, and slack forward. I want to break down in tears but scream out in anger. Every emotion for every shitty thing in my life is finally pouring out of me like an overflowing stream.

A knock on the door breaks me away from my thoughts, and I sniffle, wiping my nose with my arm. The door opens, and I hear someone walk in. I shut my eyes and release a breath at his scent.

"Trey let me in," Kyle whispers into the darkness of my bedroom. I vaguely see his hand held out to me. "Come here."

I shake my head. "I need to get this out."

He nods, but instead of leaving, he slides down the wall and sits next to me. "Then, get it out."

He doesn't talk or touch me again. He sits there, assuring me I'm not alone, until I fall asleep.

When I wake up, he's gone.

CHAPTER THIRTY
CHLOE

Gloria's funeral was two days ago.

I've kept to myself, and Trey has done the same—playing video games and Netflix-bingeing. My phone keeps alerting me with reminders to call the social worker regarding Trey, but when I pick up the phone to do it, I can't. I'm scared. The fear of what she'll tell me knocks back my energy into making the call. I'm biding my time until they come knocking on the door, and I'll ready to fight like hell when they do.

My shoulders tense when I hear the doorbell ring, and my legs feel weak when I walk to the door. I question myself on answering when I look through the peephole, and worry seeps through me when I answer.

Nancy Lane is standing in front of me.

My breath catches in my throat while I wait for her to speak. I'm at a loss for words.

"Hi, Chloe," she bursts out in a sweet tone, "Can we talk?"

I blink, and it takes me a moment to reply. "Sure."

This is it.

This is where she tells Trey to pack his bags and leave me.

I lead her into my living room, and neither one of us is relaxed when we sit on the couch.

She cuts straight to the point. "I'm aware Claudia informed you that Michael and I felt it was in Trey's best interest if we raised him."

I grimace and ball my knuckles. "She did, and I respectively disagree." I'm biting back the angry words I want to scream at her.

"It seems you're not the only one."

Her response surprises me.

"I'm sorry ... what?"

Her eyes are glossy, and she places a finger underneath her nose as she tilts her head down. "I want to apologize." She blinks away tears. "I'm sorry if I'm being too emotional. Kyle came to talk to me. He explained that you've been the sole caretaker for Trey, that, since he was a baby, it's always been you. He asked me how I'd feel if someone tried to take my children away from me, and his words made me understand. My heart hurts if I caused you any pain. I only wanted to help Trey, but I understand now that helping him is having you. Trey can stay with you. Michael and I will not be pursuing any type of custody battle, and we have no issue with helping if need be—whether it be money, school assistance, anything like that. We're here." She sucks in a breath. "And, when you two feel comfortable, I'd love to get to know him. So would his brother and sisters."

Tears fill my eyes. "Thank you," I blurt out, my voice thick with emotions, so many damn emotions. "Thank you so much." I pull in a breath and wipe away my tears before clearing my throat. "And I'm sorry ... for keeping everything from you ... and, uh ... taking money away from your family."

She shakes her head. "Honey, you did that for those kids. Michael told me he had the checks made out to you because he knew you'd do the right thing and that you stopped accepting them when you had enough money to help them yourself. You doing that, even against your better judgment, only further proves how much you care for them." She grabs my hand and squeezes it. "And I am so, *so very sorry* about your loss."

We're both crying as we stand, and she wraps her arms around me before leaving. "My door is always open." She hands me a piece of paper when we separate. "Here's my number. If you need anything, Chloe, please let me know."

I sniffle. "Thank you again."

She gives me one last look before leaving. "Now, I understand why my son loves you so much." She sighs. "With four children, I try to steer clear of their love lives, but Kyle cares for you deeply. He's not perfect, and sometimes, he doesn't think before he speaks. But he's ready to take on every broken piece of you, and hopefully, you're willing to do the same with him."

CHAPTER THIRTY-ONE

KYLE

I've told Chloe good morning for the past week.

I'm not greeted with curse words or finger signals.

I get a small glimmer of a smile and a bowed head.

That's it.

I should appreciate her lack of telling me to fuck off but don't. It further proves every light inside her has dimmed.

My family's disdain toward Chloe has lowered. We sat down after the funeral and all came to the understanding that she's not the bad person; he is.

I haven't forgiven my father, but I am giving him credit for stepping up. When he realized my mother was finally going to walk away, it sucker-punched him. My mom ignored his infidelities before because they were hidden, but when they were released in the open, that did her in. Not to mention, he produced a child with his mistress *years ago*. My siblings and I had begged her to leave him, but she didn't want to lose her family. I didn't agree with her decision, but I accepted it because I love her. She asked us to work on not hating our father, so for her, I've tried to keep a straight face and not punch him when he's around. But no matter what, I'll never have respect for him.

I slam the door shut after getting into the car with Gage. He's my best friend, but lately, he's proven to be more than that. He was there for Gloria's funeral, and that was a big step for him. Gage isn't one who frequents funerals, especially children's funerals, after what he experienced in Chicago. He came for me. He kicked away those fears for me.

He jerks his head toward Chloe's house. "Have you gone over and talked to her yet?"

He asks this every day.

I give him the same reply every day.

I shake my head and rub at my eyes. If you don't count my good mornings, then no. "I'm not sure what to say."

"She hasn't mentioned your mom's visit to her?"

"No."

"Use it as a conversation starter. Knock on her door and deliver the news as if you didn't know your mom had paid her a visit. You wanted to make sure she knew."

I blow out a breath. "I'm giving her time to grieve."

"You are one patient man."

"Hey there. New job?"

Trey is squatted down and sliding cans on a lower shelf in a grocery aisle at Garfield's. The last time I saw him here was for shoplifting, and now, they've given him a job.

Good for him.

Trey looks up at me with a nod before standing up. "Yeah. I need something to help pass my time before my mind goes crazy." His voice lowers. "I don't have a little sister to look after anymore, so it's all I think about in my downtime."

I've debated on reaching out to Trey after the funeral. I told them my door is open, so when they're ready, I'm ready.

I give him a hopeful look. "I'm sorry, buddy. My door is always open if you want to talk or hang out," I offer again.

He smiles and plays with the collar of his red work shirt. "I'm sorry for what I said when I eavesdropped on the conversation about your parents wanting custody of me. I was pissed. It was nothing against you."

I smile. "Don't worry about it."

He kicks his feet against the ground. "But I'm down for whatever. I got a new number."

He fishes his phone from his pocket. I grab mine, and we recite our numbers to each other.

"You know," he starts with hesitation, "I've always wanted a big brother."

I wink. "You have one now."

He grins wider before pointing to my cart. "That's a lot of food."

"My parents are having a dinner on Christmas. You're more than welcome to come with me if you'd like."

"Maybe. Aunt Chloe is making dinner on Christmas."

"That's scary," I joke.

He laughs. "I know, right? She wants us to have a traditional Christmas dinner." He pauses, and all friendliness on his face has disappeared and is replaced with sadness. "I'm worried about her. Gloria and I always spent the day with her, and now …"

I nod in response. "You be there for her, okay?"

"I'm trying my hardest to."

———

Trey texts me the next day.

He asked Chloe if it was okay for him to hang out with me, and she approved.

We go out for pizza, and I take him to the arcade. We have a blast. He says Melanie has been hanging out at the house to keep Chloe's spirits up. He's still worried about her, and he knows she's hiding her sadness.

We brainstorm, coming up with ideas to help her through her pain.

CHAPTER THIRTY-TWO

CHLOE

Christmas has never been exciting for me.

The holidays were never bright and cheery, growing up. When I was younger, I didn't know how I always managed to be on the naughty list. No matter how good I acted, Santa never visited our house. I never received coal either, so it was a confusing time for me. I promised myself that Trey and Gloria would never doubt where they stood with Santa. I worked my ass off to give them a decent Christmas every year.

This year, I've made an entire Christmas dinner with more food than Trey and I could eat in a month.

"I wish she were here with us," Trey mutters when I hand him his first gift. He frowns at the box, as if it's wrong for him to open it.

My brows scrunch together when he drops the box and grabs his phone after it beeps with a text message.

"Oh, yeah," he says. "I forgot to tell you that Mr. Garfield said they had extra pies at the market that are close to expiring, so they're dropping them off."

Trey brought up getting a job to me three days after Gloria's funeral. He needed a hobby to take his mind off his mother going to prison and his sister's death. I agreed and was surprised when he told me he'd been hired at Garfield's Grocery.

I'm doing the same. I work as often as I can and considered looking into a second job—not for financial reasons, but to keep my mind off my problems as well. Melanie has made it her mission to be my sidekick at all times, and even though I act like it's driving me crazy, I appreciate her company.

Then, there's Kyle. I feel terrible for not thanking him for talking to his mother. It's a bitch move on my part, but I'm terrified. He hasn't reached out since the night he consoled me and then disappeared, which I don't blame him for.

I sigh. Tomorrow, I'm going to his house and apologizing for my outburst, for kicking him out of my house, for not telling him every-thing about his father, and for not giving him a hug for saving me from the heartache of losing Trey.

I uncross my legs and stand up from the floor. "Aw, that's nice of them."

He pulls on his boots. "Can you give me a hand? They're old and it's snowing, so we should probably help them."

"Of course."

I put my shoes on and throw on a coat. "Are they not here yet?" I ask, shivering when we walk outside.

Trey is typing on his phone. "Hold on. They're texting me now."

I raise a brow in confusion. "The Garfields know how to text?"

He doesn't answer me, and seconds later, the abrupt sound of his voice cuts through the morning air. The deep voice brims with an overflow of emotions.

"Merry Christmas to the girl I love!"

My attention sweeps over to Kyle's porch to find him standing there, shirtless, wearing only his gray sweatpants, looking the same as he did every day before we started our relationship. A Santa hat is on his head, and I can't hold back my burst of laughter—my first loud, belly-aching laughter I've had in months.

"You're going to get hypothermia!" I yell back in exchange for, *Fuck off.*

He hops down the stairs, and Trey is beaming from the sidelines. Their setup is playing out smoothly.

"If I get hypothermia," he says when he reaches me, "I'm blaming you, babe."

I press my hand against my chest. "On me? It's not my fault you enjoy flaunting your naked self around in the freezing cold."

I can see his breath releasing into the cold. "Please be honest with me, Chloe. That's all I want for Christmas, and your honesty will provide me the energy to make my way back inside. Otherwise, I'll probably freeze outside and die."

I shake my head, still laughing. "I can't believe I'm even entertaining this."

He grabs me by my waist, and his chest is freezing. "Tell me how you feel about me, Chloe. No bullshit. Look at me and tell me you don't care about me the way I care about you."

I gulp, and my heart races so hard that I'm waiting for it to fall out of my chest. "I ... I don't care about you, Kyle."

His face falls.

"I mean ... I do ... but I *more* than care about you."

A smile takes over his face. "Say it."

I cover my face with my hands. "Oh my God. I can't believe I'm about to declare my love to a half-naked man sporting a Santa hat, who looks like he should be featured in an X-rated Christmas calendar."

He takes my hand and kisses the top. "I'm more than happy to get you a calendar with my pictures in them."

A tear falls down my cheek, and his finger is cold when he wipes it away.

"I love you," I say with no hesitation, regret, or unease.

He stares down at me, his white teeth showing as he grins wildly. "And, damn, do I love you."

He tilts his head down and kisses me. He pulls away and inspects me, and then his lips hit mine again.

I glance back at Trey while smiling. "I take it, there are no pies?"

Trey shrugs. "They must have forgotten to stop on their way home."

"Did you say pie?" Kyle chimes in. "Weird, I have *plenty* of them in my house." He snags my hand in his and leads me toward his porch while calling out for Trey to come on.

"Did your mom make the pies?" I ask when we make it inside.

Kyle grins. "Would you think any different? I told you, I want to always impress you, not give you food poisoning."

———

"I got you something," Kyle says.

After we devoured the sweets Kyle had brought home from his family Christmas dinner, we went to the living room to watch Christmas movies.

He hops off the couch and walks barefoot to his bedroom while Trey snores in the background.

"You … you didn't have to do that," I say when he hands me a small box.

"I know I didn't. I *wanted* to."

I stare at it, moving the box around and inspecting it, before undoing the bow. I gulp, unsure of why I'm so nervous about opening a present. It's a jewelry box. My heart races when I pop it open.

Nestled inside is a necklace.

I pull it out, playing with the thin string, and inspect it. I cover my mouth to conceal my whimper, and tears flood my cheeks. On the necklace hangs a heart pendent that says *Mother* and inscribed are Trey's and Gloria's names.

"It's beautiful. Thank you," I whisper.

Kyle's face is filled with pride, and he nods toward Trey. "He helped me pick it out. He said he's always seen you as his mother, not anyone else, and we knew nothing better would suit you."

I frown, and he uses his thumb to gently rid me of my tears. "I didn't buy you a gift."

He tips his head down to kiss my lips. "Don't worry," he says against them in a low tone. "You can give me mine later."

The thought of him touching me, of being in his bed, of us

together again, sparks happiness inside me. If Trey wasn't sleeping on the other side of the sectional, I'd be straddling Kyle right now.

I blush. "You can't joke around about that even if he is asleep."

He draws back with a grin. "Huh? I want a night full of you repeating you love me *over and over* again. That's what I want as my gift."

I chuckle. "This conversation is mirroring one of those Hallmark movies we just watched."

"I'll take it because Hallmark movies always end up with a happily ever after."

CHAPTER THIRTY-THREE
CHLOE

TWO MONTHS LATER

Even though today is Trey's birthday, you'd think, with the excitement beaming from me, it was mine.

"It's official," Trey says. "You're my mother."

Tears fall from my eyes.

When we finally opened gifts on Christmas, Trey slipped me a letter, asking me to adopt him. Kyle talked to his parents, and Michael agreed to sign over custody to me. Trey still wants to get to know his family, but he wanted to make sure he was always *my son*. I'd been reluctant on adopting him for years in hopes that Claudia would change, but Trey deserves a good mother who loves and appreciates him.

I shut my eyes as a tear slips down my face. I wish I could've done the same for Gloria, wish I'd done it years ago. It's bittersweet, celebrating being Trey's parent while also wishing you could've done the same with his sister.

Kyle wraps his arm around my shoulders and walks with us. "You know, since we're in the county building, we can go upstairs and get married."

I throw my head back and laugh. "You always make jokes."

He squeezes my side. "No joking. You say the word, and I'm throwing you over my shoulder and making you my wife. Absolutely no fucking joke about that."

———

"I'm nervous," Trey says from the backseat of Kyle's Jeep. "I'm meeting a brother and sisters I never knew I had."

"Hey, you met me before," Kyle says in an attempt to lighten his nervousness.

"Yes, but you were super cool when we first met."

Kyle elbows me from the driver's side while I'm in the passenger seat. "Listen to that. He knows I'm super cool."

I shake my head. "He's calling you *super cool* because you got him out of a shoplifting charge."

Kyle's grin drops. "Ah, man, and here I thought, we were best friends."

Trey smacks his shoulder. "Trust me, dude; we are best friends. Any other cop would've arrested me with no questions asked. You never made me feel like anything but a normal kid."

Happiness radiates through my chest—the opposite of how I thought it'd be when we got here. I'm going inside, facing Nancy and Michael while we share a dinner. Michael and Nancy reached out, and before we threw Trey into the mix, we had a meeting at Kyle's house. Michael apologized. I accepted but will never forgive him for the pain he'd caused my family. Trey needs a father, and he's working on accepting Michael not being there for him before.

We're taking chances in our lives.

Losing Gloria convinced me to take a step back and realize what I wanted in life—to stop being scared and be happy.

We count to three before getting out of the Jeep, and Trey looks around in awe at the home.

We see Sierra first when we walk in. She's skipping down the stairs with her boyfriend trailing behind her.

"I don't understand why you keep hanging out with Maliki," he mutters behind her. "You close the bar with him every night, and it's not even your job."

"He's my friend. Get over it," she snaps.

Her boyfriend snorts. "I bet you wouldn't be okay with me having a friend who was a girl."

Their conversation ends when they notice us.

"What's up, big and little brother?" she greets.

I cover my face to stop the joyful tears. She's treating Trey as if he's one of them and not creating any awkwardness.

"I'm Sierra, the best sister in the world," she adds.

"Hell yes!" Rex comes roaring through next. "I'm your big bro, Rex. If you think Kyle is cool, prepared to be shocked by the increased coolness factor of me!"

I glance at Trey, expecting him to be nervous, but he's smiling from ear to ear.

Dinner goes by smoothly. I don't share words with Michael, but he acknowledges Trey and isn't acting like an asshole, like the first time I had dinner here. Kyle said he's changed since news of his affair broke out. Nancy was done, her children supporting her when she called a divorce lawyer, and it opened Michael's eyes.

By the time we're loading back into the Jeep, Trey and Rex have plans to go to the arcade tomorrow.

———

Kyle slides into bed next to me after we finish brushing our teeth. We're shoulder-to-shoulder as we lean back against the headboard.

He stares ahead when he speaks. "I know you just adopted Trey, but you told me you wanted another child as well. *Children,* if I'm certain."

My attention shoots straight to him, and my eyes meet his green ones. I clutch my stomach and swallow without saying a word.

He doesn't stop for my reply. "I did some research and got in touch with organizations I know through the force." He turns, opens the nightstand on his side, and eases a folder from inside it. "Here's a list of babies in need of adoption. There are other options, Chloe, *so many* other options, and I will be by your side on any path you go on."

I cover my mouth, my hands shaking as I open the green folder, and tears glisten in my eyes. "You did all this … for me?"

"Yes, because I love you more than I've loved anyone in my life. You own every part of me, and I'd love nothing more than to create a family with you, a life with you, with us turning old and gray together. I want us to live together, so I can always say my good mornings from *our* bed."

The tears fall, landing on the paperwork on the folder, and I set it aside to curl into his arms. "Thank you, Kyle. You are everything to me. I never believed in love, never thought I'd have it, until you barreled through my insecurities."

He kisses the top of my head, my nose, before tilting my chin up to kiss me on the lips. "Also, let me know when you're ready to be my wife." He winks. "They say it makes it *much* easier to adopt when you're married."

I grin and shuffle through the folder. "Get me a folder with a marriage license to sign, and I'm game."

JUST ROOMMATES

CHAPTER ONE
SIERRA

AGE FIFTEEN

"Show me your ID."

I'm startled by the edgy voice, and my path is blocked when a powerful body stands in front of me.

Oh shit.

On my What Could Go Wrong list, this is at the top.

I shift to the right, planning to make a run for it, but he cuts me off.

Please don't be him.

If it's him, I'll die of embarrassment right here at his feet. At least the last person I'll see before meeting death is good eye candy.

My heartbeat rages out of control while I nervously lift my gaze. I gulp when my eyes set on a face darkened with frustration.

If this is a dream, it's not how I imagined one starring him would go.

It was more along the lines of me seducing him. Kissing. Us naked.

We've never crossed paths, but I know who *he* is.

Maliki Bridges, the owner of the Down Home Pub, the bar my eighteen-year-old ass snuck into.

A wave of light-headedness hits me—not from the liquor, but his presence.

I'm going to kill Ellie.

This was all her genius idea.

"We'll totally be fine, chicken," she insisted while we sipped wine coolers in her parents' basement. "Leo said as long as we stay in the corner with his friends, we're as good as gold."

There wasn't much else to do in our small town of Blue Beech, Iowa, so I stupidly changed clothes, tugged on a black baseball cap, and put on a fresh coat of red lipstick—all attempts at looking old enough to hang out in a bar.

Our plan was running smoothly. The guys ordered our drinks from the bar and carried them to us. It was all fun and games until I needed a restroom break.

And that's what brought me here—scrunched in a narrow, dimly lit hallway with a hot and very pissed off man.

Maliki crosses his arms and taps his foot. "I'm waiting."

I start to respond but shut my mouth at the realization that I'm holding a drink.

"Shit," I hiss under my breath—although it comes out louder than what I intended.

I shove the glass behind my back, and his glare hardens, as if I were a child.

Okay, or the teenager I am.

The clamor of other bar patrons fades away, and my heart races as I give myself an internal pep talk. I blow out a long breath and give him my signature *I'm innocent* smile—my *get out of jail* smirk, as Ellie calls it. It carries a high success rate of my parents' cluelessness to me doing shit like this.

I dramatically gasp, my open hand flying to my chest. "Oh my God! I must've forgotten it. I swear, with the four kiddos at home, I always forget something."

The irritation on his face doesn't falter.

I'm a terrible fucking liar.

Four kids? Really?

I should've gone with one … one and a half.

"ID," he demands again, his tone destroying any playfulness in mine.

Get out of jail smirk *crashed and burned.*

I reluctantly unzip my bag and retrieve what he wants, knowing damn well it'll make my circumstances worse. If I don't give him *something*, I'm definitely getting thrown out. My smile stays intact when I hand it to him.

"You could've at least given me a fake, Princess," he says, unimpressed.

Yeah, well, I don't own one, jackass. Otherwise, I would've.

I hold back the urge to roll my eyes. "I'm …" I stutter for the right words. "I'm waiting for my *of age* ID to arrive in the mail. You see, there was an error with this one. They mailed out a new one, but my postman broke his leg … and his knee was reconstructed … so he can't walk and deliver anything to our mailbox."

Dear God.

I'm rambling.

A rambler is always guilty.

Maliki cuts me off, "Spare me the lies. Everyone in this town knows who you are." He jerks his head toward the same door I strolled through earlier, huddled between Leo's friends. "Now, let's get you back to your pink bedroom covered with posters of boy-band heart-throbs." He moves his hand in a shooing motion as if I were a bug.

Okay, seriously rude.

"You suck," I grumble but then perk up as something hits me. "I'm a paying customer." *Well, Leo's friends are paying customers.* If he knows he'll make money off me, he might let me stay.

"Tough shit," he fires back. "I can't have teenyboppers sneaking into my bar."

I twirl a finger in his direction. "You wait until I'm twenty-one. I'll be here *every day* to annoy you."

He smirks and pats my head over my hat. "I'll appreciate the business in the future, little one." He gestures to the door again. "See your legal ass in a few years. You can exit the same way you snuck in."

I'm holding it together but close to losing my shit. Not only am I nervous about getting in trouble, but this is also *Maliki Bridges.*

He's the town's bartending heartbreaker—a man no woman has tamed, no matter how hard they've tried to hold him down. Rumor is, three women have dropped to their knees and proposed *to him.* A single, attractive man in this town is rare. It's *his* choice not to settle down.

I've heard plenty of gossip about him. He's funny—which so far, I've yet to agree with—and he always offers a helping hand to anyone in need.

"Whoa! Wait!" I shriek. My drink comes into view when I dart my hands out to stop him from leading me to the door. Him seeing my strawberry daiquiri is now the least of my worries. I'm stunned when he pauses and waits for me to explain. "You can't kick me out yet!"

"*And* that's where you're wrong, Princess."

"I have no ride home."

"Isn't your Barbie Jeep waiting for you outside?"

I throw him a death stare. "The battery is dead actually." My attention drifts to Leo's friends and the empty stool I safely sat in until my bladder turned on me. "I rode with a friend."

He takes a quick glance at the guys before looking back at me. "You came with *those* little assholes?"

I chew at my bottom lip. "Just a friendly tip: you might not want to refer to your customers as *little assholes* if you want to stay in business."

He yanks the daiquiri from my hand and points to my bag with it. "Call your parents."

"Absolutely under no circumstances is that happening. I'd rather you pour that drink over my head." I lower my tone. "Do you know who my father is?"

"Sure as fuck do, *Sierra Lane.*"

"Then, you know he'll kill me if I call, asking for a ride home from *a bar.*" I swallow. "*And* given he's the mayor of this town, there's no doubt he'll make it his mission to create problems for you. He'll want this place shut down, so the innocent children of Blue Beech can't sneak into your big, bad bar."

His jaw clenches. He knows I'm right. "Call your brother then."

"He's out of town."

He rubs the back of his neck, now appearing stressed. "A friend."

I groan. "*Fine.* I'll call someone, but it'll take them time to get here." I motion toward Leo's friends. "I'll hang out over there until they do."

Ten minutes ago, Leo received a call, needing to run a quick errand. Ellie joined him, and instead of tagging along, his friends offered to keep me company.

Maliki shoves my ID into his back pocket and catches my elbow in his fist. "Nice try, Miss Teen Blue Beech. You can wait in my office until they get here. I'll grab you a coloring book to pass the time." His grip is firm as he pulls me out of the hallway and to the edge of the crowd, hiding me the same way Leo's friends did.

"Won't you taking me to your office look worse than allowing me to enjoy a few drinks?" I ask behind him, struggling to not stumble in my heels.

His gaze flashes back to me. "You're too young to be in a bar, Sierra, not too young to fuck."

I slam my mouth shut.

Fair point.

I lick my lips, hoping I don't mess up my lipstick. Unfortunately, he looks as interested in fucking me as he does in serving me drinks.

He leads me through swinging double doors and down another hallway, and then he pushes me into a cramped office. A black desk with a computer and a tattered chair are the only furniture. The door slamming shut startles me, and Maliki strides around the desk.

He opens a drawer, drags out a sheet of paper and pen, and slaps them onto the desk. "I promised coloring books, but this is all I have."

I study him up close. I've admired him from afar—once at the grocery store and another time when he was running shirtless in Town Square before I rear-ended the minivan in front of me, unable to take my eyes off him—but he's more attractive in person. Captivating.

Defined muscles are underneath his black tee that has the bar's logo on the right side of his chest. Dark stubble shadows his jaw, and his face is hard and handsome. His skin is tan—somewhat natural but also a result of being out in the sun. A backward black baseball cap covers his dark hair.

Hat twinning.

He could give any Instagram model a run for their money.

I wave off his lame offer. "Don't worry about me being entertained. I plan on snooping through your stuff as soon as you leave." I shrug with no shame.

"There are cameras in here, Pageant Queen."

"And?"

"And keep your hands off my shit."

We're interrupted by a knock on the door, and a loud voice follows on the other side. "Ki! Man, we're slammed! I need you out here!"

Maliki gestures to my phone. "Call every contact in your phone if you have to."

I release an exaggerated sigh.

He opens the door, throws me one last irritated look, and leaves.

I snatch the pen and write *Screw you, asshole* across the paper while grinning, and my snooping party starts.

Fifteen minutes later, Ellie texts, saying she's in the parking lot. Maliki says nothing as I leave, but when I peek back to the bar on my way out, he's watching me.

I add an extra skip to my step and flip him off over my shoulder.

CHAPTER TWO

SIERRA

AGE TWENTY

"ID."

Here we go again.

Like last time, I told Ellie sneaking in was a horrible idea, and also like last time, she persuaded me otherwise.

"We're home from college, and there's jack shit to do," is what she said, speaking the truth.

Leo swore on his grandmother's grave that Maliki was out of town and not playing ID regulator. No longer am I taking Leo's word on anything. I should've known the guy was trouble when he said he wasn't a dog person.

Two years have passed since my last attempt to sneak in. Maliki might think I'm old enough to drink now.

I dramatically sigh and slap the ID into his waiting hand.

Well, it's not exactly my ID.

He snorts while inspecting it. "Oh, your name is Ellie Ross now, huh?" He moves the ID from his view to gain a better look at me. "The strangest thing just happened. Minutes ago, I served a woman at the bar with the same name. That *Ellie* resembles the photo on the ID *way* more than you."

Ellie celebrated her twenty-first two months ago and got a copy of her ID, which went to yours truly. I normally have no issues using it. At the bars on campus, if you're cute, you're in. Not so much at this jackass's pub.

I shrug. "I filed a name change. It was no fun, sharing it with a beverage ending in Mist."

He holds the ID back up and studies it further, a grin twitching on his lips. "You changed not only your name, but also the color of your hair?"

"I went through a bad breakup. You can't get over a man until you change your hair."

He nods, eating up my responses. "I'll escort you out."

"I'd prefer you be a gentleman instead and *escort* me to the bar. Maybe buy me a cocktail?" I don't bother hiding my drink this time. "If I recall correctly, you told me I could've at least given you a fake last time. I followed your exact instructions."

"You took that out of context."

A flirtatious smile dances on my lips. "Let's talk compromise, shall we? How about this—we walk away from each other, pretend this chitchat didn't happen, and that you never saw me? I'll act invisible and swear not to cause any problems." I thrust my hand out, bringing up my pinkie, but drop it seconds later when he ignores it.

Maliki snatches the drink from me. "Did you drive?"

"No, Ellie did."

"Ellie, your friend, or Ellie, your alter ego?"

"I hate you," I bite out, narrowing my eyes at him.

"And I hate annoying teenagers."

"I'm not a teenager."

"I hate annoying *young women*. Is that better for your underage ass?"

"I hate annoying *old* men."

Technically, Maliki isn't that old. I don't know his exact age, but I'd guess around thirty. Ten years older than me isn't ancient, but dude was learning multiplication when I was pulled from the womb.

He smirks, now looking more humored. "How much have you

had to drink to give you enough balls to talk shit to me in my own bar?"

Crap. I internally forehead-slap myself. *Play nice.* "Only a few. I'm not planning to get wasted and dance on the bar." I point to my glass in his hand. "I'll make this my last. I promise."

"And who the fuck served you?"

"Ellie Ross."

I should've done a one-eighty and hightailed it when I spotted Maliki behind the bar. Instead, I made Ellie play waitress and deliver my drinks to our table. Like last time, I sat in the corner. And also like last time, I had to abandon my spot for a restroom break. I shouldn't be punished for being a few months shy of turning twenty-one. It's not like I'm asking Sir Checks-ID-a-Lot to fill my sippy cup to the brim with vodka.

He takes off his hat and runs his fingers through his thick hair. "Jesus. You need to stop thinking you're a grown-up."

"I *am* a grown-up." I count down my reasons of argument on my fingers. "I'm legally old enough to play the lottery, buy cigarettes, and hell, even do porn."

He cocks his head to the side. "Interesting. I'd love to witness your father's face if the last one ever happens."

"So, deal?" I hold my hand out once more, this time for him to shake.

Again, he ignores it.

It falls slack to my side.

"As I explained before, you might be old enough to place bets and fuck, but you're too young to drink, Pageant Queen."

I yank the ID from him. "I've changed my mind. You won't be blessed with my business when I turn twenty-one. My money will be spent elsewhere."

"Perfect." He pinches the bridge of his nose. "Now, this is the part where you call someone to pick you up. You know the drill."

"Kyle motherfucking Lane!"

I gasp, and my chest tightens at the sound of the name yelled.

"Jesus fucking Christ," Maliki mutters under his breath, scrubbing a hand over his stressed face.

I see Kyle—my overprotective, older, police-officer brother—strolling through the bar with a cocky smile.

Kyle is cool but not cool enough to be okay with my being here. And even though Maliki wasn't the one serving me booze, he'll be held responsible. It's *his* bar.

My gaze swings back to the pissed off, broad-shouldered man, and his expression confirms we share the concern. He grips my hand and rushes us to his office. The door shuts, and I spin around, scowling at him.

"Call the person who picked you up last time you were a pain in my ass. You have an hour, Princess, or I'm ratting you out to your brother."

"You wouldn't dare," I hiss.

Maliki can easily snitch on me. He owes me nothing. And my money is on Kyle believing him.

He stares at me in challenge. "Care to find out?" His voice drips with an authority that causes me to shiver.

I gulp, turning quiet while figuring out my next move.

"Call someone, Sierra. Don't make me cause problems and tell your brother what you do in your spare time when he orders a beer from me in five minutes."

He starts to leave, but I stop him.

"The person who picked me up last time was *Ellie Ross*. The real Ellie Ross," I explain in exasperation. "And she's the person I rode with tonight. She's hammered, so I need another plan."

There's no Uber here, and my mom is friends with the only taxi driver in town.

"You have no other friends?"

"Not one willing to leave because I'm getting booted."

He grabs a remote from the desk, seeming to accept my answer, and tosses it to me.

The only changes to the office since my last visit are the TV on a wall and a wide sofa lining another.

I play with the remote in my hands, taking his gesture as a surrender in not tattling on me. "I see you glammed the place up."

"I don't know what the fuck that means, but sure." Tension rides his face. He has a crowded bar and has to deal with me *again*.

I fall heavily onto the chair and prop my feet on the desk. "How's your Netflix watch list?"

"I don't know. I don't watch TV."

Who doesn't watch TV?

I point to the TV with the remote. "You have a smart TV."

"When I'm in here, I work."

"Why did you buy it?"

He blows out an annoyed breath. Answering my questions is the last thing he wants to do, but I don't want to lose his company. I enjoy pushing his buttons, and hanging out in an office alone isn't much of a party.

"My sister works here and occasionally brings my cartoon-loving niece." With that, he whips around, cursing under his breath, and leaves.

I open Netflix, select *That '70s Show*, and take off my leather jacket before shuffling to the couch. When I drag my phone from my bag, it's dead.

Shit.

I yawn.

I'll watch one episode and then rummage through his drawers for a charger.

My eyes slowly shut as I relax.

———

A tap on my shoulder startles me awake.

My head shoots up and connects with something hard. That something hard is someone's chin. The strong chin-holder and I simultaneously groan. I massage my head when he pulls away. When I peek up from the couch, I expect to find Maliki at maximum annoyance.

Instead, he looks drained. His bar tee is wrinkled and drink-stained.

"All right, Princess. Time for you to go home," he says.

I comb my fingers through my ratty couch-head hair, and my stomach drops. "My phone died. I'll call someone and wait outside until they get here."

Hopefully, there's someone sober with Ellie.

He extends his hand, helping me up, and retreats a step to give me room to walk around him. I snatch my jacket from the chair, yank it over my shoulders, and shove one arm in, stopping when he speaks.

"I'll take you home."

I gape at him, and my jacket falls loose on my uncovered arm. "Is that smart for me to get in the car with someone I don't know? Stranger danger and all?"

Who am I kidding? I've allowed him to force me into an office in the back of a bar twice. I've long surpassed smart decisions with him.

He shrugs. "You can walk, but I'd rather you not. Your choice."

"All right, but I'd make a terrible hostage. My dad would tell you to keep me, and I'm very demanding. You'd be forced to bring me hot wings and a hair straightener and provide plenty of company."

He snorts. "Me kidnapping you is nothing you'll ever need to worry about, Jailbait."

"Jailbait? I'm *so* not jailbait."

"You are jailbait. And trouble. The trouble of rich parents making a guy's life a living hell for talking to their precious daughter."

He's not wrong. My father would flip his shit.

"Come on. I'm wiped."

I follow him out of the office to a door with a bright Exit light shining above it. The silence tells me the bar is closed.

"What time is it?" I ask when he holds the creaky door open for me.

We step out into an ill-lit, vacant back lot of the bar. I'm a twenty-year-old woman catching a ride with a stranger after a night of drinking, but I'm not alarmed. Call me twisted for being thrilled to spend time with this man even if it risks dying.

Okay, I doubt he's a serial killer, but I live for dramatics.

"A little after two," he answers.

Good thing I'm staying at Ellie's tonight. My mother would have the police—aka my brother—searching for me.

Speaking of Ellie …

Did she not realize her best friend was nowhere to be seen?

I tighten my jacket around myself, my heeled boots crunching against the gravel, and follow him the short distance to a running car, the chilly breeze smashing into me.

"Do you have a phone charger?" I ask behind him.

He nods but doesn't glance back at me. "In the car."

He opens the driver's door to the black Camaro, and I do the same with the passenger side. We slide into our seats at the same time. I run my hands over my arms, grateful he heated the car.

I wait quietly when he opens the glove compartment, grabs a charger, and gives it to me. "Thank you."

He shifts the car into reverse but doesn't move from the parking spot. "You going to give me your address?"

"God, no," I rush out. "Do you want me sent to an all-girls' college?"

"I don't know much about being sent to one, but it sounds like an overdramatic sorority girl like you wouldn't like it." He shakes his head and smiles. "I'm amazed your parents haven't already shipped you off somewhere. I wouldn't have predicted their daughter dearest to be such a rebel."

"Trust me, neither did they."

He reverses out of the parking spot, his arm settling at the top of my seat. "Is it an act of rebellion? Desire for attention?"

"Neither. It's me being me."

I'm half-tempted to shine my phone in his direction to see the expression on his face.

Which reminds me …

I clumsily plug my phone into the charger. As soon as it powers on, I text Ellie.

Me: What the hell? I know you always forget shit, but I was hoping that stopped at your best friend!

My phone beeps seconds later.

Ellie: Calm down, drama queen. I watched you follow the hot bartender you have a thing for to the back.

Me: I do not have a thing for him!

Ellie: Yeah, okay. I'll make you a doctor's appointment for pretendinitis tomorrow.

Me: That doesn't clarify why you left me! YOU NEVER LEAVE A MAN BEHIND!

Ellie: Chill out. He let me check on you twice, and you were snoozing. Your brother and Leo hung out all night. When I tried figuring out an escape plan, Maliki offered to take you. I've been waiting up for you to call, so I can let you in.

Me: He could've severed my head off!

Ellie: My sister used to bang him. He's not into that kinky shit.

Me: I hate you. We're broken up.

Ellie: I'll make you waffles in the morning and buy you a new candle.

Me: Two candles, and you'd better have Nutella.

Ellie: Fine, two candles, and duh. Do I still need to wait up, or are you staying the night with him?

Me: I'm on my way. He doesn't have a kink for chicks who can't legally drink either.

Ellie: What a shame.

"You going to tell me where we're headed?" Maliki asks, breaking me away from texting.

I drop my phone into my lap. "Ellie's."

"And where does Ellie live?"

"You should know since you've banged her sister."

"It's weird you're assuming and entertained with my sexual history, Jailbait."

I bite the inside of my cheek. "That's what Ellie said."

"If Ellie said it, it must be true."

I shift in my seat to face him and cross my arms. "Are you saying it's not true?"

He leaves the parking lot, not answering my question, and drives toward Ellie's house—confirming the sister-screwing. I've never been a fan of Ellie's older sister. Chick once spit gum in my hair. The fact that she slept with Maliki makes me hate her more.

"You know, I found condoms when I searched through your office last time."

He taps his fingers against the steering wheel and keeps his eyes on the road. "I know."

My mouth falls open. "You watched the cameras?" I rack my brain over everything I did that night, praying it wasn't anything embarrassing. I talked plenty of shit about him to Ellie. If there was audio, there's no doubt he heard me.

"I wanted to make sure you didn't rob me."

"Sadly, I didn't find any money."

"Good. That means my hiding places are legit."

"Your condom hiding places are trash."

"Not wanting to stash them in places I have to search out to find." He chuckles. "I also saw you stole a few for yourself."

"Just in case."

He finally glances over at me. "You're trouble, Jailbait—a pageant princess with a crooked crown and leather jacket."

I grin. "I'm surprised you're just figuring that out."

CHAPTER THREE

AGE TWENTY-ONE

I walk into Down Home Pub, a smile filled with confidence and determination on my face.

It feels almost like home—a home I've never exactly been welcomed in.

Call me the unwanted stepchild of Down Home Pub.

Except, now, this rejected stepchild has the upper hand.

A group of sorority girls who aren't excited to spend their night in a hole-in-the-wall bar are behind me. Not only is the pub an hour from the city, but there's also no expensive DJ, VIP section, or bottle service.

I laugh to myself while picturing the look on Maliki's face if someone requested a VIP section. He'd probably throw them out faster than he tried me.

I pause to give the bar a once-over. It's the first time I've had the chance to look around since I always ducked and hid before. There's a long wood bar with beer taps at the rear of the room. Behind the bar is a shelved brick wall. Liquor bottles fill the top shelf, and glasses of various sizes line the bottom. People are huddled around pub tables cluttered with food and drinks. The small space looks near capacity.

Finally.

I'm the winner in this game.

No booting me tonight.

I'm ready for an evening loaded with drinking and smugly throwing my age in Maliki's face.

The best fucking birthday ever.

I find the pain-in-my-ass bartender in seconds and beeline toward the side of the bar he's manning, excitement shooting through me. There's a crowd waiting to be served around him. I ignore the dirty looks I receive when cutting my way to the front of the line.

I mutter, "Birthday girl," a few times, but their glares don't lessen.

I need a stiff drink after listening to my friends whine about coming here. I tuned them out, wondering what he'd do when he saw me.

No doubt he'll ask for my ID. I plan to throw it at him and prove I'm a big girl now. No more *Jailbait, Pageant Queen, Teenager* mocking.

I admire the sight of him before he notices me, and if I saw myself in the mirror, there'd be lust flickering in my green eyes. I lick my lips. His hair has grown out since I saw him last, and the expanse of his chest looks wider. His olive skin is still as smooth, and I'm tempted to ask him for his skincare routine. A backward baseball hat covers his hair, he's wearing his signature bar tee, and his cheeks are still sporting light stubble.

He blinks a few times when his attention cuts to me and meanders my way in no rush.

Huh. I expected him to bombard me with an ID demand.

"I'll have a vodka tonic, please," I order when he reaches me.

His mood is unreadable. "Sorry, did you say an organic juice box?"

"*Fine,* give me an organic juice *with* a shot of vodka."

"I'll need to see a *legit* ID for that. A *real* one."

I crack a smile on my matte red lips and raise my arm, holding the ID between two fingers.

He raises an eyebrow, his lips tilting into a sliver of a smirk, and takes it from me. That smirk grows as he inspects it. "Motherfucking finally."

Pride rocks through me. I open my mouth to answer but am shoved into the bar.

"Hot bartender!" Louise, a sorority sister, yells, interrupting us. "I need shots and then more shots after that. You ever heard of Buttery Nipples?"

I stifle a laugh and shoot Louise a dirty look. *This is so not a Buttery Nipple place, Louise.*

"Heard of them? Yes. Made them? Fuck no," Maliki replies.

"Body shots then?" Louise fires back with a pout of her lower lip. "I promise to let you do one off me."

Hell no. Not on my watch.

Chick isn't coming anywhere near *my* Maliki.

I shove Louise's shoulder. "Go away. You're embarrassing yourself."

"What?" she draws out in a whiny voice. "Dude is hot." She clicks her tongue and points to him while backing away. "Buttery Nipples!"

Maliki shakes his head, clearly not offended. He's probably used to attention like this.

He sweeps his gaze over me, inching forward and settling his palms on the bar in front of me. "What can I get you, birthday girl?"

"Surprise me, *but* don't make it a Buttery Nipple."

"I'll make you something better than that or anything you've ever had." He smirks, pushes himself back, and turns on his heel.

"Seriously—I'll say it louder for the sorority girls in the back—you two have a thing for each other," Ellie says next to me.

I didn't even notice her presence. Call it the Maliki Effect. Everything around me fades away when he's around.

"Whatever," I mutter, rolling my eyes.

She clips her black strands behind her ear. "Ask him to take you to the office you've hung out in so many times. Tell him how excited you've been to see him like you've told me *all fucking month* long."

"I was excited to turn twenty-one and finally show him up."

"Yeah, okay," she replies sarcastically, bumping her hip against mine. "I won't interrupt your flirt-fest, and if any of these sorority girls try to sink their claws in him, I'll trip a bitch. Get your flirt on, girlfriend."

With that, she walks away.

Ellie attends Iowa State with me but called me batshit crazy when I suggested she join my sorority. Joining was a requirement for me. Luckily for her, her parents are more easy going than mine and not obsessed with their image.

I glance back to Maliki.

He pops a black straw into a glass, adds an orange slice garnish, and drops it in front of me. "Legal looks good on you, Princess."

The short red dress and strappy nude heels I'm wearing don't fit into the relaxed atmosphere, but I don't care. I wanted to look sexy tonight … *for him.*

I tap my nails against the beat-up bar. "I warned you I'd come on my twenty-first. It was necessary for me to fulfill that promise *and* throw it in your face."

"I thought you'd come back to rob me of condoms again." He tilts his head to the side and studies me. "We've never shared a conversation this calm here."

I laugh. "I know! I might find out you're as fun as people say."

He stands taller and slightly parts his lips. "Oh, trust me, I'm plenty of fun."

"Nothing I've received from you screams fun, so that needs to be proven to me." I stir my drink, take a sip, and moan when pulling away. "Holy shit. This is delicious. What's in it?"

He raises his chin. "None of your business."

"You can't *not* tell me what's in my drink. Isn't that against bartender code of conduct?"

"Alcohol. There's alcohol in it."

"You're one of *those* bartenders." I take another drink and swish it around in my mouth. "Whiskey." Another sip. "Southern Comfort?"

He stares at me, unblinking.

"Seriously?" I curl my lips around the straw, our eye contact steady, and take another sip. "Definitely SoCo and orange juice."

He slightly nods while grinning. "A girl knows her whiskey."

"A girl knows her whiskey." I take another drink and raise a brow. "Gin?"

"Possibly."

"Definitely gin. What else am I missing?"

"If I told you, I'd have to kill you."

"Oh God, never say that around me again. Your age is showing. My *father* says that."

He throws out his arms. "Hey, everyone fucking says that!"

I hold my glass in the air. "Keep these bad boys coming, bartender. By the end of the night, I'll figure out the entire ingredient list. Maybe I'll even throw in some tips to make it better."

The bar is packed, but he's not taking orders from anyone. He holds up a finger when they call his name, his eyes drinking me in as if I were his cocktail. Satisfaction hits me, and my cheeks blush. I'm the one who's holding his attention.

"Consider yourself special because I made you that drink. That's normally not my style." He rubs his hands together. "Now, I'd love to continue this guessing game, but customers are waiting. Go drink and enjoy your night."

I frown, not wanting to leave him. I grab my drink, but he stops me from turning around.

"One more thing, Jailbait."

My knees weaken when he comes closer. Mere inches separate us. I inhale his scent—cinnamon and spice—and nearly die when he drops his head, his lips brushing my ear.

"Tell me, birthday girl," he whispers.

I gulp. *Do not fall on your ass. Breathe.* "What?" I stammer.

"Who is the dude at the table behind you, shooting me a murderous glare? Does he know you came here for me?"

My nails dig into the bar, ruining my fresh manicure, and I shiver as something rushes through me that shouldn't—desire.

I was so hooked on Maliki that I forgot about Devin. I hate that I lose our contact when I peek back at Devin. His jaw is clenched, and his eyes are fixed on us.

Shit.

He invited himself tonight. We're each other's exclusive booty calls —not hooking up with other people yet not sharing love devotions.

I shrug, glancing back to Maliki. "He's kinda, sorta my boyfriend."

"Kinda, sorta?" he questions. "How the fuck is someone kinda, sorta your boyfriend?"

"I mean … we haven't made anything official."

"Some words of advice, Sierra: a man who wants you will never let you say he's kinda, sorta your boyfriend." He catches my chin and swipes his thumb over my lower lip. "This is on me, Jailbait. Go dump your kinda, sorta boyfriend and have yourself a great fucking birthday."

CHAPTER FOUR
SIERRA

AGE TWENTY-TWO

I stride into Down Home Pub, and per usual, I head straight to Maliki. It's early evening, and the night crowd hasn't hit the place yet. That gives me plenty of time to annoy him before customers arrive with drink demands.

I drop onto a stool and watch him pour a beer for a brooding customer. He nods when the man pays him, and then his eyes meet mine. We share a smile—mine no doubt loaded with goofiness. He snags a cleaning towel, takes the few steps separating us, and stops in front of me. He leans back on his heels and waits for me to speak.

I shift my weight in the stool. "Guess what."

He dries his hands on the towel. "Who knows with you, Jailbait?"

"I moved home!"

He chuckles. "Oh boy, that's fucking trouble. We should alert the authorities."

"Don't act like you're not secretly thrilled I'll be able to annoy you more," I say with more dignity than someone borderline stalking him should.

I snatch a peanut from the chrome bucket on the bar, crack open the shell, and pop the nut into my mouth.

When I came home on breaks, I always headed straight to the pub to see him. I ordered all my drinks from him, ditched my friends to hang out at the bar with him, and spent more time here than at home.

Unfortunately, that doesn't mean we've shared in-depth discussions. The bar stays busy, and most locals order from him rather than the other bartenders. We make small conversation until he's called away again.

"Oh, princess, I can't wait." He inches closer, provoking my breathing to hitch, and softens his tone. "What made you come home?" His smile widens. "You want to see me every day, don't you? I love that you find me irresistible."

Thank God the bar hides the view of me clenching my thighs underneath my maxi dress. This is Maliki's game. He loves fucking with my head. He'll get closer, whisper in my ear, and then back away to serve a customer, a shit-eating grin on his face. The ass knows I'm attracted to him.

I roll my eyes and toss a shell at him. "You're so arrogant. Gee, I don't know, maybe I moved home because"—I hold a finger to the corner of my lips—"my family lives here. That's a mighty ego you wield there, bartender. You should drink some of it off."

"Your family *and me*," he corrects with a smirk.

Am I that transparent?

For as long as I can remember, I swore I'd never live in Blue Beech as an adult. My hometown was too small, too stuffy, but that plan changed a month ago. I graduated from college a semester early, and instead of apartment-searching in the city, I packed my stuff and came home. After being gone for four years, a girl needed some familiarity.

I straighten my back and clear my throat. "I've experienced the party life, and now, I'm ready to get a job and act like an actual adult."

He chuckles. "It's weird, seeing you mature, Jailbait. It seems like only yesterday you were in here, all doe-eyed and innocent with your strawberry daiquiri."

"Hey, I'm very mature, thank you very much. Just yesterday, I scheduled my own dentist appointment."

"Oh shit, look at you, all grown-up and changing the world by assuring you're cavity-free. Maybe next week, you'll advance to grocery shopping." He pauses, holds up a finger, and winks. "Hold up. I bet you're back for my drinks. They don't make them like me in the city, do they? I've ruined you for all other bartenders."

"I hate to pop your drink-making ego, but the booze selection in the city is *much larger.*" I smirk. "I'll give you some pointers."

Down Home Pub doesn't boast an expansive drink list—beer by the bottle and draft, mixed drinks, shots, and a few select wines. Nothing too fancy. There aren't any special house cocktails, but there's also no demand for it.

He shakes his head. "Eh, not interested. You can keep testing what I give you though."

Sometimes, Maliki gives me drinks to taste-test. I've never had one I didn't like.

I roll my eyes. "God, you're boring."

"For someone who claims I'm boring, you sure seem to enjoy yourself around me."

"I love drinking your *boring* drinks." I shrug. "'Tis all."

"You love my company, babe," he talks while starting a drink. "There are two sides of the bar. Mikey is free, and I guarantee he won't have a problem serving you. He's more your age and always up for a good time. Hell, he's probably more entertaining than I am. Why don't you go bug him?"

I scrunch up my nose. "*Ew.* Mikey sleeps with any woman who can count to ten."

He chuckles. "It's eleven now."

"Aw, I'm glad he's upped his standards."

Maliki drops my favorite drink in front of me, a playful grin on his face, and turns to help another customer.

I hate this part. The part where I share him with them.

He returns when he's finished serving their needy asses.

"You moving back in with your parents?" he asks.

"Unfortunately, yes. That's something I'm not looking forward to. I plan to find an apartment, but everyone knows there aren't many open rentals in this town."

"And the boyfriend?"

I lower my head and take a long sip of my drink. "It's, uh …" I gulp it down and sigh before clarifying, "Still complicated."

He nods.

Devin begged me to stay with him until he graduated. When I didn't, we agreed to spend time away from each other—physically, that is. We still talk, and he mentioned he was searching for apartments between Blue Beech and the town he had grown up in. I told him he was nuts, thinking we could move in together. My parents would cut me if I moved in with a man before marriage.

When I peek back up at Maliki, his attention is on me. Mine is on him. He's wearing his signature Down Home Pub tee and a backward baseball cap.

He raises a brow. "Sierra is single then?"

I shrug. "Kinda, sorta."

"What did I tell you about the kinda, sorta shit?" he asks in a scold-like manner.

Instead of making me another drink containing alcohol, I'm given a glass of water.

I play with the straw, jabbing a piece of ice. "We're taking a break."

I can't stop myself from admiring his arms when he crosses them. Infatuation barrels through my blood. It's absurd how drawn I am to him.

"I'm no expert, but couples taking *breaks* from each other isn't a sign of a healthy relationship, Jailbait."

"Exactly. I'm *jailbait*. We're young."

"Twenty-two isn't young, princess."

"How old were you when you acquired the bar?"

"Twenty-nine."

"Were you ready to settle down at my age?"

"Fuck no."

"Exactly! Why does everyone like to give out advice but never take their own?"

"I also wouldn't string you along if I didn't know what I wanted. I'd be straight up and ask you to be straight up in return."

We're interrupted by my phone beeping with a text.

"Ugh, it's my mother," I say, reading it.

He strokes his face stubble. "Why's that an issue? You love your mom."

"She's throwing a welcome-home party for me." I grimace. "All the folks of Blue Beech can't wait to see me and ask three thousand questions." I get up with a huff and rub my brow to ward off the impending headache. "Most of them ask why I'm still single, just as you did."

He holds his hands up. "Hey, babe, I'm not telling you to get hitched to some frat boy just to please people."

My phone beeps again, my mother asking if I've picked out what I'm wearing. I hold up the phone to show him the text. "See! She already wants to know what I'm wearing!"

"What will you be wearing?" he asks suggestively with a smirk.

"Clothes." I click my tongue against the roof of my mouth. "Maybe a dress with no panties." I grin when his eyes widen and his jaw flexes. "You'll probs see me later when I come to drink the party away." I wiggle my fingers in a wave. "Bug you later, bestie."

―――――

"I swear to motherfucking God, I'd better not see your ass on *Dateline*," Ellie says. "I refuse to do an interview, talking about the girl you were before becoming obsessed with that man behind the bar."

I press my hand to my chest and fake offense. "What are you talking about?" I bump my shoulder against hers. "You'd better never go on *Dateline* and tell my secrets."

"Never. I'm referring to my friend being annoying on *my* birthday because she's daydreaming about the bartender dicking up her vagina." She shoots me a grin of amusement.

"*Or* this friend is staring at the bar, debating on what her next drink will be."

This isn't the first time we've had this discussion. I've lost count of the number of times she's told me to ask Maliki out. I question if she's started smoking crack. Maliki would turn me down, and I'd never step foot into the pub again.

That can't happen, and not to mention, a relationship would never work with us. We're too different. So, I'll admire him from afar like he's a handbag in a store I can't afford.

She tugs her hair into a tight ponytail. "Honey, you spend more time here than your own home *and* with your boyfriend. Do your parents know this?"

"Nope. They think I'm working crazy hours, *which is true* with my new job."

"Does Devin know about your favorite pastime and why you keep pushing him away?"

"Hey, I don't push him away," I lie.

She snorts. "Dude has brought up marriage to you like ninety thousand times, and you brush him off. If that's not pushing someone away, I don't know what is."

"We're too young to get married." I chug my drink. "Are *you* ready to get married?"

"That's a big *hell no*."

Tamara, our waitress, returns to our table with another round of drinks. "Maliki asked me to drop these off."

She throws me a wary look identical to the ones the other bar employees give me. The waitresses and Maliki's sister, Liz, aren't my biggest fans.

I signal to them. "Oh no, we didn't order these."

Ellie shoves my shoulder, giving me a dirty look. "Of course we did." She side-eyes me when Tamara shrugs and walks away. "What is wrong with you? You never turn down free drinks. Living with your parents again fucks with your head." A quick smile spreads across her lips as if something hits her. "I mean, we know you'll only take free drinks from the bartender though because you're in love with him."

I roll my eyes, a pain forming in my throat. "You've lost your mind."

———

4 MONTHS LATER

"Any plans later?" Maliki asks.

"Nope," I answer. "Unless you count hanging out here."

Instead of replying, Maliki focuses his attention on something behind me. When his eyes narrow, I shift in my chair to find what's suddenly pissed him off.

I wince.

What the hell?

Maliki tenses when Devin meets us at the bar.

My kinda, sorta boyfriend slings an arm over my shoulders and kisses my cheek. "Hey, babe."

Devin looks like he came straight from the office—sporting khaki slacks, a white button-up shirt, and chestnut-colored Sperry slide-ons. Ever since he graduated and moved home, he comes around more.

The two men I'm attracted to couldn't be more opposite.

I cringe and force a smile. Devin's kiss isn't what has upset me. It's *why* he kissed me, acting as if I were his possession. It's a reminder to Maliki that I'm not his.

Last night, Devin emailed links of possible condos to look at, and his father offered me an interior design position at his building firm, to which I accepted.

My breathing accelerates, and I grow more flustered by the second.

How rude would it be to shrug him off?

"What are you doing here?" I ask.

He tugs me closer, giving me a tight squeeze, and feigns ignorance that Maliki is here. "Corbin said you and Ellie were here. I had a break in my schedule and wanted to surprise you." His hand creeps to my waist. "I've missed you, and I needed to see your gorgeous face. *Plus,* I found a condo you'll love."

This is when I jerk away from him. He knows I can't move in with him, but again, *Maliki.*

After my twenty-first, Devin questioned me about Maliki for weeks—asking how I knew him, if I had a thing for him, if we'd ever hooked up, if I was into older men. He accused me of flirting with

Maliki, but I never entertained the conversation. Devin and I weren't in a committed relationship then.

I grind my teeth and twist in my stool. "We've had this discussion."

Maliki snatches my half-empty glass from the bar and walks away, shaking his head in irritation.

Devin grins at the loss of Maliki. "Sorry, I needed to clear the air, so we could enjoy our night."

"I wasn't aware Ellie invited you," I mutter.

"She invited Corbin, who then called me." He shoots me an accusatory look for my lack of invite to him.

Corbin is Devin's cousin and Ellie's new boyfriend. I fixed them up after she broke up with Leo.

Devin captures my hand, and I hop off the stool, allowing him to lead me to Ellie and Louis's table, wishing I could return to my stool and stay with Maliki.

Maliki is glaring at us when I turn around, and me mouthing, *I'm sorry*, to him further pisses him off.

He turns his back to me, wanders over to a woman, and talks to her for the rest of the night. He doesn't look at me again the entire night, and it infuriates me.

I fake interest in conversations but have no clue what anyone has said. The drink Devin brought me earlier—one he'd ordered from Maliki and complained he was an asshole to him while doing so—is half-full and watered down. For the first time, I'm relieved when Devin asks if I'm ready to leave Down Home Pub.

Devin walks me outside and kisses me good night, and we walk to our cars. Instead of leaving as he does, I slump down in my seat.

I'll stick around and reflect for a moment.

Settle down from the anxiety of the night.

Screw Devin for pulling a power move like that.

It's nearing last call, and I question my sanity as I watch each minute tick by. When the time hits one fifty-five and I notice people leaving, I wander back into the bar, fear surging through me.

Stupid, stupid girl.

Maliki sets down the bottle in his hand and stares at me in question. "Did you forget something?"

As I hoped, the place is almost empty with the few lingering people gathering up their belongings and heading toward the door.

I shake my head, and a brief silence passes over us while he waits for me to explain why I'm here. "I thought you might need help cleaning up."

"You thought I might need help cleaning up?" he slowly repeats. "How much did you drink?"

"Not enough." I move further into the bar, praying he won't kick me out—something he's never had an issue with. "Even if you don't want me to clean, can we hang out?" I hop onto the bar and swing my legs back and forth in an attempt to prevent them from shaking.

He shrugs, circles around the bar, and starts placing stools on pub tables. "I'm always up for pleasant company."

He considers my company pleasant.

Yay!

I jump off to help him, and when I can't take the silence any longer, I blurt out the last question I should, "You don't like Devin, do you?"

He practically throws the next stool onto the table, and it slides forward. "You won't like my answer to that."

I grab a stool, but my lifting skills are nowhere near as graceful as his. Things are heavy. "Why not?" *Why am I asking this when I already know the answer?*

He collects dirty glasses, deposits them onto the bar, and snatches a rag to wipe a table down. "I don't see you with him long-term. He's a wet blanket that'll drain the light inside you. I fucking dread that happening."

I understand his reasoning. My brothers disclosed the same worry, wording it differently. They don't know Devin like I do. He's a different person around me.

We met at a function my sorority threw with his fraternity. I was so frustrated that day. The guys stood around while us girls did the work but not Devin. He grabbed the ribbons I was hanging, stepped onto the ladder, and helped me. He was goofy, sweet, and funny in his own way, and he spoiled me with attention. We shared a few classes and had regular study sessions that led to hook-ups.

The problem is, the more Devin hangs around his father and frat friends, the more he takes shape to them. He's now judgmental and less understanding. He prefers spending time at his parents' country club while I prefer spending time here.

I halt at the table I'm at and play with the back of the ripped stool, unsure of how to respond.

"Do *you* like your kinda, sorta boyfriend, Sierra?" he fires back.

"Of course I do."

His eyes darken. "Why are you here with me instead of with him then?"

His question almost knocks me on my ass.

"He has an early morning tomorrow."

He comes closer, his focus on me growing stronger. "Again, why are you here and not in bed with him?"

Even though I want to, even though I *need* to, I don't break our eye contact. I wish the pub weren't so underlit. I want a better view of him, want to observe everything that's him. I don't have an answer to his question. Not an honest one.

I run my sweaty hands down my jeans. "I wanted to hang out with a friend. With our history, we should consider ourselves friends."

He laughs, not buying my answer. "Yes, we're such excellent *friends.*"

CHAPTER FIVE
SIERRA

"You're quiet tonight," Maliki says, restocking beers into the cooler.

Me helping him close is now a regular routine.

I relax on the bar, crossing my ankles and holding them out in front of me while watching him work.

"How many women have you slept with?" the abrupt question rushes out of my mouth before I can stop myself.

Tonight, I don't have a care in the world. Devin and I argued earlier, and all my fucks left with the last drink Maliki poured me.

For years, I've wondered but never had the guts to ask. There's no missing the women who look him up and down like he's a snack they can't wait to devour. They flirt with him, write their numbers on bar napkins, and touch him in ways I wish I could. My fantasies are appalling, provided I'm in a relationship, but that doesn't stop me from resenting them.

Maliki pauses, sets the beer in his hand on the bar, and roams his eyes over me. "What?"

Oh, he heard me.

"How many women have you had sex with?"

He shrugs and returns to the cooler. "I don't know."

"You don't know how many women you've slept with?" I slowly say, unhappy with his answer.

Maliki blowing off my question isn't surprising. He never ventures into personal territory. We make small talk, like what we did during the day or movies, and he shares crazy customer stories with me.

"Nope," he bites out, crouching down to get the last crate.

I scrunch up my face. "That's weird."

Exhaustion fills his eyes as he casts them on me. "How's that weird? I don't keep a fucking tally, Sierra." Irritation burns along with his words.

"It's a lot then, huh?"

He shuts the cooler with extra force. "I'm not clear what your definition of *a lot* is."

"A lot ..." I waver, struggling to strike the perfect words. "I don't think I've slept with *that* many guys. It's most likely a smaller number than yours. It's—"

He shoots his hand up and interrupts me, his voice cold, "I don't care how many men you've slept with." He shakes his head, turns away, and opens the register. He jams cash into it and slams it shut. "Why are we having this talk?"

"I was hoping we could get to know each other better." *I'm also jealous, insecure, and confused with my life.*

He leans against the wall and scowls at me. "Sierra, I know your favorite color, favorite food, favorite fucking movie. I don't need your sex list or care to know your goddamn favorite sex position."

I cross my arms. "What if I want to know yours?"

"Is there a reason you're asking me this tonight?"

I tug at the top of my shirt, the room heating up. "I just ... I don't know ... I don't know if I'm good in bed."

"Good in bed?"

I nod and drum my fingers against the bar. *Stop talking. Stop talking. Do not pass go and spill your guts to him.*

I stupidly pass go and tell him, "Devin." I clear my throat. "We used to have sex all the time. I mean, *all the time.*"

I'm stopped by Maliki talking over me, "Okay, got that fucking point across."

I gulp. "It seems like he's always too busy to … *you know*." My voice weakens. "I don't want to be that needy, annoying girlfriend, but it's weird."

I've already had this chat with Ellie, who insisted Devin is busy with work. I need a man's perspective, and God knows, I can't ask my brothers.

He grinds his teeth. "I've said countless times, he's a dumb shit. I don't get what you see in him."

"I bet you're awesome at sex." I slap my hand over my mouth. *Oh my God. I did not say that.*

Maliki grimacing confirms I definitely said that. "I'm not talking about sex with you."

"Why?" I blurt out. "Maybe I need some tips." I cover my mouth again. *That wasn't supposed to pass go either.*

"The only tips I have are given to me after serving someone a drink."

"I'm serious, Maliki. There has to be something wrong with me."

He stares at me for a moment, looking almost disgusted. "Tell your boyfriend to pay me a visit, and I'll give him some tips. Number one: stop being a fucking dumbass."

My ponytail falls loose when I throw my head back, my blonde strands cascading down my shoulders. "Let's forget how much you hate him for a minute, okay? Devin and I have dated off and on since college, *but* he hooked up with other women when we were on our breaks." I lose Maliki's gaze as tears prick at my eyes. "Maybe I'm not as satisfying as those other women were. We had an argument tonight, and he demanded to know how many men I'd slept with while we were separated. I told him the truth—*zero*. He refused to answer when I asked him the same. We fought more, and he confessed to sleeping with six women while we had been broken up."

"Allegedly broken up," he cuts in, his tone sharp. "What's the point of this story, Sierra? That your boyfriend is fucking trash? News flash: we already knew that."

"I'm over that. We weren't together then. I'm worried that I'm boring *now* and that those women were better at sex than I am."

He scoffs. "Doubt that, princess."

"What about the women you've slept with? What do they do during sex? What do you do to them?"

Let's be honest. My question is more than wanting reassurance that I don't suck in the sack. I crave to know more about Maliki, to find out what he's giving other women that I'll never have.

"Find another man to have this conversation with because it won't be me."

I perk myself up, my voice turning fake cheerful. "Come on. We're ole buddies, ole pals. Tell me."

"No," he snaps.

"*Please,*" I sing out, unsure of why I'm so desperate for his answer.

I gasp when he erases the distance between us and rests his palms on the bar on each side of my waist.

"What do you want me to tell you, Sierra?" He smells of lime and mint as he stares down at me in impatience. "Do you want to know how a woman writhes underneath me while I finger her until she comes?" He half-whispers, half-hisses, "Do you need me to brag about how hard I fuck women or love to eat pussy? Is that what the fuck you're asking for? *Why?*"

I swallow as tears burn my eyes. My breathing matches my racing heartbeat.

"I sure as fuck don't want to hear about you fucking another man." He pushes off the bar when I don't explain myself and remains in front of me, a wild look in his eyes.

He told me to stop pushing, and I didn't.

I'm not giving up now either.

"Why not? Why don't you want to talk about this with me?"

"It's not the relationship we have. You want to talk sex? Call one of your sorority sisters."

My chest tightens, and I solemnly look at him. "But ..." *No, don't pull away. Don't.*

"Quit pushing it, Sierra."

I open my mouth to continue this argument … or whatever it is, but I shut it when my phone rings. We both look down at it resting on the counter next to me. He curses at the same time I tense. Devin's name along with a selfie of us flash across my screen.

Maliki shakes his head while stepping away from me. "I'm drained, and I have an early delivery tomorrow. Go ask your boyfriend why he's slept with so many women, break or no fucking break, and why you're seeking out this conversation with another man about how you don't feel stacked up to those women. Do you need a ride home, or do you want to call him?"

I shake my head. "I'll call Ellie."

He doesn't wait for me to answer while stalking across the bar. I text Ellie, and thankfully, she can be here in five minutes. I'm fighting tears as he walks to the other side of the bar and fake focuses on paperwork.

He looks at me with sharp eyes when I tell him Ellie is here and holds his palm to the base of my back while silently walking me outside. He nods hello to Ellie, helps me into the car, and slams the door without a word. I watch him as she pulls away.

His arms are flexed, his face is red, and his knuckles are balled into fists. He shakes his head, releases his fists, and walks inside.

I don't know if I'm crying over my fight with Devin or over my fight with Maliki.

Maliki. Most definitely Maliki.

———

Maliki has been avoiding me since our argument.

When I order drinks, he gives them to me and walks away, saying as little as possible. He has, however, made it clear that another bartender is helping him close from now on, hinting that my company isn't needed … isn't wanted. I was wrong for pushing the conversation, and I'm now paying for it with the cost of our friendship.

That's changing tonight.

I need him.

For reasons unknown, he's who I run to. I trust him, and trust isn't easily given out by me. I don't trust people I've known my entire life, and tonight, my family was betrayed.

Devin wouldn't understand. His family is structured and clean cut. Scandals and secrets don't supply their closets.

The bar closed twenty minutes ago, and the parking lot is empty. It's a weeknight and raining, so the night was probably slow. I jerk my hoodie over my head, wipe away the tears I cried on the ride here, and jump out of my car. Hard downpour smacks into me as I rush to the door of Down Home.

It's locked.

I knock.

No answer.

I pound harder and call out his name.

I stumble forward when the door shoots open, and Maliki catches me in his arms to stop me from falling. He swiftly locks the door behind us and shoves my head into his shoulder as I break down. He rubs my back, walking us further into the bar. Instead of dropping me onto a stool, he carries me to the back, up a flight of stairs, and into an apartment.

He kicks the door shut with his foot and carefully settles me on a black leather sofa. I peek up at him standing above me, knowing my eyes are puffy and black mascara is matted to my face, aware I'm the picture of a hot mess.

I wipe my cheeks with shaking hands.

I'm pissed. I'm hurt. I want to kill a man I love.

"My dad," I whisper before raising my voice. "He's …"

"I know. I was going to call you after I finished closing." He sinks to his knees and stares up at me, pushing soaked strands of hair away from my face. His shirt is wet from my tears. "Have you talked to him?"

I shake my head. "I waited in his office for hours, but it was useless. He's not dumb enough to come home until this scandal passes. I gave up and drove here." *Came to you.*

He wipes away my mascara smudges. "Come on. Let's get you changed into dry clothes, and then we can talk."

I nod, my body relaxing. I run my eyes over the room that no doubt belongs to him when he leaves. It's tidy and simple, only a few pieces of furniture. It's clear he doesn't spend much time here.

Seconds later, Maliki returns with clothes in his arms.

He gives them to me and points to an open door. "Bathroom is there."

Yawning, I change into a tall, baggy bar tee and an extra-large pair of black sweatpants that sag, even after tying them tight around my waist. I don't glance in the mirror or attempt to fix myself up. It'll only make me feel uglier.

He's on the couch when I come out. I settle next to him and spill every secret I've learned about my father tonight, stumbling over my own words every so often.

My father had an affair resulting in an illegitimate child. That illegitimate child is my brother's girlfriend's nephew.

I sob while explaining how heartbroken my mother is, and my lips quiver when I grit out how I can never look at my father the same. I never want to see him again after he damaged our family.

When I'm done, a weight is lifted from my shoulders. Maliki sat and listened, not interrupting or advising me on how to feel. He stands, walks to the kitchen, and pours me a glass of water.

I take the glass from him. "You've been dodging me."

"I've been busy," he says.

"Bullshit." I'm dealing with lies from my dad. I won't accept them from him, too. "Ever since that stupid sex conversation, you've hardly spoken to me."

"That night proved a friendship between us wasn't a wise idea. We're too different, Sierra, and you have your own relationship issues to work out."

Us being friends is necessary for my sanity, for my heart. No words from anyone I've spoken to tonight were as comforting as being with Maliki. It's been hell, not seeing him.

"I swear, no more sex or relationship talk. I'll even sweep the floors, and we'll act like it never took place."

He smirks. "You enjoy my company, don't you? Your boyfriend is so fucking stale that you'd rather be around me."

I roll my eyes. "Oh my God, someone needs to make himself a humble drink."

———

"Sierra, listen to me. Do not go inside," Ellie urges over the phone.

"What? Why?" I ask.

"The news about your engagement has spread all over town. Your mother told everyone at the benefit breakfast this morning. There's no way it hasn't hit Down Home—that it hasn't hit Maliki—and from how well I know you, I'm sure you haven't told him."

I twist the diamond ring on my finger and bow my head. He should've known before any random person.

Devin proposed ten days ago, and since then, I've been terrified of seeing Maliki. I've also been miserable, not seeing him. He should've found out from me, face-to-face.

I couldn't do it though.

I knew what he'd do.

He'd grill me about my saying yes. Give me shit. He'd see straight through me and rip out every uncertainty I possessed about marrying Devin, throwing them at me.

That's what Maliki does. He makes me tackle my truths, which fucking terrifies me.

My voice cracks, my stomach rolling as a chill hits me. "I should've told him myself."

"Trust me, he doesn't want to see you. Babe, I hate to tell you this, but it's in your best interest to put your closing nights with Maliki to rest if you marry Devin."

I force a laugh. "Oh my God! Maliki won't care. We're *friends*. He's made that clear from day one." *Lies.*

In the pit of my stomach, heart of my soul, I know Maliki will most definitely care.

Ellie releases a worried sigh. "Tell me then, what would you feel if Maliki got engaged?"

I swallow down the curses ready to fly out of my mouth. "I mean, I wouldn't like it." *I'd fucking riot.*

"Bullshit." Her tone turns sharp. "I'm ordering you right now to turn around, leave that parking lot, and arrive early to your cake-testing appointment with your mother."

My mother has started wedding planning. Hell, she might've started the day Devin asked my parents for permission to marry me. Devin proposed in front of our families, making it hard for me to say anything but yes.

I planned to wait a few years until our nuptials, but then I saw my mother's face and heard the excitement in her voice while she talked about locations, flowers, and dresses. I didn't have the heart to tell her to relax and give me time. I missed her smile too much.

It's not that I don't care about Devin. I don't doubt my future with Devin or his feelings. Even with our relationship issues, I don't see Devin breaking my heart.

Maliki? He's never had a stable relationship.

Hell, he's never shown interest in having one with me or anyone.

We're friends. Period.

I need to accept that.

Moving on will help me.

"I'm going in," I tell Ellie.

"No! Do not make me drive up there and drag you out as if I were your mother! I won't allow you to make an ass of yourself."

"Good-bye, bestie."

She's still threatening me when I hang up.

Eyes are pinned to me when I walk into the pub, and I focus on bringing one foot in front of the other, fearful of tripping. I'm light-headed before even reaching Maliki.

I should be happy.

I'm engaged!

"Well, well, look who it is," Maliki deadpans, meeting me at the front of the bar as if he's been waiting for me. "The future Mrs. Kinda Sorta."

"Not funny," I grumble, dropping onto a stool.

"You know what else isn't funny? Marrying someone you don't love." His lips curl back in disgust. "But hey, what do I know about love? I've never had a healthy relationship like you where I break up with a person a few dozen times." His response is precisely how I imagined.

I sigh, my shoulders rolling forward. "It's complicated."

"Complicated?" His eyes widen. "He proposed. You said yes. And, now, you're wearing a diamond on your finger. That isn't complicated, Sierra."

I can't stop myself from drifting my hand upward and admiring the ring. Devin did a fantastic job. The view of Maliki's bitter smile when I look back at him erases all the happiness of my new accessory.

"In fact, why don't I make you a celebratory drink? What about The Heartbreaker? That's the future of your joke of a marriage."

My eyes burn, and a tear slips from the corner of my eye. My hair conceals that side of my face, so I don't bother wiping it. He can't know he's not the only one doubting this marriage.

"Don't, okay?" I muster out.

He lifts his arms and snarls. "Don't what? Tell you you're stupid for saying yes? I don't fucking lie, Sierra." He stops and drops his voice when he notices people are staring. "If you want someone to believe in your sham of a relationship, it won't be me." He slams his hand down on the bar and backs away. "When's the big day? According to what I've heard, you're putting something together quick."

I nod and level my eyes on him. "It'll be a short engagement."

He cringes and comes closer. "Holy shit, you're pregnant. You're pregnant, and your parents are forcing you to marry him."

"What?" I shriek. "No!" I hold my hand out and control my breathing. "Look, my mother hasn't been this happy in years. *Years*, Maliki."

"Buy her a fucking puppy. Don't marry someone to make her happy. That's the dumbest shit I've ever heard."

"Maliki," I breathe out.

"I have a job to get back to. Enjoy the married life."

———

Maliki isn't here tonight.

That's odd.

He always works Friday nights.

Mikey is running one side of the bar, and Liz is working the other. Liz has made it clear she doesn't support my closing parties with Maliki. Well, my *past* closing parties with Maliki, given we haven't talked in weeks.

I'm ready to move to Mikey's side and ask where Maliki is, but I'm stopped by Liz.

"He's not here tonight," she states, irritated.

She doesn't bother asking if I need a drink. She knows why I'm here.

Liz has the same dark hair as Maliki but with softer features and kinder eyes. Well, kinder when they're directed at anyone but me. She's older than Maliki, and according to him, she moved into the mother role when theirs left.

"Stay away from my brother."

"What?" I stutter out in surprise.

"You sent him an invite to your stupid wedding." She gives me a frigid stare. "That was pretty fucking shitty, you know."

This is what I was scared of.

She's right.

I wavered on inviting Maliki to the wedding. Would it piss him off to invite him … or *not* invite him? I was unsure but finally mailed the invite. Maliki ignoring my text, asking if I could stop by the bar, gave me my answer. He's pissed.

I muster up the courage to defend myself even though I feel like an absolute ass, like Ellie said. Guilt consumes me.

"It'd have been shitty not to invite him."

"You're so clueless."

"Excuse me?"

"You're marrying another man, but you come here to hang out with one you're *not* marrying. Is that not a warning that, *I don't know,* you shouldn't get married?" She taps her temple.

She's right, but the wedding is paid for, family member flights are booked, and my mother is over the moon.

"Can you tell him I stopped by?"

"Nope."

All righty then. I clench my fingers around my phone. It's been in my hand all night while I've waited for a reply from him.

"No offense, but you're a selfish brat," she continues without allowing me a chance to speak. "Grow up. You can't have your cake and eat it, too." She gives me a tight-lipped smile. "Have a good night, and leave my brother the hell alone."

———

I have cold feet.

Not ones I can fix with tugging on a pair of comfy UGGs.

Cold feet about marrying Devin.

The night before our wedding.

The closer it gets, the more nervous I get.

Devin is nice. Sensible. Secure.

Maliki is wild. My future with him would be a mystery.

That's *if* he'd even want anything more than just friendship.

When we used to close together, he made it clear that we were staying in the friend zone.

But I can't marry Devin when my heart isn't one hundred percent with him and wants someone else.

I texted Maliki an hour ago, but he hasn't replied. He's turned into a master of avoiding me. Every night I went to the bar, Liz said he was gone.

Until now.

Earlier, as my stalker ass had done for the past week, I drove past the bar's back lot. Tonight, Maliki's car is parked in his spot.

He's back.

It's a sign, and him being home is all I can think about. When I went over last-minute arrangements with my wedding planner, I merely nodded, not paying attention to what changes she'd made. I canceled the bridesmaid sleepover at my house, claiming I wasn't feeling well, and told my mother I needed alone time.

I need to see him. I'm about to turn my life upside down.

I unlock the door to the pub and walk in. Maliki gave me a key pre-engagement. Sometimes, I would come to the bar after closing and let myself in.

The jukebox is statically playing a song I don't know, and I don't see Maliki.

Weird.

He usually turns off the music promptly at closing, in need of peace.

What's also weird is, the bar isn't cleaned. Trash litters the tables and floor, the stools are randomly thrown around the room, and the bar top isn't wiped down. I slip the keys into my purse and head toward his office, hoping to find him there.

I freeze when I hear it.

"Yes! Harder!"

It's a woman's voice. A woman's *breathless* voice.

Nausea rises up my throat, but I talk myself down. Whoever is in the office is fucking, but it can be anyone—Mikey, Liz, or hell, even a cook.

I'm praying for any of those alternatives to Maliki as I stupidly migrate closer to the office.

"Oh my God, Maliki!" she cries out. "Your dick is amazing!"

Well, there goes that hope.

"Fuck," a man groans out. *Maliki* groans out.

My heart splinters into shattered fragments, and I can barely breathe as I push myself to continue in their direction. The echo of smacking skin is screaming at me in warning to run, but I can't.

I have to see.

I cover my mouth, in fear of vomiting and making a noise. The office door is cracked open, and my weirdo self peeks through the narrow crack.

A dark-haired woman is spread naked on the desk. Maliki is standing between her long, tan legs, just as exposed. Their moans continue, and I can't walk away.

Then, my attention shifts to only him. His chest is beautifully sculpted with muscles, and sweat glistens his abdomen. I can detect his cock pumping in and out of her, but the desk cuts off my view from eyeing anything lower.

The desk moves with each thrust as he wildly fucks her. He reaches forward to skim his palms up her chest and squeezes her breasts—breasts that are fuller than mine.

I'm comparing every inch of myself to this woman.

"Shit, I've missed you," she moans. "I love you so damn much."

She lifts herself up on an elbow, reaching for him, and he leans down, smashing his mouth to hers, devouring her.

Tears hit my eyes. I've never experienced hurt so hard. I taste bile and anger and hate toward Maliki and this mystery bitch for taking what I crave to be mine.

You can't be mad.

He doesn't belong to you.

You did this.

I was stupid and played games.

I should've told him how I felt. It's too late now. He's having sex with a woman, kissing her, and she told him she loved him. There is a connection between the two. They've had sex before. That's why he's been avoiding me—not for the invitation, but because he has a girlfriend.

Even though I can be arrested for watching them, even though it's ripping me apart, I can't turn away.

That changes when my phone rings, the ringtone blaring.

Everyone stops.

Oh. My. Fucking. God.

This is not happening right now.

I jump backward as I shakily tug my phone from my pocket, careful not to drop it, and silence the stupid thing. I don't look back while sprinting out of the bar as if Michael Myers were chasing me.

If Maliki pulls up the camera footage to find who was creeping on him, I'm moving out of Blue Beech for good.

CHAPTER SIX
SIERRA

THREE MONTHS LATER

Loud knocking on my front door wakes me up.

I yawn and check the time on my alarm clock.

Five a.m.?

No, thank you.

They can wait until regular waking hours.

Whoever's banging on the door doesn't agree with the waiting game and only pounds harder. I push off my blanket, expletives falling from my lips, and stomp into the living room.

"Chillax!" I yell. "I'm coming!"

I grip the doorknob but withdraw a step when my name is called on the other side.

Hell to the no.

This isn't going down at five in the fucking morning.

I attempt to calm my breathing—failing miserably—and the knocking persists.

I'm hallucinating.

This is a dream.

Only one way for me to find out. I stand on my tiptoes and check the peephole.

Nope. Not dreaming.

It's him.

Shit!

This can't happen now.

I need time to prepare myself before facing him—words need fine-tuned, an outfit chosen, and a minimum of three hours of meditation done.

Maybe if I don't answer, he'll give up.

I count to twenty, and the knocking doesn't cease. He gives me no choice but to answer unless I want my neighbors to call the cops on him. They're assholes like that. It's no biggie for them to have wild sex all night, but it's a crime for me to jam to Britney in the morning.

I swing open the door, air knocking from my lungs, and cover my mouth in fear of vomiting. Maliki is standing in front of me, and even though it's been months, he looks the same. Well, except he's now wearing clothes and not sticking his penis in another woman. I shudder, my stomach knotting at the memory of seeing him and her.

Our eyes meet, and he doesn't look happy to see me.

Why is he here then?

My hand drops from my mouth, and I rest against the doorframe, hoping it makes me look collected when, in actuality, it's so I don't fall on my ass. I wait for him to explain his unexpected wake-up call.

"You've been avoiding me," he states.

No shit, Sherlock.

"You know why." I'm shocked at my honesty, surprised I didn't throw out excuses like I've been working late or I had to wash my hair.

After my wedding, Maliki texted me with a simple, *Congrats.* I didn't have the guts to reply. He sent another text after I returned from my honeymoon, and I wanted to throw my phone as I read it. He'd watched the camera footage and seen me watching them that night. An apology was added in his text, but he didn't fail to add a jab after it, claiming I had no right to be angry with him because I was climbing into another man's bed at night.

That time, I didn't reply out of anger.

Our friendship is over.

There's no moving past my marriage and his office-screwing.

He scoffs, "Because I was with another woman?"

He had a brief fling with the woman he'd screwed that night, according to Ellie. She had been appointed my Maliki informant. Just because I refused to step foot into Down Home or reply to his texts didn't mean I couldn't keep tabs on him. Two weeks ago, she told me the chick was no longer coming around.

"Yep," I clip out.

"You're pissed at me for sleeping with another woman. Meanwhile, Sierra dearest, you were fucking *engaged* to another man."

"And, now, I'm *married* to that man." *Why did I find it necessary to define that?* It was a blow to compete with his asshole attitude.

"Wrong. You *were* married to him."

I wince. "Excuse me?"

He motions toward the inside of my condo. "Get dressed. We're leaving."

This is when I realize I didn't change before answering, not that he gave me a chance to. I'm wearing the pub shirt he gave me the night I came to him after the news broke about my father's affair and short strawberry-patterned boy shorts. I don't know why I'm wearing the shirt, given our fallout, but I'm blaming it on the comfort of it.

I cross my arms to cover the shirt. "I'm not going anywhere with you."

He juts out his chin. "Get fucking dressed, Sierra."

"What's going on? I work in three hours."

"I'll return you in time."

I sigh. "You're not taking no for an answer, are you?"

"Nope."

I wave him inside. "*Fine.* Give me ten to brush my teeth and change clothes."

"Nice shirt, by the way," he remarks as I head toward my bedroom.

My back stiffens, and I don't bother looking back at him. "I'm behind on laundry."

"Liar."

What is happening?

Confusion crackles inside me as I get dressed in leggings and a baggy sweatshirt, tug my hair into a messy bun, and slide on flip-flops. I'm worried his visit has something to do with Devin. Swear to God, my husband had better not have done anything stupid enough for me to castrate him for.

Maliki is holding a gold-framed photo when I return to the living room. My wedding photo.

I clap my hands. "We need to make this quick."

He gives the picture one last glare and sets it facedown onto the table. "After you."

I hop down each step and spot Maliki's Camaro as soon as we hit the parking lot. I inhale a deep breath when I get in, attempting to pick up the scent of a woman as if I were a golden retriever. All I detect is the rich amber of Maliki's cologne.

Maliki doesn't say a word, and I tug my phone from my purse. There's a text from Ellie, a voice mail from my mother, and nothing from Devin. I talked to him before I went to bed last night.

I respond to Ellie's text and drop my phone in my lap. As much as I want to call Devin, I can't. Not yet. When I peek up, I notice we're driving out of Blue Beech.

"Whoa, where are we going?"

Maliki keeps his eyes on the road and doesn't say a word.

That only pisses me off further. "I want goddamn answers, Maliki, or I'm jumping out of this car."

His fingers clench around the steering wheel, and he still stares ahead, as if he were waiting for something to run out in front of us. "Trust me on this. No matter what's happened between us, you know damn well you can trust me."

"Are you kidnapping me?"

"Negative. If I recall, you once told me you'd make the worst hostage—something about hot wings and hair shit. Not dealing with those problems."

I can't help but smile at the memory.

He scrubs a hand over the stubble of his cheek. "Do you love him?"

I stare blankly in his direction, his question taking me aback. "Who? Devin?"

"No, the other man you're married to."

I punch his arm. "I forgot how irritating you are."

He rubs the spot I hit, and relief hits me when he finally glances my way. "You love how irritating I am. Just like I love how fucking irritating you are."

Momentarily, in my mind, our situation dissipates, and I shut my eyes, savoring his compliment.

Then, I remember I'm married.

I adjust my ring and fix my eyes on the solitary princess cut diamond.

"Seriously," I say. "What is this about?"

"Answer my question." Aggravation is in his voice again. "Do you love him?"

"Obviously. I wouldn't have married someone I didn't love."

"Do you love him or the idea of him?"

"This is ridiculous. Take me home. I have better things to do than defend my marriage."

"You'd better not defend it after today."

"Please, stop talking in code … or circles … or whatever the hell you're doing. I'm getting pretty dizzy over here. Did I tell you about my motion sickness? Blue Beech Fair 1999, the Tilt-A-Whirl had me puking up pink cotton candy all night."

"You want straight up?" he grinds out in a raised voice. "Your husband was partying last night at a bar. I saw him there."

His response doesn't bother me and isn't what I expected.

"I'm well aware he was at a bachelor party," I deadpan.

His irritation grows. "Are you also *well aware* he was fucking another woman at that bachelor party?"

Disbelief rushes through me. I struggle to breathe, struggle to think … hell, I even struggle to remember my own name.

No way. I open my mouth to protest, but fear constricts me from speaking.

Our relationship isn't perfect, but since our wedding, Devin has been the model husband. I've never doubted my trust in him. There have been no signs of an affair—no whispering in the other room or a passcode on his phone, none of the signs my friends have busted their husbands with.

"You're lying," I accuse when I manage to gather words.

He isn't.

Maliki wouldn't drag me through this torture if it wasn't true, no matter how tattered our friendship is.

He winces in frustration, appearing almost pained at me doubting him. "Do you think I'd do this for shits and giggles? I was there last night and witnessed it."

I shake my head as a tear trickles down my cheek. "No."

"Good, but I want you to see it for yourself, so the little cocksucker can't lie his way out of it."

"What do you mean, see it?" I gape at him, horrified. "Jesus, please tell me there's not a sex tape or something like that, and that's how you know about this."

"A sex tape? I hope the fuck not." His face twists into a line of disgust. "Do I have proof without seeing his weasel dick? Affirmative."

I'm so lost.

My stomach tightens at his failure to elaborate, and I'm afraid to ask for details. I snatch my phone with sweaty hands, unlock it, and scroll to my husband's name. Him not coming home last night didn't worry me. He'd rented a hotel room for him and his friends the night of his party. I'd expected it. Hell, I'd *helped* him pack his overnight bag.

I shake my head, powering off my phone, and toss it into my bag. I'll ask his side of the story after seeing this *evidence.*

We don't speak the rest of the ride, and twenty minutes later, Maliki pulls into the parking lot of the Twisted Fox Bar. It's a newer establishment in the surrounding county and tends to drag in the younger crowd. Devin comes here to hang out with friends ... and this is where the bachelor party was last night.

Maliki picks up his phone from a cupholder and calls someone. "Hey, man. We're here." He nods a few times and ends the call.

We step out of the car, and he leads me to the entrance of the building. The door is unlocked. A man behind the bar is the only person here. He looks around the same age as Maliki and was here the few times I came with Devin.

He circles the bar and comes our way. He has light-brown hair, and even though he's on the slimmer side, he's hot.

Maliki lifts his chin. "Yo, Cohen." He jerks his head toward me. "This is Sierra."

I politely wave at Cohen, and he responds with a sympathetic smile before telling us to follow him.

He takes us through the kitchen until we reach an office with a desk covered with two large computer monitors. Reality strikes me when Cohen sits in the chair by the desk.

Cohen is showing me the evidence of Devin cheating.

I'm not prepared for this.

I stay in the doorway, watching Cohen punch a few buttons on the keyboard and turn to Maliki, a curious look on his face.

"You sure she wants to see this?" he asks.

"She needs to," Maliki replies.

I hold up my hand. "Uh, *she* is standing right here."

Cohen only nods and puts his attention back to the computer.

Maliki curls his arm over my shoulders and steers me to stand behind Cohen. I gulp and resist the urge to shut my eyes.

This has to happen.

When Cohen pulls up the bar's camera footage, I immediately spot Devin. My belly knots with panic while I watch him take shots with friends. Then, he's talking to a woman at the bar, and he buys her a drink. My hands curl and press against my stomach. I recite two quick prayers—the first that I'm not about to see my husband cheat and the other that I don't vomit on Cohen's head.

I grip the back of the chair and tense when Devin turns stupid.

Oh, this motherfucker.

He grabs the woman's hand and takes her to the restroom. Even though Cohen speeds up the time, I'm aware of how much has passed. Fifteen minutes later, I watch my husband exit the restroom, buckling his pants, with the woman lagging behind him.

"That motherfucking asshole," I bite out. "And that two-faced tramp."

Cohen drops his head back to look at me. "You know her?"

"She was a sorority sister. Louise." My attention shifts to Maliki. "The bitch who asked you for Buttery Nipples on my birthday."

"Never trust a chick who drinks Buttery Nipples," Cohen comments.

I never got along with Louise. One night, Devin drunkenly confessed she'd slid into his DMs during one of our *breaks* but swore he'd ignored it. I doubt that now.

I bury my face in my hands. "Well, if this isn't humiliating."

"For him," Maliki says, gently squeezing my shoulders. "Not you."

I twist out of his hold to face him. "Why?" My voice shakes. "Why did you show me this?"

I move when Cohen wheels his chair away from the desk and springs to his feet.

"I'll leave you two to do whatever," he says.

I wait until Cohen disappears through the doorway before speaking.

My chin trembles.

Don't cry.

Don't you dare cry.

"Why?" I ask again, fighting to keep my voice calm.

Maliki raises his hands next to his head in a mind-blown motion. "Are you shitting me? What did you expect me to do? Sit back in my chair at the back of the bar and let him fuck around on you?"

I stammer for the right words.

"Do whatever you want with the information, but you needed to know. Whether you stay with the cheating bastard is your call." He stops me when I turn around to leave. "Oh, and don't be surprised if he has a black eye when you see him."

CHAPTER SEVEN
SIERRA

I'm pacing the living room, wiping tears away as they fall, while waiting for my cheating bastard of a husband to come home.

My life will change when he walks in.

I'll be divorced before reaching my thirties.

Hell, I'll be divorced before making it to our first anniversary.

The video of him and Louise has consumed my every thought. I had two glasses of wine for breakfast after Maliki dropped me off at home—attempts to erase the memory of the video, but it didn't help.

Maliki asked if I needed help packing or if I wanted him to give Devin another black eye.

Do I stay or go?

I stop when the front door opens.

This is it.

There's never been a longer silence in my life as I wait for Devin to come into the living room. I clutch my stomach, nausea creeping in, and suck in a life-changing breath. Suddenly, I'm struggling to find the words I prepared, the words I held back from calling and screaming at him over the phone.

My lip trembles when he comes into view in what seems like slow motion.

"Hey, babe," he greets, gripping his overnight bag.

My plan to handle this rationally flies out the window, and I grab our wedding photo, hurling it toward him. His eyes bulge, and he shuffles back a step, barely dodging it.

"Shit," he rasps, looking from the frame to me. "Is it that time of the month?"

There's no regret on his face. Had Maliki not told me, I would've never suspected him cheating. His hair is combed over in the same style he's worn since college, his clothes are wrinkle-free, and he shows no symptoms of a hangover. There is a slight discoloration beneath his eye —a bruise that wasn't there yesterday. The black eye Maliki mentioned.

"You cheated on me?" I scream, my hands shaking. "You cheated on me with Louise?"

His face pales, and he drops his bag to the floor. "What the fuck? Who told you that?"

"Maliki. His friend works at the Twisted Fox." I make a sweeping gesture toward his face. "The man who gave you the black eye."

His hand lifts to his eye. "That fucker hates me and hit me for no reason." He sneers, an attempt to cover his lies, but his shoulders droop. "I'm insulted you'd believe him over me. I've never made you doubt my love for you."

"There are cameras there." My voice raises. "I saw you with her!"

"I swear, it's not what it looked like."

"Oh, come on! I'm *insulted* you'd think I'd believe that lie."

He extends his arms out and steps closer. "I'm sorry! I was drunk." He focuses his eyes on me and expels an audible breath. "It's eating me alive that I hurt you."

"I can see it's really *eating you alive.*"

"It was a bachelor party. It's not the first time a man has accidentally hooked up with a woman at one."

Oh, that's his argument?

I grab another frame, and he dodges it flying toward him again.

"That's supposed to make me feel better?"

He takes another step toward me.

I take one back.

"*Please,* baby," he pleads. "We've had so many years. Don't let this fuckup—my *only* fuckup—tear us apart. It won't happen again. I swear it."

"No, you tore us apart." Fear and hurt spiral through me, and I pick up my bag from the couch. "I can't even look at you."

He catches my arm, turning me to face him, and guilt surfaces on his features. I swallow, hurting while watching his face contort in pain, and it torments me not to console him.

I mean, he is my husband.

I care about him.

Not enough to stay though.

I jerk out of his hold.

"Please," he whispers. "I made a mistake."

I remove my wedding ring and allow it to fall to the floor. "And I made a mistake in marrying you."

He calls my name when I walk out.

———

"Tell me you left his sorry ass."

I didn't know where to go.

My mom would know something was wrong. My brothers would want to kick Devin's ass. Not that he doesn't deserve an ass-kicking, but today, all I want to do is clear my mind of my husband cheating. I don't want them to know yet. I need time to process it myself before hearing their relationship advice.

Stay with him.

Leave him.

Kill him.

I drop my purse onto the bar and fall down on a stool.

"I left his sorry ass." I fight to keep my voice steady and confident even though I'm near losing it.

Being back at Down Home seems surreal. It looks the same, smells the same, *feels* the same, like I never stopped coming.

Maliki beams with pride while standing behind the bar. "Where do you go from here?"

"No idea. Not only did we live together, but I also work for his father. I'm now homeless, possibly unemployed, and husbandless. *Yay.*"

Moving in with my parents is a *hell no.* They're working to move on from my father's infidelities. Ellie lives with Corbin. No doubt Devin would show up there, wanting to talk.

I press my forehead against the bar and groan. "I'm so screwed."

"I can help you in the housing and employment department. As for the husband position, you'll have to seek help elsewhere," Maliki says.

I lift my head to see the seriousness on his face. "Trust me, I don't even want to sweat about a husband."

He nods. "Good girl. You need to get rid of the one you have now." He rubs his hands together before ducking down and grabbing me a bottle of water. "The guest bedroom in my apartment is open, and you can work here."

Whoa. Definitely wasn't expecting that.

"That's …" I unscrew the bottle cap and take a drink. "That's …"

"An offer, Sierra. Take it or leave it." He's not insulted by my response. "I'm helping a friend."

Friend.

I raise a brow. "Is that what we are? Friends again?"

"We've always been friends … after you quit being annoying and sneaking into my bar."

I sigh. "I appreciate the offer but don't know if it's a stellar idea."

"If you change your mind, let me know."

———

"I swear on my shoe collection, that asshole isn't stepping foot in my apartment," Ellie says after I decline her offer to stay at her apartment. "You won't need to worry about seeing him because I'll kick his ass before he makes it through the front door."

I called an hour ago and asked her to meet me at our favorite taco joint outside of town. She was as stunned as I was when I broke the news about Devin and Louise's restroom field trip. I'd been nervous about going out in public, in fear of a breakdown, but I've stayed strong.

Each time I almost cry, I take a tequila shot instead.

It's working perfectly.

"While I appreciate your loyalty, kicking his ass will only lead to problems with you and Corbin," I tell her.

She lifts her margarita. "Corbin will be lucky if I allow him to hang out with a man who has no issues with banging tramps in restrooms."

"I'll figure something out. If worse comes to worse, I'll be at your doorstep."

Do I tell her about Maliki's offer?

Nope.

She'll go into full freak-out mode. It wouldn't surprise me if she suggested I screw Maliki, tape it, and then send the video to Devin. Ellie loves a good revenge.

"You swear?"

I nod. "I swear."

"What are your options then? Moving home?"

"Not if I can help it. Hopefully, I can find a rental."

"Good luck with that in Blue Beech. Finding a rental there is like snagging a golden ticket to Wonka's factory. The people never leave their homes. They pass them down through generations like bad genetics."

I press my palms to my temples. "Ugh, I know."

"Where are you crashing tonight? The offer is open for my place even if it's only temporary."

I chew on my lower lip, tasting the lingering tequila. "Undecided. Can you drop me off at Down Home? I told Maliki I'd help him close and then ask Kyle if I can crash at his place."

She grins. "She runs to her prince in bartending armor."

I throw a chip at her. "Shut up. I'm not running to anyone."

"You are *so* running to him. And no judgments over here, babe. Maliki is hot and will have no problem fucking every thought of Devin the Douche Bag out of you."

I gulp down the rest of my margarita. "There will be no sex with him. We're friends. I'm comfortable talking to him."

"Gee, thanks, *best friend.* I'm all for you running to him for sex, *but* I'm the one you're supposed to feel the most comfortable talking to."

"Trust me, you know way more about me than he does. It's just …" I pause, struggling to define my relationship with Maliki. "We have this weird friendship."

"Turn it into a fuckship, and I won't be offended by you going to him and not me."

"God, I love yet also hate you."

She pushes her shoulders up and smirks. "You love me." She motions for our waiter. "Now, let's get you good and drunk before you go to your future fuck buddy."

I lower my voice. "I'm not even divorced yet!"

She shakes her head. "Devin set the marriage bar when he stuck his pencil dick into a sorority tramp."

The waiter comes, and she orders us another round of margaritas.

And two shots of tequila.

———

"Your closing partner has arrived," Ellie announces while helping me walk—no, *stumble* into Down Home.

I had four margaritas and lost count of how many shots I downed during dinner. My purse swings from my shoulder while I dangle off Ellie's. I can walk. It's just easier to do it with help.

What a way to celebrate your husband cheating.

A few loners are settled around the bar, vacant stools between them, and my vision is too fuzzy to make out who they are. Chances are they know me though.

Everyone knows me in this godforsaken town.

They'll hear about Devin's restroom scandal. It'll become the scandal of the year—right behind my father's.

Keepin' it classy in the Lane family.

"And she's wasted," Maliki says, rounding the bar to meet us.

"Wasted and asking for you," Ellie clarifies. "I trust you'll take care of her?"

"Always." Maliki wraps his arms around my shoulders, relieving Ellie of my weight, and pulls me into him.

"Perfect!" Ellie kisses my cheek. "You two kids have fun."

She leaves and heads to the parking lot where Corbin is waiting. I'd reluctantly let him pick us up from the restaurant. At first, I was afraid he'd tell Devin my business, but Ellie swore on her firstborn— my future godchild—that he wouldn't.

Maliki guides me to the corner of the bar and assists me onto a stool. "I'm insulted you drank somewhere else. What's wrong with my liquor?"

"I needed to get away from Blue Beech," I answer.

"I get that."

"And I'm not drunk. I'm tipsy. I can say my ABCs and recite every word of 'Toxic.' " My words are slurred, but I trust Maliki can understand me. He's regularly around wasted people. Drunken gibberish is his second language.

He chuckles. "I'm happy tipsy you remembers her Britney Spears songs."

"Damn straight. And I'm impressed, Bridges. Im-freaking-pressed."

He raises a brow in question.

"You know who sings 'Toxic.' It makes me like you more."

He laughs. "Nice to know." He squeezes my arm and steps away. "I'll grab you a water and food to sober you up."

I gulp, realizing how dry my mouth is. "Water—yes, please. Food —God, no. I devoured enough chips and queso to feed a small country."

I rub my forehead and drag my phone from my purse. I turned it off hours ago after Devin wouldn't stop calling and texting. You can only hit the *fuck you* button so many times before you lose your mind.

I glare at it for a moment and then slide it away from me, up the bar. When I turn it on, no doubt dozens of texts from Devin will pop up. I'll make Ellie delete them later.

"Drink this." Maliki passes me a water. "And eat this." A basket of fries comes my way next.

I pick up the water and chug it. Luckily, Mikey is working with Maliki tonight and is helping the few customers here. In an hour, the crowd will grow, and Maliki won't be able to give me his full attention like this.

He leans back on his heels. "It's nice, seeing you back here. It'd better become a regular sight again, princess."

Don't say it. Don't say it.

"That depends."

I said it.

"Depends on what?"

The alcohol makes me brave. "If you're screwing women on desks."

He winces, surprised at my response, but quickly recovers. "I promise, no other women when you're here."

"And what if I'm not here with you?" I capture an ice cube from my water, bite into it, and chew it before sucking it into my mouth. Water drips down my chin.

Maliki's smile drops, and he tilts his head to the side, as if he's studying me. I grab another cube and do the same thing. The aroma of his cologne wafts through my nostrils, and I gasp when he comes forward, his large hand cupping my chin. His finger sweeps across my skin, smoothing away the water, and every muscle in my body tenses.

My lips quiver, and me gasping breaks him away from touching me. He pulls back, placing distance between us, as if he'd temporary slipped faking that we were only friends.

He clears his throat. "Did you decide where you'll stay?"

"Nope." I snatch a fry and shove it into my mouth, wondering if I made a mistake in coming here.

The home I grew up in wasn't happy—still isn't. And now, thanks to my brother's new girlfriend, the entire town knows our business. They talk in hushed whispers about my father cheating on my mother and how his mistress is now incarcerated. Thank God I dodged the cheating husband bullet before Devin knocked up another woman.

"Where do you plan to sleep then?" Maliki asks, annoyance clear in his tone.

"In my car," I answer with a shrug and chomp on another fry.

"The fuck you are."

I don't actually plan to sleep in my car. The backseat of my Lexus is roomy, but I can't park somewhere and not expect to be murdered.

I had multiple motives in coming here tonight.

"Calm down, killer," I say, growing flustered. "Is your, uh …"

"Spit it out," Maliki demands even though I can tell he's aware of what I'm about to ask.

"Is your roomie offer still open?"

"For you? Absolutely. For anyone else? Fuck no."

I run my tongue over my lips, blushing and feeling special that it's only open *for me.* I play with the splintered wood of the bar, now feeling shy. "Thank you. I need to get my stuff from Devin's."

"I can do that for you."

"Horrible idea. He hates you."

"And I hate the little asshole. If we didn't share a common interest, I wouldn't give a shit about him."

I snort. "And what common interest could you two possibly share?"

"You." The word slips from his lips in seconds—confident and strong.

My eyes shoot to his face, our contact locking, and I swear to God, I almost fall off my stool as he stares at me with hooded eyes.

"Oh …" I frown when our eye contact slips, him doing the pulling away—*again.* "Ellie offered to help, but I'm not sure if that's a smart idea. She's also on the list of people who want to kick Devin's ass."

"That's probably a pretty fucking long list."

Mikey turns up the volume on the TV when a boxing match

starts, and I look around the bar, noticing how busy it is now. It's always packed on fight nights.

Maliki flashes a smile. "Come on. I'll help you upstairs, and you can make yourself at home."

I yawn, shaking my head. "No. I promised to help you tonight."

"You'll be no help, trust me. We can resume our closing parties tomorrow."

He helps me off the stool and claims my hand in his. Dizziness rushes through me as he walks me upstairs to his apartment. It smells of fresh lemon cleaning products and him—a delectable scent. It's clean, like last time. He doesn't drop my hand until he shuts the door behind us.

He strolls down a hall, opens a door, and does a ta-da gesture. "This is your new bedroom."

It's smaller than what I'm used to, and the bed is only a full, but it's either this or sleeping in my car. The biggest benefit of staying here is Maliki's company. That compensates for the lack of space.

I point to the bed that's complete with a blue plaid comforter and matching pillows. "That thing had better be comfortable," I joke.

"Babe, anything is more comfortable than sleeping next to cheating slime."

Truth.

He moves to the side, allowing me entry into the room. "I'll grab you something to sleep in."

I look down when he leaves the room and pull at the hem of my silk blouse that I paired with black leather-like leggings and studded gold sandals. I collapse onto the bed and kick off my shoes, exhausted. I need a decent night's sleep, so I can figure out where I'm going from here.

Maliki returns with a change of clothes, but I've already slipped underneath the blankets.

"I'm too lazy to change," I say around a yawn.

He chuckles, taking a seat on the edge of the bed. "That's the best kind of drunk. I'll be downstairs if you need anything. Call. Text. Come down."

I nod, giving him a shy smile. "Thank you."

My breath knocks against my lungs when he reaches forward, clips a fallen strand of hair away from my face, and tilts his head to the side. "I don't get it."

I blink, shuddering at his touch. "Get what?"

"How a man could cheat on you."

CHAPTER EIGHT
MALIKI

I'm a dumbass.

That's the only excuse I have for inviting her to be my new roommate.

Sierra Lane is an itch I've been struggling to scratch for years.

The first time the barely legal eighteen-year-old snuck into my bar, I owned it less than a year. I had been stressed about pouring all my savings into a business I wasn't sure would survive. On top of that, an employee pulled a no-call, no-show. I was headed to my office to find a replacement, and there she was.

I knew her. Everyone did. Her parents showed her off at every town event.

The first thought when I saw her shouldn't have been how gorgeous she was while I followed her path. I wasn't sure of her age, but I knew it wasn't old enough to be in a bar. When we got face-to-face, I took in her every feature. Her face was slightly sun-kissed, and the only hint of makeup she wore was red lipstick. A sprinkle of faint freckles scattered along her cheeks, and I loved that she didn't cover them up.

She stared at me with wide, innocent eyes. I knew she was used to getting her way as she tried to talk me out of not kicking her out. I'd wondered if I was the first person to tell her no—though technically, I hadn't done that either.

As much as our cat-and-mouse game pisses me off, it also entertains the fuck out of me. And since then, every time she's stepped into my bar, my heart speeds up. It's more than arousal that crashes through me when she plops her pretty ass onto a stool. She pushes my buttons and never fails to make me laugh, and nothing is more attractive than seeing her possessiveness come out when other women flirt with me. I hold myself back from telling her I don't want them, that I want *her*.

The issue is, I shouldn't.

She's too young for me, we come from different backgrounds, and it'd never work. We're infatuated with each other—and that's how it'll stay. We'll never pass that.

"Care to explain why Rebel Barbie is dragging an expensive-looking suitcase up to your apartment?" Liz asks, storming into my office.

There are two entrances into the apartment—an entrance on the other side of the building with stairs that lead straight to the apartment and another at the back of the bar. I'll remind Sierra to use the side entrance for more privacy.

Liz is scowling at me when I look up from my paperwork, prepared to hear her bitch my head off. For unknown reasons, she doesn't like Sierra. Liz said she doesn't want me to get hurt even though I've made it clear that my relationship with Sierra is strictly platonic.

I lean back in my chair and rest my arms behind my neck. "She left her husband, had nowhere to go, so I offered the guest bedroom until she figures it out."

"Have you lost your fucking mind?"

I shrug. *Yes. Yes, I have.*

"She has money, and her family is royalty here. She can find a rental in a day, *or* I'm sure she has friends or family who wouldn't mind her staying with them."

"*Her parents* have money, not her, and she doesn't want to stay with anyone else." I rub the back of my neck. "Why are you concerned? Do you plan on moving back in?"

We grew up in the apartment above the bar. Every childhood memory I have is there—good and bad. My dad moved to Florida after signing the bar over to me, and Liz and my niece left a year later. Now, it's just me—not that I'm complaining. I've declined all rental offers until Sierra. Hell, hers was an offer *from me.*

I was shocked when I threw out the invitation. I enjoy my space and privacy since I'm surrounded by people all the time. Customers love nothing more than coming to the bar and venting out their sad songs to the bartender. It's a motherfucking cliché.

"Negative," she answers. "My concern is *you.*"

"You have no reason to worry about me."

"I made it clear she was bad news when she played *Little Miss Helper,* and it's an even worse idea to play house with her. If she's too busy having brunch and manicures with her friends, I'll gladly look up rentals for her."

Shit. The wrath of my big sister has never been pretty.

"Be nice to her," I warn.

She pinches her lips together. "I'll *try* to, but I won't keep my mouth shut if it goes south."

"Nothing is going south." Except for my hand to my dick plenty of times while masturbating to the thought of Sierra in the other room.

"Yeah, yeah. Now, we have another order of business."

"What's up?"

"I'm visiting Dad."

Just the mention of him spikes my blood pressure. "What now?"

After my mother left years ago, my father has relied on his children too much, especially Liz. He moved to Florida after meeting a woman on Match.com, and they broke up a year later. Instead of coming home, he decided to stay there—a smart move. He doesn't do well in Blue Beech. There are too many memories of my mother.

"He has a new girlfriend, and things went south." She sighs. "Okay, maybe not another girlfriend."

"You're losing me."

"He got married."

"What?"

"He eloped without telling anyone."

"Let me guess; shit fell apart?"

"You know it."

"So, he needs help cleaning up the mess, and you're running to his rescue?"

"Yes."

"Nothing new there," I mutter.

Her face softens. Liz is protective and the biggest cheerleader of our family not falling apart. "He's a heartbroken man, Maliki."

"He's a grown-ass man who's been *heartbroken* for over a decade, and might I remind you, his *heartbreak* is from his bullshit actions. It's time for him to quit whining over the past. He doesn't deserve pity from anyone. He was a dick to Mom, chose his career over the family, and didn't realize his mistakes until after he lost her. Fuck, I take that back. He still doesn't own up to those mistakes."

"Give him a break, okay? Don't you care? He's *our father*."

"It's not that I don't care. We can't change him, and our only choice is to either continue to worry about it or move on." I stand up from the chair and head toward the door. "Me? I'm choosing to move on."

"It's not as easy to move on for some people as it is with you."

"Let me know if you need any advice on learning how to."

"You'll be the one asking *me* for advice when Blondie ruins you." She taps my shoulder. "Don't do anything stupid while I'm gone, and stay away from her the best you can. The chick was trouble back then and more trouble now."

———

"You're making progress," I say.

Sierra smiles up at me with a shirt and a hanger in her hand. "I'm working on it. Ellie gave me a ride to the restaurant to get my car, so I at least have the clothes I took yesterday. I'll start rental-hunting tomorrow but will most likely have to search out of town."

I'm in no rush for her to leave, but that can change. I've spent time with her in the bar, but nothing more than that. She might be messy as fuck or do some weird shit.

"Oh!" She snaps her fingers. "How much is rent?"

I rest my back against the wall. "Zero dollars."

"I can't live here for *zero dollars*."

"Sure, you can."

"Give me a number to write on a check."

"Zero dollars." I smile in amusement. "I wouldn't waste the paper, but if you want, I'll take that and that only."

"That's taking *nothing*."

I push off the wall and tap her door with my knuckle. "Get settled. I work tonight, but if you need anything, call or come down. The kitchen, both here and in the bar, is open if you're hungry."

"I need to run more errands, and then I'll be back."

"Sounds good."

"I might come keep you company tonight."

"I have no problem with that."

Sierra doesn't show during my shift, and when I go upstairs after closing, her bedroom door is open. She's lying horizontally on the bed, sleeping, and the TV is on. I hesitate, unsure if I should wake her. I don't. Instead, I snag the blanket off the couch and drape it over her.

CHAPTER NINE
SIERRA

"I hope you don't mind. I'm a stress-cleaner."

That's what I tell Maliki when he strolls into the kitchen to find me scrubbing the counters. I've already organized the closet and cleaned the guest bedroom and bathroom, and I'm finishing the kitchen. If he hadn't been sleeping, I'd have already dragged the vacuum out.

Stress-cleaning is a gift passed down from my mother. She cleaned when she was worried—a constant occurrence—and my brothers would hardly pick up their dirty laundry, so I helped. Now, I get the same relief from a deep scrubbing.

I glance at the time. It's one in the afternoon, and Maliki is just waking up. That's not a shocker though, given his job requires him to stay up all night.

I drink in the sight of him standing in front of me, shirtless. He's wearing gray sweatshorts that hang low on his waist. His hair is a wild mess, and his eyes are still half-asleep.

"You'll get no complaints from me," he says.

"Although I'm disappointed there wasn't much to clean. I've never seen a guy's house so spotless."

He drags out a stool from under the island and sits. "One of the waitresses likes the extra cash and cleans the place once a week."

I slowly nod, uncertain of how I feel about someone else up in my space.

"I'll tell her to steer clear of your bedroom."

"No," I rush out. "Totally unnecessary."

"Your face dropped at the mention of her. Either you don't want her around your shit or her in the apartment. Which one?"

"Both." I perk up. "How about this? I'll clean for the both of us. I'm not paying rent. It's the least I can do."

"All right, but let me know if you change your mind."

I jerk my thumb toward my chest. "Stress-cleaner, remember?"

He frowns. "I hope living here won't cause you any stress, *so* let me know if you change your mind."

"I will." *I won't.*

The three waitresses who work at the pub are gorgeous, and I've seen them flirt with my new roomie aplenty. I'm the only one allowed to do that in this apartment now.

At least, that's what I want.

Oh my God.

I'm jealous.

Jesus.

I can't be jealous. I'm *married.*

"You don't work today?" His question breaks me away from my thoughts.

"I quit my job." I called in the day I learned about Devin's affair and haven't returned.

He leans inward and clasps his hands together.

"I'm not irresponsible for not putting in my two weeks." I'm uncertain why I feel the need to defend myself. "I tried, but his mother rattled on about forgiveness. *Then,* she used my parents' situation as an example, which *totally* pissed me off." The only thing I'm forgiving is my heart for being so damn dumb, trusting him. "I'm also not fond of working with an ex."

It sucks, losing my job. His father's firm was reputable and had a notable client list, and the pay was great. It'll be difficult, finding something like that in Blue Beech, so I'll have to look in surrounding towns.

"Any other job prospects?"

"I've had a few," I answer with a frown.

"Why do you look unhappy about that?"

"None of them are jobs I want." All of them are part-time gigs that'll hardly pay my grocery bills. I have money in savings, but that's for finding a new place. "Not to mention, the pay sucks. The demand for an interior designer in this town is practically nonexistent." Some residents haven't updated their homes in decades.

"I'll hire you to renovate the pub."

My breathing catches. "What?"

"The pub hasn't been updated in fuck knows how long. Renovate it … work your magic."

Excitement ripples through me, causing me to grin, and I squeal, clapping my hands. "I would *love* that! I've already thought of ideas of how I'd change things if ever given the opportunity." I needed something to do to pass the time when Maliki left me to make someone a drink.

I suddenly remember the conversation I planned to have with him this morning. Even with his offer, one job won't exactly load my bank account. Plus, I can't charge him as much as Devin's dad did his clients.

"You know …" I pause. "I have my bartending license."

He stills. "What?"

"I have my bartending license. I bartended on campus my senior year for extra cash."

Even though my parents paid my tuition and a chunk of my bills, I worked two jobs. Most of that money went toward the down payment for the condo.

"Your parents were okay with that?" he asks skeptically, raising his brows.

"Hell no."

My father would've flipped his shit.

A grin twitches at his lips. "How'd you manage to hide that from them?"

"Told them I was tutoring." I hold up a finger. "Which, technically, wasn't a lie. I was tutoring. It just wasn't where most of my cash came from."

"What about now? If I hire you, there's no lying about tutoring. This is a small town, princess ... and you're *you*."

"Their opinions are the least of my worries. My father ruined our family name with his little affair, so I can't do any worse damage. Plus, a change would be nice." *I'll also be able to hang out with you.*

He taps the countertop. "Lucky for you, my sister is leaving for a few weeks. You can take her bartending shifts. When she comes back, I'll have to move you to waitressing."

Shit. I forgot about Liz.

He laughs, as if catching on to my thoughts. "Don't worry. I told her to be nice."

Ugh, I'm not three. You don't have to force someone to be nice to me. "So, I'm hired?"

A slight smile hits his lips. "Why not? Looks like you scored yourself two jobs today."

"When do I start?" I ask eagerly.

"Whenever you want. I planned to ask Mikey to cover her shift tonight if you're game?"

"That works." It'll take my mind away from the chaos of my life. I give him a wide grin and bounce on my tiptoes.

He laughs. "Look at you, Jailbait. You're redecorating the pub, slinging drinks, and cleaning like a boss. Is there anything you can't do?"

"Keep a man."

"No. A man can't keep you."

"Any brilliant ideas yet?" Maliki asks, stopping next to me.

I grin. "You have no idea how many I'll pitch to you. You might regret hiring me."

"As long as you don't remove the authenticity and create a replica of the club you worked in the city, I trust you."

"I'd never."

With the little clients I've had, I've never forced my styles onto them. They tell me what they're looking for, and I bounce ideas off that.

"It needs to keep that easygoing vibe. And brace yourself … there's shopping."

"Shopping?" He groans dramatically. "Don't I write you a check, and you do all the work?"

"We can do it that way, but I don't suggest it. This is your bar, your baby, Maliki. I prefer you have a voice in the changes. You're looking at it for the rest of your life, not me." I signal to the empty bar. "I promise, nothing crazy." I clap him on the back. "We'll look at paint, furniture, decor. It'll be fun."

"Oh fuck, I'm going to regret this, aren't I?"

"Hiring me is one of the smartest moves you've ever made."

I proceed around the room, jotting down ideas, for an hour. When I'm finished, Maliki gives me a tour of the bar and explains everything that happens behind the scenes. I'm shown where all the alcohol is stocked, he introduces me to the kitchen staff, and I ask him countless questions.

When we're finished, he curves an arm around my shoulders and drags me into his side. "Welcome to the Down Home Pub team, princess."

I was smart, making my first night during the week. I'll have time to adapt before the weekend comes.

This is the only place in Blue Beech if you're looking for fun or seeking to drink away your sorrows. Like every bar, the pub has its heartbroken, drunks, and partiers.

The pub is nothing like the club I worked in. It's relaxed compared to crazy coeds who just turned old enough for their first shot of vodka. There was no relaxing at the club like it is at Down Home—no sharing a quiet, deep conversation.

The prying eyes come as soon as my shift starts. The pub is hosting a pool tournament tonight that usually brings in a decent crowd—meaning more people seeing me and the higher the chances my parents find out about my new job. I'm already dreading the phone call.

"You okay over there?" Maliki calls over from his side of the bar.

"I'd be better if someone ordered a drink from me," I answer with a sense of rejection.

Nearly every customer has ordered from Maliki, avoiding me as if I had the plague. Either they don't trust my drink-making skills—which is a joke, considering the drinks served here are basic as hell—or they're scared of my father finding out I served them. I've already spotted a few of his employees.

He nods in understanding. "Give it a few shifts. It was the same when I started working with my dad. They're comfortable with me."

I hold my hand up and cross my fingers. "Let's hope so. Otherwise, I'm coming over there and making their drinks without their permission."

"What the hell are you doing here?"

The glass I'm holding crashes to the floor when Liz steps into the bar area. Her hands are parked on her skinny hips, and her usual snarl toward me is darker. I lean down and scramble to pick up the pieces of glass.

Great. Already dropping shit on my first day.

Maliki comes up behind her, towering over her small frame, and his eyes set on me. "I gave her a job."

Liz backs away to face him and shakes her head. "Last time I checked, we weren't hiring."

"Someone needs to cover your shifts while you're in Florida," Maliki replies sharply.

I twist to grab a rag from a shelf to stop the glass from cutting me as I clean up and focus on their standoff.

"Have Mikey cover them," Liz says, raising her voice. "Not a girl who's probably never stepped foot behind a bar."

I rise and toss the shards of glass into the trash. "I worked in one of the busiest clubs in the state."

The glare shot in my direction tells me she either didn't expect that answer or for me to defend myself.

Her face tightens. "Of course you have, Barbie." She rolls her eyes, turning her back to me, and continues yelling at Maliki, "What happens when I come back?"

"She'll serve," Maliki bites out. His eyes drift to me in reassurance and then return to his sister. "Now, unless you have business to discuss other than my employees, I don't want to hear it."

"Whatever," Liz huffs out. "Fuck up our family business because you're thinking with your dick."

Maliki's jaw tightens in frustration. "It's *my* business, and I'll do with it as I fucking please."

"Wow," she draws out. "We're going there now, huh? I'll be back in a few weeks. Oh, and consider this my resignation."

She storms away, and Maliki is running his hand over the stubble of his jaw when his eyes snap to me.

I smooth down my tank top and rush out my words. "You can fire me. I don't want to cause friction between you and your sister."

He chuckles, the stress slowly fading from his face. "Appreciate it, but Liz *resigns* once a month."

He squats down to clean up the remnants of glass I missed. I didn't exactly want to crawl around on the floor by their legs.

He tosses the pieces into the trash can, and a relaxed smile crosses his face. "Now, get to work before I write you up."

I salute him, and he drifts back to his side of the bar.

"Your brother is going to kick your ass, and I'll take a Bud Light, please."

I shift my attention from Maliki to Gage—Kyle's best friend since childhood. They're partners on the Blue Beech police force.

I groan. "Please tell me he's not coming."

"Last I heard, he was," he answers with a smirk.

"Perfect."

I was so concerned about my parents' reaction to my job that I didn't think about my brothers. Rex, my younger one, won't give two shits about it. He'll probably ask me to make him a drink. But Kyle, as the overprotective older brother, won't be happy.

"I take it, he doesn't know about this new gig of yours?" Gage asks.

"Nope, so I'd appreciate it if you kept your lips sealed and led him to Maliki's side of the bar … or better yet, inform him the bar has shut down for the night and he can stay home." I smile, reach into the cooler for his beer, and hand it to him. "Don't forget my generous tip."

He slaps cash onto the bar. "This is a shitshow I can't wait to see."

I nod. "Facts."

"Then, why do it?"

"I need money to, I don't know, not starve to death."

"Seems legit." He swipes his beer from the bar. "I'll make sure to order my drinks from you, so you can have a cheeseburger tomorrow."

I roll my eyes. "Very funny."

His phone beeps. He reads the screen, laughs, and shows it to me. "Oh, he's most definitely coming."

Kyle: Is my sister working there?

My mouth turns dry, and I pour myself a water while groaning. "Great. The masses have already started gossiping."

He slaps his palm against the bar. "Good luck, little one."

I chug the water and refill my glass. Just as I'm about to finish it off, Kyle bursts through the crowd.

"You. Me. Talking now." He shoots his thumb toward the kitchen area.

My gaze darts toward Maliki, who gives me a silent nod, as if he knew Kyle would show up. I slam down my water and circle around the bar. Kyle is talking behind me, but I ignore him and take us to the back office.

I slam the door shut when we make it there. "Seriously? You're going to get me fired!" I haven't finished one shift, and I'm already bringing drama into the workplace.

My brother looks nothing like me. His hair is darker, taking after my father. He's built, strong, but he has nothing on Maliki.

Sorry, big brother.

He folds his arms over his chest and places his glare on me. "A. Maliki won't fire you. B. What the fuck is going on? Since when are you a bartender?"

I swallow hard, tears approaching. "Devin cheated on me."

"That son of a bitch," he hisses, straightening his stance. "Good."

"Good? How the hell is my husband cheating on me *good*?"

"I can kick his ass now. He's always annoyed me."

"Seriously, Kyle, don't touch him."

His face tightens. "I should've known he was a joke when he wore loafers to a barbeque." He balls up his fist. "I'm going to kill him."

Even though he works in law enforcement, he'd have no problem roughing Devin up. Being the oldest, he's protective of our family, especially now with everything that happened. His relationship with a woman who carries serious baggage has made him more vigilant.

"You're not killing anyone," I say. "Last I heard, inmates don't like police officers in their block. Do you know how bored you'd be when they stuck you in solitary confinement?"

My joke eases some of the tension on his face, and he blows out a breath that calms him further.

"Thanks for the tip, little sister, but I won't go to prison for punching him a few times."

"I want it to be done and move on with my life."

"So, you found out your husband cheated, and instead of coming to your family, you ran to Maliki?"

That does sound crappy. It takes me a moment to reply to his question. "Yep," I finally croak out.

He's mentioned how much time I spend with Maliki several times, and I've always blown him off—the same as with everyone.

His shoulders loosen, and with each minute that passes, the more he eases. "You're in better hands with Maliki anyway."

"Me and Maliki … we're not—"

He cracks a smile. "Not yet."

I shove his chest. "Hey, I'm still married—only a few days separated."

"I'm not saying marry the dude. He's an awesome guy, a good friend to you, and from what I've heard, he's a wonderful fucking boss." He whistles and jerks his head toward the door. "Now, come on. Let's see how well you serve a beer."

I glance back at him. "With extra spit."

———

"Ki, I'm out of here!" Tamara calls out while scooping up her tips and shoving them into her purse. "What time do you want me to come over tomorrow?"

I drop my towel on the bar, and my blood turns colder than the beers chilling in the cooler behind me.

Excuse me?

Tamara is one of the gorgeous waitresses. Her boobs are bigger than mine, her curves are sexier, and I don't know anything about her. She's an outsider who lives in the next town over. She also has taken up flirting with Maliki as a second job.

My attention shoots to Maliki, who's on his side of the bar, ridding it of empty glasses and baskets of bar food.

He takes off his hat and scratches his head. "Tomorrow doesn't work. Let's try again later this week."

She nods, smiling brightly at him. "Just text me."

She uses three fingers to wave good-bye to me, and I turn the dirty look I'm giving her into a fake smile while doing the same wave. She doesn't deserve my animosity, but I can't stand watching her flirt with him.

Maliki walks her out and locks the bar when he comes back in. That's one thing I respect about him. He walks his female employees to their cars at night. He cares about the people who work for him.

"Why are you shooting murderous glares at my waitress?" he asks.

I pull in a breath and set my attention on cleaning the bar. "Do I need to find somewhere to go *later this week* when she comes over?"

"She cleans the apartment."

"Oh." The annoyed expression remains on my face. His answer still hasn't put me at ease.

"Why do you still look pissed, even after I explained that?"

"Does she do more than *clean your apartment*? Is there a particular time I should steer clear of the apartment, so you and her can have privacy *to clean*?"

"All she does is *clean,* so there's no need for privacy. Is there a reason we're having this conversation?"

I shrug. "Just in case we have people over to—"

"Ahh," he cuts in. "In case I have someone over to fuck." He leans back against a pub table, crosses his arms, and releases a laughter filled with edge. "Are you going to have guys over to fuck? Do we need to set up schedules?"

"What? No." I stare at him, baffled.

"Then, why is this coming up?"

"*I'm* not planning on sleeping with anyone in your apartment."

"Appreciate that."

"I don't want to be a buzzkill for you and … your women."

"I won't bring a woman home while you're there, okay?"

"So, what?" I grimace. "You'll go to their house?"

"Why are you asking so many questions?"

"I told you, I'm curious."

"Do you not want someone to come over because you don't want me with anyone else other than you?" He tilts his head to the side.

Yes. "How would you feel if I was going to another man's house and sexing it up?" I mirror his head tilt.

"You can do whatever you want, Sierra." He shoots me a frustrated look. "You've done that for a while now."

CHAPTER TEN

MALIKI

"Now that you've slept on it, how was your first shift?" I ask Sierra, strolling into the kitchen. "Still want to work with me?"

She's wearing a tight, ribbed tank top with a sports bra underneath that shows just the right amount of cleavage and black leggings. Her blonde hair is swept back into a ponytail, and her face is makeup free—my favorite look on her.

The view of Sierra early in the morning is the best goddamn view ever.

Scratch that. Even though I'll never see it, I'm sure the best goddamn view of her is waking up next to her in bed.

Thank fuck she gave up on asking me irrelevant questions about Tamara and bringing other women home when we finished closing last night. I'd never pull that shit with her here. From what it seems, Sierra believes I've screwed every woman who's flirted with me at the bar. Little does she know. I've wanted to punch every man who looks at her with desire while ordering his drinks. As the night turned later, people grew more comfortable, heading to her side of the bar.

She cracks an egg into a skillet. "I liked it, so no quitting from this girl." She grabs a bottle of coconut water and takes a long swig. "Egg?"

"Sure."

She cracks another egg. "How do you like them?"

"However you want to make them. I'm not picky."

"What if I add pickles and mustard to them?"

I scrunch up my face. *The fuck?* "Do you add pickles and mustard to them?"

"No, but you didn't know that. That could have been how I liked my eggs, and then you'd be stuck with them for breakfast."

I chuckle. "You are the most random person I know."

She grins and holds up her spatula. "Over easy eggs coming right up."

"Sans pickles and mustard?"

"You shall see," she sings out.

I circle the island to start a cup of coffee in the Keurig. "How'd the chat with your brother go?" I talked to Kyle after his conversation with Sierra and assured him I'd look out for her.

"It surprised him, is all."

"And your parents?"

"I have three missed calls from my father and eight from my mom. They know something. Whether it's my new job or my leaving Devin, I have no idea."

"You'll have to tell them eventually."

"I know. I'm visiting them after this afternoon. Devin is out of town this weekend with his father for a work thing. I texted Kyle this morning and asked if he could help me move my things out." She stops. "Shoot, I forgot to ask for my schedule. Do I work tonight?"

I shake my head. "Nope. We have the night off."

"Oh, cool." She places the eggs on the two plates next to her and slides one along with a fork in front of me. "Do you have any plans?"

"I'm having beers with some friends."

She leans in, not bothering to touch her food, and places her elbows on the counter. "Do I know them?"

She doesn't realize it, but her stance is giving me an even better view of her cleavage. She doesn't have large boobs, but they're also not small. My hands wouldn't be full if I played with them.

I shove another bite into my mouth, hoping it distracts me from brainstorming about the things I could do to those breasts.

When I glance back to her face, she's waiting for me to answer. *Shit.* I forgot she'd asked me a question.

"My friend Cohen."

She flinches. "The guy from Twisted Fox?"

"Yes, that guy."

She nods back and bites into her lower lip, looking disappointed. "Ahh ... well, have fun."

CHAPTER ELEVEN
SIERRA

"I can't believe Devin is so stupid," my mom says, squeezing a lemon into a pitcher of lemonade. Even though her face is twisted in disgust, you'd guess she was referring to a sunny day. She has the sweetest voice I've ever heard, and no matter how angry she gets, it never rises or changes. "What a little asshole."

I crack a smile. "Oh my God!" I smack her arm as I walk past her and snag a cookie. "Mom!"

"What?" she asks, wiping her hands down her flowered apron. "He hurt you."

She was waiting for answers as soon as I walked through the front door. She'd made my favorite cookies—cookies and cream cheesecake —and she was starting on the lemonade—also my favorite. She consoles through stomachs, claiming cookies and hot meals always make someone feel *a little* happier.

Nancy Lane is the sweetest woman you'll ever meet. If someone is sick, she's at their doorstep with chicken soup. If a family is in need of charity, she not only pulls out her checkbook, but she's also at the family's side, taking a list of anything they need.

I didn't bother taking my time to break the news. I blurted out, "Devin cheated," when I walked in.

She knew what to do—immediately wrapping me up in a hug as I cried for the ending of my marriage. Then, she told me she had cookies waiting for me.

She was right.

It did make me feel better.

Her calling Devin a little asshole puts a cherry on top.

Nancy Lane is not someone who curses on the regular.

She frowns. "I was so excited for you to get married. Maybe I pushed you too hard, and you should've waited. I should've known he was wrong for you." She sniffles. "Mothers are supposed to know these things."

I kiss her cheek. "Don't worry. I threw something at his head." I bite into a cookie and savor its yumminess. "Healthy communication at its finest."

She circles her fingers around the handle of the pitcher, grabbing a few glasses, and I snag the plate of cookies while following her to the kitchen table. We sit down where my sister, Cassidy, is texting on her phone. She's home from college—most likely so that my mom can do her laundry and send her back with food, so she doesn't starve.

"Did you ask him why he did it?" my mom asks.

"He slept with someone because he was thinking with the scrawny thing between his legs. That's the only explanation I have." I pour myself a glass of lemonade. "No, wait. He told me it wasn't so bad because it happened at a *bachelor party*."

Cassidy drops her phone. "Ew. That's really what happens at bachelor parties? I thought that was just in the movies." She shudders. "Devin seriously sucks."

"No, honey," my mom says. "That isn't what happens at all bachelor parties."

Cassidy and I took after our mom in the looks department—blonde hair, lighter eyes, somewhat on the short side.

Even for her age, my mom is beautiful. She's made it a full-time job to run charities, help people, work in the kitchen, and keep up with her appearance. She wears makeup and dresses up more than I do.

"Never get married," I tell Cassidy, snatching another cookie. It seems leaving my husband has led me to turn to carbs, making Devin an even bigger bastard.

"Hey now, marriage is a beautiful thing," my mom argues. "It's just … sadly, some aren't respectful to their vows."

I reach out and capture her hand, lightly squeezing it, and see the compassion in her eyes. Right now, we're both suffering through infidelities, but I'd take on my mom's hurt over mine any day. Her heart is too big for this pain.

I cringe, wondering but too afraid to ask how she can look at dad, knowing what he did. I always saw her as this strong woman and was so proud when she threatened my father with a divorce. Then, I cried the day she told me she changed her mind and was taking him back. As much as I love my father, she didn't deserve that, and he doesn't deserve a woman as amazing as her.

"Now that I've decided I'm never getting married," Cassidy says, shooting her attention to me, "what's going on with you and the hot bartender? Eight people asked me about it at the gym this morning." She pours herself a glass of lemonade. "And let me put it out there that Maliki Bridges is so much hotter than Devin."

"Oh my God. People your age are talking about me?"

She shrugs. "You know it's a small town, and you're getting it on with the town's hottest bachelor. People will talk."

"Cassidy!" my mom shrieks, her tone having a sprinkle of warning in it.

"What?" she asks. "I bet he wouldn't cheat at a bachelor party."

I point to her bookbag on the floor. "Go study."

She shakes her head, pulls out her ponytail, and glides her hand through her hair. "No, this conversation is so much juicier than Anatomy."

My mom's awareness slides back to me, her features loaded with concern. "Now that you've scared your sister out of marriage, we need to talk about your new job. Devin said you quit his father's company, and word is, you've not only switched jobs, but also moved in with Maliki?" She touches her face and pauses, as if she's thinking. "Now, honey, you know I don't judge, but we didn't spend thousands of dollars in education for you to end up working in a hole-in-the-wall bar. I don't look down on those in the service industry, but I never want my daughter around drunk people. I've read plenty of crime books. Most serial killers prey on women at bars."

"Yep! I just saw this Netflix documentary. That crap is *creepy*," Cassidy cuts in and shuts her mouth when my mom shoots her a disapproving look.

"Cassidy, go study, text, take selfies, something," she says.

She raises her hands high in surrender. "All right, I'll keep my mouth shut, but I'm staying. I love hearing lectures that aren't pointed in my direction."

"Mom, it's a transition period until I find another job," I say in my best voice of reassurance. "I'm using my degree and renovating the pub, so technically, that's my job. The bartending is for extra cash to get a new place."

"You can stay here. Your room is always open. Plus, you know your father and I will help you with any financial issues you're having."

"I'm a grown woman. I'm not moving in with my parents *or* taking money from you."

"Can I volunteer as tribute with the cash offer?" Cassidy interjects.

Instead of answering her, my mom keeps her focus on me. "Why not? I make amazing banana nut bread, you'll always have a hot breakfast, and I'm sure I keep a home cleaner than a bachelor."

"I'll let you know if I change my mind, okay? But right now, I need to do this on my own. It's time for me to figure out this new chapter in my life."

"You're not on your own if you're living with another man." Her words are gentle, but her blow is harsh. She's trying her hardest to sound sweet, but it's what she's feeling at the moment.

"We're friends."

"I know you, honey. You wouldn't just move in with someone like that."

"We have separate bedrooms. It's nothing different than when I lived in the dorms at college. I'm renting a room from him. That's it."

Cassidy snorts. "For now."

"You're right. I'm sure you weren't an angel in college." Mom wiggles her finger at me. "And you have fun explaining that to your father. Maliki's family doesn't have the best reputation in town."

"Right now, neither does our family. Maliki is a loyal man, and I trust him more than I did my own husband."

———

Kyle scrubs his hands together and surveys the living room of my condo—well, *old* condo. "Is that it?" He peeks over at me. "We're leaving everything else, right?"

"Yes. All I want is my personal stuff," I answer.

Rex groans and thrusts his arms out toward the living room. "Come on, sis. Take the TV. The couch. *Something.* That cheating bastard didn't pay for all this shit himself."

He's right. I paid for half of everything—the down payment, the furniture, the bills. When the divorce papers are drawn up, I'll insist we sell the condo and split the profit.

Easy-peasy.

Ending this divorce shouldn't be a challenge.

"I don't have anywhere to put it," I answer. Nor do I want the memories of shit I shared with Devin. I'd rather buy new furniture.

"You know," Rex sings, "I wouldn't mind storing that sixty-inch flat screen in my living room." He shrugs. "I'm that nice of a brother."

I roll my eyes. "*Fine,* you can have the *bedroom* TV."

"Hell yeah," Rex says. His gaze darts around the room again. "What about the fine china? I could use something classier than paper plates."

"*Oh my God,* you can have the dishes."

"And the fridge?"

"Jesus, you're not taking the fridge." I push his shoulder. "Come on. I'll treat you to pizza for being the muscles."

"Pizza sounds awesome," Rex says, snapping his fingers. "And speaking of pizza, you have to let your baby brother have that kick-ass pizza oven."

"What the hell?" Kyle says. "That was my wedding gift."

Rex slaps Kyle's stomach. "If I recall, you told her you had the same one and fucking loved it. Your ass doesn't need another."

"*Fine*, you can have the pizza oven too," I tell him.

———

"How'd you find out Devin cheated?" Rex asks, taking a bite of his pizza.

Fred's Pizzeria is the only pizza joint in town, but even if it wasn't, it's still where I'd always come. They have the best pizza, subs, and garlic bread. If you're looking to stuff yourself with carbs—which, apparently, is my new hobby—Fred's is the place to go.

I saw the eyes on us when we walked in. That, or I'm so paranoid that I'm convinced anyone who looks in my direction knows what happened with Devin, as if a neon sign were shining above my head.

I take a drink before answering, "He was at a bachelor party and wasn't smart enough to know that people talk. He had a restroom break with another woman, and when they came out, it was obvious what had happened."

Rex smooths a hand over his mouth in an attempt to hide a smirk. "He could've been drunk and needed help finding his small dick."

I tear off a piece of crust and toss it at him, giving him the dirtiest look I can muster. "I hate you."

He holds up his hand. "Jesus, no more bread-throwing, crazy woman. You know I'm kidding." He leans back and relaxes in his booth. "I was never a Devin fan, so no love lost there. He was lame, and hopefully, your next boyfriend"—he stops to dramatically cough and covers his mouth—"Maliki"—another cough—"has somewhat of a sense of humor."

I chew on my bottom lip. "Hey, he wasn't that lame." I ignore the Maliki comment. Everyone is calling Devin lame, so what does that make me for marrying him? Lame, too?

Rex snags his drink and takes a sip. "You were complacent with him. He did what you wanted … had no balls."

"He had enough balls to cheat," I fire back.

"He hardly challenged you, and I know from growing up with your mean ass that you love being challenged. Sure, you liked him, but he was the easy way, not *love*, love."

Frustration rattles through me. Not at my brother, but at being so blind. Marrying Devin was a mistake.

I level my elbow on Kyle's shoulder, who's next to me in the booth, and narrow my eyes on Rex across from us. "Okay, Dr. Drew, how are you such an expert on relationships? You've never even had a serious girlfriend."

"Coaches don't play, sister." He shrugs and pops a pepperoni in his mouth.

I roll my eyes. "You're dying old and alone."

"No, I'll have my booty calls at my funeral, crying at my casket, sad that their favorite screw bit the big one."

I glance over at Kyle. "Swear to God, you're taking care of him when the nursing home kicks him out for bad behavior."

My arm falls when Kyle shifts to look at me. "Nope, dear sister. He'll shack up with you, considering you'll both be single."

"I hate you too," I grumble, pushing my hand over his hair, messing it up as he attempts to pull away.

"Where are we moving your shit, by the way?" Rex asks.

"You moved my stuff all day and never thought to ask that?" I reply.

Kyle chuckles, shaking his head. He borrowed Gage's truck, and after dinner, we're dropping off what I'm not taking to Maliki's at the storage unit I rented.

A wide grin spreads across Rex's face. "I was too busy staking out the residence for shit I wanted you to give me."

I roll my eyes.

"You still haven't answered my question," Rex continues. "Are you moving home? I have an extra bedroom at my place if you want to crash there."

"Hang out with your college buddies?" I ask. "I appreciate the offer, baby bro, but that's a hard no."

"You know the offer still stands to stay with me," Kyle says.

"Your place is full," I say. "Not to mention, you have so much happening with Chloe and Trey. It'll be uncomfortable for everyone there."

Chloe is Kyle's girlfriend, and Trey is her nephew. Trey is also our half-brother. Chloe never told Kyle that my dad was Trey's father, even after they started dating. Our family found out at the same time as everyone in town. All thanks to Chloe's sister, Monica's boyfriend shouting it out for everyone to hear. That was the night I went to Maliki. The night our family changed. Now, Trey comes around from time to time. Kyle and him are close, given they live together, and Rex bombarded himself into Trey's life, wanting a relationship with him. Rex felt bad for him, that he'd been handed such a shitty life, and wanted to change that. My brothers have taken him under their wing.

"So, Mom and Dad's it is," Rex says, sipping his Coke.

I shake my head.

His lips form a wide grin. "I know where this is headed. You're moving in with your side boy toy. I dig it." He dramatically waggles his eyebrows.

"Shut up. I don't have a side boy toy."

Rex snorts. "Who is Maliki to you then, huh? Even when you were with Devin, you had a thing for him."

"We'll be roommates for a minute. That's it," I answer.

"Holy shit, so you *are* moving in with him."

"It isn't like that," I argue.

"Keep your head straight, sis," Kyle says. "Maliki is cool, but as long as I've known him, he doesn't do committed relationships. You're already dealing with a broken heart, and I have a feeling a broken heart from him will be harder on you." He shakes his head. "Ki won't let it get that far though, so you shouldn't have anything to worry about."

Kyle's warning tugs at my heart. He's not only right about Maliki not doing a committed relationship, but he's also spot-on with how Maliki has the ability to pulverize my heart.

He did it that night I found him in his office.

It's a bad idea, moving in with him, but any opportunity I get to be around him, I'll take, consequences be damned.

"Not to mention, you'd be hooking up with your roommate and *boss*," Rex adds.

I groan. "Can we stop talking about my love life now and move on to someone else's?"

"Trust me, you don't want to talk about mine," Kyle says. "We'll be here all night."

I smile over at my big brother. "But you and Chloe are happy now, so that's all that matters." I clap his shoulder. "How are things with the adoption agency coming?"

He releases a stressed breath, gritting his teeth. "We're trying, but with her family's history, it's proving difficult." A grim expression falls across his face.

This isn't the place to discuss his relationship.

So, on to Rex.

"Looks like we're moving on to you, little brother."

Kyle snorts. "The only love life he has is the one with his hand."

"Lies," I sing out, tilting my head toward Rex. "He's going to marry Carolina."

Kyle snorts again. "Carolina is too smart to marry him."

"I'm right here, assholes," Rex chimes in, furrowing his brows. "And no, I'm not marrying Carolina."

"Kyle is right," I say. "She is too smart to marry you. You should've taken your chance in high school, but it's probs too late now."

"We never dated because we're best friends," Rex grits out.

Carolina is a touchy subject for him. They've been best friends since high school, and he's more protective of her than he is of his own sisters. I've never seen my brother care about someone so much. There's no doubt the love for each other is there between them, but Rex is scared to ruin their friendship.

"Best friends who secretly love each other." I angle my gaze toward him. "You just wait. I'm calling it right here, right now. You'll be with her before you hit your thirties."

"I don't know," Kyle says. "I think he ruined his chance."

"Both of you can fuck off," Rex grumbles.

I come to the Twisted Fox when I need a beer and peace away from my customers. You can't enjoy a relaxing drink in your own bar. Clients and employees are demanding even if you tell them you're off for the night.

That's why Cohen and I have a thing.

I come here when I need away from the chaos.

Down Home is his destination when he needs space from here.

It's like our bars are friends, too.

Tonight, neither one of us is working, so I sit down at a table. Cohen comes strolling through the bar, navigating around his customers, holding a beer in each hand. He slides one to me, twists his stool around, and straddles it backward, resting his arms on the back.

"How's everything at the bar?" is the first question he asks.

It's our version of, *What's up, man?*

"Busy as hell," I answer. "We're out of the red and pulling in a respectful revenue."

I finally started turning a decent profit two years ago. I'd managed a bar before this. The owner had given me complete control, and I doubled the revenue, reduced expenses, and raised his Yelp rating two stars. I worked myself to death at that bar for one goal: to own my own.

Everything changed when Liz called, crying.

She'd rooted through my father's mail, and what she discovered wasn't pretty. He had the bar in a financial mess, held countless loans and liens against it, and if he didn't write a hefty check to the bank in seven days, he'd lose it. It wasn't my issue, was what I told her. I didn't want the bar, didn't want to move back to Blue Beech, didn't want to clean up our father's goddamn mess.

Liz was determined to keep it in the family and decided she'd try to take over. She tried and struggled—struggled to secure loans with her less than average credit score and lack of funds. I love my sister and didn't want to see her kill herself to make the bar work, so I paid the debt and took over.

Pissed, I'd hardly spoken a word to my father when he sold it to me, but now, I'm glad I did it.

Cohen shifts in his stool, making himself comfortable. "Remember when we talked about launching a bar together?" He shuts his eyes in recollection. "Look at us now, owning our own and some might say in competition with each other."

"Shut the fuck up. You're not my competition," I say, kicking his foot with my Converse.

Cohen and our friend, Archer, asked me for the go-ahead prior to opening the bar. Some might be pissed if their friends opened a bar thirty minutes away from theirs, but I was happy for their success. Cohen and I had dreamed of having our own business, and here we are, fulfilling that goal. Plus, I get to hang out with my best friend all the time.

He shrugs. "We should revisit the idea sometime."

"It's poor timing right now. My hands are full, getting the place back up and running. Plus, I'm renovating and upgrading my shit."

Not only am I having Sierra redo the face of the bar, but I'm also purchasing new kegs, kitchen appliances, and upgrading my taps. I'm not the founding father of Down Home, but I can still make it mine. I've considered a remodel for a while, but hiring Sierra has gotten the ball rolling.

He nods slightly while grinning. "That's awesome, man. I'm fucking happy for you."

He raises his beer into a cheers motion, and I clank mine against his.

I met Cohen through a woman I dated. He dated her best friend. He worked at another bar in the city, a lame-ass one, and I hired him where I worked. That was eight years ago, and we've been friends since. If there's anyone who understands me, it's him. We grew up in bars, and now, we eat, sleep, and breathe our businesses.

He snaps his fingers a few times and grabs his beer. "Oh, I meant to ask you, what happened with the chick and cheating husband?" He takes a long swig of his drink.

Oh shit.

I didn't think of Cohen asking me about Sierra. I came here to clear my head and get a grip on the situation.

There goes that.

"She, uh … moved into my place."

He spits out the beer in his mouth, liquid spewing on his lap and the table. He snatches a few napkins and cleans the mess, laughing. "Are you shitting me?"

I shake my head.

"You've never let anyone move into your place. Your mother-fucking ass wouldn't even let one of our best friends move in."

"Her losing her place of residence wasn't her choice. Finn, on the other hand, was kicked out as a result of banging his roommate's sister."

Finn is a friend and also works at Twisted Fox.

He rolls his eyes. "Yeah, yeah. Now, let's return to the fun subject of you and your hot new roomie. I'm sure you'll have no problem screwing the hurt from her cheating husband right out of her."

I reach forward to push his shoulder. "We're not fucking. We're simply roommates, and she's helping me renovate the bar."

He drags his hand through his hair. "You must know her pretty damn well to let her move in. You were also pissed enough that you beat the dude's ass like he'd just cheated on your little sister. Is she a friend's sister? Why do you care so much about her?"

I contemplate my next move and scratch my cheek while looking away from him. "Do you remember when I used to tell you about the teenage brat who kept sneaking into the bar?"

He smirks. "Holy shit! That's her?"

I nod. "That's her."

He smacks his knee. "Man, I told you that something would happen with her someday. She's not even your type."

I massage my neck, suddenly feeling tense. "I have a type?"

"You for sure have a type."

I raise a brow.

"Emotionally unavailable, like you, is your type. Women who are fine without wanting more from you. I don't get that vibe from her. Hell man, she's married."

"Soon-to-be divorced."

"You sure about that?"

I nod. "Positive."

I don't tell him how well I know Sierra—that I know how fucking strong she is and that she won't take Devin's punk ass back.

At least, I hope not.

———

I toss my keys onto the kitchen island and head into the living room where I hear the TV playing. I shove my hands into my pockets when I see Sierra slouched on the couch. Her legs are drawn to her chest, and she's staring at the screen as if it were the most fascinating thing in the world.

It's a fucking vacuum infomercial.

She peeks back at me over her shoulder, her eyes red and puffy.

Shit.

"You were out late," she deadpans.

I should've canceled my plans with Cohen and stayed with her, but damn, she seemed fine. It surprised me with how relaxed she's been the past few days, given her situation. I just found out Sierra is a closet crier. She waits until she's alone to expose her wounds.

I swallow a few times, guilt rising up my spine, and level my voice. "It's midnight. I'm normally not in bed until four in the morning. This is early for me."

That only grants me a sullen look. "Did you have fun with your friends?"

I'm sure I had more fun than her. She looks like someone ran over her dog.

I proceed further into the room to face her. "It ended up being only me and Cohen hanging out."

The initial plan was drinking in the city with our other friends, but I didn't want to leave Sierra alone all night. When I told Cohen I wanted something more chill, he stayed behind with me.

She repeatedly nods. It almost makes her look like she's rocking back and forth.

"What about you? Did you do anything?"

Her face falls more. "I talked to my mom, and then my brothers helped me move." She rubs at her tired eyes. "Other than having my entire life overturned, nothing."

She needs a friend, and I wonder why she didn't call Ellie. That chick seems to be the Robin to her Batman.

Looks like I'm her Robin tonight.

I crash on the other end of the couch, giving her plenty of space. "Did you get everything out of the condo?"

She chews on her lower lip to block it from trembling. "I did."

"And have you talked to him?"

"He's called a few times, but I've dodged his calls. He knows about me working at the bar and had the guts to accuse *me* of cheating on him with you." She drops her legs and snorts. "I didn't even bother replying. I hope he thinks I'm screwing your brains out, so he can feel as stupid as I do."

My head jerks back. "Screwing my brains out, huh?" My dick stirs. *Why does she have to say shit like that?*

"You know what I mean."

"It can be arranged, if you'd like."

Our eyes briefly meet until she breaks contact by rolling hers. "Whatever. I annoy you."

"True. You're right. I shouldn't screw an annoying woman's brains out."

"So, is that what you were doing tonight?"

"Screwing an annoying woman's brains out? Negative."

"What *were* you doing then?"

"Hanging out with Cohen."

She sucks in what sounds like an aggravated breath. "You already said that." She yawns. "I've had a long day. I'll see you later."

I capture her arm when she gets up, stopping her. "Don't bullshit me, Sierra."

She sinks back against the cushions. "What are you talking about?"

"I'm talking about your rounded-ass questions you ask in some code that I'm supposed to understand, and then you get pissed when I don't speak in code right back. I had drinks with a friend."

"So you told me."

"Why are you upset about that?"

"I'm not."

"Bullshit."

She throws her head back. "I don't know why I am, honestly." She shrugs, tears hitting her eyes.

"Again, speaking in code."

"I hoped maybe as roommates, we'd hang out or something." She shakes her head and slaps her forehead. "Oh my God, that sounds so stupid and immature."

I stand, walk to the kitchen, and grab two beers from the fridge. My next stop is the pantry where I snag a bag of kettle corn and chips. I reach into the freezer, pull out a container of ice cream, and open the drawer for two spoons.

"What are you doing?" she draws out, her attention bobbing from me and the snacks clutched in my hold when I return.

I plop back down on the couch, closer to her this time, and the chips fall between us. "If you want to hang out with me, just say it." I hand her a spoon and the tub of ice cream. "I bought this at the store earlier. Mint chocolate chip is still your favorite, right?"

She nods as a blush hits her cheeks.

"Good. Now, pick something to watch. I'm exhausted, and I can't promise to stay awake long, but I'm here. I'll always be here."

CHAPTER THIRTEEN
SIERRA

Tonight is my first weekend shift.

Maliki briefed me this morning on what to expect. A live band is performing, so no doubt we'll be busy. He answered my last-minute questions. We reviewed drinks and prices. I'd used a cheat sheet my first night, but I won't have time for that.

He'll change the ice and kegs—thank God. The last time I attempted to change a keg, it doused me, and I smelled like stale booze all night.

Maliki is on his side of the bar, prepping his area, when I get downstairs. Even though it's not that long of a bar, when working, it's almost like we're in two different worlds. I slip my bottle opener into my jean shorts pocket and start setting up my space.

The jukebox plays in the background as I slice my garnishes, restock my straws, and get all my supplies in place. Everything needs organized, so this shift slips by with ease. So many people have shown their doubt about me working here, and I need to prove I know what I'm doing.

People don't come to Down Home only for the drinks and kick-ass bar food. What brings them here is the live music, events, atmosphere, and of course, the old-fashioned dance floor. I've witnessed sad souls with downcast eyes walk onto that dance floor, and when they return, their smiles could light up the room.

The atmosphere unwinds you.

That's why I love it here so much.

Well, that, *and* Maliki.

I don't stress about fitting in here like I do at a benefit dinner with my parents or when hanging out with Devin at a country club. My hair can be messy, my clothes casual, and no one bats an eye.

There are a few customers already here, mainly on Maliki's side, and when a customer plops in front of me, I take his order.

Jack and Coke. Bacon cheeseburger and onion rings.

I yell his order to the kitchen and start his drink. After handing it to him, I return to cutting my lemons.

"You look fucking gorgeous tonight."

I get a whiff of his cologne when Maliki stands behind me. I love how he smells. It's clean but masculine. I focus on my task, frazzled, and don't glance back at him. Every muscle in my body convulses as his chest hits my back, and I shiver when his cold hand brushes my hair away from it, his fingers slightly running along my neck.

Oh my God. Oh my God.

I squeeze my thighs together, and my heart clunks against my ribs. If only I were brave enough to grind against him, but there are people around, and public rejection doesn't sound like a great time. I grip the knife in one hand and use the other to clutch the bar while struggling to control my breathing.

I don't know what to expect when I turn around to face him.

Maliki retreats a step, his eyes wide and focused on my fingers

I meet his gaze and realize I'm still holding the knife.

"Shit," I mutter, dropping it onto the bar. "Totally wasn't about to go all stabby on you." I sigh and run my hands down my shorts. "And thank you."

I'm wearing cutoff jean shorts that my mom would call inappropriate and have my bar shirt tied around my waist, revealing a hint of midriff. A shiny, new pair of pink Doc Martens are on my feet.

"I have to make those tips," I add.

He chuckles. "I see. You're trying to steal my cash because you're cute."

He doesn't seem anywhere as worked up as I am about our little encounter. Meanwhile, my heart is banging batshit crazy.

"Damn straight." How I'm speaking is beyond me.

I bite into my tongue, holding myself back from mentioning how hot he looks tonight with his hat, torn jeans, and boots. I don't because it'd make things awkward. Maliki knows how to play off his flirting. Me? I'm a disaster. It always comes out wrong. We're working together all night, so it's in my best interest to not make it weird.

But he isn't making it easy with the whispers in the ear and touching.

He levels his eyes on me, as if he's about to break news I don't want to hear. "There's a bachelor party tonight. I would've given you a heads-up, but I just found out. You cool with that?"

"Of course." I pat his chest a few times and fake a smile. I'm not *exactly* okay with it, but I'll deal. "I'm a professional, Maliki. I mean, I might kick a dude in the junk and kick him out if I see him cheating on his wife, but other than that, I'm peachy." I shrug, grab my knife, and slam it into the cutting board.

He laughs, smoothing his hand over his jaw. "Please don't kick anyone out. That's my job, remember?"

"I learned from the best."

Our attention flashes to the opening of the kitchen when someone calls his name.

"Let me know if you need anything," Maliki says. "I have all your stuff in your area, so you won't need to search for anything."

"Maliki, you don't have to do that. It's *my* job."

"And?"

"You don't help Mikey set up his space. People will think you're giving me preferential treatment."

"Sierra, if someone *doesn't* think I'm giving you preferential treatment, they're dumb and should be fired."

"I'm serious," I whine with frustration.

He smiles, showing off his bright white teeth. "Look, you're my friend, roommate, and … someone I like to look after." He glances to the ceiling, either searching for the right word or asking God for an answer. "Little sister?"

Oh, hell no.

He didn't just pull the little-sister card.

"Oh my God. Never refer to me as your little sister again."

"That's not how I meant it. What I'm saying is, it's obvious I help you as much as I can and watch over you." He shrugs. "That's it."

"While I appreciate that, I don't want other employees talking shit about me."

"They won't." He chuckles. "Not to your face."

I kick my boots against the floor. "I already know they hate me."

His voice lowers. "They thought it was weird." Irritation flashes along his features. "Just like I'm protective of you, so are my employees of me. Not as much, but they are."

I blink at him. "Protective of you for what?"

"Over me hanging out with a woman who has a boyfriend at home."

His face falls as if he remembers every time I left him and went to Devin. Shame crushes through me.

Why did I do that to him? Why did I do that to myself?

He clears his throat. "I need to get back to work. Holler if you need anything."

He walks away, his strides long, as if he wants to put as much distance between us as he can.

Guilt, so much fucking guilt, shatters through me.

I've already spilled a beer on myself and messed up three orders.

One waitress keeps shooting me death glares.

The other is giving Maliki all her orders after my screwup.

So much for proving myself tonight.

I'm blaming it on my conversation with Maliki. It completely threw me off my game.

I know when the bachelor party arrives. They come straight in my direction and are annoying as hell. With every shot, they have a stupid saying.

"Here's to losing your freedom!"

"To having your balls on a leash!"

"To having only one pussy for the rest of your life!"

I'm positive Satan invented bachelor parties.

I'm never getting married again.

CHAPTER FOURTEEN
MALIKI

The bar is slammed tonight.

Money is flowing.

People are enjoying themselves.

Normally, I wouldn't complain.

It's what you want in your business.

What I don't want is every motherfucking man flirting and drooling over my new bartender, roommate, my … whatever the fuck Sierra is to me.

Friend?

I shake my head, attempting to clear my thoughts, but it doesn't help.

Shit.

Now, I wish I hadn't started the *no drinking on the job* rule.

My night is a circle of actions.

Ask someone what they want. Look at Sierra. Make their drink. Look at Sierra. Give them their drink. Look at Sierra.

She's smiling, and the men love it. No doubt she's killing it with tips, but she isn't overly flirty or eating up the attention. What drives me insane is that they perceive her friendliness as interest.

Yeah, fucking right.

I've seen Sierra flirt.

I know what it looks like when she's interested in someone.

Because she does it with me.

She's flirted with me since her illegal ass sauntered into my bar. At first, it was almost comical. She couldn't flirt worth shit, and though I was drawn to her, I never planned on anything developing with us. She was legal and, even though she tried to hide it, innocent.

So damn innocent.

Some men love innocence.

Me? Not so much.

Innocence leads to confusion.

Innocence wants more from you than a simple fuck here and there.

Innocence gets their heart broken.

So, yeah, that's why I steer clear of innocent blondes.

Although, Sierra isn't exactly innocent anymore.

I've done a decent job of controlling myself until I see a guy take hold of her elbow. Sierra jerks away, and he grabs her again—this time with a creepy-ass smirk.

All I see is red as I drop the glass in my hand and charge over to them. I'm at her side in seconds, and I reach across the bar to shove him away.

"What the fuck, dude?" the guy yells, catching his balance.

I point to him. "Keep your filthy-ass hands off my employees."

He gets closer, and the booze on his breath reeks. "Dude, I was only talking to her."

I don't have time for this bullshit. "You order your drinks from me the rest of the night, do you hear me?"

The scrawny guy perks up his chest—an attempt to look intimidating, but it does the opposite. "How do you know she doesn't want me to touch her? She's been teasing me all night."

Sierra rolls her eyes, not bothering to look my way, and grabs the guy another beer. "Here." She hands it to him. "I'll add it to your tab."

"Thanks, gorgeous." He winks at her and turns his attention to me. He tips his glass my way, swings around, and walks away.

Sierra smacks her arm into my stomach to block me from jumping across the bar and kicking his ass.

Her eyes are narrowed when she looks at me. "This is your bar, Maliki. You can't pull that with customers."

"I can if they're making you uncomfortable," I grind out.

"I can handle my own." She blows out a noisy breath and crosses her arms.

"Doesn't mean you have to or will under my watch."

"Oh, really?" Anger burns across her face, which confuses the fuck out of me. "Maybe you shouldn't be hanging out with a woman you've hooked up with *on my watch*." She scoffs. "*Literally*."

"What?"

She makes a sweeping gesture toward the woman parked in the corner on my side of the bar.

Oh fuck.

"I recognize her," she hisses. "She might not be moaning your name while you're banging her on your desk, but I saw her. That's the woman you were screwing the night I came over."

Oh, so she wants to talk about that night.

I've been dying to do this.

This is the wrong place, wrong time, but here goes.

"Why did you come here that night?" My tone is even, and I lower my arm to stop her from ducking underneath it and scurrying away. "We hadn't talked in fuck knows how long. In fact, it was the night before *your wedding*."

She clenches her slender jaw, and a blush rises up her cheeks. "It doesn't matter."

"If it doesn't matter, then why don't you tell me?"

"We have a crowd of people waiting. I have men to flirt with." Her lips curl. "And you have a woman you've fucked to serve." She smacks my shoulder. "Gotta run, boss."

I fasten my hand around her arm, stopping her again. "Why did you come to the bar?" I grit out, wanting the answer more than my next breath.

She came for a reason. A woman doesn't visit another man the night before her wedding for no goddamn reason.

"Tell me."

She wriggles free from my grasp and looks away from me. "I needed a drink."

"You needed a drink?" I snort. "Bull-fucking-shit. Your husband might have bought your lies, but I see right through you."

She shrugs, her voice almost sounding resentful. "Whatever. I need to get back to work and make some cash."

Reality slaps me, reminding me again this isn't the place. I shake my head and return to my customers. Penny grins and signals to her empty glass.

Penny works for one of my beer distributors. We clicked, went out a few times, and fucked a whole lot of times. That ran smooth for nearly a year. I'd made it clear I wasn't looking for a relationship, and everything was perfect until she developed feelings and hit me with the L-word. She'd said it numerous times during sex—those don't count—but never over a meal. So, I had to end things with her.

We didn't talk for months before the eve of Sierra's wedding. She randomly showed up, and I needed to clear my head—to forget about Sierra.

And because I kept needing to forget about Sierra, I used Penny as that buffer—until I realized it wasn't fair to her. I haven't seen her since the night I broke it off, though we both left in an understanding that we'd remain friends.

I didn't invite her tonight, haven't spoken to her in months, but I can't kick her out. She's done nothing wrong.

Friends don't ignore friends, but I've tried to stay clear of her the best I can tonight. It's difficult, considering she keeps ordering drinks and food.

I make her a vodka soda, and before I get the chance to walk away, she seizes my arm in her hand, her fingers dancing along my skin, and leans forward, her cleavage spilling out.

"Are you doing anything tonight?" she whispers.

"Working and then crashing," I answer, bored.

"You want some company?"

"Nope. I'm pretty tired."

"Oh, come on. You never turn me down when I'm in town, and we need to catch up. It's been a while."

I jerk away and take a step back. It's just my luck that when I glance to the other side of the bar, Sierra's attention is pinned to us. Her face is pinched together as she gives me a stony glare.

Of motherfucking course.

"I've been busy," I practically fume.

She narrows her brown eyes at me. "What's up with you?"

"Nothing."

She motions to Sierra. "Is there funny business going on with you and prep-academy girl over there?" She laughs. "Where did you find her? She looks like she belongs anywhere but here."

I grimace at the truth in her observation. She's right. Sierra doesn't belong in a run-down bar like this.

"I don't know what you're talking about," I say, feigning disinterest. "She's my employee, and I want to make sure she's okay." The last thing I need is Penny starting shit with Sierra.

Her eyes latch on to Sierra, who's turned our back to us, and her face turns guarded. "Liar. You've been undressing her all night, staring at her ass, slamming shit around anytime a man talks to her. I know what it looks like to want someone. You've given me those looks *plenty* of times."

The way I've looked at her will never match how I look at Sierra. Never.

"I'm busy, Penny," I say. "Enjoy your night."

She sighs loudly and doesn't speak until I shift on my heels to leave. "What a shame. A man like you falling for a woman like her."

I whip around. "The fuck is that supposed to mean?"

"I know who she is." She plays with a toothpick in her mouth and grins. "The mayor's daughter. She might fuck you, Maliki, but she'll never keep you."

"And you could never keep me, Penny."

Fuck this night.

I wish Liz or Mikey were here. I'd ask them to take over, so I could go upstairs, have a drink, throw something, run a mile.

Anything to forget Penny's words.

Anything to stop thinking about a woman I can't have.

———

"Sit your cute ass down. You've had a long night."

The bar is closed, and it seems working the rest of the night has cooled off Sierra. And me. Neither one of us has mentioned Penny, and I have no issue with that.

Sierra snorts. "Uh, you did most of the work and were here earlier than me, meaning you've had a longer night."

My attention fixes on her, and I fight with myself on whether to say what I want to tell her. Against my better judgment, because I feel it needs to be said, I do. "You know, you don't have to work here. I'll loan you the money, help out, whatever to get you back on your feet. If you need an advance for the bar renovation, I can do that, too."

She winces. "Where is this coming from?" She's silent for a few moments. "Is this your way of telling me you don't want me working here? Did your spread-legged friend convince you I don't belong here?" She tosses the rag she was cleaning the bar with down into the sink.

I love seeing pissed off, attitude-filled Sierra.

Not so much when it's thrown at me.

"Penny?" I shake my head. *Just when I hoped we could go without mentioning her.* "Penny has nothing to do with this. What I mean is, you can find something better for yourself … for your image."

"Fuck my image," she seethes. "And fuck you for letting your fuck buddy, *Penny*, change your mind about me. If I'm a burden to you, I'll move my needing-a-better-image ass out. If you don't want me around for whatever lame reason you're thinking, I'll quit." She shakes her head and sucks in a deep breath to keep her voice steady. "I mean, I don't understand why she's so bothered with my working here. I'm not stopping her from screwing you again. Call her over." She flicks her hand through the air and slides it over the middle of the bar. "Fuck her right here, right now if you want."

I've never seen Sierra so pissed off, and it's fucking hot as hell.

My cock jerks in my jeans. Not with the thought of fucking Penny there, but with the idea of seeing Sierra spread wide, allowing me to have my way with her. Sierra's back hits the bar when I crowd toward her.

"Is that what you want?" I say, out of patience. "For me to fuck her right here, right now, in front of you?"

Her eyes widen, my words startling her, and she chews on her lower lip. "Not particularly, but it's whatever. There's nothing between us, right?" She nudges my shoulder, but I stay firm in my spot, only inches away from her. "No, you'll screw every other woman in this town though."

A mix of emotions flashes across Sierra's gorgeous face—frustration, desire, hunger. I wouldn't be surprised if mine resembled the same.

I lean in, my lips touching her cheek. "What's up with your fascination with my sex life?"

She gasps when I cup my hands on the sides of her waist and prop her up onto the bar—exactly where she told me to fuck Penny. Her legs spread, producing the perfect amount of space for me as I shift between them. She shudders, goose bumps fluttering over her skin, when my hand settles on her thigh.

Her attention drifts to my hand, but I don't move it, and she fights to keep her voice steady. "I'm not *obsessed* with your sex life."

"Yes, you are."

"Call me crazy for being curious about the chick you boned in your office, which I'm sure wasn't the first time that happened. Hell, you've probably screwed her on this bar."

I remain silent.

It's the truth.

"Wow," she says. She shoves me back, drops off the bar, shudders, and scrapes her hand over her body. "Let me get the whore germs off me—both yours and hers."

I clench my hands. "Do I ask you if you've slept with anyone who comes in here?"

She flings her arms up, and she's so close that her hand almost smacks me. "I've hardly touched anyone in this godforsaken town!"

"Good."

"Unlike *you.*"

"Babe, you have no idea what I've done with who, so quit that imagination floating through your brain and stop assuming I'm fucking every woman who smiles at me." I draw out a breath. "You know, I'm a little confused on why you even care."

I move closer, and she backs into the bar again. She doesn't stop me from repeating my actions from earlier—grabbing her waist, hoisting her onto the bar, and sliding my body between her toned legs.

I capture the back of her neck, dragging her closer to my face, and my fingers caress her skin. "Do you want to be one of those women, Sierra? Is that why you care so much?"

Her breaths come out in tiny pants. Her eyes flash down to mine and turn wild as they drink me in. She's turned on, and *fuck,* so am I.

I ease my hand down her neck, cupping her chin, and I tilt it away, giving me space to brush my lips along the curve of her jaw. Her skin is soft against my lips. I skim kisses up her neck, feeling her chest hitch against mine, and suck on the spot below her ear. I sink my fingers into her bare thighs and spread her legs wider, noticing a flash of her panties underneath her short shorts.

This is a bad fucking idea.

It's a line I swore I'd never cross with her.

I'm not the man for her. She needs a professional, nine-to-five man who wears fucking loafers. Not me, not a man destined to spend his life here and a man who can't give her the life her parents have all these years.

"Is that it?" I ask, my voice harsh as I whisper against her skin. I can feel my dick growing harder with every touch. "Is that why you're so pissed off?"

She trembles. "I work here. That's why."

"Bullshit." I pull back, my hands tightening on her thighs. "I can read you like my favorite book, Sierra. I see you—the real you—and as much as you fight to hide every thought running through that pretty little head from me, I see it. Let me give you an example: Right now, I see how pissed you are at me." I lower my tone. "I also see how much you want me."

She reaches down to dig her fingers into my hand resting on her thigh. "You're so full of yourself."

I raise a brow, staring up at her. "Am I lying?"

"Maybe I can see through you. Maybe you're the one who wants me."

"Trust me, you can't read me."

She laughs. "Oh, but I can. Do you think I don't notice your jealousy as much as mine? That I don't see how you have to snap yourself out of your feelings for me? You want me as much as I want you, Maliki. The problem is, you're too chickenshit to do anything about it."

"Too chickenshit?"

"Too fucking chickenshit."

My lips crash into hers.

Chickenshit, my ass.

We moan, and just as I start to taste her, just as my tongue enters her mouth, a loud banging blares through the room.

What the fuck?

My phone rings.

The bar phone rings.

Someone bangs on the bar door and is yelling behind it.

I make out something along the lines of, "Forgot my wallet!"

"Fucking hell," I grumble, pulling away from her.

The first time I've tasted her, and it gets interrupted like this.

Is this a sign we shouldn't cross this line?

We both catch our breaths, and I wipe my arm along my face while stalking to the door. I'm half-tempted to tell the person to fuck off, but they won't stop fucking knocking.

I unlock the door ... and in walks Penny.

You've got to be shitting me.

I hear Sierra curse under her breath.

She hops off the bar and practically snarls in my direction. "It's been a long night. You should probably help her find her *wallet.*"

She glares while passing us on her way back to the apartment, and I pray it's not to pack her bags and leave.

As much as I want to chase her, I have to get rid of Penny first.

"Well played," I tell Penny, working my jaw.

She raises her brows. "What do you mean?"

"Come on. You *forgot* your wallet?"

She shrugs. "I was hoping you'd changed your mind. I didn't know she'd be here with you, doing … whatever you two were doing."

"We were closing the bar."

"You were about to fuck her in the same place you'd fucked me."

I snarl. She's right. I was about to screw Sierra where I'd screwed countless other women.

"She's not for you, Maliki." Her hand splays across my shoulder.

I push her away. "Just because we've fucked a few times doesn't mean shit. Just because your mouth has been around my dick doesn't mean you know me."

"When she breaks your heart, you know my number."

CHAPTER FIFTEEN
SIERRA

I throw down my bag, tear off my clothes, and step in the shower.

Tears hit my eyes as soon as Penny walked in, but I blinked them away. I couldn't cry in front of her—in front of *them*.

What if he brings her to his bedroom?

I shake my head. He wouldn't do that after what happened on the bar.

I throw my loofah onto the bathtub floor and kick it for good measure. I'm reminded of Maliki's touch as I wash my hair. It was too good to be true. Just when I succeeded in proving he couldn't hide his feelings for me any longer, she interrupted.

No matter what, there's always someone coming between us.

Maliki is seated on my bed when I walk into my room. I screech and tighten my towel around my chest.

"I wanted to assure you I wasn't fucking anyone." He stands. "Get some sleep."

With that, he turns around and leaves.

"Maliki, wait."

"Go to bed, Sierra," is all he growls out.

———

"Shit."

I'm late.

With all that transpired last night, I failed to set my alarm for brunch.

I pull a dress over my head, ridding it of wrinkles with my hands, and slip on red wedges. I brush my teeth, braid my hair, and am out the door in minutes. I want to go to this brunch like I want to have mimosas with Louise.

Thank God Maliki is nowhere to be seen. I can't face him yet.

"You're late," is how my father greets me when I sit down at the table.

"I overslept," I say around a yawn.

"If you weren't working at a *bar*, you wouldn't have overslept."

I snatch the carafe of orange juice and pour myself a glass. "I'm not having this discussion." My gaze bounces to my mom's. "I told Mom to inform you of that."

"Oh, she did all right, *but* you're my daughter," he answers with a huff.

He hates not calling the shots, but his life has changed since his affair was exposed. His ass is on the line in every aspect of his life—his career, his family. Hell, even my grandparents are pissed at him. Right now, my father has no one on his side.

My mom brushes her hand against his arm. "Honey, let's wait until after we eat."

"Yeah, Dad. We don't want your sour mood to affect our French toast and eggs," Rex adds with a smirk.

A vein pulses in my dad's neck, and no doubt, he wants to give Rex an ass-chewing, but he stares at me with intent. "We will talk about this."

"Can't wait," I mutter, spreading my napkin on my lap.

I was once a daddy's girl. He wasn't perfect, but he was my dad— the man who fought the monsters in my closet and taught me to ride a bike. Somewhere between me growing up and him growing more successful, he changed—a man I no longer knew but still loved. No matter what, I stood by his side, stood up for him, until he destroyed my mother's heart.

I eat my breakfast while listening to my father rattle on about town developments and my mom about her latest fundraiser. When breakfast is finished and our stomachs are full, I help my mom clean up, moving as slow as I can to delay this unnecessary talk with my dad.

"All right, Sierra, my office," my father says, stepping into the kitchen and straightening his shirt cuffs.

I roll my eyes, follow him to the office, and speak before he has time to shut the door, "Look, whatever you say won't change my mind about working at the bar. I'm working there, and that's final."

The door clicks shut, and he circles his desk, looking more powerful when he sits in the executive chair. My father is a handsome man who's aged well. He's tall with dark hair, only a few sprinkles of gray strands, and he possesses enough confidence you'd guess he was in his twenties. He's wearing a black suit, black tie, and the Rolex that was passed down from his grandfather.

"Not only is working there inappropriate for the mayor's daughter, but it's also dangerous, Sierra."

"You know what else is inappropriate for the town mayor? Cheating on his wife."

He flicks his finger my way. "Touché. This isn't an attempt for me to control you. Maliki's life is darker than the sunshine you're used to, honey."

"Weird. Maliki is my sunshine every time I'm having a shit day, crying over *your* indiscretions and being cheated on. He makes me happy. Do you remember the last guy you *approved* of? He cheated on me in the restroom of a bar." I start pacing in front of him. "And I'm not even dating Maliki. I'm working for him. So, for that reason and our friendship, I'll take *cloudy days* with him because …"

"You have feelings for him?"

I gulp. "Friendship feelings."

He nods. "Be careful."

"I always am."

"That kid, his life wasn't easy. His mother was—" He stops speaking.

"Was what?"

"Mentally ill—in and out of psychiatric facilities—and his father's workplace didn't help the situation. She was paranoid of infidelity, became obsessed with it, and couldn't handle her life—according to your mother, who attempted to mentor her. She tried helping Kelly, but couldn't."

I cross my arms. "Children don't have to take after their parents. I'm nothing like you."

He winces, knowing that wasn't a compliment. "I love you, but I don't want you to be with a man like me, Sierra. I know what a man who can't be held down is—*I'm* one of those men—and it's hard for us. We hurt people." He rests his elbows on the desk. "Your mother filed for divorce."

I stop my pacing to look at him. "What?"

"I wanted to be the one to tell you."

"Why?"

"She fears she's setting a bad example and that you'll take Devin back because she didn't leave me. I suppose we were delaying the inevitable. When she told me about Devin's cheating, I wanted to kill him for hurting you. Your mother reminded me it was no different than my actions. I hurt my wife, my children, and betrayed the town that voted for me. I have to face the consequences for that."

My head is spinning. "What happens now?" *This can't be real. He didn't say that.*

"I'll work on redeeming myself."

"And while you're doing that, let me work on who I want to be."

He lifts a brow. "Which is?"

"Happy."

He nods. "I'll shut my mouth, sit down, and realize I'm not perfect."

"Finally."

Him staring down in shame hurts my heart, and I move around the desk to kiss his cheek. He's a ruthless man, but I love him.

"I'll see you soon, okay?" I tell him.

He nods. "You call me if you need anything. *Anything*. I'm sleeping in my office, but it's time I find somewhere to move permanently. I'm letting your mother keep the house."

———

I unlock the door of the apartment and walk in, finding it empty. I haven't spoken to Maliki since the girl he desk-banged showed up last night.

Speaking of last night …

What in the ever-loving hell was that?

We kissed.

Maliki Bridges finally kissed me.

For years, I'd wanted to feel his lips against mine.

And it happened with terrible timing.

I was married, and Penny showed up.

Did I overreact last night?

Maybe.

Maliki isn't mine. I have no claim to him.

I have no right to be upset, but I can't stop imagining Penny returning for round two … two hundred … who knows how many times they've banged?

She wasn't startled, seeing me—a clear sign she was staking her claim and making it known they had history.

When I go to the bar in search of him, it's empty. My next stop is the dreaded office—somewhere I haven't stepped foot in since that night. The door is shut. I knock and wait until he calls for me to come in. He pulls away from the paperwork on the desk when he sees me, straightening in his chair, almost appearing as if he's a boss intending to scold an employee.

There's no roadmap for where this conversation will lead. I'm a married woman, frustrated at him over another woman. I'm in the wrong and mortified by my feelings.

"Hey," he says, realizing I'm a mute weirdo gawking at him.

"Hi," I nearly whisper, shutting the door.

"Look, about Penny," he begins.

"Ah, good ole Penny." The mockery falls from my lips in contempt. My eyes shoot from him to the desk, and I cringe. "Okay, I can't talk to you in here." I put my hand up and gulp away the disgust rising.

His gaze shoots around the room in confusion. "What? Why?"

"That desk. I can't even look at it after your whole … sexcapade with *Penny*."

He leans back in his chair and fastens his hands together behind his head. "You mean, after you spied on me?"

"I didn't spy on you."

"I watched the cameras. You didn't take a peek and then scurry along—which, I might add, a sane person would have done. You stayed and enjoyed the show. A show that wasn't yours to watch."

I stutter for the right words. "I was … shocked … horrified … frozen in place." I cross my arms. "Don't twist this around on me. You should've advised me not to work last night if you knew she was returning for another go at desk-fucking."

"I didn't know she was coming last night, *nor* did I invite her to come later. Do you think *forgot my wallet* is code for sex? I was as surprised and pissed as you."

"I wasn't pissed."

"You were pissed. Jealousy looks sexy on you."

"Excuse me? I wasn't jealous of her." I was, but I snort to make myself sound more believable. "I was annoyed, is all." *Irritated that you had my panties wet, offering me something I'd wanted for years, and then bam, Penny the Penis-Blocker showed up.* "I'll be upstairs. We can have this chitchat then."

He drops his arms and shifts in his chair. "Look, I'm sorry." A self-satisfied smile hits his lips. "Not that I have much to atone for."

"Then, you're not apologizing, Fake Apology Giver."

"I'm apologizing for Penny's behavior. I did nothing wrong."

"You're right. You shouldn't have to apologize for desk-banging chicks."

"Don't make it sound like cheap porn."

"It sure looked like cheap porn. If it walks like a duck, talks like a duck, then it's cheap duck porn."

"You're impossible," he mutters. "It was much better quality than *porn*. Yes, I had sex with Penny. No, I won't do it again. It's settled. Let's move forward."

I scrape my hands together. "Conversation over."

I spin around in my wedges and feel Maliki behind me as I dash upstairs. I leave the door open for him and plop down on a stool at the island.

"Now that that's over, you want to tell me what else is on your mind?"

I love how he's not afraid to dig into my feelings, not afraid of me bringing my issues to him. "My parents are divorcing."

Why I'm so overwhelmed is weird. I was happy when my mom said she was leaving my father after news of his affair came out and pissed when she decided to stay.

Now, I feel numb.

Two divorces are happening in my family this year—mine and my parents'.

He stands on the other side of the island. "I'm sorry."

"I ..." I stop to clear my throat. "It might be my fault."

"The fuck it is. Everyone in this town knows your father is to blame." He shakes his head. "Don't you dare think that."

"*Yes*, but my mom didn't leave him after she found out about the affair. She's leaving in fear of setting a bad example to her daughters."

"Does her staying with him set a nice example?"

"Every situation is different."

He nods. "I agree."

"It's ... *ugh*. It'll be weird, them not being together, you know?"

"Yeah. It was the same when my mom left, but it became our new normal."

My mouth falls open.

Holy shit. Is Maliki getting personal with me?

Do I act like I know what my father told me?

"When did your mom leave you?"

"Yes. When I was six and my sister was nine." His face is blank, offering me not an ounce of emotion.

"Did she tell you she was leaving?"

"Nope. I came home one day, and all her shit was gone. She never came back."

"Do you know where she is now?"

He shakes his head. "I don't care to know. She chose to leave, to not take us with her, and never come back. That's it. I won't fight for anyone's love. She did what a mother should never do, regardless of the situation."

I want more.

I want everything personal he has to offer.

"Why did she leave?"

"I don't know. Years ago, when we were moving my dad's shit, we found her good-bye letter. She blamed it on the bar, on my father making it a priority over his family and not showering her with enough attention. He needed to find out what it was like, taking care of a family, is what she said. I was furious with my father and blamed him for everything. In actuality, it was both of their fault. Her letter proved she didn't deserve me looking for her." He shifts his weight from one foot to the other, shaking his head, and offers his hand. "Come on. We've had enough depressing shit for one day. Let's do something fun."

I perk up in my stool. "Like what?"

"You pick."

"Well …" I draw out.

"Oh shit. Did I stick my foot in my mouth?"

"How about we go shopping for bar selections?"

He shrugs. "Why not? It's a perfect day to get out of town."

I slide off my stool. "Let me change really quick."

He snaps his fingers to stop me. "Cohen is having a barbeque tonight at his house. Come with me."

"Really?"

"Yeah, it'll be fun."

I nod, a smile taking over my face. I walk out of the kitchen and skip to my bedroom when I'm out of his sight.

CHAPTER SIXTEEN
SIERRA

"First things first," I say, whipping around and walking backward facing Maliki. "The desk has to go bye-bye."

He tilts his head to the side. "What's wrong with my desk?"

"What's wrong with it is, you banged Penny and who knows how many other women on it."

My answer captures the attention of an elderly couple passing by. The woman gasps, clasping her hand over her mouth as if I were straddling Maliki instead of making small talk, and then moves her hand over her heart. She shakes her head, snatches the man's hand, and pulls him away.

Maliki shakes his head. "You can't trash my desk for that reason."

"Do you possess a sentimental attachment to said desk other than it being your go-to spot for screwing? Family heirloom?" I tsk him. "Which would be disrespectful as fuck to your elders."

"No, Sierra. I'm not having sex on family heirlooms."

Another odd glance comes our way from a passerby. I should've brought this up in the car.

He drops his tone. "Why do you care about the desk so much?"

Because I've been falling in love with you since I was eighteen.

I clear my throat and shrug. "I don't want to hang out with your sex juices if I ever work in your office."

"Sex juices?" A grin plays at his lips. "You're nuts, and please never use the term *sex juices* again."

"Whatever." I loop my arm through his and lead us to the office furniture department in the store we're in. "New desk, here we come." When we reach the spot, I twirl on my heels and gesture to the options. "What look are we going for, Mr. Bridges?"

He scratches his head, and instead of searching out a desk, he fixes his attention on me. "You pick. You're the one demanding it be replaced."

"All righty, I see this is an area you're giving me creative control on." I grab his hand and walk us through the aisles.

"As long as it's not pink or covered in sequins, which seems to be my niece's style, I'm good."

"I wouldn't do that to your desk. The stools, on the other hand …" I grin back at him. "This might be the time to mention, they most definitely have sequins."

He shakes his head, a smile tugging at his lips. "You're such a pain in my ass."

"Get used to it."

"Trust me, I did years ago."

I steal his hat, put it on, and point to a desk. "I like this one. It screams, *Maliki!*"

It's a basic black desk with open drawers. My favorite part is, it looks uncomfortable. That should ward off women from spread-eagling across it.

"Sold." He snatches his hat back.

———

"Cohen works at the Twisted Fox, right?" I ask from the passenger seat of his car.

We're on our way to the barbeque. Our shopping trip ended with us ordering the uncomfortable desk and office chair, and we have a book of floor and paint samples.

He nods. "He co-owns it with a few of our other friends."

I stiffen in my seat. "We're not going there, are we?"

He shakes his head. "No, it's at his house. I wouldn't have invited you if it were there. It's me and some friends. That's it."

"Cool." I can't believe I'm meeting his friends—friends who aren't in Blue Beech.

Maliki moved out of Blue Beech years ago but came back when he took over the bar. All I knew was, he wanted out of the small town like I did and then was brought back—our reasons different. His was to save the family business. Mine was being around familiarity, my mom, and … *him*.

———

"Do I look okay?" I inspect my shorts, white tank, and red wedges I'm wearing.

Maliki slides his sunglasses off his face and sweeps his gaze over me. "You look perfect."

I grab the handle but pause while taking in the home we're parked in front of. It's a small brick ranch with a bright yellow door and black shutters. The driveway is packed with cars and a motorcycle.

I exhale an uneasy breath. "What am I walking into?"

The excitement of meeting his friends has shifted into nervousness. I'm normally outgoing, the girl who strikes up conversation with others, but Devin's cheating has changed me. I don't want to talk to people or go out in public. I feel taken advantage of, humiliated, and manipulated. My trust in people sucks.

At least we're not in Blue Beech.

"Walking into?" Maliki repeats. "You're walking into a chill barbeque with my friends. This isn't one of your parents' social events. Don't worry about being anyone but yourself."

I rub the back of my neck. "Has Cohen told anyone how we met?"

"Doubt it. Cohen has more shit to worry about than gossiping."

I relax in my seat. "I've decided I already like Cohen."

He pats my thigh, giving it a gentle squeeze. "Don't worry. Just have fun."

———

Maliki's arm is draped over my shoulders, and I'm pulled into his side when we walk into Cohen's backyard. The gesture shocked me, given he hardly touches me when we hang out. His arm fits around me perfectly, as if it belongs there. I could walk in his hold for the rest of my life and never want to pull away.

"Ki! My man!"

Cohen grins when he sees us, shuts the grill in front of him, and comes our way. "Glad you could make it *and* bring gorgeous company."

I give the backyard a once-over. A group of girls are settled at a table, consumed in conversation, and three men are lagging behind Cohen, moving toward us.

"You must be Sierra," Cohen says when he reaches us. "Maliki said you were coming, and he's told me so much about you. Welcome to my home."

Maliki was right. Cohen is acting as if I were a total stranger.

I laugh, a blush rising up my cheeks. "Whatever he's told you are lies."

Cohen motions toward me and looks at the guys. "Do you remember the youngster who kept sneaking into Maliki's bar?"

"Yes," one brown-haired man draws out, a lollipop in his mouth.

Another guy's mouth drops open. "Holy hell! This is her?" He shakes his head with wide eyes. "I fucking love this shit."

"Sure is," Cohen replies. "This is Sierra."

He introduces the guys.

Lollipop guy is Silas.

The *holy shit* one is Finn.

The only one not sporting a smile is Archer.

I give them a wave. "Hey."

Cohen wraps his hands around his mouth and yells to the girls, "Georgia! Come here!"

A short blonde rises from her seat and narrows her eyes in our direction. "This'd better be good. We were having a deep discussion about *The Bachelor*."

"Trust me, it's so much better than that stupid-ass show!" Finn calls out.

"No, it's not," Maliki shouts. "Stay your ass over there!"

Georgia, I'm assuming, proceeds our way, and Cohen signals to me as soon as she joins us. "This is Sierra, aka the underage girl who kept sneaking into Ki's bar."

I hold my hand up to correct him. "Hey now, I was never underage. I was eighteen."

"Eighteen is underage to drink, babe," Maliki says with a hint of a smirk.

"She means not underage to screw," Georgia says, rolling her eyes and grinning at Maliki. "I so called you and her having a thing." Her attention drifts to me, her smile still intact. "I don't know you, but I already like you for the hell you put him through."

Maliki's arm drops from my shoulders. "First off, I never talked about her to you. Your nosy ass eavesdropped on me talking about it with Cohen. I needed advice on what to do other than call the cops on her."

Georgia dismissively waves her hand in his direction. "Shut up. You would've never called the cops on her."

"Eh, he threatened to plenty of times," I inform them, replaying all the times he said that in my mind. "Even threatened to call my parents."

"Shit, dude, not the parent threat," Finn cuts in. "I thought you were cooler than that."

Maliki flips him off.

I shake Georgia's hand when she introduces herself. She's gorgeous, and her look is total nineties. Pink glitter is on her eyelids, and her blonde hair is pulled into two buns at the top of her head. From the smile on her face and the friendliness in her voice, I already like her.

"I hope you brought an appetite," she says. "We have plenty of food."

I eye the food on the picnic tables.

Shoot. It looks like a pitch-in.

"I'm sorry," I rush out. "Maliki sprang this on me at the last minute, or I would've brought something." *Great.* Already making a bad impression.

"Don't worry," Silas says. "We have plenty."

"Maliki already paid me for you two," Georgia says. "They pay, and I normally make—with the exception of the grill stuff."

Maliki's arm returns to my shoulders as we follow her, but I'm pulled away when Georgia snatches my hand.

"I'll introduce you to the girls." Her attention lands on Maliki. "I promise to bring her back."

I nod when Maliki gives me a questioning look and allow Georgia to lead the way.

"She'd better like me when she comes back, you little shit-talker!" Maliki yells behind us.

"I can't make any promises!" Georgia laughs.

When we reach the table, two women smile invitingly, and I take the chair next to Georgia.

"I'm Lola." Lola is a fair-skinned girl with sleek, middle-parted hair.

"And I'm Grace." Grace's name matches her perfectly. Her strawberry-blonde hair is braided into a crown around her head, and she's wearing a loose white dress.

"Sierra." I smile. "I came with Maliki."

Their grins widen.

"Oh, we noticed," Lola comments.

"Do you date Cohen?" I ask Georgia.

"God, no," she replies, scrunching up her face. "He's my brother." She shifts in her seat. "And these are my besties. None of the guys have girlfriends. They're all too chickenshit to have anyone *tying them down.*"

Her eyes narrow toward the guys, and I follow her gaze, trying to single out the victim of her glare but can't.

Hmm. Definitely a story there.

"Guys who work in bars," Grace says, soft-spoken, and squeezes Georgia's arm. "It's what you get with them."

Lola clears her throat and motions to me.

"Oh shoot," Grace sputters out. "I didn't mean it like that. *Some* of them. Maliki isn't like that. He doesn't bring different women with him to every barbeque."

"Heck, the man hasn't brought a woman with him, period," Georgia states matter-of-factly. "Until you."

"And that's before we banned them from bringing girls," Grace chimes in.

"Banned?" My gaze darts to each girl in nervousness. "Was he not supposed to bring me?" *I'm so kicking his ass.*

Lola shakes her head. "No, you're totally fine. There was an issue a few years back with one of Finn's girls. She was friends with Cohen's baby mama and talking hella shit about him. It didn't slide well with Georgia, obviously."

I gape at them. "Wait, Cohen has a kid?"

Grace nods. "Noah."

I give the yard a once-over, not spotting anyone under the age of twenty in sight. "Is he here?"

"No," Georgia replies, checking her watch. "His aunt is dropping him off soon."

My mind is spiraling with so many questions. "What about the mom? Is she here?"

Obviously not, but it's the best way I thought to bring her up.

Grace grimaces. "Heather sucks."

I shoot a glance to Georgia. "Why?"

Her pink lips curl in disgust. "A few months before she was due, out of nowhere, she told Cohen she wanted to put Noah up for adoption. Cohen begged her not to, promising to accept all responsibilities and custody. As soon as she gave birth, she ran off to Vegas. Cohen kept his word, is an amazing father, and hasn't spoken to Heather once. Noah has met her a few times when he's been with Jamie but doesn't know who she is to him." She sneers in disgust. "We prefer to keep it that way to protect him."

My stomach clenches. *How could someone do that to their child? Poor Cohen.*

"Wow," I draw out, my eyes glued to Georgia. "Who's Jamie?"

"Heather's sister," Georgia answers. "She has a relationship with Noah."

I peek over at Cohen. "That sounds like one giant ball of headaches."

Georgia shrugs and grabs her beer. "Not really. We're grateful for Heather's absence."

As if in perfect timing, a little boy races into the backyard, tennis shoes stomping against the grass, and takes over everyone's attention.

"Dad!" he shouts, clutching something in his hand and holding it in the air. "You won't believe what Jamie bought me!"

Affection spreads over Cohen's face, and he releases a *humph* when the boy jumps into his arms, squeezing him into a tight hug.

Noah holds the item on display when he's dropped to his feet. "It's an iPod!"

The kid is adorable—a little Cohen with his brown hair and small frame.

Noah's smile can't be contained as he jumps up and down. "It's blue!"

Cohen bends down on one knee to Noah's level. "That's so neat, buddy!"

"Hey, Jamie!" Georgia shouts, causing my attention to slide to a tall brunette woman coming our way.

"Hey," she replies around a yawn.

"You want to stick around?" Georgia offers.

Jamie shakes her head. "I'm working a double tomorrow and in dire need of sleep."

"That's awesome that you're a doctor." Grace shudders. "Blood makes me squeamish."

"Everything makes you squeamish," Finn says, crouching behind her and ruffling his hands through her hair, disheveling her braid.

"Especially you." She reaches up, sticks her palm in his face, and nudges him away.

Cohen and Noah run over to us.

"An iPod?" Cohen asks Jamie. "You didn't have to do that. You spoil him too much."

Jamie laughs—a forced one. "It's for selfish reasons, so I can Face-Time him."

"You always FaceTime me to talk to him. It's never been a problem," Cohen responds with a hint of a frown.

Her face is expressionless. "You're busy sometimes."

He winces before checking himself. "We have plenty of food." His hands sweep toward the table. "Stay."

"Thanks for the offer, but I can't." She bends down to hug Noah. "Make sure you call me, okay?"

Noah hugs her back and then salutes her. "You got it!"

She kisses his head and tells everyone good-bye.

"She is *pissed* at you," Georgia sings when Jamie disappears from the yard.

"She's not *pissed at me*," Cohen imitates in her high-pitched voice.

"Why's she pissed at you?" Grace asks.

"She FaceTimed Cohen to talk to Noah the other day, and some chick answered, asking Jamie twenty-one questions about who she was." Georgia rolls her eyes and shoots a glare at Cohen. "That's why she bought the iPod."

"I need to quit telling you stuff," Cohen mutters.

He shakes his head, grabs Noah, and throws him over his shoulder. Noah breaks out in loud laughter, holding on around his neck when Cohen takes off running.

"Are he and Jamie a thing?" I ask Lola when he's out of earshot.

She shakes her head, scraping a hand through her hair. "They totes should be, but Cohen is too chickenshit."

"You have to admit, it'd be confusing for Noah," Grace chimes in.

"Love is love," Georgia inputs.

Both girls stare at her in sadness.

"Yes, and men are stupid," Grace says while Lola nods in agreement.

I jerk my head back when Maliki comes behind me and whispers in my ear, "You doing okay?"

My stomach flutters. "Yes." There's a slight rise in my voice.

He squeezes my shoulders. "Let me know if you need anything *or* if these heathens give you too much trouble."

The three of them tell him to screw off in three different ways.

"Uncle Maliki!"

Maliki turns as Noah charges toward him and hops on his back.

"I've missed you so much!"

"I've missed you more," Maliki replies with a cheerfulness in his tone I've never heard.

Noah holds on to him as Maliki jogs over to the guys playing cornhole and drops Noah to his feet. They go to one board, and Cohen and Finn take the other. They play while Archer sits in a chair, a beer in his hand, and watches them. Correction: he watches Georgia while pretending to pay attention to the game.

"You two are cute," Georgia says.

"Huh?" I ask, turning to look at her.

She points back and forth from Maliki and me. "You and Ki. You're cute together."

Her comment startles me.

"Oh, no. We're friends."

"For now," Lola chirps. "I've seen Maliki around women at bars, and believe me, babe, he's never checked to make sure they're okay."

"He's also never looked at them like he does you," Georgia adds. "You two will definitely be banging."

I shake my head, wishing I could hide the blush creeping up my cheeks, as tingles sweep up my back and face.

They wouldn't say that if they knew I was still married.

———

Maliki plants his hand on my shoulders. "You ready to eat?"

My stomach growls at the mention of food. "Yes, I'm starving."

He holds out his hand, helping me from my chair, and I follow him to the table covered with food. It all looks delicious, and I take one of everything. When I'm finished making my plate and I head back to the table, Archer is in my seat next to Georgia. She's glaring at him, and he shakes his head, chugging his beer. There's only one chair open at the table, so Maliki leads me to a separate two-top table.

"I can't believe you told them about me sneaking into the bar," I say as soon as we sit.

Maliki pops the top of his beer and leans back in his chair. "I wanted Cohen's opinion. It's not like I could ask anyone in Blue Beech, seeing it was you and word would've spread like wildfire. I needed someone to vent to."

"I'm delighted I was on your mind."

"Can I sit with Uncle Maliki?" Noah yells, charging toward us without waiting for an answer.

"Sure," Cohen answers, heading our way with two plates in his hand.

I push to my feet. "I'll find him a chair."

"Unnecessary," Maliki mutters, anchoring his large hands around my waist and dragging me onto his lap. "This one is big enough for two."

Holy shit. Holy shit. Holy shit.

I'm on his lap.

My heart freezes and then pounds like it's prepared to jump out of my chest, so I can hand it over to him. My mind scrambles in so many directions that I'm waiting for it to explode. Maliki is a different man outside of Blue Beech, and I love this Maliki.

Noah falls into my chair when Maliki gestures for him to take it. Cohen drops Noah's plate on the table and sets a bottle of root beer next to it. When his gaze travels to us, he quirks a brow, smiles, and pushes my plate to me.

"Who are you?" Noah asks, kicking his feet against the chair legs when Cohen leaves.

I grin. "I'm Sierra. Who are *you?*"

His attention stays on me. "I'm Noah. Are you Uncle Maliki's girlfriend?"

Maliki rests his hand on my thigh, causing me to take a moment to answer him.

I shake my head, wishing I could curse Maliki. "No, I'm his friend."

Noah scrunches up his face. "You sure look like his girlfriend."

We are in need of a subject change, pronto, and Maliki isn't jumping to stop him from asking these awkward questions.

I pick up my fork. "How old are you, Noah?"

He holds up a hand. "Five *but* almost six."

"Wow, you're old."

"Yes, he is," Maliki says. "I'm waiting for him to sprout some gray hair."

Noah straightens in his chair. "No! That isn't happening until I'm ninety-two hundred."

Maliki chuckles. "Ninety-two hundred, huh?"

"Yes." He grabs his hot dog and points to Maliki with it. "Don't forget you promised to do something fun with me for my birthday."

"I haven't forgotten," Maliki replies.

Noah looks over at me and scuffs his chair closer. "You want to come?"

My back straightens, causing Maliki to jerk behind me. "I'll see if I can."

"You have to since you're his girlfriend," Noah argues.

"I'm not—"

Maliki squeezes my thigh. "Just go with it. You won't change his mind," he whispers into my ear with a slight chuckle.

His hand doesn't move as he changes the subject and asks Noah if he's excited to start school. Noah says yes. Then, he proceeds to talk about his favorite TV show and toys, and he shows off his iPod. When he takes the last bite of his hot dog, he asks Cohen for a cookie. Cohen says yes, and he darts in his direction.

I reclaim my seat and slide my plate to my side.

"You're good with kids," I say, popping a chip in my mouth.

Maliki raises his brow in question. "Did you expect me to be awful with them?"

"No … just some guys aren't."

"Kids are cool. My niece and Liz lived with me before she moved in with her husband."

I click my tongue against the roof of my mouth. "Do you want kids someday?"

"Possibly. It's complicated, having a family with the lifestyle and career I live. My father proved that."

"Then, why did you go into that occupation?"

"It's what I've always known, and I wanted to be a business owner." He shrugs. "But eventually, I'll entertain the idea. I want to make certain I can give them a stable home."

"That means, you'll have to settle down long enough to have a child with someone."

"Yes, it does."

"Do you ever see yourself … you know … doing that? You're not exactly young."

"Nor am I exactly old." He laughs. "According to Noah, I have up to ninety-two hundred years before I start turning gray."

I toss a chip at him. "Shut up."

We're interrupted by Georgia calling our names.

"All right, you two lovers, time for me to beat your asses in cornhole. It's you two against Archer and me."

"Archer is playing cornhole?" Maliki asks with shock.

She lifts her chin, fighting back a smile. "I'm forcing him." She snaps her fingers. "Now, chop-chop, before he changes his mind."

I lean across the table. "I've never played cornhole."

"It's easy," Maliki says. "Just follow my lead."

"Prepare for us to lose."

———

"Your friends are nice," I say during our ride home.

Spending the day with Maliki wiped out all my family and divorce worries. I didn't think about Devin or my dad or what the hell my future holds. I'm struggling to mask the happiness from tonight rolling through me. I want to savor these moments with Maliki and never forget them—in case the day comes when they stop.

The day *will* come when they stop.

So, for now, I'm going to stay on this ride with him before he kicks me off.

We lost at cornhole … all four games, even when we played against Noah and Cohen. That's right. My ass couldn't even beat a five-year-old at the game. Our night ended with a bonfire and smores. I've never enjoyed myself so much at a barbeque.

Maliki's eyes stay on the road. "They are."

"Georgia invited me to the next one. Hopefully, you'll be in attendance, too."

He chuckles and parks in the rear parking lot, cutting the ignition. "Oh, it's like that now, huh? *Hopefully*, I'll be there?"

"Damn straight."

"Come anytime, and consider Georgia's invite a big deal. She's normally not as receiving to women brought to our barbeques as she was with you."

"Really? Why?"

"She's protective of the people she cares about."

We get out of the car and step into the night, the bright security light glowing above us. I unlock the door, head up the stairs, and flip on lights with Maliki trailing behind me.

"Have you and her ever …"

He shakes his head. "I see her as a little sister. Cohen is a brother to me, and even if I were attracted to her romantically, I'd never touch her. He practically raised Georgia. Hell, he waited a year until introducing us to her—post threatening to rip our balls out one by one if we touched her."

I bite my lips to hide my smile. "And none of the others have?"

He tosses his keys onto the island. "Nope."

"Has she tried with any of them?"

"Don't know. Not my business, and if you learn any different, don't tell me. I refuse to be swept up in that shitstorm."

"Gotcha. I like her and the girls."

"Watch it though. They're quite the troublemakers."

I open the fridge for a bottle of water, my back facing him. "They're convinced we're going to have sex."

"Oh, really?" There's no difference in his tone, and I'm too scared to face him.

"Really," I say around a gulp.

"Do you agree?"

My back straightens, chills running up my spine, and I return the water to the fridge. Hell, I need something stronger. I go to snag a bottle of wine but stop when he keeps talking.

"Look at me, Sierra." His voice has pivoted, now controlled, deep, and demanding.

I do as I was told, shutting the fridge and leaning back against it. His brown eyes are fixated on me, his face hardened, jaw clenched. I've never felt so on display, nor has my pulse been so strong.

"Would you have sex with me?" His smirk is loaded with confidence. He knows my answer. "Answer me straight up."

Act cool.

Act normal.

I gape at him while pulling myself together. "I mean … if you wanted to have sex with me."

"You think I wouldn't want to have sex with you?"

There's no doubt we're attracted to each other.

That we want each other.

I shrug, struggling to answer him without a shaky voice. "You've never seemed interested in my advances, and it'd make our relationship … complicated. It could ruin it, and I never want that to happen." I sigh. "You don't do relationships, and I'm not sure I can have sex and not want more."

The smirk hasn't left his face. "Anything else?"

"Nope. That's it."

He circles the island, invading my space, and stops a few steps away. "Interesting."

"What does *interesting* mean?" I blow out a long breath, my face flushing. "See! I've made it awkward now! Exactly what I didn't want!"

I'd love to have his lips on mine again, to feel his body pressed against mine, but it's not worth losing him.

I gasp when he wipes out the space separating us, captures my waist with his strong hands, and tugs me into him. I lose a breath when the erection straining against his jeans rubs against my core.

He cradles my face in his hands. "I can't believe you'd doubt me wanting you."

And his mouth meets mine.

CHAPTER SEVENTEEN

MALIKI

Sierra tastes fucking sweet.

Sweet but not as innocent as I imagined.

Spending time with her today was incredible.

She met my friends. They loved her. She loved them. Maybe she does fit in my world.

I kiss her roughly, lacking the restraint I should have but don't.

We've delayed this for too long.

She tastes like sweet chocolate and marshmallows when my tongue slips into her mouth, devouring her. My dick stirs when she moans into my mouth.

I've never been so turned on, just making out with a woman.

I need more.

My lips stay on hers while she stays pressed against the fridge. Goose bumps run up her skin when I turn her to rest her back against a wall. My hand nearly shakes when it eases up her tank. Her skin is soft, so damn soft.

"Maliki." My name releases from her lips in a moan, and Jesus fuck, the things that does to me … to my dick.

I cup her breast, thrill rippling through me, and grind against her, rotating my hips.

As a mood killer, a reminder she's married zips through me, urging my dick to calm down, but I shove the thought away.

Fuck that.

She's mine.

Has been since the day her young ass walked into my bar, drinking a goddamn strawberry daiquiri.

"I need you," she breathes out, attempting to wedge her hand between the tight space of our bodies.

I swoop my hand down, snatching her wrist, and stop her.

"Not yet." I fasten her arms above her head and sweep my tongue over her lower lip.

I get to play first.

"Oh my God," she hisses as I drop kisses along her neck, sucking on her soft skin as if it's my favorite snack.

I need more.

"Sierra." My voice is so strained; I hardly recognize it.

"What?" She parts her legs and hooks one around my waist. "I need you, Maliki."

"The first time I fuck you won't be against a wall."

"Why not?" She rubs against me. "Sounds like the perfect plan to me."

"I want to do so many things to your body, and this wall will fuck with my plans. We'll save wall sex for later."

She groans in annoyance.

I chuckle, loving how desperate she is for me. "Do you know what happens now?"

"You pull down your pants and shove your cock inside me?"

"I'm unpinning you, and you're going to strut your sexy ass to my bedroom."

"And you'll join me?"

I unhand her and caress her cheek. "Is that even a goddamn question?" I fall back a step, giving her space, and clench my fists to stop myself from touching her.

She stares at me with confidence as she passes, her hand lightly brushing against my cock, a smirk hitting her lips.

Shiiiit.

"Goddamn, that ass." I dart my finger over my lips and catch my breath.

She stops mid-step to glance back at me. "Imagine the things you could do with it."

I'm behind her, my eyes roaming every inch of the back of her—her ass, her thighs, her back, her hair. I can't wait to wrap my fist around those blonde strands.

I adjust myself in my jeans, my dick throbbing so hard and pleading to be freed. It's never suffered through so much foreplay hell, and damn, we haven't even reached the good shit yet—only making out and dry-humping like two teenagers after a homecoming dance.

I flip on the light to find her standing at the foot of my bed with a wicked smile on her lips.

I stay in the doorway. "Have you thought about this before?"

She nods.

"You, in my bedroom?"

She nods again, sweeping her eyes down my body. Her smile grows when she stops at my erection straining against my jeans.

My dick screams at me to quit playing games.

I advance closer. "What did we do?"

"Fucked." The word pops from her full lips with no delay.

Shit.

I crowd her. "Is that the best you have for me? We *fucked?*"

She shivers when I stop in front of her. Not another word leaves my mouth as I glide my hands up her shirt and cup her breasts. My cock thickens at the sight of her nipples peeking through the thin fabric.

I tug at the bottom of her top. "This has to go."

She raises her arms with no hesitancy, allowing me to drag it over her head, and I drop it at our feet. Next, I unhook her bra, her breasts spilling out.

"You're beautiful," I comment, stroking a hand over her nipple.

She shuts her eyes, exhaling a deep breath.

"More beautiful than I imagined, baby." I tilt my head down and blow against her nipple, capturing it in my mouth and sucking hard.

I move to her other nipple, peeking up at her when she suppresses a moan, and softly bite the tip. I suck and bite each of her breasts. They're on the small side, and I tend to be a boob man, but I've never seen breasts so perfect.

I can't wait to put my hands and tongue on every inch of her.

"Now, tell me about your thoughts ... about us *fucking*. What did I do with you?" I sink to my knees without granting her the chance to respond. "Did I do this?"

She curses my name as I pop the button of her shorts open and unzip them.

"Please, fuck me," she begs.

I trace my finger along the edge of her panties. "Mmm ... such filthy words spilling from a pageant queen's mouth."

She grasps my hair when I yank her panties down and kicks them off her feet. "Not a pageant queen, and trust me, this mouth isn't sweet."

I brush my finger along her thigh. "I can't wait to find out how dirty that mouth is."

I also can't wait to get my tongue inside her.

My mouth waters.

I have to taste her.

She trembles, her legs weakening at my first lick, and I grip her ass to prevent her from falling.

"I want you inside me," she pleads. "Do you know how long I've waited for this?"

Does she know how long I've waited to get my tongue between her legs?

I flick her clit with my tongue and hook her leg over my shoulder.

"Every part of you is beautiful." I glide my finger through her folds, back and forth. "You are soaked, baby."

I suck on her clit, drawing a path through her slit with my tongue, and plunge it inside her. She gasps my name, her heels digging into my back.

It's the greatest sound I've ever heard.

I skim my hands up her legs, resting them on her ass. I rise onto my feet, confirming she's steady, and take a step back to admire her.

She's perfection.

I'm impressed at my willpower of not shoving her on the floor and fucking her right here, hard and raw.

She deserves better than wall-fucking and floor-fucking our first time.

She deserves my bed, me taking it slow and worshipping her body.

"Now that you've tasted me, it's only fair I do the same," she says, setting her sharp eyes on me.

I wipe my bottom lip and stand. "How about you lie down and let me have my way with you?"

"Fine, undress then."

She sits on the edge of the bed, her gaze fastened on me, as I shed my shirt and then lower my hands to my belt.

"Jesus, you're slow." She slaps my hand away and reaches for my buckle, and her hands are quick as she undoes it, shoving my jeans and boxer briefs down. "You're, uh … huge," she rasps.

I chuckle. "That's what every man likes to hear. Way to boost my ego before I give you my cock."

She bites into her lip.

"Lie down. I'll get you ready."

She scoots her ass up the bed and drops to her back when I crawl over her.

I slide a finger inside her, not wasting a second. "How many times have you gotten wet, thinking about my cock inside you?"

"You have no idea." She arches her back when I slip another finger in.

I rub her clit. "Trust me, I do." My number is much higher than hers.

"How many times have you jacked off, thinking about me?"

"Too many fucking times to count."

She leans forward, reaching for my cock, and I draw my fingers out of her to fall back against the bed, allowing her to stroke my throbbing cock. She grips it tight, her manicured fingers looking perfect around my cock as she jerks me.

"We've waited too long, Maliki," she says, squeezing the tip.

I pull back, my cock twitching at the loss of her touch, and open my nightstand for a condom, putting it on. I stare down at her—her eyes filled with longing, a small smile on her lips—and my heart rages in my chest. Her legs part wider as I settle myself between them, and she quivers when I drop a kiss to her soft lips.

I swipe my finger across her jaw and grin when her stomach muscles clench. I skim my hand down her neck, between her breasts, and stop at her clit, slowly rubbing it.

We drag in a breath when I position myself at her opening.

The first time I slide inside her is fucking bliss.

She's tight. Perfect. Too perfect for me.

"You feel amazing," I grind out, taking my time as I move in and out of her.

I'll stay inside her for as long as she'll let me.

"No, you feel incredible," she moans out. "I never knew sex could feel *this* good."

Her words give me chills, and I fight back the impulse to pound into her.

If I fuck her as hard as I'm craving to, I'm bound to bust quick.

I maintain a steady pace, my balls smacking against her ass each time I edge in deeper.

"Please," she begs. "Please, fuck me harder."

I grin. "There's that dirty mouth."

"Do you know how long I've wondered about what it'd be like to sleep with you?"

I slow my thrusts more. "How long?"

"Since you kicked me out the first time. I wished you had taken me to your office and let me seduce you."

And slower.

Our words release between pants.

"Seduce me at eighteen?"

Her hips tilt up and grind against my cock. "Just because I was a teenager didn't mean I was a virgin … didn't mean I wasn't attracted to you. I imagined you fucking me better than this."

"Oh, really?" I fuck her harder.

Her arms shoot up. "Yes, just like that."

"Always getting your way."

Satisfaction lights up her gorgeous face.

I quicken my thrusts while struggling to last as long as possible, but her dirty talk isn't helping.

"Yes, just like that." She moans. *"Oh my God. Don't stop."*

With every word, I pound harder.

With every moan, I grow closer.

The bed creaks, hitting the wall, and our moans are so loud. I wouldn't be surprised if the people downstairs hear us.

Let them know who she belongs to.

All I care about is the beautiful woman underneath me—pleasing her, making her happy, making her mine if for only one night.

I flick her clit with the tip of my finger.

"I'm close," she breathes out.

Seconds later, her back arches as she screams out my name.

Four thrusts later, I'm spent, spilling out into the condom, and, *"Fuck, baby,"* leaves my lips as they meet hers.

"I was going to call off my wedding," Sierra says the moment we drop to our backs.

Fuck.

She couldn't even give a man a minute to catch his breath before throwing that bomb on him.

I still. "What?"

"The night before my wedding, when I came to the bar, it was to tell you I was calling it off."

Chills hit me, and I remain silent while turning on my side, my eyes traveling over her naked body. I imagined her being in my bed so many times, jacked off on these very sheets as my imagination grew wild, but never did those include conversations about her marriage.

I should've stopped her from marrying him. We should've ended the game we played for years. I would've never seen her in my bar with an engagement ring wrapped around her finger, and she'd never have watched me fuck another woman. We suffered and risked our happiness out of fear. If we had skipped the games, we would've been here years ago.

I have her now.

And I'm not letting anything or anyone stand in our way.

"Instead of thinking about Devin that night, you consumed me. I went to the bar to tell you I wanted us to turn into an *us* and had for years." She shifts on her side, mirroring my position, and rests her cheek in her hand on her pillow.

She's beautiful. Her cheeks flush as she stares at me with sleepy eyes. Her tangled hair is feathered against the pillow. I love how they're all evidence of what we did. I massage her slender shoulder, and she shivers when I skim my hand down her waist, hauling her closer.

Her warm, naked body against mine is heaven.

She hesitates, questioning if it's wise to venture into this conversation after I was just inside her. I don't want my mistake to ruin this moment with her.

Sex with Sierra is the best I've ever had.

Hell, we went vanilla and fucked in a bed, but no one compares to her.

"When I saw you with her, it killed me." Her voice and body tighten. "I didn't know what to think, what to do, but like I took thinking about you the night before my wedding as a sign, I believed seeing you with her was one too—proof we weren't meant to be. It was a warning you were a man who couldn't keep it in his pants or give me the type of relationship I needed. I was heartbroken, angry, and embarrassed for assuming I could walk into the bar and change everything between us."

"But even after all that, you married him."

She shuts her eyes. "I did."

"Why didn't you tell me?" I trace a finger over the soft skin of her thigh. "Come to me?"

"I couldn't face you after that. All I'd see was you screwing her on that desk."

"And all those years, I couldn't rid the sight of him kissing you and touching you in my bar. You'd be with me and then go to bed with him."

"I know. I'm sorry. I was stupid."

"I ditched town the week of your wedding to clear my head but returned that night. Not going to lie, in the back of my mind, I was hoping you'd come to me. Then, Devin showed up as a pregame to his bachelor party. I knew he was there to rub it in my face, that you'd chosen him, and it killed me. Penny showed up, and … well, you know the rest."

"I was selfish—from the moment I sent you the invite to the wedding, thinking you'd come."

"That invite was a waste of paper. I burned it in the pizza oven."

She laughs.

"Did you think about me when you fucked him the night of your wedding?" I take her chin in my free hand, stopping her from looking away.

"I did," she whispers.

I snake my hand down her waist, pulling her leg up over my thigh, and peer at her. "I thought about you when I was with her, too."

She rises, her hand going to my chest to push me down, and straddles me. I groan, throwing my head back, as she grinds down, her bare pussy against my hard cock.

I cup her breast. "Ride me how you wanted that night. Fuck me how we would've. Give me what we should've had."

She bites into her lip, grabs a condom from my nightstand at my direction, and then fucks me hard.

"Don't stop," I mutter.

"Don't make me."

"I love looking at you like this," I say, smacking her ass. "All mine."

CHAPTER EIGHTEEN

SIERRA

I've hardly slept.

Every time my eyes attempt to shut, I force them back open, scared of falling asleep and waking up to discover this was all a dream.

Our legs are tangled, and Maliki's bulge presses against my ass as he stirs in his sleep.

His arms tighten around my waist.

"Good morning," he grumbles into my neck, running his hand up and down my leg.

"Morning," I squeak out.

He rests his hand on my waist and falls to his back, taking me with him, and situates me so I'm straddling him. He reaches out to clip a strand of my bedhead hair behind my ear, his gaze concentrating on me.

I settle my hand on his bare chest and release a deep, weighted sigh.

"What's wrong?" he asks.

It's always better to rip the Band-Aid fast.

Here goes.

"Do you regret what happened last night?"

He squeezes my waist. "Why in the living fuck would you think that?" He reaches up, sliding his hands over the curve of my jaw, and cups my chin when I attempt to break eye contact.

"From the beginning, you've made it clear you A.) aren't interested in a relationship like that with me and B.) aren't interested in a relationship, *period.*"

"I didn't want to corrupt you."

"Corrupt me?"

He nods. "We come from different sides of the tracks. At first, not going to lie, in my eyes, you were a young teen getting her rocks off on being rebellious against mommy and daddy."

"Wow," I draw out, my brows scrunching. "I'm thrilled you thought so highly of me."

"Hey, that was my first impression."

I squirm, the panties I slipped on after our last round rubbing against his bare cock. I'm not as comfortable naked as he is. "What do you think about me now?"

He tips his head back when I shift back and forth and groans. "Even when I met you and thought you were rebellious, I thought you were sexy and funny. I still think those things along with how amazing you are, and I'm so glad you walked into my bar that night."

I grin. "Corrupt me."

He leans back to snag a condom from the nightstand, and my breathing heightens as he puts it on. He wastes no time sliding my panties to the side, slipping his cock inside me, and I have the best morning sex of my life.

———

I grimace when I read the text.

Devin: We need to talk. You're still my wife.

I was so occupied with my parents' issues, my new jobs, and Maliki that I neglected the husband situation.

That's right. I forgot I was married.

Or maybe I've put it in the back of my mind, so I don't have to tackle the whole divorce thing.

"What's up?" Maliki asks.

"Devin texted me."

He frowns. "And?"

I cover my face with my hands. "This is humiliating."

"Why?"

"Uh … I'm married."

He scratches his cheek. "You're divorcing him, *right*?"

"Yes."

"Good." He takes a bite of a carrot and points to my phone. "Text him back and tell him that."

I ignore the text and shut off my phone.

———

Tonight is my first shift of working with Maliki since we had sex.

I'm like a lovesick teen.

Our eyes briefly catch when I peek over at him and grin.

"You slept with him, didn't you?"

I shift my attention back to Ellie, who's perched on a stool, nursing a glass of wine. We haven't hung out since dinner the day I left Devin.

I make a poor attempt of hiding my grin with my hand.

She laughs, reaching across the bar and slapping my arm. "You hooker! You screwed him and didn't tell me, your best friend. What the hell?"

I blow out a long breath, still unable to rid myself of my smile. "I can't call you *in front of him*. That convo needs to be saved for when we're alone."

"Uh, you can trek your little ass to the bathroom and call me … or at least shoot your girl a text. It's rude and against friendship rules for me to find out at the same time as all these wasted people here."

I jerk my head back. "Wait, what?"

She rolls her eyes. "It's obvious. You're eye-fucking him, and he does the same between every drink he makes."

I perk up, my heart leaping. "Really?"

She whistles. "Girl, you've got it bad. He has it bad. I demand every single detail, please and thank you."

"I'm off tomorrow. Margaritas?"

"Can't. I'm babysitting."

I raise a brow. "Someone trusts you with their kid?"

"It's my niece, so if I lose her or something, I won't go to jail." She shrugs. "My sister is moving home, and I was given the option to babysit or help move. Considering physical labor isn't my jam, I chose babysit." Her eyes brighten. "Oh, *instead* of drinks, you can have the pleasure of helping me. You've volunteered with kiddos. You know how to change diapers and all that stuff."

I shake my head, fighting a grin. "I'm not changing diapers."

"*Kidding.* The little heathen is, like, six. Consider it practice for when you and Maliki make little ones."

I hold my palm up. "Seriously, don't go there."

"Oh, I'm going there." She grins and then downs her wine.

———

"Ellie said it's obvious we had sex," I tell Maliki. "That everyone at the bar knows."

We're closing as usual, but tonight, it's different. We exchange flirtatious glances and brush against each other as we cross paths.

He chuckles, his lips stretching into a broad smile. "Then, maybe you shouldn't eye-fuck me all night, huh?" He steps closer and pokes the tip of my nose. "That makes it obvious."

"Oh, *puh-lease*. You eye-fucked me all night. And not only tonight but *every night*."

"I won't dispute that." He spans his arm around my waist. "You know what's nice?"

I shiver when his hand wanders to my ass. "What?"

"Now, I can do more than eye-fuck you."

I grin. "Oh, yes, that's definitely nice." I encircle my arms around his neck to tug him my way.

He bows his head, brushing a gentle kiss over my lips. "I have an idea."

"Hmm?"

"You. Me. The apartment. We'll save the closing for later." He swoops his tongue into my mouth to suck on mine.

"Why wait?" I peek down and notice the erection through his jeans.

His hands leave me when I hop onto the bar—the same place he pinned and kissed me the night Penny ruined our moment.

He raises a brow but doesn't speak.

I pat the bar and signal for him to come closer with my finger. "I want you to screw me here."

"Sierra." My name leaves his lips in warning, and he exhales audibly.

"Maliki." I imitate his tone. "Finish what you started before *she* showed up. Let me mark my territory. Now, when you look at this spot, you'll be reminded of me—where you laid me onto my back and fucked me until I couldn't breathe."

"Shit," he hisses through clenched teeth and advances a step, stopping in front of me and standing tall. He snags my waist and tugs me to the edge of the bar, my core rubbing against his hardness. He releases my waist, his hand drifting up my side and shoulder, and he moves my hair to the side, his lips brushing against my ear. "How do you want it, baby?"

I rub my thighs together, feeling my wet panties, and desire screams through me.

"Fuck me hard, right here, right now. Own me, Maliki." The words exit my mouth in harsh gasps.

He wraps my hair in his fist, tugging it back. "Jailbait, I've owned you since you were eighteen."

I lick my top lip and lean forward until my mouth is almost resting against his. "Prove it."

His lips claim mine, heavy and heated, and he widens my legs, giving him enough space to stand between them. He tightens his hold on my hair, yanking my head back, and his lips roam my neck.

My pulse beats hard in every spot he kisses and licks. I struggle to breathe when he grabs my ankles and pulls me toward him, my ass hanging off the bar.

"I hate when you wear these short shorts," he says. "It drives my imagination wild, thinking about licking and sucking your tight pussy." He rakes a finger across my core over my jeans. "Is that why you wear them? To torture me?"

I lower my head to stare at him, his eyes mischievous as they harden on me. "Maybe."

His mouth replaces his hand, resting his lips on my jeans and blowing on them. I open my mouth to beg him for more, but his hands are faster than my words.

In seconds, he has my shorts unbuckled and shoves them along with my panties down my legs. I help him drag them off my feet, and he falls to his knees, resting my thighs on his shoulders. I squirm when his hand squeezes my ass, holding me still, and his tongue dives deep inside me.

My nails dig into the bar and move to his hair, pulling at the strands while he plunges his tongue deep inside me, playing with my clit, and then his fingers meet his tongue.

The roughness of the bar is hard against my back. I'll be sore tomorrow, but I don't care.

I dig my heels into his back and beg for more.

Then, I gasp because I can't take it anymore.

My skin tingles against the wood when I arch my back, and my body trembles as I release onto his tongue.

He lifts, wiping his hand across his mouth, and I shake my head.

"I can't handle it anymore." Deep breaths leave my stomach. "You can't … there's no way I can … Jesus, that was incredible."

His hands rest on my knees, and he carefully settles my legs back down. "You can."

He snatches a condom from his wallet before dropping his pants, his dick hard and long as it comes into my view, and it twitches as he places it at my opening.

"You want me to own you with this cock here?" he asks, raising a brow.

I gyrate my hips, pleading with him, and grab his ass to come closer. I wrap my fingers around his cock, raise my hips, and position him at my opening.

He's moving too damn slow.

He waits, allowing me to take control, and throws his head back when I push in the tip. His eyes fixate on my hand as I play with myself with his cock, moving in just an inch, and his breathing is harsh and ragged, but he doesn't thrust himself in. He lets me play my game as he grows harder and harder underneath my fingers.

I release his cock, my hands running up his chest, and cup his shoulders.

Then, he grabs my ass, holding me up, and pushes inside me.

It's the best damn feeling everywhere.

Maybe because we're doing it here—a forbidden place.

Maybe because I know he's had other women here, and I want to erase them.

Maybe because I've sat at this bar, night after night, fantasizing about this that I never want him to stop as he plunges in and out of me.

Sweat builds along his forehead, his gaze pinned on our connection.

"God, you feel so good," I moan.

His attention flicks up to meet my eyes. "You're perfect, Sierra. So tight and so perfect."

It doesn't take long until his thrusts turn harder and faster, my hips moving at the same speed as we slam into each other. My eyes shut, my head dropping back, and I yell out his name while collapsing against the bar.

He continues his thrusting, groaning, until he releases inside me.

Our breathing echoes through the bar.

It takes a moment to gain control of myself. "That was amazing."

He gives me a quick peck. "You're amazing."

CHAPTER NINETEEN

MALIKI

"I'm back," Liz sings, walking into my office. "How big of a mess are you in with troublemaking Barbie?"

"Don't call her that." I narrow my eyes at her from my desk.

Two weeks have passed since Sierra and I had sex.

It's been a fucking amazing two weeks.

Liz shuts the door. "Your answer tells me she hasn't broken your heart yet."

I recline in my chair, crossing my legs, and play with the pen in my hand. "How's Dad?"

"He's Dad. He and the wifey reconciled, and she's surprisingly not terrible."

"What happened to divorcing her?"

"It was his fault for their issues. He was scared she'd leave him like Mom did and pulled away. They talked and seem okay now."

"Good." I fidget with the pen between my fingers. "I have something to tell you."

"What's up?"

I massage the back of my neck. "I'm renovating the bar."

"Oh, cool." She smiles. "I'd love to help."

"Actually—"

Sierra walks in mid-sentence, her hands filled with a notebook and paint samples. Liz's smile wipes off her face, turning into a glare.

Without bothering to glance up, Sierra starts talking, "So, I've gone back and forth with the taupe color you picked—and by picked, I mean, pointed and said, 'That one,' without bothering to look at other options. I don't see it working with the floor we ordered. I know you like it, but *blugh*. I promise to find something better. You'll love it."

All the color drains from Liz's face while Sierra continues her rambling.

"I also have furniture options, and stop me if I'm going too far, but *maybe* we can tear down a wall?"

Liz's gaze pings from her to me. "Tear down a wall?" she shrieks.

The notebook drops from Sierra's hand, paint samples fluttering on the floor, and her eyes shoot straight to me in panic.

"When you said renovating, I took that as a fresh paint job," Liz spits out.

"We are doing new paint," Sierra remarks.

Liz shoots her a hard look. "I meant, not changing everything."

"*Technically*, we're not changing everything," Sierra answers. "We're preserving the bones of the bar, just altering a few things, making them better."

"The bar doesn't need to *get better*." Liz turns back to me, her face serious. "Why wasn't this discussed with me?"

"Liz, not here, not now," I caution.

"I'll go … look at other ideas," Sierra mutters.

I tilt my head her way with a small smile, and she backs away, hurrying out of the room.

"What will you hire her for next? To sleep with you?" Liz seethes as soon as Sierra disappears.

"Don't go there." My tone is harsh. "Leave Sierra alone."

"You've already slept with her, haven't you? Jesus, Maliki!"

"That's none of your fucking business."

"You're making a mistake."

"Then, it will be my mistake. I'm a big boy."

"You're going to let her ruin our family's legacy."

"Our family's legacy?" I explode. "What legacy is there to be proud of, Liz? The one where our mother was clinically depressed and regularly institutionalized? Or is it when she abandoned her family? Is it our father neglecting to care for his children as he should have, passing that responsibility on to you, or when he nearly went bankrupt and lost this *legacy?* What goddamn legacy are you referring to?"

Her face softens at my hard blow. "You know what I mean. The bar has been in our family for generations without any *renovations*, and you never mentioned changing anything until *she* came along."

"Let me remind you, I rescued this bar from going under." I slam my hand on the desk. "I didn't want it. You knew that, but you begged me to come home and save it—to keep it in the family and make it my own. That's what I'm doing. If you have such an issue with it, I'll gladly sell it to you."

"You're an asshole." She stomps out, the door slamming behind her.

———

"Am I fired?" Sierra asks.

I took a breather in my office before coming out.

How dare Liz throw out *family legacy* bullshit.

"No," I answer.

"Maliki, I don't want you and your sister arguing over me."

"We're not. We're arguing because she's stubborn and she was rude to you." I kiss the top of her head, smelling her strawberry shampoo. "Don't worry about Liz. She'll get over it."

She looks up at me. "Or kill me in my sleep. Does she have a key to my bedroom?"

"Your bedroom is in my bedroom now, and no, she doesn't."

She frowns, sighing. "You know what I mean."

I lean down and press my lips against hers. "Don't"—another kiss—"worry"—another kiss—"about"—another kiss—"her."

CHAPTER TWENTY

"It's been forever since I've been here," I say, walking into Ellie's apartment.

"You've neglected your bestie while on Operation Dodge Your Husband," she teases.

"A successful mission so far. Has he been here?" I assured Ellie I don't expect her to stop Devin from coming over. It's not fair to Corbin.

"A few times." Her tone softens. "He misses you."

"Ellie," I warn.

She holds up her hand, palm facing me. "I'm not suggesting you take him back. I'm simply reporting what I've seen when he's here with Corbin. I don't want you to get back with him, *but* there is no doubt he regrets cheating."

My throat burns. No matter what, I care about Devin, but not only can I *not* forgive him, but I also can't walk away from Maliki.

We're interrupted by a small brown-haired girl wearing a yellow sundress and a daisy clip in her hair. "Aunt Ellie's friend!" A smile beams on her face when I spot her sitting on the floor behind the coffee table, surrounded by crayons and coloring books. She holds up a book, showing off a picture of a princess scribbled with different colors, and squeals in excitement. "Look what I colored!"

I lean down to her level and take a long look at it. "Oh my goodness! That's so pretty!"

She sits up straight and giggles.

"See, you're better with kids," Ellie comments. "I'll whip up some mac and cheese while you watch her not color in the lines."

I shake my head. "You're awful."

"I know." She shrugs and heads to the kitchen.

"And make me a bowl!" I call out behind her. I plop down next to the tot, grab a coloring book from the stack, and snag a few crayons. I open the book and flip to a picture with Barbie and Ken.

"I'm Molly." Her voice is bubbly as she grips a crayon and shows it to me. "Purple is my favorite color!"

I choose a crayon and grin. "I'm Sierra." My voice lowers as I lean in closer. "And guess what."

She giggles. "What?"

"Purple is my favorite, too."

Her face brightens. "Really?"

I nod. "Really."

"Will you be my friend?"

I bump my shoulder against hers. "Uh, duh."

"Yay! We can play dolls after this."

———

"I've always loved watching you with kids."

I glance away from the TV to find Devin standing behind me. "What are you doing here?"

Molly looks between the two of us, curiosity swimming in her eyes. I can't exactly be rude to him in front of her.

He points to the patio with his chin. "Can we talk?"

Hell no. "Sure."

I stand, and he follows me outside.

His shoulders are tense when he shuts the door behind us, and his scowl hits me. "I've called you nonstop, Sierra. I'm your husband. I know you're angry with me, but at least show me respect and answer my calls. Hear me out."

I cross my arms. "You cheated on me. What do you expect? I don't want to talk to you. I don't want to see you."

"What do I expect? I expect you to at least hold a goddamn conversation with me. You're my wife! We got married, exchanged vows, promised to love each for the rest of our lives—for better or worse." His words come out in forced restraint.

I scoff. "*For better or worse* doesn't excuse you sticking your penis in Louise."

"It was *once*. One fucking time, and I was drunk. *Please*. I've given you time. Hell, I've even sat back while people walk around, saying you're screwing Maliki. *Him*. Out of all people, you had to run to him."

"I'm not talking about Maliki with you."

"Are you sleeping with him?" he grits out.

"That's none of your concern."

He drops down on a chair, taking my hand, and a sob leaves him, surprising me. Sadness clutches my heart. I've never seen Devin this emotional.

He scrubs a hand over his face and uses his free hand to point to Molly through the window.

"You see that little girl in there?" he asks. "We were supposed to have that. How many times did we talk about kids in our future?"

I jerk my hand back, unable to look at him as tears swell in my eyes.

His shoulders slump. "I fucked up, and I'm sorry. Whatever you did with him, it's in the past. We'll start fresh and consider this a speed bump in our marriage, act like it never happened."

I shut my eyes for a moment, an attempt to hold myself together. I can't flip my shit with Molly watching us. "You can't have a family with a man you don't trust."

He scowls and releases a spiteful laugh. "You think *he'll* give you a family? Where would you raise your children? In an apartment above a place filled with drunks? You're worried about trusting me. What do you think you'll get with the town's biggest bachelor, huh? He lives in that bar, and we've both seen how well he attracts the ladies. Do you honestly think he'll stay faithful or that he'll even *want* a family?"

"Don't go there."

His words hit too close to home. That's what happened with Maliki's mom—she couldn't handle being the bar owner's wife—and the girls at the barbeque said the same about bartenders.

"I'm owning up to my fuckup and begging you. Let's go to counseling. I'll do whatever you want to make this work. *Please.* I don't want to lose you."

Tears fall from my eyes. "I can't … maybe this means we weren't meant for each other."

He shakes his head in disdain. "You haven't filed yet. That has to mean something."

"I haven't had a chance to."

"I won't sign."

I retreat a step. "Don't do that."

"Do what?"

"Drag this out."

His eyes darken in frustration. "I'll fight for my marriage."

"You should've fought for it then!"

He abruptly stands. "You'll never have a family with him. Think about that before throwing everything you've ever wanted away. You know where to find me, and I swear to God, I'll forget anything you did with him if you come back to me." His lips graze my forehead, and the patio door squeaks when he opens it to leave.

I fall back in his abandoned chair and wrestle with Devin's words running through my mind. He made valid points. Maliki said his job would interfere with having children, and he couldn't give them a stable home. I sniffle, wiping the tears from my eyes, and catch my breath.

"Are you okay?"

I inhale a breath and look over at the door where the tiny voice came from. Molly has it open a few inches, enough room for her head to poke through, and holds the handle in hesitation. She waits until I give her a head nod and opens the door all the way, stepping on the porch with me.

"I'm fine, sweetie," I answer, fighting back sniffles.

She wraps her arms around me. "My daddy says to always hug people when they're sad and crying. It'll make them happy again."

I hug her back.

Maliki is older than me and has never settled down with a woman, never mentioned living anywhere but his apartment, never seemed to want to move on from the bachelor life.

Where will our relationship be in a month?

Six weeks?

A year?

Will we even have one?

———

Liz is behind the bar when I walk in.

Great.

I've already dealt with Devin today.

Now, her.

We've rarely been around each other without Maliki around, and she's made it clear she's not a fan of mine—his presence or not.

I should've taken the back entrance, but I wasn't sure if Maliki was working.

She sourly stares at me while setting the clipboard in her hand onto the bar. I twist on my toes to head upstairs, but her voice stops me.

"You know how long I've wanted to bitch-slap you?"

Whoa. I expected an insult, smart-ass comment, definitely not bitch-slap talk.

"No, but you do it, and I'll slap you back," I quip.

"I see why my brother is infatuated with you." Her tone is surprisingly sincere as a hint of a smile presses against her lips.

Whoa. I didn't expected that ... whatever it was ... either.

I hitch my purse onto my shoulder. "Will there be any bitch-slapping going down?"

She shakes her head. "Maliki would never talk to me again if I laid a hand on you."

I stay quiet, unsure of where she's going with this uncomfortable-as-hell conversation.

She lifts her chin. "Are you divorcing him?"

I nod. "Yes."

"My brother is in love with you."

I retreat a step, wincing, and force a laugh. "I don't know about that." Another laugh. *Please sound amused, not scared that she might be wrong.*

"I do. I know him, and he's in love with you. He might not admit it, but when you got married, it nearly broke him. Make him happy. He deserves it."

"You're crazy," I stammer.

I have no doubt Maliki cares about and is attracted to me. He's told me how much he wants to be together, *but* I'm still unsure of where our relationship stands. Does he even know how to have a relationship?

"No, you're blind or too afraid to admit it like he is. You're scared he'll break your heart like your ex, but that won't be Maliki. If you were another woman, eh, I wouldn't say that, but it's you. My brother has been obsessed with you for years."

I gulp, unable to form the right words.

"In other news, I'm extending my leave from the bar. The bartending job is all yours for as long as you'd like."

I smile weakly. "Thank you … for letting me keep my job."

She picks up her clipboard. "You're welcome. He's upstairs."

I walk up to the apartment and find Maliki in the bedroom, undressing, his well-defined back facing me. I gulp when he pulls his pants up.

I step forward, wrapping my arms around his waist, and hug him from behind. "Hey you."

After what Liz told me, I should be on top of the world, but I still can't stop thinking about Devin's words.

I rest my head in the crook of his shoulder, and he turns to kiss me.

"Hey, how was your day with Ellie?"

"We babysat." I pause to hold up a finger. "I babysat while Ellie watched me and texted."

He chuckles, grabbing his shirt and pulling it over his head, causing me to frown. Now that I've seen him without his clothes on, it's my favorite sight. Like a child, I hate when he takes my favorite show away.

"Who trusted you with their kid?"

"Hey, I'm exceptional with kids, thank you very much. It was her niece, Jessa's daughter. You remember her; you two had a thing."

He throws his head back and groans. "You never neglect to bring up the *few* women I've had *a thing* with."

"I'm certain there are more than *a few* that I know nothing about."

Maliki has always been quiet about his history with women. All I know is, he's never had a serious relationship.

He grimaces. "I haven't spoken to Jessa in years. It's been months since I touched Penny. Hell, since I've slept with anyone but you. Trust me on this, Sierra. *Please.* I'm not like Devin or your father." He wraps his arms around me, his mouth meeting mine, and smiles against my lips. "You're all I want. All I need."

CHAPTER TWENTY-ONE
MALIKI

I'm drinking a cup of coffee when Sierra walks into the kitchen, whistling with a pep in her step.

I set my mug down and raise a brow.

She's always been eager and ecstatic, but after Devin's cheating, it's faded out some, and I hate that.

"So … I did a thing," she reveals, her tone bubbly.

"Yeah, and what kind of thing?"

"I met with an attorney and filed for divorce."

I jerk my head back. Not what I was expecting, but *motherfucking yes.*

Excitement spirals through me. All of my doubts of Sierra going back to Devin and us being a fling have vanished. Her filing has opened the gates of us developing a deeper relationship than sex.

Fuck, who am I kidding?

Our relationship has always been more than sex.

We formed a deep connection before I even touched her.

My grin is so large that I'm surprised it hasn't fallen off my face.

"Let's celebrate. I'll take you out."

"Really?" Happiness and surprise register on her face.

It hits me that we haven't done much outside of hanging out at the bar and the apartment. Sure, we went shopping and to Cohen's but nothing like a date. She deserves more from me.

I nod. "Really."

She skips around the island to plant a kiss on my cheek. "I can't wait."

Devin cheating might've broken her heart, but it's the best damn thing to happen to mine. I was right all along. He wasn't the man for her.

I am.

———

I fasten my gaze on Sierra sitting across the table. "Mikey won't stop pestering me about renting my apartment. He's driving thirty minutes back and forth to work and whining about his lack of sleep and gas money."

Tonight has been incredible, and we're only at the beginning. I brought her to Clayton's, a five-star restaurant outside of Blue Beech. Clayton's is the preferred spot for anniversaries, proposals, birthdays, and celebrations.

And tonight, we're fucking celebrating.

Sierra is cutting the Devin cord, and I can't wait to throw that sucker away.

"You'd better tell Mikey I'll crack a bottle over his head if he attempts to steal my roommate position," she replies.

Shit. She's not going where I wanted this conversation to go.

Mikey won't steal her roommate position.

He'll move in. We'll move out.

"We're more than roommates," I correct.

She taps the tip of her chin. "Right ... we're ... bedmates?"

"More than that, too."

She looks damn gorgeous tonight. She doesn't dress up much around me, given the bar is so laid-back, and I love the casual look on her, but she looks stunning. I nearly fell on my face when she walked out of the bathroom in a short red dress that showed plenty of leg and strappy black heels, and her hair is down in loose curls. Her lips are painted a bright red. The lipstick seems to be the only makeup she wears.

I can't wait for the day that red lipstick stains my cock.

I shift in my chair, just thinking about it.

I'm ready to explain my reasoning for bringing Mikey's whining up, but as soon as I open my mouth, she's already talking.

"Have you ever had a relationship?"

"No," I respond without hesitation. "Well … not before you."

My honesty startles her, her bright lips lifting into a wild grin. "Are you saying …"

"Am I saying we're in a relationship? Yes." I cock my head to the side. "If that's okay with you?"

She gapes at me. "We're doing this for real?"

I don't know who's more excited—her or me. This is a serious step for me—wanting a relationship. I couldn't see myself doing this with anyone but her.

"You're divorcing Devin, correct?" I ask.

"Absolutely," she rushes out.

"Then, it's settled."

"Holy shit," she whispers. "I'm in a relationship with Maliki Bridges. My teenage fantasies have come true."

I chuckle. "Oh, really?" I fold my hands together, rest them on the table, and lean closer. "Did you write about me in your diary?"

"Yes." Her voice turns soft and almost childish. "*Dear Diary, Maliki smiled at me today.*" She cracks a flirtatious smile. "*Dear Diary, Maliki said he hates annoying teenagers, and I'm an annoying teenager.*"

"You have to admit, you were an annoying teenager."

"You have to admit, you were an annoying bar owner," she counters with amusement. "And that you drank before you turned twenty-one."

"I won't deny that."

"See! Why was it such a big deal for me to drink?" She snatches up her martini, gives me a *cheers,* and takes a long sip with a smirk.

"The difference is, my dad was the owner then and didn't care if I drank. I owned the bar when you tried and *did* care."

She rolls her eyes and drops her empty glass onto the table. "FYI, and side note, I am a high-maintenance girlfriend. Just wanted to give you a heads-up. This is your first test: I'm drinking *a lot* of martinis tonight. I might be annoying."

"And I don't give a shit. High maintenance, annoying—which I have dealt with for years, mind you—or not, you're still mine."

———

"I can't eat for another week," Sierra declares when we walk out of Clayton's, dodging bodies in the busy crowd.

We've run into three people from Blue Beech, and luckily, Sierra had drank enough martinis that she didn't stress about what they thought about her being married.

Me? I couldn't care less.

Let them report back to Devin.

"Even if it's an ice cube," she goes on, "I'll die." Her head falls back in a groan. "And thank goodness you barely drank, so you can be DD tonight, *boyfriend.*"

I grin like a motherfucker at her last word.

I gape down at her as she stays in my hold. "You're going to regret drinking so many martinis tomorrow, *girlfriend.*"

She wobbles in her heels a bit, and I tighten my arms around her shoulders, keeping her from falling.

"Nope. I'll be ecstatic I drank all those martinis." She licks her lips. "Martinis are my jam, and I can't wait to bring more recipes to the pub. I'll turn all the beer and whiskey drinkers into champagne and martini connoisseurs."

I chuckle. "Good luck with that, babe."

I hand the valet our slip and focus on her, admiring the woman who's become everything to me, while she babbles on about different martinis—something along the lines of Key Lime and Blood Oranges.

This damn woman has buried herself so deep in my fucking veins that there's no way I can cut her out.

I wave off the valet when he goes to help her into the car, doing it myself, and rush over to the driver's side.

"I wonder if the bar is busy tonight," she comments, leaning back in her seat.

"We won't know until tomorrow when I check the figures," I say, pulling out of the parking lot.

"Ah … the boss won't be going down to check on business?" She gasps. "I can't believe Maliki, the workaholic, will let that slide for a night."

"The boss won't even be in the building." Even though it's dark and she most likely can't see me, I smirk her way. "Tonight, it's you and me, babe. No bar chaos, no employees, nothing other than room service and us relaxing in a hotel suite."

She perks up in her seat. "Seriously?"

I nod, loving how excited she is. I should've spoiled her like this sooner. I'll have to make up for my lack of taking her out.

"Uh, shit," she mutters, and by her tone, I wasn't supposed to hear that.

"What's up?"

She shakes her head. "Nothing."

"Sierra," I warn.

"I don't want to feel like a Debbie Downer, and I know I won't be wearing any clothes tonight—"

"Correct on that assessment," I can't help but chime in.

"I'm worried about tomorrow. This dress and heels aren't exactly comfortable to wear then."

"I packed a bag while you were showering."

"You went through my things?"

"Don't worry. I wasn't *too* nosy … didn't find your diary filled with *I Heart Maliki* and *Mrs. Bridges* written between hearts."

She laughs. "I can't wait to write in that journal about how I sucked and then straddled your dick tonight."

"Jesus." I grip the steering wheel tighter in fear of driving off the road. "You can't say that shit to me when I'm already struggling to pay attention."

Good thing the hotel is only minutes away.

————

Sierra's mouth is on mine as soon as we walk into the hotel room.

I suck in a breath as her drunken hands fumble with my belt.

The bags I'm holding drop out of mine, hitting the floor.

Yes.

The hotel room was an amazing idea.

I flip on the light.

She backs me toward the bed, and my heart nearly gives out when she shoves my pants down. Her lips have never met my cock, and my heart quickens from me just thinking about it.

She drops to her knees and tugs down my pants, and my swollen cock springs free.

Shit. I might come before she even puts me in her mouth.

She peeks up at me, a teasing smile on her lips before she licks them. I groan when she wraps her lips around the crown of my dick and takes me all the way in, the tip of my cock hitting the back of her throat as she starts sucking me.

The best goddamn blow job I've ever had.

I dig my fingers into the bed while watching my cock move in and out of her mouth. I suck in a breath, grab her hair, and pump my hips to the same pace she's sucking.

I'm close.

As bad as I want to see her swallow my cum, I need to be inside her more.

"Stop sucking me and take off your clothes," I rasp out. "Then, fuck me."

As I grab a condom, I see her lipstick on my dick and grin.

I waste no time slipping on the condom as she gets naked.

She straddles my cock and rides me.
My life has never been perfect.
Never will be perfect.
But Sierra has made it damn near close.
Too bad I don't know it's going to all fall apart.

CHAPTER TWENTY-TWO
MALIKI

I'm searching real estate online while Sierra is shopping with her mom. To say the market blows in Blue Beech is an understatement. Finding a place might take a while, so I haven't mentioned anything to Sierra yet.

No matter what, I'll find a new home for us. We need privacy and space from the bar. From experience, this isn't a stable place to raise a family either.

That's right.

I'm already thinking about having a family with her.

I want her to be my wife and the mother of my children.

I never thought that was something I'd say.

I shut my laptop and drop it next to me at the sound of a knock on the door. I don't get very many visitors here, given it's in the back lot and most people see me at the bar.

I open the door to find the last person I expected.

She gapes at me, her face brimming with stress.

What the fuck?

I have no clue why she's here or what to say.

"Hey, Maliki," she says, looking high-strung.

I cross my arms. "Jessa, this is a surprise."

She scowls at my harsh tone. "Can I come in?"

"Sure." I retreat a step while doubting if it's a good idea, making sure there's ample space between us, and shut the door. "What's up?"

"I need to tell you something."

"So, tell me."

"I, uh …"

Jesus. She needs to stop this stuttering shit and explain herself. I can't risk Sierra coming in and seeing her here.

I snap my fingers in her face. "What do you need to tell me?"

I'm acting rude, which is unnecessary, but why is she standing, speechless. in my doorway? Her uneasiness makes me worry she's about to start some shit. The faster she explains why she's here, the faster I can go back to house-hunting.

Until something hits me.

An abrupt wave of nausea smacks into me. "Is Sierra okay?" It's reaching, but if something is wrong with her, Ellie could've asked Jessa to relay the message.

"Sierra?" She glances around the apartment. "Why are you worried about my sister's friend?"

"Why else would you be here?"

"*Again,* why do you care about her?"

"Cut to the chase and spit it out, Jessa. I have shit to do that doesn't involve your manipulative games."

"Manipulative games?" She snorts. "I'm manipulative? You're the one worried about a *married* woman. I see your type hasn't changed."

"I had no idea you were in a relationship when we fucked," I seethe. "You and Pete were off and on as much as you changed your panties." I clench my jaw. "*Now,* for the umpteenth time, why are you here?"

"There's something I've been hiding from you."

"Tell me what this *something* is."

"You have a child," she blurts out.

I explode in laughter. "Good one. Did Devin put you up to this?"

"It's true." She shakes her head and pinches her lips together. "I got pregnant when we were sleeping together."

I rub the back of my neck. "Bullshit. I always wrapped up." Sierra is the only woman I've gone raw in.

She continues shaking her head while firing back her argument that I'm her baby daddy. "Tom Petty concert. The backseat of your car."

My mind scrambles back to that night.

Broken condom. *Shit.*

She promised she was on the pill.

"I got pregnant." She rocks back on her heels. "By the time I found out, I was back with Pete."

I hold my hand up, swallowing loud, and sink into a chair at the kitchen table, growing light-headed. "I'm so fucking lost right now."

She takes the seat across from me. "Pete would've left me if I was pregnant with another man's baby, so I told him she was his. Our relationship was solid, and I knew a relationship with you was off the table because you're ... well, *you.*"

"Jump to the part where I have a child," I grind out. "And why I'm just now finding out."

She slightly lifts her chin. "She's six years old. Pete's mother has never been a fan of mine and always questioned the paternity of Molly. She took it upon herself to swab my daughter's cheek and send it to one of those stupid mail-in labs. Pete found out the truth and filed for divorce. Now, I'm back in Blue Beech, and you deserve to know the truth."

"Oh, *after* Pete left you, I deserve the truth. How fucking convenient is that?"

"I'm telling the truth, Maliki!"

"You've always been a liar, Jessa."

"I swear, I'm not lying."

"Just because she's not Pete's doesn't mean she's mine. Who knows how many men you slept with behind our backs?"

"She's yours. One hundred percent. You might think I'm a vindictive bitch, but I love my daughter."

I grind my teeth and keep an eye on the door, as if I'm waiting for

Sierra to walk into this mess. "If you loved her so much, you would've told me years ago, so she wouldn't be fatherless."

"She had a father. Pete. You and Pete were the only men I slept with, *and* I was only screwing you during the time. Believe me, I knew you'd treat me like this and still told you."

"I want a paternity test," I bite out.

"That's no problem."

Her answer falls from her lips in seconds, shocking me.

Maybe she is telling the truth.

She stands and runs her hands over her black dress. She rests them on the table with a stern look on her face. "And FYI, if you're screwing my sister's friend, be careful. She was arguing with her husband the other day while watching Molly. She cried, and they kissed. If I were you, I'd check on your sidepiece." She stops to put her finger to the corner of her mouth. "Or are you her sidepiece, given she's married?"

I fight with myself from throwing whatever I can grab across the room. Too much is being flung at me.

I might have a child.

Sierra was with Devin.

They kissed.

My hands shake as I maintain my composure. "All I'm talking to you about is a paternity test. Otherwise, keep your mouth shut about my life."

"I'll figure it out and get back with you."

I nod.

I'm speechless.

She leaves without another word, and as soon as the door shuts behind her, I snatch a coffee cup on the table and chuck it across the room.

I'm not believing anything until I see results.

But if it comes out positive, that means she's hidden this part of my life from me for six years.

I calculate the timeline of my relationship with Jessa while cleaning up the glass and then slump down on the couch, staring at the wall.

Jessa has always been a fan of games. We went to high school together, fucked a few times, and then I moved away. We reconnected a few years later and fucked some more. Since I wasn't living in Blue Beech, I didn't know she was engaged to Pete.

"Off and on," is what she said, and I was young and dumb and ran with the *off*, thinking with my dick.

We fucked, plain and simple, and I cut her off when she turned crazy.

I rise to my feet, pour myself a drink, and return to the couch. My mind drifts to Sierra and what Jessa said about her being with Devin at Ellie's. She never mentioned their encounter.

Why would she hide that from me?

I'm being smacked with too many bombshells.

I might be a father.

Jesus fucking Christ.

———

Sierra stops dead in front of me and presses her lips against mine. "Sorry I'm late. Please don't fire me, boss man."

Please don't leave me if Jessa's telling the truth.

I kiss her again. "Only if you make up for your tardiness later."

She flips her straight hair over her shoulder. "Duh."

I grab a towel and smack her ass with it. "Now, get to work."

She salutes me, bends down, and smacks my ass in return. "I missed you today."

As much as I don't want to ruin the mood, the words have been resting on the tip of my tongue since Jessa left. "Jessa said you and Devin had a moment at Ellie's. You never told me that."

She freezes in step. "Jessa? What were you doing, talking to Jessa?"

Shit. "She came into the bar before you got here, you late one, you, and told me." I hate lying to her.

"Well, Jessa can kiss my ass because she's lying." Her face reddens. "She probably wants to start screwing you again now that her husband left her unfaithful ass."

I wish I weren't avoiding her gaze, but I can't look at her. I'm afraid she'll see the lies in my eyes. "Why'd he leave her?"

She shrugs with a frown. "Something about her lying to him about being the father of their daughter. It's sad because the little girl is so adorable, and now, Jessa stuck her into this weird position of not knowing who her dad is." She kisses my cheek. "Be happy you dodged that bullet."

"Trust me, I am." *At least I thought I'd dodged it.*

"Yep, because then you met me. By the way, Devin was begging me to stay with him at Ellie's. I made it clear I wasn't and then filed for divorce the next day. That lying tramp can kiss my ass, and she'd better stay away from you."

"I love when you get all territorial."

CHAPTER TWENTY-THREE

MALIKI

TWO WEEKS LATER

My hands shake as I stare at the envelope—the paternity results. The day after Jessa broke the news, we went to get a paternity test. She brought her—maybe *our*—daughter in first and left, and then I went in. It isn't healthy to include the little girl until paternity is established. Jessa could be lying, and the little girl is already confused after learning the man she believed to be her dad for years isn't. I need to be positive before breaking the news and further confusing her.

Jessa called the bar, looking for me this morning, which resulted in a glare from Liz. I ordered Jessa to never do it again and reluctantly gave her my phone number. She's already texted me five times.

I decided not to tell Sierra until the results came. Our relationship is perfect, and I'm scared this news will lead to problems, given she can't stand Jessa. She wouldn't be happy to find out Jessa is the mother of my child.

I pace back and forth and then tear it open.

I lose my breath as I read … *99.9% positive paternity.*

I drop the paper on the floor.

Holy fuck.

I'm her father.

CHAPTER TWENTY-FOUR
SIERRA

"All right, I'll let you know. Love you."

I bite the inside of my cheek when I hang up the phone, setting it on the couch next to me and scowling at it as if it were evil. I'm lost on what to do.

"Not a good call?" Maliki asks, strolling into the living room and handing me a coffee mug.

We had our morning shower, and he went on coffee duty while I returned the missed call from my father.

I slouch against the cushion. "I have yet to decide."

He moves my phone and takes its place. "What's up?"

"My dad found an apartment. I can move in by the end of the week."

The room turns mute until Maliki clears his throat. "You can stay here for as long as you want. You know that, right?"

I nod. "It's just … we're not exactly *just roommates* anymore. What if things change between us? I'll end up in the same situation as I was with Devin." My situation was better with Devin. We co-owned the condo. I could've stayed, but here? It's Maliki's. I have no claim.

"The only turn our relationship will take is in the right direction of growing stronger."

"No one plans for relationships to fall apart. Devin *didn't* plan to cheat when we married."

I didn't *plan* on divorcing him after three months of marriage.

My father didn't *plan* on cheating on my mother.

I trust Maliki, but never say never.

His jaw clenches. "You and Devin didn't work out because you belong with me, not him."

I scrub my hand over my face. "My father needs an answer by the end of the day, or the landlord will rent to someone else. It's the only place available, and if I don't take it, who knows how long it'll take for another one to open up?"

"What if we rent it together?"

My mouth falls open. *Together? As in him moving out of the apartment?* I grin at the thought of us being in our own new space, but then reality crashes through.

I shake my head. "The only reason the apartment was offered is because the landlord is an associate of my father's. My father wouldn't allow him to rent to *us*, nor would he be okay with you staying there."

He nods in disappointment. "It's your decision, babe. If it counts for anything, I want you here as much as I can get you. If you're scared of breaking up and need a backup plan, go ahead. I won't be upset. As for me? I'm not doing anything to fuck this up. Now that I have you, I won't risk losing the woman I love."

"What?" Good thing I'm sitting, or his words would've knocked me on my ass. I stare down at my lap, studying my hands, unsure if I'm fighting back a smile or a sob.

"Look at me, Sierra."

That's Maliki's thing—always wanting me to look at him, to keep that eye contact. He wants to read me—read my eyes, my heart, every emotion bleeding through me.

When I do, there's a tenderness on his face I've never seen. His eyes are soft with affection when our eyes meet. Maliki has never been a softie.

He smiles. "Even with you being a pain in my ass, I fell in love with you."

"Really?"

He nods. "I think it's been obvious for a while."

I laugh. "And I think it's been obvious I love you."

His voice turns arrogant as he cracks a giant grin. "Oh, babe, I know."

I roll my eyes. "Shove it."

He wraps his arms around my shoulders, drags me into him, and kisses the top of my head. "This is the best way for us to say it—romance with a hint of sarcasm and teasing."

"That's our style." I grin. "You know what else is our style?"

"Hmm …"

I pull away, and he relaxes against the couch when I straddle him. I skim my hands up and down his chest and lean forward until our lips are nearly touching. "You've had feelings for me for a long time."

He gulps. "Probably. I was just too pissed at myself for wanting an eighteen-year-old."

I gasp when his hand falls to my ass, catching it and pulling me into him. "I was *grown*."

He clenches his jaw while I grind against him. "Yes, eighteen—old enough to gamble and do porn is what you said. You don't understand what those words did to me."

My lips part as he cups my chin and brings my mouth to his.

"I wanted to make a point," I whisper against them.

"And you certainly did with my imagination."

I gulp when he teases my top lip with his tongue. "Good thing because I love you, too, and I'm sick of feeling like a stalker."

"It was fun, being stalked by you." His hands anchor on my waist to pull me to my feet.

I'm hardly stable when he throws me over his shoulder and heads toward the bedroom.

"Let me show you what you'd be missing every day if you left. Don't think I won't do *plenty* of convincing with my tongue on the matter."

———

Three hours later, when I'm good and orgasmed out, I call my father back.

"I'm not taking the apartment," I blurt out when he answers.

Maliki loves me.

He said those three incredible words and then brought me to his—no, *our* bed and made love to me with his fingers, his tongue, and his cock.

"Sierra," he cautions. "Don't be foolish."

Am I being stupid?

I won't turn my back on this with Maliki.

Let's hope it doesn't come back to bite me in the ass.

"I want to be with him."

"How about you be with him *while* having your own place?"

"Look on the bright side. I'll save money on rent."

Hopefully, this persuades the man who's a spitting image of *money talks.* He's a lover of the dollar, so maybe he'll understand from that perspective.

"I'll pay your rent until you get on your feet. Problem solved," he promptly fires back.

"Dad …"

"Don't *Dad* me. What excuse do you have now?"

"I'm happy, living with him."

He blows out an exhausted breath. "This is a mistake. Let's hope I can find you something when you change your mind."

"I won't."

"Don't be so sure of that."

"*Gosh,* quit being so negative on love."

"I have a meeting and have to go. Love you. You have by the end of the day to change your mind. Think about it."

"Love you, too."

CHAPTER TWENTY-FIVE
MALIKI

Three days have passed since I learned I'm a father, and I still haven't wrapped my mind around it.

What's worse is that I've been an absentee father, thanks to Jessa.

I hate her and now have to figure out a co-parenting plan.

After Sierra leaves, I give Jessa permission to come over.

I've kept my phone off when I'm with Sierra because Jessa has made it her mission to blow it up.

It's such a dick move.

Sierra told me she loved me.

We made love.

And now, I'm letting Jessa step into our home.

But what else can I do?

I sure as shit can't meet her in public or in the bar. This needs to stay private until we make a plan.

This isn't an easy fix.

My daughter thought a different man was her father for years, and now, I'm supposed to walk in and say, *Surprise! I'm your dad.*

An annoying smirk is on Jessa's face when she drops the results onto the table. "I told you, asshole."

I pluck the paper back up, fuming, and point to my chest with it. "I'm the asshole? Not you for hiding the fact I have a goddamn daughter? Not only that, but you also made her believe she had a different father for years! How fucked up is that, Jessa?"

"You didn't want me!" she shrieks.

"That doesn't mean I wouldn't want her!"

"Oh, please," she sneers. "You, a father, especially at that time? You would've said you weren't ready."

"Fuck off. Don't say that shit." Anger spreads through my body. "Where do we go from here?" Enough with the bullshit. We need to figure out the *now* shit.

"You tell me. Apparently, you're calling the shots and not answering my calls. Do you want to be in her life?"

Is that even a question? "Fuck yes, I want to be in my daughter's life."

"What about your little girlfriend, huh? Have you told her yet?" She rolls her eyes and shifts her weight from one foot to the other. "God, I hate seeing her around Ellie's. I do everything in my power to avoid it."

"Trust me, I'm sure she does the same with you."

She perks up, a sly grin on her face. "Does that mean she knows?"

"None of your business." I rest my elbow on the table and rub my forehead with both hands, warding off the Jessa-ache.

"Oh, she doesn't. This will be interesting. Want to tell her together?"

"Shut the fuck up," I grind out.

"When do you want to meet Molly?" She parks her hands on her slender hips.

"We need to ease her into this." *Shit. I need to ease into it myself.* "She knows Pete isn't her father?"

She nods. "She doesn't know about you yet. She's asked a few times who her *real* dad is, but I want us to do it together. Until I find a home, I'm staying at my grandparents' while they're in Florida. You can come over tonight and meet her. Six o'clock okay?"

"Sure. I'll be there. Do I need to bring anything?"

She licks her lips. "A bottle of wine would be nice."

"Our daughter doesn't need wine for me to visit her," I sternly reply.

"Whatever." Her gaze flicks upward. "It would be nice for me to get through this stressful night."

I walk her to the door. "Good-bye, Jessa."

She waves with too much enthusiasm. "See you tonight."

———

I hate myself.

"Hey, babe," I say to Sierra over the phone.

"Hey," she chirps. "I'm about to head home. Do you need anything while I'm out?"

Home. She's coming home, and I'm about to fucking lie to her.

A sour taste sets in my mouth. "I'm good. I wanted to let you know that I'm not working tonight." I need to leave before she gets here. I can't face her.

"Uh-oh, the boss is calling in?" she teases.

I force myself to chuckle. "Cohen needs help at the Twisted Fox." I cringe at how easily the lie comes out. "They're short-staffed, and the others are on vacation."

I went through lies all day today. I need to tell Sierra about my daughter, but things are so damn good between us. Not to mention, she turned down an apartment for me. She was right. It'd put her in the same position as Devin. I need to figure out the perfect path to spring this on her and pray she doesn't freak out.

Shit.

Not only is the change to our lives a daughter, but it also involves Jessa—a chick she can't stand.

Fuck. I don't even know why I'm hiding it.

I'm a pussy. That's it.

"You can't have Mikey do it?" she asks, snapping me away from my worries.

"It's too hard, explaining the ropes on a night shift. I helped Cohen open his bar and know my way around it."

I hear the disappointment in her tone. "Oh, okay. I'll see you later then. If you need an extra hand, I don't mind tagging along."

"I'll ask him and let you know, okay? Love you."

"Love you, too."

I hate myself more when I hang up.

Even worse, I have a message from Jessa giving me the address with a smile-face emoji.

———

I'm sweating bullets.

My mind is scrambling.

I'm suffering from more anxiety than I have in my entire life.

I'm about to meet my daughter.

My heart races as I park down the road from Jessa's grandparents. I don't need anyone seeing my car there.

I gulp, my hands sweating when I knock on the door.

It swings open, and I jerk back as soon as I see her.

She's beautiful.

My daughter has dark hair, identical to mine. It's pulled into tight French braids with red bows on the end of each one. She's wearing a purple unicorn shirt, polka-dot pants, and unicorn slippers.

Her mouth pops into an eager smile. "Hi! Who are you? Mommy tells me not to answer the door for strangers, but sometimes, it's a Girl Scout selling cookies. I *love* Girl Scout cookies, and I told Mommy I want to be one, so I can eat all the cookies in the world."

Holy shit.

She's adorable.

"But you're a boy, and boys aren't allowed to be Girl Scouts. You have no cookies. Bye-bye."

I stop her from shutting the door.

"Whoa, I'm a friend of your mom's, and sadly, I don't have cookies. I'll bring some next time though."

A friend?

Way to confuse her more.

She wavers and keeps the door cracked. "Mom!" she yells. "There's a man without cookies at the door! He said he's your friend!"

Jessa comes to the door with a wineglass in her hand. "Molly, honey, this is Maliki, the friend I told you was coming to dinner."

Dinner? I didn't agree to fucking dinner.

Jessa is wearing a tight red dress, baring plenty of cleavage, is barefoot, and her hair is pulled into a tight ponytail. There's no denying she's an attractive woman. It's what drew me to her and caused me to fuck her so many times. I ignored her craziness in exchange for her hotness.

"Come in," Jessa says, waving me in, and Molly stands behind her. "I didn't see you pull up."

"I parked down the street."

"Of course. You don't want anyone to see you."

My heart leaps when Molly bounds down the hallway. I follow her into the living room where she has coloring books sprawled over the coffee table and dolls lined up the couch. I glance at Jessa in hesitation, asking for permission, and she smiles with a head nod in Molly's direction.

My steps are slow, and I settle down next to Molly on the floor, keeping distance between us. "Whatcha doin'?"

"Coloring," she says, stating the obvious while snatching a crayon.

Her head tilts to the side as she colors a unicorn the same color as the one on her shirt.

"What are you coloring?"

She holds up the book and points to it with the crayon. "This is a unicorn and the castle she lives in."

I control my shaky breath. "Wow, you color really well."

"Thank you! I've been practicing real hard because I'm going to start school soon! My daddy said I need to color in the lines before I go!" She drops the crayon and frowns. "Well ..." Her eyes shoot to Jessa. "My old daddy said that. He doesn't want to be my daddy anymore."

I inhale a breath, and Jessa rushes over to squat down next to Molly.

"Honey, I told you that's not true."

Tears fill her eyes. "I don't know why I don't have a daddy … but Mommy said I'll get another one."

I freeze, and swear to God, tears prick at my eyes.

Jessa fucked this up before giving me a chance.

My gaze flicks upward to give Jessa a glare.

She turns away, her attention returning to Molly, as she wipes loose strands falling from her braids away from her face.

I stand.

"Honey, why don't you finish coloring your picture, and Mommy will be right back, okay?"

"Okay," Molly says in a soft-spoken voice.

I follow Jessa into the kitchen. I keep my voice low, but there's no hiding the anger in it. "You're confusing the shit out of her! A different daddy? Where's she expecting to get one? From goddamn Santa Claus?"

She holds her hand up toward me. "Chill out. What was I supposed to do? She wouldn't stop begging to call Pete, and he doesn't want to talk to either of us. I needed to find a way to explain his absence. Otherwise, she thought I was keeping her away from him."

"There were better ways."

"You know of a better plan, Mr. Sudden Parent?"

"Don't do that." I scrub a hand over my face. "You're right. I don't know."

"You should thank me. I made it easier for you. Now, she knows Pete isn't her dad, and you won't have to explain that to her." She smiles as if her plan is gold and won't further fuck up our daughter's head.

"Where do we go from here then? Since you have it figured out?"

"I made dinner. Let's eat, conversate, help her get comfortable with you, and go from there."

———

Jessa made over-boiled spaghetti and burned garlic bread.

I hardly touched my food while listening to Molly, my daughter —*fuck*, it's weird saying that. Sauce is on her face as she rambles about enjoying dance and how she wants to be a cheerleader and then an astronaut when she grows up.

I nod, captivated by her every word, not wanting to miss one.

"What do you think?" Jessa asks, pouring herself another glass of wine after we clean up after dinner.

I've turned down a glass of wine or whiskey five times. Molly has gone back to her coloring in the living room.

"I think she's ready," she adds, shocking me.

"You do?"

She nods.

I trail behind Jessa into the living room. She asks Molly to sit on the couch and takes the seat next to her.

"Sweetie, do you remember when I said you have a different daddy?" I've never heard Jessa speak so soft.

Damn, she went straight for it.

Molly blinks at her in disbelief and rubs her eyes. "Yes …" She drops her hands and rests them in her lap. "But … I don't know why Daddy can't be my daddy anymore. I liked him being my daddy. I love him!" Her cheeks turn red as tears fall down them.

Tears hit Jessa's eyes, and she hurriedly wipes them away. I have no doubt she loves our child.

They cry while I struggle to control my own emotions.

Struggle to not console them.

I knew this would be hard, but I didn't think it'd be this painful.

My heart knocks against my chest while breaking at the same time for the little girl I hardly know. I'm livid with Jessa but also with myself.

What if she's telling the truth of knowing I wouldn't have wanted anything to do with Molly?

Regret slams into me like a headache.

Jessa pulls Molly into a hug and mouths to me, *Tell her.*

I respond with a *what the fuck* look.

I'm the last person who knows how to do this.

I move closer and sink to my knees in front of them.

Is it too early?

Hell yes, it is.

It's too late to stop now.

I suck in a breath to stop my tears, focusing on Molly, and scratch my neck. I don't speak until she pulls out of Jessa's arms.

"Molly." I pause to clear my throat. "I know what your mom said is confusing. I was confused when she told me, too. You loved your daddy, and I know he loved you. But you also have another daddy who loves you, and that's me."

Molly's eyes widen in more disbelief. "Huh?"

"Honey, Maliki is your real daddy," Jessa explains more confidently. "Pete was what we call a stepdad. He was your daddy when Mommy was married to him." She kisses the top of her head. "You have two daddies, and Maliki will be yours from now on, okay?"

From what it seems, Pete was a good father to her.

Until he tossed her out of his life as if she meant nothing.

It'll look like I took that away from her.

Shit!

Molly gapes at me with brown eyes, her mouth open. All I can manage to give in return is a lame attempt at a reassuring smile.

I feel so guilty.

I hate myself.

Hate Jessa.

Her tears don't stop. "So … you're my daddy now?"

I nod. "I am."

"What if I want my old daddy back?"

My eyes are damp.

I want to fucking kill Jessa for putting us through this.

"Sweetie, this is your *real* daddy," Jessa stresses.

Molly frowns, and that makes a man feel like shit. "My *real* daddy?"

"He's always been your daddy," Jessa goes on.

Her eyes pin to me. "Why weren't you my daddy before? Where was you when I was smaller?"

Jessa squeezes her. "He didn't know he was your daddy, and that's Mommy's fault." She takes Molly's small hand in hers. "I'm so sorry, honey."

Wow.

Shock rushes through me at Jessa's honesty—for her taking the blame.

We wait for what feels like forever for Molly's response.

She sniffles, her face unreadable. "Can I have my doll, please?" Every ounce of the excitement she's had all evening vanishes.

I frown.

Jessa nods, handing her a doll, and Molly grips it to her chest while sprinting down the hall.

"That didn't go over so well," Jessa whispers.

I stand and shake my head in disbelief. It wasn't supposed to go down like this. "Way to confuse a six-year-old."

She sighs. "It went better than I'd expected. Sure, she'll have questions, but she's more in shock and scared than anything."

I stumble back a step. "Scared of me?"

"No, of the situation. I bring in a stranger and say, *Hey, here's your father, not the one you've called Daddy for years.* She needs to spend time with you, not see you as a stranger. She needs familiarity."

"I agree." I sit down, drop my head between my legs, and calm my anger before lifting it. "It would've been much easier had you told me in the beginning."

Her eyes downcast. "It's over. We can't change what happened."

"My daughter thinks another man is her father," I hiss. "Why did you hide it?"

"What was I supposed to tell Pete? I was pregnant with another man's child but wanted to be with him? He would've left me."

"Speaking of Pete, what about him? I'm sure he's on the birth certificate as the father. That's another issue."

She shakes her head. "He's heartbroken, and he refuses to see her. He says it hurts too much and has already filed for divorce. He's done with both of us."

"Ah, he left you, and now, I'm your next option. What you did was inexcusable."

Sadness cloaks her face. "She deserves a family like she had before."

"Let me make this clear: this does not mean we'll be a *family*. I can hardly look at you for hiding this from me, but I have to for my daughter. A daughter I hardly know because of your selfishness."

"I'm sorry, Maliki! If I could take it back, I would."

I only shake my head.

"I loved you, you know. Then, you left me."

"We were young, dumb, and I had my own shit to deal with. *You* had your own shit to deal with."

She rolls her eyes. "Too young and dumb? Look at who you're dating. Someone young and dumb."

I sneer at her. My heart clenches, reminding me how I lied to Sierra tonight. "Don't. Don't even fucking bring up or disrespect Sierra."

"I have a say of who's around my child."

"Sierra is part of my life. Molly is now part of my life. Eventually, they'll interconnect."

"Let's confuse her more." She throws her arms up in the air. "Here's your new dad *and* his girlfriend."

We need a subject change.

"Why don't we stop talking about my girlfriend and check on our daughter?"

Jessa rises. "Follow me. I know how to fix this."

I follow her into a bedroom with a full-size bed where more dolls take residence next to Molly. Her eyes are puffy, and she doesn't look up when we walk in.

"Molly, honey, how about some ice cream?" Jessa asks.

Molly's head flies up as if Jessa had told her the Easter Bunny were here. She wipes away the snot under her nose and grins. "Really?"

"Really. It was your dad's idea. He wants to make you a bowl."

Molly's attention flies to me, and I grin. "Come on. We'll make your favorite kind."

She drops the doll and jumps to her feet. "Can we watch cartoons while eating our ice cream?"

"Sure," I answer.

Ice cream makes her happy.

I need to remember that.

Shit, I'll spend every dollar I have on ice cream if it makes her feel better.

We make giant bowls, and she grins when I sit next to her on the couch.

———

I'm woken up by my phone buzzing in my pocket. When I glance down to retrieve it, I find Jessa snuggled in my lap, nearly on top of me. She's awake with the remote in her hand.

"What the fuck?" I snap. "Why didn't you wake me?"

She peeks up at me with puckered lips and innocent eyes. "I didn't want to be rude. You looked exhausted and in need of sleep."

I shift to stand, but she moves quicker and straddles my lap.

Jesus Christ.

"Why don't you stay here tonight?" She rotates her hips, her lips nuzzling into my neck, and I nearly vomit.

If her goal is to get my dick hard, she's confused.

"Jessa," I bite out, "I don't want to push you off my lap, but if you don't get up in the next five seconds, I will."

She moans and rolls her hips.

I grab her ass and dump her onto the floor.

Her eyes bulge, staring up at me, flustered, from the floor when I stand.

"I warned you."

She brings herself up while huffing, "Where does she think you are tonight anyway?"

"None of your business." I tug my phone from my pocket, my pulse quickening. "When can I see Molly next?" I can't wait until she becomes comfortable enough with me that I won't have to deal with Jessa around.

"Whenever you want. Maybe you can have lunch with us tomorrow?" She holds up her finger. "Oh! We're going to the city in a few days to shop for school clothes. She's nervous about going to school. Maybe it'll be a good experience for you to bond, and you can put her at ease."

I nod. "Email me the details. I don't want you texting me anymore. Lunch tomorrow sounds good."

"Email, huh? You'd better tell Sierra dearest before she catches you in your lies."

I point to her, fuming. "Stop with the fucking Sierra talk. I won't say it again."

"Why? If you're so *serious*, why won't you tell her? Are you ashamed of our daughter?"

"I'll see you tomorrow." I halt, noticing Molly isn't on the couch, which means Jessa put her in bed while I was sleeping.

When I walk out the door, I check my phone.

Cohen's text is what woke me up.

I scroll down the screen.

My stomach drops.

Six texts from Sierra.

I check the time.

It's after midnight.

Fuck!

CHAPTER TWENTY-SIX

SIERRA

I *trust him.*

That's what I repeat to myself while waiting for Maliki to come home. I wish he'd asked me to take his shift tonight instead of Mikey. It would've calmed my nervous thoughts.

I attempt to work on designs for the bar but can't concentrate.

He's hiding something from me.

I could've tagged along with him to Twisted Fox, and the panic in his voice told me he didn't want me anywhere near that bar tonight.

Why?

I've texted him a few times and received one reply, saying he was busy and would be home around nine o'clock when a replacement came.

Nine o'clock was three hours ago.

I don't call or text him again.

Screw that.

I shut my computer, debating on sleeping in the guest bedroom tonight. I decide otherwise as I yawn, plug in my charger, and climb into bed, worry dancing through me.

I fidget, staring at the alarm clock, watching the night grow later and later.

I stiffen when I hear the front door unlock and then open. I remain still and silent, listening as he walks into the room, undresses, and slides into bed.

His arms wrap around my waist, and he pulls me into his chest.

I twist away.

Fuck that.

"What the hell, Sierra?" he bursts out.

I whip around as he lifts and shove his chest. "You tell me! You're coming home from the same bar my husband cheated on me at, smelling like some cheap whore's perfume." Spit flies with my words. "At least Devin had the decency to hide it."

He moves away to turn the lamp on.

We're on our knees, staring at each other in shock.

"You honestly think I'd hurt you like that?" He holds his finger up, his brows furrowing. "And your soon-to-be *ex-husband*. Let's get that straight right fucking now. I have nothing to *have the decency* to hide."

"And I'm your soon-to-be ex-whatever-I am," I fire back with venom in my words.

His chest hitches. "Don't say that shit."

"I want to see Cohen's tapes," I challenge, resulting in him flinching.

"You don't trust me. *Wow.*"

"Not when you come home this late. *Wow.*"

He runs his hands through his hair. "I swear to you, on everything, I'd never cheat on you. If I ever even thought about touching another woman, I'd end things between us first."

Tears trickle down my face, sticking my hair to my face, and he brushes the strands aside.

"I love you. I fucking love you to no end and will never jeopardize losing you. Do you hear me?" He catches my chin in his hand, forcing me to look at him, and massages my face with his fingers.

I swallow rapidly. "Okay." As much as I want to carry on this conversation, I'm drained and terrified of where our relationship will go from here.

I've wanted Maliki for as long as I can remember, and he's already slipping away.

I sniffle. "Please don't play me for a fool."

"Never happening." His jaw flexes, and he drops his hand from my face. He gives me a quick peck on the lips and pulls himself out of bed.

"Where are you going?" I rush out, crawling to the edge of the bed, wishing the desperation weren't there.

His jaw remains clenched. "Shower. I apparently smell like some women's cheap perfume, and I'm not about to bring that shit into our bed."

He kisses the top of my head, and nausea balls up into my stomach as I lie back down, my back facing the bathroom.

Maliki's arms wrap around me again when he returns. He smells like clean soap, and his hair is wet. His lips brush against my ear. "Please trust me, baby." He drops kisses along my neck. "I've never given you a reason not to."

I don't push him away this time. "You've also never done anything this sketchy."

His hand slips between my legs, and I wish I didn't spread them wider.

"Why would I want another woman when I have this?" He sinks two fingers inside me. "When I come home to this? You're all I want."

He grabs my jaw, pulling my head back to kiss me.

I let him.

Even though I don't believe him.

I gasp when he slides himself inside me.

Even though I don't believe him.

I allow him to make love to me.

Even though I don't believe him.

I'm on the road of heartbreak again, but I can't seem to jump off the ride like I did with Devin.

———

The next morning, Maliki makes love to me.

He's gone all day, supposedly at the Twisted Fox, but he makes it back in time to work at the pub.

Weird.

———

This morning, he gives me an orgasm before dropping his bomb.

He makes us breakfast before ruining my day.

"Hey, babe," he says, giving me a quick peck on the lips and sitting across from me at the table. "I'm going to the city to sample new product with Cohen. Liz offered to cover my shift, so you'll be working with her tonight. I won't be gone late."

I take a bite of toast and consider what response to give while chewing.

Rip him a new asshole?

Act like everything is okay?

Leave him?

"That's cool," is what I choose to go with as an idea pops into my head. I keep my tone calm. "I've put off going to the mall. I need some makeup and bras. I'll ask Mikey to take my shift. It shouldn't be a problem. He always wants money, and we can make a day of it. Maybe have dinner when you're done."

This is a test.

He drops his bacon, startled, and scoots his plate away from him. "Make me a list. I'll pick up whatever you need. We'll make a date to go into the city sometime next week. Sound good?"

Hell no.

"Make you a list of *bras and makeup* I need?" I deadpan.

He nods, refusing to meet my gaze, and plucks a slice of bacon from his plate.

I roll my eyes and am the next one to push my plate up the table. "I need to shower."

He stiffens in his chair and stops chewing. "We showered an hour ago."

"Yeah, well, I didn't think you'd lie to me an hour ago."

He curses as I walk away but doesn't stop me.

CHAPTER TWENTY-SEVEN
MALIKI

"You're shitting me," Cohen says over the phone after I tell him about Molly.

I had to give him a heads-up. I need a favor.

I shake my head even though he can't see me. "Nope."

"Wow," is all he says, stretching the word out for seconds.

Cohen is the only person I've told. No one in my family knows. I have to handle my own shock and come to terms with everything before releasing the news into the world. Cohen won't ask as many questions as Sierra and my sister.

At least, I hope not.

I've never exactly held a secret this large.

I followed Sierra when she stomped away from breakfast to shower. She wouldn't listen to a word I said as I went into detail about this stupid-ass nonexistent product I was lying about testing. She turned away, giving me her back, as I begged her to trust me. I debated joining her, thawing out her cold behavior with an orgasm, but wasn't going to risk a razor to my balls.

I will fix this.

I will tell her.

I don't know why I'm being so chickenshit.

As bad as I want to stay here with her, shower with her, work with her, I also want to see my daughter.

The more relaxed Molly becomes with me, the faster I can kick hanging out with Jessa to the curb.

"What did Sierra say?" His question breaks me away from my thoughts.

I scratch my head. "I, uh … haven't told her yet."

"Now, you've really got to be shitting me. What the fuck, Ki? Did you break up?"

"No, we're good. I'm waiting for the right time."

"Not only have you known about this for weeks, but you also told me before her? I understand you're inexperienced in the relationship department, but that's not how one functions—a healthy one, at least. Hiding you have a kid sure as fuck isn't healthy! Think about this: her ex cheated on her. The longer you hide this, the worse damage it'll cause."

I've never heard Cohen so pissed off at me.

"I need to ask for a favor," I remark, desperate to switch the subject.

"Don't ask me to participate in your lies."

"I'm not doing anything wrong," I hiss. "I'm going shopping with them, and I need you to cover for me."

"Fuck you."

"Please. I'm going through some shit, but I want to get to know my daughter."

"Fine, but when this comes back to bite you in the ass, I don't want to hear you whine about losing her."

I spent yesterday with Molly playing board games and was introduced to her stuffed animals. I haven't known her long, but she's already growing into my heart.

I'm building a relationship with my daughter while my relationship with Sierra is crumbling.

———

Even though I told Sierra that Liz is covering my shift tonight, I haven't asked my sister yet.

"Hey, can you cover for me tonight?" I ask Liz, walking into the bar.

Liz drops the clipboard she's doing inventory with onto the bar. "Why?"

"Cohen and I are looking at new whiskey in the city. We won't be gone long, just for the day." And just like that, another lie slips from my lips so easily.

She shakes her head. "I call bullshit."

"I call not bullshit." I crack a smile in an attempt to lighten the mood. It doesn't work.

"I know when you're lying to me."

Do I tell her?

"You had another woman call the bar the other day, acting shady, and there's tension with you and Sierra." She shakes her head, staring at me in near disgust. "Here I thought, she'd be the one playing you, yet it seems to be the other way around."

I flinch at the truth in her words. "I'm not playing her."

"What's going on then?"

Here goes.

I start pacing. "Do you remember Jessa?"

"Bitch-face Jessa? Yes."

I stop to face her. "I got her pregnant."

She falls back a step, her back knocking into the shelves, and thankfully, nothing falls. "What do you mean, you got her pregnant?"

I shake my head, nerves rippling in my stomach. "Not recently. In the past, when we used to hook up. She came over a few weeks ago and broke the news. I have a daughter."

"And you believe her?" she says with a laugh and a snort.

"I didn't until I got a paternity test."

"Holy shit." She releases a hard breath. "Have you told Sierra?"

"Not yet," I croak out.

She throws a towel at me, and I barely dodge it. I deserve to get hit though.

"You're an idiot," she snaps. "You can't hide something like that from her. What would you do if it were the other way around?"

"I doubt Sierra will find out she has a secret baby she never knew about."

"Shut up, dick. You know what I mean. This is a big deal. It changes your life and everything around it."

I bow my head. "Trust me, I know."

She walks around the table, slumps onto a stool, and gestures for me to do the same. "What are you going to do? Does she know you're her dad?"

I hoist myself on the stool next to her and nod. "I met her the other day. It's hard on the both of us. She'd thought another man was her father for years."

Her hand flies to her chest. "Whoa, that's messed up." She pats my back with a stern look on her face. "You'd better tell Sierra. News travels fast in Blue Beech."

Another person knows.

And I still haven't told Sierra.

———

All the madness of my day vanishes when Molly races toward me with a glowing smile on her face.

She jumps up and down. "I can't wait for us to go shopping today! Mommy said I can get new clothes." She stops and claps her hands. "She said we can look at American Girl dolls, too! I've wanted one for forever and ever."

I had Jessa meet me at a gas station twenty minutes out of Blue Beech. She smiles and gives me a hug when she sees me. I grit, patting her shoulder, and pull away as fast as I can.

"Do you think she can ride with me?" I ask.

"I thought we could ride together," Jessa says.

"Yes!" Molly squeals. "Let's all ride together in the cool car!"

I groan, covering my face. "All right. We'll ride together."

Fuck my life.

We pack into the Camaro, and as soon as I turn the radio on to get through this hell of a ride with her, Jessa leans forward and changes the station. I've never been so annoyed with someone. Spending time with Molly is supposed to be fun, but Jessa is driving me nuts, and I haven't even pulled out of the parking lot.

The good to come out of Jessa's music changing is Molly starts animatedly singing in the backseat.

I check my phone when a text comes through.

Cohen: I still vote you tell Sierra.

I groan.

"Is that your girlfriend?" Jessa asks. "It's not safe, texting and driving, *especially with our daughter* in the car."

I drop my phone in my lap and clench the steering wheel.

God, why are you testing me?

When Jessa realizes I'm not going to talk about Sierra, she stretches her legs out and sighs. "Molly needs some clothes, and she asked for an American Girl doll. Do you mind paying for them?"

I shake my head. "That's no problem."

She nods. "We'll need to figure out child support payments, too."

I nod. "I'll call my attorney and have her get in touch with you."

She bites into her lower lip. "I'm broke, Maliki, so the more you can help us, the better. I was a stay-at-home mom, and now, without Pete, I have no income."

I don't mind supporting Molly.

"Start looking for a job then," I remark.

"As soon as she starts school, I will. I want her to make a smooth transition."

———

I buy Molly four new outfits, new tennis shoes, and an American Girl doll.

We grab lunch in the food court, and Molly holds my hand and skips as we walk out to the parking garage to leave.

"You know what would be fun?" Jessa asks.

Never having to speak to you again.

"If we stayed in the city tonight," she continues when I don't answer. She turns to look at Molly in the backseat, a smile on her face. "Wouldn't that be fun, honey?"

"Yes!" Molly squeals.

Fucking great.

"No," I grit out without looking at Molly. I can't see the disappointment on her face.

This is where I draw the fucking line.

"Oh, come on." Jessa smacks my arm with a laugh. "It'll be fun." She whips around to look at Molly again. "Ask Daddy pretty please for us to stay in the city."

What the flying fuck?

CHAPTER TWENTY-EIGHT

SIERRA

"I think Maliki is sick of me," I say. "We've been a *thing* for three months. Maybe that's his cutoff time. He can't handle a relationship this long."

"Are you on drugs?" Ellie asks. "It's clear how much he loves you when I see you two together. You've been into each other for years."

"He's acting shady."

I shrugged off all Maliki's attempts at conversation while I re-showered.

I don't like liars.

He stuck around until I got out, kissed me, and left.

Since then, I've restrained from texting or calling him.

He texted twice, asking what I was doing.

I've ignored them.

What's he doing? is the better question.

"I love you," Ellie carries on, "but you don't trust anyone because of Devin cheating, which is understandable."

I take a lengthy drink of water and settle the bottle down on the table. "Maybe you're right."

"I'm always right." She grins and pops a cracker in her mouth.

Even if he isn't cheating like Devin, he's hiding something.

Our conversation is cut short by Corbin *and* Devin walking into the apartment.

Devin stops, his eyes dilating when he notices me. "Shit, Sierra. I didn't know you were here."

He appears in better shape than I saw him last. He hasn't attempted to contact me again since our patio talk. Maybe he's moving on like me.

My chest caves. *I hope not with Louise.*

Ellie scowls at Devin before shifting the look to Corbin.

Corbin flings up his arms. "We didn't know you were here! Ellie never told me she was coming over. I thought the coast was clear."

"It's fine." I swish my hand in the air. "I was about to leave anyway."

"You don't have to do that. The cheater can go," Ellie replies.

"I need to work," I comment, rising up from my chair and grabbing my keys.

"I'll walk you out," Devin offers.

"Not necessary." I glance at Ellie. "I'll call you later."

I say good-bye to them and don't stop Devin as he walks behind me.

"I don't want to sign, Sierra," he says as soon as we make it outside.

I swing around to glare at him. "Please, it's over." I can't deal with him on top of this Maliki madness.

"You're in love with him, aren't you?" His voice loses power at the end, and his eyes are gentle as I meet them with mine. "You don't want to be with me because of him."

My stomach knots. "This isn't about him. This is about your unfaithfulness. We'd still be together had you not done what you did. Maliki has nothing to do with this. Us not being together is all on you."

His broad chest hitches. "You're right."

He turns around without another word and walks to his BMW, shaking his head. He leans into the seat, opens the glove compartment, and grabs a folder. I stay silent as he drags the forms from the folder, a pen falling out, and goes to the last page.

I stagger back a step when he places the paper against my car and signs it.

"Here you go," he says, holding it out to me. "Be prepared for him to fuck you over worse than I did." He falters a step after I take them. "We could've made it work. Think about that before you sign and throw us away."

He goes back inside the apartment without another word.

I rest my back against my car, catching my breath, as my heart twists in my chest.

"Be prepared for him to fuck you over worse than I did."

Devin already knows what's coming.

I study the divorce papers when I slide into my car.

Am I doing the right thing?

I toss them into my passenger seat and call Maliki.

No answer.

———

The crowd has died down when Maliki gets to the bar.

Relief strikes through me that he's here.

Anger follows next.

I shouldn't have been afraid he wouldn't come home tonight.

That's not a healthy relationship.

He drops a kiss on my cheek, says, "Hey, babe," and runs upstairs for a quick shower.

When he's finished, he comes down and does paperwork in the corner, keeping his eyes on me.

I'm drained when my shift ends, and I ask him to close with Mikey, so I can shower. I slide into bed without waiting for him to come up.

When he does, he wraps his arms around me, as always.

"I wasn't sure you'd come home tonight," I whisper into the darkness.

His arm twitches, his body stiffening against mine. "What?"

"It seems you're doing everything in your power to avoid me."

His lips trickle down my neck. "I love you, Sierra. You believe me, right?"

I nod.

"Whatever you're gathering in that pretty little head of yours, it's not what you think."

"Why are you being sketchy?"

"I'm working it out. I promise."

"Let me help you."

"You being here helps me."

I'm too exhausted to argue.

CHAPTER TWENTY-NINE
MALIKI

This has to stop.

Sierra is breaking down with each day I carry on this lie.

She hardly speaks to me in the morning.

I feel like a piece-of-shit boyfriend.

No, I *am* a piece-of-shit boyfriend.

What happened after the mall trip proved this will only get worse.

I'm still pissed about Jessa's sleepover attempt, causing me to look like a jackass in front of Molly. No exaggeration, I declined sixteen times.

I was fuming the rest of the way home.

It got worse *when* I got to the bar and saw the crestfallen look on Sierra's face.

The words are sitting on the tip of my tongue, but I can't set them free.

I almost did last night, but it wasn't the right time.

The right place.

The right way.

I can't do it while she's slinging drinks.

I can't do it after she's wiped out from a long night.

I grab my phone.

This shit is long overdue.

No more lying or sneaking around.
She'll be pissed, but I hope she understands.
Me: Date night tonight?
Sierra: Ooh, sounds good! I've missed you.
Me: A night in the city?
Sierra: That sounds perfect.

CHAPTER THIRTY
MALIKI

"What's that smile for?" Ellie asks.

The eager grin hasn't left my face since Maliki texted me. "Maliki and I are going out for the night."

Her smile grows just as wide. "Does that excitement mean he's no longer being Shady McShaderson?"

My smile falters an inch. "Somewhat, but I see this as promising." I shake my head. "I've been dumb, waiting this long to demand answers."

"I don't see him cheating on you. He looks at you like you own his world."

"I'm not as worried about cheating as I am him wanting to break up with me. I'm scared he wants to end our relationship, and since he doesn't know how, he'll pull away until I cut the cord."

"Doubt the man is taking you on a date to break up with you. Stop being paranoid."

"I'm sick of you telling me to stop being paranoid."

"Then, stop being paranoid."

"Aunt Ellie!"

Molly comes running into the kitchen, an eager smile glued to her face. She wraps her arms around Ellie's legs, and Ellie squeezes her shoulders.

"Hey, I didn't know you were coming over," she says.

"I need you to babysit." I hear her grating voice before seeing her. "Mom isn't home, and I need to run errands."

"Okay," Ellie says to Jessa. "A heads-up would've been nice."

"I texted, but you didn't answer," Jessa fires back. "Molly asked to hang out with you."

"I'm watching cartoons!" Molly says before rushing into the living room.

"It won't be long," Jessa continues. She turns to leave but halts when her eyes meet mine. "Oh, hey, Sierra."

I narrow my eyes at the smugness in her tone. "Uh, hey. How's your moving going?"

My mama taught me never to act rude … unless someone pisses you off. So far, Jessa hasn't hit that level.

She fidgets with her necklace. "Oh, it's going. I thought it'd be terrible, moving home, but I've enjoyed catching up with *old friends.*"

"That's good." *Please stop talking to me.*

She smirks. "How's Maliki today?"

What the fuck? "He's fine." I still. "Why?"

She slaps her hand through the air. "I haven't heard from him since last night. I know we had a long day yesterday, but we normally talk every day, so this is unusual. I might stop by the apartment and make sure he's okay."

My ears ring, my stomach knotting. I've never been a violent person, but I want to punch her in the face.

"What are you talking about?" I snap.

She releases a mocking laugh. "He still hasn't told you we hang out?"

"Hang out where?"

"At my house … sometimes his apartment." She shrugs. "Whichever is more convenient."

"Excuse me?" I shriek. "He went to *your house?*"

She nods. "Not yesterday though. We went to the city, had lunch, spent time together."

Ellie slides between us, and my stomach sinks.

"What are you doing, Jessa?" she asks, her tone filled with warning. "Don't come into my home and play games with my best friend."

I rest my hand against my chest while doing a shitty job of controlling my breathing, controlling my aching heart, and restraining myself from not clawing her eyes out.

"I'm not the one playing games." Jessa cackles, sharpening her attention on me. "Why are you so offended the father of my child was at my house?"

"What?" Ellie and I scream simultaneously.

Ellie aims her finger toward the door. "Leave. I'll watch Molly."

Jessa laughs, pleased with herself, and ignores Ellie. "You don't know yet, do you?" She squints, a hard smile passing over her lips. "I've told him to tell you for weeks now, but that's how Maliki is, you know? So secretive, lets no one in. That's why it didn't work out with us last time, but we're doing better now that we're older."

I shut my eyes. *No. No. This isn't happening.*

He would've told me if he had a kid.

My eyes tighten. "Nice try."

Jessa scoffs. "I'm serious. He's Molly's father." All eyes are on her when she drops her bag on the counter, rummages through it, and pulls out an envelope. She slaps it down next to me. "Don't believe me? See for yourself."

It takes everything I have to control my hands from shaking when I pick up the envelope and pull out the paper.

I read it once.

Twice.

Another time for good measure.

I see his name.

He's a 99.9% match.

Molly's cartoon in the background is the only sound in the apartment.

I check the date on the test. It was done over three weeks ago, and he never told me.

Three weeks!

Hell, he's known for longer since that's when he had the test.

The secrecy makes sense now.

"How did you get this?" I stammer, hating how weak I sound.

"I went to his apartment, of course," Jessa answers. "He's spruced up the place, hasn't he?" Her hands go to her chest. "We normally hang out at my place though. There's more room."

I grip the paper. "Stay the fuck away from my boyfriend."

"Boyfriend for how much longer?"

I take a step toward her, nearly in her face. "I'd be a bigger bitch if your daughter wasn't here."

Ellie squeezes between us again, and we both stumble back.

"It's okay," Jessa says over Ellie's shoulder. "It's not like she'll see you around much."

"Jessa, stop!" Ellie yells.

Jessa doesn't. "Where do you think he was the other night when he came home late?"

My face falls.

Jessa grins, knowing she hit a spot.

It was her perfume.

It was her scent he went to the shower to wash off.

It all makes sense.

I shove the paper in my bag and storm past her.

"Hey!" Jessa shouts behind me. "You can't take that!"

Ellie is calling my name as I leave her apartment and sprint to my car.

———

I storm into the bar with the paternity test in my hand.

"Oh shit," Liz yelps, standing next to Maliki at the bar.

Maliki's eyes are wide, all the blood draining from his face, and he scrubs a hand over it.

"We need to talk," I grind out.

He nods, and I lead the way to our apartment.

No, *his* apartment.

An apartment he allowed Jessa to come into who knows how many times.

I shove the paper into his chest as soon as he shuts the door and faces me. "Care to explain this?"

He doesn't bother looking at the paper as it floats to the floor.

He knows what it is.

"I planned to tell you tonight," he says.

I scoff. "You *planned* to tell me the day I confronted you? How convenient. Why wasn't I told weeks ago?"

"I had to know if she was mine."

"You've known she was yours for a while. Not only did you keep this from me, but you've also been hanging out with Jessa behind my back." Tears sting the backs of my eyes. "You came home, smelling like her perfume. You were never helping Cohen, were you? You weren't in the city with him. You were with her."

"I was with my daughter," he corrects, grinding his teeth.

"And her!"

"I had no choice!" His voice rises. "Molly didn't know me! I couldn't walk in and expect her to be comfortable. Jessa had to be there."

"You could've told me." I choke back a sob. "I would've helped you work through it. I would've been with you like a *girlfriend* should."

He draws in a breath, his body tensing. "It was complicated."

My pulse slams into my throat as all rationality flies out the door. "I can't." I shuffle back a step. "I can't do this."

He winces. "Can't do what? Be with a man who has a child?"

Hell no. I won't allow him to turn this around on me.

It's my turn to raise my voice. "No, be with a man I don't trust."

He scowls. "You don't trust me?" His shoulders straighten. "Before this, I never lied to you. Not once. Hell, Sierra, you're fucking married, and I've accepted that!"

"Not for long. The divorce will be finalized this week." My answer is firm. Flat. No expression shown.

He blinks. "What?"

"Devin signed the divorce papers. You'd know that if you came around."

His face softens. "Why didn't you tell me?"

That flat voice rises a few notches. Okay, a lot of notches. "Why didn't you tell me you had a child?"

"I was scared it'd become an issue, like it fucking is right now. You're young, Sierra."

"Screw you. Don't you dare use that as an excuse for your fuck-up!" My chin trembles, my voice shaky. "I'd have accepted you in any way I could have you—daughter, no daughter, twenty damn daughters. I would've held my arm out and helped with your baggage because you've accepted mine, but that acceptance ends at lying." My voice cracks. "I should've known when you came back smelling like her, when you went MIA for hours, when you weren't working in your own goddamn bar!" Tears swim in my eyes, and I jerk my head to the side, wishing I could rid myself of them. "You and Jessa can make yourselves a happy little family and stay the hell away from me."

Maliki's eyes glaze over. "I don't want Jessa."

"Yet you've been secretly hanging out with her."

"Don't do this. Don't fucking walk away from us, Sierra."

I whip around, and he's on my trail as I storm toward the bedroom. I scoop up what folded clothes I see, not even caring what they are, and shove them into my bag, overfilling it. Items fall, but I don't care.

Like with Devin, I'll buy new shit.

Maliki stays at my heels as I leave the room, pleas falling from his mouth. "Don't do this. Don't fucking walk away from us."

I don't stop until I'm at the door.

That's when I face him.

And when I nearly break down.

No, I *do* break down.

Our sad eyes meet, neither one of us wanting to be the first to waver.

Disappointment swims in his.

I don't know if that disappointment is toward me for leaving or himself for lying, for doing this to us.

"I thought you were different," I finally whisper.

His eyes shut. "I am." He swallows hard. "I thought you loved me enough not to walk away because I have a daughter."

I point to him, tears blurring my eyes, and my anger resurfaces. "Fuck you! Don't you goddamn dare try that excuse to make yourself feel better." I shake my head and snort. "I always fall for the cheaters."

"I'm not a goddamn cheater," he grinds out. "She tried, but I stopped her before it went anywhere."

I withdraw a step, nearly tripping over myself, my back hitting the door. "She *tried*?"

"Sierra—"

I cut him off, "Let me put this in perspective. How would you feel if I told you I went to the condo and Devin *tried* to fuck me? You'd want to know, wouldn't you?"

"Fuck yes!"

"Exactly!"

His hand curls around my arm when I turn to leave. "Please," he begs. "Don't do this, baby."

I shake my head, sobbing.

"Don't throw us away like this." His voice breaks. "Please, for the love of God, drop your bag and don't leave me."

I attempt to control my sniffles. "We need time apart, and you can spend that time getting to know your daughter."

His hold softens on me, his hand massaging my arm. "I can be with you and spend time with her."

I shake my head and jerk away from him. "I'm sorry."

"You're walking away the second there's a bump in our relationship. I'm going through some shit, and I stayed by your side when you were going through the same."

"You wouldn't have been by my side if it involved still being around Devin."

"Our circumstances are different."

"True, you have a woman from your past who had your baby,

claiming you're sleeping together. Just like Devin, you don't care about trust in relationships. I learned my lesson with men I can't trust. You need time to spend with your daughter. Do that."

I can't believe I gave up my apartment for a man.

I'm never doing that shit again.

Lesson fucking learned.

And with that, I walk out with tears falling down my cheeks.

CHAPTER THIRTY-ONE
MALIKI

I've never been a man who fails.

Who quits.

I'm learning today I'm also a man not afraid to beg the woman he loves not to leave him.

My pulse drums against my throat as I follow Sierra down the stairs and through the bar, biting my tongue to keep my mouth shut in front of customers. As soon as we're outside, customers be damned, I'm still pleading with her.

Begging her not to leave.

She doesn't stop until she makes it to her Lexus. "Maliki, just—"

Weight settles on my heart as I take in the hurt on her face.

I did this to her.

Now, I need to fix it.

"Look at you!" I yell. "Neither one of us wants this! I've never made you doubt my feelings for you, my loyalty to you. Not once!"

"Until today. Why did you smell like her? Why were you there until after midnight?"

"Don't fucking believe her lies," I hiss, lowering my voice as people start walking into the bar.

Her sadness swerves into anger. "You might've turned her down then, but what about the next time and the next? When you're with her, *seeing your daughter*, all I'll think about is whether you're sleeping with her. Had you not hidden this or stayed at her house until midnight, things would be different. I don't trust you and refuse to let myself go through that pain again. You lied about this, something I would've understood. Who knows what else you've lied about?"

I duck my head down to her level, my arms spreading to each side of her body, my hands resting on her car. "Please."

She shoves me away, opens her door, and gets in.

She leaves me.

As fast as Sierra railroaded herself into my life, she's walked out.

———

Liz is waiting for me in my apartment.

I don't know how long I stayed in the parking lot, praying she'd come back, but all I saw were customers ready to have a good time.

I've called.

I've texted.

I've left voice mails.

She's gone.

I should've never hidden it.

That much is obvious.

I didn't know what to do. I'd never had to answer to anyone, to explain to anyone, never shared a life like I did with her.

"I told you this would blow back in your face," Liz says, frustration in her tone.

"She left. You should be happy." I plod around her and yank a bottle of vodka from the cabinet.

"*Please*, I don't feel sorry for you. I feel sorry for her."

In seconds, a shot glass is in my hand, and I fill it to the rim with vodka. "I thought you hated her."

One shot down.

She pushes her hands into her pockets. "Me, too, but now, I hate you. I thought she'd hurt you, not the other way around. You, my dumbass brother, are to blame for losing her."

Another shot knocked back.

I'd offer Liz some, but who knows how long I'll be drowning in my pity?

I slam my glass down. "I did it because I didn't want her to worry about me with Jessa. She was already having trust issues. I fucking did it because I finally had a woman I'd wanted for years and was afraid of losing her."

She snatches the glass from me, pours herself a shot, and downs it. "All of those reasons are what made her leave. Had you told her about Jessa and your daughter, she'd be here. You were a dumbass."

Another shot.

"How did she find out?" she asks.

"Fucking Jessa," I answer through clenched teeth.

"I never liked her. I might've hated her more than I did Sierra back then."

"Join the club."

"You'd better go rip Jessa a new fucking asshole."

"Trust me, I plan to."

"When do I get to meet the little one?"

"Now that the news is out, whenever, I guess."

Another goddamn shot.

———

Calling her drunk is a bad idea.

Fuck good ideas.

I've already proven I exceed at bad fucking ideas.

"What the fuck is wrong with you?" I scream at Jessa over the phone.

"I've been waiting for your call," she replies.

I slam the shot glass on the island.

"She needed to know, and you didn't have the balls to tell her. It's not like I went to Ellie's, planning to break the news, but she was there, and I figured, *Why not?*" Her voice is chipper. Goddamn chipper after ruining my life.

Why not?

Her words only fuel the fire burning inside me.

"You're telling me, you walked around with a copy of our paternity test?" *That's some weird, manipulative shit.*

"I never took it out of my purse."

I stay quiet.

"When will we see you next? Molly has been asking about you all day. I thought it was smart to wait on your phone call, given what happened."

"My attorney will be in touch." No longer will I be a participant in her mind games.

"What?"

"I'm establishing rights to my daughter. I want to see her without you breathing down my neck. You keep making shit complicated, and I'm a simple man. Molly knows who I am now, and I can see her without you."

"I want us to be a family. Molly deserves that."

The vodka is close to coming up while I listen to the phoniness in her voice. "Get it through that dense skull of yours that there will never be an *us.*"

"She left you, didn't she? I told you Little Miss Perfect wouldn't accept this. Hell, I'm sure she never intended to stay with you. You were the bad-boy fling before she went back to her straitlaced husband. He cheated, and she wanted to play, too. Don't think I haven't over-heard them talk."

I pull my phone away to find Liz calling.

"Gotta go." I hang up with Jessa and answer Liz's call.

"Hey," she says timidly.

"What's up?"

"Sierra's brother is here to collect her things. Is it okay to let him up?"

"Yeah."

I hang up.

She really is walking away.

Seconds later, there's a knock at my door.

I'm not sure which brother I'll find on the other side.

"Dude, you fucked up," a kid I don't recognize says, walking into the apartment, uninvited, his shoulder hitting mine.

Since I know Kyle, I'm guessing this is Rex.

"I'm well aware," I grumble. "I need you to talk to her for me."

He shakes his head. "Dude, I don't know you or what happened or what to tell you. What I do know is my sister's trust in people is shit, and beware, she holds grudges like a motherfucker now. I don't know if there's any talking to her that can be done to change her mind. You saw how quickly she left Devin's ass. She doesn't play games."

"Ask her to call me."

"You hurt my sister. I'm not relaying shit."

The little shit has a mouth on him for being twenty pounds less than me.

I clench my fists. Punching her brother won't get me back in her good graces.

"Look, dude," he says, noticing the switch in my mood, "give her a few days. We all know she loves you. It just depends on how much."

I give him her bags, making sure I don't pack *everything,* and search for another shot glass when he leaves.

———

Working was a bad idea.

I'm near as drunk as the people ordering drinks from me.

But hey, I can work under pressure ... under alcohol ... under heartbreak.

I have to work, or I'll go nuts upstairs, thinking about her.

I've always thrived on solidarity and silence, but suddenly, I hate it.

The man who never needed anyone needs *her.*

I miss her—her presence, her scent, her laughter.

I miss my rebellious princess—the woman who pushed my

buttons from our first meeting, who challenges me and pushes a smile out of me more in one day than I used to in months.

I miss her when I close the bar.

I miss her when I slide into bed.

I miss her and can't fucking sleep.

CHAPTER THIRTY-TWO

Three days have passed since I walked away from Maliki.

Three long, miserable-as-hell days.

He keeps calling.

I keep ignoring.

"Hey, babe," Ellie says, walking into Rex's apartment with ice cream, hot wings, and wine. She glances around. "Your little bro's pad isn't as bad as I imagined." She drops all her items, including hand sanitizer, on the floor next to the couch.

I called my father and asked if the apartment he'd offered was available. It wasn't. I needed a place to stay and asked Rex if his offer was still open. My baby brother doesn't ask questions. I'm closer to him than any of my other siblings.

He shares the three-bedroom apartment with another roommate, who welcomed me with open arms. It's a total bachelor pad with large TVs, video games, and movie posters as the wall decor, *but* they do keep it clean and are respectful.

I hop up from the couch to put the ice cream in the freezer and grab two plates from the set Devin's uncle gifted us on our wedding. Next, I open a drawer for the wine opener and snag two wineglasses.

Instead of avoiding Ellie's apartment in fear of running into Devin, it's now Jessa I'm dodging.

Ellie blows out a long breath when I hand her a plate. "Damn, am I in one crappy position."

I open the bottle of wine and pour myself a full glass. "I don't expect you to take my side over Jessa's."

"She's in the wrong though."

I gulp down my entire glass and pour hers. "You really didn't know he was Molly's dad?" The question has been lingering in my head since Jessa's big reveal.

From Ellie's reaction when Jessa broke the news, it seemed Ellie was clueless, but I never know. She could've been protecting her family.

"Hell no. I would've told you the moment I found out. My sister led our entire family to believe Pete was Molly's dad. Hell, she made it seem like what she and Maliki had was just a fling. I told you my sister had slept with him. That wasn't a secret. I never knew it was more than that, and I definitely didn't know my niece was his. I can't believe I missed it though. I mean, he looks nothing like Pete."

I nod even though I don't know Pete.

I do feel bad for the guy though.

Not only did he think Molly was his, but he also had to deal with Jessa on the regular.

I shiver, just thinking about it.

"Have your parents said anything about me?" I ask.

"Jessa and I got into a screaming match at my parents', and she called me unfaithful because I'm friends with *the enemy*. She told them about Maliki and you, and it was a shock to everyone. The way she did it was shitty, and I hope this doesn't change our relationship."

"I hope so, too." I drop two wings onto my plate. "I can't believe your sister and I are fighting over the same man."

She crosses her legs. "Technically, you're not. Maliki doesn't even see Jessa because he loves you."

The problem is, he has to see her.

———

"Hey, honey."

I smile up at my father from my chair and stand to hug him.

He wraps me tight, patting my back, and straightens his suit before taking the chair across from me.

"I'm searching for an apartment for you," he says, diving straight in with no good-morning chat. "I offered the last guy nearly double in rent, but he said no. When you sign a lease, it's hard to back out."

He pauses when the waitress comes to take our order.

"I can look outside town," he continues when she leaves. "Leaving Blue Beech for a while might help you."

I nod, taking a sip of my orange juice. "You're right."

He frowns. "I hate seeing you like this."

"Like what?"

His face creases in concern. "Sad. Heartbroken. It seems it keeps happening to you."

"There's nothing—"

He cuts me off, "I know when something is wrong with my daughter. Is this about Devin or Maliki?"

My cheeks blush. "There's no way I'm discussing my love life with you."

He holds up his hand. "Tell me what they did, and I'll offer my opinion. I'm the epitome of a bad man. I'll let you know if they stack up or if there's reason behind their actions."

"It's Maliki. He has a secret kid ... *just like you.*"

I recoil in my chair, my appetite disappearing, and notice the change in my father as well. He holds his hand to his lips, shuts his eyes, and then slowly opens them back up.

My situation is so similar to my mom's.

Maliki has a child and kept it a secret.

Sure, there are a lot more differences than similarities, but my broken heart can't stop comparing the two.

He raises a brow, finally speaking, "Maliki has a kid?"

I nod. "A daughter."

"Did he know about her?"

"No."

"That changes things. Our situations aren't similar."

CHAPTER THIRTY-THREE
SIERRA

Two weeks have passed since my fallout with Maliki.

"Your brother and I totally understand if you don't want to come," Chloe says. "It won't hurt our feelings."

Her engagement party is tonight.

At Down Home.

I wave off her offer. "No, it's fine. I'll avoid Maliki. Everything will be good."

Yeah, right.

I fake a smile.

"What's going on with the bar's remodel?" she asks.

"All the hard work is done. We already selected flooring and paint. The contractors were scheduled, and I sent copies to Liz. The contractors will show up, do their job, and I'll check on them while Maliki is gone from the bar. Liz has agreed for me to come in on his days off."

"Maliki is okay with that?"

I shrug. "Don't know. Don't care."

Lies.

Chloe whistles. "Oh Lordy, your life is becoming more interesting than mine."

"Why the frown, new roomie?"

Josh, Rex's *and* my roommate, crashes next to me on the couch, a wild grin on his face.

Rex glances up from his video game—a video game he's *developing*. "Boy problems." He pauses his game, tosses the controller to the side, and turns to face us. "Maliki problems."

I wince, just hearing his name.

It possesses so many good and bad memories.

"You going to the party tonight?" Rex asks.

I nod.

"You sure that's a good idea?"

It's stupid, but as I have for so many years, I'm going there even though it's a bad idea. I've become a professional at ignoring warnings to steer clear of Down Home Pub.

"I can't miss my brother's engagement party because of boy problems, and it's not like I hate Maliki." I wrinkle my nose. "We just aren't right for each other."

Wrong.

We are right for each other.

You can be right for someone and it still not work out.

Romeo and Juliet.

Cleopatra and Mark Antony.

Minus the whole dying thing.

"Maliki," Josh says, breaking me away from my thoughts. "He's the bartender at Down Home, right?"

"Yep," Rex answers for me.

He didn't ask questions when I texted him that I was moving into his spare bedroom, nor did he when I asked him to pick up my stuff from Maliki's. All he did was tell me he was here if I needed to talk.

That's the thing with my brother. He puts up this funny, not-give-a-shit act, but deep down, he's one of the most caring men I know.

Josh props his feet onto the coffee table, his eyes cutting to me. "Want to know of a good way to get your mind off him?"

Yes, please. "Nope," is what I answer though.

Josh drinks cheap beer, pisses with the bathroom door open, and has an obsession with *The Sopranos*. Not taking relationship advice from him.

He thrusts his thumbs into his chest. "This guy."

I swat my hand through the air. "Go away before I call your mother."

"*Shit,* if I bagged a girl like you, my mother would be a very happy woman."

"And mine would have a heart attack."

"Shut up. That's my sister," Rex says in agitation.

Josh ignores Rex. "What did Maliki do? Want me to beat him up?"

A smile tugs at my lips at the same time Rex snorts and says, "Maliki would squash you, dude."

Again, Josh ignores Rex. "You've had an older man. A guy your age. Why not try a younger one this time around?"

"I wish I could tell you to go home," I tell him.

He scoots closer to curve an arm around my shoulders. "I am home, babe."

I roll my eyes and shove him away.

Josh looks at Rex. "It sucks you can't go out tonight, man. We need to score you a fake."

Rex shrugs. "It's all good. I have plans with Carolina."

"Ah, sweet Carolina," Josh sings. "That's my girl right there."

"She's not shit to you," Rex growls with a glare.

Josh glances at me. "I warned Rex if he doesn't make his move on her in six months, I'm asking her out."

Rex tenses. "You'll be smothered in your goddamn sleep."

"Why aren't you two a thing?" I ask, happy the attention is off me. "I've never understood that."

"She's my best friend, and I don't do girlfriends well. I won't ruin what we have because I'm a dumbass when it comes to relationships."

"Yet you won't let me ask her out," Josh says. "You also don't want *anyone else* to have her."

"Yes, because none of you pricks deserve her."

"Neither does someone afraid to ask her out."

"Fuck off." Rex turns around and goes back to his video game.

My father wasn't happy when he found out Rex had swapped out his political science major to computer science, but I'm proud of him. He has a dorm at Iowa State, but since he only has classes three days a week, he commutes from his apartment. He hasn't even graduated and already scored an internship at some huge tech company.

Josh twists to look at me. "If you need a make-him-jealous man, I'm your boy."

Rex isn't old enough to get into bars yet, but Josh is. They met each other at Iowa State, kicked it off, and became roommates. Josh is cool and flirtatious as hell but means no harm.

"Dude, be careful," Rex says. "Maliki will kick your ass."

CHAPTER THIRTY-FOUR
MALIKI

Saturdays are the pub's busiest nights.

I hoped the bustling crowd would hinder my thoughts of Sierra—and then I remembered her brother's engagement party is *here* tonight.

I've been scanning the bar all night, unsure if Sierra is coming. I've spotted a few of Kyle's friends and her cousin but no sign of her. She might sit this one out. I frown, hating my bullshit might prevent her from celebrating with her brother.

It's been a tough week overall and a busy week for my phone, given how many times I've called and texted Sierra … and dodged Jessa's phone calls. It pisses me off how damn quick Sierra threw us away when she'd fought for us for so long.

That's not me placing all the blame on her.

This is all my fault.

I was stupid, and Sierra is afraid of getting hurt again.

Sierra hasn't returned to the bar since she walked away from me. Although she's talked to Liz. How the fuck that happened is beyond me, but Liz knows the schedule of the renovation, and she agreed to take all of Sierra's shifts. Liz has taken Sierra's side in our breakup.

I'm numb as I move around the bar, going about my regular routine.

A vodka and Sprite.

Bud Light.

Corona.

A guy from high school mentioning an old memory.

I yell out an order for a basket of hot wings to the kitchen.

Same shit, different shift.

Only Sierra isn't here.

I got so used to us working together. The bar feels hollow without her.

My back goes straight, and I overpour the drink I'm making when I see her. I don't move, nearly in shock, when she comes to the bar.

I walk away, ignoring a customer, and meet her, wishing the bar didn't divide us.

She's more anxious than she was the first time I busted her here.

"Hi," she says, her voice nearly a whisper.

She looks damn gorgeous.

She also looks tired.

My chest caves in, as I know that tiredness is most likely from my dumbass actions.

I stare at her, tongue-tied for a moment, scrambling for the right words to not fuck this up.

"Are you ready to come home?" I decide to go with a playful tone. "Or are you here to get your job back?" I'm trying to stay composed, but my heart is heavy as it constricts in my chest.

"I'll pass," she says with unreadable eyes. "I'm here for the party, and I don't want it to be weird between us. I'll order all my drinks from Liz and steer clear of this side." She gestures toward my area of the bar.

"Why did you come over here then?"

"To give you a heads-up."

"I call bullshit."

"Whatever, Maliki. Call bullshit all you want, but it's the truth."

I open my mouth to explain why I'm calling bullshit, but I'm cut off when she keeps talking.

"Also, I don't know if Liz told you, but everything is scheduled for the remodel. I'm doing all my communication through her." Her lips are pressed into a firm line.

Liz already shared this info with me.

I fix my stare on her. "Liz doesn't own the bar. *I do.* Not communicating with your client is unprofessional."

She narrows her eyes at me. "Whatever. I'll maintain a *professional* relationship until the remodel is over. I've appointed Liz as my assistant, so all communication will go through her. How's that?"

"I'd much rather deal with the woman I *hired.*"

"Don't make this difficult."

Trust me, I'm trying hard not to.

I pinch the bridge of my nose. "I miss you, Sierra. We need to talk about this. I know you're young, but—"

She inches up her hand, stopping me. "Nope, don't blame this on my *age.* I'm smart enough to know not to get hurt again."

"If you get hurt again, it won't be by me."

"You already have. I won't take that risk again."

I gulp in an exasperated breath. "Anytime you're in a relationship with someone, you risk heartbreak. Have another relationship, but you can't guarantee it won't happen again. With me, you have a fucking guarantee I'll do everything in my power to never hurt you again. I've never made you doubt my feelings for you. Never. Remember that."

"Maliki—" Her eyes narrow as she stares over my shoulder.

"Hey, babe," Jessa says behind me, and I shit you not, I'm shocked my back doesn't break with how tense my spine goes. "Molly is knocked out. Do you want me to bring your dinner down?"

My pulse slams into my neck, and my eyes don't leave Sierra.

"Wow," Sierra snarls. "Never doubt you, huh?" Her fingers dig into the wood of the bar.

"It's not what it looks like." The words slowly leave my mouth.

She scoffs, "Piss off, Maliki."

I hop over the bar when she turns to leave, knocking down napkins and baskets of food, and follow her. I call her name louder with every step through the bar. When we make it to a clearing, I snatch her wrist and whip her around to face me.

She smacks my hand and wriggles out of my hold. "Don't. I'm here for my brother and Chloe. I won't let our drama ruin their party. This isn't happening tonight."

"Well, well, look what we have here." A hipster-looking dude comes up and slings an arm around her shoulders, blind to what he's walked into. "My hot-ass roommate."

What the hell?

My temples throb.

Sierra tenses before relaxing when he drags her into his scrawny-ass chest.

"Who the fuck is this?" My voice thunders through the bar, catching the attention of customers around us.

Luckily, there's a band playing that covers some of my anger.

The dude has the balls to hold out his hand. "Josh." He cocks his head toward Sierra. "New roommate. New friend. Hopefully, future boyfriend."

My hands clench.

"Josh," Sierra drags out in warning. "Now isn't the time."

The smirk on the dude's face drops when he sees the temper in mine.

He pulls away, takes a glance at me, and squeezes her arm. "I'll be at Kyle's table."

"Your new roommate?" I hiss when he walks away.

She nods. "I'm staying with Rex and him." Her lips twitch into a smile, and I wince at her sudden mood change. "Will you make me a drink? Liz looks busy over there."

My brows crinkle. "Sure."

Her smile stays intact as we walk back to the bar. "Tequila."

I pour her a shot.

She knocks it back. "Two more."

I pour her two more.

Her smile turns cold. "Thanks. I can't wait to take these with Josh." She grabs one in each hand and smirks. "Enjoy Jessa's gross dinner."

My eyes stay pinned to her as she walks straight to Josh's table and hands him the shot, and they take them together.

I march over to Liz. "I'm taking five."

She nods, her eyes moving to Sierra.

Asshole's arm is back around her.

Liz squeezes my shoulder. "She's doing it to piss you off. She wants to hurt you like you did her."

"I'm well aware." *It's fucking working.*

———

Molly is crashed out on the couch, and Jessa is in the kitchen, not making shit when I walk into the apartment.

"I warned you not to pull that shit," I bite out.

My attorney hasn't come through with the custody paperwork yet, so I'm still tortured by Jessa when I visit with Molly. She came over for pizza before my shift, Jessa's annoying ass right behind her. We hung out, and she asked to stay and finish the movie we'd been watching. I figured they would've left by now.

"What shit?" she asks, playing coy.

"That stunt you pulled when you saw me talking to Sierra."

She releases a hard laugh. "God, Maliki, it's time for you to say good-bye to your little sorority-girl fling. She won't be with someone like you long-term. Stop wasting your time. She's been friends with my sister since they were kids. I've seen the guys she dates, the ones she's brought over for group dates in my parents' basement. They aren't you. You're a rebound."

"You need to leave," I grit out.

She reaches out, brushing her hand over my arm, and I jerk away in disgust. Her face falls. She's not used to being turned down.

"Come on, Maliki. We had something—good times, hot sex."

"That was in the past. You were a *fling.* That's it. I want a relationship with Molly, but you? I want nothing to do with. I've been nice, but you've played nothing but games. All I want from you is to be mature and co-parent with me."

"Molly needs a stable home, and my grandparents are returning this weekend. There's not enough room for the two of us there without being too cramped." It's as if she didn't hear what I'd just told her.

"If you feel you can't provide somewhere for Molly to stay, she can live with me. *Only her.* Not you. If you need a place to live other than your parents', I can help you find an apartment, but you're not moving in with me."

"You have a guest bedroom."

"It isn't available for you."

———

I hug Molly good-bye, knock back a shot of whiskey, and return to the bar. I've left Liz long enough to deal with the craziness tonight and feel like an asshole.

I immediately shoot my attention to Sierra.

She's at the same table with her douche-bag roommate.

He holds up his shot glass and gestures to Sierra with it. "She's coming home with me tonight, gentlemen!" he drunkenly slurs. "Be jealous!"

I charge toward the kitchen, open the door, and yell inside, "Mikey! You're on bar duty!"

I leave without waiting for a reply. Mikey needed extra cash, so I told him he could work in the kitchen. Thank fuck I did that and can bail from this place.

"I'm out of here," I tell Liz.

I can't make a scene here. Can't punch a dude in the face here.

I'm a business owner, a father. I have to change my mindset about shit.

The asshole kisses her cheek next.

On second thought, fuck this shit.

CHAPTER THIRTY-FIVE
SIERRA

"Oh shit," is all I hear Chloe say before Maliki captures my elbow, hoists me up from my stool, and hauls me outside, the crowd watching with curious eyes.

"What do you think you're doing?" he snarls, unclasping me when we make it to the edge of the parking lot.

What does he think he's doing?

"Enjoying my night," I fire back.

"Bullshit." Temper flashes in his eyes. "You're *enjoying* making me miserable."

Yes, that, too.

I internally shrug.

He deserves it.

I've been miserable since our breakup. It only seems fitting it's the same for him.

"Whatever. You know nothing," I somewhat slur, realizing how much I've had to drink now that I'm standing, no longer supported by the barstool. "Better yet, maybe I should play games with you like you did me."

He thrusts a hand through his hair. "Jesus Christ, you're plastered."

"That's your fault."

"*My fault?* I didn't shove those drinks down your throat."

"I never planned to drink this much, but I needed to erase the image of your baby mama, the one you were … whatever with behind my back, coming down from *your* apartment." I struggle to keep my voice strong, and it cracks near the end. Heartbreak clutched at my heart when I saw Jessa.

He shakes his head. "What happened with Jessa isn't what you think."

I flick my hand through the air. "I don't care. I'm leaving."

"You're not going home with that kid, FYI."

"*Excuse you*, that's where I live, FYI."

He stands tall with his arms crossed. "You're drunk. He's drunk. Not happening."

"I'll sleep where I damn well please." I tap my finger against my lip. "Hmm … maybe I should sleep with my *new* roommate. This one might not break my heart."

"Do you want to be responsible for that kid getting his ass kicked?" His pissed off glare lifts into a smile. "Not to mention, he's too young for your liking."

I want to slap that stupid smirk off his face. My head throbs, and the liquor is making its strike to my brain. "Where am I supposed to sleep then, huh?" I regret my question as soon as it drops from my lips.

"You can crash in the guest room."

I release a cold laugh. "Oh, yes, that sounds like a blast. Maybe I can eat Jessa's dinner to sober myself up. Is she still up there?"

"Jessa came over *with Molly*, so I could visit with *Molly*. I don't give a shit about Jessa. Barely spoke to her until after she pulled that shit. She said it to provoke you, and you fell for the bait."

I scoff, "Whatever."

"I'm already taking care of one kid, Sierra. Don't act like that."

"Screw you," I hiss, turning and walking around the building. "I can't believe I was dumb enough to fall for every word that came out of your lying mouth. I swear, it's always the cute ones. Cute guys break your heart. I need to switch up my type, pronto."

He grabs my arm, stopping me from walking back into the pub, and leads us toward the apartment. I don't jerk away, but I do throw a string of curses alongside each step we make.

He releases me when we make it to the stairs, standing behind me, and blocking me from going back to the parking lot.

Fuck it.

I turn and stomp up the stairs. He remains quiet while following behind me as I swing open the door that leads to the apartment stairs, surprised it's unlocked.

"You had me walking around, looking like a fool." My stomps grow louder and harder when I make it to the apartment, my muttering continuing, "You're like every man in my life—like my father, Devin—"

I'm abruptly cut off, and I yelp when Maliki grips my shoulders and twists me around to face him.

His face is inches away from mine, his dark eyes settled on mine. "Don't you dare compare me to them."

I shove him back, destroying our eye contact. He can't witness my impending tears.

"Why? You're no different." I retreat another step and stare up at the ceiling, blinking and silently yelling at my emotions to stop being such a pansy.

"You and I both know I'm nothing like that. I *never* touched anyone but you when we were together."

I dip my chin after I've calmed down the tears and bumped up the anger, catching on to the past tense of his words. "Oh, but what about now that we're not together?"

"Still haven't touched anyone. Don't want to touch anyone." He raises his arms. "Now that we have that cleared up, drink some water and sleep that bullshit off. We'll talk in the morning."

"Fine," I snap, maintaining my stomping game into the living room. I kick off my shoes, snatch the pillows on the couch, and hurl them across the room. Next, I start grabbing cushions and chucking them.

"What are you doing?"

"Sleeping, like you told me to." I throw the last cushion down.

"No way am I sleeping in a bed you could've screwed her in." My drunken mind doesn't believe him. My wonderful, pessimistic friend —aka tequila—is screaming he's a liar. "I don't want to sleep here, but it seems it's the only choice I have, considering you threatened physical violence on my new roomie."

He stays quiet, standing in the corner, and I drop down on the couch.

I suck in a breath. My intoxicated anger has shifted to intoxicated sadness. "Why did you make me do it?"

"Do what?" he asks in a strangled voice.

"Make me fall in love with you." I sniffle, a failed attempt to suppress my tears.

"I should ask you the same." He releases a hard sigh. " There's no damn reason for us not to be together."

I lift my head, and my back is stiff as I sit against the bare couch. "Losing Devin was nowhere near as painful as losing you. I offered you too much of my heart." Tears swell in my eyes, and I wipe them away with the back of my arm. "I would've accepted you having a daughter, accepted her into my heart, because she's a part of you, and I love every part of you. You never gave me that chance, and now, we'll never have that chance again."

"Sierra," he gently says.

I stretch on the couch to my side, turning my back to him. "Forget it. I'm over it, and I need sleep."

All I hear is a sharp sigh from him, and the room turns miserably silent.

Minutes pass.

No words.

Did he leave?

I reposition myself, still facing the rear of the couch but allowing myself to peek behind my back.

My throat tightens when I see Maliki sitting on the floor by my feet, his elbow resting on his knee as he massages his forehead.

The air turns heavy as we remain quiet—a silence that's too loud.

Finally, I yawn, my eyes feeling weighted as I shut them.

I don't know how much time passes before he lifts me in his arms and puts me in his bed.

I'm too exhausted to fight it.

———

My throat is dry and scratchy when I wake up.

My pounding head is calling me an idiot.

I rub my forehead and glance around his bedroom.

Relentless jerk.

He's nowhere to be seen, but I hear clattering in the kitchen. I slide out of bed, brush my teeth with the toothbrush Maliki didn't give Rex, and rub my sleepy eyes decorated with old mascara off with a washcloth.

I make a stop at his closet, snag one of his tees, and find a pair of my panties in the drawer I was using. Yes, I'm walking out half-naked, but whatever. It's nothing he hasn't seen.

Maliki's head rises, his attention moving from the sizzling pan to me when I wander into the kitchen.

How much shit-talking did I do last night?

I don't realize those words actually left my mouth until Maliki answers me.

"Oh, you definitely expressed yourself, Jailbait." He forks out bacon strips from the pan and drops them onto a plate with a napkin covering it. He grabs another pan and cracks two eggs inside it.

"Oh, we're back to Jailbait now, huh?"

He turns to snag a water bottle from the fridge, motions for me to sit, and slides the bottle to me when I do. "Drink this."

"All right, Dr. Hangover. Do you know how many times I've been plastered? *Way more drunk* than I was last night?" Sorority life hurts your liver.

"I won't dispute that, but next time, make sure you're only plastered around me."

"I thought drunk people annoyed you?"

He scoops the egg on a plate, drops a few bacon strips on it, and hands it to me. "They do. You're not just a person to me, so I don't mind."

I slump down in my stool and start eating.

I miss you.

And just like the shit-talking comment, that wasn't supposed to come out either.

He doesn't eat. He just stares at me, leveling his elbows on the island, even though he made himself a plate. "Fix it then. Pack your shit and move back in."

"You need time."

"I need you."

"You've had a serious life change," is my next argument.

"Still doesn't change the fact that I need you. If anything, *this* is when I need you the most—when I'm going through some shit."

"I wish you had needed me when everything started," I mutter. "Or at least told me."

"If I could take it back, I would."

"But you can't."

His face falls. "Tell me this, do you trust me?"

I swallow.

"Do you trust me, Sierra?"

I shake my head. "I don't trust anyone anymore." Not my family, not my exes, not even the lady at Sephora when I went there last week.

My new life philosophy is, *Don't trust anyone.* Maybe I should get it tattooed.

His lips twist downward. "Never doubt your trust in me."

I pick up my fork but drop it seconds later. "I never doubted you before, but you can't honestly stand there and defend what you did, say that it didn't hurt our trust."

He nods. "You're right, but I'd never jeopardize my relationship with you for her or any other woman. I promise."

"Maybe you want to have your cake and eat it, too?"

"Wrong. I wouldn't be pushing through these problems, begging you not to leave me, if I didn't love you, if I wanted another woman."

"I know," I whisper. I take a large bite, wishing for this conversation to be over. My head needs to be clear when we sit down and have a mature talk about our relationship.

"How's staying at Rex's?"

"Not as disgusting as I thought it'd be. He's actually pretty clean."

"And the other guy? The roommate?"

I keep my focus on my eggs. "What about him?"

"Don't play coy with me."

I glance up at him. "What if I was fucking him?"

He flinches. "Excuse me?"

"What if I was fucking him?"

His face hardens. "Don't fuck with me, Sierra." His fork clangs against the plate when he drops it and circles the island, grabbing my stool and swiveling it so I'm facing him. "If you want a boy who plays beer pong with his friends and doesn't know how to please anyone but himself, go right ahead, but we know that's not what you want. Is it?" He rests his hands on my thighs.

My stomach turns inside out as I struggle to control my composure. "I said nothing about *dating him*. I've stopped confusing sex with love."

He releases a harsh laugh. "Then, why are you here, huh? Why were you in *my* bed last night and not his bunk bed with Spider-Man sheets?"

"I hate you, and in case you forgot, I was taken into your bed unwillingly."

He travels a hand up to my chin, raising it, and tightens his hand resting on my thigh, smirking. "You would've rather been in his bed last night?"

I gulp. "Yep."

I'm not sure how the sneaky jerk does it, but somehow, someway, he—or his hands—convinces me to stand at the same time his mouth meets mine.

His tongue slides into my mouth, tasting like coffee and vanilla and a man I've missed so damn much. Our knees knock into each other's as he backs me against the same wall we visited the first night we had sex. That memory only turns me on more.

Seconds ago, I was lying about wanting for sleeping with another man.

Now, he's drifting his hand up my shirt, his fingers exploring my stomach.

"You want to be in *my* bed. Not his. You're lying. Admit it," he grinds out against my mouth, his hand dipping to the band of my panties, panties that are soaked and waiting for his hands, his mouth, his cock—anything of him.

I ignore him, and his hands move when I pull his sweatshorts down.

"Admit you're lying," he repeats, slightly pulling away.

I don't.

He yanks up his pants, taking a step back. "Then, no dick for you."

"Are you kidding me?" I snap, my heart picking up speed.

"Nope." He's fighting to control his breathing, control his hands from touching me, and there's no controlling his erection.

I shove him back. "I don't want to touch anyone but you, you bastard. You want to know why?" I don't wait for him to answer. "'Cause I fucking love you!"

He grins. "There's my girl."

I squeal when he grips my waist, lifts me into his arms—my legs wrapping around him—and walks us to the bedroom. I'm thrown onto the bed, bouncing up while he undresses. He crawls up the bed, pulling my shirt off, and slips my panties to the side, two of his fingers diving inside me. My back arches as he works me, and right as I'm about to lose it, he pulls them away along with my panties and positions himself between my legs.

I moan when he shoves himself inside me.

"The only girl I want in my bed." He pulls out and slams inside me.

"The only woman I ever want to be inside." Another thrust.

"The only woman I'll ever love." Another thrust.

"The only woman I want to spend the rest of my life with."

His slams get so rough, so hard, as if he's pushing his words deeper and deeper inside me so I have no choice but to believe them.

Being inside Sierra again is like going back to heaven after being punished in hell.

There's no damn way I'll ever want any woman over her.

She's perfect—stubborn as hell but goddamn perfect.

We're sweaty against the sheets, attempting to catch our breaths, but each time I push myself inside her, we lose them again.

She hooks her legs around the indent of my hips, drawing me closer, and digs her heels into my back when I obey.

"Your nails," I say.

She pushes her chest against mine, her mouth hitting mine, and rakes her nails down my back.

I grind my teeth.

I love when she marks me.

If she leaves me after this, I'll have the marks of her being here again, if even for a few days. I feel her pussy clench against my dick as her nails claw at my skin, and she yells out my name.

"*Fuck*, you feel good," I groan with my release.

When her eyes open, I brush her hair from her face and stare down at her.

"Jesus, you're beautiful. Thank you for letting me touch something so perfect," I whisper.

———

"You ready to hand out more truths?" I ask Sierra while she sucks in a few breaths and falls down on her back next to me.

She takes a moment before glancing over at me. "Hmm? What truths?" She narrows her eyes. "You can't make me orgasm like that and then expect a deep conversation. That's cheating."

I chuckle. "I can give you another one, sentence by sentence, if you'd like?"

She throws her head back "Oh my God. I would die, and then we couldn't have that conversation. I'll take an hour-by-hour orgasm."

"I'll give you whatever you want."

She grabs the blanket and draws it up our naked bodies. "I'll actually take sleep and *then* another orgasm." She yawns. "Can we save all serious talk until then?"

I pull her into me, taking a chance, and she has no problem with snuggling into my side.

All the tension I had of losing her releases.

She's mine, and I'll hand her every damn secret, every thought in my head, every move I make if it means keeping her.

———

I made her hot wings.

Correction: I went down to the kitchen and asked the cook to make her hot wings.

They're her favorite, and she deserves as many of her favorites I can give her for making me so goddamn happy.

I set the basket in front of her, and a thought hits me.

"So, are we made up?" I ask with an eager smile. "I gave you the truth, orgasms, *and* hot wings. There's no way you can turn a man down after that."

She swallows her bite and cleans her hand with a napkin before answering, "If we do this, it needs to be complete honesty going forward." She grabs another wing, dips it in ranch, and takes a bite.

"Complete honesty," I agree with a nod. "I owe you an apology. I should've never kept secrets from you, especially one of that magnitude. Hiding that from you and hanging out with Jessa behind your back was fucking stupid." I blow out a breath. "I was scared to tell you, for fear of losing you. I needed the right plan. It needed to be at the right time, and whenever I tried to convince myself it was, I would chicken the fuck out."

"You really were planning to drop the bomb on the dinner date?"

I nod. "I figured if I wined and dined you, you'd surely accept it. Plus, I'd give you orgasms." I wink.

"Had you revealed you were hanging out with Jessa behind my back, I would've thrown that wine at you." She wipes the sauce off her mouth. "You know I wasn't upset about you having a daughter, right? It was the whole secrecy and Jessa part that hurt me."

She's not lying. Sierra has too much heart to do that. I only said that to cast the blame on someone else even though I was in the wrong.

"I want you there with me," I say. "In Molly's and my life."

She grins. "She's such a cute girl. When I babysat with Ellie, she was so sweet."

I smile at her words. "She is. Jessa is worried about her starting school in a new town. We enrolled her in dance, so hopefully, she'll meet some friends before the year starts."

"Call someone who has a daughter her age." She stops to think. "What about Dallas Barnes? His daughter is a total sweetheart and looks to be around Molly's age. She's always at events with her grandparents, given they're so involved. Maybe we can schedule a playdate. I'll ask my brother to see if we can set something up."

"I don't know why I waited to tell you for so long. You're already perfect at helping me with this."

———

A self-satisfied smile is on Sierra's face as she kicks her feet against the floor. "I told you this flooring would be amazing. *Plus,* the maintenance is child's play compared to hardwood."

I was reluctant on switching over to tile. Tile can make a room appear cold. The pub isn't cold. It's a relaxing experience. Sierra, the determined woman she is, found tile that looks exactly like wood. I wasn't even able to tell when she first showed me. No more constant worrying about spills causing damage.

I do a once-over of the bar. It looks so damn good. I've lost count of the number of times I tried calling her to tell her that when we weren't talking. She did a kick-ass job—from the flooring to the paint scheme and the furniture. She had the brick walls behind the bar painted, changing from red to a subtle gray. That same color brick is wrapped around the outside of the bar, and she left the tops untouched to keep the authenticity. The new kitchen appliances were installed a few days ago as well as the kegs. The new taps are coming tomorrow, and I can't fucking wait.

"And the paint matches *perfectly*," she sings out. "We *are* missing the furniture *you* said you'd assemble."

"I didn't think it'd be that complicated. I opened the boxes and found five thousand pieces. How the hell do they think that's cool?"

She settles her gaze on me, attempting to put off a serious look but it fails when a smile cracks along her lips. "I told you so."

I wrap my arm around her shoulders. "Care to help a man assemble furniture?"

She dramatically groans. "I guess."

I smack her ass. "I love you."

CHAPTER THIRTY-SEVEN
SIERRA

"I swear, Jessa won't be showing up here," Ellie says, snagging a doughnut and dropping it onto her plate.

We haven't seen each other in days. I've been swept up in Maliki, moving my things back to his apartment, which wasn't much, and wrapping up the bar's remodel. I have a busy week ahead of me and came over to spend time with her this morning, doughnuts and pineapple smoothies in hand.

"She's still not talking to me over the whole *I'm hanging out with the enemy* nonsense." She lifts her chin and rolls her eyes. "I've never been tight with her. Hell, I'm closer to you than her, and she's in the wrong. So, the enemy is who I shall hang out with."

"It doesn't matter. I'll see her later today." I take a gulp of my smoothie to hide the dread on my face. "We're hanging out with Molly later."

She drops the doughnut in her hand. "Holy hell. You're meeting Molly as *the girlfriend?*"

"Sure am."

I'm nervous about seeing Molly, and I would rather shave off my eyebrows than be around Jessa. Fingers crossed I won't see her since we're picking Molly up and taking her out for the day. Jessa tried weaseling her way into tagging along with Maliki, but he wasn't having it.

"This is a big step! I'm happy for you!"

I pick at my doughnut. "I don't know why I'm nervous. I've babysat her with you. It's not like she's a stranger."

"You're nervous because you'll be her stepmom one day."

My eyes widen. "I don't know about that."

"I do."

———

My knees are bouncing as I sit in the passenger seat.

"I hate I wasn't here for you last time," I tell Maliki.

He briefly glances at me before returning his eyes to the road. "It might've been for the best. Jessa broke the news to Molly terribly. She sprang it on her without warning. Molly was upset and confused."

Of course Jessa did.

My heart aches for them. "It probably would've done more harm than good. I would've been another person added to the confusion."

He nods. "She's comfortable with me now, and I've talked about you with her."

"I'm sure Jessa loved that."

"I've started tuning out Jessa when it's not Molly-related." He hesitates before continuing, "I forgot to explain the day I went to the city without you. I took Molly shopping for clothes and a doll."

That's random.

But I did say no more secrets.

"Way to piss me off more about Jessa right before I see her."

He chuckles. "Yeah, bad move on my part to start throwing out confessions right now. I just don't want everything out in the open, so anytime I think of one, I'll clear that shit up fast."

"Appreciate that."

He pulls up to Jessa's parents' house. After their grandparents returned, Jessa moved in with them. I had been here countless times during my childhood with Ellie.

He shifts the car in park. "Ready?"

"Absolutely." No longer is nervousness crashing through. I'm excited to hang out with the little girl who will be such a huge part in our lives.

The front door opens after Maliki knocks, and Molly stands in front of us with an eager grin spread along her face. Her eyes travel from Maliki to me, her smile growing wider.

"I remember you!" she squeals. "You're Auntie Ellie's friend! Sierra! You were nice and colored with me!"

I blink at her, taking in the similarities between her and Maliki.

I see it.

She has his nose.

His lips.

I grin down at her. "And I remember you! You color so well and watch the best cartoons!"

I like kids. My mom had our family regularly volunteer with them, growing up. It's one of the best things she ever did for us. All my siblings have hearts of gold when it comes to children.

She hops from one foot to the other. "Are you my daddy's girlfriend?"

"What's she doing here?" Jessa snaps, coming to the door, standing next to Molly, and breaking our warm vibe. Her arms are crossed as she fixes a glare toward me.

I ignore her, not even firing a fake smile her way. Today is about having fun with Molly.

"I don't know if Molly should go, given you brought your flavor of the week. I made it clear I want to be careful who my daughter is around," Jessa barks before anyone replies.

"You had no issue when Sierra babysat her with Ellie," Maliki hisses.

"That's different. She was Ellie's friend, not her new father's *girlfriend.*"

Maliki tenses at the *new father* blow. "I won't argue with you in front of her. We can talk later." He leans down to Molly's height. "Ready to go?"

Molly squeezes between her mom and grabs Maliki's hand. "Yes!"

She skips hand in hand with Maliki to the car.

I don't peek back at Jessa, but there's no doubt she'd stick a knife in my back if she could.

———

Maliki helps Molly into her seat before we get in and turns to look at her. "Did you decide what you want to do today?" He told Molly she could choose.

Molly straightens in her seat. "Can we go to the movies, and can I get a gigantic bucket of popcorn, and then can we paint my nails like Sierra's, and then she can maybe braid my hair later? I *love* my hair braided."

Maliki eyes me in question.

I twist back in my seat to smile at her. "Sounds like we have a plan."

She's giggling when we turn around, and I snatch my phone from my purse to check movie times. The theater is thirty minutes away, so we have plenty of time to decide. I rattle off the movies and let her pick.

We raid the concession stand when we get to the theater, scoring a bucket of buttery popcorn, M&M's, Mike & Ike, and slushies.

Molly will definitely be in a sugar coma.

With me right alongside her.

Molly takes the seat between me and Maliki, and I can't help but crack a smile at Maliki. He's about to sit through a two-hour-long animated children's film for his daughter. He doesn't complain once, even when he watches the movie trailer with a horrified look on his face.

As soon as I fall down in my seat, I pour the M&M's into the popcorn and offer it to Molly.

"I've never had that before," she says, glancing up at me with an arched brow.

I push the bucket closer. "It's the best. I promise."

She grabs a handful, and her eyes brighten as she swallows it down. She immediately goes for another handful.

Maliki shakes his head at us with a smile.

Molly turns to look at Maliki. "You want to try some?"

His smile grows. "I'll let you two have it all."

"Your dad doesn't appreciate the art of sprinkling sugar on top of everything," I whisper to her, and she breaks out in laughter.

————

Molly taps her chin. "Hmm … there are *way* too many colors. I can't pick only one." She does another scan of my nail polish collection. "Can I pick however many I want?"

"Yes, ma'am, *but* we have to stop at ten." I wiggle my fingers in the air. "Unless you have an extra thumb somewhere." I grab her hand to inspect it.

She bursts into giggles. "No!"

She spins to look at Maliki. He's in the chair, watching us. *Beauty and the Beast* is playing in the background, there's an array of fingernail polish bottles scattered around us, and Molly's hair is braided into four braids.

"Can you paint my nails while Sierra does my toenails?" she asks him.

My mouth falls open.

Maliki shifts in his seat. "Sure, but I can't promise they'll look pretty."

"It's okay. If they don't, Sierra can redo them."

I laugh, my hand going to my stomach, as Molly hands him ten bottles and another for "glitter on top."

————

"I think it went well with the exception of Jessa losing her shit when she saw me," I say after we drop Molly off at home.

To minimize the baby-mama drama, I gave Molly a hug at the car and stayed behind while Maliki walked her to the door. I wouldn't let Jessa taint the fun we'd had today.

I grin over at him. "I learned something else about you today."

"Yeah? What's that?"

"You are a terrible nail-painter."

"Yes, I've been told that by a six-year-old."

CHAPTER THIRTY-EIGHT

MALIKI

I groan when the name flashes across my phone.

If only I didn't have to answer.

I briefly wonder when is too young for a phone.

Noah has an iPod.

Maybe I can do the same with Molly and tell Jessa to only call on emergencies or to set up visitation.

"Hello?" I answer.

"I don't want that whore around my daughter," is the first thing she says.

Jesus. I scrub my hand over my face.

Jessa's bullshit isn't what I want to deal with today.

"First things first. Don't you refer to Sierra like that again, do you hear me? Don't you mutter a bad word about her to me, or we'll have serious issues," I snap.

She scoffs, "She's married, for God's sake. What does that teach our daughter?"

My stomach drops. I hate being reminded that Sierra married someone other than me. "The divorce papers have been signed by both her and Devin," I bite out, shaking my head. "Not that I need to explain shit to you about my relationship, so unless you called about Molly, it's time for us to hang up."

"Uh, yes, you do need to explain and ask my approval if you want to see your daughter."

I clench my fingers around my phone. "Take me to court, Jessa. I fucking dare you."

I don't tell her, but my attorney is already drafting a document. I want Molly's last name changed to mine, three days a week of visitation, and a set child-support payment. But if Jessa wants to play games with me, I don't mind asking for more.

I hang up and shop for an iPod online.

———

"Hey, man."

I turn to find Dallas Barnes hopping onto a stool at the bar. "Hey. What can I get you?"

It sucks Dallas doesn't frequent the pub as often as he used to, but it's for a good reason. He went through a rough patch after his wife died from breast cancer. Not only was he going through hell, but he also had to take care of his daughter.

So, on the days his daughter, Maven, was with her grandmother, Dallas would come here to drown his sorrows. Sometimes, we talked. Sometimes, we gave each other a head nod, and I gave him his space. He's a good man who found love again. We were all surprised as hell when Willow came into town, pregnant with his baby after a one-night stand. She was a town outsider but helped replace Dallas's pain with happiness.

He smiles. "Whiskey, neat."

I make his drink and set it in front of him. "How's the family? Kiddos?"

"Good." A shit-eating grin spreads along his lips as he thrums his fingers against the glass. "Speaking of kids ..."

Ah shit, here it comes.

"Word has hit town, I take it?"

He nods. "Word has definitely hit town, thanks to your baby mama. She did things *way* different than Willow." He shakes his head.

"Sierra told Lauren your little one is around Maven's age and starting school here. Maybe Maven can put her at ease, having a friend there." He takes a drink and laughs into his glass before pulling it back. "Want to schedule a playdate?"

I chuckle. "Look at us, scheduling fucking playdates."

"Playdates are the easy part. You wait until you're singing along with Disney songs and having tea with stuffed bunnies and—I shit you not—holding straight conversations with them. Winnie-the-Pooh loves extra honey with his tea, and her American Girl doll prefers coffee with extra cream." He takes a drink. "And be careful about the people you have her around. My pain in the ass sister is the one who introduced her to coffee."

"Lauren does love to stir up trouble."

"That she does. I told her to wait until her little one grew older. I'll be getting her right back."

I pour him another drink and hand it to him, lowering my voice. "How'd you do it? Raise a daughter by yourself?"

Technically, I have Jessa but don't consider her a part of my team until she cooperates with co-parenting and keeps her opinions to herself. I understand her concern, but it's not like Sierra's a bad person, nor did Jessa have an issue with her being around Molly until she found out I was dating her.

Dallas raises his glass and his brow at the same time. "You're not raising her on your own. You have Sierra."

CHAPTER THIRTY-NINE

MALIKI

"Is Jessa coming to the festival?"

I shrug at Sierra's question. "Maybe."

Didn't ask. Don't care.

I tend to tune Jessa out when she's not talking about Molly, but I might've caught the end of her saying she was coming.

"She has a new boyfriend and has been too busy making his life more miserable than mine. I'll take it," I add.

Jessa has become tolerable now that she's grasped Sierra isn't going anywhere. The signed custody agreement and the new boyfriend have helped, too.

"Good riddance," Sierra mutters. She aims to steer clear of Jessa as often as she can.

We turn around when Molly comes into the kitchen.

"You ready for the festival?" I ask.

"Yes!" Her excitement dies down, her smile replaced with a frown. "I won't have any friends there to play with me though." Her attention shoots to Sierra. "Will you play with me?"

"Duh," Sierra replies. "There will be a lot of kids there. I bet you nine million dollars you'll meet new friends and then ditch me to hang out with them."

"No way. I *love* hanging out with you. You and Aunt Ellie are my best friends in the whole wide world," Molly argues.

"You and Ellie are my best friends in the whole wide world," Sierra replies.

"Hey, what about me?" My palm goes to my chest as I fake offense. "Don't I get a friendship bracelet in this mix?"

Molly shakes her head. "You don't paint your nails, Dad. You have to do girl stuff to be best friends. You're my dad who gives me pizza and takes me swimming!"

Dad. It still sounds surreal, being called that.

I'm a dad.

It took Molly a while to call me that—understandable—and the first time she did, swear to fucking God, it was music to my ears. My chest lightened, and I held myself back from jumping in the air with a raised fist.

We get into the car and make the short drive to the benefit festival. Dallas texted me the other day and invited us. His family is throwing it to benefit a local who was recently diagnosed with cancer.

It'll be my first time at a benefit.

I've donated bar gift cards to them but never *attended* one.

It's a family thing—full of fried food, face-painting, and children's games.

Not a pastime for a bachelor.

We park in a lot separated by orange cones, and I help Molly out of the car. She walks at my side, swinging her arms up and down while naming off everything she wants to eat and do and see.

For a small town, there's a full house—well, full parking lot and clubhouse. The local pizza shop owner is playing DJ, blasting some kid shit I've never heard. It might be the music Dallas was talking about—Disney stuff.

Chloe swings her arms in the air to get our attention and waves us over to their crowded table.

Chloe and Kyle.

Willow and Dallas.

Lauren and Gage. Gage is Kyle's best friend and partner at the station.

The six of them are seated at the table.

I've known the guys for as long as I can remember. It's nice, seeing them all happy.

Maven, Dallas's his little girl, is sitting next to him. She grins wildly when she sees us.

"Hi!" she chirps, her eyes on Molly as she waves with a caramel apple in her hand. She pats the seat Dallas is occupying next to her with her free hand. "Come sit by me. My daddy got an extra caramel apple, and you can have it."

Dallas moves down a seat and slides his old one out for Molly to sit. Molly peeks over to me, and I nod. Her eyes are wide as she scurries over to Maven and jumps in the open seat.

"I'm Maven," she says, scooting the plate with the caramel apple to her. "I like your hair." She flips her attention to Willow, Dallas's girlfriend, on the other side of her. "Can you do my hair like that tomorrow?"

Willow smiles. "Sure."

Sierra and I take a seat. Maven dances in her chair while eating her apple, and after a few minutes, I notice Molly doing the same, caramel on the side of her face. I'm so excited to see Molly so comfortable that I'm close to dancing in my damn chair, too.

If someone had told me this was what my life would be, I would've laughed and kicked their wrong ass out of my bar.

Conversation is happening around us, but my focus is on Molly and the glowing smile on her face.

"There's a jump house," Maven announces after finishing her apple. "After you're done eating, we can go play in it! They're so fun!"

Molly keeps on grinning while chomping on her apple.

The little tykes have sticky hands when Maven asks permission for them to go play.

Dallas and I nod at the same time.

Maven grabs Molly's hand, and they run toward the bounce house, joining the group of children.

I suck in a concerned breath, my eyes glued to my little girl.

This is the first time I've had her and she's *away* from me. Even if it is only across a yard, I'm still nervous.

What if she gets bullied?

What if someone kidnaps her?

What if someone accidentally kicks her in the face in that jump house?

"Relax," Dallas says, as if he were reading my mind. "I promise they're not as breakable as you think."

Willow nods. "Just wait until you have a little one. You'll truly be crazy and uptight. I'm pretty sure I'll be the epitome of one of those helicopter moms."

I glance over at Sierra, and her attention is on Molly, too.

I beam with pride.

I can't wait to have babies with her.

"I'll be there, right beside you," Lauren adds. "I thought being a nurse would make me more easygoing, but nope, I'm paranoid."

Gage throws his head back. "You have no idea."

My focus switches to Rex when he plops down in Maven's abandoned chair.

"Hey, what are you doing here?" Sierra asks.

"Carolina," is all he says while looking exhausted.

Sierra glances around. "Where is she?"

"Volunteering around here somewhere," he answers, rolling his neck back and forth. "She forced me to come do all the heavy lifting."

"Speaking of Carolina," Kyle says, unable to control his grin as we all watch Carolina come our way, a stern face pointed toward Rex.

"Oh shit," Rex says, rubbing a hand against his brow. "I might be in trouble."

"Hey, Carolina," Lauren sings.

Carolina smiles and waves at us before whipping her attention to Rex.

Rex throws his arms up. "Hey! Don't get mad at a man for taking a break and saying hello to his family!" He taps his thigh. "You can sit and chat if you want."

She pushes up her glasses before flipping him the bird.

Rex rises from his chair. "I'll see you guys when my boss lets me clock out." He throws his arm over her shoulders as they walk away.

"Are they a thing?" Chloe asks, her eyes on them.

Sierra shakes her head. "I wish they were. Rex is too chicken to pull the trigger."

Our Rex talk is interrupted by Maven and Molly storming in our direction, and I tense up, waiting for Molly to fall, break a leg, scrape a knee—something with how fast she's moving.

She makes it to us, safe and sound.

"We need ice cream money!" Maven shouts. "Pretty, pretty please!"

"And face-painting money!" Molly adds, sticking out her lower lip. "I want to get a unicorn face!"

"All right," Dallas groans. "You talked me into it."

He hands Maven money while I do the same with Molly as she jumps up and down in front of me.

They take off running, hand in hand.

That settles my heart.

Willow bumps Sierra's shoulder. "Forewarning: that paint is a pain in the ass to get off their face."

CHAPTER FORTY

"Where are we going?" I ask, rolling down the passenger window and sticking my head out like a little Chihuahua when Maliki turns onto a road that doesn't lead to Down Home.

"I have an idea," is his explanation as he continues driving.

I pull my head back into the car. "What kind of idea?"

"A good idea."

"I have an idea. How about you stop being vague?"

He chuckles and keeps his eyes on the road, not revealing said idea. I'm jabbering on about how I hate when he's vague and secretive, and I'm not a person who has patience when he pulls in the drive of an old farmhouse. It belonged to our town librarian before she passed a few months ago—in the library, not the house. Otherwise, I would be telling him to cut and run.

I don't do ghosts.

The home has been vacant since her death, and my mom mentioned it was recently listed for sale.

He shifts the car in park, cutting the engine. "I spoke with a realtor who found a few homes for us to view. If you're not a fan of this one, we can check out the others, but my vote is here."

His vote?

I cock my head to the side. "Your vote for what?"

He gestures toward the home. "Come on. Let's take a look."

We get out of the car at the same time and walk toward the front porch. It's a beautiful wraparound, begging for rocking chairs and children running around with lemonade in their hands.

I close my eyes, visualizing the scene.

"Tell me if you hate the house *or* the idea I'm about to pitch," he says before raising his hands as if he were staring through a camera lens. "You're an expert on beautifying older places without removing the authenticity of them. What do you think about buying and renovating it together?"

My heart dances in my chest.

This is the sweetest thing anyone has ever done for me.

He's mentioned moving from the apartment a few times, and as much as the idea thrills me, I've never pushed it since finding real estate here is difficult.

I clasp my hand around his forearm. "You have no idea how much I'd love that." I kiss his arm before catching his hand in mine and moving around the yard. "I could make this a home for us." I eyeball everything—from the foundation to the windows to the brick—taking mental notes of the makeover I'd give it.

Maliki leads me up to the porch and punches in the code on the padlock when we're finished looking outside.

I fall in love with it more when we walk into the foyer.

The bones of the home are beautiful, sturdy, and the ideas rushing through my brain ignite me. I continue my babbling—knocking down walls, changing windows, updating cabinets—while he laughs.

I lose his hold when we hit the fourth bedroom and whip around. "This can be Molly's bedroom. She can help me design it. I'll turn her into a little designer, just like me."

His lips smack into mine. "Does this mean it's a yes?"

I jump into his arms. "It's definitely a yes."

CHAPTER FORTY-ONE

SIERRA

6 MONTHS LATER

"Have you seen my tutu? I can't find my tutu?" Molly yells from her bedroom.

"I'll check the laundry!" I shout.

I glance around the house in awe of my work as I walk through the kitchen and living room—as I've done so many times.

I love our new home.

We spent so many hours creating it into a place perfect for us … for our family.

Our home renovation gave me remodel jobs. As people saw it, they wanted to do the same in their homes. I'm remodeling two homes now, and I have a six-month waiting list.

I sift through the folded laundry. "Found it!" I hold it up and rush to her bedroom.

It's pink and ballerina-themed with a sparkling chandelier hanging from the ceiling.

"Do you have your bag?" I ask.

She nods and shoves the tutu into it when I hand it to her.

Jessa is picking her up for dance class. Our co-parenting has improved. We attend Molly's recitals and school functions without a glare sent in my direction. The new boyfriend is nice and definitely tames her.

Maliki and I kiss her good-bye, and she runs out to Jessa's waiting car.

I flop down on the couch and yawn. "Have I mentioned how comfy this thing is?"

One thing I was adamant on was a comfy couch. Growing up, we always had stiff, expensive furniture that felt like cardboard. Our sectional is pillow-topped, making you never want to get up.

Maliki chuckles and falls next to me. "You pick the best, babe."

I turn to rest my head on his lap and look up at him with a smirk. "Yes, I know this. Care to send any more compliments my way? I'll take them all."

He runs his hand through my hair—one of my favorite things he does—and I shut my eyes. "I'm so happy we're out of the pub apartment. I would've settled for a hard couch to have this peace with you. Plus, this home provides us with plenty of room for little ones."

My eyes fly open. "Little ones? Really? More than just Molly?"

He continues massaging my head. "If that's what you want. I know I do."

"Uh, I would have your baby right now."

His hand stops, moving to my face, and he cups my chin. "I'd make a baby with you right now."

He leans back when I rise to straddle him.

"Look at me, taming the wild bartender," I say, winding my arms around his neck.

He strokes my cheek. "Look at me, claiming the sexiest, smartest, most amazing woman in the world."

I place my hand over the one resting on my face. "I love you."

He kisses the tip of my nose. "I fucking love you."

"Now that the sweet stuff is out of the way, can we jump into the baby-making? I'm all for that, please and thank you."

He picks me up under my elbows and tosses me back onto the couch but stops, his lips tilting into a grin. "I forgot to show you what I found. You're going to love this."

I raise a brow. "Probably not as much as us having sex right now."

He tugs something out of his back pocket. "I was going through the rest of my office boxes and look at what I found."

He holds it up, and I see my young face.

"Oh my God, shut up!" It's my driver's license he confiscated when I snuck into his bar at eighteen.

"Damn, look at that sexy woman." He holds it out to inspect it. "I think we should frame it. We'll say it's the day Daddy met Mommy."

I grin. "I like that. Now, let's start trying."

JUST
FRIENDS

CHAPTER ONE
CAROLINA

HIGH SCHOOL—SOPHOMORE YEAR

"I'll pay you fifty bucks to write my English paper."

I slam my locker shut before shifting to face the brave soul who asked that.

I don't cheat.

I don't break rules.

Everyone knows this.

He's casually leaning against the locker next to mine. A smirk is spread across his face, as if he expects me to squeal in delight that he's asking me for a favor.

Not happening, homeboy.

Homeboy is Rex Lane.

Our school's arrogant fuckboy.

A guy I'm *not* writing a paper for.

I mock his smile. "I'll *charge* you fifty bucks not to rat you out for homework bribery."

"Homework bribery?" He flashes a brighter *I'm a nice guy; do what I'm asking* grin.

I firmly nod. "Yes." I motion down the hallway. "Now, go away.

Having this stupid conversation with you is wasting my valuable study time."

I count on my rudeness to scare him off, but when his eyes brighten in amusement, I know I'm wrong.

Crap.

I have two high school goals in life:

1. Become class valedictorian.
2. Do not gain Rex's or any popular guy's attention.

Luckily, he caught me after the class bell rang, so no one is around to witness this unfortunate encounter.

"Come on, Carolina," he pleads. "Prove to me the rumors about you aren't true."

I stiffen. "Rumors?" I deliver a stern look. "What rumors?"

I mind my business. Don't gossip. Stay in my lane.

All of this to prevent rumors from circulating about me.

He licks his lips, leaning in closer, and lowers his voice. "The rumors that you have a stick up your ass and lack personality."

This jerk.

There might be a stick up my ass, but I'm going to shove my foot up his.

I narrow my eyes, and my response releases in a hiss, "Really? You want to talk about rumors? Maybe I should believe the rumors about *you.*"

"The rumors that say I'm cool as fuck? A terrific lay? Fucking hilarious?"

Our high school halls flood with rumors about him.

The one that he sports an overinflated ego is officially confirmed.

"Negative," I reply. "The rumors that you're a sucky lay with a small penis."

This is a lie—a rumor I've never heard—but hey, if he wants to talk crap, so can I.

"Lies, babe, all lies. I'm more than happy to present the evidence to back up my claim." He retreats a step, dropping his hand to the crotch of his jeans, and tugs at his zipper.

I do another quick scan of the hallway before loudly snorting. "You won't do it."

He flinches, that smug smile slipping off his lips. "Huh?"

"You won't do it." I nod toward his crotch. "You won't unzip your pants and *present your evidence*." I park my hands on my waist and kick my foot out.

He gapes at me, speechless.

"Pull it out or go away." I dismissively wave my hand. "I have a test in ten minutes, and you, standing in front of me with your hand on your junk, aren't helping me ace it. Go beg another girl to write your paper because you lack a brain … and according to the girls' locker room gossip, a decent penis size."

He drops his hand from his crotch, his smile returning. "Looks like Little Miss Innocent might not be as uptight as she leads on. There's some personality hidden underneath those awful, itchy-looking sweaters of yours." He makes a show of eyeing me up and down.

I opt out of giving him hell over the *uptight* comment. The faster he goes away, the better.

"No, she has a low annoyance tolerance."

He steeples his hands into a praying motion. "Say yes to writing my paper, and then you can go about your studying, sweater-wearing ways."

"No."

"Sixty bucks *and* a bonus of proving I'm well-endowed when we're in private."

I dramatically gag. "Gross." As much as I don't want to deal with him, I could use the cash. "Seventy-five, and I'll *help* you write the paper, but you're doing it yourself. I don't cheat." I signal to his jeans. "And keep your micropenis to yourself. I'd rather fail every class than have you prove you're *well-endowed*."

"Paying you to *help* me write the paper defeats the point of paying you."

"*Really*? With that brilliance of yours, you shouldn't need me to write your paper."

He laughs.

"Why are you even asking me? You're in line—*behind me*—to be class valedictorian. You can easily write your own paper." I reach forward to pat his shoulder. "I have faith in you, petite-penis buddy."

"Never said I couldn't write the boring-ass paper. I'd just rather not. I'm a busy guy who doesn't give two shits about Shakespeare."

"Eighty dollars," I blurt out.

"Eighty? What the fuck? You can't up the ante like that."

"I can, and the longer you waste my time, the higher the price." I can't believe I'm agreeing to this, but hey, money talks. "Eighty dollars. Meet me at the library after school."

"The library sucks. My house."

I shake my head. "You're high if you think I'm going to your house."

"If I'm paying eighty dollars, which is fucking insane, at least give a guy the privacy of his own home."

I thrust my finger toward him. "You'd better not try any funny business."

He rubs his palms together. "This is homework, Carolina. Get your virginal mind out of the gutter."

My last class of the day is AP English.

It's also Rex's.

This gives him the opportunity to stalk me out of class, to my locker, and out to the parking lot while I ignore him.

Classmates call out his name, give him head nods, and say hi as we pass them. Interest floods their faces when their eyes cut to me. It's not that I'm the class weirdo—although, as I learned today, I apparently have a stick up my ass.

High school kids are so original.

I'm more along the lines of the class do-gooder who aces every test and spends her free time volunteering.

Oh, and I'm also the preacher's daughter.

Rex definitely isn't preacher's daughter's friend material.

Hell, he doesn't even fit into his role of the mayor's son.

"Where's your car?" he asks, strolling next to me and scanning the parking lot.

I look away, embarrassment striking me. "I don't have one."

My parents gave me the option of waiting until my sister graduated and passing her car down to me or buying one myself. Considering my cash flow is zilch, waiting for hers it is.

A whiff of fresh soap and citrus hits me when he slings his arm over my shoulders.

"You ride the bus?"

I shift out of his hold. "I ride with my sister."

"Tell her you don't need a ride today." He returns his arm to my shoulders and spins us toward the opposite side of the parking lot. "Today is your lucky day, sweetheart. You get to ride with me."

"Hard pass." Surprisingly, I don't shove him away while he leads me to a newer model black Dodge Challenger.

"Come on, Lina. It'd be pretty selfish to have your sister drive you when you could ride with me."

"Don't call me that," I grumble.

His arm falls, and he ups his pace to turn around and stare at me, walking backward. "What?"

"Lina. No one calls me that." I immediately regret telling him this.

He rubs his thumb over his bottom lip. "I'm for fucking sure calling you Lina now. It'll be our thing, babe."

"Ugh, and don't call me babe either."

"Lina babe, when you tell me not to do something, it only makes me want to do it more."

"Then, it's only fair for me to give you a nickname." I tap my finger against the side of my mouth. "I'm going with … Needle Dick." There's no stopping my lips from cracking into a smile.

He points at the car. "Get your ridiculous nickname-giving ass into my car and stop insulting my dick before I really do show you."

"You've already proven you're too chicken in the hallway."

"Of course, I can't pull my dick out at school. My parents would kill me if I got caught showing off my cock like I was at the school's talent show."

I snort. "That would require you to have talent."

He smirks. "Oh, babe, I have *plenty* of talents. My first trick will be to show you how to pull that stick out of your ass."

"So I can stick it up yours?"

"I like this little attitude of yours. It's hot."

He digs out his keys from the pocket of his jeans and unlocks the car. I hop into the passenger seat with no argument. He's right. Not only would my sister bitch on the entire drive to Rex's, but she'd also charge me gas money for having to go out of her way.

I settle into the leather seat while Rex pulls out of the parking lot. He thrums his fingers on the steering wheel to the beat of a Snoop Dogg song. I use this chance to take in everything that is him.

What's fascinating about Rex is, he's not your typical popular guy —the ones you see in movies and read about in books. He's not the star athlete or the prom king or the school's notorious bad boy. His personality is what draws people to him. He's fun, cocky, and laid-back. Everyone either wants to be his friend or his girlfriend.

That is, everyone except yours truly.

I don't need that kind of distraction in my life.

Rex is also crazy smart. He spends most of his time in the computer programming lab and has even been called into the school office to fix technical issues. Rumor has it, he's also hacked into the system before.

He's tall, at least six feet, and he towered over my small frame when we walked through the parking lot. He might not play sports, but he's more toned than our quarterback. His hair is a coppery-brown and cut short. Two dimples pop out of his cheeks when he smiles, and the asymmetry of his face is flawless.

He's also rich. I'm reminded of this when he pulls into the

driveway of his mansion of a home. It's the biggest in their neighborhood, and it has a giant yard and impeccable landscaping. The Lane family is considered the most affluent in our small town of Blue Beech, Iowa.

Rex shifts the car into park and steals my attention from the home when he clears his throat. "That sure was a fun ride. I've never been checked out by a preacher's daughter before."

My eyes widen.

Oh dear God.

Was I that obvious?

"That's it. Take me home," I demand. "I don't check out guys. I was simply observing the guy I'm going to be stuck with for the next few hours."

"Too late. We have a paper to write, Lina babe."

He kills the engine to the car, circles it, and opens my door as I'm debating my next move.

Go in or leave.

I smack away his waiting hand, and he moves out of the way. With a scoff, I follow him into the house. As soon as we make it through the front door, he captures my hand in his, and I nearly fall on my face when he starts pulling me up the stairs.

"My bedroom is up here," he says.

I jerk back, causing him to stop. "I'm not going into your bedroom."

He glances back at me, blinking. "Yes, you are."

"No, I'm—"

I'm cut off when he grabs my hand again, tightening his grip, and stupidly, I don't fight him this time. He steers us down a long hallway and into a bedroom.

It's a spacious room, larger than my parents' master, and surprisingly clean. Three of the walls are painted a dark red, and the other is black. Against the black wall is a sleek metal bed with a black comforter on top. It's different than any guy's room I've seen before.

Granted, I normally don't hang out in guys' bedrooms.

There's a mini fridge in the corner, a massive desk with three monitors on top, and a TV above a black console. A collection of gaming devices and games clutter the stand.

I lose his hold when he shuts the door behind us.

"Seriously?" I snap, crossing my arms. "You have no boundaries."

He grins, showing off his bright white teeth. "My mom said that can be a great trait in life."

"For who? Serial killers?"

"For guys asking girls to do their homework."

He walks around me to the mini fridge, opens it, and peeks up at me. "What's your drink of choice, Lina? Water? Pepsi? Tequila?"

I roll my eyes, pushing my black-rimmed glasses up my nose. "You don't have tequila in there." This calling-his-bluff game is fun.

"I beg to differ." He clicks his tongue against the roof of his mouth. "It's in a Gatorade bottle, tucked into the very back so no one sees it."

Yeah, right.

Today, I'm feeling gutsy.

"Give me a tequila shot then."

He squints in my direction. "You're fucking with me."

I shake my head. "I'll need it to get through an afternoon of hanging out with you."

He grins, pushing his arm into the fridge, and pulls out a bottle.

Maybe calling his bluff wasn't the smartest idea.

We're not at school where he can be expelled for doing something like this.

We're in his *bedroom.*

I gulp when I see the bottle, focusing on the amber-tinted liquid inside that's most definitely not Gatorade.

Way to call his bluff, Carolina.

Now, he's calling yours.

Time to gear up and taste tequila for the first time.

The room is quiet as he stands. His eyes are fastened on me while he slowly unscrews the orange cap and holds the bottle out to me.

I'll be damned if I let him win this … game? Whatever it is.

Nausea cartwheels in my stomach, and I haven't even taken a

drink. Lord knows how it'll feel after I do. I inhale a deep, determined breath.

I got this.

I've never drunk tequila, but I've had wine.

It can't be that different, right?

Deciding it's done doing gymnastics, my stomach tightens, as if it's preparing itself, when I snatch the bottle from him. I grip it and drag it to my lips. Right before I do anything drastic, my back stiffens, and I frown at the same time.

"How many people have taken a drink from this bottle?" I question. "I'm not about to contract some STD."

He chuckles, signaling to the bottle. "The only person who's drunk from that bottle is me." He pauses, snaps his fingers, and points at me. "And you, in a minute."

I narrow my eyes at him. "You better not be lying."

His hands go to his chest, feigning offense. "Lina, my sweet Lina, I'm heartbroken you don't trust me."

I gulp again.

Here goes nothing.

I can do this.

Before I chicken out, I take a quick swig of the tequila. My eyes slam shut, blocking me from witnessing his reaction, and my teeth clench as I swallow down the most disgusting thing I've ever tasted. There's no stopping my body from shuddering. I hold in a deep breath out of fear of puking it up.

When I open my eyes, I immediately roll them.

A huge grin is spread across Rex's shocked face.

He whistles and leans back on his heels. "*Damn, Lina.* Either you have a secret wild side, which I'd fucking love, or I'm bringing it out of you, which I'd also fucking love."

I shrug. "You'll never know."

I inhale a deep breath, dragging up as much nerve as I can, and take another sip to prove myself. My throat burns as if it were on fire, and I smile with pride as soon as I swallow it down.

"It's your turn, Needle Dick." I extend the bottle back to him.

"Look at me, corrupting you." He grabs it, *cheers* me, and takes a gulp. "I can't wait to do it more."

Little do I know, walking into Rex's bedroom will change everything.

Rex Lane will take over my life.

He'll steal my heart.

I'll steal his.

Only we won't know what to do with what we've taken.

CHAPTER TWO

REX

HIGH SCHOOL—JUNIOR YEAR

"Yo, Lane, I need a favor," Murphy calls out, slapping me on the back while strolling past me in the guys' locker room.

I tug on my T-shirt. "What's up?"

He stops at a locker a few down from mine, opens it, and turns my way. "Put in a good word for me with Carolina." A sly grin passes over his flushed, freckled face. Dude was struggling to hit twenty push-ups in gym class earlier. "You two are tight and all, right?"

A sour taste fills my mouth. Carolina Adams has always stayed in her own withdrawn world, but little by little, I've been tugging her into mine. That tugging has shone attention on her since we spend so much time together. That's when I want to push her back into her world, away from the just-surpassed-puberty douche bags like Murphy.

"Sorry, dude. I have no good words to say," I answer with a shrug.

He groans, throwing his head back. "Come on. Do your boy a favor."

Murphy is not *my boy.* The only time I've been around him outside of school is in passing at parties. He's a lightweight who brags *and lies* about hooking up with girls. No way in hell am I letting him near Carolina.

"Why do you want me to lie to her?"

He produces an overeager smile. "I'm asking her to prom."

The fuck he is.

"No, you're not," I say with warning.

"Yes, I am," he fires back, irritation growing in his tone.

"She already has a date. *Me*. Ask someone else."

I snatch my bag from the bench and walk away without a backward glance. When I'm in the hall, I drag my phone from my back pocket, open my texts, and hit Carolina's name.

Correction: the name she changed her contact to.

Me: Meet me at my car after school. I'm taking you home.

The Smartest and Coolest Girl in the World: Okay, Mr. Bossy. What's up?

Me: It's too much to text. My fingers hurt. They had quite the workout last night.

The Smartest and Coolest Girl in the World: Gross. If you meant for that to be a sex joke, it was weak sauce.

I can't help but chuckle.

Me: See you at my car, you pain in the ass.

———

A year has passed since Carolina *helped* me write my paper.

Help meaning, we put off writing it and hung out instead. We watched TV. I taught her how to play my favorite video games, and we ate as if we were on death row and it was our last dinner.

Day after day, we hung out with the intention of writing that dumbass paper. I ended up writing it myself in twenty minutes and still scored an A.

Who said doing shit half-assed never got anyone anywhere?

After I turned in the paper, we kept hanging out, and somehow, we became friends—which was a fucking shock to us and everyone.

She introduced me to chick flicks, and I introduced her to a thing called having fun—like taking her to parties, where she wasn't allowed to leave my side. I've brought her out of her shell, and she's calmed me.

Somehow, in some-fucking-way, we click.

I'm a dude who doesn't want to get in her panties.

She's a chick who doesn't want to bang me.

There are no expectations between us.

We study. Watch movies. Go out for pizza.

She has dinner at my house at least two nights a week.

My mom fucking loves her.

Her parents, however, aren't my biggest fans, but they keep their mouths shut because my family donates a shit-ton of money to her father's church. Carolina hasn't been banned from hanging out with me yet, but that doesn't mean Pastor Adams hasn't attempted to sway her view of me.

I grin when I find her at my car with a stack of books balanced in her arms. She's wearing one of her signature sweaters, skinny jeans, and flats that tie up to her ankles. The sweater looks itchy and is ugly as hell, but I've learned to love them. A string of fake pearls lines her neck, and her deep black hair is straight, hitting her shoulders.

"What was *so* important that you had to text me *during* class?" she snaps when I reach her. "Mrs. Heath confiscated my phone in front of everyone *and* wrote me a warning."

"Screw Mrs. Heath." I grab her books from her arms. "Tell her you're my best friend next time she pulls that shit. Guarantee she'll hand it back in seconds."

"What does that mean?" She scrunches up her nose. "Your family might be the Kennedys of Blue Beech, but I'd suggest you calm that ego down, good sir." She turns around and gets into the Charger while I toss her books into the back seat before getting into the driver's side.

"It means, Mrs. Heath *attempted* to confiscate my phone once. I made a compelling argument. She gave it back. Not to sound like a dick, but she's scared of me."

"Uh, that does make you sound like a dick."

I shrug, starting the car.

"Are you going to tell me what your *compelling* argument was?" She makes a sour face. "God, *please* tell me you didn't sleep with her. She's married and as old as your mom!"

"Hell no. Married cougars aren't my type. They tend to be too bossy. All I simply said was, I was sure her husband would love to know what her favorite after-school activity was."

"Which is?" She cocks her head to the side. "Isn't she the tennis coach?"

"She's bumping uglies with the PE teacher."

"*Gross.*" She sticks out her tongue. "Doesn't he have a wife and, like, five kids?"

I nod. "Sure does."

"How do you always know these things? You know everyone's business."

I shrug. "I watch people. I pay attention. Not to mention, I work on the school's cameras sometimes." I poke her shoulder. "Don't think I haven't seen Clint Evans stopping by your locker between periods."

Her eyes widen, a blush rising up her cheeks, and she shoves my side. "Oh my God! You spy on me?"

"Nope." I struggle to fight back a smile. "I'm making sure the school is a safe environment for my fellow peers to learn."

"I'm so sure that's where your *concern* is."

"And not to put poor little Clint on blast, *but* dude calls his mother *mommy* when they're on the phone." I exaggeratedly shudder. "Some weird shit there. I wouldn't take on that kid."

"You're seriously terrible, you know that?" Her lips twitch into a smile. "Don't pick on Clint for being a mommy's boy when I'm sure you have no problem with girls being daddy's girls."

"Oh, man, you set yourself up for this one. For your information, I do dislike chicks calling their fathers *daddy* because it's what I prefer they call me in the bedroom."

She shoves my shoulder. "I don't know why I talk to you."

"I'm your favorite person in the world, that's why." I shake my head, clapping my hands. "Now, let's step away from the daddy talk and move on to serious business. Grab your planner, sweetheart. Pencil me in to pick you up three Saturdays from now. Seven o'clock."

"Okay," she drags out. "What's up with the preplanning?"

"Prom night. Let me know the color of your dress, so we can do all that matchy-matchy bullshit."

"Excuse me?" She scowls in my direction. "You can't just *tell me* I'm going to prom with you." She throws her arms up, her voice nearing hysteria, like the boring romance movies she forces me to watch. "You didn't even ask!"

"No need for me to ask. You're going to prom with me."

"What if I don't want to go with you? You didn't even give me a promposal!"

"Tough shit. You won't find a better date. Not to mention, I'm the only guy in this school who won't try to weasel his inexperienced dick into your virginal panties." He raises his brows. "If you want a promposal, I'll get one of those banners that fly in the sky or some shit."

"You're so romantic." She crosses her arms, pouting her glossy pink lips. "Have you ever thought that I don't want my panties to stay virginal? *Maybe* I want to change that on prom night."

"Maybe you've lost your goddamn mind." I clear my throat, and my voice grows deeper. "You're my date. Your panties will remain untouched." I jerk my thumb toward her planner in the back seat. "Put it in there, circle it with a red marker, and don't forget."

She huffs. "What about Leanne, the girl you've *already* asked to prom?"

Shit. I fucking forgot about Leanne. "She can either be your sister-date or kick rocks."

"I am *not* having a sister-date!" she shrieks.

"Looks like she'll be kicking rocks then. I'll bribe her to go with someone else."

Murphy is available.

"I can't believe I speak to you."

"You. Me. Prom." I lean over and kiss her cheek. "My mom is making tacos tonight. You coming over for dinner?"

"Ugh, fine, but I'm only coming for her and the tacos."

CHAPTER THREE

REX

HIGH SCHOOL—SENIOR YEAR

I pause my game at the sound of a knock on my bedroom door.

"Come in," I call out.

When the door opens, I expect to find my mom, asking for dirty laundry or if I've decided on which college I'm going to attend.

Nope and nope.

My back straightens in my chair when Carolina walks in.

Relief settles inside me. Lately, she's been distant, blaming it on finals, scholarships, and college acceptance letters. I have no doubt she's stressed. Her parents put too much pressure on her to be perfect, and it pisses me off.

I blink, adjusting my eyes to her in the faint light coming from my desk lamp, as she shuts the door.

"Did you try to call?" I ask, tossing the controller in my hand to the side.

She shakes her head, and my stomach drops as I focus on her. She reminds me of a nervous cub who lost her mother as she fidgets with her bracelet and then her earrings and then pulls at the end of her ponytail.

The fuck?

I stand from my chair. "Is everything okay?"

Her fidgeting stops as she draws in a breath and plays with the button of her sweater. "I want you to take my virginity." The words fall from her mouth so casually, like she's asking me to watch a movie, not confiscate her fucking V-card.

There's no stopping the laughter that rolls out of me. "Good one."

She shoots me a frustrated glare. "I'm serious. I want you to take my virginity. *Tonight.*"

I pinch the bridge of my nose. "Quit fucking with me."

We've talked about her virginity—mainly me teasing and telling her to keep it forever—but she's never suggested *I* take the damn thing before. She's either messing with me or lost her mind.

Conversation change, pronto.

"Want to order a pizza? Watch a movie?"

"Screw pizza," she snaps. "I'm not going to college a virgin."

"Why not? You should stay a virgin forever."

Don't get me wrong. It's not that I haven't imagined having sex with Carolina. I've imagined sex with her a fucking lot.

In the shower with my hand on my cock.

In bed with my hand on my cock.

When we're hanging out and I have to fight to keep from getting hard.

It wasn't like that in the beginning. Sure, I thought she was cute, but I only saw her as a friend. As we grew closer and older, my attraction developed. Everything about Carolina is perfect. She has the biggest heart I've ever known, and once you cut through her shyness, she's pretty funny. She's too gorgeous for her own damn good—a one-of-a-kind beauty hiding behind her glasses and sweaters.

I've come to love those damn sweaters.

Bought her two for Christmas.

No lie, I'd love to throw her on my bed and give her what she's asking.

But I can't.

Sleeping with Carolina is a line I'll never cross.

She's my person.

She knows me better than anyone, and I'll be damned if I give that up to temporarily get my dick wet.

"I've thought about this for a while, and I've made my decision." She exhales a sharp breath. "I don't want it to be with some random guy, and I trust you more than anyone, Rex."

I clench my fists, standing only inches from her.

How can she come here and ask me that?

How can she put me in this position?

"I'm not taking your virginity." My tone is sharp. My body is tense.

"Fine." Her tone mimics mine. "I'll find someone else to take it."

I grind my teeth when she turns to leave, and I move faster than I ever have before in my life. I catch her elbow, hauling her deeper into my bedroom and away from the door.

I tilt my head down, glaring at her while my hand is still latched on to her elbow, and my lips meet her ear as I speak. "Don't do this. Don't be stupid."

"Do what I'm asking then."

"No," I bite out.

She jerks out of my hold and pushes my chest. "Why?" she hisses. "You screw girls on the regular. It's nothing out of the ordinary for you —rinse, wash, repeat. Act like I'm a random girl you've texted for a week and met up with at a party to bang."

"You're not some random girl I've texted for a week." *You're everything to me.*

She's also fucking insane. Carolina has officially lost her goddamn mind.

She quietly stares at me for a moment.

Thank fuck.

I think I've won this … talk, argument, whatever the fuck it is.

She proves me wrong when she falls back a step and starts unbuttoning her sweater.

Motherfucker.

"Carolina," I warn.

She ignores me, and the sweater falls to her feet, giving me the sight of her chest in only a plain black bra. I lose a breath, my heart beating wildly, and my stomach knots in nervousness. Just as I'm about to bend down and scoop up her sweater to hand it back, I stop.

I'm frozen in place as she unbuttons her jeans.

"Carolina," I warn again, this time harsher.

I hate that my dick twitches as I eye her. I cover my crotch with my palm, mentally telling it to calm down.

I'm not being very persuasive.

To neither it nor Carolina.

"Rex," she says, mimicking my tone again. "Do it, or I'll find someone else."

My nostrils flare at the thought of someone else *doing it.* My bedroom seems ten times smaller as we stare at each other.

Her breathing is heavy.

Mine is deep.

She's waiting for me to give her what she wants.

I'm waiting for her to change her mind.

She won't change her mind.

I know Carolina, and I know when she's determined. This is determined Carolina.

I've never seen her so determined in her life.

I'm so fucked.

She tilts her head to the side. "So … can we start now?"

Jesus.

"I don't want this to come between us," I croak out.

"It won't. We'll act like it never happened." She's so damn sure of herself.

"*Why* are we doing it then?"

She shrugs, and I scrub a hand over my face when she unzips her jeans.

Nervous of falling on my ass, I sit on the edge of my bed. My eyes fasten to her as she wiggles out of her jeans, and I gulp at the reveal of her black boy shorts. I've seen her in a bikini plenty of times when she's come over to swim. It's hard, but I've always done a decent job of not gawking at her.

It's more intimate in here than in my backyard.

We're in my bedroom. She's stripping in front of me.

And she looks fucking breathtaking.

I can't help myself from taking in every inch of her. Her skin is tan. Her straight hair is pulled into a tight ponytail, showing off the perfect angles of her face. Since the light is limited, I can't see as much as I'd like, but I see enough to want more of her. Her breasts are full, and I eye her curves, unable to stop myself from running my tongue along my bottom lip.

"*Please, Rex*," she whispers. "Do it for me."

We don't mutter a word when I stand. I keep a safe distance between us as I try to figure out a plan.

We're doing this.

Having sex.

I'm going to take my best friend's virginity.

My heart pounds as I clear my throat. "I'm not sure how to even start this."

Why do I feel like the virgin here?

"Do whatever you normally do," she says with confidence, as if *I* were the one losing my virginity. "Part A goes into Part B." One of her hands forms an O while she sticks a finger through it with the other. "We both took sex ed."

"Okay, let's not refer to sex like we're following directions to assemble furniture." I draw in a nervous breath. "And if I do what I *normally* do, it'll get more *intimate*. I don't just stick Part A into Part B."

She flinches, her lips forming an O, similar to what her hand did. "Oh."

She takes small steps backward to my bed, throws back the comforter, and slips underneath the sheets. I'm speechless when she takes off her glasses and sets them on my nightstand.

Not exactly a compliment when a chick takes off her glasses before sex.

Please change your mind. Please change your mind.

I chew on my lower lip while shuffling my feet on the floor. My heart has never beat so hard. I'm sure I look frenzied as fuck.

She eyes me in expectation. "Get naked. Get on top of me. We'll have sex." She waves her hand through the air. "You don't have to make it special, kiss me, or any of that nonsense. Just stick your … *penis* into my vagina, pop my cherry, and we'll be all good."

"Jesus, Lina!" I run my hands through my hair. "That's not how it works."

"Uh, yes, it is. I'm a virgin, not dumb." She taps her palm against the bed. "Let's do this."

My dick twitches and is growing harder by the second. I'm shocked she hasn't mentioned the hard-on showing through my sweatpants.

I pull at the roots of my hair. "Swear to me, this won't change anything between us."

"I swear it."

I inhale deep breaths before tugging off my T-shirt and locking my door. Her eyes are pinned to me when I drop my sweatpants, and I give myself a silent pep talk to keep my cool through this. I hesitate when my fingers hit the band of my boxer briefs, deciding to keep them on for now.

Her coffee-brown eyes meet mine as I climb onto the bed, anxiety slithering through me like a snake. The confident demeanor she's worn is melting away.

I pull back. "We can stop." *I have no damn problem with that.*

She frantically shakes her head and shifts in place. "No. Keep going."

I pull the comforter back, and she squirms underneath me as I crawl over her. A breath catches in my throat when I reach out, trailing a finger down her body and then between her legs.

She tenses, squeezing her legs together and trapping my finger. "What are you doing?"

"Getting you ready," I explain, resting my hand on her thigh.

"What? Why?" I can hear the horror lacing her questions.

"I can't just shove my dick inside you, Carolina." My voice thickens. "The wetter you are, the less it'll hurt. I want to make this comfortable for you, and that calls for foreplay."

Her chest hitches. "Oh … then I guess we can do a quick foreplay."

I shake my head, unable to fight back my smile. *Who says, we can do a quick foreplay?*

She spreads her legs wide, giving me permission, and I'm surprised my hand isn't shaking as I drag it between her legs. I rake a finger between her slit, moving it back and forth before circling it around her clit.

She gasps when I slowly push a finger inside her.

My dick aches. She's so goddamn tight.

"Relax," I whisper, waiting for her to do as I said before moving.

I hold back until her shoulders slump against the sheets and her muscles ease before I stroke her. The more I stroke her, the more she relaxes.

"Has anyone ever done this to you?" I rasp, keeping my eyes on her.

Her eyes have been closed since the first thrust of my finger, and I've been waiting for them to open.

"Once," she whispers, her legs trembling, and a sense of satisfaction hits me when she starts moving against my hand. "It was never like this. Never *felt* like this."

My satisfaction is hit with anger.

Who the fuck did she let in her panties, and how can I find him to kick his ass?

I quicken my thrusts and hesitate before adding another finger and massaging her clit. With how tight she is, sex will be painful for her. I want to make this as comfortable as I can, to make her feel good. I don't want her to have the typical *losing my virginity sucked, hurt, and I didn't get off* experience.

My mouth waters. As badly as I want to drop my head between her legs and taste her, I hold back.

We're already crossing one fucking serious line.

That's enough.

I love the sound of her soft moans floating through my bedroom.

"You okay?" I ask around a gulp.

She nods, and her voice is scratchy when she replies, "I think I'm ready. Do you have a condom?"

I want to keep stroking her, keep playing with her, to get her off, but I only nod. I rub her clit a few more times and then carefully draw my fingers out of her. I can't hold myself back from dropping a single kiss onto her stomach. I bring my hand into a fist, release it, and reach over her, snagging a condom from my nightstand.

Her eyes dart to mine as I pull down my briefs, my cock popping free, and then she shyly looks away as I slide on the condom. She stiffens, and her eyes slam shut when I align myself at her center.

"Carolina, you have to look at me," I say. I'm as nervous as she is.

She opens one eye at a time.

"Are you sure you want to do this?" I ask. "We can back out."

"Positive," she firmly answers.

I take a deep breath. I wasn't expecting this tonight—to have this load of pressure dropped onto me. She's handing me something so precious to her, trusting me to do it right, and I don't want to let her down.

I can't believe we're doing this.

I grab her hips, tilting them up, and gently slide inside her.

I can't stop myself from groaning.

Fuck. She feels like heaven.

I slide in deeper and stop. "You good?"

She nods, forcing a small smile even though I can sense her pain.

I move again. "Still good?"

Another nod, tension clear on her face.

I halt. "Switch spots with me."

She winces. "Huh?"

"It'll be less painful if you're on top. You can control how much of me you take," I explain, slowly pulling out of her.

She reaches forward and grabs me around the back, her nails digging into my skin to stop me from moving. "I can't … get on top of you." She gestures to our connection with her free hand. "This is fine. We'll stay like this."

My voice softens. "Tell me if you change your mind or if it hurts too much."

I notice a faint smile on her lips, and her hand briefly rubs my back before dropping.

"I trust you, Rex. I trust you more than anyone."

I softly squeeze her hips and thrust all the way in, causing her back to arch and a gasp to leave her. I stop again, giving her time to adjust to my size, and I gulp as her tightness overwhelms me.

My head spins while I slowly push in and out of her. My pace is not only to lessen her pain. I'm also fighting to stop myself from busting inside her in seconds. I smile like a motherfucker when I notice it's starting to feel good for her. Her hips move up to meet mine, and she moans.

I want to run my hands up her stomach, push up her bra, and play with her breasts, but I can't. This is purely sex. Nothing more. So, I play with her clit instead.

She moans again, setting me off.

My face goes to her neck as I quicken my thrusts.

I hold back from telling her how fucking perfect she feels.

How tight she is.

How much I love being inside her.

My hips jerk, and I move faster yet also cautiously, still not wanting to hurt her. I'm close to reaching my brink, but I *need* to make her feel good. I rotate my hips and mentally give myself a high five when a high-pitched moan leaves her, and she grinds against me.

It's somewhat of an orgasm.

Not a full yell-out-my-name one, but there's more pleasure there than pain.

This is when I can't stop myself from bucking forward faster. Shocking us both, I smash my mouth to hers as I come. My lips move from hers to her ear, sprinkling kisses along the way, and I bury my face in her neck.

"*Fuck*, Lina," I groan, exploding into the condom, shivering.

My hands rest at each side of her head as I pull back, and I glance down at her, both of us catching our breaths.

Her lips tilt into a shy smile. "Thank you."

I return the smile. "It was my pleasure."

It was a bad idea, but I love that I was her first.

That she gave me that.

I also hate her for it.

Now, I know what it feels like to be inside her.

No matter what she said, our relationship will change.

Carolina has ruined other girls for me, but I have to fight it.

We can't have that type of relationship.

"Now, I can't breathe," she says with an awkward laugh, breaking me away from my thoughts.

I pull back, noticing I'm still giving her some of my weight, and rise. I grab my boxer briefs, go to my bathroom to get rid of the condom in the trash, and turn on the light when I return to my bedroom.

Carolina pulls the sheets up her chest before sitting up while I tug on my briefs.

"Oh my God!" she suddenly gasps, her hand flying to her mouth.

My attention moves to what she's looking at.

Blood on the sheets.

It's not a lot, but it's there.

"It's fine," I say gently. "I'll throw them in the wash. No big deal."

"What … what about your mom?" she stutters out.

"I'll do them myself. She won't even see, and if she does, I won't tell her it was you."

She nods.

I bend down and kiss her forehead. "Like it never happened."

"Like it never happened," she repeats.

I just took my best friend's virginity.

And now, I'm supposed to act like it wasn't the best fucking moment of my life.

CHAPTER FOUR
CAROLINA

COLLEGE—SOPHOMORE YEAR

"**P**retty, pretty please come out with me tonight," my dormmate, Margie, begs.

I open my mouth to tell her I'll pass when my phone beeps with a text from Rex.

My Main Man—I did *not* put this as his name: **Sorry, Lina babe. I've already made plans. We're going out tonight for Nigel's b-day. I can come by later if you're awake, or tomorrow night, I'm all yours.**

His response shouldn't piss me off as much as it does, but tonight's the second Friday he's had *other plans*. Sure, expecting him to hang out with me every weekend isn't fair, but damn it, he should hang out with me every weekend.

Call me codependent; I don't care.

Rex has always been my security blanket.

I was here without him for a semester last year while he deferred, undecided on his major. Undecided meaning, he spent that semester arguing with his parents. They wanted him to go into law or politics. He didn't. It'd always been the plan for the Lane boys to follow in their father's footsteps. Kyle, his older brother, sank half of that dream when he dropped out of school to become a police officer.

His drop out pushed their pressure onto Rex.

I can't picture Rex as an attorney or in politics.

It'd bore him to death.

His parents eventually grasped there was no changing his mind, and being obsessed with their image, they found him not attending college more embarrassing than him majoring in computer science.

He now attends Iowa State with me.

Having him here has been a relief. My first semester, I was either driving home to Blue Beech regularly or he was making the two-hour trek, so we could see each other.

Him being here has helped with the loneliness of my college life.

Him being here has also fueled a spark of jealousy inside me.

The dating pond was small in our high school.

Here, it's a freaking ocean.

Panic spills through me every time I catch a girl hitting on Rex. The fear that one of them could possibly be the girl who changes his life, who steals his heart and takes him from me. Even though he denies it, one day, I'll lose him to another woman.

It's no party, being in love with your best friend, let me tell you.

Rex has been anti-relationship since the first day we hung out. His parents' dysfunctional marriage has him convinced that relationships are toxic and nothing but forced expectations. He's so afraid of failure, of ending up like his father, that he pushes away at any mention of the word *commitment*.

My friendship with Rex is the longest relationship he's ever had.

He's not a fan of relationships.

I'm not a fan of getting my heart broken.

Friends it is with us.

Even after giving him my virginity, I've never expected more from him. That night, he changed the sheets while I went to the bathroom, and we awkwardly said our good nights. The next day, we acted like it never happened. Neither one of us has muttered a word about the night I randomly walked into his room and demanded he take my V-card.

Margie snapping her fingers in front of my face breaks me away from the *I'm pissed at Rex* thoughts. "You. Me. Going out. Your sad face says you need a drink, and I will gladly help with that."

When I first met Margie—a bleached blonde wearing a miniskirt and suede knee-high boots—I thought there was no way we'd get along and that I was in for a miserable year.

I was so wrong.

Margie is a girlfriend I wish I'd had in high school.

She's popular, but she always tries to include me in everything she does.

"Hey," I argue. "I don't have a sad face." I force my lips into a smile.

"You're definitely sporting a sad face." She plops down on the side of my bed. "You know what goes well with sad faces?"

"I have a feeling you're about to tell me, and it's not going to be a proven fact," I grumble.

"Alcohol. It'll turn that frown upside down." Her tone turns into a whine. "Come on. You've gone out with me a total of three times—"

"You're keeping track?" I interrupt.

"Yes, so I can hold it against you every time you say no."

"All right." I dramatically sigh. "You talked me into it."

She tilts her head to the side, as if she didn't hear me correctly. "Huh?"

I shrug. "Having fun tonight sounds better than Netflix."

She leaps up from the bed, squealing, and then breaks into an obnoxious dance. "Girls' night! We're going to have so much fun; you'll be begging me to go out every night!"

Doubt that.

The less people-ing in my life, the better.

I change out of my sweats into a snake-print minidress. Margie forced me to go shopping with her after we met. As soon as we walked into the boutique, my eyes went straight to this dress. She snatched it from my hands before pushing me into a dressing room and handing it back, insisting I try it on. The dress is hot—not something I'd normally wear since party attire isn't needed much in my life. When I refused to buy it, she did and hung it up in my closet *just in case*.

That *just in case* is happening tonight, apparently.

"And put these on, too," she says, shoving strappy black heels into my hands. "You're going to look so hot." She whistles when I'm finished. "*Day-um.* It looks even hotter on you now than it did in the boutique. I'm going to have the sexiest wingwoman tonight."

I run a hand down the dress with a satisfied smile. "Thank you. I still need to pay you back for it."

She waves off my response. "Consider it a dorm-warming gift. Now, put on some makeup, and let's blow this joint. Lewis, the guy with dreads down the hall, is having predrinks in his room. We'll pregame and then go party-hopping."

I nod, quickly putting in my contacts, swiping on mascara, and adding light-pink gloss to my lips. She grabs my hand as soon as I slide the lip gloss into my bag and hauls me down the hallway.

The fact that I don't break an ankle in the heels is a miracle.

I still have the rest of the night to worry about it, though.

I'm not the most coordinated person wearing flats, so fingers crossed I don't bust my ass.

"Margie, you brought a friend!" a guy calls out when we walk in.

His dreads are a sure sign he's Lewis. I've also passed him in the hall a few times since our dorm is coed.

Rex isn't a fan of my *coed* living situation and has suggested I request a transfer more times than I can count.

I notice three guys and a girl in the corner of the room, their attention glued to their phones.

Lewis shuts the door and points at me. "I've seen you before. You're in my Social Science class."

I nod and offer a friendly smile.

"For that, I'm making you a drink."

He takes the few steps to a desk covered with alcohol bottles and sodas. My eyes widen as he hurriedly pours vodka into a red Solo cup and adds a splash of Pepsi. He has a dopey smile on his face when he hands it to me.

Margie plucks it from my hand in seconds. "You're not drinking this." She gives it back to Lewis, pats my shoulder, and grabs a bottle of beer from the other desk. "Here, this is much more your style, babe."

My style is actually tequila. It's the drink Rex and I secretly and frequently sipped on in his room, straight out of Gatorade bottles.

Margie points at me. "Don't take anything from anyone while we're out tonight."

Margie reminds me of Rex.

Apparently, I have an affinity for people who like to boss me around.

"I'm a big girl," I say. "Older than you as a matter of fact."

"Is that why you go to bed at the same time as my grandma?" Her face turns serious. "Carolina, I love you and all, but you fail at the party scene. Lewis could've handed you roofied mouthwash, and you would've trusted him and drunk it."

"Okay, you're rude," I mutter.

"Stay by my side. Don't accept drinks from creeps. Steer clear of frat guys."

"I'll do my best not to drink drugged Listerine, Mom."

She kisses my cheek. "That's my girl."

———

The house is crowded when we walk in. A different song pounds from every room, and my shoulders bump into people when I follow Margie into the kitchen.

"You fucking suck!"

I wheel around, finding a group of people crowded around a beat-up, graffitied beer pong table. A guy at the far end grabs a red Solo cup and chugs down the remnants in seconds.

"Here, drink this," Margie says, pushing a cup in my direction.

"I'm sorry," I say, peeking up and batting my eyes at her. "My mother told me not to accept drinks from creeps."

"Good practice, babe," she says, tapping the top of my head. She tips her cup toward the table and calls out, "We've got next game!"

Oh, heck no.

"I'm *so* not playing beer pong," I hiss.

"You're *so* playing beer pong," she corrects, authority-like. "I don't care if you suck. I'll take one for the team because I know you'll have fun." She gives me a sappy grin. "Suck all you want, and I'll still be your friend. I mean, I'll be a *very drunk friend* but still a good one."

I sip on my beer as she proceeds to explain the rules of beer pong while we wait for the guys to finish up their game. I shake my head when she asks if I have any questions.

I gulp, fighting with myself on how to play this out.

"I'll go first," Margie says as we take our spots at the end of the table. "Just watch what I do, okay?"

I nod. "Got it."

"Do we have a newbie in the house?" our opponent, a guy sporting an overgrown man bun, asks from across the table. Even though his question was directed at me, his eyes are fixed on Margie, his face masked with desire. "Does that mean you're trying to get drunk tonight, babe?"

"Shut up," Margie says, pulling her shiny hair into a ponytail before blowing them a kiss. "Prepare to lose, assholes."

She wastes no time before grabbing a white ping-pong ball and tossing it toward them, and the group yells when it lands in the cup in front of him with a *plop*.

The guy laughs and *cheers* her before downing his drink.

He takes his turn, and the ball drops into one of our cups.

Margie drinks her cup before handing me the ball. "You got this."

"I got this." I sigh to myself, drawing in the confident smirks smothered on our opponents' faces, fully expecting me to miss.

I lift my hand, gracefully sending my ball in their direction, and it sinks into their middle cup.

Margie squeals, grabbing my arm and jumping up and down before smirking at them. "Drink up, boys."

"Beginner's luck," man-bun dude yells.

"I never said I was a *beginner*," I retort. "That's what you get for *assuming.*"

"Holy shit," man-bun's partner says—a scrawny guy with a shaved head. "I think I love her."

He gulps down his drink.

Makes his next shot.

I drink.

Just like with tequila, Rex is a beer pong fan—a *big* one—and he taught me how to play a mean game with him. One of our classmates always held bonfires in his field and beer pong tournaments in his parents' barn. Rex demanded I be his partner every time, and I learned the game. We were the reigning champs until we graduated.

People might think I'm a prude who doesn't have fun, but they don't know me.

I'm not me with other people, not in my comfort zone like I am with Rex.

He gets me, and when someone gets you, you're not afraid to take risks.

———

I'm on my fourth game of beer pong.

Margie and I have won every time, and even though we've been kicking ass, our opponents don't suck. They've hit enough cups to give me a slight buzz, which I'm thankful for.

It's clouding my thoughts about Rex ditching me.

I bring the cup to my lips … and then nearly choke when it's pulled away mid-sip.

"What the fuck are you doing here?"

My heartbeat triples in speed when I see a fuming Rex in front of me. I don't get the chance to ask what he thinks he's doing before he captures my elbow in his hand and pulls me through the crowd. He doesn't release me until we're outside and away from the madness.

"What the fuck are you doing here?" he repeats, stepping closer.

Oh, hell no.

He doesn't get to act like he can be the only one to have fun.

"I'm here for the same reason you are—to party and drink," I answer with a huff. "And screw you. How dare you drag me out of there like you're my father!"

It's dark, and the only light around us is the faint one coming from the porch light.

I can't witness the anger on his face.

I can hear it, though.

Irritation slides along every word, and tension fills his sharp breaths. "I told you, if you go to a party, I go with you."

Even though he can't see it, I scowl at him. "Weird. You don't ask for *my* permission to attend parties."

"That's different," he grumbles. "And you know it."

"How?"

"I'm a dude, and you're … well, you."

I angrily open my crossbody bag, pull out my phone, and ignore the texts he sent me an hour ago. "I'm *me*? Let me interrupt this broadcast to Google the definition of *women's rights* for you where it says I can do whatever the hell I want."

I groan when he snatches the phone, turns on the flashlight, and shines it down on me. I wince at the bright light, hating that he's putting me on display.

"I know enough about that, considering the endless documentaries you've made me watch about it," he replies.

"Obviously, I need to make you watch more."

"I do this to keep you safe, Carolina," he says. Some of his frustration slips, and a hint of gentleness comes through. "Not to be an overbearing asshole."

My eyes rise to meet his. "Safe from what? Having a good time?"

"No, safe from date-rape drugs, from dudes who take advantage of tipsy chicks, from you putting yourself in dangerous situations. I'm your best friend, and it's my job to watch over you."

"*Huh*. Maybe as your best friend, I want to keep you safe. Maybe I don't want you to get date-raped." I sigh. "If you want to be my cockblock, Lane, then I'll be yours. I'll be blocking vaginas left and right tonight." I do a show of dramatically elbowing the air on each side.

He rubs the back of his neck with his free hand. "Not funny."

"You know what isn't funny? Having a double-standard friendship." I hate that my eyes turn glossy. Normally, I'm not this sensitive, but I miss him, and I'm mad at him, and we rarely argue. "It's not fair, Rex."

"Shit," he bites out. "Don't cry."

"I'm not. My eyes are irritated from your bullshit. Seems I'm allergic."

He chuckles before holding out his hand. "Come on. I'll drive you back to your dorm."

I slap his hand away. "Nuh-uh, mister. I'm staying here and having fun, and then I'll ride back with Margie's friend."

He shakes his head. "Nice try. I'm driving you back. If you're good, I'll stop and get you an ice cream cone."

"This isn't funny," I seethe.

Rex always tries to make light of every situation because serious talks aren't his thing. I can only imagine what we look like—standing to the side of the yard at a party, arguing like a drunk couple where the girlfriend found her frat boyfriend cheating.

I snatch my phone from his hand, catching him off guard, and aim the light on him. "I'm not a child or your little sister. I'm old enough to take care of myself."

I was wrong about him being frustrated.

Now that I can see his face, every emotion shows.

He's downright pissed.

His eyes narrow as he steps closer. "You're drinking and dressed like that." He bites into his lower lip while moving his gaze down my body. "Where did you even get that dress? I've never seen it, and *trust me*, I'd remember it."

"You don't see me all the time."

"Enough times to know you haven't worn it before."

"Rex!"

I shift over to look past him and find a blonde on the porch. She yells his name again, her hand resting against her forehead as she scans the yard for him. Rex doesn't bother turning around to look at her; his intense eyes are closed in on me, as if we were the only people in this yard.

"Lina," he says softly.

"Rex!" the chick yells his name again.

I snarl in aggravation. *Why is she looking for him? Did he come with her?*

Rex might be overprotective of me, but that doesn't mean I don't want to keep an eye on him. Sometimes, I hate myself for it—like right now, when there's a girl yelling his name, wanting him to go back and hang out with her.

Hang out with her. Not with me.

I push him back. "You have a party to get to, and so do I."

He steps to the side, stopping me. "Fuck the party. You're more important."

"What will you do then?" I throw my arm out toward the porch. "Take me back to my dorm, come back, and then hook up with the chick on the porch who's looking for you?"

"I don't know," he replies, his voice on edge. "I didn't have a plan, considering I didn't know you'd be here. My biggest priority at the moment is to return you to your dorm, safe—"

I cut him off, "You're a jerk."

It's his turn to cut me off. "If you'd let me finish my goddamn sentence, I was going to say, *unless* you want me to stay and hang out with you."

"I don't want you to pity hang out with me." My voice is strained.

He looks at the sky. "*Fuck!*" His attention flickers back to me. "I don't know how much you've had to drink, but what the hell? Why are you acting like this?"

"Like what exactly?" I give him a death stare.

"Like a totally different Carolina."

"Maybe this is *me*. The new Carolina." I step to the other side of him, so he's no longer blocking me, and I walk past him, pushing the phone back into my purse without bothering to turn the flashlight off. "This Carolina is going to drink some more and maybe find a guy to look for her from the porch."

I sound like a total brat, but how dare him!

His arm circles my waist, and he pulls me back. "*This* Rex is not going to allow that shit."

I shove him away. "Jesus. Overbearing much?"

He groans. "Fine, go have fun with your friends." He shoves his finger through the air in the direction of the house. "But I'm staying here."

I scoff. "I don't need a babysitter."

"I won't be up your ass, but you're not staying here by yourself." His tone is half-calm, half-bossy. "When you're done having fun, I'll take you back to your dorm."

"Carolina!"

This time, it's my name being called out from the porch. Also, this time, Rex and I both look at the porch. Margie is standing next to the girl who has been looking for Rex.

Margie's head turns to Rex. "Rex! Piss off! I need my partner back. We had a good winning streak going on."

I use this as a quick exit plan.

"I'll talk to you later," I say, rushing away from him and scurrying up the porch steps, stumbling a bit in my heels.

Margie grins when I make it to her.

Rex calls out my name, and I don't look back while following Margie into the house.

———

I'm being watched.

I *hate* being watched.

Rex's whiskey-colored eyes have been burning into me since he returned to the house with a scowl on his face and leaned back against the wall, giving him the perfect view of the kitchen. He sips on his beer while focusing on me, as if I'm his favorite show. Holey black jeans hang low on his waist, and he's sporting gray slip-on Chucks and a black leather jacket over a blue tee. A light scruff covers his cheeks and strong jaw, and his toffee-colored hair is messily pushed back.

Rex Lane doesn't look anything like a man who plays video games on the regular.

Margie and I have continued to play beer pong, but luckily, our opponents are getting drunker, so we don't have to drink as much.

I fight the urge to stare back at him and am proud of myself for only stealing quick glances every few minutes. My heart nearly stops during one of these peeks. I miss my shot, startled at the sight of the skinny blonde from the porch standing in front of him, her back to me. He's sharing his attention between her and me now, and I clench my fist around the ball. When it's my turn, I can't stop myself from hurling the ball across the room, my aim directed at him.

It lands at his feet. Blondie spins to glare at me, and I only shrug. Rex shakes his head, raising a brow, fully aware my cup miss wasn't an accident.

I look away when Margie taps my shoulder. "Carolina, stop playing dodgeball with Blondie and get your ass over there to claim your man."

I force a laugh, a sick feeling in my stomach. "He's not my man."

"He comes to our dorm enough that someone would think he's your man. He dragged you out of this party, claiming you as his."

"Or he thinks he's my father."

I grit my teeth as the girl lifts on her tiptoes to whisper in his ear, her hand caressing his jaw. He nods, as if he were listening, but his eyes are back on me.

"I say, you go punch him in the balls for even entertaining her," Margie comments.

My shoulders slump. "He's my best friend."

She scoffs. "You need to quit being blind if you think you're only friends."

My eyes water when Rex's attention leaves me longer than it has all night as he offers the girl a flirtatious smile. He's nodding, laughing at what she's saying, and she steps in closer, their bodies nearly rubbing against each other. I'm well aware Rex has an active sex life, but when he's with me, he's with *me*.

Blondie kissing the side of his mouth is my undoing.

"I'm out of here," I say. "I'll Uber home."

I can't stop myself from looking at them again. Blondie's arm is wrapped around his neck now.

"No, I'll get Kara," Margie says. "She's the DD tonight, so she's probably ready to dip anyway. No one likes their DD nights."

I nod, tapping the side of my eyes to stop crying. Rex will probably take Blondie home tonight and screw her brains out. I shut my eyes when memories of the night he *screwed* me push through my mind. Even though I'd sworn it wouldn't change anything, I'll never forget every way he touched me and how my body responded. I'd had other guys touch me, finger me, but no one has ever made me feel as good as Rex did.

It was like he knew me in every way.

In my perfect world, I'd be kissing his mouth. He'd be taking me back to his place. We'd spend the rest of the night naked in his bed.

Too bad my world isn't perfect.

Margie takes my hand, and we walk outside.

"I told you I was taking you home, Carolina!" Rex yells behind me when we hit the sidewalk and walk toward Kara's Honda Civic.

"I told you I'm riding with my friends," I reply without looking back at him. I know him well enough to know he's following me.

Margie whips us around, and Rex is only inches away, the streetlight shining over us.

"Look, Rex, she's hanging out with her girlfriends tonight. We need to gossip about what a dumbass you're being. I promise to take good care of her."

"I know how to take care of her better than anyone," he snaps, but he's not looking at Margie. He's looking at me.

Guilt creeps through my blood at the torture on his face. I want to pull away from Margie and let Rex take me home, but I have to stop depending on him. I can't sit at home on Friday nights when he's busy and sulk about it. We're in college now, and our relationship has changed.

"Rex," I say around a sigh. "I'm going straight back to the dorm."

He shuts his eyes, defeat covering his features. "Text me when you get back then. I'll be at your doorstep if I don't hear back from you in an hour."

"Uh, stalker much?" Kara cuts in behind us.

I didn't even notice she'd stopped with us.

"Uh, best friend much?" Rex says, mocking her voice without even giving her a glance. He tips his head down and kisses my forehead. "I hope you had fun tonight, Lina babe. Text me next time you go out, but you're not wearing that fucking dress, FYI."

"Hater," Margie sings out. "Don't get mad at other guys for wanting something you're too chicken to touch."

He slams his mouth shut, fighting to control his smart-ass response. His palm falls at the base of my back as he walks us to Kara's car, and he stands in place as we pull away.

Is he going back to the party?

To Blondie?

I clench my fingers in my lap, just thinking about it.

"We need to make a quick pit stop at the grocery store," Margie demands from the front seat. "We need snacks on snacks on snacks."

"I agree!" Kara says.

"I can definitely use some ice cream," I add.

Kara drives us to the small convenience store on campus, and we get out, laughing.

"You're on ice cream duty," Margie instructs me. She points at Kara. "You're potato chips." She points at herself with her thumb. "And I'm on candy."

"Got it," I say, and we all head in the direction of our items.

My stomach growls when I hit the ice cream aisle, and I scan the endless choices. I'm in the middle of narrowing down my options to three when I jump at the sound of the masculine voice.

"You're sure out late, and by the way, you look gorgeous."

I put my hand against my chest, startled, and smile when I see the familiar man. Familiar as in I've seen him plenty of times around campus, but not familiar enough that we've had a conversation. He looks hot, wearing a green shirt and fitted black sweatpants—nothing like I've seen him in before. His short brown hair is wet as though he's just gotten out of the shower.

My cheeks blush, and I look down to hide the cheesy smile on my face. "I think it should be the other way around." I gain control of myself and meet his eyes again. They're a light blue, round, and I could stare at them forever. "I should comment that *you're* out late." I nervously laugh. "I'm a college student. It's code to stay out late."

Okay, not usually mine, but whatever.

He returns the laugh and nods toward the freezer. "Looks like we both had an ice cream craving tonight."

I nod. "Sure did. There's no better way to end the day than with ice cream."

He turns to consider his options and steps closer to me. "What's your favorite?"

"I don't think there's such a thing as a favorite ice cream. Bad question to ask someone."

He peeks down at me, his upper lip curling into a smirk, and then shoves his hands into his pockets. "It isn't a bad question. In fact, it's your typical first-date question."

"I haven't had many first dates to actually know if that's a fact or something you just made up."

"Oh, come on." He bumps his shoulder against mine. "An extremely smart and gorgeous girl like you? I doubt that."

"Eh, I prefer to study." It shocks me that I feel so comfortable in his presence. I'm normally not into small talk, and I never thought I'd be so chill talking to this man—a man I've heard so many girls on campus drool over.

"You going to tell me your favorite, or do I need to ask you out on a first date to get my answer?"

I snort. "Good one."

"I'm serious, Carolina."

This time, when I peer up at him, there's no smirk on his face.

"Are you sure ..." I gulp, lowering my voice. "Are you sure that's appropriate?"

"Probably not, but I'm good at keeping secrets." He reaches across me, his arm brushing against my chest, and opens the freezer door. "Now, choose your favorite for me and tell me when you're free."

I hesitate, wondering if I'm batshit crazy. "Okay." My answer comes out in a whisper.

Why not? Maybe I need to step out of my box with other people.

I'm fighting back a smile as I dip underneath his arm, grab a mint chocolate chip, and hand it to him. I rest my back against the freezer when he shuts the door behind me. He tucks the ice cream under his armpit and leans into me, his lips close to mine.

"Carolina!"

We both pull back at Margie yelling my name from the next aisle. "What are you, milking the cow over there? Pick something, and let's go!"

"Give me your number," he rushes out, tugging his phone from his pocket.

A smile is smothered across my face as I give it to him.

"You'd better get back to your friend," he says, reaching out and skimming his hand over my jaw. "Hopefully, I'll see you soon."

Oh my God.

Swoon.

I keep my back against the freezer door, watching him as he disappears down the aisle, and then grab the ice cream. We load up on snacks and go back to the dorm.

As soon as I change into my pajamas and take a giant bite of ice cream, my phone beeps with a text.

Unknown Number: You're right. Mint chocolate chip is the best. When are you available?

I grin, shove my spoon in the container, and hurriedly text back.

Me: Friday night?

Unknown Number: Perfect.

Maybe this girl needs to change her college life.

Try something exciting.

I almost put my phone on the charger and finish my ice cream before crashing, but then I remember I need to text Rex. There's no doubt he'll show up here if I don't.

Me: I'm home, safe and sound.
My Main Man: Good. I apologize if I was being an ass tonight.
Me: It's okay.
My Main Man: Good night, babe. Love you.
Me: Night. Love you, too.

CHAPTER FIVE

Carolina has been the master of call-dodging lately.

Come to think of it, she's been distant all week, ever since our stupid spat at that lame-ass party.

I texted her this morning, asking her what she was doing. It's the weekend, so she doesn't have class, and I want to hang out. After receiving no response, I asked if she wanted to get pizza. An hour later, I called. My next text was asking her what the fuck her deal was. That also went ignored.

Something is up.

She never ignores me. Even when she's pissed, she always at least replies with a smart-ass GIF.

A sick feeling settles in my stomach, a heavy dread falling over me.

Is this it?

Where college drags us apart and I lose her?

I clench my fists.

I think the fuck not.

Carolina and I are lifers, friends until the end. I don't give two shits what a future boyfriend or husband or any guy I'm going to hate who comes in the picture says about it. Carolina won't have to worry about that on my end. There will never be a woman who breaks our bond, who kicks her out of my life.

Some might say that's selfish of me, but I don't care.

It's not that I've forbidden Carolina to have a boyfriend. I can't pull that shit. I just want her to hold back for as long as possible. I'm not ready to put up a fight to not lose her yet. It scares me too damn much.

When I knock on her dorm door, I don't expect her to answer dressed like every man's wet dream—or at least, my regularly scheduled wet dream ... of her.

The short jean miniskirt she's wearing shows off every curve of her body, a white shirt hangs off one shoulder, and she's wearing some type of heel shit that isn't exactly a heel.

Platforms?

Shit. My sister wears them ...

Wedges.

They're wedges.

Unlike my sister, Carolina isn't a frequent wedges wearer.

At least, *my* Carolina isn't.

Maybe shit has changed. She did say she was a *new* Carolina.

I just hope to fuck this *new* Carolina doesn't leave me.

"Damn, where are you going?" I bite into my lower lip.

Her dark hair is down—unlike my usual Carolina who regularly sports it in a messy bun. She's wearing makeup—her bubblegum pink lipstick drawing my attention to her plump lips—and she replaced her glasses with contacts, showing off her coffee-brown eyes. Her standing in front of me, looking sexy as hell, reminds me of her outfit of choice at the party.

Carolina's sweaters have started disappearing. I miss those ugly-ass things.

I suppress a moan, and my cock jerks in my sweats, reminding me of how much I want her ... as more than a damn friend. When we had sex, when she insisted it wouldn't change anything between us, it didn't.

Well, it didn't change the dynamic of our relationship.

We still hang out, talk, and are normal around each other as if it never happened.

Emotionally, it has changed me.

I'll never forget the happiness shooting through me when she laid down on my bed and trusted me with something she'd held on to for so long. The perfect feeling of sliding in and out of her will stick with me until I take my last breath. That night, I knew Carolina would never be just a friend, but I also knew I needed to act like she was. It was the best and most awkward sex I've had in my life.

I'm a stupid guy.

Selfish at times.

I'd take her heart, sure, and I'd make her come a few times, but I could never give her everything she deserved. She's a romantic. She wants the marriage, the family, the man who knows how to be in a relationship, and that isn't me. So, I play it cool when we're together, acting as though she doesn't hold me by my heart and balls. I love her enough to never fuck her again, but that doesn't mean I don't imagine her naked and moaning my name.

But when she's dressed like *this*, fuck, it's hard not to reach out and touch her. It's hard, not telling her how amazing her body is and how I'd love to have her again.

"I'm going out with a friend," she answers with a slight shrug, like it's something she does on the regular.

"A friend?" I look around her to peek into her room, searching for this *friend*. "Is it Margie?"

God, let it please be Margie. Please fucking be Margie.

Also, God, one more request: please also don't let it be Margie dragging her to another party.

I like Margie. She's cool people, and I know her intentions of getting Carolina to enjoy college life are pure. I just wish it were going bowling or shopping, not partying with dudes who look at her with sex eyes.

"No, I have more than one friend, you know," she replies with a frown.

She turns, giving me space to walk into her room. For the first time, I feel uninvited in here.

I've lost count of how many chicks I've ditched to be with Carolina.

She knows every damn move I make.

Yet here she is, acting as though she doesn't owe me the same, that she doesn't need to explain that she's most likely going out with a guy —a stupid jackass not worthy of having her. I can't stop myself from clenching my fist.

"Then, what friend?" I question … okay, more like interrogate.

She pulls at the hem of her skirt. "A *friend*," she stresses.

"You're sure dressed up to hang out with just *a friend*. And why do you keep putting so much emphasis on the word *friend?*" My clenched fist releases to hold two fingers in the air. "You have two friends: me and Margie. So, obviously, this friend"—I cover my mouth and cough —"*douche bag*—isn't one of them."

"I have other friends from class, and I like to be cute sometimes. Sue me."

"Bullshit," I spit, unaware of how aware she is of my jealousy. "You have a date." My stomach turns.

I don't like this. I don't like this at all.

Why this is making me so sick to my stomach, I have no idea.

Oh, wait. Yes, I do.

It's because I'm fucking in love with my best fucking friend, and I never want to share her.

"It's a hangout," she says.

"A hangout with a dude?" I correct with irritation.

"*Fine.* I'm going on a date. You happy now, Daddy?"

"Hey now." I can't help my voice from turning playful. "You know how I feel about chicks calling me daddy in bed."

Oh fuck. Now, I'm thinking about her calling someone else daddy in bed. Playfulness ejected.

"Good thing all we do is *sleep* in your bed, so that's something you'll never have to worry about."

Except once, is what I want to tell her. One time, we did more than sleep in my bed.

I collapse onto her bed, making myself comfortable, and refrain from pulling her down with me. I snatch a pillow and place it behind my head. "So, who's the lucky guy?"

She pushes her phone into her purse. "Just a guy from class. No big deal."

"What class, hmm?"

"None of Your Business 101."

I snap my fingers. "How about this? Cancel your plans and hang out with me instead."

She shakes her head. "Nope."

I throw my head back. "Fine, but give me his name."

She parks her hands on her hips. "You don't need a name. You don't give me the names of all the girls you hook up with."

I perk up, my back stiffening. "Oh, so now, you're *hooking* up with him, not just going out on a date?" *What the flying fuck? No. No. I am not allowing this.*

"You're annoying," she grumbles, taking a last look in the mirror and fluffing out her hair.

"Still waiting for that name." I tap my finger against my watch.

"Still not going to give it to you."

I jump to my feet. "What if something happens to you? What if he's a serial killer or some shit? I'll need to know who you were with, so I can kill him."

"I doubt he's going to murder me," she deadpans.

"You never know." My voice turns serious, and I beat her to her doorway, blocking her from moving into the hallway. "When you get in the car, take a picture of his driver's license and send it to me."

She holds her palm up. "Uh, no. That's not weird or anything."

"It's normal. My sister did it in college with her friends. The dude will know there's evidence you were with him, and I'll have the info to hunt him down and chop off his balls if he lays a hand on you."

"I don't badger you about your dates."

"A.) I don't date. B.) I wouldn't give a shit telling you who I was going out with."

She crosses her arms. "Move it, Rex. I need to go."

I scoot to the side, and she walks past me. I stay on her heels as we move down the hallway, down the stairwell, and out to the parking lot.

"Whoa, dude isn't even picking you up?" I say when she tugs her car key from her purse. "He already sucks."

"Oh my God," she groans, throwing her head back. "Go away."

Rushing in front of her, I turn around and walk backward while still talking. "Look, text the guy, tell him you realized I'd give you a better time than he could, and let's do something. Your choice. Anything you want." I sound close to begging.

"No, Rex," she says sternly. "Go party, like you have all the times you've ditched me lately."

I wince. "The fuck? I've never ditched you. On the *few times* I've gone to parties, I've always told you that's what I was doing. I've never made plans with you and then bailed on them."

"And I didn't make plans with you tonight, so I'm not ditching." She looks down at her phone when it beeps with a text. "I have to go."

I move to her side, keeping at her pace, my words quickly falling from my mouth—almost in desperation. I have a bad feeling about this. "Pizza sure sounds fucking killer right now, don't you think?"

She doesn't reply.

"He's not even picking you up." I snort. "Some stand-up dude."

She turns around, her face softening. "Rex, I'll be back later, okay? Don't worry about me. I'll be fine."

I swallow.

There's no changing her mind.

Just as the night we had sex, I know determined Carolina.

This is determined Carolina.

Fuck!

She gets into her car, and I knock on the window.

As soon as she rolls it down, I poke my head through. "Text me when you get home."

She nods. "I will."

"Or I'll—"

"I know," she interrupts. "Or you'll be knocking on my door."

I turn my head to kiss her on the cheek. "Have fun tonight, I guess."

My shoulders slump as I watch her pull out of the parking lot. I've never felt so fucking defeated, and I don't know why I'm *this* bothered. She's gone on a few dates before, but something doesn't seem right with this one.

It's all fun and games, dating around in college … until it's your best friend doing it.

My phone beeps with a text message from the chick I was talking with at the party. After Carolina left, I went back in for five minutes before bailing. Clarissa stopped me before I did, and we exchanged numbers.

Clarissa: Hey, want to get together? I'm still salty about you leaving the party early.

Me: Nah, not today. Rain check?

Clarissa: Rain check. Let me know if you change your mind.

I need to be available in case Carolina A.) calls me, needing a ride or to be saved or for me to beat up the dude, or B.) makes it back to her dorm, safe and sound.

When I get back to my dorm, I order a pizza, turn on the TV, flip through channels, and decide on *20/20*. It's Friday night, and I don't give two shits about being at a party. I give all the shits about wanting to be with Carolina. I can't stop myself from texting her.

Me: On a scale of 1–10, how lame is your date?

No answer. I wait fifteen minutes and text again.

Me: You must've fallen asleep because he's lame AF. I'll call you in 10 to wake you up.

She texts back a minute later.

The Smartest and Coolest Girl in the World: I can't text. It's rude!

Me: Sure you can. I do it all the time.

The pizza I ordered arrives, and I walk down to the lobby to grab it. I text her a picture of it as soon as I'm back in my room. Chicken and pepperoni—her favorite.

Me: You're really turning down this? Yum, yum. I won't save you any.

No response.

I eat my pizza, watch a few shows, and text her an hour later.

Me: The streetlights are about to come on. I expect you to be home, or you're grounded.

The Smartest and Coolest Girl in the World: You're going to ruin my date!

Me: That's my mission.

The Smartest and Coolest Girl in the World: Officially signing off.

Me: Officially waiting for you to realize the date is a bust.

Two hours later.

The Smartest and Coolest Girl in the World: Home, Daddy.

Swear to God, my heartbeat lowers a good twelve beats. *Thank God.*

Me: I might have to change my stance on that word. I like it from you.

The Smartest and Coolest Girl in the World: You're nuts.

Me: Get some rest. You're mine tomorrow.

CHAPTER SIX

REX

SIX MONTHS LATER
COLLEGE—JUNIOR YEAR

My phone ringing wakes me up.

Carolina.

It's after midnight.

We haven't talked today. Hell, even though we still talk almost daily, it's not like it used to be. I'm losing her to this secret douche bag she's dating, who she'll tell me nothing about. Even Margie is clueless to her new boy toy.

She put a passcode on her phone, but considering I know everything about her, I figured it out. I crossed personal boundaries and went through her text messages. His Contact was saved under *James*— like that's easy to narrow down.

I shuddered as I read through a few *sext* messages, and just as I was hitting his Contact information, Carolina walked back into the room.

I haven't gone through her phone since. It only makes me sick to my stomach, thinking about her talking to him.

"Hello?" I hurriedly answer.

"Hey," she says on the other line.

I jump out of bed the moment I hear her sobs through the phone.

"I'm outside your dorm. Can I come in?" she asks.

I don't stay at my dorm much because I fucking hate it. I like my personal space. I only have class a few days a week and normally commute back and forth from my apartment in Blue Beech, but lately —maybe because it's my worry over Carolina—I've been sleeping here the past two weeks. She's changed—ditching me, dodging my calls, even Margie said she doesn't come home some nights. Margie called last weekend and said she left with a suitcase, and no one heard from her all weekend.

"I'm coming," I rush out, pulling on a pair of shorts, not bothering with a shirt or shoes.

I run down the hallway and stairs. I throw open the door and find her standing outside in the rain.

Fuck!

She runs into my arms, and I wrap them around her while walking her inside. She's soaked and shaking as she cries in my arms in the lobby.

"What's going on?" I ask, trembling in anger and fear. "What the fuck happened? Did someone hurt you?"

She buries her face in my neck. "Not here," she whispers in my ear.

I hoist her up, and she wraps her legs around my waist while I take us upstairs. I left my door unlocked, so I walk in and set her down on my bed, keeping the light off.

"Lina babe, what's going on?" I ask, a knot in my throat. Every muscle in my body is tense. "Did someone hurt you?"

"Yes," she answers in a whisper.

"What?" The knot thickens.

"It's not like that," she says, sensing my anger. "No one ... *hurt me*, hurt me." She covers her face with her hands. "This is embarrassing."

"I can take embarrassing." I reach up and move the hands from her face, running my finger along her jaw, wiping away drops of rain and tears. "Tell me."

She sniffles, looking away from me. "You have to promise not to judge me ... or get mad."

"Lina, you know I'll never judge you for shit. I'll have your back, no matter what."

She inhales a deep breath and then breaks my fucking heart.

I clench my fist, wishing I could break a motherfucker's neck.

CHAPTER SEVEN

CAROLINA

SIX MONTHS LATER

"I need chocolate chip cookies, babe, and I need them stat," Rex shouts, bursting through the front door of my loft. "*Mmm … I smell them. Perfect timing.*"

My gaze moves from the TV to him. "What you need is to learn how to knock."

He takes the few steps to my couch, collapses onto it, and throws his arm over the back while making himself comfortable. "I have a key." He holds up said key, grins arrogantly, and shoves it into the pocket of his jeans. "No need to knock."

I have a key to his place. He has a key to mine.

Rex claimed it was a stipulation of our friendship to have copies of each other's keys when I moved into the loft above my older sister's garage. I declared it insanity *and* an invasion of privacy when he *stole* my key, went to Home Depot, and had a copy made.

After what happened at school, I was afraid my relationship with Rex would change. I'd started pushing him away due to an outside influence putting thoughts into my head.

"You honestly think you'll stay friends?"

"He's going to leave you as soon as he finds a girlfriend."

"Push him away before he does you."

I'd stupidly listened to someone I shouldn't have.

The night I went to his dorm, I had no idea what to expect. All I knew was that I needed him, and like the best friend he is, he wrapped me in his arms, telling me everything would be okay. It was dumb of me to doubt him. We've always accepted each other wholeheartedly in our friendship. It'd take a lot for me to kick him out of my life, and I think it's the same for him with me.

As he says, we're lifers—*C&R For-fucking-ever.*

He suggested we get it tatted. I told him he was nuts.

I hadn't realized how strong our bond was until that night. He was there for me. Under all the humor and ego is one of the sincerest people I know.

I sit cross-legged, shifting in my spot, and give him my full attention. "I'll be sure to have the locks changed," I reply, knowing damn well I won't.

His signature crew haircut has grown out on the top, long and sticking up—his everyday look. He's sporting dark jeans, a black shirt, and white sneakers. Casual is Rex's style.

"What happened?" I question.

Cookies are our go-to when we're having a bad day.

Correction: us hanging out and cookies are our go-to when we're having a bad day.

"This game," he explains, blowing out a stressed breath, "it's kicking my ass. I can't be in my apartment right now, or I'll throw the console through the window."

My face softens at his admission. Rex has worked his butt off on developing this game, and it means so much to him. Not only for his own self-gratification, but to also prove wrong everyone who's doubted him for his career choice—those who claim he lazily sits at home, playing video games all day.

Eight months ago, on a whim, he sent in a demo of the game he'd been designing to one of the largest names in the industry. They loved it—which was no surprise to me. They gave him an advance and a year to finish it. Lately, he's been stressing, wanting the final product to be perfect.

"I've also missed you," he adds with a wink. "You never told me how your date with the douche bag went."

"Why do you call every guy I go on a date with a douche bag?" I ask, raising a brow. "You don't even know him."

The date was a bust. We went to dinner, had zilch in common, and haven't talked since. I only went because my sister had set it up without asking, and I would've felt bad, saying no. I'd rather have my ear bitten off Mike Tyson–style than hit the dating scene again. Technically, I've never hit the dating scene. My first serious relationship was hidden.

The sucky thing about a secret relationship?

No one knows you're heartbroken when it ends. You can't use a broken heart as an excuse to hide away in your loft or, say, drop out of college.

Okay, I didn't *exactly* drop out of college over a broken heart.

It's more complicated than that.

There are more twists and turns than my heart being shattered.

"I call them douche bags because they're lame, boring, and bad for you," Rex explains matter-of-factly.

"You're one to talk." I roll my eyes. "Who's your flavor of the week?"

Rex hasn't changed his mind about a relationship. Since we're open books to each other, I know why he runs from them. He doesn't think he's capable of having a normal relationship. He doesn't trust anyone other than his mother—he did correct himself, adding me to that list after I scowled at him for not including me—and he thinks love makes people weak. He grew up around his parents' toxic marriage, and he saw the pain his mother endured in the name of love as his father cheated.

He scratches his scruffy cheek. "Hmm … I'd say chocolate chip." Mischief flashes in his eyes. "Next week, you can whip me up some Snickerdoodle."

I can't help but laugh. "Sucks for you. All the chocolate chip have been eaten by this girl." I poke myself in the chest with my thumb.

"Lies, my dear Lina, all lies. You *always* save me cookies. It's in our friendship handbook." He squeezes my thigh, smacks a kiss onto my cheek, and rises from the couch. "You love me too much to withhold them."

He's right. I always make extra for him, *especially* chocolate chip.

They're his favorite.

He goes to my kitchenette, and I don't bother glancing back at him as I hear him opening cabinets.

After I dropped out of school, I stayed at Rex's apartment for two weeks. I was terrified to tell my parents and had to build up the guts to break the news. Rex offered to go with me, but it would've only made them angrier. They would've somehow pointed the blame at him.

My mother cried. My father threatened to cut me off. *Technically,* he did cut me off. I'm now responsible for every bill—phone, rent, car insurance. My sister, Tricia, stepped in and offered me the loft above her garage. It's roomy, with plenty of space for one person. I have a small bedroom, a living room, a bathroom, and a kitchenette. On the plus side, it's larger than my dorm room. It also came furnished with a queen-size bed, a couch, and a TV. I've added a few special touches—bright purple throw pillows, numerous photos of Rex and me, and a large bookshelf I filled with my favorite novels.

Tricia doesn't charge me rent, but I still need money to eat and for basic essentials, so I got a job waiting tables at Shirley's Diner. The money isn't great, but it will hold me over until I decide my next step, which is to eventually look into online classes.

"Uh-oh," Rex draws out, stepping into my view. A plate of cookies is in one hand, and a bottle of wine is in the other. An *empty* bottle of wine. He snags a cookie before setting the plate and wine on the table in front of the couch. "Cookies *and* wine. Who pissed my girl off today?"

"I don't want to talk about it," I grumble.

I'm not a big drinker even though I'm twenty-one now, and doing it at home isn't a normal thing for me, but it's been a day. Rex knows that I only pull out a bottle of wine when my stress level is high.

"Tough shit." He plops back down on the couch, closer to me this time, with concern etched across his face. "You force me to talk about my problems, giving my dude Dr. Phil a run for his money." He cocks his head to the side, studying me, and takes a bite of his cookie. "What's on your mind?"

I twist in my spot, snatching the glass of wine resting on the end table behind me. "You remember my cousin Faye?" I gulp down the remainder of wine. A good amount of alcohol needs to be in my system to even say her name.

He nods, swallowing down his bite before answering, "Chick who couldn't handle one beer without puking it up and then went and tattled on us for having said beers? The one who was a major bitch to you until I set her straight?"

"The one and only."

"What about her?"

"She's getting married."

He loudly whistles. "Damn, poor guy. How much did her parents pay him to put up with her evil ass?"

A laugh escapes me. Rex always adds humor to my crappy situations.

"She invited me to her wedding in Texas."

"And?" He grabs another cookie.

"And not only do I not want to attend, but I'm also lacking a date."

"Ahh … Douche Bags 'R' Us doesn't have any availability for that day, huh?"

I snatch the half-eaten cookie from his hand. "No cookies for smart-asses." I shove the entire thing into my mouth and expressively munch on it.

He chuckles. "I know you enjoy my slobber and all, but you don't have to resort to stealing my cookies. Just ask me to make out with you."

I shoot him a glare. "I'm burning our friendship bracelets."

"Good thing I have letter beads and strings to make new ones." He holds up his wrist, showing off his bracelet that matches mine. They're not beaded or cheesy, just leather bands with our initials on them. It was a Christmas gift from me. "I have plenty with your initials."

"Yeah, that's not creepy or anything."

"Oh, really?" He smirks. "Says the girl who's stolen nearly my entire wardrobe."

"Your clothes are comfy." I shrug before swatting my hand through the air. "*Anyway*, back to the wedding."

"Your sister will be there. Say you want to sit at her table. Or simple, don't go. Why are you even stressing?"

"I'm sorry, but did you forget who my parents are? They'd kill me. And my sister is friends with Faye. They'll be hanging out, sharing smiles—all that annoying stuff."

"Eh, I doubt a preacher would kill his daughter. It'd be bad for his image."

I toss my head back. "They're all about supporting your loved ones —*blah, blah*, vomit, *blah*."

I set down my empty wineglass, wishing I could pour another, but I only bought one bottle at the store. I hadn't expected my mother to spring this on me at the last minute. Hell, I didn't even receive a personal invite. Faye couldn't care less if I showed up to her wedding. Lord knows, she won't be receiving an invite to mine. Tattletales have no room in my big day.

"Are you aware of the worst thing about attending weddings solo?"

"Nope," Rex answers, a sly smile arching on his lips. "Although I have a feeling you're about to tell me—all dramatic and shit."

"Everyone asks why I'm single!" I throw my arms in the air. "Even the kids! Shoot, even my grandmother, who suffers from dementia and doesn't remember anyone in our family, *except* her single granddaughter." I wince. "Do you know how miserable the singles table is?"

"Can't say I do. Never had to sit at one."

"Of course you haven't." I glower in annoyance. "That will change when you're eighty and you have no one because you're *so scared* of relationships and too old for a quick fling."

"Eh, I'll take my chances." He ruffles his hands through my hair, giving me a playful grin. "Who knows? We might be single at eighty together, hanging out in the nursing home, stirring up trouble. We'll have our own singles table. It'll be lit."

"Sounds like a better time than going to this godforsaken wedding."

"I'll go with you."

I narrow my eyes at him. "Funny."

Rex offering to tag along isn't surprising. We're each other's side-kicks. I'm there when he has to deal with his father, whose favorite hobby is giving Rex the third degree ... and cheating on his mother.

He and Rex don't exactly see eye to eye—haven't since Rex was a teen.

"No joke," he says. "I'll go. When is it?"

"This weekend." I wrinkle my nose. "It's short notice, and I know you have a lot going on."

"I'm coming. I need a break, and you need a date."

His phone vibrates, and I see the name Megan flash across the screen when he pulls it from his pocket.

"Your skank is calling," I comment, leaning over and making a show of reading it.

"Any girl can wait when I'm with you. You know you're my favorite. My best friend comes before anyone."

He declines the call and eats another cookie.

———

Rex grabs my carry-on bag from me and throws it over his shoulder as we walk through the automatic glass doors. "Does my favorite girl still hate flying?"

I rode with my parents to the airport ... unwillingly, and Rex met us here. My parents insisted on the carpooling, demanding we discuss my life plans, and they know I can't jump out of a moving car to avoid their overbearing questions. Car rides with them are more dreadful than having my pinkie nail ripped off, and it's turned worse now that I dropped out of college and moved back to Blue Beech.

"The preacher's daughter doesn't make reckless decisions like that."

"She doesn't have secrets."

Oh, man, if only they knew the stupid stuff this preacher's daughter did.

Nausea fills me at the thought of my parents finding out. It'd ruin them, their name, and they'd never look at me the same. To keep this from happening, I have to play someone else's game and am at his mercy. Thankfully, it hasn't been as bad lately as it was at first. I keep this secret so tucked away that Rex doesn't even know.

He's my ride or die, and I don't think he'd walk away from me if he ever were to find out. The problem is, I know Rex well enough to know he'd jump in and try to fix the situation. Him doing that would only make things worse.

"Sure do," I answer, strolling next to him through the airport.

"Good thing I upgraded you to first class." He peeks back at my parents walking behind us. "I also upgraded the 'rents. Maybe it'll convince them to like me."

"Hey, they like you," I halfway lie.

When I mentioned Rex was coming—while on the way to the airport—they weren't happy, *but* they also weren't pissed. They've been vocal about their issues with Rex and our friendship ... or *dependency*, in their words. They think Rex is the reason I dropped out of school. It was the other way around. Rex had begged me to stay in school, but he supported my decision in the end.

He scoffs. "They like *my family*, so they put up with me."

"How did you even upgrade us?" I ask, walking around a group of parents yelling at their kids to hurry it up, and I take our place in the check-in line. "You don't know our ticket numbers."

"*Au contraire*, Lina. I know your email password, which led me to your ticket information because your father forwarded the info to you."

"Seriously?"

He shrugs with no shame. "You haven't changed it since senior year. You should probably do that, for security reasons and all."

When my mother finds out about her seat upgrade, she's ecstatic. My father, not so much. He argues with the attendant, then Rex, and then my mother to change it back. My mother finally rips him a new one and says it is insulting to Rex's kind gesture. Since my mom tends to make the rules in our family, he caves, shooting a glare at Rex.

"How did you know my password senior year?" I ask while my father continues to complain to my mother behind us.

Rex shrugs again. "I don't remember. I was probably bored."

"You know no boundaries." This is something I tell him on the regular.

"I do want to put in a request for you to change that password. I can't believe it's still *The_Future_Mrs_Jonas*. You know none of those guys are single anymore, right?"

I roll my eyes. "I'm concerned you know the love life of the Jonas brothers."

"I'm concerned you thought you'd marry one. If you need help, I'm a great password creator. I'm thinking …" He fakes deep thinking, running his palm over his chin. "*Rex's_biggest_fan*. It suits you better."

If my parents weren't behind us, I'd kick my foot out and trip him.

"It's an old email and hasn't been high on my priority list. I suggest you find a new hobby because your password ideas are worse than the *Game of Thrones* finale." I rub my forehead before yawning. "It's too early for me to deal with you right now. I need coffee, snacks, and Tylenol PM to knock my ass out."

"You want something that'll keep you up but then also something that'll make you sleep? Sounds like a legit plan you thought out well. New plan: coffee, snacks. No Tylenol PM for you." He ruffles his hand through my hair, screwing up the messy bun I took a full ten minutes to perfect. "I can't be sitting next to you while you're drooling and dreaming about me. It's also a short flight. You don't want to show up all cracked out on cough meds."

I hold up a finger. "A.) I don't drool." I hold up another. "B.) Sounds like the perfect plan for me."

We get coffee, snacks, and unfortunately no Tylenol PM before heading to our terminal. Luckily, we don't have a long wait before boarding the plane. They welcome first class, and the flight attendant doesn't fail to check Rex out as we take our seats. Rex grins and winks at her as he makes himself comfortable next to me in the aisle seat.

"All right," he says after the flirty flight attendant quits giving him googly eyes and starts to actually do her job. "How are we playing this?"

I take a sip of my iced coffee, blinking. "Playing what?"

He leans into me and lowers his voice. "Am I the best friend? Boyfriend? Wedding date? What's my role here?"

His role? I pull back in confusion. "Uh, my best friend."

He draws in closer to me. "Just the best friend?"

"Just the best friend," I slowly repeat.

"Gotcha. If anything changes, let me know."

What the …?

"Do you want to act like you're someone else?" I draw out.

"No, I want to make sure you know I have your back and won't let anyone give you any shit. If they want to know why you don't have a boyfriend—which, from what you've told me, is a regular question from them—say it's me. I'm game." He tears open a bag of chips, snags one, and offers them to me.

I shake my head. "I can't lie to my family and say we're dating."

"Sure, you can. Think about it. If you change your mind, I'm all up for role-playing."

I chew on the edge of my straw. "I'm sure you're all for role-playing."

"Eh, it's usually not my kink, but I'll do it for you. I have your back if vultures come your way, talking shit." He tips his head down and takes a sip of my coffee while it's in my hand.

———

"Aw, Carolina brought her best friend as her date. How cute," Faye, my bitch-faced cousin, announces when we walk into the banquet room.

Dread clouds my mind when she steps in front of Rex and me, her irritating girl squad behind her. Her diarrhea-colored hair is pulled into a high ponytail, and she's wearing a white dress that hits her knees. Across that white dress is a sash that says, *Bride!*

How annoying.

Everyone here knows she's the bride, considering it's *her* wedding.

This hell wedding is a weekend affair. Tonight, we endure dinner. Tomorrow, we'll suffer through lunch and then the wedding.

I slapped Faye in the face when I was fourteen because she'd ripped apart my favorite book.

Got grounded for a month and my phone taken away.

It was worth it.

My parents added that I'd be grounded for the rest of my life if I touched her again. They said that in front of her, so Frightening Faye knew she could bully me more since being grounded for the rest of my life didn't sound like a party. Lucky for me, she moved away her freshman year.

Unlucky for me, she came back a week during the summers to visit my grandparents. One year, my parents demanded I allow her to tag along with me to Rex's house. She flirted with him the entire time and made fun of my one-piece bathing suit, so Rex kicked her out, making his mom drive her home. That was when I knew Rex would always have my back. He could've easily ditched me and hooked up with Faye, but he knew my history with her. Shoot, he hardly muttered a word to her with the exception of telling her to leave his damn house and never come back.

I stiffen, holding in a breath, while racking my brain for the perfect comeback.

"She brought her *boyfriend*," Rex abruptly corrects next to me. His arm wraps around my waist, and he pulls me in closer to him, my hip hitting his.

Faye's mouth drops open. Her eyes and finger ping back and forth between Rex and me ... between my apparent *boyfriend* and me. When she finally speaks, her words are choked out, "You two are—"

"Dating? In love? Sure fucking am," Rex says to her with no hesitation. He stares down at me, a tender smile spreading across his face. "We're much more than friends, but we do agree on one thing: we are fucking cute." His gaze turns nasty when he looks back at Faye. "I knew you'd be so happy for your cousin to find love. Maybe we'll invite you to our wedding." He makes a show of looking around the ballroom. "It'll probably be less stuffy than this shit, so it might not be your thing."

Oh my God.

I'm struggling to hold back not only my surprise, but also my laughter. *This* is why Rex mentioned pretending we're in a relationship. He knew Faye would give me shit for bringing him.

Faye stares at us, speechless, before stammering out words, "I, uh … need to find my fiancé."

"Good idea," Rex says, turning us away from her and capturing my hand in his. "I'm in desperate need of some alone time with my girlfriend."

Rex's grip is firm as he leads me out of the room and into a deserted hallway before releasing me.

I hold up my hands, my palms facing him. "*Whoa.* I thought we weren't playing the dating thing."

He tilts his head, as if he's studying me, and I do the same.

Faye's shock of us dating isn't surprising. Rex is the complete opposite of me. I'm wearing a black dress with a white collar, looking like Wednesday Addams, and my black-rimmed glasses. It was necessary for me to wear black in mourning of her husband losing his soul. I didn't shower before coming to the dinner, so my hair is half-straight, half-looking crazy.

Rex is wearing a black button-down shirt and dark jeans, his hair perfect even though he hasn't touched it since this morning.

"We did say that," he answers, shoving his hands into his pockets. "That changed. Fuck her. No way will I listen to her talk shit about you. She would've given you hell all weekend for being solo." His dark eyes level on me. "This weekend, you're my girlfriend."

"Uh ..." I draw out. "We have some issues with this game, *boyfriend*."

He arches a brow. "Which are?"

"First and foremost, we're sleeping in separate rooms."

"Easy fix," he says with a relaxed smile before it turns boyish. "I'm being a gentleman, respecting your 'rents. Your dad is a preacher. Of course we're not sleeping together." His grin moves from boyish to cocky. "I have motherfucking values, Carolina."

"They won't buy it." I shake my head and nervously walk circles around him. "This is so stupid."

He grabs my hand, spinning me around to face him. "We'll share a room then. It's not like we haven't shared a bed. Shit, I took your virginity."

I push his shoulder, feeling a deep blush ride up my cheeks, and force myself not to cover my face. "Oh my God! Shut up!" I frantically glance around the hallway, and my response comes out in a low hiss, "People can hear you!"

"We're dating, babe. They already assume we're fucking." He reaches out and runs his hand over my chin, causing me to shiver. "Now, come on, my sexy-ass girlfriend. We have a dinner to get to."

That's the first time he's brought up taking my virginity. I'm still shocked at myself for building up the courage to ask him that night. Like I told him, I didn't want to go to college, hauling around my V-card, yet I also had no interest in handing it over to a random guy.

I trusted Rex to be careful with me, to make me comfortable.

He knew I was a virgin and wouldn't make fun of me for my inexperience.

The best decision I ever made was letting Rex Lane take my virginity.

Well, the best decision for my vagina.

Not the best decision for my heart.

This rehearsal dinner is stuck up as fuck.

I come from money. Not trying to sound like a pretentious asshole, but my family is the wealthiest in Blue Beech. I've never acted as snobby as these people, and they're not nearly as rich as my family.

My family's money isn't my money, obviously. I never take advantage of that or run to them for exuberant amounts of cash. They paid for college, but when I decided to move into my own apartment, that was on me. I make most of my income from winning video game tournaments.

But no matter how much money I have had or will ever have, I'd never look down at people like they are—with the exception of Carolina's parents. Most of the people, including good ole Faye, are treating the servers like shit, complaining about the food, and as soon as one family member turns their back, someone is already talking shit about them.

No wonder Carolina didn't want to come.

They made a show when they realized they had to move around seating arrangements to make room for me.

"We didn't think she'd have a plus-one," Faye's mother said, her over-injected lips giving my new girlfriend a mocking smile.

Her family members are firing off question after question, as if trying to catch us on our lie. They're so desperate; it's sad. It's easy, playing this game because we know everything about each other. We've done so much boyfriend-girlfriend shit together even though we can never be boyfriend-girlfriend.

I can't cross that line because I can't lose her.

She's one of the most important people in my life.

The rehearsal dinner is in the banquet hall of the hotel we're staying in. It's also where we're having brunch in the morning, and the wedding will be held outside the hotel in the garden.

"That was dreadful," she mutters when dinner is finished and we head back to our rooms. "Thank God you came. I would've smothered myself with my napkin." She blows out a breath and loops her arm through mine. "We need to get out of here before they play another round of Twenty Questions. Swear to God, they were more interested in our love life than the bride and groom's."

Carolina isn't much of a touchy-feely person, except with me, which makes me feel so damn special. It took her a while to warm up to me and my charm. Now, she has no problem leaning into me, sticking her feet in my lap, and resting her head on my shoulder when she's tired and we're watching a movie.

Me, on the other hand? I started the whole arm-over-the-shoulders shit as soon we talked. Like she says, I have no boundaries when it comes to her—with the exception of *never, ever, ever* having sex with her again. That is the only boundary … and hurting her.

"Our love life, huh?" I ask, and she tucks her face into my chest, not wanting to have the conversation of me calling her out for her *love life* comment. "It's simple, why they paid more attention to us. The bride and groom are lame as fuck. No one cares about them."

She pulls back to playfully slap my stomach. "Rex! You're going to get us kicked out of the wedding."

We disconnect after stepping into the elevator, and I hit our floor number. Since her parents had already booked her room, I had to bribe the hotel manager to put me next to her.

"I don't think you'd have a problem with them booting us," I comment as the elevator doors close. I lean back against the wall and cross my arms, staring at her.

She looks gorgeous. It's always hard for me to keep my touches platonic, but it's fucking hell when she dresses up. Her dress hardly shows off any skin—and by hardly, I mean, the bottom of her legs, ankles, and arms. My cock twitches as I remember how perfect she looks under that dress. With every friendly touch I give her, there's not-so-clean thoughts behind it on my end. I'm proud of how strong I am for holding back.

At dinner, she pulled her black hair into a ponytail, showing off the neck I'd shoved my face in after I came inside her. All I thought about during the main course was how soft her skin would be as I kissed that neck … how she'd react to my lips on her.

She lights up every damn room she walks into, and I hate how much people give her shit for being her. She doesn't have a boyfriend because she's selective—*thank fuck*—and I respect that she's picky.

"True, *but* my parents would," she says, cutting me out of my thoughts.

She's right. Her parents are all about family and doing the right thing. They're also strict and expect Carolina to be perfect. That's one issue I have with them. Carolina was always stressed about school because they put so much pressure on her. She wasn't allowed to get a bad grade or miss homework because they were focused on her scoring a scholarship. She got a B on a paper once—a fucking *B*—and her parents lost their shit. She'd hung out with me the night before, and they blamed it on our friendship.

We shuffle out of the elevator when we hit our floor, and she digs through her clutch for her key card.

"Are you coming in and hanging out?" she asks while unlocking it.

"Only if you promise not to fall asleep in ten minutes."

She glances back at me as we walk into the room. "I can't make any promises. Stress makes me sleepy, and my stress meter is in the double red."

I flip on the light. "Stop being stressed then. Who gives a fuck what these people think?"

She sighs. "I know."

I snatch the extra key card lying on the desk. "I'm taking this."

She falls down onto the bed and drags her heels off her feet. "Huh?"

I hold up the card. "This is my copy." I open my wallet, pull out my extra key card, and drop it where hers was. "Here's my spare for you." I stick my new key into my pocket. "In case I need to get into your room or you need to get into mine."

"Gotcha." She jerks her head toward the bathroom. "Let me change first."

"Same. I'll be right back." I run to my room and change into gray sweats and a tee.

When I return to her room, she's walking out of the bathroom, wearing similar sweats and an oversize tee with our high school's logo on it.

Technically, they're *my* pajamas since both items used to belong to me. Swear to God, every time she stays over, another piece of my clothing goes missing. My attempts at getting them back have stopped because I never win.

I grin. "I'm going to have to start charging you for your theft," I say, falling down onto her bed, lying on my side, and holding my head up with my elbow. I might complain, but secretly, I love seeing her in my clothes.

She rolls her eyes. "Yeah, right." She tugs at the bottom of my shirt. "They don't make women's clothes this comfy. Therefore, your clothes are my clothes."

She makes herself comfortable next to me, her back against the headboard, and turns on the TV to *Live PD*.

It's our favorite show.

Twenty minutes later, Carolina is knocked out.

I chuckle to myself and carefully slide off the bed, not wanting to wake her. I throw the covers over her, kiss her forehead, and then go back to my room. As soon as I walk in, my phone rings.

"Hello?" I answer.

"Hey, little bro," Sierra, my older sister, says on the other line. "Are you busy tomorrow? I think my computer is on crack, and it needs you to take it to rehab. I can't access any of my clients' files."

"Sorry, sis, but I'm in Texas with Carolina all weekend," I reply.

"Oh, I like," she gushes.

Everyone in my family is Team Rex and Carolina Need to Date. There isn't one person who dislikes her. In fact, sometimes, I think they like her better than me.

"Shut up," I grumble.

My grumpiness doesn't faze her.

"What are you doing? Couples retreat?"

"Piss off. She had a family wedding and didn't want to go alone."

"I wish you two would start dating. You pretty much already act like husband and wife; it'd just have more *benefits*."

I make a gagging noise. "Gross. You're my sister."

She laughs.

I yawn. "I'm wiped. I'll look at your computer when I get home."

We say our good nights, and I notice a text from the chick I've been hanging out with lately.

I ignore it.

Ever since Carolina came to me, heartbroken, it's been hard for me to be around other women. I always want to make sure she's okay. I hate seeing her hurt, and it kills me when I think about her falling for a complete scumbag who took advantage of her.

I hate how much I care about her but can't imagine her not being in my life.

I love Carolina Adams, and there's nothing I can do about it because I wouldn't survive losing her.

CHAPTER NINE

Rex isn't answering my calls.

If he overslept, I'm kicking his ass.

All eyes have been on us since his relationship announcement. If we're late, there will no doubt be more gossip. I brainstorm on possible excuses for our tardiness.

We overslept.

Had wild morning sex.

Got it on in the shower.

Okay, I need to stop with the sex cop-outs.

Overslept it is.

It's boring but convincing.

Rex is a night owl and works on his video games at night. Players are most active at night, and he chats with the gamers testing his game. Last night after dinner, I set the alarm on his phone, so he wouldn't oversleep, but it wouldn't surprise me if he slept through it.

I call him again.

No answer.

I slide on my heels.

Call him again.

No answer.

I grab my clutch and check my reflection in the mirror. I woke up early to give myself enough time to get ready for brunch before the wedding. My hair is straightened and parted down the middle. I'm wearing my contacts, and I did my makeup. My dress and heels are black again.

I take both key cards from the dresser and head to Rex's room. After banging on the door six times with no answer, I shrug, unlock the door, and let myself in.

"You'd better wake your butt up!" I shout before lowering my voice in case any of his room neighbors are family. "No way am I facing these people alone, *especially* before food and coffee are in my system!"

The door slams shut behind me. His bed is empty, the blankets and sheets rustled, and I spot his phone charging on the nightstand. I toss my clutch onto the bed and move to the bathroom when I hear the shower running. The door is ajar, and just as I'm about to yell at him to hurry it up, I freeze. My mouth drops open, my fingers flying to my parted lips, and I stumble back.

Oh my freaking God.

My heart thrashes against my chest at the sight.

A slight fog is steamed over the glass shower door, but I see him. I fixate on the lean, powerful body as water cascades down his every muscle. Rex isn't only showering. No, his hand is wrapped around his hard cock, lazily stroking it. When his fingers reach the head, he turns his grip while releasing a deep, guttural groan. His free hand is flattened against the tiled shower wall, and his head is tipped down, concentrated on his stroking.

It's the hottest thing I've ever seen.

My fingers move from my lips to my throat, caressing it.

I wish I could join him.

I smack myself in the forehead.

That can't happen, Carolina.

My nipples ache when his hand speeds up and his moans release in harsh pants. I press my thighs together, a heavy throb hitting me, and my fingertips tingle with the need to slide into my panties. Rex is so focused on his pleasure; maybe he wouldn't notice me pleasuring myself back.

I smack myself in the forehead again to knock some sense into me.

No! Bad Carolina!

No touching yourself while your best friend jacks off.

Watching him is terrible enough.

Invasion of privacy much?

What do I do?

Run out of here?

Yes. Walk away!

My heart tightens when his head drops back, and he moans out his release. His next moan snaps me out of my *Rex is jacking off in front of me* trance. I gain control of my thoughts, and my breathing is labored as I scurry to the bed. I can't stop myself from rubbing my thighs together, wishing I could run to my room and relieve myself.

I've always been attracted to Rex.

I've always wanted him.

I've never wanted him as bad as this though.

I need to pull myself together and not act like I watched him jerk off when he comes out.

Cool. Calm. Collected.

My hands shake when I collect my phone from my clutch and pretend to concentrate on the screen, not bothering to unlock it, when the shower turns off.

"Jesus, Carolina!" Rex bursts out when he strides into the bedroom. "You scared the shit out of me."

He's wearing only a towel that covers his bottom half. Water drips down his six-pack, and my eyes close in on the V that trails down to the cock I was stalking seconds ago.

My pulse races, and there's no doubt my cheeks are flushed red.

Do not look like you were just watching him jack off in the shower.

I chew on my lip and can't look him in the eye. "Uh ..." I scramble for words, and they come out between rapid breaths. "I came to wake you up. I just got here. I sat down, haven't moved from this spot. Didn't realize you were in the shower ... most definitely didn't see anything." I pat the bed with shaking fingers. "I've been right here, on my phone, waiting for you to get out. I didn't want to be rude and interrupt your shower. You know how rude shower interruptions are?"

He eyeballs me strangely. "What's up with you? Why are you rambling?"

He's as calm as a cucumber. The worry he caught me watching him fades. All I need to do now is act natural, so he doesn't suspect his best friend is a creep.

Now that I'm in the clear, my goal is erasing the memory of him in the shower from my mind.

Yeah, probably not happening.

My gaze flicks to his, and I fidget with my ring. "I'm a rambler. You know this."

"True, but only when you're nervous," he replies with a pointed look.

"I'm nervous about this stupid wedding."

He rakes his hand through his damp hair and nods, accepting my excuse. "Let me get dressed. I'll be ready in fifteen."

He steps forward to kiss me on top of my head, and I nearly lose my shit. Since I'm sitting, his barely covered junk is smack dab in front of my face. My mouth waters. When we had sex, I never looked at his cock. If I had *seen* the size, I would've chickened out.

I hold in a breath when he pulls back, and my eyes follow him as he travels across the room. He gathers his suit from the closet and takes it to the bathroom. Thoughts of him naked in there stay in my mind, causing me to blush.

Will I always think about him naked now?

There's no better approach to get my mind out of the gutter than to talk to my parents. I send my mom a text, saying we'll be down in twenty minutes and to save us two seats. Rex returning in his suit, looking as hot as ever, doesn't help control my desire for him. The black suit is tailored to his body. I smile. I told him I was doing all black, and he matched me.

Rex throws his arm over my shoulders. "Let's do this."

My voice is raspy when I reply, "Let's do this."

The same hand he was stroking his cock with finds my hand, and my cheeks change from a blush to bright red.

———

"I don't believe it," my cousin, Lindsay, sneers after cornering me in the restroom.

I hit the cousin jackpot because Lindsay is just as evil as Faye. They're cousin besties. At least with Faye, I only have to see her here. Lindsay lives in Blue Beech. She's two years younger than me and gorgeous, but her attitude makes her hideous. I do my best to avoid her. Some people love living in a small town because their family is there.

Me? Not so much.

Don't get me wrong. I love my parents and sister.

And my grams—minus the whole constantly-asking-why-I'm-single thing.

That's pretty much it.

"What are you talking about?" I ask even though I have an inkling where this is going.

"I don't believe you are *dating* Rex," she practically snarls. "Unless it's been for, like, ten minutes, you're lying. He was having sleepovers with my roommate recently." She tilts her head to the side, a phony smile working over her lips. "There was *no* mention of a girlfriend."

Ugh. I have to deal with this before they've even delivered brunch to the table?

"It's new," I answer, proud of how relaxed I sound. "I know all about his past sleepovers with your roomie. It was *twice,* five months ago, when we weren't dating." I tilt my head to the side, imitating her earlier position.

She snorts. "Whatever. Everyone knows Rex will do anything for you, like, say, *pretend* to be your boyfriend because you can't get one yourself."

It's not that I *can't* get a boyfriend. Guys ask me out, but they're never anyone I see myself sharing a future with.

Why waste my time?

I clench my fists. *My parents can't ground me for smacking chicks now.*

"Piss off," I snarl. "Go back to the guy you're playing side-chick with while he shares a bed with his wife every night."

Normally, I'm not a snotty bitch, but my cousins bring out the best in me.

I push past her, leave the restroom, and order a mimosa as soon as I sit down.

Time to get buzzed in celebration of Faye's love.

CHAPTER TEN

I squeeze Carolina's thigh in an attempt to stop her laughter—or at least calm it down—and I tilt my head down to whisper in her ear, "Carolina."

She snorts between laughs. "They seriously did *not* just call each other their pet names in their vows." She shoves her face into my neck to mask her giggles. "I can't. Oh my God, I can't."

"Shh …" I repeat.

Scowls turn in our direction.

"*And* terrible pet names at that," she adds.

Goose bumps rise along my skin when her wet lips brush against my neck.

"Do me a favor." She draws back to peek up at me. "If you ever hear me call a boyfriend Tubba Wubba, I give you permission to drown me in your parents' pool."

It's a struggle to hold back my chuckles. "You're going to get us kicked out."

Disapproving looks come from the people in our row, and I reply with an apologetic one.

"Good." Carolina lowers her voice. "This wedding is lame, and the Tubba Wubba newlyweds need their alone time."

She's not wrong. This wedding has been a complete joke. The

bride's walk down the aisle was a fifteen-minute affair, and their vows have been a good twenty minutes. How no one is sleeping is beyond me.

"How many mimosas have you had?" I ask.

"Not enough to let me forget those god-awful vows," she answers around a hiccup.

I grab her neck when she laughs louder and pull her face against my chest again. "I can't take you anywhere."

I've missed goofy Carolina.

She glances up at me after getting a handle on herself and taps my chest. "Technically, I brought you."

"Fine, I can't tag along with you anywhere."

While everybody is focused on the wedding, we're in our own little world.

Good thing we sat in the back.

———

Carolina talks a lot of shit about me flirting when she does a fair share of it herself.

Only she doesn't realize she's doing it.

Call me selfish, but I've scared off every friend who's shown interest in her.

They don't deserve her.

I left her alone for five minutes to get our drinks, and some lame dick has stolen my chair. A lame dick sporting an ill-fitting gray striped suit like he's some D-list mob boss.

I place our drinks in front of him on the table and wrap my arms around Carolina's shoulders from behind while she sits in her chair. "Hey, baby."

She smiles up at me. "Hi."

I hold my hand out for Lame Dick to shake and refrain from ripping it off his fucking arm when he does. "I'm Rex, her boyfriend."

Lame Dick's eyes widen. "Ah, dude, I didn't know."

He knew.

He's been eye-fucking her all day, and since Carolina is my girl-friend this weekend, I've touched her and acted like her boyfriend.

"Now, you do." My attention moves to Carolina as I offer her my hand. "Dance with me."

She grins. "Oh, I guess."

I pull her to her feet and turn her around, so we're facing each other as soon as we hit the dance floor. I drag her close, my palms resting against the base of her back. Turns out, she wasn't drunk on mimosas. She was only tipsy, and I made her suck down water as soon as the wedding ceremony ended. Her tipsiness has nearly worn off.

My chest constricts as I stare down at her and release what's been on the tip of my tongue all day. "You're the most gorgeous girl here."

She's wearing her contacts, showing off her round brown eyes. Her black dress hugs every curve of her body, and curves is something Carolina has plenty of. Her heels don't bring her near to my height. She's short, which I love because it's easy to drag her head into my chest and kiss the top of her head.

It's one of my favorite things to do.

No matter what, I love my hands on her—whether it's an arm around the shoulders or hugging her face into my chest. I'm happy as hell that, on this trip, I get to do more than a simple arm draped around the shoulders, and I've been taking full advantage of that. Tonight, I'm being as handsy as I want.

I drop a hand to her waist, drawing her closer, and my other goes to her hand, weaving our fingers together as we dance.

She laughs when a sappy country song plays. "You have to say that. You're my best friend."

"And for the time being, your *boyfriend*," I correct. "I don't have to say that either. It's the truth. If I were at the singles table and looking for a girl to corrupt, I would've done what the douche bag wearing the lame suit did and came to your table to hit on you."

Her hand briefly leaves mine when she slaps my shoulder. "He was harmless."

I raise a brow. "He wasn't harmless. He was talking to *my* girlfriend."

"I wasn't interested in him." She wraps her arms around my neck, resting them on my shoulders, and laughs again—this time louder. "I don't even know *how* to flirt."

She tips her head forward, her eyes meeting mine, and I brush my lips against her forehead.

"Oh, babe," I say around a chuckle, "you most definitely know how to flirt. You just don't realize you're flirting."

She rolls her eyes. "Whatever."

"You do." My grip tightens on her hips. "When you laugh at something someone says, your face is bright and shows how real you are. When you speak, you allow every emotion to pour out of you. Your amazing heart shows in every move you make, and someone would be dumb not to want that in their life." I run my hands up and down her waist, and she shivers beneath my fingers. "I haven't seen you flirt much, but I know when you're doing it."

Lies. She's flirted with me plenty of times, but I haven't seen her do it much with other guys.

"My flirt game sucks," she mutters.

Heat creeps up my neck as she strokes the back of it with her fingers.

"Thank you for coming," she says, her voice filled with tenderness. "I would've been miserable without you."

I smile. "It's my best-friend duty. You need me? I'm there."

She laughs. "What's my best-friend duty?"

I arch a brow, considering my options. "Hmm … I'll have to get back to you on that."

"Oh God," she groans. "It's going to be video games, isn't it?"

"Possibly." I squeeze her hips. "You love my video games."

She grins up at me. "I love that you named the best woman character Carolina."

"I actually changed that. You're now the big, bad villain."

She pinches the back of my neck, and I jerk forward.

"Whatever." Her fingers rub the spot she pinched. "I thank the gods that you tried to bribe me that day. I would've been sitting miserable in the corner."

"I thank the gods you gave me shit and allowed me to corrupt you."

The music stops, and I dip her back.

"Thanks for the dance, Tubba Wubba."

She narrows her eyes at me when I drag her back up. "I'm poisoning your cookies, FYI."

———

My elbow is grabbed on my way back to Carolina after a restroom break.

"Hey, handsome," a high-pitched voice purrs—trying and desperately failing at being seductive.

Lindsay, a girl from school *and* another one of Carolina's cousins, stands in front of me.

Poor Carolina was blessed with some demon-ass family members.

Lindsay brushes a strand of brown hair behind her ear and thrusts her chest forward. "It's so sweet of you to come with Carolina and play her date."

I pluck her fingers off me as if she has Ebola and glare at her. "No, I came because I'm *dating* Carolina. No playing here."

She rolls her eyes. "*Please.* Everyone knows you'll do anything for her—be her prom date, take her on pity dates, *fake* being in a relationship with her—for God knows what reason."

My jaw clenches. "I take her out on dates because I love her, not for fucking pity."

"You play the part *so well,*" she throws back, "yet not once have you kissed her … not on the lips at least." With this, she puckers her lips and kicks out her foot, showing her bare leg through the slit of her green dress. "Not to mention, you were in my roommate's bed not too long ago. Did you forget about that? Either you were cheating on Carolina *or,* as I suspect, you're lying so that she doesn't look pitiful, hence the pity date."

"Your roommate was more of a pity date than Carolina will ever be," I snarl, my nostrils flaring.

How dare she call Carolina a fucking pity.

"As for you," I go on, "you've flirted with me *how many times* and haven't managed to snag yourself a pity date?"

I hate being a dick, but fuck this.

Fuck them for treating Carolina like shit when she has a heart of gold. When Lindsay's mother was down with shingles for a month, Carolina put together a fundraiser dinner for her. She also made cookies for them countless times and dropped them off at her house.

Scorn passes over Lindsay's face, and just as she's about to speak, my name being called cuts her off.

"Hey! Rex!"

I glance back to find Carolina's father, Rick, along with two other men approaching me.

Shit!

I scan the room for Carolina and grind my teeth when I spot the group of women circled around her. All conversation is aimed in her direction, and my body turns rigid when she gulps down a glass of champagne in one swig.

Goddamn it!

Carolina is a terrible drinker.

She has a low tolerance and doesn't know her limit.

Shockingly, Carolina's parents haven't interrogated her about our dating lie, although she hasn't spent much alone time with them. No doubt they'll drill her with questions when they have her by herself.

"What do you think, Rex?"

I'm broken away from my Carolina trance when the man next to me claps.

"Huh?" I ask, sweeping my attention over to the men.

"I asked your thoughts on violence in video games." The man gestures to Rick. "He said you develop video games."

"I don't have much to say on that matter," I answer with annoyance while searching the room for Carolina when I don't see her with the women anymore.

I spot her at the bar in the corner of the room, taking a shot, and the bartender is pouring another. I don't give them another word before turning on my heel and speed-walking in her direction. Before I get the chance to confiscate her next shot, she knocks it back.

"Hey, babe," I greet, sliding my arms around her waist.

"Hey," she half-slurs, signaling to the bartender for another.

I hold up my hand, stopping him. "She's good, bro."

"She's not, *bro*," she corrects with an eye roll. "Make it a double." Her palm slaps the counter. "And get my friend one—sorry, my *boyfriend* one." She flicks her hand in the air. "Not a double for him. His job is to take care of me tonight, and one needs to be sober to do that."

I clutch her elbow and tug her away from the bar, and she's talking shit as I walk us toward the exit.

"How much have you had to drink?" I question, swinging her around to face me.

She holds two fingers apart from each other and squints one eye to focus on them. "Just a *wee* bit."

"How much is a *wee* bit?"

She wrinkles her nose, her hand dropping to her side. "I lost count at the third glass of champagne and second shot of ..." Her finger goes to her lower lip, and she clicks her tongue against the roof of her mouth. "Vodka maybe? It was something in a glass."

"Jesus," I hiss. "I leave you alone for five minutes."

"Wrong. You left me alone for *fifteen* ... with the sharks." The *sharks* are the overbearing women in her family.

I raise my arms, apology spilling over my face. "I was cornered on my way back!"

"People already think we're lying about being together. Let's just prove them right." Carolina also gets snarky when she drinks.

I reach out my hand. "Come on. Let's go to your room."

She smacks it away. "Let's get *me* back to the bar, and *you* can go back to chatting with my cousin."

Perfect. She saw me talking to Lindsay.

"We're not doing this here." I grip her hand, make sure she's steady, and weave us through the people.

"Bye, Rex! Call me sometime!"

Carolina halts at Lindsay's farewell. Knowing this might be a shit-show, I attempt to pull her away, but Carolina stands firm.

Lindsay is dumb enough to continue taunting Carolina, and she chirps out her words. "It was *so* nice seeing you and catching up. Want to hang out tomorrow? Grab breakfast?"

"Fuck you," Carolina snarls, startling everyone. She points at me while holding strong eye contact with Lindsay. "You look dumb, hitting on a guy who's coming to *my* room. He might've entertained your corner conversation for five minutes, but he entertains *my bed*." She holds her middle finger up. "I win."

I bite back my laughter. "Jesus, let's get you out of here."

Thankfully, she allows me to take her to the elevator, and her eyes are narrowed at me the entire ride. When we hit our floor, I take her key from my pocket and unlock the door.

"Entertain your bed, huh?" I ask as soon as we walk into the room and tilt my head toward the bed. "Is this the bed I'm doing that in?"

She falls back against the mattress and starts taking her heels off, tossing them across the room. "I have no idea what I meant, but it sounded better in my head."

"It sounded like you told her I was going to fuck you in that bed of yours." My cock hardens at the thought.

"I have no regrets. We're dating, so it's assumed we're banging, considering you're … well, *you*."

"I won't take that as an insult." I clap my hands and rub them together. "Where are your pajamas?"

Her head jerks toward the dresser. "Folded in that thing."

"Of course they are, you organized freak, you."

"Hey," she whines. "An organized life is a happy life." She releases a heavy sigh. "When you were in the restroom, they asked me why I dropped out of school in sixteen different ways." All the playfulness and snark in her tone has dissolved, sadness clouding her features.

"What'd you say?"

She shuts her eyes, a slow breath releasing from her chest. "My mind went blank. I might've said something about joining the circus."

I stare at her in regret. "I'll never leave you with those vultures again. Promise."

"I can handle myself."

"Never said you couldn't, but tonight, you chose alcohol to help you. Replace me with alcohol next time, okay?" *Replace me with alcohol every time.*

She salutes me, a glimmer of a smile on her lips. "Got it, captain."

I sift through her drawer, and my heart jolts as I ease out an unfamiliar item. "Now, my sweet Carolina, I thought I'd seen all your pajamas. Turns out, you've been hiding these." I hold the nearly see-through blue lacy teddy in the air.

A blush covers her face before she buries it in her hands. "You're not supposed to see that! It's for bedroom eyes only!"

I hold it out, inspecting it. "Next time you spend the night, your ass had better be wearing this."

"Not happening." Her hands leave her face, and she shakes her head. "It's uncomfortable and meant to be quickly taken off. Then, it stays off."

I lean back against the dresser, crossing my ankles, and lift the teddy in the air. "Why'd you bring it? *Who* did you plan to wear it for ... or take it off for?" My mouth turns dry at my question.

Did she plan on hooking up with someone here?

She sucks on her lower lip. "I don't know ... in case I met someone. I didn't plan for you to play my boyfriend."

I hold a finger up. "Stop right there, young lady. You're either going to make me jealous or have my imagination running wild." *Too late.* I run my fingers over the lace while my mind starts racing of thoughts in her wearing this teddy.

She grabs a pillow and throws it at me. "Whatever. You'd see me as one of your guy friends wearing that."

"You've never been more wrong in your life," I grumble around a gulp after dodging the pillow.

"What if I wear it now?"

I snort. "Funny."

"I'm serious."

"You're drunk."

"Isn't that what a *girlfriend* would do? And this weekend, I'm your *girlfriend*." Challenge spills along her words. "Oh, wait. You can't be my boyfriend if you were screwing Lindsay's roommate not too long ago."

I shove the teddy back into one drawer and open the one underneath it, finding a pair of sweats and a white tank top. "That's why you're pissed?"

"Duh. My date has been screwing other women."

"Screwed. Haven't touched her roommate in months, *and* I'm not touching anyone here. Since when do you believe your cousins? What the hell?"

"Forget it," she huffs out.

I set her pajamas on the edge of the bed and rest my knee next to them, halfway crawling up the mattress until our faces are only inches apart. Cupping hers with both my hands, I run my thumb over her soft, freckle-kissed cheek and then pull myself up. "Now, stand and get your pajamas on."

"Fine," she whines, sliding off the bed, "but I need you to unzip me."

A shiver runs up my spine when I stand behind her and stare at the zipper running down the back of her dress. The room turns silent; the only sound I hear is my raging heartbeat. My fingers are tense when I grab the zipper of her dress, dragging it down, and the dress pools around her feet in what seems like slow motion. I draw in a breath, unable to stop myself from taking her in.

Jesus.

Standing in front of me is my best friend … wearing only a nude-colored thong. Her skin warms at my touch as I stupidly and bravely brush my fingers along her waist. Her breathing shudders, and she grinds back into me, rubbing her ass against the erection I shouldn't have.

"Rex," she whispers.

I fight with myself on why I'm being such an idiot when I skim my hand along the bottom of her bare breast. *Why the hell wasn't she wearing a bra?* Good thing I didn't know, or it's all I would've thought about tonight.

She tilts her head to the side. "My necklace."

As my fingers stroke the bottom of her breast, I use my other hand to sweep her hair off her shoulder and unclasp the pearl necklace I bought her for Christmas. Our connection stays when I carefully set the necklace onto the bed. Never has my heart pounded so intensely when I replace my hand resting on her neck with my lips, skimming them along her soft skin.

"Tell me to stop," I hiss. "Fuck, Lina. Tell me."

CHAPTER ELEVEN
CAROLINA

"*Tell me to stop. Fuck, Lina. Tell me.*"

My heart races at Rex's pleas, but I'm selfish. That word isn't leaving my lips tonight. I don't want him to stop. I want more—of his touch, of his lips, of everything that is him. The deep breaths pulling from his chest and his erection pressing against my back confirm I'm not alone in my desire.

His lips linger at the curve of my neck while he waits for me to push him away, to say *no*. When his hand grazes the underside of my breast again, I can't stop myself from grinding my ass against him.

Big mistake.

Huge.

All this in Julia Roberts's voice.

It's as if my move wakes his restraint and slaps him in the face with reality.

His hands drop from my body as if I'd caught fire, and he jerks away, fleeing to the other side of the room. I glance back over my shoulder to find him resting against the dresser, agony lining his features, and he presses a fist against his lips.

"Shit, Carolina," he finally chokes out. "I'm so damn sorry."

A brief silence passes, as if we're both battling our next move. My back stays to him while I stand by the bed. Rejection doesn't exactly make a girl want to put her boobs on display. He already has a view of my bare butt.

My gaze sharpens when he slowly eases my way and swipes the tee off the bed. A brief pause happens before he advances a step farther. I can't stop myself from laughing when he slips the shirt over my head, and as soon as the job is done, he promptly returns to his side of the room. When I turn around, there's no missing the anguish on his face.

He frowns, dragging a hand through his thick hair, and releases a long breath of frustration. "That wasn't cool. I'm sorry."

I shift from one foot to the other, pulling at the bottom of the shirt while chewing on my lower lip. "You have nothing to be sorry about, Rex." Heat creeps up my cheeks. "In fact, I highly encourage you to keep touching me. *Don't* stop."

He gapes at me. "You're drunk. Not happening."

"I'm not drunk. I'm tipsy." I smirk. "It won't be the first time I've had tipsy sex."

His upper lip snarls, and his words leave in a deep hiss. "Don't even think about going on about that shit." His tone hardens. "Conversation change, motherfucking pronto."

I gesture down my body. "I'm standing upright with no assistance from you, nor am I slurring my words or puking my guts out. I'm not drunk." To further prove my point, I hold a leg up, standing on only one while doing my best to balance myself, before repeating it with the other leg. I end my move with a ta-da gesture.

My awesome skill doesn't change his mind.

"I'm not ruining us by having sex." He rubs the nape of his neck while cursing under his breath.

"Just like with my virginity, we'll act like it never happened," I argue.

Why do I suddenly want this so much?

Is it because I spied on him while he jerked off, and I can't stop seeing it in my mind?

Or because I'm having such a good time with the boyfriend-girlfriend game we're playing, and I want it in real life?

Is it the alcohol giving me the bravery?

I'd say a mix of the three.

He stepped up and played boyfriend.

Defended me.

I love and want Rex for all those reasons and more.

Who cares if it'll change our relationship?

It might even make it stronger.

"We're not teenagers," he fires back. "There's no acting like it didn't happen. Shit has changed, and shit *will* change for the worse if we cross that line. I guarantee it."

I pout my lips. "*Please.* I promise, no changing us."

Rex has always had a weakness for my whining.

"No." His voice is stern as he pinches the bridge of his nose. "Come on. Let's get your pajamas on, so you can get some sleep. You're going to feel like shit in the morning."

Nope.

I was taught not to give up so easily.

I cross my arms. "I need a shower."

He blinks. "Excuse me?"

"I need a shower."

"Take a shower then."

"Since I'm so *drunk*, I probably need your help." My imagination flickers to watching him in the shower earlier, and my skin tingles at the thought of us sharing one.

"Shower in the morning when you're sober."

"You can stop telling me what to do now." I plow my hands into my hair before dragging the strands out. "I need to wash this hairspray out."

"Stick your head in the sink and wash it out."

"Um, negative. I might drown."

He groans. "Fine."

I grin.

He shifts to the side, making room so I can pass him, and I peek back to check that he's following me and not making a run for it.

Let him run.

I have a key to his room, and I'll just take a shower in his bathroom.

See how much he likes the idea of switching keys then.

He trails behind me … looking as though he's on the way to a torture chamber instead of a fun shower.

That's awesome.

I frown, my stomach twisting, and stop in my tracks, causing him to trip into me.

What if he truly doesn't want to sleep with me?

What if he's not attracted to me like that, and he's using our friendship as a cop-out, as a vagina block?

Oh my God.

There's no doubt I was a sucky lay when we banged, but you can't blame a girl. *I was a virgin!*

He should understand I was a sex newbie, but maybe he thinks I'll lie there like a boring starfish again.

But what the heck? I was nervous!

Surely, he's taken that into account of my suckiness.

He grabs my waist before either of us face-plants, pushes me into the bathroom, and remains in the doorway—displeasure on his face. His eyes are everywhere but on me when I pull my shirt over my head and drop it to the tiled floor. My nipples harden at my sudden nakedness. I slide down my panties, curious where this courage is coming from. His eyes stay pinned to the ceiling as if he were waiting for it to collapse on us.

I open the shower door while frowning at him for not offering the attention I'm seeking. I clear my throat and bend down to turn on the water, but *nothing.*

The ceiling is apparently more exciting than my naked body.

What does a girl have to do to get ogled around here?

"Uh … can you help me inside?" I ask.

His dark eyes *finally* cut to me, and he frowns while taking in my naked body. "It's best you shower tomorrow."

"Nope," I quip before holding out my hand and wiggling it. "Help, please and thank you."

He takes two steps forward, erasing the distance between us, catches my hand, and assists me in the shower. My shoulders relax when the warm water hits my skin. I tilt my head back, allowing the water to stream down my face. When I'm good and soaked, I wipe the water from my face, smooth back my hair, and stare at him in expectation—ready for him to join me.

The door is cracked, and he's standing outside it. His head is tipped down, his focus now on his feet, and him wearing his suit is a sure sign he's not shower ready.

"Seriously?" I groan. "How are you going to help me shower from *out there?*"

He lifts his gaze, but it still doesn't roam over my body. "You asked for help. Not for me to join you."

Don't two and two go together?

"I wasn't aware clarification was necessary." I clear my throat and deepen my voice. "This is a formal invitation for you, Rex Lane, to join me for a warm shower. Snacks will be provided, and you get a complimentary wash."

"Invitation respectively declined."

"You can't stand there with the door open!"

"Tell me when you need help, and I'll stick my hand in the shower." He shrugs. "Simple."

"*Okay,* Stretch Armstrong, that's absurd."

"Not absurd. Smart."

"All right then. I need help."

When he sticks his hand into the shower, I grab it and pull his body halfway in with me. Before he gets the opportunity to yank back, I capture his ear with two fingers.

"Get your butt in this shower right now, Rex Peyton Lane!"

This is the most awkward conversation we've ever had.

Hell, this is the most awkward conversation I've had, period.

He attempts to pull away, but I tighten my ear-hold.

"Are you seriously grabbing my damn ear right now, Carolina? This is best-friend abuse!"

"Absolutely." I press my nails into his skin before releasing him. "Now, get your butt in here. You're letting all the cold air in, and next time, I'll pinch something more sensitive than an ear."

He shakes his head, his voice strained. "I can't do that."

"You have two feet. Yes, you can."

He signals to my body. "Are you serious? You, in there, naked and wet in front of me, and you expect me to keep my hands to myself?" He repeatedly shakes his head. "I'm not taking any chances."

I grin, proud of myself.

Seduction plan working.

One point, Carolina.

"I need help with my hair, and I'm not getting out of this shower until you do it."

He's as stunned as I am that I'm being this bold.

Champagne and not being miserable at the singles table gives me courage, I see.

"Fine."

He shoves off his jacket, discards his tie, and plucks off his shoes, one by one, before removing his socks. I stand there, unmoving and shivering while he rolls his pants up.

"Scoot over," he instructs.

"Seriously?" I ask, falling back a step when his large body joins me —him wearing his pants and white button-up. "Your clothes will be soaked."

He shuts the shower door, deep breaths expelling from his muscular chest, while we stand inches apart. "If these clothes come off, something will happen that shouldn't. This way"—he signals down his body—"there's a barrier between us, and my cock will stay to himself."

I frown and slump my shoulders. "Will something happening between us be *that* stupid?"

"Yes." There's no hesitation in his answer.

"Why?" I gulp, terrified of hearing his response.

I should've never fought for this shower party.

"You aren't someone who has sex just to have sex … only for the pleasure."

I've never seen his face or heard his tone so gentle as he continues, "It's not in your heart, in your soul, to have random sex. You want a relationship, and that's something I can't do because I'll fuck it up." His eyes squeeze shut, as if his words pained him.

"Rex," I whisper, "you're a good guy. You don't know what you're capable of. How can you knock commitment without trying it first?"

Yes, ladies and gentlemen, this convo is happening in the shower.

Me totally naked.

Him fully dressed.

His eyes drink in my face, and he presses his icy palms to my cheeks, cradling my face. If we weren't standing so close, I wouldn't make out his words. "I'm a good guy as a friend. In a relationship, not so much."

My heart aches at the pain on his face. "You don't know that."

He shakes his head. "I refuse to lose you for my stupidity. You mean too much to me. You're the first person I talk to when I wake up and the last person I talk to before I go to sleep. I called you before anyone when I got my game offer—before my family. I want to spend every damn minute with you I can. If I touched you, if I fucked you, and screw everything up—which I would—I wouldn't have that anymore. If you were some random chick, I wouldn't hold back, but I am because I love you. I hold myself back day after fucking day because I will never, ever in my goddamn life fucking hurt you."

I nod as tears slip down my cheeks alongside the water. "Okay. I'm sorry."

His lips brush the top of my head. "Nothing to be sorry about." He chuckles. "Now, turn around, so I can wash your hair, you pain in my ass."

I can't help but laugh while doing what he instructed.

"Help a guy out here," he comments from behind me. "There are four bottles of different shit in here. Which one's shampoo?"

My shoulders shake when I laugh again before handing him the shampoo.

"Mmm … this shit smells good. I'm jacking it for my next shower."

My knees weaken at the mention of him taking another shower. He massages the shampoo through my hair better than my hairdresser, and as the sound of water falling takes over the air, shame grips me. I was unfair to push him into the position I did.

"You're on your own with the body washing," he says after rinsing out my hair. "Since you're only *tipsy*, I think you can handle it."

I grab the washcloth from him, cleaning myself off, and then shriek at the sudden coldness. When I twist round, he's walking out of the shower. His clothes are dripping wet, and he snags a towel from the hook, opening it wide. Carefully, I step out of the shower, and he drapes the towel around my shivering body, drying me and being careful not to touch anything over PG-rated.

"Will you at least stay with me tonight?" I whisper as he slips my shirt back over my head before releasing the towel.

The shirt reaches my knees, and he doesn't get any glimpses of my goods.

Not that I didn't have them on display earlier.

He awkwardly wraps the towel around my hair, doing a terrible job, but I'll give him an A for effort. "Only if you keep your hands to yourself, tipsy shower girl."

I feign annoyance with a huff. "All right."

He exits the bathroom, comes back with my pajama pants, and hands them to me. When we return to the room, I hop onto the bed while he starts taking off his clothes.

"Oh, so *now*, you want to get naked," I comment, unwrapping the towel from my hair and licking my lips as his shirt falls from his broad shoulders.

He drops his pants, wearing only his boxer briefs, and then scans the room.

"You should've thought that through," I remark. "Feel free to wear the teddy you found earlier."

He chuckles. "I'm certain there're sweats of mine somewhere in here." He starts rummaging through the drawers before finding my favorite pair of his sweatpants and turning toward the bathroom.

"Wait!" I toss him the towel to take back with him and then make myself comfortable in bed as he disappears.

"You're going to feel like shit tomorrow," he says, walking back in before joining me in bed.

Facts.

I twist on my side, scoot closer, and rest my head on his shoulder. "I know, and you're going to take care of me."

He blows out a long, exaggerated breath. "Fine, but I want *two* batches of cookies when we get home."

I pat his chest as my heart warms. "I love you, best friend."

He swings his arm around me. "And I love you."

How can Rex think he'd be such a horrible boyfriend when he's been the best friend a girl could ask for?

He takes care of me, makes me feel special, and would do anything for me. He's an amazing man, and from what I experienced this weekend, he would be an amazing boyfriend.

I sigh. *One of these days, he'll realize that.*

He'll realize it with another girl and leave me in the dust.

Unless ... I become that girl who wakes him up.

CHAPTER TWELVE

Carolina is asleep when I wake up.

Carefully, I pull my arm off her, grab my wallet and keycard, and tiptoe out of her room. I'll come back and grab my suit later.

I'm struggling to wrap my head around last night. When I slid into bed with her, my fingers tingled as I remembered how they'd felt when running along her soft skin while I helped her undress.

I should've kept my hands to myself.

My stupidity is what started last night.

When I noticed she wasn't wearing a bra, I should've walked away.

Instead, I became a dumbass, and my dumbass move lit a fire inside Carolina … a fire I had to fight like hell to put out. It was torture, turning her down. My hands balled into fists as I kept my eyes everywhere but on her body while in the shower. When I washed her hair, there was no stopping the few quick glances I took. Her perfect, round ass was so close to my cock … warning me but also tempting me with how easily I could've bent her over and taken her from behind.

And boy, was it a motherfucking challenge.

I'm not sure what got into her last night—*definitely not me …*

unfortunately—but the only other time I've seen that side of her was the night I took her virginity.

I couldn't …

I can't.

Losing Carolina scares me more than being in love with her.

My hands have to stay to myself, so she remains in my life.

Softly, I shut the door behind me, walking into the hallway, and head to my room.

"Morning."

I still at the sharp morning greeting.

Oh shit.

The air is thick as I turn on my heel to face Pastor Adams. The crease in his forehead and disapproving expression on his face confirm he thinks I'm doing the walk of shame from his daughter's room.

If he only knew.

I straighten and slap on a cheerful grin. "Good morning, Pastor Adams." I gulp, stopping myself from adding, *This isn't what it looks like.*

The shorter our conversation, the better.

Thank fuck I changed out of my suit last night.

Me wearing sweatpants looks far more believable that I slept in my room than me sneaking out in my suit.

My grin stays intact as I jerk my head toward Carolina's room. "I ran over to wake Carolina up and ask what she wanted for breakfast."

"Oh, really?" His lips press together in a grimace.

He's calling bullshit.

I look him in the eyes, establishing I'm not a rude little shit who spent all night banging his daughter. "Yes, sir."

He cocks his head to the side, his face twisting in displeasure. "What did she say?"

"She doesn't feel well."

"She's sick?"

I nod.

Carolina owes me a shit-ton of cookies.

I'm lying to a preacher.

Okay, Lord up above, it's not a full lie.

She will feel like shit when she wakes up.

He advances a step. "I should check on her."

My hand darts out as I rush closer to stop him from knocking on her door. "She went back to sleep and asked me to wake her in an hour."

He fixes a hard stare on me. "Why don't we have breakfast then? We can bring Carolina back something when we're finished. It's no fun to eat by yourself, and my wife is at the spa this morning."

I jerk back, a sudden headache slamming into me.

Oh, man.

Not a coffee date with my fake girlfriend's father.

How do I get out of this?

"Uh, yeah, sure," I mutter, knowing I can't decline without looking like an asshole. "Let me get dressed."

"Good idea," he deadpans and stops me as I whip around. "I suggest you refrain from roaming public hallways shirtless in the future … especially on a Sunday morning. It's disrespectful."

I peek back at him. "Appreciate the advice."

I shuffle into my room, change into jeans and a shirt, brush my teeth, and hurry back into the hallway where he's waiting. I was hoping he'd bailed on me. We make small talk while taking the elevator downstairs to the restaurant. Lucky for me, we have plenty of time for this coffee chat since our flight doesn't depart until this afternoon.

"For someone who's been close to my daughter for years and is now *dating her*, you sure don't come around often," he says as we sit down at the two-person table, and he smooths a napkin over his lap. "We've never shared a one-on-one conversation."

He's right.

Even in high school, Carolina came to my house when we hung out. Sometimes, her parents knew of her whereabouts, and other times, she told them she was studying at the library.

Carolina's exact words about hanging out at her house after I suggested it was, "We'll have to sit in the living room on different couches and watch a documentary about the sins of having sex before marriage."

The preacher is an old-school man. He's around my father's age, but unlike my father, his age shows. He's slender, a man who wears loafers on the regular, and his brown hair is peppered with gray strands. He's been the preacher of the town church for as long as I can remember. They're a religious family with strict rules and deep values. He's a good man who'd probably be more welcoming to me had Carolina and I not been such great friends … and boyfriend and girl-friend now.

How are we going to fake break up without me looking like an ass?

With my reputation, everyone will assume it was my fault, and I'll look like an even bigger asshole for breaking the heart of the preacher's daughter.

"We haven't, sir," I answer to his one-on-one time comment and pause, allowing him to take lead on this torturous chat.

"You don't frequent church," he sternly adds. "And no need to call me sir. I'm Rick."

"I've been busy with my job and school—"

He cuts me off, "You never attended when you were in your teens either with the exception of holidays."

"You're right." No need to dispute facts. It'll only make me look dumb.

Our waiter, Bobby, arrives at our table to save me from this awkwardness and takes our order. As soon as Bobby leaves, Rick is back to his interrogation.

"Is there a reason for that?"

"No."

Bobby comes back with Rick's coffee and my espresso—because I'm extra—and sets them in front of us. "Your order was put in and will be out shortly."

We both thank him.

"How are your parents doing?" Rick asks, pouring creamer into his coffee.

I'm unsure of which conversation I want to avoid more—me and Carolina or my shitshow of a family.

"Good." I take a long sip of my espresso, wishing I'd declined his breakfast offer. I should've told him I was sick, too. I'd planned to take the morning to digest what had happened with Carolina. Now, I'll be digesting last night and this conversation with Rick.

"How are you coping with their divorce?"

I never asked for this counseling session.

"Coping perfectly fine," I reply at the reminder of what an asshole my father is. "My mother is a strong woman and did the right thing." She should've divorced him a long-ass time ago.

"You think that's the right decision to make?" He raises a brow. "Giving everything up?"

I focus on my drink, avoiding eye contact to shield my annoyance. "When someone hurts you as much as my father did my mother … *my family*, then yes, I excuse her for leaving him. He cheated and hid secrets too large to heal from."

He waits until I look at him again before replying, "You know, I counseled them before she made the final decision to proceed with the divorce. I tried to help them reconcile."

Why is he telling me this shit?

Shouldn't he have to keep that confidential?

"Marriage is sacred," he goes on.

My hand clenches around the handle of my mug. "I agree."

"Do you plan to marry my daughter?"

I choke on my drink, and it takes me a moment to swallow and clear my throat before I can reply, "What?"

"You are dating my daughter now, correct?" His face tightens, as if the thought pains him.

"Yes." *And I love her.*

"What are your intentions with her? Marriage? A quick fling?"

My pulse races as I work my answer through my mind before relaying it. "I care about Carolina. She's been my best friend for years."

"Best friend? What about girlfriend?"

"It's new. We're trying it out. We've had feelings for each other for years, and we decided it was dumb to keep holding ourselves back from happiness."

Uh-oh. This fake relationship will definitely be following us home to Blue Beech.

"Do you plan on breaking her heart?" Worry is etched along every feature on his face. This interrogation isn't him being an asshole; it's him protecting his daughter's heart.

I repeatedly shake my head. "No, of course not. It's never my intention to hurt Carolina—*ever.*"

"She's in love with you." There's no bullshit in his tone.

I go quiet for a moment. I know she loves me, but I pretend to be blind about it.

"This is typically the part where boyfriends say they love their girlfriend back."

I stutter for the right words. "I love Carolina. She's the most amazing person I know."

My answer doesn't satisfy him. "I'll ask again, what are your intentions with my daughter?"

"For us to be happy."

He leans back in his chair, his eyes suspicious, and points at me, moving his finger back and forth. "Guys like you, they don't date the preacher's daughter."

I can't help but scowl. "Carolina is more than just a preacher's daughter, and I don't think it's fair to put that label on her."

Bobby becomes my favorite person when he interrupts us again with our food. Dude is getting a good-ass tip from me this morning.

Hopefully, Rick worries more about his food than talking to me.

I splash hot sauce onto my Spanish omelet and take a large bite.

"Tell me why Carolina dropped out of school," Rick urges, not even giving his pancakes a glance.

I swallow down my bite. "She didn't feel it was right for her."

"She had no issues her freshman year." He takes a drink of coffee and wipes his mouth. "Out of nowhere, she decided to drop out and move home. Was it for you? Did something happen to her?"

I understand his concern. I had one hundred questions for

Carolina. She answered some, lied about some, and refused to answer the others.

"Carolina hasn't told me the entire truth on why she moved home," I honestly answer. "Whatever she's going through, I hope she'll open up to us when she's ready."

He frowns. "Don't break my daughter's heart, Rex."

"I won't." *I'll try not to.*

"And I expect the next time I catch you sneaking out of her room, it's after you're married," he says, giving me a pointed look. "My daughter has values."

With that, he pours an excessive amount of syrup on his pancakes and takes a large bite.

———

I have a doughnut in one hand and a coffee in the other as I stroll into Carolina's hotel room.

"Rise and shine," I call out.

After my wonderful and not-at-all-awkward breakfast with her father, I ran to my room and showered.

Carolina yawns while sitting up in the bed. "Quit being so perky." Another yawn. "It's too early for that." Her hair is a tangled mess, there's dried slobber on the side of her mouth, and even with the shower, there're still blotches of mascara under one eye. She's a gorgeous, hot mess.

I hold the doughnut bag and coffee up. "I brought food for your hungover self. I'd be nice to this perky dude."

"All right," she groans. "Thank you. Carbs is just what the doctor ordered."

"Or what the preacher ordered." I hand her the bag and a napkin before placing the coffee on the nightstand next to her. "Your dad picked it out for you."

She stills, just as she's about to take a bite of the doughnut. "My dad?"

I plop down on the edge of the bed by her feet. "Yep. We had breakfast."

"You had breakfast with my dad," she drags out.

"Sure did. It was quite a blast, let me tell you. We drank mimosas and took tequila shots. He sure enjoyed the hair of the dog."

She stretches her leg out to kick me. "You're such a liar."

"About the shots, yes. About us having breakfast, no. He wanted to have coffee with his daughter's new boyfriend to tell him not to break your heart." I leave out the questions about future marriage and why she left school.

Her eyes widen, the doughnut falling onto the bag in her lap, and her hand cups her mouth. "Oh my God! I forgot about our boyfriend-girlfriend game. What happens when we get home? How are we going to break up?"

I poke her foot. "Let's say you cheated on me."

"What? No! You're not blaming the breakup on *me*."

"Oh, and I'm supposed to take the blame?" I point at myself and shake my head. "I'm not being the bad guy." I scratch my cheek. "There are reasons other than cheating. We can say you joined a nunnery. You join, no one suspects anything, and all will be right in the world."

"You need to stop suggesting I join a nunnery. Not happening." She shoves a bite of the doughnut into her mouth.

"Why? Your father probably has some great connections."

She rolls her eyes, chewing. "You just want me to stay single and non-sexually active for the rest of my life."

"Fine, no cheating or nunnery. We'll say we're better off as friends."

She throws her head back. "It's way too early to discuss our fake breakup for our fake relationship."

I nod in agreement. "Your head hurt?"

I'm acting as normal as I can.

Does she remember what happened last night?

She wasn't drunk. I definitely won't be bringing that shit up, though.

"Nope." She finishes off her doughnut.

"Liar."

"Ibuprofen, please." She points at her bag. "Left pocket."

I snatch her bag, grab the ibuprofen, snag a bottle of water from the mini fridge, and hand them to her.

"Thank you," she says, swallowing the pills down.

She hands me the water, and I set it on the nightstand next to her coffee.

"Our flight leaves in a few hours," I inform her, sitting back down on the side of the bed. "I'm shocked you're not packed and ready to go yet."

"Last night drained all the life out of me. I can't wait to go home."

———

"Back to reality," Carolina says after we land and stroll through the airport. "I never thought I'd be so excited to be home from a vacation." She holds up her hand to correct herself. "Technically, it was a *hell-cation.*"

We took an Uber to the airport with her parents this morning, and Carolina tried her hardest not to appear hungover. The disapproving glances her father shot her way proved her convincing skills sucked ass.

I bump my shoulder against hers. "Rude to say that to the person who accompanied you on the trip."

"Fine." She bumps my shoulder back. "It would've been a *hell-cation* had you not been there. Seriously, thank you for coming, Rex."

"I'll always have your back … until you break up with me later." I press my hand to my heart. "I'm already putting together a broken-heart playlist."

She rolls her eyes. "You're breaking up with me. I've been brain-storming for the perfect story."

"Too late. I've already made the decision. You're into some kinky shit in the bedroom that's *way* out of my comfort zone." I struggle to hold in a laugh. "I refuse to let you spank me with whips and give you a golden shower."

"Oh my God," she gasps, slapping my arm, and she casts a glance at her sister walking a few feet behind us. "What is wrong with you?

My sister is right there, and you know how much of a tattletale she is. I can't have my parents thinking I want you to pee on me!"

I chuckle. "I highly doubt your parents know what a golden shower is."

"Uh … you ever heard of Google?"

"Google?" I stroke my chin. "What is this Google you speak of?"

She hitches her bag up higher on her shoulder. "I like your idea, but it needs to be switched around. *I* was the one who refused the peeing thing."

"I see we're having some creative differences here. Time to find a better approach. You riding home with me? We can talk about the best way to break up."

"Duh. My parents already know." She blows out a long breath. "I'm definitely not sharing another ride with them."

"How did you know I'd let you ride home with me? Maybe your boyfriend needs some alone time."

"Don't care. I'm riding with you. Get over it."

I chuckle. "I love it when you're bossy."

There might've been some awkward times during our trip—like, say, when she got naked and asked me to shower with her—but I'm sad it's over. Not that I won't be spending more time with Carolina back home, but it was nice to be able to touch her without it appearing weird. I was her boyfriend in Texas. It was my job to be all touchy-feely. If only I could do it here in Blue Beech.

Our vacation is over.

Our fake relationship will end.

Our lives will go back to normal.

Neither of us has muttered a word about the shower incident, and I'm hoping it stays that way. I already felt bad enough about turning her down. Carolina doesn't put herself out there like that; it's not in her nature. It was rough to say no, but it was also satisfying to know she trusts me enough to pull herself out of her comfort zone. Sure, she was drunk, but had I been some random dude, she would've never dropped her panties in front of me.

At least, I hope not.

We grab our luggage, and Carolina turns her parents down for a ride four times before we finally say good-bye and walk to my car in the parking garage.

"Have I mentioned how much I love this car?" she says after we throw our luggage in the trunk and get in. "It's so much fancier than mine. You just keep getting more tech savvy."

"An electric car is not tech savvy," I argue from the driver's side as we pull out of the parking spot.

She stretches out her legs. "In our small town, anything above a gas-hogging truck, Jeep, or minivan is tech savvy."

"Which is why, Lina babe, I don't suggest it. Finding charging stations is a bitch."

I fucking love my Tesla. It took me a while to finally make the plunge and buy it, but it'd been my dream car for years. After I signed my contract with the development company for my game, I sold the Charger and bought the Tesla. The next item on my list is purchasing a home after my lease ends.

"I'm too poor to buy a new car anyway," she says with a frown. "I might stay poor for the rest of my life since I dropped out of school … says my parents."

I gulp, gripping the steering wheel as I glance over at her. "Do you think you'll ever tell them the truth?" *Do you think you'll ever tell me the entire truth?*

"Who knows?" She wrinkles her nose. "Maybe in thirty years." She shakes her head while turning her attention out the window. "It's embarrassing. I'm stupid."

"Hey," I say softly. "You're not stupid. You were taken advantage of."

"My stupidity is more than just him." She casts me a nervous glance. "It's him, what happened with Margie, *all* of it. I feel stupid, weak, and wish I could go back in time."

My stomach sinks at the heartbreak in her voice, and I wish I could wrap her in my arms, hold her tight, and let her know it'll be okay … as I've done so many damn times since that bastard did what he did.

"My parents wouldn't understand *being taken advantage of* because I made that stupid choice," she continues. "It was a consequence of my decision. None of this would've happened had I not been irresponsible … had I not been too scared to tell the truth and stopped hiding it."

Yet she's still hiding it.

"Has living at your sister's improved?"

At first, Tricia gave her shit for dropping out, which is bullshit. Tricia didn't go to college. She married her high school sweetheart right out of school and started a family. Her parents approved of that, but they don't approve of Carolina waitressing and getting her shit together. Her sister hasn't failed to remind her how much work and money their parents put into Carolina's education.

"A little," she replies. "I stay in the loft as much as I can when I'm there. When she makes her surprise visits *for girl talk*, I agree with her, so she'll go." She shrugs. "What can I do? I'm not going to be a bitch. She's giving me free rent, for goodness' sake, and losing money by not renting it to anyone else. I can handle a little lecturing for that."

"The offer to move in with me is still open," I say.

She shakes her head. "Hearing my sister's lectures is better than being around you and your women."

"Oh, come on." I crack a smile. "You act like I'm with a different woman every night. Hell, I spend nearly half of my time hanging out with you and the other working on my fame."

She laughs when I glance her way and smirk.

"You're at my apartment more than your own anyway," I add. "It'd be no different."

I've offered the spare bedroom in my apartment to her several times. I'd love for her to be my roommate, for me to be able to watch over her and hang out with her more.

"On the days we're not together, you're with another chick, not working on your fame—unless it's to be Blue Beech's biggest man-whore even though you've already won the title." She waggles her finger in my direction. "Don't forget, I've been there on numerous occasions when random chicks show up at your doorstep."

"I didn't know *numerous* meant twice," I correct. "And I made them leave."

My other nickname for Carolina is the Exaggerator Queen. She always multiplies everything I do by at least five. Two chicks show up, and she'll say it's ten. I tell her I've had sex with one chick, and she says I've had sex with five.

"Are you going home or to my place?" I ask when the *Welcome to Blue Beech, Iowa* sign comes into view.

"Home for now," she replies. "I might come by later. I need to unpack, do laundry, take a long bath, and get over this stupid hangover."

I nod and head toward her sister's house. "Text me in a bit … with a breakup text."

She sighs. "Not happening, homeboy."

A playful groan leaves my throat. "At least send your boyfriend a picture of you in the bath." I slam my mouth shut as soon as I say the words, and I want to slap myself.

Teasing Carolina whenever she said she was taking a bath was one of my favorite pastimes, but now, after the shower incident, bath sexting references are a terrible idea.

Her face pales, confirming she no doubt remembers what happened last night. "Not …" she stutters. "Not happening."

I force myself to sound as playful as I can. "Kidding, my sweet girlfriend."

CHAPTER THIRTEEN
CAROLINA

Hangovers are a bitch.

Turns out, while around distant relatives you don't like, drinking helps you tolerate them. It also turns out that drinking will convince you that attempting to seduce your best friend in a hotel room is a fantastic idea.

Damn you, alcohol. You're the best friend who's also a bad influence.

Good for the mind but bad for the hormones.

Rex was thankfully smart enough not to mention last night. He knows I'd die of embarrassment, and he'd lose his favorite cookie-maker. As much as I'd like to forget last night, I can't. All I'm doing while taking my bath is asking myself, *Why?*

Why did I enjoy our boyfriend-girlfriend game so much?

Why, even as awkward as I feel now, wouldn't I mind if he came barging in here, asking me to share my bath?

Why? Why? Why?

These past few months have been hard on me and on my heart, but Rex has been by my side every step of the way. He goes beyond the best-friend title, and sometimes, I wish he'd move into the boyfriend title.

I love him so damn much.

If only things were different.

If only he believed in love.

I understand he doesn't want to break my heart. I've seen him struggle with women—struggle when they begged him to give them more than a quick screw, struggle to cut them off, struggle to put himself out there. As much as I love him rejecting them, I wish he hadn't turned me down the same way.

When I get out of the bathtub, I drop my towel and get dressed into my pajamas. On my way back to my bedroom, I snatch my phone and hop into my comfy bed. As soon as I glance at the screen, nausea fills my stomach more than this damn hangover.

Margie: Hey! My birthday is next week. We're having a dinner at El Pacinos! Tacos and margaritas are calling our names. Please come!

So many emotions flood through me as I stare at her text message —envy, guilt, and sadness. A tear slides down my cheek as I contemplate whether to reply. Some days, I do. Some days, I don't.

Me: I have plans. Sorry.

Seconds later, my phone vibrates.

Margie: Come on, Carolina. Talk to me. You said I didn't do anything to piss you off, but all you do is blow me off. You left the dorm without even saying good-bye!

She's right. Rex and his roommate, Josh, went to my dorm and packed up my things, and I haven't been back.

Me: I've been busy working, and campus is such a long drive.

Margie: I can come there. Girls' night this weekend?

Me: Not this weekend. I'll get back with you.

Margie: Whatever. I'll just stop reaching out.

I sigh, wishing I had the guts to say more.

I haven't talked to Margie since I dropped out. When I disappeared from my dorm, she called and texted every day. I never answer her calls, but I text back, telling her I am busy or have a lot going on. I blow her off every time she asks to hang out.

After plugging my phone into the charger, I tuck myself into bed. My head might feel better after sixteen hours of sleep.

"Good morning, honey! How was your trip?" Shirley asks, her voice cheerful and loud when I walk into the diner bright and early.

Shirley is the owner of the diner I work for and waitressed here for years before her mother passed it down to her. She's a dark-skinned woman in her sixties who's a kind soul full of wisdom. I frequently studied here for hours in high school while eating slices of her famous pie. She never complained about me taking up a table, nor did she fail to slide a free slice in front of me—cherry, my favorite. She attends my father's church regularly and is a frequent donor of everything sweet.

"I think I'm in need of a vacation from that vacation," I grumble, grabbing an apron and tying it around my waist.

She laughs. "Oh, family weddings. They're always so fun."

"And also depressing," I add with a frown.

When I moved back to Blue Beech, my father offered me a job at the church, but I declined. Working for him is a bad idea. I'd hear his lecturing forty hours a week, and he'd watch every move I made. I still volunteer for functions at the church on my time off, but I can pick and choose those dates. They're normally when my father is busy or in a public place.

Shirley's Diner has been a staple in our town for decades. It has cute '50s-themed décor—complete with classic red booths, black-and-white-checkered floors, and bright teal walls. The most popular part of the diner is the silver counter in the front with a glass case filled with slices of pie in every flavor imaginable. Shirley makes them herself every night, and I stay over to help sometimes. It's the least I can do for her since she gave me a job and donates so many of them to the charity dinners I throw.

"Your boyfriend is in your booth," Candy, another waitress, sings while skipping into the kitchen.

Rex and his family have always been regulars at the diner, but he's here nearly half of my shifts and sits in the same booth in my section every time. On these days, he wakes up earlier than usual, brings his laptop to work, and eats. He also leaves me crazy tips, to which I try to shove back into his hand, pockets, shirt—wherever there's a crevice on him—but he won't allow it. He knows how hard up for cash I am. He also knows I won't take any money from him, so this is his way of helping me out.

"He's not my boyfriend," I reply.

Candy rolls her eyes while Shirley laughs in the background. "He's *so* your boyfriend."

"Sweetie, sooner or later, that boy will be your *husband*," Shirley gushes. "You two need to do some growing up." A grin takes over her wrinkled face. "You wait and see."

"Shirley, I'm beginning to think you're crazy," I remark, shaking my head.

"Not crazy, honey, just wise." She squeezes my shoulder.

I push my notepad into my apron, drag my hair into a ponytail, and rub at my tired eyes.

"Good morning, Lina babe," Rex greets as soon as I come into his view. He's wearing a black baseball hat that covers his bedhead and a loose gray sweatshirt. "I'm a little offended you told them I wasn't your boyfriend."

Thankfully, since the diner only opened an hour ago, nearly all the booths are empty, and no one is hearing this boyfriend talk. Rex is sprawled out in his booth, his closed laptop on the other side of the table. An elderly couple—Candy's grandparents—are situated in a booth in her section, and a few police officers are immersed in conversation at the counter.

"What?" I ask when I reach him. "How'd you hear that?"

"I not only like this booth because it's in your section, but I can also hear *all* the kitchen talk. You ladies are loud as hell when you gossip about me." He arches a brow. "It seems to be your favorite subject back there. Wait until they find out I was granted the role of being your boyfriend over the weekend and we have still yet to break up."

"Oh God, get over yourself," I grumble.

I'm clueless on how to tell my parents we broke up. We should've thought about this following us home when we started the stupid charade. No matter what, when I tell my parents we broke up, they'll blame it on Rex. Even if I say it was my decision, there will be no changing their mind. They've seen Rex as a bad influence all these years and me as their innocent little princess—except for the whole dropping out of school. My innocence status dropped a few notches after that.

He stretches his legs out and smiles. "Have I mentioned how much I love you in that uniform?"

"Yes," I say with a groan. "Every day I serve you."

Our uniforms stay with the '50s theme—red-and-white-striped dress with a white apron and white shoes. We all sport them with the exception of Shirley, who's retired from the outfit and wears a tee sporting the diner's logo. Last week, we jokingly started a petition to change our uniforms, and she said she'd consider the change.

"I'll have my usual, my hot candy cane-striped waitress." He doesn't even bother to open his menu. "And a coffee."

I leave to start his order, and when I return to his booth, his laptop is open in front of him. I drop a handful of sugar packets onto the table before setting his coffee down. Rex has a sweet tooth—hence why he loves my cookies.

"Aunt Lina!"

I glance back to see my nephew, Henry, barreling my way, and I nearly stumble back when he hugs my legs, peeking up at me with a bright smile. A Superman cape is tied around his neck, and his sneakers light up with every move he makes.

"We came to see you for breakfast!" he beams. "Grammy said I can get smiley-face pancakes!"

I bend to squeeze him into a hug and see my sister coming our way with my two-year-old niece, Addy, on her hip.

Tricia's gaze pings from me to Rex in the booth, her eyes widening in interest. "Oh, hey, your boyfriend came to see you this morning. How cute."

I can't tell if her comment is a compliment or a dig. My sister is a hard person to read and isn't a Rex fan. He hooked up with one of her friends in high school and then never called her back after the sixteen voicemails said friend left. She needs to get over it. She's married with children now.

Tricia and I weren't close growing up. My parents were strict with every move I made but not with Tricia. She had more freedom and could get away with mediocre grades, and my parents accepted her choice not to attend college. After I moved into her loft, our relationship has improved, but we're definitely not best friends. She's also taken on the hobby of finding me a man to marry.

Trailing Tricia is my mother, the expression on her face even more unreadable than Tricia's tone.

"Did you say boyfriend?" Candy squeals, rushing our way. She is nearly jumping up and down when she reaches us. "Carolina keeps denying it!"

"Oh, they're together all right," Tricia confirms. "They made it official over the weekend at our cousin's wedding."

My eyes flash to Rex's in a *help me* look.

"Isn't that right?" my sister adds skeptically, her gaze pointed at Rex as if this is a test.

"That's right," Rex answers, shutting his laptop and sliding it away from him. "We've been keeping it on the down-low for this very reason—to stop people from gossiping and making a big deal about it. It's new, and no matter what, we'll always be best friends first."

What the heck did we get ourselves into?

"Mom! Pancakes!" Henry squeals, interrupting this awful moment and stealing everyone's attention.

Kiddo is getting extra pancakes today.

Henry rushes toward the booth, sliding down to the wall, and Shirley already has a high chair ready to go for Addy when Tricia sits down next to him.

"Hi, sweetie," my mom says, giving me a peck on the cheek before moving her attention to Rex and giving him a wholesome smile. "Good morning, Rex."

"Morning, Mrs. Adams," he says with a grin before gesturing to his booth. "You guys are more than welcome to join me."

"You're so sweet," she replies. "We have a handful over there that might be too noisy for you this early in the morning. I can't promise that you wouldn't be wearing Henry's pancakes by the end of the meal."

Rex chuckles.

"Be over in a minute to take your order," I rush out to her before this gets weirder.

"Perfect, honey."

"Holy shit," I hiss to Rex as soon as she's out of earshot. "We need a plan, *pronto*, to break up this relationship."

Rex taps his fingers against the table. "We should've thought about the post-wedding aftermath."

I squeeze into the seat across from him and lean in closer, lowering my voice. "It's simple. You broke up with me."

He rests his elbows on the table. "The fuck it is. I'm not being the bad guy in this fake breakup. *You*"—he points at me—"broke up with" —he thrusts his thumb toward him—"me."

"Fine," I groan, throwing my hands up while he relaxes back against the booth and grabs his coffee. "I'll say it's because you couldn't sexually please me. I can work with that."

He tilts his mug toward me. "Yeah, go tell your preacher father that I couldn't sexually please you. No one in this town will believe you."

I scoff. "Why?" I do a sweeping gesture of the diner. "Because all the women here know what it feels like to be sexually pleased by you since you've slept with everyone in this town with a vagina?"

"Nope." He takes a loud sip of his coffee. "I haven't slept with Candy or Shirley—"

I cut him off. "Really?"

"What? You insinuated I've slept with all the women in town. I haven't slept with your sister—"

I interrupt again, "Thank God for that."

"Or your mother."

I snatch the knife from his side of the table. "I'm going to stab you and get fired from this job."

He stretches his arms along the booth. "There isn't one person in here who I've slept with." He pauses and lifts a finger. "Well, except for you." He clicks his tongue against the roof of his mouth. "I've also never shared a shower with any of them." He does the same motion as before. "*Except for you.*"

I cross my arms, heat creeping up my cheeks. *Oh no. He's not bringing this up for the first time here.* "Oh, you mean the shower where you were too wimpy to get naked?"

"Not a wimp. I was the only smart one in that shower," he says, his voice thick.

"Wimp," I snap back.

His dark brows furrow. "Drunk ass."

I jump up from my seat. "I need to get back to work. I'll be sure to spit on your waffles."

He licks his lips. "I love your spit."

I roll my eyes. "Quit the flirting. It's been made known that your flirting leads to nothing but boring showers."

He tenses. "That shower was definitely not boring."

"It was for me. You couldn't even look at me." I'm struggling to keep my voice low. I'm also struggling not to bop him in the head with the menu on the side of his table.

"Trust me, my dick got hard with every peek I made. When I saw your ass in the shower in front of me, I nearly died." He holds up his coffee. "Can I get a refill, please?"

I blink at him, ready to see my heart fall at my feet as it rages against my chest.

"Extra cream," he adds, licking his lips and thrusting the cup closer my way.

Just as I'm struggling to come up with a reply, Henry calls my name. I pivot on my heel, trying to catch my breath, and look at him.

"We're ready to order!" he calls out. "I need lots and lots of syrup with my pancakes, please!"

"Sugar-free syrup," Tricia adds.

"You'd better go help them," Rex adds with an annoying chuckle.

I slide his coffee mug along his table, leaving it there, and stroll over to take their order. On my way back to the kitchen, I swipe Rex's mug from his table without saying a word.

"I'm so jealous," Candy squeals after I call out my orders to the cooks. "Why would you want to hide being in a relationship with *Rex Lane*? He's so hot."

I went to high school with Candy. She was part of the popular crowd and wasn't that nice then, but she's been cool since I started here. I *somewhat* think of her as a friend. She only irks me when it comes to Rex and how she makes a big deal about him being here.

The rest of my shift goes smoothly. I bring Rex his coffee refill and breakfast, and he thankfully doesn't mention our shower party of no fun again.

CHAPTER FOURTEEN

"Thank God you're here," Maliki comments when he answers the door.

It's late. I've been up, working on my game, and then Sierra texted me, reminding me about her computer. She instructed me to text Maliki when I was here and not to knock since Molly would most likely be sleeping.

Their house was recently remodeled and looks awesome. Sierra is an interior designer, so she had the most say in the changes. Maliki stepped to the side, letting her create her dream home for them.

"She's been whining about her computer nonstop," he adds as I follow him into the living room.

Sierra is on the couch, and next to her is a sleeping Molly, her head resting on Sierra's lap.

"Oh, shut it," Sierra chimes in. "I have not."

Maliki nods toward Molly. "I'll put her to bed."

Sierra nods and plants a kiss on Molly's forehead before Maliki scoops his daughter up in his arms and carries her down the long hallway.

"Let me grab my laptop," Sierra says, pulling herself up and plodding barefoot to the kitchen while I relax on the couch.

Maliki returns at the same time she hands it over to me. He's cool as shit, and he owns the only bar in our town—Down Home Pub. He took it over years back when his father nearly went bankrupt and then moved to Florida. My sister works with him, bartending a few nights a week, but now that her interior design company has taken off, she's cut down on her hours.

"How was your lovers' trip?" Sierra asks, her and Maliki sitting next to each other. She turns, resting her back to his side, and he tucks his arm around her waist.

It's time like these when I wonder in the back of my mind if I'm capable of having that. Sure, Carolina and I *snuggle* sometimes, but this is more than snuggling. There's a certain intimacy, and the love they have for each other bleeds off them. Briefly, I wonder what it looks like when Carolina lies against me like that. Does our ... *friendship ... our love* bleed off us?

"It wasn't a lovers' trip," I scold, opening her laptop and powering it on.

Sierra tilts her back and smiles up at Maliki. "Aw, babe, do you remember when we were friends and tried to hide that we were in love with each other?"

Maliki's arm tightens around her, and he brushes his thumb against her cheek with his free hand. "Yep, and what a waste. Imagine all the extra time we could've had if we had stopped pussyfooting around."

Sierra lifts her head while they look at me with expectation.

I switch my attention to the laptop, hitting keys. "No pussyfooting around. I don't get what no one understands about us being only friends."

Fuck. Why is this all I've been hearing about lately?

Maliki chuckles, shaking his head. "Quit giving him shit, babe. He'll figure it out eventually."

Sierra groans. "Hopefully, it doesn't take him too long. Remember what happened when you didn't step up?"

He frowns. "Don't remind me."

"I got *married.*" She stresses every syllable as the words leave her mouth before focusing on me. "Do you want Carolina to marry someone else, Rex?"

I rub at the sudden tension in my neck, the thought hitting me like a headache. "Carolina isn't getting married."

I fucking hope not.

"How do you know?" Sierra continues, as if her mission tonight is to piss me off. "*I* got married."

"She won't," I grind out, contemplating whether to change her password and the language to Chinese in revenge for her taunting.

I love my sister, and I know she means well. We've always been the closest, but she's a pain in the ass.

"Are you saying that because you don't want her to get married?"

"Jesus, babe," Maliki cuts in, shooting me a sympathetic stare while giving her a gentle squeeze. "You're going to make his head explode."

She sighs. "I want to see my baby bro happy, and he needs to stop being dumb."

I hold up her computer, arching a brow. "The one who can't figure out her computer is calling me dumb?"

"Learn from my mistakes, little bro." She skims her fingers along Maliki's arm. "Don't you think they'd be cute, babe?"

"So cute," Maliki says, mocking her voice. "Fucking adorable."

"Funny," she deadpans. "Remember who you sleep next to at night."

Their relationship story is pretty damn entertaining. Maliki used to kick my sister out of his bar whenever she was underage and tried to sneak in. It became a thing to them. They're so opposite—my sister being the rebellious sorority princess and Maliki being the bartending bad boy who hated commitment. I admire their relationship so damn much.

Maliki smacks a kiss against the top of her head. "The best damn woman in the world is who I sleep next to at night."

I gag. "Gross. You two save your flirtfest for later." I drop the laptop onto the couch and stand. "Computer is fixed."

"Oh, sweet Carolina, ba, ba, ba!" Josh sings when Carolina walks into our apartment.

He does it every damn time.

"Shut up and leave her alone," I grumble in annoyance, pausing my game.

Josh is cool. We shared a few classes together at Iowa State and were partners on a project. He's a few years older than me, clean, not *that much* of a pain in the ass, and he pays rent on time. The only times I consider kicking him out is when it comes to Carolina. He—along with every-fucking-body else—gives me shit about our relationship and has threatened to ask her out one too many times. He won't. There would be an eviction notice on his bedroom door as soon as the words left his mouth.

He's your typical hipster who wears beanies over his shoulder-length hair that he pulls into a man bun most of the time, he sports a scruffy beard, and his closet is packed with flannels in every color.

"Damn," he grumbles, attempting to fight back a smug smile. "Can't a man say hi?"

"You didn't say hi." I divert my attention to Carolina. "You hungry? I ordered a pizza."

She worked a double today and is always hangry when she gets off work.

She licks her lips. "Yum. You da best."

I grin. "Well aware of that, babe."

She looks damn adorable when she strolls into the living room—wearing a loose, flower-patterned dress that isn't made to look as sexy as it does on her. It shows a hint of cleavage, causing me to gulp as I remember the night in the hotel room.

Fuck. Will I ever forget that night?

She kicks off her white flip-flops on her way to the couch and takes the open seat next to me, tucking her legs underneath her ass. "How many levels do you need to finish? Are you still stuck?"

I love that she asks this. Hardly anyone—except for her, my

mother, my sister, and Josh—asks about my game. They're the only ones who take it seriously and understand how important it is to me, how much I love it. Carolina has been on this game's journey since nearly day one—hearing me throw out idea after idea, change shit, work on levels, and beg gamers to give it a try.

She listens, understands, and offers advice about my game. Not too many chicks are comfortable with hanging out with a guy who plays video games as much as I do. Either that or they *fake* being into it, not even knowing the difference between my game and Fortnight.

Carolina does because she genuinely cares.

"I'm slowly getting out of my slump," I reply, unpausing it and hitting buttons on the controller. "It was too easy, breaking through a few levels. I needed to make it harder." I've been working nonstop for twelve hours, only taking bathroom and food breaks.

Thank fuck Josh isn't a big TV watcher. I like testing in the living room rather than my bedroom.

"Attaboy! I'm so proud of you!" She gestures to the screen. "How you do all this—create, design, code. It's so amazing."

I fasten my free arm around her back and drag her closer to my side. "Thanks, Mom."

She shoves my shoulder, causing my character to die. "Shut up and take my compliment."

"Looks like it's easy to die when a chick is touching you," Josh says from the chair next to me. "You have that going for you. Include a hot girl to distract them in every game."

I flip him off.

He laughs. "You fools coming out tonight?"

"No way," Carolina answers around a yawn. "I'm beat, and I work the morning shift tomorrow."

"Losers," he teases, winking at Carolina.

I narrow my eyes at him and hold up the controller—a silent warning that it'll hit him in the face if he continues his annoying-ass flirting.

I turn my attention to Carolina. "Looks like it's you and me tonight."

Josh jumps up from his chair, snaps his fingers, and pings his finger back and forth between me and Carolina. "Good. You two kids do something bad."

I flip him off again as he walks away, his laughter booming through the apartment.

CHAPTER FIFTEEN
CAROLINA

I tug my phone from my apron when it vibrates, and my heart sinks when I read the text from the last person I want to talk to. He's the man I hate and who's made my life a living hell.

James: You can't keep ignoring me.

My fingers are close to shaking as I hit the reply button.

Me: I'm not ignoring you.

James: Let me correct myself. You can't keep avoiding me.

I roll my eyes. He didn't correct himself. *Avoiding* and *ignoring* are the same thing.

Me: Whatever. What do you want?

James: Don't forget who has the upper hand here.

My jaw hurts as I grit my teeth at his threat, and I wish I were brave enough to do something. Call me weak … a coward … but fighting him on this will lead to serious consequences.

I've found there are two ways to appease him:

1. Agree.
2. Stroke his ego.

My phone beeps again.

James: I want to see you.

Me: I've been swamped with work.

James: Yet you had time to fly to Texas.

Me: Are you following me?

I glance around my surroundings in the diner's kitchen even though there's no way he's in here. From now on, I'll be looking over my shoulder with every move I make. I came home with the thought he'd never make the drive here. Hopefully, I wasn't wrong.

James: No. I saw your little boyfriend posted it on Instagram.

He's following Rex?

He hates Rex.

Me.

That's why he's following Rex.

To follow me since I blocked him.

Just as I'm about to reply with expletives that'll piss him off more, I'm saved by a text from Rex.

My Main Man: Going to Down Home tonight. Come with?

Me: Sounds good to me.

My problems slip from my thoughts when I'm with Rex. I also feel safe with him.

My Main Man: You want me to scoop you up?

Me: 9:00?

My Main Man: See you then.

I untie my apron, drop my phone into my purse, and head back to the loft without replying to James's message. My guess is he's drinking, in a mood and feeling sorry for himself, or having girl problems. He reaches out whenever one of those problems happens, bugs me for a day, and then disappears for a while … and then the cycle starts over a few weeks later.

Whenever possible, I have Rex pick me up when we go out—because I'm selfish. That way, he can't bring another woman home with him. Sure, she could always go to his house after, but I tend to invite myself over and hang out with him. Not that he's ever said no. Not once has he ever brought home a woman when he's with me.

Rex is seen around town as the rebellious, rich kid.

His reputation always makes me laugh. Hell, I believed it, too, before we became friends.

He's considered *rebellious* because he does what he wants, he has never had a serious girlfriend, nor has he been interested in one, and he defies his father with every move.

Rex doesn't care about that rep and hardly shows anyone who he really is. We've learned each other's secrets, flaws, skeletons, and secret traits.

Which is why we're in love with each other.

Rex knows this.

I know it.

It's just easier for us to play pretend.

———

Damn, Lina, Rex says, strolling into my living room. "You look hot."

I lower my gaze to my white summer dress and strappy brown sandals. Summer dresses are my go-to outfit. They're comfy, cute, and effortless to pull together—my style. I've never been one to keep up with trends, and my parents were strict with what I wore growing up.

My contacts are in, my hair halfway up, halfway down, and I have a hint of makeup on.

I shyly grin.

Rex complimenting me isn't new.

My dress could be a paper bag, and he'd still flatter me.

Having a best friend who pumps up your ego on the regular is fun.

"Thank you." I snatch my pink sweater from the edge of the couch and drag it over my shoulders. "You don't look so bad yourself."

His walnut-colored hair is messy. Envy hits me of how simple his hair routine is. All he does is run gel through it, spiking it up, and he's all set. A gray moto jacket fits his muscular shoulders perfectly, a thin white tee underneath it, and his black jeans have rips down the front.

He playfully pops the collar of his jacket. "Yeah, I know."

I snort and smack his stomach on my way to grab my crossbody bag. "Geesh, how has your head not exploded from all that ego you carry in there? Must be because your brain is so puny."

"Weird." He chuckles. "You sure have no problem taking compliments that boost your ego."

"That's different."

"Do explain how it's different."

"I don't pop my collar like a 2002 rap song and say, 'I know.'" I mimic his collar-popping gesture. "I politely say thanks without letting it go to my fat, smug head."

He's laughing as he opens the door, and he follows me down the outside stairs to the driveway.

This week was a rough one. A drink will help dim my problems … dim my secrets. I duck into his car after he opens the door for me, and then he goes to his side. The ride to Down Home is short, and the parking lot is packed when we pull in. The pub is the place to go for a good time and to relax. Even when it's a full house, the setting unwinds you. Sierra remodeled the bar and made it her goal for the customers to feel like they're at home, sharing drinks with friends.

Music playing from the live band hits us when we walk in, and Rex's hand finds mine before he leads us to a crowded table in the center of the room. He steals two unoccupied stools from another table and brings them to ours, gesturing for me to sit in one while taking the other. When I sit, he tugs me closer, and I settle back while doing a once-over of our table.

Rex's brother, Kyle, is across from me with his arm slung over his girlfriend, Chloe's, shoulders while he sips on a beer. Their history has always fascinated me. They hated each other in high school, became neighbors, and are now in a serious relationship. It's been a rough ride for them with Chloe being involved in their family drama. I'll never forget the night Rex called me, ignited with a fury I'd never heard from him before, when he found Chloe's secret. It was some soap-opera, Jerry Springer drama.

Chloe is chatting it up with Lauren Barnes, who's sitting next to her. I've admired Lauren for years. Her family has never failed to help me with any charity or benefit dinner I bring to them. The Barnes family is one of the kindest families in Blue Beech. Her fiancé and Kyle's best friend, Gage, is next to her. They were high school sweethearts, and everyone was waiting for their marriage announcement, but instead, Lauren broke his heart. He returned a few years later with no intention of rekindling with Lauren. That didn't last long, considering they have a baby girl together.

Lately, Rex prefers to hang out with his family and brother's friends than the people we went to school with. Since they're chill and always accepting of me, I have no issue with that.

"Hey, Carolina," Sierra greets from the other side of me, a friendly smirk on her face.

I smile at her. "Hey!" I signal to the crowd. "It's a full house tonight."

She nods. "Sure is."

"No hey for your little bro?" Rex asks her.

Sierra wiggles her fingers in an exaggerated wave. "Hello, my pain-in-the-ass brother."

"Carolina," Kyle says, setting his beer down. The resemblance between him and Rex is crazy. "I love when you come with my brother. You tame him."

"Fake news," Rex argues. "I tame her."

Kyle snorts. Sierra scoffs. Gage laughs.

I pat Rex's head. "I keep him in line like a good little boy."

The waitress stopping by to take our order interrupts our conversation. Rex and I order two Jack and Cokes, and he adds in an order of nachos supreme for us to share—my favorite.

"You're not working tonight?" I ask Sierra.

She shakes her head. "Nope. I've been overloaded with work, so Maliki hired a part-time bartender to cover for me."

She shoves a hand through her blonde hair before pulling it into a high ponytail.

Sierra is gorgeous. She was nicknamed the Pageant Queen of Blue Beech, growing up. Okay, the *rebellious* Pageant Queen of Blue Beech, since she acted out like it was her job. After becoming single, she took a job working at the pub with Maliki before starting her own interior design business.

Her gaze moves past my shoulders, and I shift in my chair, following her attention to Maliki pouring a beer behind the bar. Maliki is hot—there's no denying that—with his dark hair, muscles, and facial scruff. He's older, in his thirties, and he was known as a ladies' man who'd never settle down. Word was, he swore serious relationships weren't his thing, but Sierra came into his life. He changed for her, going from a ladies' man to one of the best boyfriends I've seen.

I love their love, but it also scares the shit out of me.

It proves people who think they're not capable of love are.

What happens when Rex finds the woman to change him?

His heart is big enough for commitment, for him to be someone's everything and make her his everything. That fear just needs to be broken.

"Is it hard for him to relax when he owns the place?" I ask, turning back to Sierra.

"Definitely," she answers. "It's better now that we don't live above the bar anymore. It's not as easy as running downstairs to check on things."

She sips on her pink cocktail. Down Home was never big on cocktails. It was more of a beer and hard liquor establishment until Sierra came into the picture.

I nod in understanding. "I get that. It was difficult for my father to separate family and work with us living next door to the church."

We spent more time there than at home since my father was the preacher and my mother ran the after-school program.

The waitress comes back with our nachos and drinks, and Rex has her start a tab for us. Rex was a huge partier since high school, and it only worsened his first year of college, but now that he's doing so well with his game, he's cut down on the drinking. A hungover brain isn't a productive brain. It's frustrating that people don't notice the change in him—the maturity evolution is what I've named it, to which he always responds with an eye roll.

One of those people being his father, Michael Lane. He lives his life with the belief that all Rex does is party and waste his life away. Since Rex avoids as much contact with him as possible, he doesn't bother correcting him. Michael has always been friendly with me, but he's a jackass to Rex, which pisses me off. I force smiles but never go out of my way to start a conversation with him when I attend dinners at Rex's house.

Call it rude. Whatever.

Anyone who treats Rex like crap is a sucky person in my book.

Rex takes a swig of his beer before peering at me. "I'mma run to the restroom. Save me some nachos." His hand brushes along my shoulders as he walks away.

Chloe updates everyone on her and Kyle's adoption journey and reveals they're considering becoming foster parents while waiting for approval.

I'm mid-nacho-chomp when Rex is walking back from the restroom, and I nearly choke on the chip when a woman stands in front of him, blocking his way. I pinch my lips together, nausea swirling inside my stomach, and shove the nacho basket up the table.

"Don't worry about her," Sierra comments, bumping her shoulder against mine as I painfully gawk at Rex and Blockzilla. "He doesn't want her."

My eyes narrow when the girl slides her hand up his arm. "Rex wants any woman who looks in his direction."

Flirty women are a constant when we go out. They attempt to force themselves onto him while I play indifferent and fake that it doesn't hurt my heart. Rex never entertains it, but that still doesn't stop my envy.

"No, babe, he wants you." Sierra releases a heavy sigh. "He's scared. Maliki was like that. He just needed a little convincing."

I transfer my attention to Sierra. "Convincing how?"

I halfway know the answer to my question. She and Maliki played a cat-and-mouse game for years, ever since she was eighteen and snuck into his bar.

She nudges her head toward where Rex is standing, but I stop myself from looking back. "Call him out on his bullshit. Call him a chickenshit until he stops acting like a chickenshit. And if all else fails, date someone else. Scare him into getting his head out of his ass."

"You and Maliki are different than me and Rex. We've been friends for years. Plus, you're bolder than I am. I'm pretty much a chickenshit, too."

"You're a total badass, and my brother is head over heels for you. He's just too stupid to admit it."

She throws her arm out, motioning toward Rex, and I brace myself to be upset as I peek over at him. He's ditched the girl and dodging bodies while heading in our direction.

"See!" she cries out. "Y-O-U!"

Rex takes his place by my side again, interrupting our conversation, and Sierra glances up at Maliki with a grin when he joins us and says hi to everyone. He kisses Sierra, whispering words against her mouth, and they become disgustingly cute.

"Another one of your women?" I question Rex, a frown on my face before I shove a nacho into my mouth.

"Nope," he replies with a straight face.

I narrow my eyes at him.

"What?" He shrugs. "She asked if I'd buy her a drink. I said no. She then asked if she could buy me a drink. I respectively declined like the gentleman I am and walked away." He shrugs again. "No biggie."

"I'm amazed you didn't take her up on her offer," I grumble.

"Not interested. I'd never ditch you for another chick."

"Oh. My. Freaking. God!"

Her shrill voice hits me right before Candy comes into our view. She halts at our table, as if someone hit the brakes on her legs.

I dip my head down and cover half my face with my hand, fully aware she's about to make a scene.

"If it's not the happy couple making it official!" she shrieks. She pouts out her lower lip when her green eyes cut to Rex. "It sucks you're off the market, but I'm happy someone nice like Carolina snagged you!" Her words come out in a slight slur. "She's a keeper. Don't you go breaking her heart, or I'll break your thumbs! And it's hard to play video games without thumbs."

This is not happening.

Out of all places, she announces it in front of a crowd of people.

Every muscle in my body stiffens, my heart clamoring against my chest while I struggle not to freak the hell out. Rex's hand sweeps underneath the table, settling on my thigh, and he tenderly squeezes it.

"What?" nearly everybody at the table asks in their own manner.

It takes me a moment to uncover my face, and my gaze swiftly darts around the table, taking in everyone's response. Excitement. Happiness. Curiosity. Not one person appears pissed as their attention bounces back and forth from me to Rex.

"Whoa, did I miss something?" Kyle asks. "Is it finally happening?" He gestures between me and Rex. "Did you two finally get your heads out of your asses and admit you're in love?"

"Sure did!" Candy answers for us with extra pep in her voice. "You should've seen them at the diner." She folds her hands over her chest. "*Swoon!*"

We were so not swoon.

Sierra eagerly focuses on me. "Tell me everything."

"Details!" Chloe adds.

"How'd this happen?" Lauren yelps.

I stare at Rex in horror.

Oh my God. Oh my God.

How are we getting out of this?

It's not only my parents we have to create a breakup story for. It's now pretty much the entire town. And when it happens, most of them will give Rex hell for it, placing all the blame on him.

Rex's hand stays on my thigh as he speaks, "This is why we kept it on the down-low." He motions toward the table. "We didn't want this shit to happen—you clowns making a big deal about it." His hand leaves my thigh, and he curves his arm around my shoulders, dragging me closer to him. "Yes, we're trying something new."

"I love it." Sierra beams.

"Kiss!" Candy yells. "Now that the cat is out of the bag, you should totally kiss!"

I want to kill Candy.

No more picking up any extra shifts for her.

Her voice rises as she starts pumping her fist into the air. "Kiss! Kiss! Kiss!"

Kyle joins in on her chanting … then Chloe … then Lauren … and then the rest of the damn bar.

My mind goes blank when Rex cups the back of my head.

"Might as well make the crowd happy." His mouth crashes against mine.

Screams erupt across the bar, and clapping ensues.

Rex doesn't give me a quick peck. No, his soft lips part, and his tongue plunges into my mouth, teasingly stroking against mine. He tastes like beer and salt. His hand knots into my hair, and he yanks me closer, his mouth claiming me as his girlfriend.

My cheeks are on fire.

I'm making out with Rex in front of everyone.

And it doesn't feel pretend.

The. Best. Kiss. Ever.

It's life-changing.

Friendship-changing.

We're so screwed.

All the commotion around us is drowned out as he devours my mouth.

I'm clueless as to how much time passes before he tears away from me.

He tenderly kisses the tip of my nose.

I shiver when his cheek touches mine, and he whispers in my ear, "FYI, I'm not ending this. Figure out how you're going to break my heart." His tongue runs along the edge of my lobe, and I tighten my thighs. "You taste delicious, by the way."

This friendship just got a lot more complicated.

———

Rex doesn't ask if I want to go home as he drives to his apartment.

He knows me well enough to know the answer.

Hanging out with him is more enjoyable than hanging out in the loft solo.

Tonight was a shitshow, to say the least. I'd expected a simple night out of having drinks, not for every resident of Blue Beech to believe we're dating.

Rex stuck to water the rest of the night since he was driving. Like at the wedding, he played the boyfriend role perfectly—further confirmation he's capable of commitment even if he doesn't believe it himself. It was as if Candy hit a switch in him tonight. His hand never left me after our kiss—whether it was on my hip, my shoulder, or my thigh. He kissed my cheek a few times, but there was no more mouth action.

Thank God.

Had it been like the first one, there would have been a decent chance I'd lose my mind and straddle him in front of everyone because I was so turned on.

I toss my sweater on the back of the couch and kick my sandals off when we walk into his apartment. His three-bedroom place screams total bachelor pad. Rex has the master bedroom with an attached bathroom, Josh has the second bedroom, and the third is empty for a new roommate. Rex is picky about who he rents to.

He tosses his keys onto the coffee table while I run to his bathroom. I glance around his room on the way there. It matches his personality perfectly. One wall is painted a deep red while the other three are black. A black-and-white canvas painting is hung over his bed along with video game and cinema posters. I grin when I pass the picture of us from graduation on his nightstand.

When I leave the bathroom, Rex is in the kitchen, standing in front of the open fridge.

"Yo, drink?" he shouts over his back while snagging a bottle of water.

"H2O, please!" I join him in the kitchen while he grabs another bottle and shuts the fridge.

His jacket is off, his feet bare, and his thin white tee shows off his muscular arms. Just because Rex isn't built like a bodybuilder with bulging arms doesn't mean he isn't fit. He's tall and lean. I love how he towers over me.

When he comes closer, my pulse races as I remember our kiss, him touching me at the bar, and of him in the shower, stroking himself.

"Are you still worried about your game?" I ask when he hands me the water.

He leans back against the counter, his forehead scrunching. "Every damn day."

My heart breaks at the stress on his face. "I'm sorry. Anything I can do to help?"

The offer grants me a smile.

"You help me every time we hang out—calming me and shit," he says.

"I'm your personal Xanax, huh?" My words come out in a laugh.

"Pretty much." He chugs down half his water.

"Let me check it out." I stroll into the living room, him lagging behind me, and drop my water onto the floor before grabbing a gaming remote. "It's been a hot minute since I've played, but my amazing skills haven't been forgotten." *Hopefully.* I pop a squat onto the carpeted floor and stretch my legs out in front of me.

Rex powers on the TV and game console.

I beam with pride when the game's home screen pops up on the TV, displaying the characters, and I point at the TV with the remote. "That princess had still better be me."

"You think I'd risk you kicking my ass if I changed it?"

"You'd never change it anyway."

He cocks his head to the side, smirking. "I might when you break up with me."

I roll my eyes. "You'd better not when *you* break up with *me.* You can make the character dudes hotter in case my character wants to date one of them."

"Hotter character dudes, huh?"

"Damn straight," I answer with a firm nod.

His hand rests over his heart. "Ouch. You're already breaking my heart."

Shock storms through me when he sits behind me, spreading his legs to each side of my body, and he slowly drags me between them until my back hits his solid chest.

I peek back at him, struggling to remain confident. "Nope. I told you I wouldn't be the heartbreaker. You made it worse with that kiss of yours." My gaze swings back to the TV. "What was up with that?"

He pushes my hair behind my shoulder and runs his fingers through the strands. "They were fucking chanting for us to. How suspect would it look for a happy couple to be that reluctant to kiss?"

"Why do you care if it's believable?" I question. "You refused to touch me at the hotel, but now, you're making out with me in public?" The game beeps when I touch the start button, and I shake my head as my level begins. "Mixed signals alert."

"Confused best-friend alert," he grumbles.

Whoa.

"What?" My fingers freeze, causing my character to die. "What are you saying?"

"I struggle daily to protect our friendship, but why do I crave to kiss you now that I've had a taste? I want to touch you." He blows out a ragged breath. "*Fuck*, Carolina. You have no idea how badly I want to touch you … to tell you I love us playing boyfriend and girlfriend."

"Then do it," I dare.

He buries his nose in my hair. "It's not that simple, Lina."

Rejection is the third party in this friendship of ours.

Sierra's advice from the bar zips through my thoughts

I hold the controller in my sweaty palm and am proud of myself for staying composed. "It's okay. You're not my type anyway."

His chest moves behind me as he laughs. "Oh, really? I'm not your type now, huh?"

"Nope. To be honest, you never have been."

"You begging to share a shower and for me to touch you sure screamed I was your type."

"Desperation. My vagina gets needy when I drink."

"Mmhmm. Tell me then, what's your type?"

"A guy not scared to share showers." I pause, drawing in a gutsy breath. "A guy who isn't afraid to touch me."

His chest presses against my back, and his hand slips from my hair to my thigh, inching underneath the hem of my dress. He does this silently, not a word being muttered out of his mouth.

Tonight, I will be bold.

"Someone who isn't afraid of taking chances," I continue around a gulp.

His free hand drops to my other thigh.

"Someone who isn't afraid to slide their hand higher."

His voice is raspy when he speaks, "We're playing with fire, Carolina."

Yes—a fire that has the capacity to not only incinerate our friendship, but also our hearts.

But I'm done with not taking risks.

Done searching for a guy who'll never compare to what I feel for Rex.

"If we're going to fake a relationship, might as well take advantage of the relationship perks."

A wave of pleasure smacks into me when I rub the bottom of my butt against him, feeling his growing erection. He's turned on *by me.*

He steals the remote, hits the start button, and hands it back to me while the game loads. "Play."

"What?"

I'm offering sex on the table, and he wants me to play a damn video game?

I know he loves it and all, but *what the heck?*

"Play. The. Game." His hand eases underneath my dress. "Don't die, and I won't stop."

I clutch the controller in my hands and stare at the screen. *How does he expect me to play while he's doing that?*

My fingers shake while he caresses my bare skin. The game hasn't changed much, and I'm on the first level, so this shouldn't be so hard. I'm playing at a slow pace and still alive.

I spread my legs wider, a silent plea for more, and he takes the hint—skimming his hand higher while the other stays rested. My eyes are heavy, and I fight not to shut them while he explores me—this time dipping between my thighs but not going where I need him.

I stop when his thumb slips underneath my panties.

A combination of a chuckle and a groan escapes him. "Keep playing, baby."

I shake my head while reluctantly doing what he demanded. "Are you serious? Not possible."

"Pass this level. Get an orgasm."

What a reward … if only it wasn't freaking impossible.

I spare my character from dying at the last minute. "Pass a level, and you have sex with me?"

His lips brush my ear, and I can feel his heart thumping wildly against my back. "Three levels."

To give me more incentive to pass the damn level, he slips his hand into my panties and cups me between my legs, the heel of his hand brushing against my clit.

My fingers slam against the remote buttons as I buck my hips forward. "Jesus, you're making a girl beg and play video games all for the D?"

"Sure am." He sinks a finger inside me, and my back arches against him. "You're so wet for me."

"Don't get too cocky. It might be for the guy in the game."

"Keep playing." He adds another finger.

"There's no way," I moan while he slowly strokes me.

"I'll make you come so hard if you beat the level. I promise."

I groan in defeat when my character dies and toss the controller to the side.

"Game over," he says, dragging his fingers out of me.

My hand shoots between my legs to stop him, and I press it tighter against me. I've never been so turned on in my life. I jerk my hips forward while using his hand to manipulate how I want it while moaning, and I hope he doesn't pull away when I release him.

He doesn't.

He groans in my ear, pressing a palm against my stomach, and roughly drags me into him, thrusting against me.

He balls up my dress in his fist and hoists it up until my butt is showing.

"Holy fuck," he hisses around a low groan, shoving another finger inside me, and my nails dig into his hand. "Move up."

I relax my hold on him and moan at the loss of his fingers ... and then again when I'm pushed forward on my hands and knees in front of him.

I moan, my head dropping, as he smooths his hand over my ass before massaging it.

"So much for my strong willpower," he says, sliding my panties to the side before sinking two hard fingers back into my wet core.

I rake my nails against the carpet, and he situates himself behind me.

I'm close.

So close.

I match his every thrust. "Oh my God!" I cry out. "I'm about to come!"

"Yeah," he says. "I feel you tightening around my fingers."

The pleasure amplifies when he finds my clit again.

"The motherfucking party is here!"

My heart stops so quick that I don't know how I'm not dead when Josh barges into the apartment with a flock of people behind him. Rex's fingers slide out of me in seconds, and he falls down, pulling me onto his lap. The controller is shoved back into my hand, and he starts the game back up.

Our breathing doesn't match people who were innocently playing video games.

More along the lines of Zumba ... or *sex.*

Josh freezes, taking in the scene. "Oh fuck." His eyes widen before he turns on his heel to face the group. "Let's grab some grub. I'm fucking starving."

"What?" a woman whines. "Order a pizza here or something. I'm not paying for another Uber."

Josh snaps his fingers and creates a zipping noise before pointing at the kitchen. "Let's do shots in the kitchen then! I have some grade-A tequila in there, and we can order a pizza."

Luckily, they follow him into the kitchen, and Rex pulls us up as soon as they disappear. I'm silent when he takes my hand, and we scurry down the hall to his bedroom. He releases me as soon as the door shuts behind us. When I turn around to face him, he's resting his back against the door, his hand to his chest as he catches his breath.

"I declare myself a winner since we were interrupted," I comment.

Technically, I died before they showed up, but this argument sounds better for a possible orgasm.

"How about I be the winner as I give you the best orgasm you've ever had?" He doesn't give me time to answer as he stalks forward, his face covered with need, and crushes his mouth against mine.

CHAPTER SIXTEEN

REX

*B*ad idea. *Bad fucking idea.*

That is what my brain is telling me.

Keep kissing her.

That's what my dick is telling me.

Love her.

That is what my heart is telling me.

Will we regret this tomorrow?

We're at our breaking point—putting it all on the line for this attraction we've fought for too many years.

Heat rushes through my veins as I cup her soft cheeks and devour her mouth in a way I've never kissed a woman. But then again, I've never wanted anyone so damn much in my life.

Our kiss is impulsive. Heated. Urgent.

Our desire is finally being freed from its cage.

I tune out the music blasting in the living room—most likely a courtesy from Josh to drown out any noise that might escape my bedroom. He deserves a thank you later. No doubt he'll demand my gratitude be rewarded with details on what he walked into. That's not fucking happening. Convincing him nothing happened will be a bitch, though, considering Carolina was on her hands and knees, her dress shoved up to her waist, while my fingers were inside her.

Pretty fucking hard to dispute that.

I snarl at the thought of him seeing her so exposed and sink my teeth into her lower lip. Carolina moans in response, and I hiss as she returns the favor, her bite sharper than mine. I wouldn't be surprised if she drew blood. It's a fucking struggle to breathe when I break our connection to retreat a step.

Her cheeks are flushed, her lips swollen, as she stands in front of me. Our eyes lock—hers overflowing with anticipation and hunger, matching mine.

I squeeze my eyes shut, coming to grips with what's about to happen. "What do you want, Carolina?"

"You," she breathes out. "I want you." She reaches down, grabs the hem of her dress, and pulls it over her head. She stares at me with confidence while providing the view of the woman who means everything to me.

Every ounce of tension in my body releases, all my fucks fly out the window, and I rub the tip of my thumb along my lower lip. There's no stopping my hand from dropping to my crotch to adjust my erection through my jeans even though there's no hiding how hard I am.

A beam of satisfaction floods her features. Her lips part as she reaches behind her back to unsnap her bra, and she tosses it to the side. I stifle a groan when her next move is to shimmy out of her soft pink panties.

Carolina is standing in the middle of my bedroom with her perfect, petite body on full display for me. Her breasts are fuller than they were in high school, and I gulp at the thought of tasting them. Her hips are curvier. It blows my mind that she's offering me something so damn precious.

I don't deserve it.

I've never deserved Carolina.

Yet here I am, jeopardizing it all.

My eyes cut to the limited view of her pussy, and my mouth waters.

"I keep making all the moves." Her words snap me out of imagining all the things I want to do to her. "It's your turn, Rex."

Whoa. She's making the moves?

I'm certain I was the one with my fingers shoved inside her pussy, but if making a move is what she needs from me, I'll make a goddamn move—a move that'll have her moaning and squirming underneath me.

She raises a brow in challenge, a daring smile dancing on her moist lips.

I wipe out the small distance dividing us, my hands finding her hips, and tip my head down. "You know I'm not one to turn down a challenge."

She grins deviously. "I know."

My lips crash into hers again and never separate as I walk us to my bed. She squeals when I bend my arms, my hands cupping her armpits, and I playfully toss her onto the bed. She wastes no time sliding up the bed, making room for me to join her, and rises to her knees. I join her, my pulse pounding with every move, and fall to mine.

As soon as I'm settled, she frantically pulls my shirt over my head and flings it across the room. "All of it." Her fingers start fumbling with the zipper of my jeans. "Right now."

I curl my fingers around her wrist, nudging her hand away, and do the job for her. I drop my pants along with my boxer briefs down and kick them off my feet. Her beautiful brown eyes widen when it's her turn to eye-fuck me, her gaze lingering on my cock.

She leans forward, her ass coming off the bed a few inches, to circle her arms around my neck and tug me closer. We make out slowly, and I take my sweet time kissing her—nipping at her lips, sucking on the tip of her tongue—all while she grinds against my thigh, panting.

This is it.

Our lips stay connected as I settle her onto her back, her dark hair nearly blending with my black pillow, and I crawl up the bed. I use my legs to spread hers and slip between them. A quiet moan escapes her when I bury my head in the crook of her neck, kissing my way down it. I cup her breast with my large palm while my mouth continues its journey. My lips replace my hand the moment it reaches her nipple, drawing the tiny bud into my mouth, twirling my tongue around it, and then sucking hard.

"Holy crap," she releases in a loud hiss while writhing underneath me. "More. *Please.*"

With no warning, I give her what she's demanding and thrust two fingers inside her warmth. Her pussy is soaked, which makes it easier to glide my fingers in and out of her tightness because, Lord … she's so fucking tight that I can barely fit the two in. Satisfaction hits me of how turned on she is.

Because of me.

Her pussy is this wet in response to how much she wants me.

Fuck, if this isn't about to make me come already.

I tilt my head and gently suck on her swollen clit. Her legs rise at the knees to each side of me, and her body quivers as I brush my tongue into her slit, licking it alongside my fingers. Her back arches, a desperate cry escaping her when I withdraw my fingers. Her cries change from desperate to strained when I replace them with my tongue, pushing it deep inside her.

"Jesus," she bursts out, bucking against my face. "Don't stop."

Curses fly out of my mouth as I lick and suck her pussy, my thumb climbing to her clit and massaging it in gentle circles.

"More," she urges.

I eat her pussy harder, and her hand falls to my hair when I add my fingers to the mix again. It fucking hurts, the way she's clutching at the roots, but I'll handle it. I'll deal with anything to give her the best orgasm of her life.

"Please," she begs breathlessly. "Quit holding back and have sex with me already."

It kills me, but I ignore her pleas.

Her moans grow louder, and the hard breaths knocking from her lungs tell me she's close to reaching her brink.

I briefly pull away to peek up at her before going back to work. "Come on my tongue, baby."

As if my words set her off, her back flies off the bed, and she holds my head in place. Her legs tremble as she lets herself go, and I deliver a simple kiss on her clit before lifting my head.

"Holy wow," she gasps, catching her breath. "Now, have sex with me."

I jerk back, stupidly shocked at her words momentarily. She was begging me to fuck her only minutes ago.

I chuckle, shaking my head, and suck on the fingers that were inside her before responding, "Not happening tonight. I got you off. Don't be selfish."

"*You're* the one being selfish," she argues with a hint of a frown as she points her chin toward my hard-as-a-rock cock pressed against her thigh. "If anything, you need this more than I do."

My knees nearly buckle when she wraps her fist around my dick, and I can't stop myself from jerking forward.

"I'm not fucking you with a house full of people," I grit out, throwing my head back as she starts stroking me.

"I'll be quiet," she whispers. "You can cover my mouth with the same hand that was in my vagina."

Holy hell.

Where did this Carolina come from?

As much as I crave to push her down and fuck her hard, we're not ready for that step.

My hand swoops down, wrapping around her wrist to stop her. "It's okay. This was for you."

"Trust me," she says around a snort, stroking me faster. "This will most definitely be for me, too."

My cock twitches, begging me to give her the go-ahead, and my mouth drops open as I move closer to offer better access. She seizes that opportunity to rise to her knees and shove me onto my back. I don't have time to argue before she wraps her warm lips around my hard dick and sucks on the tip, and I nearly bust when she takes my entire length into her mouth. It's my turn to thrust my hips up, feeding my cock to her as she draws it in and out of her mouth, swirling her tongue around my tip.

It doesn't take long before a surge of pleasure zips through me, and my balls tighten.

"I'm about to come," I warn in case she isn't a swallower.

She only sucks harder as if she can't wait to taste me.

My hips jerk forward, every nerve in my cock awakened as I explode in her mouth.

"Holy fuck," I seethe, still coming down from the high of the best damn blow job ever. "That was amazing."

She sits back, her butt hitting the back of her legs, and affection spills over her features. "When can we do it again?"

My lips tilt up in a grin, and I give her a raspy laugh.

Maybe this is what we were destined to be.

Best friends.

Temporary lovers.

Then, I'll lose her.

Our lives will never be the same.

We're risking it all for sex.

———

For the first time ever, I'm awake before Carolina.

The morning sun shines through my bedroom blinds, offering me the view of her tucked comfortably at my side. I'm on my back, and she's on her stomach. One of her legs is slung over my hips, and her arm is draped across my bare chest.

We've shared a bed plenty of times, but it's different this morning.

We gave each other oral last night.

One of my old high school T-shirts is bunched up at her waist, granting me a peek of her white boy shorts and the bottom cheeks of her plump ass. She grabbed a pair last night from the drawer in my dresser she assigned to herself, which is now overflowing with panties and bralettes.

She stirs, showing off more of her ass, and her body shifts more on top of me. My dick hardens as I recall what took place in this bed— her shoving me onto my back and sucking my cock as if her life depended on it. The taste of her is on my tongue.

There's no going back from this.

We weren't drunk.

There's no blaming it on the alcohol or pretending it didn't happen.

All morning, I've stressed over what this means for our relationship.

I need to know where Carolina's head is.

After her mind-blowing blow job, I kissed her and jumped out of bed. Otherwise, I would've ended up fucking her. She joined me in getting dressed, stealing another one of my tees, and swapped her contacts for glasses.

Josh's guests usually spend the night, and my door was locked, but I wasn't risking anyone seeing her naked.

There's no containing my cheesy smile when she wakes up, and her eyes soften when they see me.

"Good morning, sunshine," I chime.

"Morning," she says sleepily, not alarmed at our position.

"How'd you sleep?"

"Wonderful actually." She grins. "It's been a while since I slept over."

"A while as in a few days ago at the hotel."

"Since I've slept *over*, not shared a bed with you."

"I guess it missed you."

She repositions herself and props her chin on my chest, staring up at me. "Want to talk about the elephant in the room?"

"Here, I considered you the shy one."

"I am … except around you." She pokes me in the chest. "It's your fault, making me hang out with you all the time."

"Hey, this isn't a one-way street. Somehow, you know every detail of my life, you force me to watch shows about desperate housewives banging their lawn boys, and you insisted you teach me how to bake."

She laughs. "I'm an evil woman."

"Damn straight you are."

Thank fuck we're comfortable. Normally, I don't do sleepovers in fear of suffering through the morning after. If I ever do stay over, I leave early without breakfast or conversation.

"What will we be walking into when we leave the room?" she asks.

"Huh?"

"Josh and his friends were sure having fun last night."

"More fun than us?"

A blush rides up her forehead. "Eh, doubt that."

I wrap a strand of her hair around my finger. "Like me, Josh is picky about our houseguests. One guy is his cousin, the other is a girl he's steadily dating, and then her friend."

"Josh has been steadily dating someone?"

"Shocking, huh? They've been off and on for a minute and are *on* right now. She and her friend are cool."

A silence passes as she gawks at me. "Do you ... ever hang out with her friend?"

"No." I tuck the strand of hair I've been playing with behind her ear. "I haven't slept with her."

"How'd you know that's what I was thinking?"

"I always know what's going on in that pretty head of yours."

She slaps my chest. "I hate you."

"You love me." I roll us over, settling her on her back and staring down at her. "Is this real life right now?" My gaze travels down her body.

She pinches me. "You feel that?"

I flinch. "Uh ... yeah?"

"Then, yes, it's real life." She briefly looks away before she frowns, her eyes meeting mine. "Why wouldn't you have sex with me? Was last night a one-time thing?" She smacks her forehead. "I'm so confused."

"That makes two of us."

"You wouldn't have sex with me last night, though. Why? You don't give other girls a hard time about it."

"You're not any other girl, Carolina."

"What are we then? Friends with benefits?"

"We're way beyond friends with benefits. I can nine thousand percent confirm that."

"Super-best friends with oral benefits?"

"Wrong again."

"Is it because you think I suck at sex?"

"What? Why would you think that'd crossed my mind? As a matter of fact, you're pretty damn hot in bed."

"I was boring when we had sex in high school."

"You mean, when you were a *virgin*?" I stroke her jaw with my free hand. "I didn't expect you to be a pro at sex or for it not to be awkward. We were teenagers."

"Still, no doubt it sucked for you."

I scoff. "Did you forget I came? I was worried it'd sucked for you."

"Yes, it was painful, but you were gentle with me."

I'll always be gentle with you.

We're interrupted by her stomach grumbling.

"Breakfast?" I ask, pulling away from her.

"I'm starving."

"Do you work today?"

She shakes her head. "I have the spaghetti dinner fundraiser to raise money for the after-school program at church." She motions back and forth between us. "*We* have the fundraiser dinner. I told you to mark it in your calendar."

I forgot.

"I wait for your reminders," I grumble.

"This is also a reminder that you're helping me make the cookies."

I groan. "How many again?"

"Only two hundred. Lauren and her mom are making the other two hundred, and Shirley is making the pies."

"Jesus. We haven't done that many in a few years."

I nod. "Yep, so get ready."

One of Carolina's hobbies is hosting fundraisers. She's done countless silent auctions and dinners for people, organizations, or the church's needs. I love how much she loves helping others. I tag along, helping and allowing her to boss me around.

Her stomach growls again, and I hop off my bed.

"Let's get food in your belly."

CHAPTER SEVENTEEN
CAROLINA

"Good morning, lovebirds," Josh bursts out when we walk into the kitchen.

"Don't start," Rex warns.

Josh holds up his hands. "Hey, I'm happy for you! I've waited a long time for this moment. I'm a proud mama bear here."

"Waited for what moment?" I ask, diverting my attention into the kitchen.

He makes a sweeping gesture to Rex and me. "You two to bang."

Rex shoves his shoulder when he passes him. "We didn't bang."

Josh scoffs. "All right. I've waited a long time for you to *hook up*."

"Who says we hooked up?" Rex fires back.

"Your guilty-ass faces when I busted you in the living room." Josh raises his brows.

"We were playing video games," I explain, looking as guilty as he said we did last night.

What I'm wearing doesn't help our argument—Rex's tee, a pair of his sweats—and my hair resembles a rat's nest.

Josh opens his mouth to reply, but everyone's attention shoots to the tall blonde strolling into the kitchen, wearing a shirt that hits her knees.

She stands on her tiptoes and snags a mug from the cabinet before glancing at me, wearing an amused smile on her face. "You must be Carolina."

"Yes?" I answer in confusion.

She points at Rex. "He's in love with you."

"Told you!" Josh shouts.

"Every convo we've had, he's mentioned you." She tips her mug my way. "We order pizza; he tells us your favorite is chicken and pepperoni. We watch a show; he informs us how many episodes he's seen *with you*. Girl, I know enough about you that we could be best friends." Her smile grows. "I'm Angelica."

I offer a friendly wave. "I'm Carolina … although it seems you already know that."

The fridge shuts, and Josh holds up a carton of eggs.

"Is the happy couple hungry this morning?" he says. "I'm making French toast!"

"I'll never turn down French toast," I reply.

Josh starts pulling out ingredients while Angelica grabs a pan. Rex squeezes between them in the narrow space, snatches two mugs, and makes our coffee—adding the perfect amount of sugar and almond milk.

"I'm waiting for Rex to tell me that French toast is your favorite," Angelica jokes.

"Pancakes are her favorite," Rex inputs. "Extra syrup. Add bananas if possible."

He sets down a mug in front of me and winks, and my heart melts.

————

"I have an excellent idea," Rex says when we finish unloading groceries in my sister's kitchen. "You bake. I taste-test." He tips his head toward Tricia's kitchen table with a boyish smile beaming on his full lips. "I'll sit here, watch the master do her work, and then make sure they're scrumptious when finished."

I deposit the bags into the recycling bin. "Nice try, but no. You're the assistant baker today." I tug two aprons from the drawer and toss him a pink one printed with yellow rubber duckies.

"Can't blame a man for trying." He ties the apron around him with amusement. "I like this look."

After devouring Josh's French toast and evading questions from him and Angelica, we cleaned up and went to the grocery store for the cookie ingredients. Rex offered his kitchen, but room is limited there. Tricia's has more counter space and top-of-the-line appliances. We'll also be left alone since she and the family went away for the weekend.

It's been a while since I've baked this large of a batch. I'm a bit rusty and grateful Rex is helping.

"I will let you lick the bowl in reward for your help," I offer, strolling around the kitchen while gathering all the needed supplies.

He gives me a satisfied smile. "I love when you let me lick things."

The measuring cup slips out of my hand, crashing onto the floor, and I bend down to retrieve it. Normally, I'd roll my eyes and throw a dish towel at him—something along those lines—but his words hit a different spot. Not annoyance. Desire. He's right. *I do* love it when he licks things, but I'm too shy to tell him that.

When I rise, I replace the cup in my hand with an oven mitt and slap him on the side of the head, wishing desire weren't igniting through me. I'm supposed to be making cookies for my church fundraiser, and all I want to do is fall back onto my knees and taste-test him.

He exaggeratedly flinches with a satisfied smile on his face at flustering me.

"All right, what flavors are we baking up today, boss woman?" He scrubs his hands together.

I swoop my hand toward the ingredients. "Chocolate chip."

He snatches the bag of chocolate chips. "I call those."

"Oatmeal raisin."

He gags. "You can't do oatmeal raisin."

"What? Why?"

"People who make oatmeal raisin cookies deserve to be in prison."

He stands taller. "Here us chocolate chip lovers are, minding our business and snagging a cookie, only to bite into it and discover it has wrinkled-ass grapes inside." He flicks the box of raisins along the island with his fingers. "And people wonder why I have trust issues."

"You have trust issues because you get too much in your head." I drag the raisins back and hold them up. "You're getting raisins. We need variety."

He scans the ingredients. "What are our other options? Peanut butter? Snickerdoodles?"

"None. Everyone has confirmed what they're bringing. I'm responsible for chocolate chip and oatmeal raisin."

"All right, but don't let anyone think I helped you with that disgrace of a cookie. I'm making the chocolate chip, and I will give you the honors of eating the nasty raisin dough."

"You're too overdramatic."

"I take my cookies very seriously, Lina. You know this."

"Yeah, yeah, yeah," I mutter.

"I'll be on sugar duty." He snags the sugar jar.

I pluck it out of his hand. "*I* will be on sugar duty." I set it on the other side of me on the counter, away from him, and waggle my finger in the air. "Remember last time I let you be on sugar duty?"

"Yes, they were heavenly."

"No, they weren't."

His palm goes to his heart. "You sure know how to hurt a man's baking ego."

"You put *way* too much sugar in them. They tasted horrible." I hand him the carton of eggs. "You're on batter-mixing duty."

"Well, if that isn't damn boring," he grumbles, opening the carton.

———

Four hours later, the house smells like a bakery, and the cookies are done.

I rub my hands together before turning around and washing them. "I need to shower and get ready."

Rex nods, and I swallow back my laughter at the flour handprint on his face from me tapping his cheek earlier. He tried to wipe it away with the back of his arm, and I was such a good friend and held back from telling him he missed it.

"Same," Rex says, throwing the last of our trash into the can. "Do you want me to pick you up or meet you there?"

"You can meet me there," I reply.

"Cool. I'll help load these into your car."

He carries most of the containers, and we stack them into my back seat before he kisses me on the cheek and says good-bye. I rush upstairs to shower egg yolk and flour off myself and start undressing when my phone beeps with a text.

James: Have dinner with me.

The high I've been riding from hanging out with Rex is wiped away, and the thought of having dinner with James makes me gag. I debate on not answering him, but like always, I do.

Me: Busy with a fundraiser tonight.

James: Can I come?

This time, I nearly heave up the few cookies I taste-tested.

Me: No. My parents will be there.

James: That's rude. Isn't it time to introduce me to your family?

I want to introduce him to my family like I want McDonald's to stop serving their fizzy Cokes.

Me: What do you want?

James: For you to stop hanging out with him. To stop fucking him.

Repulsion shakes through me. *Him* is Rex. I hate when James brings him into our mess.

Me: Stop. We're just friends.

James: Better be.

I toss my phone onto my bathroom counter with tears pricking my eyes. I can't ask Rex to make his Instagram private, or he'll question me. If I ask him to block James, he'll assume he's messing with me. My mouth will stay shut, my secrets hidden, and I'll keep dealing with James the best I can by pacifying him.

Eventually, he'll get tired of me.
Hopefully.

———

I arrive at the church two hours early to set everything up.

The weather is on our side today, the sun shining bright with a slight breeze. The fundraiser is being held in the parking lot. My biggest goal during these events is to keep the kids entertained, so I made sure it was near the playground, I ordered a bounce house, and the elementary school principal agreed to attend dressed up as a clown.

Food and money have been donated, and from what I've seen on Facebook, the fundraiser should pull in a decent crowd, which is typical. Blue Beech citizens love their church, food, socializing ... and *gossiping.*

The after-school program is a great cause. Years ago, my mother started it, and she runs it for free along with other volunteers. The church provides free childcare to children until parents can pick them up after work.

People are arriving, searching for seats while children run through the parking lot toward the bounce house.

"Hey," Rex says at the same time his arms wrap around my waist from behind.

His arms don't move as I turn around to face him.

"Hey." A hint of shyness is in my tone, surprising me since I'm always myself around him.

Then again, we've also never hung out in public the day after his face was between my legs.

He looks as hot as ever today with his black shirt and knee-length ripped black shorts with frayed ends. His hair is messy, per usual, and I can't stop myself from running a thumb over the stubble coating his jaw.

What happened last night exposed the attraction we'd hidden for too long. It's freeing now that everything is out in the open, and pride swells through me over the thought that he trusts me enough to take this step together.

My shoulders slump.

What is this step?

A quick speed bump of us hooking up, and that's all it'll ever lead to?

Tonight, I'm asking him. We've always been open and honest in our relationship. Even when we were holding back from anything physical, we knew the feelings were there—that there was so much love that it'd take a heavy chain saw to break it.

Only inches separate us, and his hands trail down my waist before tugging at the hem of my green dress. "I like this."

I peek up at him, biting the corner of my lip, wrapped in the zone of him. "Thank you."

He nuzzles his face into my neck. "I wish I could take it off."

That makes two of us.

I rub my thighs together, and he laughs when I push my body into him.

"Maybe later?"

The contagious grin on his face causes me to do the same when he pulls his head away, his hands still wrapped around my waist. "Are we having another sleepover tonight?"

Heat shoots up my neck. "If you want? Maybe we can play video games again?"

Excitement lines his features, and he chuckles before dragging me into his chest and pressing his lips to the top of my head. When he pulls back a bit, we stare at each other in hesitation, curious on our next move. Rex owns it by dipping his head down and pressing his lips against my mouth this time.

"I'd love another round of video games."

"Carolina!"

I jump back at the sound of my father's voice as he's stalking in our direction.

Shoot!

We were so wrapped up in our own world that I not only forgot there were other volunteers and my father here, but I was also close to making out with Rex at my church.

My dad will have a field day with this one.

A lecture is coming as soon as we're alone.

CHAPTER EIGHTEEN

Pastor Adams is positively putting a bad word in for me with God. He's doing a sucky-ass job of hiding his frustration while strolling in our direction.

My kiss with Carolina was hardly a peck, but from his heated face, you'd think Carolina was straddling me, naked, on the teeter-totter.

While delivering my best face of innocence, I shove my hand out when he reaches us. "Pastor Adams. It's nice to see you again."

He shakes my hand, his firm tight, while his lips form an irritated frown. "Rex, I appreciate you coming."

"Anything I can do to help," I reply with a big, friendly smile.

Rick's gaze shifts to Carolina, and he jerks his chin toward the other side of the parking lot. "Your mom needs your help with the donation baskets."

Carolina's cheeks are as red as the roses I bought for her birthday this year. "Of course." She signals toward the tables. "Let me wrap this up, and I'll be right there."

"Nah, I got it," I say, waving my hand toward a table covered in baskets. "Go help your mom."

"Thank you," Carolina says, shooting me an apprehensive glance before turning her attention back to her father.

The fundraiser reminds me of a mini carnival. A large pavilion is set up over the tables and chairs. The children have plenty to entertain them—playground, jump house, clown, and a DJ blasting kid shit. Carolina arranged a silent auction, and those entering the spaghetti cook-off are arranging their food placements. I raise a brow when I spot the dunk tank. Mr. Rogers, the old high school football coach, was the dunk tank dude, but he recently moved.

Who's taking his place?

I situate the tables and chairs exactly how Carolina does every time, and she returns minutes after I'm finished.

"Perfect timing. Show up right when the hard work is done," I joke.

"You're so hilarious." She rolls her eyes while walking away, waving me to follow her. "Come on, my favorite helper. I have the perfect job for you."

I follow her, having no shame in checking out her ass. "What's this job?"

"You'll see," she sing-songs.

"That's scary. Last time you said that, you auctioned me off for a date, forcing me to endure dinner with the town's cat lady."

"Ms. Gorgman is sweet." Her voice is full of sarcasm.

"She asked for her cake to go with the intention of me licking it off her later—verbatim." I shudder, reliving the moment in my head.

"Oh, please. I doubt it was the first time you licked food off a woman."

"Not cake, and most definitely not off a sixty-five-year-old woman who has the stench of cat piss."

"Lucky for you, it's not a date auction."

"Better not, or be prepared to drop your savings to buy a date with your boy." I signal down my body. "You know this sells for big money."

She scoffs. "Calm down, Casanova. Your job is way better than paid dates."

When she stops, a groan leaves me.

"The dunk tank? Not fucking happening." I make a circle around my head. "Do you know how long it takes to perfect this look?"

"Five minutes," she deadpans.

Next argument point coming. "I don't have dry clothes to change into."

"You're covered. I brought some of yours from the loft."

"I love how well you planned this out without telling me." My finger moves to my chin, tapping it, as her face floods with delight. "If I recall correctly, whenever I ask for my clothes back, you say once they make it to your place, they're no longer mine. Sorry, babe, but I can't change into *your* clothes. It looks like you'll be sitting your pretty ass in that tank."

The thing looks like a death trap with the wire net around the tank and the red target on the bright yellow backstop.

It's her turn to signal to her hair. "It takes me a good hour to do this work of art." She grins, slapping my shoulder. "I win. Follow me, and I'll show you where to change and shower when you're done."

"Fine," I grumble. "I'm only doing this because I love your ass."

She grins wildly. "I know."

How does she always manage to talk me into this shit?

———

I've been chilling in the dunk tank for a good thirty minutes, and I have yet to go underwater.

One reason might be that only kids have played.

I'm ninety percent sure that will change when Molly hands Maliki the ball.

Shit.

"Dude," I blurt out, shifting in the uneasy wooden seat, the ice-cold water up to my knees. "Hand the ball back to the kid, and I'll buy you a round of beers." I pause to hold up four fingers. "Make that four rounds."

Today's goal is to not get wet.

Maliki turns his hat backward, throwing the ball up in the air and catching it. "Did you forget that I own a bar and get my beer for dirt cheap?"

"Fifty bucks then!"

He continues tossing the ball in the air.

"I'll give you permission to marry my sister."

"He doesn't need your permission," Sierra pipes in before throwing her attention to Maliki. "Dunk him."

"Why don't you allow me the honors?"

The crowd, filled with grown-ups and children, part as Rick comes through, all dramatic and shit. He stops in front of Maliki and holds out his hand. Maliki shoots me an apologetic look before passing the ball to Rick. My eyes widen when Rick faces me, and the serious expression on his face confirms he's determined to make this shot.

I'm unclear why Pastor Adams has a beef with me, but I thought after our breakfast, we were cool.

"Dad," Carolina warns, catching on to the tension.

"What?" Rick asks, acting clueless. "It's a game." His eyes flash my way, meeting mine. "Right, Rex?"

"Just a game," I repeat, hoping he's never been an avid baseball player. "Let him have at it."

Everyone's attention is on us as they watch my girlfriend's dad stretch his arm back as if he were throwing the winning pitch at the World Series and then chucks the ball toward the target. The crowd jumping up and down notifies me he's going to hit the target, and seconds later, my seat collapses, dropping me into the pit of freezing water.

"Holy shit," I can't stop from yelling as I come up for air before standing.

Rick doesn't pay me another glance while handing the ball to Maliki. "Your turn." Without waiting for his response, he spins around and walks away.

Aren't pastors supposed to be understanding, kind people?

That'd better have been a truce.

Maliki raises a brow in my direction as I shiver like a wet dog. "Seems you're bonding well with your future father-in-law."

"Never had a better relationship," I reply, my teeth chattering as I wrap my arms around my body.

———

"Thank you for getting wet for me."

Carolina is leaning against a wall in the hallway when I step out of the church restroom, wearing fresh, dry clothes.

Lucky for me, after being dunked by her father, my job ended. Carolina had a towel waiting for me when I jumped out of the tank, and I wrapped it around my body while rushing inside the church, barefoot. She was behind me, asking for a volunteer to be the next dunk tank victim, but no takers were speaking up. Not surprising. I doubt my fall looked enjoyable.

I drop the bag of clothes onto the floor and run my hands through my damp hair. "Next time, put me at the kissing booth."

She shakes her head, pushing off the wall. "Never happening, so don't get your hopes up."

"Why not?" I pick up the bag and throw it over my shoulder, walking in step with her. "Would you be jealous?"

We turn down a hall, passing volunteers, and my hand finds hers, weaving our fingers together.

Us doing this is more comfortable than I ever thought it'd be.

It might be only holding hands, something we've done countless times, *but* it's more than platonic now.

She looks up at me with a radiant smile. "Absolutely, and you'd be the same if it were the other way around."

"Nah, I'd cut in line and buy all your kisses."

I grunt when I'm pulled down a vacant hallway and pushed into a dark room. While I wrap my head around what's happening, the door slams shut behind us, and Carolina's lips hit mine.

It's a sweet kiss.

Minimal tongue.

Lasts only seconds.

Her eyes search mine as she pulls her mouth away, but she doesn't move. "I've wanted to do that since you agreed to the dunk tank."

I lick my lips to taste her. "It was my pleasure."

She snorts. "It definitely wasn't."

"You're right." I kiss the tip of her nose and stare into her beautiful eyes. "You can make it up to me later."

———

"Question."

My eyes sweep over to Carolina at her ... question. She's sitting next to me in one of the two remaining chairs we left after cleanup. I'm in the other.

It's dark, nearly ten o'clock, and the fundraiser has ended. A group of people stayed behind and helped clean up, but it's only us now. Rick has dodged me since he dunked my ass, but I remind myself to reach out to him and figure out what's on his mind. My guess is, he's unhappy that Carolina and I are so serious yet not married. For as long as I've known Carolina, she's expressed her parents stress marriage and abstinence.

I'm tired, every muscle in my body aches, and I can't wait to go home and collapse onto the couch.

"Answer," I reply, stretching my legs out in front of me.

"Can you clarify this?" She signals between us.

I raise a brow in confusion even though I'm not confused about shit. "Huh?"

"What's going on with us?" She delivers the words slowly, as if it'll take a moment for my brain to digest them.

This is what I've feared since day one.

The dreaded *what are we* talk.

It's not the first time I've been asked this question. Those discussions ended in awkwardness and me fleeing the scene.

I'm shit at expressing myself.

Shit at *clarifying* labels.

I clear my throat, scrubbing a hand over my now-sweaty forehead while gathering my thoughts before allowing them to fall from my mouth. Unlike with other women, there's no walking away from this conversation with Carolina. No matter how weird it gets, I'll have this talk with her. She deserves that.

"How about you clarify what you want us to be?" I finally say.

That's a good answer.

Whatever she wants to be, I'm game.

Her furrowed brows inform me I'm stupid, and that was not a good answer.

"Nope," she quips, shaking her head repeatedly. "We can't do that."

"Why not?" My mind races for the reasons we can do that.

She thrusts her finger into her chest. "*I* can't clarify what *you* want." Her finger points at me.

Valid point.

I want her, but I also need her help walking me through this so I don't fuck anything up.

I wrap my arm around her shoulders, and her chair rattles as I drag it closer to mine. I soften my voice as I say, "I want what you want."

Her head drops into the crook of my neck as she leans into me. "I can clarify what I want, Rex, but you're the only person who can speak for your heart, for where your head is."

"My heart is with you." The words come out effortlessly, but their meaning is massive.

I grin as she relaxes against me, and my hand strokes her arm.

"And your head?"

My hair rises on the back of my neck. It's not always the heart you have to fight. Sometimes, it's your goddamn head that fucks you up.

"My head is …" I release a heavy sigh. "I won't lie and say I know what I'm doing because I sure as hell don't. I can't promise to be perfect, but I can promise to give this everything I have."

She loses a breath when I turn her in her chair so we're facing each other, her features unreadable.

"Can you work with that?" I ask, fear storming through me.

Will that be enough for her?

A slow smile builds along her lips, settling my stomach, and her hands cup my face. "I can most definitely work with that."

———

"Perfect timing!" Josh shouts when we walk into the apartment to find him and Angelica sitting on the couch while watching TV. "Looks like we're about to have our first double date! How was the fundraiser?"

"Good," Carolina answers around a yawn. "Long."

"You have any leftover cookies?" He raises his leg to nudge a closed pizza box on the table with his foot. "I'll share pizza."

"They're in the car," Carolina answers, thrusting a thumb toward the door. "You can go grab them if you want."

I followed Carolina home after we left the church to drop off her car. She made a pit stop into the loft and packed an overnight bag, and I drove us to my place.

Josh stands. "Be right back. You two make yourself comfortable, and everyone pick a movie." He snaps his fingers and does a circling motion around the three of us. "Make it a good one, so I don't pass out."

Angelica scoots over to give us enough room on the couch, and I collapse onto the other end. Carolina falls down next to me, her body halfway on top of mine.

The remote is in Angelica's hand as she glances over at us with a raised brow. "What kind of movies do you like?"

"I have a feeling I'll be outvoted, and we're bound to watch something romantic," I comment.

Carolina rolls her eyes while patting my thigh. "Honey, don't act like you didn't get emotional during *A Walk to Remember*."

"Yes, because the girl reminded me of you!" I argue, throwing my right arm up in frustration before counting my reasoning with my fingers. "Preacher's daughter. Ugly-ass sweaters. The guy is the complete opposite of her. At the end, she dies." My attention briefly flicks to Angelica. "Spoiler alert."

A flash of understanding flashes in Carolina's eyes. "Oh shoot, I never thought about that."

"That entire week, I stressed, waiting for you to tell me you had a terminal illness and that the movie was a silent warning. Scared the shit out of me."

Angelica points at me with the remote. "You wait until you watch *The Notebook*."

"Already seen it," I reply.

"*The Fault in Our Stars*?"

I nod.

"*The Vow*?"

I nod again.

"*P.S. I Love You*?"

Another nod.

Angelica looks back at Josh when he walks in. "You need to step your movie game up, babe. Rex has watched nearly every movie that I've cried over!"

Josh plops next to her with the container of cookies in his hand and whistles through his teeth. "Dude, quit making me look bad, or I'm not sharing the pizza *or* cookies."

"Don't get mad at me for being smart," I fire back.

He snatches a cookie and takes a large bite before gagging. "Jesus! What are these?"

"Oatmeal raisin," Carolina replies around a laugh.

He sticks out his tongue, gagging again, and tosses the cookie back into the container as if it were toxic. "Why would you do that to a man? I thought they were chocolate chip."

The three of us crack up in laughter.

"Told you," I say to Carolina. "Oatmeal cookies are blasphemous."

"And banned from our apartment," Josh adds.

"What about *Save the Last Dance*?" Angelica asks, flipping through the options.

"I love that movie." Carolina peeks up at me. "You haven't seen that one."

Angelica hits play.

The movie is actually pretty damn good.

———

Josh and Angelica are knocked out when the movie credits flash across the screen.

I'm spent as my eyes dart over to Carolina snuggled in my arms. "Another movie or bed?"

She yawns loudly, standing and stretching, and I do the same.

"Bed. Definitely bed." Her attention drifts to the snoring couple. "Should we wake them?"

"Would you want to be woken up?"

"Probably." She nods. "That couch isn't very comfortable."

Josh's eyes pop open when I nudge his foot with mine.

"Hey, sleepyhead. It's bedtime."

He shakes Angelica awake, and they grumble a quick, "Good night," before sluggishly poking along down the hall. Carolina and I turn off the lights, moving to my bedroom in slow motion.

As soon as I close the bedroom door, Carolina rummages through my drawers, pulling out her favorite tee of mine. With her back to me and with no hesitation, she whips her dress over her head, causing my heart to nearly jolt out of my chest. Only seconds pass before she unsnaps her bra and slides the tee over her head. The shirt hits the top of her knees, and her nipples are poking through the thin fabric when she turns around and looks at me.

My mouth waters at the sight.

I gulp when the memory of us in the hotel room courses through my mind—of how similar the situation was and how I turned her down. I fight with myself on how to handle this. Sure, we hooked up last night, but we didn't take that final step.

No doubt that will happen if I touch her tonight.

She smiles back at me while walking to the bathroom, her hand brushing against my stomach when she passes me. I follow her, and Carolina snags the toothbrush I bought for the nights she stays over. My hand is nearly shaking as I brush mine. Her smile grows the second time she slips past me, and my knees nearly buckle when she hops into my bed and yanks the blanket up her body, stopping only inches underneath her neck.

My cock is obnoxiously hard, and there's no hiding it. The room is dead silent while I change into sweats, and the sheets are cold as I settle on my knees on the edge of the bed. She scoots over, giving me room, and I leave the bedside lamp on when I join her. My sheets still smell like her—a vanilla mixed with cherry scent.

She wastes no time in getting comfortable under my arm, resting on her hip, with her leg slung over mine.

Carolina is halfway straddling me, and I'm not freaking the fuck out.

It feels right.

Natural.

Where she belongs.

"Thank you again for everything," she says, rubbing her foot up and down my leg.

My arm swings around her waist. "Always."

I release a *hmph* when she pushes herself up to straddle me.

"I think you deserve a reward for all your hard work."

My hands settle on the tops of her thighs as I fight to control my breathing *and* not shift my hips. She's only wearing panties underneath that shirt, and her pussy covered with only panties would feel amazing against my cock.

"You normally reward me with cookies."

Yes. I'm suggesting she reward me with cookies rather than straddle me.

Fucking idiot.

She smirks, her pink lips full. "Would you rather have cookies?"

"I don't know."

Her smile wavers, confliction on her face as her gaze lowers to me, and my stomach twists at the sudden disappointment.

My hand leaves her thigh when I reach forward, pushing away a loose strand of hair away from her face. "Hey. What's up?"

She hesitates.

I slide my hand up and down her thigh in reassurance. "Come on, tell me."

Her face tightens, and she bites into her cheek. "I suck at this whole seduction thing."

A heaviness falls over me, and my voice is tender. "Trust me, babe, you don't suck at this."

She's not convinced. "You look like you'd rather me pluck your eyeballs out than be on top of you."

I tighten my grip on her to stop her from moving off me.

Here, I thought I was doing us a favor by holding back, and she thinks it's because I don't want her. As scared as I was that us being together would push her away, my constant rejection will do just as much damage, if not more.

I tilt my hips up, and she gasps when my erection presses against her core. "There's never been a question of *if* you turn me on. It's always been *if* this is a good idea."

Her eyes widen, understanding flickering on her face. "So, I *do* turn you on." The grin she was sporting minutes ago resurfaces.

The air grows thick, and I curl forward to cup the back of her head with my palm. Not a word leaves my mouth until our eyes are locked —hers with traces of every emotion.

Fear. Excitement. Love. Hurt.

We're so close that I feel her chest heaving underneath my shirt.

"I want this as much as you do, babe," I say, inches from her lips, not breaking our eye contact. "Hell, more than you do."

That gorgeous smile of hers grows larger than I've ever seen in all the years I've known her. "If I say something, do you promise not to throw me off your lap?"

Not going in the direction I thought this was going.

I arch a brow, my hands digging into her hair. "Sure?"

"I want you to take this step with me, Rex."

"Step?"

She blows out a long breath and lifts one of her hands, smoothing her palm over my face before settling it on my cheek. My mouth goes dry. Affection simmers in her eyes as we focus on nothing but each other, in our own little confused world.

Her words come out slow. Her tone soft. "Rex, you're capable of a relationship, and as someone who believes in you, who trusts you, I'm willing to put my heart on the line to prove it."

My hand covers hers resting on my cheek. "Carolina—"

She shoves my hand away to press a finger against my lips. "I'm not finished." Her finger leaves my lips and brushes my chin before she lowers her hand to my chest, tapping the spot over my heart. "This heart is capable of being a good friend, a good boyfriend, a good lover—"

"Is that what you want?" I cut in, my head spinning. "For me to be your boyfriend?" Just the thought sends a jolt of excitement through me.

Us together.

Boyfriend and girlfriend.

Lovers.

She nods. "More than anything." The serious look on her face morphs into a smirk. Her next words come out in a song, one sounding like a cheesy-ass car commercial, and she moves her shoulders from side to side in a dancing motion. "You know you want to."

She further proves her point by wiggling on top of me, rolling this romantic moment into a hungrier one filled with need for her.

"Let's do it then."

Her face brightens. "Really?"

My answer comes in the form of kissing her with everything I have.

We've lit the fuse, and I pray it doesn't burn everything we've built.

CHAPTER NINETEEN

CAROLINA

My heart thuds against my chest.

Rex's tongue slides into my mouth, giving me the taste of toothpaste.

I grind against him in his lap while we make out, feeling his erection grow harder underneath me with every movement. My skin tingles at his excitement *for me … for us.*

"I want you," I whisper into his mouth.

He draws away, locking my eyes with his, and understanding dawns on his face.

This is it.

What we've been beating around our entire friendship.

Nervousness rocks through me as I grab the waistband of his sweats. I whip a leg over his, no longer straddling him, and am on my knees when I tug at his pants. I don't make much progress before his hand wraps around my wrist, his grip firm. Just as I'm about to argue, he flips me on my back and hovers over me.

"Swear to me, Carolina," he whispers. "Swear to me, this won't change us."

I shake my head, the pillow soft under my head. "It won't change anything. I swear."

All the reluctance he's been carrying splits into hunger, and his voice is thick as he speaks, "You want to fuck me?"

What does he think I've been trying to do for the past week?

Play Yahtzee?

He leans down to whisper in my ear, "Do you remember the first time we had sex?"

His scruff rubs against my cheek, and I shiver when he pulls away.

I will until the day I die.

I nod. "Yes."

"God, I wanted to do so much more, starting with this."

Heat creeps up my spine when he pushes up my shirt, baring me to him, and palms my breast while lowering his body over mine.

"I love you in my shirts," he bites out, capturing my nipple in his fingers and lightly pinching it. "I wanted to suck on these." With the last word, he draws a nipple between his lips and sucks hard.

My hips tilt forward when he slides his tongue up and down my entire breast.

"My mouth watered to taste your pussy ... to have it on my tongue, so I could taste you all night."

Unlike our first time, I stare down at him, not wanting to miss a second of what is happening, when he slides my panties down my legs. Our eyes are locked as he carefully spreads my legs. Then, my lips between my legs part, and he sticks his tongue inside me.

Holy mother-freaking crap!

"I wanted to set you on fire while I played with your pussy. Wishing I could suck on your clit."

He does just that, wrapping his lips around my most sensitive spot and slowly sucking it, circling his lips around it in the process.

Rex is a dirty talker during sex.

I love it.

Just as I'm wrapping my mind around his tongue being between my legs, he grips my thighs, pulling my butt off the bed, and drags me into his mouth, devouring me.

I'm dizzy.

I'm trying to keep up and watch, but when he loses his hold on a thigh and curves a single finger inside me, all eye contact is over.

I'm overtaken by tingles hitting every inch of my body, and my moans take over the room.

"There's that G-spot," he says with a chuckle.

I don't have to see him to know he's sporting a smirk.

With the few guys I've done this with, it maybe lasted a good ten minutes and resulted in no orgasm, but not with Rex … no. He's passionately kissing me between my legs, fingering me, and he rides me through one orgasm … then another. At this point, I'm doubting if he's going to have sex with me or just keep getting me off, using his tongue to appease me.

I'm not complaining, but I want more.

I want him inside me.

All of him.

I sigh at the loss of his mouth, and he stares up at me.

"You were so wet and tight when I got you ready for my cock," he groans out at the memory.

I writhe underneath him. "I remem—" I stop myself from finishing. "Actually, I don't. Please remind me."

He smirks, climbing over my body, and sweat lines his forehead when his mouth returns to mine. "Now, Carolina, a man will have a complex if you don't remember how good he filled you with his dick."

I taste myself when he briefly plunges his tongue between my lips before I lose him again.

He rubs a thumb over my bottom lip—that seems to be his thing. "You want to fuck me, Carolina?"

I nod repeatedly. "Yes … please … now." My voice is so strained; I hardly recognize it.

A yelp leaves me when he rolls us over—him on his back and me on top again, his hands firmly gripping my hips.

"Then, fuck me," he grounds out, tilting his head toward the nightstand. "Condom, top drawer."

I wriggle against him a few times, hearing him release a hiss, and then stretch along the bed to the nightstand. There's a box of condoms inside the drawer. It's nearly full, XL—not surprising since I've seen his cock a few times now. It was a struggle to take him all the way in my mouth last night.

I hesitate, taking in how he's having me do all the work, and build up the courage to appear as confident as I can.

He hisses as I drag his pants down, his cock springing free, and I fumble with ripping open the condom wrapper. It's the first time a guy has asked me to do the honors.

His muscles tense when I stroke him once before rolling the condom onto his thick cock.

"Is that good?" Stupidity hits me at my question, but it's important.

Homegirl is not getting preggers over here.

My parents would really shit.

I scrub a hand over my forehead.

Why am I thinking about my parents right before having premarital sex?

"Is everything okay?" Rex asks, rising on his elbows at the change in my mood.

I nod. "Mmhmm. *More* than okay."

"Take off your shirt, so I can see all of you."

I whip it off and throw it across the room. Our moans fill the room when I align myself with his cock and slowly ease my way down, as he fills every inch of me. It's been a while since I've had sex, so there's a slight pain, and I still for a moment.

"Holy fuck," he hisses, biting hard into his lower lip. "You're tight."

I only nod while adjusting to his size.

"You good?" Rex asks.

I'm grateful he's not rushing this, that he's giving me time.

I nod again. "I'm perfect."

His hand rises, rubbing circles over my clit, making me wetter.

Turning me on even more.

Well … that's a way to get my mind off the twinge of pain.

"This will be better than the last time, I promise." I buck forward as he slows his movements on my clit.

"Every time is perfect with you, babe." His hand locks around my hip before his jerk forward.

A burst of pleasure barrels through me, my ache of pain turning into an ache of needing more of him, and I slowly grind against him.

He stays still, allowing me to take charge.

At the rotation of my hips, his rise, matching my tempo.

It doesn't take us long to find the perfect rhythm.

Sex with Rex is amazing.

Perfection.

Better than what I imagined.

I fall forward, unable to support my weight, and rest my hand onto his chest, knowing I'm close to my brink.

That slow tempo speeds up until we're going wild, all the years of sexual tension bleeding through us. My hand moves from his chest to the headboard as he drills his hips into me, his hand on my waist tighter to keep me from flying off him, and I collapse against him, moaning out my release, not caring who hears.

He thrusts violently underneath me, losing every ounce of gentle control he's ever had for me, and I gasp when he rolls us over again. As soon as I fall to my stomach, he props my hips up, his hand sliding down my back, and I level myself on my elbows, peeking back at him.

Hunger fills his face.

Need in his eyes.

Not wasting a moment of not being inside me, he fills me again, pounding into me hard and fast.

I smile as another orgasm approaches.

I'm not getting a fake Rex.

This is real.

All him.

How he is in bed.

How he likes it.

He's giving me all of him, showing me all of him.

"You feel so good, Carolina," he moans. "Do you feel how hard I am inside you?"

I gasp, fighting to control my breathing … to speak. "Yes." It's a struggle to release even that word.

"I'm going to come so hard inside you."

I slump against the bed, my body trembling as soon as my stomach hits the warm sheets, and I grin at the splotches of sweat on them.

From us being together.

I shudder as I release my orgasm, saying his name in a low whisper.

He gives me a few more thrusts before slamming into me one last time, holding me in place, and releasing a low groan, my name leaving his lips louder than his did mine.

Seconds later, he pulls out and collapses on his back next to me.

Sweat covers our bodies, the scent of sex in the room, as our chests heave in and out.

The door to our friendship has been closed and locked, the key thrown away.

There's no returning.

We're somewhere new.

Hopefully, this *new* won't ruin us.

———

We did it.

Rex and I finally had sex.

Amazing, *out of this world, will never be better with anyone else* sex.

We're tangled up in his sheets, naked, after another round this morning.

It was different than last night.

It was slow.

Every hair on my body rose, and I orgasmed in minutes as he whispered sweet things into my ear.

"You're beautiful."

"I love being inside you."

"Love how we fit together perfectly."

"You own every inch of me."

Not only is Rex a dirty talker in the bedroom, but he can also be a sweet one.

Rex props himself up on his elbow, me on my back, as he stares down at me. "What are you up to today?" He tucks a strand of hair behind my ear, and even though his eyes are tired, they're crinkled at the corners as a smile takes over his gorgeous face.

My smile is shy in return. "Working and then nothing really."

Other than regaining some energy after the workouts you've given me.

Screw a gym membership. All I need is good sex from Rex.

Sex with him is the equivalent to one week of cardio.

"Working and then hanging out with me?" he corrects.

"Duh." I groan at the sound of Bob Marley playing from the kitchen.

"Josh is up." Rex chuckles.

"At least we'll get fed well."

Reggae means Josh is cooking one of his infamous breakfasts. Sure, loud music first thing in the morning is annoying, but he makes up for it with his kitchen skills. My stomach grumbles, just thinking about it.

"We need it after last night."

"Do you think he heard us?" A blush runs over my skin.

"I'm positive all of Blue Beech heard us. You'll be getting calls about your bad behavior later." He tickles my side, causing me to burst out in laughter. "You made me work up an appetite this morning. Let's hope Josh is making pancakes."

After enduring an hour of dating questions from Josh and Angelica—their smug expressions confirming they most definitely heard us last night—we trek back to Rex's bedroom.

Rex hops in the shower, and I fall onto his bed, resting my back against his headboard. I capture my phone from the nightstand.

As badly as I wanted to join him, my legs feel like noodles.

My vagina needs a break.

My stomach drops when I pull up my notifications.

James: We need to talk.

I need to talk to him like I need to grow antlers out of my head.

The text was sent at one this morning, and I debate whether to answer.

He could've been in one of his moods.

Stupidly, I reply.

Me: No, we don't. Kick rocks.

Seconds later, my phone rings.

James calling.

My heart rages against my chest. He normally doesn't call. He prefers to type out his threats, so I don't miss them.

I decline the call.

It rings again.

Decline.

I cast a glance at the bathroom when it rings again, hearing the shower running, and my hands are shaking when I answer.

"What?" I hiss into the speaker. "Leave me alone!"

"Who is this? Why are you texting my boyfriend?"

My hand tightens around the phone at the sound of her voice.

Margie's voice, releasing in a nasty snarl.

I clear my throat and lower my tone, attempting for it to sound masculine. "Sorry. Wrong number."

Click.

The phone rings again.

James calling.

The best morning of my life—waking up, wrapped in Rex's arms—has been ruined by him. Tears slip down my cheeks, and I quickly push them away with my arm, ridding the evidence for when Rex comes back.

"Everything okay?"

The phone falls from my hand when Rex walks into the room, a towel around his waist, water droplets on his chest.

"You look like you saw a ghost," he adds, concern on his face.

I shake my head and hate myself for lying to him. "It's just Margie."

Technically, it isn't a full lie.

It was Margie.

"Still blowing her off?" He drops the towel, and my mind momentarily forgets my issues at the sight of him naked. I frown when he pulls a pair of gray sweatpants on. "Don't you think it'd be right to clear the air and tell her everything? She deserves that."

I flick my phone farther away from me on the bed as if it were poisonous. "I'm not blowing her off. I'm keeping my distance." *Same thing, but it sounds better.*

He swipes a shirt from a drawer, pulling it over his head. "It's not fair to her."

"Life isn't fair sometimes." I cross my arms. "I'm not opening that can of worms. It's better for her to think I hate her than for her to hate me."

"She wouldn't hate you."

"She called me a skank-ass ho."

"Technically, she didn't call *you* a skank-ass ho."

"Close to it."

"Not even close."

"Look, I'll reach out when I feel comfortable." I jump up from the bed with a frown on my face. "I need to get ready for work."

CHAPTER TWENTY

I broke the cardinal rule of our friendship.

I fucked Carolina.

And I have no regrets.

My heart feels closer to hers, our connection stronger, and I'm pissed I didn't take this step forever ago. It'd sure have saved us from a lot of troubles.

Fear creeps in as I doubt that we can stay this way.

There's no way in hell I'd ever hurt her, so I hope to God she doesn't stomp on my heart.

The only days I'm a morning person is when I wake up early to visit Carolina at work—less people to steal her attention away from me.

Today, I'm visiting her during the lunch shift.

I want to see my girl.

As usual, the diner is packed when I walk in. Shirley's is known for its kick-ass lunch specials. Her sandwiches are to die for.

I spot Kyle and Gage seated at Kyle's regular booth, wearing their blue uniforms. They're partners on the police force and often stop by for a quick bite while on duty. I walk down the aisle and head straight to my usual booth. I texted Carolina, asking her to keep it open for me. My plan was to surprise her, but I didn't want to lose my chance to sit in her section.

"Shirley!" I greet, stepping up to the bar. "Mind if my girl takes a lunch break?"

Shirley pinches my cheeks. "As much as I love this cute face of yours, no. We're slammed. She'll have a break in an hour after the rush dies down."

"Have lunch with us," Kyle calls out, waving me over. "She's our waitress, so you'll still be able to make googly eyes at her."

"I'm going to need that table anyway, sweetie," Shirley says. "Carolina can make some extra cash, too."

I smile, failing to mention that I'd give her a tip far larger than anyone who'll sit in that booth, and walk over to Kyle's booth. He slides over to make room for me to sit next to him. Carolina grins when she spots me and slides the guys' plates on the table in front of them.

Her attention swings to me as she wipes her forehead with the back of her arm. "Hey. I didn't think we'd be so packed today. Sorry for Shirley giving your table away, but you know it's hard to say no to her. I planned to text you when I got a sec."

"It's cool, babe." I don't bother picking up a menu and glance at the guys' plates.

Gage has the buffalo chicken.

Kyle has the grilled tenderloin.

I nod toward Gage's plate. "I'll have that. Shoestring fries. Water."

"Got it." She tucks her pen behind her ear and scurries off to the kitchen.

"You two are cute," Kyle says, grabbing the bottle of ketchup.

"Mmhmm," Gage adds, thrusting a hand through his dark hair.

Gage isn't much for conversation. He's the quiet one, and his fiancée, Lauren, is loud enough for the both of them.

We chat for a while.

Gage says he and Lauren are trying for another baby.

Kyle tells me the sale on Chloe's house fell through.

"Is it still available?" I ask, perking up in my seat. "No backup offers?"

"Still available," Kyle replies. "Know anyone who'd be interested?"

"Me."

"You want to buy her house?" Kyle draws out.

I shrug. "Why not? My lease ends in a few months. I have money saved up for a down payment."

"Look into it," Kyle says. "I'll talk to Chloe and see if there's anything we can do to help."

It'd be cool as hell to live next door to them. I wasn't close with Kyle growing up, since he was so much older, but as he's settled down, our relationship has grown stronger.

Our conversation stops when a voice comes through their police radio, telling them there's a family of raccoons stuck in a dumpster.

"Serious business," I comment as they take their last bites and wipe their mouths.

"I'd rather have that than the other," Kyle states. A wave of sadness spreads along his face as he digs his wallet from his pocket. There will never be a day Kyle doesn't remember the scene he walked into that changed his life and how he had to break the news to Chloe of her loss.

I stop him. "I got it. Go help those little critters."

Kyle nods. "Thanks, brother."

Gage slides out of the booth. "I got you next time I see you at Down Home then."

They say good-bye, and I stack their plates up before sliding them to the other side of the table. Crumpling up the napkins, I pile them on top of the plates, wanting to clean up the table as much as I can so Carolina will have less work to do.

Pulling up a book on my phone, I kick back in the booth and read until Carolina arrives with my food, setting it in front of me.

"You need anything else?" she asks.

I slide my napkin toward her. "Your number, hot waitress."

She laughs, shaking her head. "Sorry, I'm spoken for by my wonderful boyfriend."

"Lucky man." I wink.

"What he doesn't know won't hurt him, though."

"Oh, really?" I raise a brow.

She snags her pen from behind her ear, snatches the napkin, and writes something on it. Folding it up, she slides it to me. I can't stop myself from doubling over laughing when she waggles her eyebrows and then skips away in that cute little uniform of hers.

My cock stirs as I read her note.

I can't wait to get you naked tonight.

Xoxo

I shake my head and tuck the note into my pocket.

CHAPTER TWENTY-ONE
CAROLINA

"Can we try something?" I ask, wrapping my arms around Rex's neck.

"Sure?" He tips his head down, and the water from the shower blurs my view of him.

I unclasp my arms, dropping them to grab his hand and slide it between our naked bodies. His breaths turn harsh, his back straightening, when I close our fingers over his already-hard cock and move them up and down the length of him.

"You want to watch me jerk off?" he hisses through his teeth.

"Yes."

My heart gives a nervous jolt when I fall back a small step, creating a narrow space between our bodies, giving me a perfect view of us working his erection. A gasp leaves me when he tightens his hold on his dick, causing me to do the same, and his head falls back in ecstasy.

There's no taking my eyes off this … off him.

His soaked abs are strained, and the muscles in his arms tense with each movement. His thick hand, which has made me orgasm countless times, grips his cock, pumping up and down. Tingles sweep through me at the memory of the sounds he made that day.

This is it.

What I wanted to see so desperately that morning.

"Confession," I whisper, my eyes not leaving our connection.

He bows his head, his eyes fixing on me, his breathing ragged. "Let me hear it."

Our pace slows as we speak.

"When you were in the hotel …" I start before stopping in hesitation. "Before the wedding, I saw you in the shower."

Understanding dawns on his face. "You watched me jack off?"

I nod, putting more space between us.

"Fuck," he groans before sweeping his eyes up and down my body.

Thrill powers through my veins.

I want him again.

Need him.

It's never *just sex* with me and Rex.

It's love.

Mutual respect.

Feelings out of this world.

I push my wet hair away from my face to gain an unobstructed view of him.

"Tell me," he demands. "Tell me what you saw."

"Your hand on your cock." I squeeze my hand over his, feeling his thickness.

His eyes slam shut, his pace the same. "Did you wish it were yours?"

"Oh God, yes." *I've never been more turned on in my life.*

"Did you wish you could join me?"

"Yes."

"Do you like it better up close?"

"Yes," I whimper, as if the only thing functioning in my body were my hormones, and my brain can't come up with another word.

He stifles back a deep groan. "Is that why you wanted us to shower that night?"

"Yes," I whimper again, the word leaving my lips more strangled.

"Come here."

I'm not given the chance to move on my own when he grabs my

waist and tugs me to him, his hands roaming to my ass cheeks to lift me up.

"I'm not finishing on the shower floor. I'm finishing in you," he grumbles.

My legs instinctively wrap around him as he pushes me against the wall at the same time his lips crash against mine, his tongue immediately sweeping into my mouth. It doesn't take long until we're messily making out, grinding against each other.

"Fuck," he groans, his forehead meeting mine.

"What?" I ask, unable to stop my hips from grinding against him, feeling his hardness rub against me—*so close* to my core that it's driving me wild.

His head doesn't move. "I'm about to freeze my ass off to get a condom."

When he starts to separate us, I tighten my legs around his hips.

"I'm on the pill," I blurt out, my nails digging into his back.

His face is turned on and anxious as he stares down at me. "You sure?"

"Positive. Now, get inside me." I slightly lift my hips, giving him the perfect angle.

My back arches when he thrusts inside and pushes me harder into the wall.

Our mouths stay connected as we steal each other's breaths, and he screws me against the cold tiles of the shower.

———

"Do you know how perfect you are?" Rex asks, standing naked in front of me while drying me off from our shower.

I shiver in his arms, looking up at him while combing my fingers through my hair. "Nope, so you can go ahead and tell me."

He chuckles, his eyes soft as I lift mine to meet his. "That doesn't surprise me." He snatches one of his shirts from the bathroom vanity. "Arms."

I swing my arms up, and he tugs the shirt over my head. It's white, my nipples showing as my soaked hair drips onto it. "You know I love it when you pump up my ego."

He runs his cold finger down my cheek, stroking it, giving me goose bumps I don't care about. "How's this? Here's all the reasons I love you—"

My heart nearly stops when I interrupt him, "Did you … did you just say, you *love me*?"

He raises a dark brow. "Uh … yes."

"You love me?" A smile lights up my face.

A smirk flickers across his lips. "Uh … yes."

My head is spinning. "Like … you're in love with me?"

"Uh … yes."

My hand flies to my mouth as my heart bursts with joy.

His eyes brighten at my reaction. "Has that not been obvious to you for, I don't know, *years*?"

It has.

I just thought I'd never hear him say it.

That he loves me like I love him.

"It's amazing to hear you say it out loud," I explain.

"Is it now?" His smirk grows. "I'll remember that whenever I want to make you smile."

A gasp leaves my throat when he drops the towel from my body, hauls me over his shoulder, and rushes into the bedroom. I bounce on the bed after he tosses me onto it and crawls up it seconds later, in the space between my legs.

He caresses my hair while staring down at me, his forehead still beaded with water. "I should have said that a long time ago, huh?"

"Yes, definitely." I curl my legs around his hips, drawing him closer. "Same goes for me. I should've told you how much I love you."

His lips curl into a smile before he slowly kisses me.

We're wet against the sheets as he makes love to me just as slow, whispering he loves me with every thrust.

My life was empty until I met Rex.

He filled me with light.

Then, when that light began to fade, he lifted me up.

No matter what I've gone through, he's always been by my side.

My dark times are always brightened with the lightness he brings to me.

I stare up at him, watching his face flood with love and desire as he makes love to me.

I know what I need to do.

I have to fix what could break us.

———

Eventually, Rex has to shower by himself.

I don't join him. It'd probably end up with wet, sloppy sex again.

My grip on the phone is so tight that I'm shocked my fingers aren't crushing it.

This has to end.

Rex has opened up his heart to me, giving me his all.

I owe him the same.

If he were to ever find out my secrets, it'd damage our trust.

Would he hate me if I told him? Probably not.

Would he try to fix it? Yes.

Would he hate me when I told him not to? Yes.

It hurts my heart to know I'm hiding this, but he can't know.

A chill crawls up my spine, and I take a deep, steadying breath when I hit *his* name.

Me: This has to end.

It takes him less than a minute to respond.

James: No. We're not ready.

Me: I AM READY.

James: Too bad. I'm not.

I blink away tears.

Me: WHY? This is ridiculous!

James: What's ridiculous is you leaving me when I told you not to.

My anger spirals out of control as I hold myself back from throwing my phone across the room. *Screw him.*

Me: Are you kidding me? You know why I left!

I have no idea why I'm arguing. My goal is to make him happy so he leaves me alone.

James: You never gave me the time to explain myself.

Oh, he explained himself aplenty.

He texts again before I reply.

James: Meet me, and we'll talk.

Me: I'm not meeting you!

James: It's meet me or nothing.

Horror flows through me.

Meet him.

Rex will for sure ask me what's going on if I tell him I'm meeting James, but seeing him might be my final way out of this.

Me: Fine. Where?

James: Tomorrow. My place. Noon.

Oh, hell no.

Me: I'm not going to your house.

James: The bistro off-campus?

Me: Too public.

James: Public is anywhere but my house.

Me: I'll be there at noon.

James: Love you.

There's no stopping me from texting him back with my precious endearment.

Me: Go screw yourself.

James: I liked it better when you screwed me.

I throw my phone down on the bed.

I hate him so damn much, and I know he won't make it easy on me tomorrow, but I have to attempt to play nice with him. All I need is for him to sign a document.

If only it were that simple.

I've never lied to Rex before.

I've omitted the truth, yes, but never flat-out lied.

That'll change tomorrow.

CHAPTER TWENTY-TWO

"Hey, babe, what are you up to today?"

Carolina whips around at my question, giving me her back when she opens a cabinet and takes forever finding her mug of choice.

"Hanging out with my mom and Tricia," she replies, twirling around in her socks with two mugs. "We're having lunch. Shopping. Girl time. Should be done before dinner." She glances down at the floor as she makes the few steps to the coffeepot. "You?"

I shrug. "Might go for a run and then work on the game."

"Want to stay in or go out for dinner later?"

"Whatever you want."

We eat a quick breakfast, and after she kisses me good-bye, I change into my running clothes. The sun is out, a nice breeze flowing, when I run through Town Square. I'm interrupted by a good fifteen people with questions about my mother and Carolina.

Before heading back to the apartment, I make a pit stop at the local doughnut shop that has a kick-ass smoothie menu. Something with coffee in it sounds damn good. My sleep has been shit lately, and I have a long day of working on my game. Not that I'm complaining since the lack of sleep is from all the sex I've been having with Carolina. We're like two teenagers who just discovered orgasms.

I walk into the small shop, the smell of fresh baked dough and sugar smacking my face, and I stand in the busy line. People are seated around small pub tables, snacking and drinking.

"Rex! Hey, Mom! Rex is here!"

Henry comes running over to me, a doughnut in his hand and chocolate frosting on his face. Tricia is struggling to keep up with him as she pushes the stroller with Addy in it while carrying a pink smoothie in her hand.

Henry pops the final bite of his doughnut into his mouth, not muttering another word as he chews it up when Tricia reaches us.

"Hi, Rex," she greets, thrusting a napkin into Henry's hand.

"Hey, guys." I ruffle my hand through Henry's hair before turning my attention to Tricia with a polite smile.

"Can I come over and play video games today?" Henry bursts out.

"If it's okay with your mom."

Carolina brings Henry over when she babysits sometimes. He loves my video games. Plus, I feed him junk food.

Speaking of Carolina …

My eyes sweep over the shop before returning to Tricia. "Is Carolina with you?"

She shakes her head, her answer drawing out in confusion, "No … is she supposed to be?" Her eyes widen, showing the regret of asking me that question.

"She said she was hanging out with you and your mom." I step out of line when my turn comes up, losing my place, but I don't want to miss talking to Tricia for answers.

"Uh …" Tricia fumbles for words. "Maybe she and my mom had plans and forgot to tell me."

I nod. "I'll call her."

Shock and apology flood her face before passing into worry.

Carolina isn't someone who lies.

The only times she hasn't been truthful with me is when it's about *him.*

I say bye, no longer giving a shit about the smoothie, and fish my phone from my pocket as I speed-walk toward my apartment.

When I hit her name, I get no answer.

I try again.

Rings until it hits voicemail.

And again.

Not trying to be on the line of stalker shit, but what the hell is happening?

Is she hurt?

I'd think it was an emergency had she not lied about being with her sister.

She's hiding something from me.

My mind twists and turns with possible scenarios.

I shove my phone back into my shorts pocket and sprint home. I'm nearly out of breath when I get there and rush up the stairs while calling her again. Her phone is ringing when I walk into the living room.

"Dude, that thing has been ringing nonstop," Josh complains when I come into his view. "I'm half-tempted to throw it out the window."

"Is Lina here?" I rush out, searching the room how I did at the doughnut shop.

"I woke up fifteen minutes ago, but I haven't seen or heard her."

She'd have also answered her phone if she were.

Her phone rings again, the call not from me, and I find it on the nightstand when I walk into my bedroom, following the noise.

Tricia calling flashes across the screen.

The call ends before I get the chance to answer. Snatching the phone, I see tons of text messages on her screen. All of them from James.

The fuck?

I try four different passwords before succeeding in unlocking her phone. I'm an asshole for this, but she's been missing, and a bad guy from her past is texting her.

Something is up.

James is at the top of the list when I open her texts.

James: You still coming over today?

Carolina: I'll be there.

James: Wear something sexy.

I clutch the phone, ready to throw it across the room, but I stop myself since it's not mine.

It's a jackass move, but I read through their few texts. Most of the texts have been deleted, although I'm certain they're similar. I'm capable of hacking into her phone and reading them, but the thought makes me sick to my stomach.

My head spins so hard that I can hardly think straight as I continue reading the texts she sent at ten this morning.

Carolina: Leaving now. Be there in 2 hours.

James: Can't wait.

She left twenty minutes after sending that message, and an hour and a half has passed.

How has she not realized she forgot her phone?

The phone beeps with another text.

James: Where are you?

I debate on answering when another text comes.

James: I made us lunch. How far away are you?

James: Baby, answer me, so I know you're still coming.

I nearly puke at him calling her baby.

I want to throw the phone into the toilet and flush the fucker.

I hit his name to get the contact information and grab my laptop, doing a search on his phone number even though I already know who this *James* is. She broke down and told me that night she cried in my arms.

My suspicion is verified.

James Cordry.

Professor James Cordry.

Motherfucking asshole.

Why is Carolina talking to him again?

All I can do now is wait for answers.

———

Four hours later, Carolina comes barging into the apartment.

Uneasiness lines her soft features as the lies start falling from her lips. "I'm sorry if you tried calling. I lost my phone." Her eyes are red when she looks at me. "Can you use the Find My Phone feature you did last time this happened?"

My eyes darken on her, my pulse hammering in my throat as I take her in and stay seated on the couch, her phone gripped in my palm.

She's fighting to look cool, calm, and collected.

Too bad I know her well enough that she's far from that.

Guilt screams along every feature of her beautiful, lying face.

I hold the phone up. "Found it."

She releases a sigh of relief. "Thank God. I didn't want to buy a new one."

This is a shitty situation, and I feel like a shitty person.

An insecure guy who's interrogating his girlfriend about cheating.

My hand clenches around the phone, dread sinking through my veins of where this will lead. Hesitation hits me before I reply, and I take in every inch of her, searching for differences.

Her lips look plumper than when she left.

Did they kiss?

Her face is more flushed.

Did they have sex?

She barely pays me a look when she grabs the phone. "Thank you." Her tone is polite—her *church* voice is what I call it. "I'm going to change into something more comfortable."

I nod my head, my voice bitter. "By the way, how was hanging out with Professor Cordry?"

She freezes mid-turn, gaping at me. "W-what?"

My teeth grit. "You weren't with your mom and sister today."

"What are you talking about?" She grips her throat, rubbing it, catching the truth to replace it with lies.

"I ran into Tricia earlier, and you were nowhere to be found." I snap my fingers. "She didn't even know you had *plans*. Words of advice: get your story straight if you're going to lie."

"What?" she repeats, as if that were the only word she knew.

Her phone beeps, and pain flicks along her face when she glances at the screen.

I raise a brow, releasing a harsh laugh. "Is that a text from … what is the professor to you?"

My asshole is coming through, but I don't care.

Why the hell did she push us to be more than friends so much if she was still seeing him?

Was I her rebound until they got back together?

"Rex." Her lower lip trembles, and the phone drops from her hand to the floor. "It's not what it looks like."

"Explain it then," I spit. "It sure *looks like* you lied to me and went to him." I spread my legs, leaning forward, and rest my elbows onto my knees, shaking my head and feeling like a fucking fool. "You deleted most of your texts with him … out of what? Guilt? Secrecy?" I tap my temple. "Only liars have to delete shit from their phones."

"James and I … we have history." She clutches her arms around her body.

"And we fucking don't?" I burst out.

"You know what I mean, Rex."

I stand and thrust my thumb into my chest. "I was the one who held you in my arms when you were crying *over him!*" I shake my head with a snarl. "Now what, huh? You still have feelings for him? He decided he was done sticking his dick in other women and wants you back?"

"We … we needed to talk," she stammers, her face turning red.

"In person? You drove two hours to talk instead of a phone call?" I throw my arms out. "Or even a text—you know, how you've been communicating with him behind my back?"

"No." She squeezes her eyes shut. "He'd only talk to me in person." When she opens them, she blinks back tears, causing me to soften my tone.

"To do what?"

"End things."

"Didn't you end things months ago? Have you been talking to him behind my back this entire time?" The anger returns. I'm burning with so many questions.

"No …" Her eyes drop. "Sometimes."

"Jesus!" My voice is thick as it rises. "This is why I didn't want us to cross that line! I wish I'd never touched you!"

"Don't say that," she whispers, tears falling down her cheeks. "It's complicated."

"Damn it, Carolina, I can do complicated."

She looks away from me.

I pinch the bridge of my nose before moving in front of her. "What's going on? Why are you talking to him? Seeing him?"

"Because he won't give me a divorce!"

CHAPTER TWENTY-THREE
CAROLINA

SIX MONTHS EARLIER

The text on my phone has me grinning like a child on Christmas.

James: I love you, my wife. Come over.

Wife!

That grin overtakes my face at the endearment.

Me: I thought you were busy tonight?

I asked him to have dinner at his place, but he told me he had a business dinner to attend.

James: Change of plans.

Me: Just got to my dorm. Give me an hour, and I'll be there.

James: Turn around and come see me. I miss you, baby.

Me: Fine. Twenty minutes.

James: Is your roommate there?

Weird question.

Me: IDK?

James: Have you talked to her today?

Me: This morning. Why?

James: No reason. Hurry up and bring your cute ass here.

My dorm room door is unlocked, and I hear sobbing as soon as I walk in. Margie is collapsed on the floor, her back slumped against her bed, and her face is red and puffy when she peeks up at me.

"Margie?" I drop my bag and fall onto my knees next to her. "Are you okay?" Stupid question on my part considering she's a crying mess.

She sniffles, mascara running down her cheeks. "Yes …" *Sniffles.* "No."

My stomach flip-flops as bad thoughts rush my mind. "Did someone hurt you?"

She shakes her head.

"What then?"

She rubs at her eyes, smearing her makeup more, and blinks away tears. "Promise you won't judge."

I reach forward and squeeze her hand. "Promise not to judge."

She inhales a breath of courage. "I'm sleeping with a professor."

Oh, man.

That confession hits close to home.

"I take it that fell apart?" I ask in concern.

"I didn't know he was married!" she shrieks, the tears reemerging. "I was over at his house earlier and went through his phone." Her voice rises. "He was texting someone he called *My Wife*. He got married in Vegas last weekend!" She snags a flip-flop from the floor and throws it across the room. "I'm so fucking stupid!"

My body stiffens, ice chilling my veins. "What?"

"He's been sleeping with some other slut and married her," she seethes, the words spewing out like venom. She slams her palm against her chest, her cries louder. "Why wouldn't he marry me? Why'd he pick some skank-ass ho over me?"

I dread the answer before I ask the question, "Which professor?"

"It doesn't matter." She pulls her knees to her chest, resting her chin on them.

"Come on," I push. "I won't tell anyone."

Her nostrils flare, her sadness swirling into anger. "Professor Cordry. Asshole of Psychology."

My head spins, and I suck in my cheeks to hoard in my anger … my pain.

The name is a slap in the face.

My voice is thick as the words slowly leave my mouth. "I didn't know you were taking his class."

"I'm not," she replies. "We met at the coffee shop on campus. He asked me out, and my dumbass said yes."

"How long have you been seeing each other?"

"Two months."

It takes everything I have not to break down next to her.

Call it a heartbreak party.

If I lose it, she'll know everything.

I have to get out of here.

I snatch my phone and fake getting a text message before jumping to my feet. "I have to go."

I should hug her, give her a kiss on the cheek, and tell her everything is okay.

But it's not.

Nothing is okay.

There's no way I can spew out that bullshit without breaking down.

I have to see him.

I need to kick him in the balls … scream at him … and … *divorce him.*

———

"You cheating, lying scum!" I explode as soon as James answers his front door, throwing the diamond ring in his face.

The ring I only wear when we're together.

Never in public.

Not counting when we got hitched in Vegas and spent the weekend there.

Hot tears swell in my eyes.

I cried and cursed him the entire ride here.

I hate myself for how stupid I am.

"What the hell?" he asks.

He knows why I'm angry.

That's why he told me not to go to the dorm.

Why he asked if she was there.

"You're sleeping with Margie!" I shout.

"Who?" He rubs his chin, playing stupid while standing in the doorway.

I sweep my arms out, and my voice cracks. "My roommate! You're screwing her!"

"Keep your fucking voice down," he hisses.

"Screw you!"

The door swings open wider seconds before he clasps his hand around my elbow and tugs me inside, slamming the door behind us.

"Why would you do this to me?" I shriek, jerking out of his hold. "To us?"

My hands are shaking. My chin is trembling. My mind is racing.

James moves, standing tall in front of me, and shoves his hands into the pockets of his pants. "Baby, I don't know what you're talking about."

No sign of guilt or regret is on his face.

No sign of him feeling apologetic for ripping my heart out of my chest and stomping on it.

No longer do I see the man I fell for.

Now, I see a man with slicked-back dark hair, wearing an expensive button-up and black pants and a phony smile on his face.

James Cordry is a good-looking man in his thirties.

He's a smooth talker. Successful. Intelligent. A liar.

The perfect storm for a naïve woman searching for love.

I loved him. Opened up to him. Changed myself and broke my values for him.

Did things I'd never thought I'd do—all in the name of love.

I was younger, inexperienced, and allowed him to lead every step in our relationship.

I shove him away when he reaches out and attempts to take my shaking hand in his. "Don't touch me!"

"Carolina," he says sharply. "Calm down. Why are you acting so distraught?"

"Why did you tell me you were busier earlier?" I question. "Is it because you were with her?"

"I had a business meeting. It got canceled. I texted you because I wanted to be with the woman I love. The woman who said *I do* to spending the rest of her life with me."

"Liar!" I scream, slapping his hand away when he tries to touch me again. My heart knocks against my chest, breaking into pieces, and it takes everything I have in me not to fall apart in front of him. "Just tell me the truth. That's all I want from you."

He shrugs. "There's nothing to tell."

"Tell me! Be honest!"

He drags his hand through his hair. "Nothing to tell, so stop your bitching. I've had a long day, and the last thing I need is you coming in, acting like a lunatic." He shakes his head, his face burning. "Here I thought, I was in love with a grown woman, not a dramatic brat."

"I'd rather be a dramatic brat than a cheater." I glare at him in disgust. "We're done."

He stares at me, sure of himself, and laughs coldly. "Oh, Carolina, that's where you're wrong, baby. We're not done until I say we're done."

"No, James, that's where *you're* wrong," I argue with a scowl. "I'll be filing an annulment first thing in the morning."

A venomous smile crosses his face. "You do that, and I'll let everyone on campus and your *preacher father* know what a whore you are."

I inch forward and smack him across the face.

He winces, rubbing his jaw, but doesn't back away. "Don't do that again. That's your only warning."

"We're over."

He shakes his head. "You're mine."

"I was until you cheated on me." I scoff. "I'm sure she's not the only one you've been with either. I don't even want to know how many women you've screwed behind my back."

"Nah, she's the only one, and it's your fault it happened."

Startled, I stumble back a step. "Excuse me?"

"You ditched me for your little high school fuck boy. I saw Margie at the coffee shop. I didn't know she was your roommate until we fucked and she talked about you."

"Yet you kept screwing her," I seethe.

He shrugs. "She was good in bed."

I move forward to smack him again, but he catches my wrist, tightly gripping it so I'm unable to pull away.

"I told you not to do that again," he growls out.

I'm not strong enough to break his hold. "*I told you* I want a divorce. Go be with someone else."

He snorts. "I don't want someone else."

I fight him as he pulls me into his living room and shoves me onto his couch. As soon as my butt hits the cushions, I bounce up to leave, but he shoves me back down.

"Please stop," I whimper. "Let me leave."

This is a stranger to me—not the James I fell in love with.

My first boyfriend is a wolf in sheep's clothing.

"Why do you even care if we're together?" I cry out. "You can find a new girlfriend tonight!"

"You're different than the others," he says slowly … gently. "You were made for me. The other women, they wanted the thrill of *sleeping with a professor.*" He snaps his fingers and points at me, moving his finger up and down over and over again. "You, on the other hand?" He steps in closer, his feet hitting mine as I fight to control my breathing underneath him. "You love me for *me.*"

"Loved," I correct. "I'll figure out a way to forget that stupid marriage ever happened."

I go to stand again, but he pushes me back down.

"Want to know why we're not done?"

I break down when he tells me.

———

Tears. Arguing. Threats.

I spent three hours at James's house, experiencing all of the above until I promised to keep my mouth shut and he let me leave.

He's broken me in every way imaginable.

I don't even know who I am anymore.

As I grew closer with him, I became distant with Rex.

Ignored my parents' phone calls.

Skipped a few classes.

Tears return at the realization of how dumb I've been.

How blind.

As soon as I get into my car, I pull out my phone and find a text from Margie, asking when I'm coming back to the dorm.

I ignore it.

How do I explain this to her?

Tell her we've been sleeping with the same man … and I'm his wife?

James made it clear that telling anyone, especially Margie, was a big no-no.

"She's angry, and she'll get me in trouble," was what he said.

"Good," was my response.

"She spills information; I spill information," he fired back.

No telling Margie for me.

Putting my car into drive, I go to the only person who can fix me.

Regret barrels through me. If only I'd confessed to Rex during the dozens of times he begged me to tell him who I was dating, he'd have told me I was being stupid, being used, and to leave him.

Maybe I would've listened to him.

Too late now.

When James found out Rex was the hack master, he bought me a separate phone to talk to him on in case Rex wanted to look into who I was communicating with. I was betraying Rex in every way imaginable.

I'm sobbing hysterically when I call him in the dead of the night and say I'm outside his dorm.

His voice is sleepy when he tells me he's coming.

My sobs grow louder, harder, as I run through the rain to the entrance of the dorm, waiting for him … for his comfort.

The door flies open, and Rex's eyes widen, his lips snarling when he sees me.

Not wasting a second, I run into the arms of my security blanket, of the person who's been there for me and I know will never break me.

Into the arms of the person I should've trusted.

The only man I'll trust ever again.

My mind is blank as he walks me inside, and I cry in his arms.

"What's going on?" His chin is trembling in anger. "What the fuck happened? Did someone hurt you?" The arms around me tighten at his last question.

"Not here," I whisper, burying my face into his neck.

He lifts me, and I wrap my legs around his waist while he walks us up the stairs to his floor. The hallway is empty—*thank God*—and the light stays off when we land in his dorm room.

His questions start as soon as he drops me onto his bed. "Lina babe, what's going on?" His voice hardens as he asks the same question he did earlier, "Did someone hurt you?"

"Yes," I say into the darkness.

"What?"

The air grows heavy, an anger I've never seen from Rex surfacing.

"It's not like that," I rush out. "No one … *hurt me*, hurt me." I cover my face with my hands. "This is embarrassing."

He falls to his knees and removes my hands, one by one. "I can take embarrassing." He runs his finger along my jaw, wiping away drops of rain and tears. "Tell me."

I sniffle, unable to look at him, to see the disgust on his face when I tell him. "You have to promise not to judge me … or get mad."

"Lina, you know I'll never judge you for shit. I'll have your back, no matter what."

I inhale a deep breath, and my words come out exactly how they did when Margie made her confession with a few word tweaks. "I'm dating a professor."

"What?" he asks. Even though I can't make out his face all that well, I can hear the shock in his voice. "Who?"

"Professor Cordry."

"That motherfucker," he hisses. "I'm going to kick his ass."

"No, you can't," I sob.

"I can. He took advantage of you."

Leave it to Rex to think it was all James's fault, as if I had no play in it.

Everyone sees me as this perfect woman who makes smart decisions. Maybe I am smart, except when it comes to love ... to men.

I shake my head. "No ... he didn't. I'm a grown woman."

"You're a naïve college student who's never broken out of her shell," he fires back. "Big damn difference."

"We're the same age—"

He cuts me off, "It's different." He rises to his feet, grabs dry clothes, and hands me a shirt. "Get out of those wet clothes."

I pull my shirt over my head while sniffling before giving it to his hand he has held out. "Oh my God, I'm getting your bed wet." The realization hits me.

"You're cool." He hands me the bottoms next.

I undress underneath the blanket, changing into the dry clothes, and he slides into bed when I'm finished. Some of my sadness wears down when he wraps his arms around me and kisses the top of my head.

"Everything is okay. You'll be okay. You're strong."

I whisper my confessions to him.

How I met James.

How we hit it off and secretly dated.

How I found out he had been doing the same with Margie.

I don't tell him about us getting married ... or how James will always have the upper hand with me.

———

I drop out of college.

No one, except Rex, knows why.

I'm terrified of my parents' reaction.

Rex and Josh moved my things out of the dorm, and I haven't talked to Margie since the day she told me she was sleeping with James. I feel terrible, but I can't be around her without feeling guilt, without getting us in trouble.

He has dirt on us both.

I poured bleach on the phone James had bought me and then tossed it in the trash can.

All of this to get rid of him.

It's not that easy.

He knows my regular phone number. It's what we talked on until things grew serious.

I move back home to get as far away from James as possible.

There will be space between us, and maybe he'll forget about me and find someone new.

James thinks I'll come back to him because if I don't, he can ruin me.

CHAPTER TWENTY-FOUR

"Can you repeat that?" I ask, unsure I heard her correctly as my jaw falls slack. "Did you say, you're *married* to that asshole?"

My head is spinning as I digest her words.

Her gaze drops to the floor when she nods.

Certain I'm mistaken, I ask again, "You married him?"

"I did," she whispers, failing to lift her eyes.

Questions hurl through my mind so fast that I struggle to grasp one to throw at her.

"How?" I seethe. "When?"

A heavy, unrecognizable tension consumes the room, and for a moment, I'm not sure she'll answer.

She blows out a stressed breath, and her eyes are cold and teary when she raises them. I ache to stand and comfort her, wrap her in my arms, but her betrayal stops me. I need answers.

"It was a week before I broke things off with him," she explains, taking slow steps before collapsing onto the chair next to the couch, her shoulders slumping. "He took me to Vegas for a weekend, and we went clubbing with his friends. I drank a lot, and somehow, marriage came up. It sounded like a good idea at the time. I was alcohol-and love-drunk and thought we'd be together forever."

"If you were drunk, you can get an annulment. Problem solved."

She clutches her arms around her chest, and our eye contact is wiped out again when she stares at the floor, releasing a heavy sigh. "I can't do that."

"Why not?"

"It's complicated."

"Carolina, look at me, damn it," I snarl, the ache to console her returning. "You file. Sign the papers. It's done."

My job as her best friend is to be her rock.

I've taken on that role. Loved that role.

I can't be her rock if she's hurting me.

My fear of our friendship being ruined has become a reality.

"He threatened to tell my parents," is her ridiculous reply.

I scoff. "Did you think no one would find out about your marital bliss? Why'd you tie the knot if you had to keep it a secret?"

"Our plan was to wait until he was no longer my professor. Until then, we kept it low-key."

"That's the stupidest shit I've ever heard."

Those beautiful, deceitful eyes of hers widen. "Wow. Really, Rex?"

"Yes, really." I scrub my hand over my face. "Why do you care about your parents? You won't be the first person to divorce someone. They won't like it, but they'll get over it."

"He ..." She hesitates. "He said he'd grant me a divorce if ..."

I wait for her to finish but get silence. "If what?"

She swallows a few times. "If I stay away from you for a year and try to work things out with him."

"Are you kidding me?" I shake my head, anger burning through me. "Scratch my earlier statement. *That's* the stupidest shit I've ever heard." My temples throb. "Are you *considering* it?"

A sharp pain runs through me at her lack of response. Even with what my father put our family through, I've never been so hurt.

"I don't know what I'm considering!" she cries out. "All of this has just been thrown at me! I need to get my head straight. I just need time!"

"Time?" I fire back. "How long? A *year*, like he's asking?"

"I never said that's what I want," she chokes out. "I said, he *gave* me that option."

"Fuck this." I stand and pull my keys from my pocket. "Someone needs to set this asshole straight."

That someone being me.

I should've done this a long time ago.

"No!" she shrieks, jumping up from the chair and scurrying behind me, grabbing my elbow and attempting to pull me back into the living room.

I jerk out of her hold. "I'll fix this for you. I promise."

"Don't threaten him," she whimpers around her plea. *"Please* leave him alone. We can act like he doesn't exist, and eventually, he'll get tired of me and go about his way."

I blow out a frustrated breath. "If he doesn't? Will you stay married to him?"

Nothing makes sense.

Why does she give so many fucks about divorcing him?

I need answers.

Carolina won't give them to me; therefore, I'll get them from James.

I'll fix this.

She dashes in front of me when I start walking again, blocks me from the door, and takes my face in her hands. "Don't leave me." Her lips tenderly brush mine. "I need you with me, Rex."

"I'll be back in a few hours," I grind out against her mouth, my teeth catching on to her lower lip.

"Please," she begs, pulling away an inch before rubbing her thumb over my lips. "Do whatever you want tomorrow, but tonight, I need *you.* The man who'll never turn his back on me. *You*—your love, your security, your arms around me."

Tears slip down her cheeks, hitting her thumb and my lip.

"Okay," I whisper, putting my anger aside at the sight of her pain. "I'll stay."

———

Carolina promised to give me answers tonight before she left for work.

Last night, it was too fresh—my anger, her pain.

Neither of us knew what to do or where this would lead for our future.

It was like we were too scared to discuss it, to change everything between us.

There's more to this story.

Carolina's parents being disappointed isn't what's stopping her from divorcing James. She's always been scared of disappointing them, but she failed when she dropped out of school.

I'm pissed the entire drive to the university, and the lecture hall is empty when I walk in.

Exactly what I planned after pulling up his class schedule.

Professor Asshole is gathering up papers and shoving them into a brown leather briefcase. He halts, papers fluttering to the floor, when he notices me walking toward him.

He speaks before I get the chance to, his tone cool and collected, "Let me guess … you're here because of Carolina?" He whistles. "Gotta say, I'm shocked she told you."

Other than looking up his pictures the next morning after Carolina came to my dorm, crying, this is my first time I've taken a good look at him. I understand his appeal. He's tall, fit, and on the younger side. His good looks, expensive clothes, and smooth-talking personality are what draw women to him.

I don't speak until I'm standing in front of his desk, nearly in his face. "Quit playing games and give her a goddamn divorce."

A bold smirk crosses his face, and he falls back a step. "Don't tell me what to do with *my wife*."

My wife.

Those words send a spiral of anger through me.

"Wife?" I clench my jaw, my pulse skyrocketing. "Not for long."

"Oh, really?" He draws himself up to his full height, thrusting his chest out and tensing his muscles—a lame attempt at appearing intimidating. "Is that what she said? That she planned to *divorce me*? It wasn't the tune she was singing yesterday when she came to *my house*."

His house.

Dude knows how to piss another guy off; that's for sure.

What did Carolina see in this douche bag?

My ribs tighten as I hold myself back from jumping over the desk and pummeling his face in. "Yes, that's *exactly* what she said—that you won't give her a divorce and are playing mind games."

He shakes his head, a laughter filled with edge coming from him. "I don't play mind games with *my wife.*"

If this motherfucker says wife *one more time, Carolina will become a widow.*

"What do you have on her?" I ask, getting straight to the point.

"None of your business. This is between me and *my wife,* so stay away from her."

My nails bite into my palms as I clench my fists. "Listen, creep—"

He cuts me off, "How does it feel, screwing a married woman, *Rex?*"

"She doesn't want to be married to you," I fire back.

"Do you plan to date her if we divorce?"

"Yes."

"Marry her?"

"Yes."

He smiles deviously while fishing out a phone from his pocket. "Tell me something then, how would you feel ... how would your *mayor father* feel if your new girlfriend's pictures were posted online?"

I blink, and it takes my eyes a second to adjust to the screen when he shoves the phone in my face—answering all the questions I came here for.

This is why she won't leave him.

This sneaky motherfucker.

I jerk the phone from his grimy fingers, throw it on the floor, and stomp on it, shattering it to pieces underneath my Chuck Taylor.

"Are you sure you want to date my wife *now?*"

My crushing his phone doesn't seem to faze him.

Phone down.

His face to go.

I circle around the desk faster than I've ever moved in my life, grab him by his scrawny-ass throat, and slam him against the wall, pinning him into it. "You motherfucker!"

"Ah … so she didn't tell you everything."

He gasps when I tighten my hold on his neck, and it takes everything I have not to keep choking him when his face starts turning purple.

I came here to scare him.

Not to kill him.

Even though I thought of dozens of ways I wanted to kill him on the drive here.

He bends at the waist when I release, his hands resting on his knees as he inhales deep breaths, nearly choking on them when I pull away.

"Sign the divorce papers when they're delivered to you," I demand, wiping my hands down my pants and turning to leave.

He snorts coldly. "You don't think there's more where that came from?" A smug smile takes over his face. "I have plenty of pictures of her." He tips his head toward the phone. "You might've broken my phone, but I still have them *everywhere.*"

I circle his desk and snatch his iPad from it.

It breaks when I stomp on it next.

"Two devices down," he says. "*So many more* to go. I have them saved *everywhere,* waiting for Carolina to make the wrong move. If she decides to leave me for you, there will be repercussions. She belongs with me—someone mature—not a little video game–playing college kid. I might've made a few mistakes with Carolina, but she's mine."

"I don't know if Carolina has told you what I'm capable of. I will not only kick your ass, but I'll also hack into everything with your name on it—phones, computers, emails, your fucking preschool records if I have to. Every-motherfucking-thing."

"You don't think Carolina has told me how you can hack into accounts?" He rubs at his red throat. "Which, by the way, is illegal, and I'd definitely turn you in for whatever you did."

"Good luck proving it. You might be a sloppy motherfucker, but let me promise you, I'm not." Pointing at him, I narrow my eyes. "Delete every picture and leave her the fuck alone. Find another student to bang since they seem to be your type, you fucking creep."

"Or what?"

"Like I said, I'll search through everything you own."

"Are you threatening me?"

"Nope. Only telling you what I'll do. I won't stop digging into every move you make until you leave her alone."

"Fuck you," he spits.

"Prepare for me to know your every secret, Professor." I grab his briefcase, slide out the laptop inside, and hold it up. "I'll smash this up as soon as I'm finished with it."

CHAPTER TWENTY-FIVE
CAROLINA

Rex texted me two hours ago, asking if he could stop by the loft. Considering all the text messages I've received, I have a hunch I know what him coming over means. We've hardly spoken since this morning, and even then, there was an uncomfortable silence as I got ready for work at his apartment.

Maybe he needs space to decide if he still wants to date me after he found out about James.

Stupid—that's what I was for thinking I could hide my marriage from him. Then again, I didn't expect Rex to open up his heart to me like he has and take the leap with me I'd wanted for years.

I never told Rex because I thought being with him wasn't an option. All this time, I've waited for us, only to hit a roadblock—a block I have no idea when it'll open.

I've shifted in twenty-five different positions on the couch trying to get comfortable. My head throbs, my heart ready to dive out of my chest.

Honestly, I'd have no problem with that.

I'd hand it over to Rex—a promise that, no matter what, he has it.

Not James.

Not anyone else.

Him.

It'll always be his.

Right now, even though I love him, I want to kick his ass.

"Are you nuts?" I screech when he walks through the front door with his computer bag, anger on his face. "James said you went to his lecture hall and threatened him."

His visit to James shouldn't surprise me. Even after the lies, Rex will always protect me. It's what he's done our entire friendship—with my cousins, with anyone who gave me shit, and now, with James. Rex would destroy anything in the world than see me in pain.

The cold glare aimed in my direction confirms I'm not the only mad person in the room.

"Sure did," he snaps.

"Rex," I say carefully. "Please don't get involved in this. I asked you to leave it alone, and I'll figure it out."

"Figure it out?" he shouts, his eyes not leaving me. "What is your plan on *figuring it out*?"

I chew on my lower lip. "I don't exactly know that yet."

His anger heightens. Even last night, he wasn't this upset. Dread takes over my body as I wait for him to throw whatever he's pissed about at me.

James told him something.

The question is, *What did he tell him?*

"When did you plan to tell me the reason you won't divorce him is because he's blackmailing you with nude pictures?"

Good thing I'm sitting, or my knees would've given out, and I'd be crying on the floor. I'd love nothing more than to sink into these cushions and disappear. The pie I ate at work earlier is threatening to make an appearance in this argument ... talk ... whatever it is.

He told him.

I want to slice and dice James right now.

Go Lorena Bobbitt on him.

It takes me a moment to find my voice and not die in front of him. "He ... he told you?"

"He fucking showed me," he hisses through clenched teeth. "I wanted to kill the bastard."

I close my eyes as they burn with tears and choke out my answer, "He's been holding it over my head since the night we broke up."

Rex will never look at me the same way again.

"Are you shitting me?" he screams. "You've just been letting him threaten you all this time? What the hell, Carolina?"

"I didn't know what to do!" I sob.

That's right.

I was stupid and sent James naked pictures of myself.

I was even *stupider* because I didn't even cut off my face in those pictures.

James knows he has me right where he wants me—the preacher's daughter whose reputation means so much. All he's done since we broke up is threaten me with them.

"Gee, I don't know," he argues. "Ask your best fucking friend for help! That's what you could've done!"

"I knew what your *help* would be."

"I would've fixed this problem for you months ago. You wouldn't be dealing with this jackass."

I violently shake my head, swiping away tears in the process. "It won't solve it. You can't hack into every device he owns. You don't know where he has them or if he's printed them off or stored them on a random drive."

"I'll find wherever he has them."

"What if you can't?"

"I'll take matters into my own hands. I've managed to snag his IP addresses, passwords, and looked through his laptop before trashing it."

"You *stole* his laptop?"

"Borrowed it," he corrects.

"So … you're giving it back?"

"Accidentally broke it while borrowing it." He shrugs. "I'm clumsy sometimes."

"I bet." I sigh heavily. "I appreciate you wanting to help, but all I can do is ride this out until he decides he's done with me. I thought him dating Margie would help, but she broke up with him again."

He arches a brow. "He and Margie are dating again?"

I nod.

"Even after she found out he was married?"

"Apparently so. When I texted him the other day, asking for a divorce, she had his phone. I thought maybe if they'd worked things out, he'd let me off the hook. I was wrong."

Yesterday, James blamed me for their breakup since it was over my text. Annoyingly, he still has me under *My Wife*, so she doesn't know it's me.

I wish I could tell Margie everything.

As the tears come faster, I cover my face with my hands. "God, this is embarrassing."

Rex plops down next to me on the couch, grabs my shoulders so I'm facing him, and plucks my hands off, one by one. "What's embarrassing is you not trusting me enough to tell me. You know everything about me. Every secret. You'd for sure know if I got married."

The hurt is clear on his face.

Rex's problem isn't that I made a mistake.

It's that I kept it from him.

That I didn't trust him with my secret.

I gulp, my eyes meeting his. "I'm sorry."

He nods, an inch of forgiveness in his features. "Why haven't you gone to the university and reported him? You don't even have to tell them about the pictures. He'd get in trouble for marrying you; I have no doubt about that."

"You think getting him fired from his job will convince him not to revenge-porn me? It'd give him more incentive because he'd have nothing to lose."

Rex grabs his laptop from the case. "To work I go then."

I snatch it from his hands. "You can get in trouble for that. You don't think I told James you'd do that? He'll report you, especially if it's any emails from his university account."

"You have no idea of the lengths I'd go to protect you." He snags the laptop back from me. "I'll risk it all."

He opens the computer, powers it on, and starts hitting keys.

I thrust a hand through my messy hair. "Do you … are you … are we …?" My voice is low and shaky.

He glances up from the computer. "Are we what?"

"Do you hate me?"

"Nope," he answers with no hesitation. "Am I pissed as fuck at you right now? Yes. I'd never hate you for making a mistake—unless it's cheating on me." This time, he does hesitate. "Which you haven't done, correct?"

"I'd never," I rush out around a gasp. "I'd never let another man touch me. There's no way I'm ruining the one thing I've wanted for years—the person who means everything to me. That is something you'll *never* have to worry about."

He shuts his eyes. "It's killing me you're married to another man and that there's nothing I can do to convince you to change that."

"I'll figure it out, I swear."

He thrusts his thumb toward me, the expression on his face breaking from frustration to a slight smile. "Which brings me to my next point. No dick until you're no longer a married woman."

I wince. "What?"

"It'll give you more incentive to change this situation … and allow me to break some laws." He rests his palm on his chest. "As I've said before, your boy is a man of morals."

I roll my eyes. "Pfft, whatever." I shake my head, my tears starting to dry as his anger calms. I throw my head back in a groan. "I can't believe he showed you pictures of me."

He taps my thigh before leaving his hand to rest there. "Yeah, no offense, but not very smart, babe."

"So, no girl has ever sent you nudes?"

"I'm feeling it's not a good idea to answer that question."

My Rex is resurfacing. No matter how upset he is with me or how dumb my choice was, he'll never stop having my back … never fail to put a smile on my face, even in the shittiest of situations.

"Come here," he says, waving me to him, and I scoot closer. The tip of his finger lifts my chin, and his lips slowly brush mine. He speaks against them, "Never be embarrassed with me, okay? No matter what, I'll be by your side, fighting with you."

I nod, resting my hand on his cheek. "Thank you."

He kisses my lips, my cheek, the tip of my nose, and then my forehead before pulling back. "Now, turn on one of those stupid-ass romance shows you like to get your mind off the bullshit, and I'll be busy at work over here."

Tension leaves my body. "Busy hacking into James's files?"

"Files, photos, emails, text, phone calls …" He shrugs as if it's no big deal.

"That's scary you know how to do all that. You should get a job with the FBI."

"Thought about it once, but I'm not one to follow rules."

———

My eyes are sleepy, and I rub at them as Rex carries me to bed in his strong arms. I yawn loudly as he flips on my bedroom light and attentively drops my sleepy self onto the comfy bed.

He sits down on the edge of it, peering down at me as I lie on my back, and runs a finger along my cheek, slowly stroking it. "Everything will be okay, babe. All I need is honesty."

I close my eyes, relaxing at his touch, at his presence. "Nine billion percent honesty from now on. I swear it."

"Sorry, I'm going to need nine billion and one percent to be happy."

A lazy laugh escapes me. "*Fine.* Nine billion and one percent." I reach forward and slide my hand up and down his arm. "Will you stay with me tonight?"

Being in his arms is the only way I'll be able to get a wink of sleep.

His arms are my comfort blanket I never want to give up.

"Will your sister care?"

Rex has never spent the night here. Our sleepovers always happen at his place.

I shake my head in response.

"You sure?"

"Eh …"

Definitely not sure but willing to risk it.

Willing to risk anything to keep him here with me … in my bed … in my life forever.

"We can say you slept on the couch."

Scooting over, I flip the covers up to allow him enough room to join me. Realizing I'm wearing a dress, I rise to my knees and pull it over my head, now wearing only a bra and boy shorts.

Rex lifts from the bed, panic ensuing me.

He's leaving.

My hands shake as I wrap my arms around my body, my eyes glued to him as he walks to my closet.

He snags a shirt and tosses it to me. "If we're sharing a bed, put this on, please and thank you."

I raise a brow. "I'm not wearing that to bed."

"You're also not going to seduce me in your bra and panties."

"Get over it." I roll my eyes, bunch the shirt up in my hand, and toss it onto the floor before patting the bed. "It's cold, so get in here before the panties come off next."

He throws his head back. "Fuck, you kill me."

I grin mischievously.

"Get in bed. I'll be right back."

Not giving me the chance to ask what he's doing, he leaves the room. Minutes later, he returns with his laptop. Setting it on the bed, he pulls off his shirt and then his jeans, showing off his semi-erection.

I lick my lips, my mouth watering.

"Nope," he groans out, snapping his fingers before pointing at my mouth. "Keep your lip-licking and eye-fucking to yourself tonight. Not happening."

"You suck," I grumble, dramatically falling back on the bed.

He collapses next to me, pulling his computer on his lap, and rests his back against the headboard. "Yeah, yeah, yeah."

"You can take a break, you know," I comment, rising up onto my elbows and focusing on him.

His eyes go to the laptop. "I want to get as much work in as I can. This shit is time-consuming. Also, you can bet your ass, James is frantically clearing his shit right now. I need to get to everything before he does."

Guilt crashes through me as I frown. "You're taking time away from your game. That's not fair."

"I'm okay."

"What if you don't find anything?"

He shrugs, rubbing the back of his neck, kneading away his tension before going back to work. "I'll plant something on his computer then."

"Are you serious?"

"Yes," he answers sharply, not giving any more explanation.

"Rex," I start, stress in my tone. "I don't want to do this shady."

"You're not doing shit; it's me."

With that, he goes back to his work.

My eyes get heavy, all energy for an argument gone, and just before I fall asleep, what I need to do to make this right hits me.

I don't deserve this.

Rex doesn't.

Margie doesn't.

Any other girl who James has manipulated doesn't.

It's time I stand up for myself.

———

"Have you even slept?" I ask the question as my eyes slowly open to find Rex in the same spot he was in my bed last night, the computer still on his lap.

An easy smile hits my lips.

All this time, I was scared he'd leave me after finding out about James, about the photos, but he's here, by my side and ready to fight this out with me.

I've always loved my relationship with Rex, but now, it's so much more. My heart bursts with so much passion for this man.

I loved him in high school.

I tried fighting my attraction in college.

Now, there's no doubt, no fighting. This is the only man who will own my heart.

He stole my heart the day he tried bribing me to write a damn Shakespeare paper.

"Morning, sunshine," he says, paying me a quick glance, his eyes sleepy, before going back to work on the computer. "I got a few hours."

Guilt consumes me.

He's losing time to work on his video game.

Losing sleep.

All for my stupidity.

I should be the one going through James's shit. Sure, I'd need to figure out how to hack and all, but it's not fair to Rex.

I'm sitting, pulling the sheet up my chest, when he speaks again, "You know, Iowa has a law criminalizing revenge porn." He moves his gaze my way, finally giving me his full attention. "If he posts intimate or sexually graphic pictures without your knowledge, he can be criminally charged for it."

"So what? We wait until he posts the photos? We can't get him in trouble for threatening to post them?"

"I'm still looking into that, but I wanted you to know that if he does do anything with them, he can get in big trouble. We need to bring that to his attention if he doesn't already know and make it clear you will press charges against him."

"If I were to press charges ... my parents would find out."

"Yes, probably." He frowns, going back to work. "Until then, we find more blackmail."

"What if I have an idea?" I ask around a gulp.

He raises a brow, his typing paused. "Shoot."

———

Margie stares at me from across the table. "I was shocked when you texted me since you've been dodging me for months."

Same, Margie. Same.

It's what needed to be done.

No more running scared from James.

No more allowing him to control me.

He needs to go down, and unless someone steps up, he'll do it again … and again … and again to innocent women. I've decided to take on the job of breaking that cycle—or at least attempting to. First things first. I need to apologize to Margie, and then I need to ask her for a favor.

After telling Rex my plan, I texted Margie, asking her to meet with me. Whether she'd reply, I had no idea. Thankfully, she did, and three hours later, here we are, sitting at a table in the park, having coffee.

It's strange, seeing her after everything that's happened.

Neither one of us is the same as we were before James stormed into our lives.

The happiness that took permanent residence on her face when we lived together has dimmed. James stole some of her light, and I want to punch him in the face for it.

We'd cluelessly slept with the same man.

Whether she knows that, I'm not sure.

I'm taking a risk by being here. Last time we talked was when she had James's phone, and I don't know the status of their relationship. Even though James said they broke up, he could've manipulated her into getting back together. She could tell James everything I say.

I take a sip of my caramel macchiato, wishing it contained something stronger for liquid courage. "I apologize for being distant. I'm truly sorry."

Gripping her iced coffee, she leans back in her chair, focusing her blue eyes on me. "What happened, Carolina? I was so confused. I confessed a huge secret to you, I was heartbroken, and then I never saw you again."

Here goes nothing.

I'm struggling to find the right words even though I rehearsed them so many times on the drive here.

"That night"—I close my eyes, pulling in a calming breath—"when you told me about sleeping with Professor Cordry …"

"Yes?" She raises a brow, sadness spreading over her face.

"That other girl he was seeing—*his wife*—that's me."

She gapes at me, her mouth dropping open. "Wait, what?"

"We'd been sneaking around for six months and stupidly gotten married a week before you found out." The memory tears a hole in my chest. "I had no idea he'd been dating you, too. When you told me, a wave of shock hit me, and I freaked out. When I ran off, it was to confront him about the cheating."

"Wow." She cringes, resting her coffee on the table. "Did he know we were roommates?"

"He said he didn't when you met, but I don't believe anything that leaves that man's mouth." I blow out a deep breath. "We got in a fight over Rex texting me at one in the morning and didn't talk for days. I think that's when he met you."

She releases a spiteful laugh. "God, I was so flattered at the time. I was used to dating stupid frat boys, and here was this guy, making me dinner at his house instead of inviting me to parties where he did keg stands." She throws her arms out. "Why didn't you tell me?"

"When I confronted him, he threatened me with—"

"Let me guess," she cuts in. "Pictures?"

"You, too?"

She nods. "Yep. He begged me to get back together after the whole wife thing, saying they had a quick fling in Vegas and everything was over. Since then, we've been off and on—off every time I catch him with someone else. A few days ago, I found he'd been talking to women on some stupid secret app and receiving naked pictures of them, and I finally left him."

"According to Rex, he has quite the collection of nudes."

When I asked Rex if any of the photos were of Margie or other women we knew, he shook his head, saying he didn't know because he wasn't going to look through them.

"How'd Rex know?"

"He hacked into James's accounts to find information to stop him from blackmailing me."

"Oh, good old Rex," she says with a smile. "The man who'd do anything for you."

I grin at the truth in her words.

"Tell me that grin means you two finally got your heads out of your asses and admitted you're in love with each other."

I nod. "Sure did."

A genuine smile crosses her face. "I'm so happy for you, Lina!" She pauses for a moment. "I'm also sorry for calling you a skank-ass ho."

A laugh escapes me. "Since you didn't know I was the wife, I totally understand. I would've thought the same thing."

"Those words would've never left your mouth."

"I said, I would've *thought* the same thing." I blow out a breath and frown at the subject change I'm about to throw out. "So, you and James are done? You're no longer dating him?"

She shakes her head. "Dating? No. Talking? Unfortunately. He won't leave me the hell alone."

"He likes the power," I say matter-of-factly.

She nods in agreement. "The asshole sure does."

"He said if I told you what a piece of crap he was, he'd also release pictures you'd sent him." I'm unable to meet her gaze for a moment as my stomach turns. "It was a reason I was scared to tell you, but I can't keep letting him do this to women."

"I understand." She reaches forward and settles her hand over mine before giving it a tight squeeze. "His threats are brutal. It's scary, hearing them and knowing it might jeopardize my future career."

Margie's majoring in communications and journalism. With her goal of being a news anchor, a public figure, nude pictures of her online would demolish any job opportunities.

We separate when I pull away to take a long sip of my coffee. The fear of James retaliating against Margie for me exposing him terrifies me, making me question my plan. I need Margie's permission before I make any decisions. She deserves that respect from me.

"We need to band together," I say, sitting up straight in my chair. "Rex spent last night reading through James's texts and emails. There were more women he was threatening, and Rex managed to get their contact information. Legally, we have nothing on him since he hasn't gone through with his threats—"

"That we know of," she adds.

"That we know of," I repeat, my eyes meeting hers. "What we do have on our side is his profession. We can report him to the university. There's no way, if we step forward and expose him, the university will overlook it. James will get in trouble. The more women, the more they'll have to listen to us."

"What if the university doesn't do anything?"

"Rex's brother's girlfriend is a journalist." I shrug. "I'll have her write an exposé on him."

"Another problem."

I raise a brow, fully aware there can be a million problems with this plan of mine.

"If we do this, it'll piss him off more. Who's to say he won't release them out of spite?"

That's a question I've contemplated a million times.

"It's a risk we have to take," I explain around a nervous sigh. "Before I meet with the dean, who we have a meeting with in a few hours, I'll text James a web link that tells him the legal repercussions. Let's pray it works."

With Rex's parents being who they are, he had his mother reach out to the dean and schedule a meeting for us. All of this is happening so fast, and I don't know how my head isn't spinning. Not only did I contact Margie, but I've also reached out to the other women on campus.

Margie sits across from me, eyes wide and speechless as she drags her fingers through her hair—her nervous tic.

"You don't have to come," I whisper, fighting to keep my voice strong as I tap my chest. "But I'm done with being his puppet."

It takes her a moment as she sucks in a few long breaths before replying, "What's the next step?"

"We have to talk to the other women," I say, dragging my phone from my crossbody bag. "Two have already agreed to meet with me, and I'm waiting on responses from the other two. I don't know if James has pictures of them since Rex isn't a creep, but he did send them threatening texts."

I pull myself up from the chair, lean forward, and rest my palms on the table. "You in?"

Margie abruptly smiles. "I'm in. Fuck Professor Cordry."

CHAPTER TWENTY-SIX

A long yawn escapes me as I trudge into my apartment.

The exhaustion of being up all night, searching through James's shit, is hitting me.

Breaking into his phone was child's play, and it turned out, it was all I needed to discover sufficient evidence for him to get in trouble with the university.

He's made a game out of exploiting female students for the past four years. He'd meet them, date them, gain their trust, and then ask for nudes. When they declined, he'd assure them the photos were safe with him and other bullshit lines. My stomach curled, vomit pushing its way up my throat, when I read the threatening messages he'd sent to them when they attempted to break up with him. It looked like Carolina was the only one who'd gone far enough to marry him.

He's a womanizer.

A creep.

A fucking predator.

Men like him remind me of my father—manipulative and power-hungry.

Carolina is taking a risk by turning him into the university, and I'm so damn proud of her for showing that asshole her resilience.

James underestimated Carolina and the people who had her back.

His manipulation might've worked on other women, but Lina has someone who'll kill for her, die for her, break every bone in someone's body to protect her.

I can't wait for that fucker to go down.

———

The idea of catching up on sleep rolls through me, but I stop myself. I've been on standby since Carolina left this morning, and my phone has been glued to my side as I wait for an update.

I'm pouring my sixth cup of coffee when Carolina calls.

"Hey, babe," I answer. "How's it going?"

"Margie and I spoke to the other girls James harassed, and the six of us are going to the dean," she replies with hope in her voice.

Good.

Let him get what he deserves.

The hopefulness in her voice changes into worry. "We're doing this."

"I'm proud of you, babe." I wish I were there, at her side, wrapping her in my arms.

"Fingers crossed and pray to every saint that James doesn't retaliate."

Let him fucking try.

"You sure you don't want me to come with you?"

"As much as I'd love that, this is something us girls need to do together."

"I understand." I open the fridge and grab the leftover box of pizza. "I'm here if you need anything. Call. Text. Send a raven."

Her voice turns gentle. "I know, and that's why I love you so much."

It's heaven, hearing her say those words.

Sure, we've shared *I love yous* plenty of times, but it hits different when it's more than friendship.

Never did I think we'd be as intimate as we are now.

"Keep me updated." I plop down on the couch and take a bite of the cold pizza.

"I will," she says in almost a whisper.

"When are you coming home?"

"I'm going to stay at Margie's tonight, so we can catch up and be there for each other."

Even though her staying with Margie means she won't be with me, I smile. Carolina has never had many girlfriends and was thrilled when she and Margie became close. It broke her, losing that.

I nod even though she can't see me. "Good luck, baby. I love you."

"I love you, and thank you for having my back."

My hand goes to my heart. "Always."

I pause my game, tossing the controller onto the floor, when my phone rings.

Two hours have passed since I last heard from Carolina. I've refrained from calling or texting, waiting for her even though it's been killing me.

It's a dick move for frowning when it's Kyle's name on the screen, not hers.

I hit answer. "Yo."

"Hey, brother," he says. "I have good news for you."

Leaning back on the couch, I kick my feet onto the table. "I hit the lottery?"

"Even better. You can become my neighbor."

I straighten. "Really?"

"Really. I talked to Chloe, and she's willing to work with whatever you need. I'm going to text you a contact we have from the bank, so we can get you a loan."

The first thought that comes to my mind is Carolina.

Living with Carolina.

Sharing a house with her.

Letting her decorate it with all her girlie shit … but demanding she allow a few video game touches throughout the place.

It's perfect timing. My lease expires in two months, and Josh's girlfriend has been up his ass about him moving in with her.

Kyle goes on to give me price details and his contacts, and in the background, I hear Chloe say she'd love to have me as her neighbor.

There's no stopping me from chuckling. "Looks like she's more open to being my neighbor than she was with you when you moved in."

Chloe hated Kyle then, and he took great pleasure in annoying her. He'd greet her with a cheerful morning every day, and she'd respond with either a, "Fuck you," or the middle finger.

I love how she gave him so much shit and also how she managed to calm my brother down.

He needed someone to do that for him.

Like I need Carolina to be the calm to my chaos.

Us Lane boys tend to give our hearts to women nothing like us, who put us in our place and make it their mission to make us better men.

Excitement beams through me when we hang up.

Look at me.

Becoming a fucking grown-up.

CHAPTER TWENTY-SEVEN
CAROLINA

Today has been the hardest day of my life.

We sat in the dean's office and shared our stories, exposing the scars James cut into us. I go last, tears at my eyes from listening to the stories, and break down harder at the reveal of my intimate life.

Never have I been flooded with so many emotions.

Anger. Sadness. Shame.

For so long, my fear circled around being judged, but the dean, she isn't disgusted with me.

She's disgusted with James.

Two hours later, she apologizes for James's behavior and thanks us for our honesty. Asking what she planned to do with James is on the tip of my tongue, but I bite it back, letting it go for now.

I'm not sure anyone knows the answer to that yet.

"We did it," Margie says with a low sigh when we walk out of the building.

"We did it," I repeat, matching her sigh.

If you'd told me a week ago that I'd be here with Margie, giving James what he deserves, I would've said you were as nuts as him.

Rex, his love, brought out that strength in me.

I've always had it. I just needed the nudge to build it.

We leave the university and load into Margie's car.

Where else do you go after you've told on your creep of a professor who's also your husband? The store for wine, junk food, and frozen pizza.

We veg out in front of the TV, watching Netflix, and when I finally go to sleep, it's with a smile on my face because I have my friend back.

CHAPTER TWENTY-EIGHT

Two days have passed since Carolina exposed James to the dean of the university.

No one has heard from him, nor do we know whether he's been fired.

It's a waiting game.

If the university fails to make shit right, I'll take it to Chloe. She loves exposing assholes.

To get Carolina's mind off the drama, I'm taking her out tonight. I rented a hotel suite and booked a dinner reservation at Clayton's, the nicest restaurant outside of Blue Beech.

I'm showering when my phone rings, and since freezing my dick off to answer it doesn't sound fun, I ignore it.

Seconds later, it rings again.

I rinse the soap off my body, acting like I hear nothing.

The third time it fires off, I open the shower door, snag a towel, and am shivering when I grab my phone. My stomach twists when I see the name flashing across the screen, and I nearly drop it from answering so quickly.

"Hello?"

"Rex, it's Tricia," she shouts, alarm etched in her tone. "There's a man in the loft, arguing with Carolina. George is at work. I locked the kids in the house and am going in now. I thought you should know … to come here."

A chill colder than the one I had when I jumped out of the shower sweeps through my veins. "What's he driving?" Dropping my towel, I pull on clothes, not caring what they are. The phone is balanced between my shoulder and ear, and I struggle to tug on my shoes while running out of the house.

"Blue BMW."

Fucking James.

A blue BMW was registered to his name two years ago.

A deep breath leaves Tricia. "Going in now."

"Stay on the phone with me."

"Shoot!" Her voice trails off, becoming distant. "My dad is calling."

"Wait!"

The call ends.

I jump into my car, grip the steering wheel, and gun the gas. Heads turn in my direction as I speed through town.

I'll kill James if he lays a hand on her.

I'm only minutes away from Tricia's when I call Kyle.

"You at work?" I rush out when he answers.

"Yeah. What's up?"

"Carolina's crazy-ass ex showed up at her place."

"Shit. She's staying at Tricia's, right?"

"Yes."

He fills Gage in. "We're on our way."

Fingers crossed Kyle coming doesn't piss Carolina off, but he's a cop. If James pulls anything dumb, Carolina can file a police report, providing further evidence of his harassment. The drawback, though, is there'll also be evidence if I kick his ass.

I cut the wheel into Tricia's driveway, arriving before Kyle and Gage. I sprint up the stairs, hearing arguing from the loft, and burst inside without knocking.

Everyone's attention swings to me while I take in the scene. Sure enough, James is here. Carolina is standing across from him, her hands clutched to her hips, and fury covers her face. Tricia is next to her, glancing around and searching for answers.

James's bitter eyes shoot to me, a sinister smile on his lips. "Oh, look," he spits. "Your little boyfriend came to the rescue, bitch."

Not a thought stops me from rushing to him, clutching the collar of his shirt, and Tricia gasps when I punch him in the face. Last time, I was nice, only choking him a bit, but James needs to learn a bigger lesson this time.

He shuffles back a few steps, his hand curling around his nose to stop the blood from my blow. "You broke my nose, you little shit!"

I stand in front of him, blocking his view of Carolina and Tricia, and my knuckles ball into fists as I wait for his retaliation.

"James!" Carolina shrieks. "You need to get out of here."

"No, *wife,*" James barks, lifting his hand from his nose, blood now dropping onto the carpet. "I'm only getting started. How dare you go to the dean and pull that shit, you stupid fucking whore!"

His insult pushes me to advance his way again. He stumbles backward, attempting to dodge me, but I'm faster. A rough grunt leaves him when my hand wraps around his neck, and I pin him against the wall—the same way I did in his classroom.

Apparently, this is how we communicate best.

For someone who delivers threats to women like he's a mailman, he sucks ass at sticking up for himself *with men.*

He flails, gasping, and the pain he put Carolina through consumes my thoughts, causing me to tighten my hold. It isn't until Carolina tugs at my arm, sobbing my name, that I relax my grip.

"Carolina, go outside and wait for Kyle to get here," I hiss.

"We're here!" Kyle shouts.

When I glance over my shoulder, not only do I see Kyle and Gage, but Rick is also next to them.

Just great.

"Rex," Kyle draws my name out in caution. "Let him go. He'd be dumb to pull anything in front of the police."

Carolina continues to pull at my arm.

"Go to them, and I'll let him go," I tell her through gritted teeth. Never in my life has so much anger surged through me.

She nods, scurrying backward, and stops next to Kyle.

James's blood is on my arm when I release him, and he bends at the waist, panting. Not trusting him, I stand to his side, my eyes glued to him, in case he tries or says something stupid.

I've placed Kyle in a shitty situation. He's a police officer on duty, and I nearly choked a man to death in front of him. If he arrests me, I'll understand and accept the punishment. James had better be in that car next to me, though.

"What's going on here?"

My attention leaves James and cuts to Rick at the sound of his voice.

Rick's eyes darken as they level on James. "Who are you?"

"James Cordry," he answers through harsh pants, pointing at Carolina. "Her husband."

It takes everything in me not to knock his ass out.

Rick's attention darts to Carolina. "*Your husband?*"

The air turns dead, no one wanting to be the first to speak, until Tricia steps up.

"You're *married* to him?"

"She sure is," James replies with a smirk, which is blocked seconds later when he rubs his arm underneath his nose, catching drops of blood. "And she's cheating on me with this asshole." He tips his head my way.

Carolina's eyes shoot to me like an SOS signal for help.

"Their marriage is bullshit," I explain. "He's blackmailing her into staying with him."

Regret hits me at my words.

How will we explain his blackmailing without mentioning the pictures?

The loft is crowded with people, but my only concern is Carolina … and James making a stupid decision behind me.

"I'm so lost," Tricia mutters.

"That makes two of us," Rick snaps, his gaze bouncing among the three of us in this fucked-up love triangle. He throws his hand out toward Carolina. "It seems your sister is married to this man … *this stranger* … and is having an affair with Rex."

"That's right," James answers, stroking the red marks on his neck.

"I don't want to be married to you!" Carolina screams.

"How did you end up married?" Tricia asks.

"You see—"

Carolina speaks over James. "It's a long story that doesn't need to be told right now."

"A long story you had no problem telling the dean," James snarls.

"She deserved to know what kind of man you truly are!" Carolina screams.

The walls shake, everyone stopping, when Rick slams the door shut.

"That's enough," he yells. "I want answers."

"I'll give you answers," James says. "After these officers get this man away from me and arrest him."

"Rex," Kyle says, waving me over. "Move away, so he feels safe."

"Fuck him," I growl. "He doesn't deserve to feel safe."

"We don't care about him, man," Gage comments. "We'd prefer not to arrest you."

"You'd better arrest him!" James shrieks. "You witnessed him assaulting me!"

Gage looks over at Kyle. "I didn't see anything. Did you?"

Kyle shakes his head. "Must've been before we showed up."

James points at his nose. "Evidence!"

"He ran into a wall before he came in," I explain with a shrug.

"I hate when that happens," Gage says. "Now, get over here, Rex."

I shoot James a warning glare before moving, and everyone stares at him as if he were on trial.

"Dad," Carolina says, "this needs to be a private conversation."

"No need to talk in private," James blurts out. "It's quite simple, sir. Your daughter married me and now wants a divorce. Since I won't sign the papers, she's blackmailing me, lying to the dean so I'll lose my job." His eyes narrow on Carolina. "Retract your statement and tell them you lied. I'll sign the divorce papers, let your little boyfriend clear my devices, and be on my way." His voice shifts into a plea. "*Please*. I can't lose my job over this."

Carolina shakes her head. "No. I won't do that to the other women who stood strong with me to expose you. Your behavior needs stopped before you put another woman through hell."

"*Please*," James pleads. "If you don't, I'll ruin your life just as much. Don't forget, all I need to do is hit a simple button—"

Kyle grabs my shirt, stopping me from lunging at James.

"You do that, and not only will you be fired from the university, but you'll also be prosecuted," Carolina states matter-of-factly. "No longer will I allow you to threaten me. Do it, and you'll go to jail."

Defeat crosses James's face. "Please," he begs.

"Leave before I have them arrest you for being here," Carolina tells him, her voice strong and firm, before she holds a finger up. "Actually, I'll be right back."

James mutters, "Shit," under his breath while Carolina darts to her bedroom, returning seconds later with papers, a pen, and a Kleenex in her hand. I tense when she approaches him and shoves a Kleenex in his hand.

"Here," she says. "Don't want you to get blood on these."

Everyone watches her in confusion, and James wipes his nose, balling up the Kleenex in his fist when he's finished.

"Divorce papers," Carolina says, waving them in the air before shoving them into James's chest. "Sign them, or I'll have these kind officers make a police report. I'm sure you'd *really* lose your job if the university found out you came here and threatened me."

We wait for his next move, and time slows while Carolina and James have a staredown. The hate Carolina feels for the man who has put her through hell is clear on her face. Finally, James nods, snatches the pen, and walks around her to the coffee table. Bending, he signs his name.

"There you go," he says, slamming down the pen and leaving the papers on the table before adjusting his attention back to Carolina. "Happy now?"

She nods, and her voice is stone cold as she says, "Very."

"Thanks for ruining my life," he spits, his face tightening into a grimace. "I'm out of here."

I step in front of him, standing tall and cutting him off on his way to the door. "Remember what she said. Do anything stupid, and she'll press charges."

"Got it," he bites out, maneuvering around me.

Everyone shuffles out of his way, and he keeps his head down while storming out of the loft. Not a word is muttered until the door slams shut behind him.

"Well," Kyle says around clearing his throat, "looks like our work here is done."

"Yep," Gage agrees, rubbing his hands together. "We'll make sure" —his voice trails off as he gets his words straight—"that guy leaves, and then we'll be on our way."

Kyle throws me a wary look. "Let me know if you need anything or if he comes back."

"We will," I say.

They say their good-byes to everyone, and as soon as they leave, Tricia asks, "Are we talking about this now or later?"

"Later," Carolina and Rick answer at the same time.

Rick wears an unreadable expression as he pushes his hands into the pockets of his slacks and focuses on Carolina. "Please stop by the church when you have a minute."

Carolina's response comes out in a whisper. "Okay."

Rick tips his head in my direction. "Rex."

Tricia follows Rick as they leave.

Thank fuck.

Carolina needs time to process everything.

She places her palm on her chest, her hand now shaking, and her eyes glaze over. She composed her emotions, but now that everyone is gone, they're releasing. "Did that happen?" Her gaze pings around the room as if she imagined everything. "Did James really come here and tell everyone I was his wife?" She rushes over to grab the papers and holds them up. "And he ... he signed the divorce papers. How was it that easy? He's been giving me hell for months, and all of a sudden, it's —*bam!*—here you go?"

I stand behind her, wrapping my arms around her waist, and kiss her neck. "Depends on what you think *easy* is. Your dad now knows about your marriage to James."

Her shoulders slump, and she drops the papers. "It was bound to come out sometime."

"I'm shocked he gave in so easily."

"He was cornered and hadn't expected an audience, hadn't expected *the cops* to show up." She turns, and when she wraps her arms around my neck, her unease fades. "He doesn't like his secrets exposed, and a room full of people found out he'd had a relationship with me— more evidence that could get him in trouble."

My eyes meet hers. "Does that mean you're not mad at me for calling Kyle?"

"Am I embarrassed? Absolutely. Did it help my situation? Yes." She nudges her nose against mine before drawing back a few inches. "So, thank you."

"You never told me you had divorce papers."

"I had them drawn up, waiting for when he'd finally agree to sign." She groans, tilting her head back. "Gosh, I wish it hadn't happened in front of everyone. I wanted to melt right into the carpet and disappear."

I run my hands up and down her arms. "I can help with that."

She arches a brow. "Huh? Did you turn into Harry Potter?"

"No, we can disappear from town tonight. Pack a bag."

———

"You're right," Carolina says. "Getting out of town has helped clear my head."

"Glad I could help." I fold my arms behind my head, resting them against the headboard of the bed, and stare at her as I'm spread out along the soft hotel sheets.

Carolina had a bag packed within ten minutes after James's

dramatic visit. We stopped at my apartment for mine and drove to the city. Our dinner was bomb, and even though we had chocolate mousse at the restaurant, we ordered chocolate covered strawberries and champagne from room service.

Cliché? Yes.

Who cares?

All that matters is, my girl likes it.

As our relationship has grown more serious, we haven't done too many *date* things together. My goal is to change that.

She eats the last strawberry, licking chocolate from her fingers, and my dick twitches when she crawls up the bed on her hands and knees, wearing the same teddy she had the night at the hotel of Faye's wedding.

"Is it bad that I thought it was hot when you punched James?" She straddles my lap, a flirtatious smile on her plump lips.

Moving my arms, I rest my hands on her thighs. "Oh, really?"

Goose bumps travel up her skin when I run my fingers across it and push the teddy up to her waist.

"Yes, really." She tips her head down and separates her next words between kisses. "I think you deserve a reward."

I moan, bucking my hips up. "You love rewarding me."

"I definitely love rewarding you."

I pull the teddy over her head, throwing it across the room, and flip her over onto her back. When I slide into her, it's slow and gentle; it's *making love.*

"You're all mine," I moan into her mouth. "Say it."

"All yours," she gasps as I suck on her neck.

"Forever."

"Forever."

CHAPTER TWENTY-NINE

TWO MONTHS LATER

I shake out my hands, an attempt to stop my palms from sweating, and take a calming breath before opening the door.

I've never been so nervous, walking into a church.

My nose wrinkles at the scent of wood polish as I walk down the aisle separating the pews. Rick is standing on the pulpit at the head of the room. His attention moves from the Bible on the lectern to me as I grow closer.

"Pastor Adams," I greet, sliding those sweaty palms down my jeans.

I've never been a flustered person.

Nervousness isn't the norm for me.

"Rex," he says, sliding his glasses off his nose and setting them down next to the Bible. "This is quite the surprise."

Yesterday, Carolina's divorce was finalized. James had been fired from the university two weeks after Carolina talked to the dean. His story hit the news outlets, so everyone knows what a scumbag he is now. Carolina considered returning to school but ultimately decided to take online classes, unsure of her career dreams now.

"I want to marry Carolina," I blurt out before the nerves get the best of me and I pass out.

He blinks, as if he's unsure he heard me correctly. "Excuse me?"

I stand tall, straightening my shoulders. "I'm in love with your daughter, sir, and I would love nothing more than for her to be my wife."

It's old-fashioned as fuck, asking for Rick's blessing, but I want the guy to like me. My anxiousness is the fear of him saying no since he's never been a fan of mine. Sure, it'd look bad if I proposed without asking for permission … but it'll look real damn bad if I do so after he didn't give me his blessing.

Him saying no won't stop me from asking her to be my wife.

Call me an asshole.

I give no fucks.

He stares at me, his eyes unreadable, before gesturing for me to follow him. Neither of us mutters a word as we walk down a narrow hall and land in a small office. Clearing his throat, he perches on the edge of the old wooden desk, his stern eyes pinned to me, and he clasps his hands together in front of him.

"My daughter's relationship with you has always concerned me," he states.

So far, not going so well.

"I didn't like it," he continues. "With your reputation, I worried you'd hurt her or be a negative influence, but you've proven me wrong."

Shock smacks into me.

Not where I thought this convo was headed.

I stand there, not saying a word, as he keeps speaking. "You've been a pillar of strength for her, and I appreciate that." His hands unclasp, and he throws them out my way. "I apologize for judging you, for doubting your intentions, but hopefully, you understand my concern."

I only nod.

Is this a yes?

I nearly fall on my ass when he stands to hold out his hand.

"I'd love nothing more than to welcome you into our family."

Hell to the motherfucking yes.

I shake his hand, unable to contain the smile taking over my face.

CHAPTER THIRTY

"I can't believe we're moving into our own house!" I squeal, jumping up and down with the new set of keys in my hand. "We're going to decorate, and I'm going to have nine million bookshelves and a great kitchen to bake in!"

Rex's game took off, breaking nearly eight hundred million in sales *in the first week*, and there's already talks for a second one. To say I'm proud is an understatement.

A few weeks ago, he asked what I thought about us moving into Chloe's house.

Living together.

Him and me.

I was ready to start packing as soon as he asked.

Today's the big day, and lucky for us, we have a team of helpers. Maliki, Kyle, and Gage are here to assist us with the heavy loading. Also helping is Rex's half-brother, Trey, and Lauren's brothers, Dallas and Hudson. Chloe and Lauren are here, and they dragged Lauren's sisters-in-laws, Willow and Stella, here to be Team Unpack.

Before moving in, we had the walls freshly painted and new flooring installed. The new furniture we'd purchased was delivered and assembled three days ago, so all we need to do is unpack and relax in our new place.

"Man, am I going to miss my old bedroom," Trey says, standing in the doorway of the guest room before walking in and falling back onto the full-size bed.

Trey lived here with Chloe before they moved in with Kyle.

"You can spend the night here whenever you want," Rex says, patting Trey on the back when he stands.

I dodge Maliki carrying a box down the hallway and stop at the empty room that once belonged to Chloe's niece. Resting against the doorframe, I imagine the possibilities. My thoughts are broken by Rex's voice.

"Pizza is here!" he yells, paying the deliveryman and grabbing the stack of pizza boxes from him.

We move, unpack, eat pizzas, and drink beer, and six hours later, the gang leaves. It's been an exhausting day, but it was worth it.

"Have you decided what to do with the spare bedroom?" Rex asks while helping me clean up the kitchen. "I'm thinking"—a smirk passes over his face—"game room?"

I dry my hands off on a dish towel and shut the dishwasher. "I have something else in mind."

He raises a brow. "What do you mean?"

"I have a surprise for you."

"I love your surprises."

"Why?" I laugh, shaking my head. "Because they normally end up with us naked?"

He snaps his fingers, a boyish smile on his lips. "Exactly why I love them, babe."

"Hopefully, you'll like this one." I gulp before moving around him and grab my phone from the counter. Unlocking the screen, I pull up the photo I found on Pinterest. My eyes stay fixed on his face as I wait for his response, afraid to miss an expression that crosses it.

He scratches his head. "Uh ..." His eyes dart from the phone to me, back to the phone, and then to me. "A baby room?"

"A *nursery*," I correct, dragging the phone away from his puzzled face and setting it down.

His dark eyes widen. "Is this you saying you want to be my baby mama?"

I nod.

That boyish smile of his lights up as if he's on top of the world. "Seriously?"

I play with my hands, a shyness hitting me. "I know we haven't been dating that long."

Rex reaches out, grabbing my face, and runs his hand along my chin. "Are you serious, babe? We've pretty much been dating since high school."

"You're okay with us having kids?"

"Fucking ecstatic. I say we start now."

"That might not be my only surprise," I whisper.

"Two surprises? I like this."

His hand falls when I pull away. My heart gives a twist in my chest when I grab my purse and retrieve the small box I shoved in there earlier.

"Whoa," he says, his eyes zeroed in on the long stick I pull from the box. "Is that what I think it is?"

I nod again, the pregnancy test in my hand, afraid to speak as color stains my cheeks.

He advances a step, staring at me, speechless for a moment as his eyes widen. "Holy fuck … we're going to be parents?"

"We're going to be parents," I confirm.

An intoxicating grin lights up his face as he grabs mine.

There's no stopping my smile from matching his.

I've always wanted to be a wife and have children.

It'll be even better when my best friend, the man I love, is by my side.

Our eyes meet, his gleaming with excitement, and his thumb strokes my cheek. "You know what this means, right?"

"What?" I don't tell him I know exactly what it means—*me gaining weight, crankiness, spending thousands of dollars on baby stuff, having our entire lives change.*

"Your parents already think I'm corrupting you—"

I interrupt him, "They do not."

He snorts. "Wait until they find out I knocked you up out of wedlock."

"They'll get over it," I grumble, scowling.

His hands leave my face, and he gives me a quick peck on the lips before turning around.

My eyes narrow as he leaves the kitchen, disappears down the hall, and then returns with nothing.

Okay, maybe he returns with nothing physical, but his mood has shifted. Even though his excitement is clear, a wave of nervousness pours from him.

He clears his throat, and the way he's staring at me—full of affection, adoration, *love*—gives me goose bumps. "I want to return the surprise."

"Okay," I draw out.

Seconds later, when he drops down to one knee, my hand flies to my mouth, and I nearly fall on my ass. I peer down at him, taking in the man I've loved since high school—who brought me out of my shell, who made me believe I was more than just the quiet preacher's daughter—and I know that I never want to lose him.

"First comes love." There's a slight tremble in his words. "Then comes marriage … and then comes a baby in a baby carriage." He reaches up, his palm spreading out along my stomach, and rubs it.

My heart nearly explodes out of my chest when he fishes a jewelry box from his pocket.

The tremble in his voice is gone, replaced with a confidence that is full Rex. "Carolina Adams, the girl who stole my heart, who let me corrupt her with tequila the first day we hung out, and the woman who made me want to be a better man. I wouldn't be where I am now had you not been by my side every step of the way, being my biggest cheerleader and putting up with my shit. We have the love. Now, will you give me marriage before we put our baby in a carriage?"

Tears are in my eyes, my hand going back to my mouth, and this time, it's my voice that's trembling. "You have such a way with words, babe."

He grins that grin I love. "Gotta give a man credit. Now, what do you say? You're scaring the shit out of me down here."

I gesture for him to stand, then swing my arms around him as soon as he's on his feet and kiss every inch of his face, the word, "Yes," leaving my lips between each of them.

He rubs his thumb over his bottom lip when we separate. "Damn, it was easier for you to agree to be my wife than to write a Shakespeare paper."

EPILOGUE
CAROLINA

SIX YEARS LATER

I'm shaking my head, trying my hardest to act annoyed, as we walk into Sierra's backyard. "You spoil her *way* too much."

"What?" Rex asks, raising a brow.

I nod toward the sparkly pink unicorn cake in his hands. There was only supposed to be one birthday cake at the party, but Esme insisted she wanted a unicorn one.

What Esme wants, her daddy gives her.

"And River isn't spoiled?" he asks, tipping his head toward the Power Ranger cake I'm holding.

"Eh, good point," I mutter.

Like Esme, River tends to get what he wants.

"I wonder how many times this will happen," Rex says.

"This is only the beginning," I sing-song.

"Oh, the perks of having twins."

That's right.

We have twins.

I nearly fell off the ultrasound table when the tech told us. I had her check it again, just in case she'd forgotten how to count, but nope, two babies were inside me. No wonder I'd been eating so many bags of

Peanut M&M's. I was eating for three, and that required a lot of M&M's … and ice cream … and carrots dipped in salsa.

Rex gagged every time I ate the carrots.

Who would've thought the two go well together?

Pregnant Carolina—that's who.

Even though I was a terrified mess, knowing Rex would be by my side put me at ease. No matter what, together, we make a great team.

The twins are already in the backyard in their swimsuits, waiting for us to give them the go-ahead to get into the pool. We do when we notice Willow sitting at the edge of the pool with her feet in the water. She gives us a wave while she plays lifeguard. Dallas is next to her, watching the other side of the pool as the kids splash each other.

"Oh, look, another cake," Sierra comments when I set mine down on the table. Next to it is a tall three-tier cake with a dump truck on it.

"Next year, we're sharing *one cake*. I don't care how many tears are shed," Maliki says. Walking over to us, he's shaking his head, while Molly is behind him, counting down the reasons she needs an iPhone.

"Have fun convincing Rex of the one-cake rule," I comment as Rex slides a stack of plates down the table to make room for the unicorn cake.

"I'm cool with that," Rex says. "Just make sure the boys are okay with a pink cake."

"I never said it couldn't be the one that my son picks out, which it will be. I said, *one*," Maliki corrects.

"Of course," Sierra mutters with an eye roll.

A baby boom hit Blue Beech. The same day I planned to announce my pregnancy, Sierra did, too—neither one of us knowing about the other. Four days after I gave birth to Esme and River, Sierra had her baby boy, Jax. He's a mini Maliki, exactly like his daddy with dark hair and his laid-back attitude.

That same year, another three baby girls came into the Blue Beech world. Kyle and Chloe adopted Callie. The sweetest in the bunch— *sorry, Esme*—who always shares her snacks and doesn't mind being last in line. Gage and Lauren had their little girl, Ava, who's as outspoken as her mother. Then Mia came, Stella and Hudson's glamour girl, who's already a fan of makeup and handbags. Dallas and Willow's son, Easton, was also born that year. While Callie is the sweetest girl, Easton is the sweetest little boy.

Our nights out have turned into playdates. We make them fun, and it helps that Sierra created the perfect backyard oasis. They had a pool installed and a massive custom play set built, and they have a roomy outdoor grill area. The kiddos love the pool, and since there are so many of us, each couple takes one-hour shifts, watching them swim.

"Dad!" Molly whines, interrupting us. "My birthday is in two months. Let's call it an early birthday gift."

Maliki shakes his head. "I'm not buying you a phone to text Noah all night."

"That's her *boyfriend*," Jax says, running over to us in his swim trunks, Scooby-Doo floaties wrapped around him.

"Ugh, he's not my boyfriend," Molly yelps.

"But she wants him to be her boyfriend," Maven, Dallas's daughter and Molly's best friend, cuts in.

Molly shoots her a dirty look.

"I think it's cute," Sierra says, sitting down at the table. "Maliki's daughter dating his best friend's son."

"She's not dating anyone," Maliki growls.

I grab a soda and sit down next to Sierra. "Noah is Cohen's son, right?"

She nods. "He's such a sweetheart. Cohen got him a phone, and he loves texting Molly." She glares at Maliki. "He texts her on *my phone*, which means Molly always wants it." She holds her arm up. "I vote yes to the phone."

Molly jumps up and down, clapping her hands. "Yay!"

"I need to talk to Cohen about this," Maliki grumbles. "No way am I having my daughter date a kid who hits on all the waitresses at his dad's bar."

Sierra rolls his eyes. "He's a preteen."

"Preteen or not, I don't give a shit."

Rex collapses in the chair next to me with a bottle of water in his hand, and I tune out Molly, who's still presenting her cell phone argument.

I relax in my seat, watching them play in the pool. "Can you believe they're five years old?"

"Time has flown." Rex reaches out and squeezes my thigh. "I say, we make another."

———

"Time for bed," I call out.

Esme yawns, tipping her head back to look at me with sleepy eyes from where she's sitting on the floor between my legs. "But, Mommy, I'm not tired." Another yawn.

"Honey, you can barely keep your eyes open." I wrap the hair tie around her braid before kissing her forehead.

She loves when I braid her hair before going to bed, and then I undo it in the morning since she got her mama's hair—thick and dark.

"Hey! I'm not tired!" River shouts, running into the living room, clad in a Power Ranger costume.

River also inherited my thick, dark hair, but he got his height from Rex. Esme, on the other hand, is small like me.

"I wonder why you're not tired," Rex says, walking into the living room in gray sweats and a tee. "Is it because you snuck an extra slice of cake?"

"Maybe." River grins before pushing the Power Ranger mask over his face.

"There is absolutely no doubt he's your son." I laugh, shaking my head.

Rex rushes over to River, playfully throwing him over his shoulder. "This Power Ranger needs his energy to fight crime tomorrow!"

River bursts out laughing as Rex carries him to his Power Ranger–themed bedroom.

"Your turn, sweetie," I say, helping Esme to her feet.

We hold hands while walking down the hallway into the pink bedroom Rex had professionally painted with unicorns and castles. I read her a short story, kiss her good night, and turn her night-light on before leaving the room. Rex comes out of River's room at the same time, and we cross paths—me going to River's room to kiss him good night and Rex doing the same with Esme. It's our nightly routine, but we switch every night, so each one gets quality time with us alone.

We're in the same home we bought years ago, but we've talked about building a new house since Rex's games have been so successful. We've saved enough money to pay for it with cash and not have to worry about bills constantly. If we decide to expand our family, we'll definitely need more room. It'll be sad, leaving Chloe and Kyle. We've grown so close, and Esme and Callie have become close friends.

I'm in my bra and panties, my pajamas in my hand, when Rex walks into the bedroom. My mouth waters when he softly shuts the door and takes his shirt off. We heard all the *marriage changes sex* talks when we were engaged, but we're the same Rex and Carolina as we were before we said our vows. The sight of my husband never fails to turn me on.

"Stop," he demands.

I pause, raising a brow. "Huh?"

"Don't waste your time with putting those on." He erases the distance between us, wrapping his arms around my waist. "We're about to make another baby."

KEEP UP WITH THE BLUE BEECH SERIES

All books can be read as standalones

Just A Fling
(Hudson and Stella's story)
Just One Night
(Dallas and Willow's story)
Just Exes
(Gage and Lauren's story)
Just Neighbors
(Kyle and Chloe's story)
Just Roommates
(Maliki and Sierra's story)
Just Friends
(Rex and Carolina's story)

BOOKS BY CHARITY FERRELL

BLUE BEECH SERIES

(each book can be read as a standalone)

Just A Fling

Just One Night

Just Exes

Just Neighbors

Just Roommates

Just Friends

TWISTED FOX SERIES

(each book can be read as a standalone)

Stirred

Shaken

Straight Up

Chaser

Last Round

STANDALONES

Bad For You

Beneath Our Faults

Pop Rock

Pretty and Reckless

Revive Me

Wild Thoughts

RISKY DUET

Risky

Worth The Risk

ABOUT THE AUTHOR

Charity Ferrell is a Wall Street Journal and USA Today bestselling author. She resides in Indianapolis, Indiana with her boyfriend and two fur babies. Her passion is writing about broken people finding love while adding a dash of humor and heartbreak. Angst is her happy place.

When she's not writing, she's on a Starbucks run, shopping online, or spending time with her family.

www.charityferrell.com

FIND HER ON: